Robinson Crusoe

Robinson Crusoe

Daniel Defoe

Illustrations by Adam Stower

ALMA CLASSICS

ALMA CLASSICS LTD
3 Castle Yard
Richmond
Surrey TW9 1SE
United Kingdom
www.almaclassics.com

Robinson Crusoe first published in 1719
First published (without illustrations) by Alma Classics Ltd
(previously Oneworld Classics Ltd) in 2008
This new edition published by Alma Classics Ltd in 2015

Text Illustrations © Adam Stower, 2015

Cover design: nathanburtondesign.com

Extra Material © Alma Classics Ltd

Printed and bound by CPI Group (UK) Ltd, Croydon, CR0 4YY

ISBN: 978-1-84749-485-6

Contents

Preface

If ever the story of any private man's adventures in the world were worth making public, and were acceptable when published, the editor of this account thinks this will be so.

The wonders of this man's life exceed all that (he thinks) is to be found extant; the life of one man being scarce capable of a greater variety.

The story is told with modesty, with seriousness, and with a religious application of events to the uses to which wise men always apply them – namely, to the instruction of others by this example, and to justify and honour the wisdom of Providence in all the variety of our circumstances, let them happen how they will.

The editor believes the thing to be a just history of fact; neither is there any appearance of fiction in it: and however thinks, because all such things are dispatched, that the improvement of it, as well to the diversion as to the instruction of the reader, will be the same; and as such, he thinks, without further compliment to the world, he does them a great service in the publication.

Robinson Crusoe

I WAS BORN IN THE YEAR 1632, in the city of York, of a good
family, though not of that country, my father being a foreigner
of Bremen* who settled first at Hull. He got a good estate by mer-
chandise and, leaving off his trade, lived afterwards at York, from
whence he had married my mother, whose relations were named
Robinson, a very good family in that country, and from whom I
was called Robinson Kreutznaer; but by the usual corruption of
words in England, we are now called, nay, we call ourselves and
write our name Crusoe, and so my companions always called me.

I had two elder brothers, one of which was lieutenant colonel
to an English regiment of foot in Flanders, formerly commanded
by the famous Col. Lockhart, and was killed at the battle near
Dunkirk against the Spaniards. What became of my second
brother I never knew any more than my father or mother did
know what was become of me.

Being the third son of the family and not bred to any trade, my
head began to be filled very early with rambling thoughts. My
father, who was very ancient, had given me a competent share
of learning, as far as house education and a country free school
generally goes, and designed me for the law, but I would be satisfied with nothing but going to sea, and my inclination to this led
me so strongly against the will, nay, the commands of my father,

and against all the entreaties and persuasions of my mother and other friends, that there seemed to be something fatal in that propension of nature tending directly* to the life of misery which was to befall me.

My father, a wise and grave man, gave me serious and excellent counsel against what he foresaw was my design. He called me one morning into his chamber, where he was confined by the gout, and expostulated very warmly with me upon this subject. He asked me what reasons more than a mere wandering inclination I had for leaving my father's house and my native country, where I might be well-introduced, and had a prospect of raising my fortune by application and industry, with a life of ease and pleasure. He told me it was for men of desperate fortunes on one hand, or of aspiring, superior fortune on the other, who went abroad upon adventures to rise by enterprise, and make themselves famous in undertakings of a nature out of the common road; that these things were all either too far above me, or too far below me; that mine was the middle state, or what might be called the upper station of low life, which he had found by long experience was the best state in the world, the most suited to human happiness, not exposed to the miseries and hardships, the labour and sufferings of the mechanic part of mankind, and not embarrassed with the pride, luxury, ambition and envy of the upper part of mankind. He told me I might judge of the happiness of this state by this one thing: namely, that this was the state of life which all other people envied, that kings have frequently lamented the miserable consequences of being born to great things, and wished they had been placed in the middle of the two extremes, between the mean and the great; that the wise man gave his testimony to this as the just standard of true felicity, when he prayed to have neither poverty or riches.*

He bid me observe it, and I should always find that the calamities of life were shared among the upper and lower part of mankind, but that the middle station had the fewest disasters, and was not exposed to so many vicissitudes as the higher or lower part of mankind; nay, they were not subjected to so many distempers and uneasiness, either of body or mind, as those were who, by vicious living, luxury and extravagancies on one hand, or by hard labour, want of necessaries and mean or insufficient diet on the other hand, bring distempers upon themselves by the natural consequences of their way of living; that the middle station of life was calculated for all kinds of virtues and all kinds of enjoyments; that peace and plenty were the handmaids of a middle fortune; that temperance, moderation, quietness, health, society, all agreeable diversions and all desirable pleasures, were the blessings attending the middle station of life; that this way men went silently and smoothly through the world, and comfortably out of it, not embarrassed with the labours of the hands or of the head, not sold to the life of slavery for daily bread, or harassed with perplexed circumstances, which rob the soul of peace, and the body of rest; not enragèd with the passion of envy, or secret burning lust of ambition for great things, but in easy circumstances sliding gently through the world, and sensibly tasting the sweets of living without the bitter; feeling that they are happy, and learning by every day's experience to know it more sensibly.

After this, he pressed me earnestly, and in the most affectionate manner, not to play the young man, not to precipitate myself into miseries which nature and the station of life I was born in seemed to have provided against; that I was under no necessity of seeking my bread; that he would do well for me and endeavour to enter me fairly into the station of life which he had been just recommending to me; and that if I was not very easy and happy in the world, it must be my mere fate or fault that must hinder it, and that he should have nothing to answer for, having thus discharged his duty in warning me against measures which he knew would be to my hurt – in a word, that as he would do very kind things for me if I would stay and settle at home as he directed, so he would not have so much hand in my misfortunes as to give me any encouragement to go away – and to close all, he told me I had my elder brother for an example, to whom he had used the same earnest persuasions to keep him from going into the Low Country wars, but could not prevail, his young desires prompting him to run into the army, where he was killed, and though he said he would not cease to pray for me, yet he would venture to say to me that if I did take this foolish step, God would not bless me, and I would have leisure hereafter to reflect upon having neglected his counsel when there might be none to assist in my recovery.

I observed in this last part of his discourse – which was truly prophetic, though I suppose my father did not know it to be so himself – I say, I observed the tears run down his face very plentifully, and especially when he spoke of my brother who was killed; and that when he spoke of my having leisure to repent, and none to assist me, he was so moved that he broke off the discourse, and told me his heart was so full he could say no more to me.

I was sincerely affected with this discourse – as, indeed, who could be otherwise? – and I resolved not to think of going abroad any more, but to settle at home according to my father's desire. But alas! a few days wore it all off, and in short, to prevent any of my father's further importunities, in a few weeks after, I resolved to run quite away from him. However, I did not act so hastily neither as my first heat of resolution prompted, but I took my mother, at a time when I thought her a little pleasanter than ordinary, and told her that my thoughts were so entirely bent upon seeing the world that I should never settle to anything with resolution enough to go through with it, and my father had better give me his consent than force me to go without it; that I was now eighteen years old, which was too late to go apprentice to a trade, or clerk to an attorney; that I was sure if I did, I should never serve out my time, and I should certainly run away from my master before my time was out, and go to sea; and if she would speak to my father to let me go but one voyage abroad, if I came home again and did not like it, I would go no more, and I would promise by a double diligence to recover that time I had lost.

This put my mother into a great passion. She told me she knew it would be to no purpose to speak to my father upon any such subject; that he knew too well what was my interest to give his consent to anything so much for my hurt, and that she wondered how I could think of any such thing after such a discourse as I had had with my father, and such kind and tender expressions as she knew my father had used to me; and that, in short, if I would ruin myself there was no help for me, but I might depend I should never have their consent to it; that for her part she would not have so much hand in my destruction, and I should never have it to say that my mother was willing when my father was not.

Though my mother refused to move it to my father, yet as I have heard afterwards, she reported all the discourse to him, and that my father, after showing a great concern at it, said to her with a sigh, "That boy might be happy if he would stay at home, but if he goes abroad he will be the miserablest wretch that was ever born: I can give no consent to it."

It was not till almost a year after this that I broke loose, though in the meantime I continued, obstinately deaf to all proposals of settling to business, and frequently expostulating with my father and mother about their being so positively determined against what they knew my inclinations prompted me to. But being one day at Hull, where I went casually, and without any purpose of making an elopement that time – but, I say, being there, and one of my companions being going by sea to London in his father's ship, and prompting me to go with them, with the common allurement of seafaring men – namely, that it should cost me nothing for my passage – I consulted neither father or mother any more, nor so much as sent them word of it, but leaving them to hear of it as they might, without asking God's blessing, or my father's, without any consideration of circumstances or consequences, and in an ill hour, God knows, on the first of September 1651, I went on board a ship bound for London. Never any young adventurer's misfortunes, I believe, began sooner or continued longer than mine. The ship was no sooner gotten out of the Humber but the wind began to blow and the waves to rise in a most frightful manner, and as I had never been at sea before, I was most inexpressibly sick in body and terrified in my mind. I began now seriously to reflect upon what I had done, and how justly I was overtaken by the judgement of Heaven for my wicked leaving my father's house and abandoning my duty; all the good counsel of my parents, my father's tears and my mother's entreaties came now fresh into my mind, and my conscience, which was not yet come to the pitch of hardness to which it has been since, reproached me with the contempt of advice, and the breach of my duty to God and my father.

All this while the storm increased, and the sea, which I had never been upon before, went very high, though nothing like what I have seen many times since – no, nor like what I saw a few days after – but it was enough to affect me then, who was but a young sailor, and had never known anything of the matter. I expected every wave would have swallowed us up, and that every time the ship fell down, as I thought, in the trough or hollow of the sea, we should never rise more; and in this agony of mind I made many vows and resolutions that if it would please God here to spare my life this one voyage, if ever I got once my foot upon dry land again, I would go directly home to my father, and never set it into a ship again while I lived; that I would take his advice, and never run myself into such miseries as these any more. Now I saw plainly the goodness of his observations about the middle station of life: how easy, how comfortably he had lived all his days, and never had been exposed to tempests at sea or troubles onshore – and I resolved that I would, like a true repenting prodigal, go home to my father.

These wise and sober thoughts continued all the while the storm continued, and indeed some time after; but the next day the wind was abated and the sea calmer, and I began to be a little inured to it. However, I was very grave for all that day, being also a little seasick still, but towards night the weather cleared up, the wind was quite over and a charming fine evening followed; the sun went down perfectly clear and rose so the next morning, and having little or no wind and a smooth sea, the sun shining upon it, the sight was, as I thought, the most delightful that ever I saw.

I had slept well in the night, and was now no more seasick but very cheerful, looking with wonder upon the sea that was so rough and terrible the day before, and could be so calm and so pleasant in so little time after. And now, lest my good resolutions should continue, my companion, who had indeed enticed me away, comes to me. "Well, Bob," says he, clapping me on the shoulder, "how do you do after it? I warrant you were frighted, wa'n't you, last night, when it blew but a capful of wind?" "A capful d'you call it?" said I, "'twas a terrible storm." "A storm, you fool, you," replies he, "do you call that a storm? Why, it was nothing at all; give us but a good ship and sea room, and we think nothing of such a squall of wind as that – but you're but a freshwater sailor, Bob; come, let us make a bowl of punch and we'll forget all that; d'ye see what charming weather 'tis now?" To make short this sad part of my story, we went the old way of all sailors: the punch was made, and I was made drunk with it, and in that one night's wickedness I drowned all my repentance, all my reflections upon my past conduct, and all my resolutions for my future. In a word, as the sea was returned to its smoothness of surface and settled calmness by the abatement of that storm, so the hurry of my thoughts being over, my fears and apprehensions of being swallowed up by the sea being forgotten, and the current of my former desires returned, I entirely forgot the vows and promises that I made in my distress. I found indeed some intervals of reflection, and the serious thoughts did, as it were, endeavour to return again sometimes, but I shook them off, and roused myself from them as it were from a distemper, and applying myself to drink and company, soon mastered the return of those fits, for so I called them, and I had in five or six days got as complete a victory over conscience as any young fellow that resolved not to be troubled with it could desire. But I was to have another trial for it still, and Providence, as in such cases generally it does, resolved to leave me entirely without excuse. For if I would not take this for a deliverance, the next was to be such a one as the worst and most hardened wretch among us would confess both the danger and the mercy.

The sixth day of our being at sea we came into Yarmouth roads; the wind having been contrary and the weather calm, we had made but little way since the storm. Here we were obliged to come to an anchor, and here we lay, the wind continuing contrary, namely, at south-west, for seven or eight days, during which time a great many ships from Newcastle came into the same roads, as the common harbour where the ships might wait for a wind for the river.

We had not, however, rid here so long, but should have tided it up the river, but that the wind blew too fresh, and, after we had lain four or five days, blew very hard.* However, the roads being reckoned as good as a harbour, the anchorage good, and our ground tackle very strong, our men were unconcerned, and not in the least apprehensive of danger, but spent the time in rest and mirth after the manner of the sea; but the eighth day in the morning, the wind increased, and we had all hands at work to strike our topmasts and make everything snug and close, that the ship might ride as easy as possible. By noon, the sea went very high indeed, and our ship rid forecastle in, shipped several seas, and we thought once or twice our anchor had come home, upon which our master ordered out the sheet anchor; so that we rode with two anchors ahead, and the cables veered out to the bitter end.*

By this time it blew a terrible storm indeed, and now I began to see terror and amazement in the faces even of the seamen themselves. The master, though vigilant to the business of preserving the ship, yet as he went in and out of his cabin by me, I could hear him softly to himself say several times, "Lord, be merciful to us, we shall be all lost, we shall be all undone," and the like. During these first hurries I was stupid, lying still in my cabin, which was in the steerage, and cannot describe my temper. I could ill reassume the first penitence, which I had so apparently trampled upon and hardened myself against: I thought the bitterness of death had been past, and that this would be nothing too, like the first. But when the master himself came by me, as I said just now, and said we should be all lost, I was dreadfully frighted. I got up out of my cabin and looked out, but such a dismal sight I never saw: the sea went mountains high, and broke upon us every three or four minutes; when I could look about, I could see nothing but distress round us. Two ships that rid near us we found had cut their masts by the board, being deep loaden, and our men cried out that a ship which rid about a mile ahead of us was foundered. Two more ships, being driven from their anchors, were run out of the roads to sea at all adventures,* and that with not a mast standing. The light ships fared the best, as not so much labouring in the sea, but two or three of them drove, and came close by us, running away with only their spritsail out before the wind.

Towards evening the mate and boatswain begged the master of our ship to let them cut away the foremast, which he was very unwilling to, but the boatswain protesting to him that if he did not the ship would founder, he consented, and when they had cut away the foremast, the main mast stood so loose, and shook the ship so much, they were obliged to cut her away also, and make a clear deck.

Anyone may judge what a condition I must be in at all this, who was but a young sailor, and who had been in such a fright before at but a little. But if I can express at this distance the thoughts I had about me at that time, I was in tenfold more horror of mind upon account of my former convictions, and the having returned from them to the resolutions I had wickedly taken at first, than I was at death itself, and these, added to the terror of the storm, put me into such a condition that I can by no words describe it. But the worst was not come yet; the storm continued with such fury that the seamen themselves acknowledged they had never known a worse. We had a good ship, but she was deep loaden, and wallowed in the sea, that the seamen every now and then cried out she would founder. It was my advantage in one respect that I did not know what they meant by "founder" till I enquired. However, the storm was so violent that I saw what is not often seen: the master, the boatswain and some others more sensible than the rest at their prayers, and expecting every moment when the ship would go to the bottom. In the middle of the night, and under all the rest of our distresses, one of the men that had been down on purpose to see cried out we had sprung a leak; another said there was four foot water in the hold. Then all hands were called to the pump. At that very word, my heart, as I thought, died within me, and I fell backwards upon the side of my bed where I sat, into the cabin. However, the men roused me, and told me that I, that was able to do nothing before, was as well able to pump as another, at which I stirred up and went to the pump and worked very heartily. While this was doing, the master, seeing some light colliers – who, not able to ride out the storm, were obliged to slip and run away to sea and would come near us – ordered to fire a gun as a signal of distress. I, who knew nothing what that meant, was so surprised that I thought the ship had broke, or some dreadful thing had happened. In a word, I was so surprised that I fell down in a swoon. As this was a time when everybody had his own life to think of, nobody minded me, or what was become of me, but another man stepped up to the pump and, thrusting me aside with his foot, let me lie, thinking I had been dead, and it was a great while before I came to myself.

We worked on but, the water increasing in the hold, it was apparent that the ship would founder, and though the storm began to abate a little, yet as it was not possible she could swim till we might run into a port, so the master continued firing guns for help, and a light ship who had rid it out just ahead of us ventured a boat out to help us. It was with the utmost hazard the boat came near us, but it was impossible for us to get on board, or for the boat to lie near the ship side, till at last, the men rowing very heartily and venturing their lives to save ours, our men cast them a rope over the stern with a buoy to it, and then veered it out a great length, which they, after great labour and hazard, took hold of, and we hauled them close under our stern and got all into their boat. It was to no purpose for them or us after we were in the boat to think of reaching to their own ship, so all agreed to let her drive and only to pull her in towards shore as much as we could, and our master promised them that if the boat was staved upon shore he would make it good to their master; so partly rowing and partly driving, our boat bent away to the norward, sloping towards the shore almost as far as Winterton Ness.

We were not much more than a quarter of an hour out of our ship but we saw her sink, and then I understood for the first time what was meant by a ship foundering in the sea. I must acknowledge I had hardly eyes to look up when the seamen told me she was sinking, for from that moment they rather put me into the boat than that I might be said to go in, my heart was as it were dead within me, partly with fright, partly with horror of mind and the thoughts of what was yet before me.

While we were in this condition, the men yet labouring at the oar to bring the boat near the shore, we could see – when, our boat mounting the waves, we were able to see the shore – a great many people running along the shore to assist us when we should come near, but we made but slow way towards the shore, nor were we able to reach the shore, till, being past the lighthouse at Winterton, the shore falls off to the westwards towards Cromer, and so the land broke off a little the violence of the wind. Here we got in, and, though not without much difficulty, got all safe onshore, and walked afterwards on foot to Yarmouth, where, as unfortunate men, we were used with great humanity as well by the magistrates of the town, who assigned us good quarters, as by particular merchants and owners of ships, and had money given us sufficient to carry us either to London or back to Hull, as we thought fit.

Had I now had the sense to have gone back to Hull, and have gone home, I had been happy, and my father, an emblem of our Blessed Saviour's parable, had even killed the fatted calf* for me, for hearing the ship I went away in was cast away in Yarmouth road, it was a great while before he had any assurance that I was not drowned.

But my ill fate pushed me on now with an obstinacy that nothing could resist, and though I had several times loud calls from my reason and my more composed judgement to go home, yet I had no power to do it. I know not what to call this, nor will I urge that it is a secret overruling decree that hurries us on to be the instruments of our own destruction, even though it be before us, and that we rush upon it with our eyes open. Certainly nothing but some such decreed unavoidable misery attending, and which it was impossible for me to escape, could have pushed me forwards against the calm reasonings and persuasions of my most retired thoughts, and against two such visible instructions as I had met with in my first attempt.

My comrade, who had helped to harden me before, and who was the master's son, was now less forward than I; the first time he spoke to me after we were at Yarmouth – which was not till two or three days, for we were separated in the town to several quarters – I say, the first time he saw me, it appeared his tone was altered, and looking very melancholy and shaking his head, asked me how I did, and telling his father who I was, and how I had come this voyage only for a trial in order to go further abroad; his father turning to me with a very grave and concerned tone, "Young man," says he, "you ought never to go to sea any more, you ought to take this for a plain and visible token that you are not to be a seafaring man."

"Why, sir," said I, "will you go to sea no more?" "That is another case," said he. "It is my calling, and therefore my duty, but as you made this voyage for a trial, you see what a taste Heaven has given you of what you are to expect if you persist; perhaps this is all befallen us on your account, like Jonah in the ship of Tarshish.* Pray," continues he, "what are you? And on what account did you go to sea?" Upon that I told him some of my story, at the end of which he burst out with a strange kind of passion. "What had I done," says he, "that such an unhappy wretch should come into my ship? I would not set my foot in the same ship with thee again for a thousand pounds." This indeed was, as I said, an excursion of his spirits which were yet agitated by the sense of his loss, and was further than he could have authority to go. However, he afterwards talked very gravely to me, exhorted me to go back to my father, and not tempt Providence to my ruin; told me I might see a visible hand of Heaven against me, "and, young man," said he, "depend upon it, if you do not go back, wherever you go, you will meet with nothing but disasters and disappointments till your father's words are fulfilled upon you."

We parted soon after, for I made him little answer, and I saw him no more; which way he went, I know not. As for me, having some money in my pocket, I travelled to London by land, and there, as well as on the road, had many struggles with myself, what course of life I should take, and whether I should go home or go to sea.

As to going home, shame opposed the best motions that offered to my thoughts; and it immediately occurred to me how I should be laughed at among the neighbours, and should be ashamed to see, not my father and mother only, but even everybody else, from whence I have since often observed how incongruous and irrational the common temper of mankind is, especially of youth, to that reason which ought to guide them in such cases, namely, that they are not ashamed to sin, and yet are ashamed to repent; not ashamed of the action for which they ought justly to be esteemed fools, but are ashamed of the returning, which only can make them be esteemed wise men.

In this state of life, however, I remained some time, uncertain what measures to take, and what course of life to lead. An irresistible reluctance continued to going home; and as I stayed awhile, the remembrance of the distress I had been in wore off, and as that abated, the little motion I had in my desires to a return wore off with it, till at last I quite laid aside the thoughts of it and looked out for a voyage.

T HAT EVIL INFLUENCE which carried me first away from my father's house, that hurried me into the wild and indigested notion of raising my fortune, and that impressed those conceits so forcibly upon me as to make me deaf to all good advice, and to the entreaties and even command of my father; I say the same influence, whatever it was, presented the most unfortunate of all enterprises to my view, and I went on board a vessel bound to the coast of Africa, or, as our sailors vulgarly call it, a voyage to Guinea.

It was my great misfortune that in all these adventures I did not ship myself as a sailor; whereby, though I might indeed have worked a little harder than ordinary, yet at the same time I had learnt the duty and office of a foremast man, and in time might have qualified myself for a mate or lieutenant, if not for a master. But as it was always my fate to choose for the worse, so I did here; for, having money in my pocket, and good clothes upon my back, I would always go on board in the habit of a gentleman, and so I neither had any business in the ship, or learnt to do any.

It was my lot, first of all, to fall into pretty good company in London, which does not always happen to such loose and unguided young fellows as I then was, the Devil generally not omitting to lay some snare for them very early – but it was not so with me. I first fell acquainted with the master of a ship who had been on the coast of Guinea, and who, having had very good success there, was resolved to go again; and who, taking a fancy to my conversation, which was not at all disagreeable at that time, hearing me say I had a mind to see the world, told me if I would go the voyage with him I should be at no expense; I should be his messmate and his companion, and if I could carry anything with me, I should have all the advantage of it that the trade would admit, and perhaps I might meet with some encouragement.

I embraced the offer and, entering into a strict friendship with this Captain, who was an honest and plain-dealing man, I went the voyage with him, and carried a small adventure with me, which by the disinterested honesty of my friend the Captain I increased very considerably, for I carried about £40 in such toys and trifles as the Captain directed me to buy. This £40 I had mustered together by the assistance of some of my relations whom I corresponded with, and who, I believe, got my father, or at least my mother, to contribute so much as that to my first adventure.

This was the only voyage which I may say was successful in all my adventures, and which I owe to the integrity and honesty of my friend the Captain, under whom also I got a competent knowledge of the mathematics and the rules of navigation, learnt how to keep an account of the ship's course, take an observation, and in short, to understand some things that were needful to be understood by a sailor: for as he took delight to introduce me, I took delight to learn, and in a word this voyage made me both a sailor and a merchant, for I brought home 5 lbs 9 ounces of gold dust for my adventure, which yielded me in London at my return almost £300, and this filled me with those aspiring thoughts which have since so completed my ruin.

Yet even in this voyage I had my misfortunes too; particularly, that I was continually sick, being thrown into a violent calenture by the excessive heat of the climate, our principal trading being upon the coast, from the latitude of fifteen degrees north even to the line itself.*

I was now set up for a Guinea trader, and my friend, to my great misfortune, dying soon after his arrival, I resolved to go the same voyage again, and I embarked in the same vessel with one who was his mate in the former voyage, and had now got the command of the ship. This was the unhappiest voyage that ever man made, for though I did not carry quite £100 of my new-gained wealth, so that I had 200 left, and which I lodged with my friend's widow, who was very just to me, yet I fell into terrible misfortunes in this voyage, and the first was this, namely. Our ship making her course towards the Canary Islands, or rather between those islands and the African shore, was surprised in the grey of the morning by a Turkish rover of Sallee,* who gave chase to us with all the sail she could make. We crowded also as much canvas as our yards would spread, or our masts carry, to have got clear, but finding the pirate gained upon us and would certainly come up with us in a few hours, we prepared to fight, our ship having twelve guns, and the rogue eighteen. About three in the afternoon he came up with us, and bringing to by mistake just athwart our quarter, instead of athwart our stern as he intended, we brought eight of our guns to bear on that side, and poured in a broadside upon him, which made him sheer off again, after returning our fire, and pouring in also his small shot from near 200 men which he had on board. However, we had not a man touched, all our men keeping close. He prepared to attack us again, and we to defend ourselves, but laying us on board the next time upon our other quarter, he entered sixty men upon our decks, who immediately fell to cutting and hacking the decks and rigging. We plied them with small shot, half-pikes, powder chests and suchlike, and cleared our deck of them twice. However, to cut short this melancholy part of our story, our ship being disabled, and three of our men killed and eight wounded, we were obliged to yield, and were carried all prisoners into Sallee, a port belonging to the Moors.

The usage I had there was not so dreadful as at first I apprehended, nor was I carried up the country to the Emperor's court, as the rest of our men were, but I was kept by the Captain of the rover as his proper prize, and made his slave, being young and nimble and fit for his business. At this surprising change of my circumstances from a merchant to a miserable slave, I was perfectly overwhelmed, and now I looked back upon my father's prophetic discourse to me, that I should be miserable and have none to relieve me, which I thought was now so effectually brought to pass that it could not be worse; that now the hand of Heaven had overtaken me, and I was undone without redemption. But alas! this was but a taste of the misery I was to go through, as will appear in the sequel of this story.

As my new patron or master had taken me home to his house, so I was in hopes that he would take me with him when he went to sea again, believing that it would some time or other be his fate to be taken by a Spanish or Portugal man-of-war, and that then I should be set at liberty. But this hope of mine was soon taken away, for when he went to sea, he left me onshore to look after his little garden, and do the common drudgery of slaves about his house, and when he came home again from his cruise, he ordered me to lie in the cabin to look after the ship.

Here I meditated nothing but my escape, and what method I might take to effect it, but found no way that had the least probability in it. Nothing presented to make the supposition of it rational, for I had nobody to communicate it to that would embark with me; no fellow slave, no Englishman, Irishman or Scotsman there but myself, so that for two years, though I often pleased myself with the imagination, yet I never had the least encouraging prospect of putting it in practice.

After about two years, an odd circumstance presented itself which put the old thought of making some attempt for my liberty again in my head. My patron, lying at home longer than usual without fitting out his ship (which, as I heard, was for want of money), he used constantly – once or twice a week, sometimes oftener, if the weather was fair – to take the ship's pinnace, and go out into the road a-fishing; and as he always took me and a young Morisco with him to row the boat, we made him very merry, and I proved very dextrous in catching fish, insomuch that sometimes he would send me with a Moor, one of his kinsmen, and the youth – the Morisco, as they called him – to catch a dish of fish for him.

It happened one time that, going a-fishing in a stark calm morning, a fog rose so thick that though we were not half a league from the shore, we lost sight of it, and rowing we knew not whither or which way, we laboured all day and all the next night, and when the morning came we found we had pulled off to sea instead of pulling in for the shore, and that we were at least two leagues from the shore. However, we got well in again, though with a great deal of labour, and some danger, for the wind began to blow pretty fresh in the morning, but particularly we were all very hungry.

But our patron, warned by this disaster, resolved to take more care of himself for the future, and having lying by him the long-boat of our English ship they had taken, he resolved he would not go a-fishing any more without a compass and some provision, so he ordered the carpenter of his ship, who also was an English slave, to build a little stateroom or cabin in the middle of the longboat, like that of a barge, with a place to stand behind it to steer and hale home the mainsheet, and room before for a hand or two to stand and work the sails – she sailed with that we call a shoulder-of-mutton sail – and the boom gybed over the top of the cabin, which lay very snug and low, and had in it room for him to lie, with a slave or two, and a table to eat on, with some small lockers to put in some bottles of such liquor as he thought fit to drink; and particularly his bread, rice and coffee.

We went frequently out with this boat a-fishing, and as I was most dextrous to catch fish for him, he never went without me. It happened that he had appointed to go out in this boat, either for pleasure or for fish, with two or three Moors of some distinction in that place, and for whom he had provided extraordinarily, and had therefore sent on board the boat overnight a larger store of provisions than ordinary, and had ordered me to get ready three fusees with powder and shot, which were on board his ship; for that they designed some sport of fowling as well as fishing.

I got all things ready as he had directed, and waited the next morning with the boat, washed clean, her antient and pendants out, and everything to accommodate his guests, when by and by my patron came on board alone, and told me his guests had put off going, upon some business that fell out, and ordered me with the man and boy, as usual, to go out with the boat and catch them some fish, for that his friends were to sup at his house, and commanded that as soon as I had got some fish I should bring it home to his house; all which I prepared to do.

This moment my former notions of deliverance darted into my thoughts, for now I found I was like to have a little ship at my command, and my master being gone, I prepared to furnish myself, not for a fishing business, but for a voyage, though I knew not, neither did I so much as consider whither I should steer, for anywhere to get out of that place was my way.

My first contrivance was to make a pretence to speak to this Moor, to get something for our subsistence on board, for I told him we must not presume to eat of our patron's bread; he said that was true, so he brought a large basket of rusk or biscuit of their kind, and three jars with fresh water into the boat; I knew where my patron's case of bottles stood, which it was evident by the make were taken out of some English prize, and I conveyed them into the boat while the Moor was onshore, as if they had been there before, for our master: I conveyed also a great lump of beeswax into the boat, which weighed about half a hundredweight, with a parcel of twine or thread, a hatchet, a saw and a hammer, all which were of great use to us afterwards – especially the wax to make candles. Another trick I tried upon him, which he innocently came into also; his name was Ismael, who they call Muly or Moely, so I called to him, "Moely," said I, "our patroon's guns are on board the boat; can you not get a little powder and shot – it may be we may kill some alcamies" (a fowl like our curlews) "for ourselves, for I know he keeps the gunner's stores in the ship?" "Yes," says he, "I'll bring some," and accordingly he brought a great leather pouch which held about a pound and half of powder, or rather more, and another with shot, that had five or six pound, with some bullets, and put all into the boat. At the same time, I had found some powder of my master's in the great cabin, with which I filled one of the large bottles in the case, which was almost empty, pouring what was in it into another – and thus furnished with everything needful, we sailed out of the port to fish. The castle which is at the entrance of the port knew who we were, and took no notice of us, and we were not above a mile out of the port before we haled in our sail and set us down to fish. The wind blew from the NNE, which was contrary to my desire, for had it blown southerly I had been sure to have made the coast of Spain, and at least reached to the bay of Cadiz, but my resolutions were, blow which way it would, I would be gone from that horrid place where I was, and leave the rest to fate.

After we had fished some time and catched nothing, for when I had fish on my hook, I would not pull them up, that he might not see them; I said to the Moor, "This will not do, our master will not be thus served, we must stand further off." He, thinking no harm, agreed, and being in the head of the boat set the sails, and as I had the helm, I ran the boat out a league further, and then brought her to as if I would fish; when giving the boy the helm, I stepped forwards to where the Moor was, and making as if I stooped for something behind him, I took him by surprise with my arm under his twist, and tossed him clear overboard into the sea; he rise immediately, for he swam like a cork, and called to me, begged to be taken in, told me he would go all over the world with me; he swam so strong after the boat that he would have reached me very quickly, there being but little wind, upon which I stepped into the cabin, and fetching one of the fowling pieces, I presented it at him and told him I had done him no hurt, and if he would be quiet I would do him none; "but," said I, "you swim well enough to reach to the shore, and the sea is calm; make the best of your way to shore and I will do you no harm, but if you come near the boat I'll shoot you through the head, for I am resolved to have my liberty," so he turned himself about and swam for the shore, and I make no doubt but he reached it with ease, for he was an excellent swimmer.

I could ha' been content to ha' taken this Moor with me, and ha' drowned the boy, but there was no venturing to trust him. When he was gone I turned to the boy, who they called Xury, and said to him, "Xury, if you will be faithful to me I'll make you a great man, but if you will not stroke your face to be true to me" – that is, swear by Muhammad and his father's beard – "I must throw you into the sea too." The boy smiled in my face and spoke so innocently that I could not mistrust him, and swore to be faithful to me, and go all over the world with me.

While I was in view of the Moor that was swimming, I stood out directly to sea with the boat, rather stretching to windwards, that they might think me gone towards the straits' mouth (as indeed anyone that had been in their wits must ha' been supposed to do), for who would ha' supposed we were sailed on to the southwards to the truly Barbarian coast, where whole nations of Negroes were sure to surround us with their canoes and destroy us; where we could ne'er once go onshore but we should be devoured by savage beasts, or more merciless savages of humankind?

But as soon as it grew dusk in the evening, I changed my course, and steered directly south and by east, bending my course a little towards the east that I might keep in with the shore, and having a fair fresh gale of wind, and a smooth, quiet sea, I made such sail that I believe by the next day at three o'clock in the afternoon, when I first made the land, I could not be less than 150 miles south of Sallee – quite beyond the Emperor of Morocco's dominions, or indeed of any other king thereabouts, for we saw no people.

Yet such was the fright I had taken at the Moors, and the dreadful apprehensions I had of falling into their hands, that I would not stop, or go onshore, or come to an anchor (the wind continuing fair), till I had sailed in that manner five days; and then the wind shifting to the southwards, I concluded also that if any of our vessels were in chase of me, they also would now give over, so I ventured to make to the coast, and came to an anchor in the mouth of a little river, I knew not what, or where – neither what latitude, what country, what nations or what river – I neither saw or desired to see any people; the principal thing I wanted was fresh water. We came into this creek in the evening, resolving to swim onshore as soon as it was dark and discover the country, but as soon as it was quite dark, we heard such dreadful noises of the barking, roaring and howling of wild creatures of we knew not what kinds, that the poor boy was ready to die with fear, and begged of me not to go shore till day. "Well, Xury," said I, "then I won't, but it may be we may see men by day, who will be as bad to us as those lions." "Then we give them the shoot gun," says Xury, laughing, "make them run wey" – such English Xury spoke by conversing among us slaves. However, I was glad to see the boy so cheerful, and I gave him a dram (out of our patroon's case of bottles) to cheer him up. After all, Xury's advice was good, and I took it. We dropped our little anchor and lay still all night – I say still, for we slept none! – for in two or three hours we saw vast great creatures (we knew not what to call them) of many sorts come down to the seashore and run into the water, wallowing and washing themselves for the pleasure of cooling themselves, and they made such hideous howlings and yellings that I never indeed heard the like.

Xury was dreadfully frighted, and indeed so was I too, but we were both more frightened when we heard one of these mighty creatures come swimming towards our boat; we could not see him, but we might hear him by his blowing to be a monstrous, huge and furious beast; Xury said it was a lion, and it might be so for ought I know, but poor Xury cried to me to weigh anchor and row away. "No," says I, "Xury, we can slip our cable with the buoy to it and go off to sea; they cannot follow us far." I had no sooner said so but I perceived the creature (whatever it was) within two oars' length, which something surprised me; however,

I immediately stepped to the cabin door, and taking up my gun fired at him, upon which he immediately turned about and swam towards the shore again.

But it is impossible to describe the horrible noises and hideous cries and howlings that were raised, as well upon the edge of the shore as higher within the country, upon the noise or report of the gun, a thing I have some reason to believe those creatures had never heard before. This convinced me that there was no going onshore for us in the night upon that coast, and how to venture onshore in the day was another question too, for to have fallen into the hands of any of the savages had been as bad as to have fallen into the hands of lions and tigers; at least we were equally apprehensive of the danger of it.

Be that as it would, we were obliged to go onshore somewhere or other for water, for we had not a pint left in the boat; when or where to get to it was the point. Xury said if I would let him go onshore with one of the jars he would find if there was any water and bring some to me. I asked him why he would go; why I should not go and he stay in the boat; the boy answered with so much affection that made me love him ever after. Says he, "If wild mans come, they eat me, you go wey." "Well, Xury," said I, "we will both go, and if the wild mans come we will kill them – they shall eat neither of us." So I gave Xury a piece of rusk bread to eat and a dram out of our patroon's case of bottles, which I mentioned before, and we haled the boat in as near the shore as we thought was proper, and so waded onshore, carrying nothing but our arms and two jars for water.

I did not care to go out of sight of the boat, fearing the coming of canoes with savages down the river, but the boy, seeing a low place about a mile up the country, rambled to it, and by and by I saw him come running towards me. I thought he was pursued by some savage, or frighted with some wild beast, and I ran forwards towards him to help him, but when I came nearer to him, I saw something hanging over his shoulders which was a creature that he had shot, like a hare but different in colour, and longer legs; however, we were very glad of it, and it was very good meat, but the great joy that poor Xury came with was to tell me he had found good water and seen no wild mans.

But we found afterwards that we need not take such pains for water, for a little higher up the creek where we were, we found the water fresh when the tide was out, which flowed but a little way up, so we filled our jars and feasted on the hare we had killed, and prepared to go on our way, having seen no footsteps of any human creature in that part of the country.

As I had been one voyage to this coast before, I knew very well that the islands of the Canaries, and the Cape de Verd Islands also, lay not far off from the coast. But as I had no instruments to take an observation to know what latitude we were in, and did not exactly know, or at least remember, what latitude they were in, I knew not where to look for them, or when to stand off to sea towards them – otherwise I might now easily have found some of these islands. But my hope was that if I stood along this coast till I came to that part where the English traded, I should find some of their vessels upon their usual design of trade that would relieve and take us in.

By the best of my calculation, that place where I now was must be that country which, lying between the Emperor of Morocco's dominions and the Negroes', lies vast and uninhabited, except by wild beasts, the Negroes having abandoned it and gone further south for fear of the Moors; and the Moors not thinking it worth inhabiting, by reason of its barrenness – and indeed both forsaking it because of the prodigious numbers of tigers, lions, leopards and other furious creatures which harbour there, so that the Moors use it for their hunting only, where they go like an army, two or three thousand men at a time – and indeed for near a hundred miles together upon this coast, we saw nothing but a vast uninhabited country by day, and heard nothing but howlings and roaring of wild beasts by night.

Once or twice in the daytime I thought I saw the Pico of Tenerife, being the high top of the mountain Tenerife in the Canaries, and had a great mind to venture out in hopes of reaching thither, but, having tried twice, I was forced in again by contrary winds, the sea also going too high for my little vessel, so I resolved to pursue my first design and keep along the shore.

Several times I was obliged to land for fresh water after we had left this place, and once in particular, being early in the morning, we came to an anchor under a little point of land which was pretty high, and the tide beginning to flow, we lay still to go further in; Xury, whose eyes were more about him than it seems mine were, calls softly to me, and tells me that we had best go further off the shore, "for," says he, "look, yonder lies a dreadful monster on the side of that hillock fast asleep." I looked where he pointed, and saw a dreadful monster indeed, for it was a terrible great lion that lay on the side of the shore, under the shade of a piece of the hill that hung as it were a little over him. "Xury," says I, "you shall go onshore and kill him." Xury looked frighted, and said, "Me kill! He eat me at one mouth" – one mouthful he meant – however, I said no more to the boy, but bade him lie still, and I took our biggest gun, which was almost musket bore, and loaded it with a good charge of powder and with two slugs, and laid it down, then I loaded another gun with two bullets, and a third – for we had three pieces – I loaded with five smaller bullets. I took the best aim I could with the first piece to have shot him into the head, but he lay so with his leg raised a little above his nose that the slugs hit his leg about the knee, and broke the bone. He started up growling at first but, finding his leg broke, fell down again, and then got up upon three legs and gave the most hideous roar that ever I heard. I was a little surprised that I had not hit him on the head, however, I took up the second piece immediately, and though he began to move off, fired again, and shot him into the head, and had the pleasure to see him drop, and make but little noise, but lay struggling for life. Then Xury took heart, and would have me let him go onshore. "Well, go," said I, so the boy jumped into the water and, taking a little gun in one hand, swam to the shore with the other hand, and coming close to the creature, put the muzzle of the piece to his ear, and shot him into the head again, which dispatched him quite.

This was game indeed to us, but this was no food, and I was very sorry to lose three charges of powder and shot upon a creature that was good for nothing to us. However, Xury said he would have some of him, so he comes on board, and asked me to give him the hatchet. "For what, Xury?" said I. "Me cut off his head," said he. However, Xury could not cut off his head, but he cut off a foot and brought it with him, and it was a monstrous great one.

I bethought myself, however, that perhaps the skin of him might one way or other be of some value to us, and I resolved to take off his skin if I could. So Xury and I went to work with him, but Xury was much the better workman at it, for I knew very ill how to do it. Indeed, it took us up both the whole day, but at last we got off the hide of him, and spreading it on the top of our cabin, the sun effectually dried it in two days' time, and it afterwards served me to lie upon.

AFTER THIS STOP, we made on to the southwards continually for ten or twelve days, living very sparing on our provisions, which began to abate very much, and going no oftener into the shore than we were obliged to for fresh water; my design in this was to make the river Gambia or Senegal – that is to say, anywhere about the Cape de Verd, where I was in hopes to meet with some European ship – and if I did not, I knew not what course I had to take but to seek out for the islands, or perish there among the Negroes. I knew that all the ships from Europe, which sailed either to the coast or Guinea, or to Brazil, or to the East Indies, made this cape or those islands, and in a word, I put the whole of my fortune upon this single point, either that I must meet with some ship, or must perish.

When I had pursued this resolution about ten days longer, as I have said, I began to see that the land was inhabited, and in two or three places as we sailed by, we saw people stand upon the shore to look at us; we could also perceive they were quite black and stark naked. I was once inclined to ha' gone onshore to them, but Xury was my better counsellor and said to me, "No go, no go." However, I haled in nearer the shore that I might talk to them, and I found they run along the shore by me a good way; I observed they had no weapons in their hands, except one who had a long slender stick, which Xury said was a lance, and that they would throw them a great way with good aim, so I kept at a distance, but talked with them by signs as well as I could, and particularly made signs for something to eat. They beckoned to me to stop my boat, and that they would fetch me some meat; upon this I lowered the top of my sail and lay by, and two of them ran up into the country, and in less than half an hour came back and brought with them two pieces of dry flesh and some corn, such as is the produce of their country, but we neither knew what the one or the other was; however, we were willing to accept it, but how to come at it was our next dispute, for I was not for venturing onshore to them, and they were as much afraid of us, but they took a safe way for us all, for they brought it to the shore and laid it down, and went and stood a great way off till we fetched it on board, and then came close to us again.

We made signs of thanks to them, for we had nothing to make them amends, but an opportunity offered that very instant to oblige them wonderfully, for while we were lying by the shore came two mighty creatures, one pursuing the other (as we took it) with great fury from the mountains towards the sea; whether it was the male pursuing the female, or whether they were in sport or in rage, we could not tell any more than we could tell whether it was usual or strange, but I believe it was the latter, because in the first place, those ravenous creatures seldom appear but in the night; and in the second place, we found the people terribly frighted, especially the women. The man that had the lance or dart did not fly from them, but the rest did; however, as the two creatures ran directly into the water, they did not seem to offer to fall upon any of the Negroes, but plunged themselves into the sea and swam about as if they had come for their diversion. At last one of them began to come nearer our boat than at first I expected, but I lay ready for him, for I had loaded my gun with all possible expedition, and bade Xury load both the others. As soon as he came fairly within my reach, I fired, and shot him directly into the head; immediately he sunk down into the water, but rose instantly and plunged up and down as if he was struggling for life, and so indeed he was. He immediately made to the shore, but between the wound, which was his mortal hurt, and the strangling of the water, he died just before he reached the shore.

It is impossible to express the astonishment of these poor creatures at the noise and fire of my gun; some of them were even ready to die for fear, and fell down as dead with the very terror. But when they saw the creature dead and sunk in the water, and that I made signs to them to come to the shore, they took heart and came to the shore and began to search for the creature. I found him by his blood staining the water, and by the help of a rope which I slung round him and gave the Negroes to haul, they dragged him onshore, and found that it was a most curious leopard, spotted and fine to an admirable degree, and the Negroes held up their hands with admiration to think what it was I had killed him with.

The other creature, frighted with the flash of fire and the noise of the gun, swam onshore and ran up directly to the mountains from whence they came, nor could I at that distance know what it was. I found quickly the Negroes were for eating the flesh of this creature, so I was willing to have them take it as a favour from me, which, when I made signs to them that they might take him, they were very thankful for. Immediately they fell to work with him, and though they had no knife, yet with a sharpened piece of wood they took off his skin as readily and much more readily than we could have done with a knife. They offered me some of the flesh, which I declined, making as if I would give it them, but made signs for the skin, which they gave me very freely, and brought me a great deal more of their provision, which though I did not understand, yet I accepted, then made signs to them for some water and held out one of my jars to them, turning it bottom upwards to show that it was empty, and that I wanted to have it filled. They called immediately to some of their friends, and there came two women and brought a great vessel made of earth, and burnt as I suppose in the sun; this they set down for me, as before, and I sent Xury onshore with my jars, and filled them all three. The women were as stark naked as the men.

I was now furnished with roots and corn, such as it was, and water, and leaving my friendly Negroes, I made forwards for about eleven days more without offering to go near the shore, till I saw the land run out a great length into the sea, at about the distance of four or five leagues before me, and the sea being very calm, I kept a large offing to make this point. At length, doubling the point at about two leagues from the land, I saw plainly land on the other side to seaward, then I concluded, as it was most certain indeed, that this was the Cape de Verd, and those the islands called from thence Cape de Verd Islands. However, they were at a great distance, and I could not tell what I had best to do, for if I should be taken with a fresh of wind I might neither reach one or other.

In this dilemma, as I was very pensive, I stepped into the cabin and sat me down, Xury having the helm, when on a sudden the boy cried out, "Master, master, a ship with a sail," and the foolish boy was frighted out of his wits, thinking it must needs be some of his master's ships sent to pursue us, when I knew we were gotten far enough out of their reach. I jumped out of the cabin, and immediately saw not only the ship, but what she was, namely, that it was a Portuguese ship and, as I thought, was bound to the coast of Guinea for Negroes. But when I observed the course she steered, I was soon convinced they were bound some other way, and did not design to come any nearer to the shore, upon which I stretched out to sea as much as I could, resolving to speak with them if possible.

With all the sail I could make, I found I should not be able to come in their way but that they would be gone by before I could make any signal to them, but after I had crowded to the utmost, and began to despair, they – it seems – saw me by the help of their prospective glasses, and that it was some European boat, which as they supposed must belong to some ship that was lost, so they shortened sail to let me come up. I was encouraged with this, and as I had my patroon's antient on board, I made a waft of it to them for a signal of distress, and fired a gun, both which they saw – for they told me they saw the smoke, though they did not hear the gun – upon these signals they very kindly brought to, and lay by for me, and in about three hours' time I came up with them.

They asked me what I was in Portuguese and in Spanish and in French, but I understood none of them – but at last a Scots sailor who was on board called to me, and I answered him, and told him I was an Englishman, that I had made my escape out of slavery from the Moors at Sallee; then they bade me come on board, and very kindly took me in, and all my goods.

It was an inexpressible joy to me – that anyone will believe – that I was thus delivered, as I esteemed it, from such a miserable and almost hopeless condition as I was in, and I immediately offered all I had to the Captain of the ship as a return for my deliverance, but he generously told me he would take nothing from me, but that all I had should be delivered safe to me when I came to the Brazils, "for," says he, "I have saved your life on no other terms than I would be glad to be saved myself, and it may one time or other be my lot to be taken up in the same condition. Besides," said he, "when I carry you to the Brazils, so great a way from your own country, if I should take from you what you have, you will be starved there, and then I only take away what life I have given. No, no, Señor Inglese," says he ("Mr Englishman"), "I will carry you thither in charity, and those things will help you to buy your subsistence there and your passage home again."

As he was charitable in his proposal, so he was just in the performance to a title, for he ordered the seaman that none should offer to touch anything I had; then he took everything into his own possession and gave me back an exact inventory of them, that I might have them, even so much as my three earthen jars.

As to my boat, it was a very good one, and that he saw, and told me he would buy it of me for the ship's use, and asked me what I would have for it. I told him he had been so generous to me in everything, that I could not offer to make any price of the boat, but left it entirely to him, upon which he told me he would give me a note of his hand to pay me eighty pieces of eight for it at Brazil, and when it came there, if anyone offered to give more he would make it up; he offered me also sixty pieces of eight more for my boy Xury, which I was loath to take – not that I was not willing to let the Captain have him, but I was very loath to sell the poor boy's liberty, who had assisted me so faithfully in procuring my own. However, when I let him know my reason, he owned it to be just, and offered me this medium: that he would give the boy an obligation to set him free in ten years if he turned Christian – upon this, and Xury saying he was willing to go to him, I let the Captain have him.

We had a very good voyage to the Brazils, and arrived in the Bay de Todos los Santos, or All Saints' Bay, in about twenty-two days after. And now I was once more delivered from the most miserable of all conditions of life, and what to do next with myself I was now to consider.

The generous treatment the Captain gave me, I can never enough remember; he would take nothing of me for my passage, gave me twenty ducats for the leopard's skin, and forty for the lion's skin which I had in my boat, and caused everything I had in the ship to be punctually delivered me, and what I was willing to sell he bought, such as the case of bottles, two of my guns and a piece of the lump of beeswax, for I had made candles of the rest – in a word, I made about 220 pieces of eight of all my cargo, and with this stock I went onshore in the Brazils.

I had not been long here, but being recommended to the house of a good, honest man like himself, who had an *ingenio* as they call it (that is, a plantation and a sugar house), I lived with him some time, and acquainted myself by that means with the manner of their planting and making of sugar; and seeing how well the planters lived, and how they grew rich suddenly, I resolved, if I could get licence to settle there, I would turn planter among them, resolving in the meantime to find out some way to get my money which I had left in London remitted to me. To this purpose getting a kind of letter of naturalization, I purchased as much land that was uncured as my money would reach, and formed a plan for my plantation and settlement, and such a one as might be suitable to the stock which I proposed to myself to receive from England.

I had a neighbour, a Portuguese of Lisbon, but born of English parents, whose name was Wells and in much such circumstances as I was. I call him my neighbour, because his plantation lay next to mine, and we went on very sociably together. My stock was but low as well as his, and we rather planted for food than anything else for about two years. However, we began to increase, and our land began to come into order, so that the third year we planted

some tobacco, and made each of us a large piece of ground ready
for planting canes in the year to come, but we both wanted help,
and now I found more than before, I had done wrong in parting
with my boy Xury.

But alas! For me to do wrong, that never did right, was no
great wonder. I had no remedy but to go on; I was gotten into
an employment quite remote to my genius, and directly contrary to the life I delighted in, and for which I forsook my
father's house and broke through all his good advice. Nay, I
was coming into the very middle station, or upper degree of
low life, which my father advised me to before, and which if I
resolved to go on with, I might as well ha' stayed at home and
never have fatigued myself in the world as I had done, – and
I used often to say to myself, I could ha' done this as well in
England among my friends, as ha' gone 5,000 miles off to do
it among strangers and savages in a wilderness, and at such a
distance as never to hear from any part of the world that had
the least knowledge of me.

In this manner, I used to look upon my condition with the
utmost regret. I had nobody to converse with but now and then
this neighbour; no work to be done but by the labour of my
hands, and I used to say I lived just like a man cast away upon
some desolate island that has nobody there but himself. But how
just has it been, and how should all men reflect, that when they
compare their present conditions with others that are worse,
Heaven may oblige them to make the exchange, and be convinced
of their former felicity by their experience – I say, how just has it
been that the truly solitary life I reflected on in an island of mere
desolation should be my lot, who had so often unjustly compared
it with the life which I then led, in which, had I continued, I had
in all probability been exceeding prosperous and rich.

I was in some degree settled in my measures for carrying on the plantation, before my kind friend, the Captain of the ship that took me up at sea, went back, for the ship remained there in providing his loading, and preparing for his voyage, near three months, when telling him what little stock I had left behind me in London, he gave me this friendly and sincere advice: "Señor Inglese," says he, for so he always called me, "if you will give me letters and a procuration here in form to me, with orders to the person who has your money in London to send your effects to Lisbon, to such persons as I shall direct, and in such goods as are proper for this country, I will bring you the produce of them, God willing, at my return – but since human affairs are all subject to changes and disasters, I would have you give orders but for one hundred pounds sterling, which you say is half your stock, and let the hazard be run for the first, so that if it come safe, you may order the rest the same way; and if it miscarry, you may have the other half to have recourse to for your supply."

This was so wholesome advice, and looked so friendly, that I could not but be convinced it was the best course I could take, so I accordingly prepared letters to the gentlewoman with whom I had left my money, and a procuration to the Portuguese Captain, as he desired.

I wrote the English Captain's widow a full account of all my adventures: my slavery, escape and how I had met with the Portugal Captain at sea, the humanity of his behaviour, and in what condition I was now in, with all other necessary directions for my supply, and when this honest Captain came to Lisbon, he found means by some of the English merchants there to send over not the order only, but a full account of my story to a merchant at London, who represented it effectually to her – whereupon she not only delivered the money, but out of her own pocket sent the Portugal Captain a very handsome present for his humanity and charity to me.

The merchant in London, vesting this hundred pounds in English goods, such as the Captain had writ for, sent them directly to him at Lisbon, and he brought them all safe to me to the Brazils, among which, without my direction (for I was too young in my business to think of them), he had taken care to have all sorts of tools, ironwork and utensils necessary for my plantation, and which were of great use to me.

When this cargo arrived, I thought my fortunes made, for I was surprised with the joy of it, and my good steward the Captain had laid out the five pounds which my friend had sent him for a present for himself, to purchase and bring me over a servant under bond for six years' service, and would not accept of any consideration, except a little tobacco, which I would have him accept, being of my own produce.

Neither was this all, but my goods being all English manufactures, such as cloth, stuffs, baize and things particularly valuable and desirable in the country, I found means to sell them to a very great advantage, so that I might say I had more than four times the value of my first cargo, and was now infinitely beyond my poor neighbour – I mean in the advancement of my plantation: for the first thing I did, I bought me a Negro slave, and a European servant also – I mean another besides that which the Captain brought me from Lisbon.

But as abused prosperity is oftentimes made the very means of our greatest adversity, so was it with me. I went on the next year with great success in my plantation. I raised fifty great rolls of tobacco on my own ground, more than I had disposed of for necessaries among my neighbours, and these fifty rolls being each of above a hundredweight were well-cured and laid-by against the return of the fleet from Lisbon – and now, increasing in business and in wealth, my head began to be full of projects and undertakings beyond my reach, such as are indeed often the ruin of the best heads in business.

Had I continued in the station I was now in, I had room for all the happy things to have yet befallen me, for which my father so earnestly recommended a quiet retired life, and of which he had so sensibly described the middle station of life to be full of – but other things attended me, and I was still to be the wilful agent of all my own miseries, and particularly to increase my fault and double the reflections upon myself, which in my future sorrows I should have leisure to make. All these miscarriages were procured by my apparent obstinate adhering to my foolish inclination of wandering abroad and pursuing that inclination, in contradiction to the clearest views of doing myself good in a fair and plain pursuit of those prospects and those measures of life which nature and Providence concurred to present me with and to make my duty.

As I had once done thus in my breaking away from my parents, so I could not be content now, but I must go and leave the happy view I had of being a rich and thriving man in my new plantation, only to pursue a rash and immoderate desire of rising faster than the nature of the thing admitted, and thus I cast myself down again into the deepest gulf of human misery that ever man fell into, or perhaps could be consistent with life and a state of health in the world.

To come then by the just degrees to the particulars of this part of my story: you may suppose, that having now lived almost four years in the Brazils, and beginning to thrive and prosper very well upon my plantation, I had not only learnt the language, but had contracted acquaintance and friendship among my fellow planters, as well as among the merchants at St Salvadore, which was our port; and that in my discourses among them, I had frequently given them an account of my two voyages to the coast of Guinea, the manner of trading with the Negroes there, and how easy it was to purchase upon the coast, for trifles such as beads, toys, knives, scissors, hatchets, bits of glass and the like, not only gold dust, Guinea grains, elephant's teeth, etc., but Negroes, for the service of the Brazils, in great numbers.

They listened always very attentively to my discourses on these heads, but especially to that part which related to the buying Negroes, which was a trade at that time not only not far entered into, but as far as it was, had been carried on by the *asientos*, or permission, of the kings of Spain and Portugal, and engrossed in the public, so that few Negroes were brought, and those excessive dear.

It happened, being in company with some merchants and planters of my acquaintance, and talking of those things very earnestly, three of them came to me the next morning, and told me they had been musing very much upon what I had discoursed with them of the last night, and they came to make a secret proposal to me, and after enjoining me secrecy, they told me that they had a mind to fit out a ship to go to Guinea, that they had all plantations as well as I, and were straitened for nothing so much as servants; that as it was a trade that could not be carried on, because they could not publicly sell the Negroes when they came home, so they desired to make but one voyage, to bring the Negroes onshore privately, and divide them among their own plantations; and in a word, the question was whether I would go their supercargo in the ship to manage the trading part upon the coast of Guinea. And they offered me that I should have my equal share of the Negroes without providing any part of the stock.*

43

This was a fair proposal, it must be confessed, had it been made to anyone that had not had a settlement and plantation of his own to look after, which was in a fair way of coming to be very considerable, and with a good stock upon it. But for me that was thus entered and established, and had nothing to do but go on as I had begun for three or four years more, and to have sent for the other hundred pound from England, and who in that time, and with that little addition, could scarce ha' failed of being worth three or four thousand pounds sterling, and that increasing too; for me to think of such a voyage was the most preposterous thing that ever man in such circumstances could be guilty of.

But I, that was born to be my own destroyer, could no more resist the offer than I could restrain my first rambling designs when my father's good counsel was lost upon me. In a word, I told them I would go with all my heart, if they would undertake to look after my plantation in my absence, and would dispose of it to such as I should direct if I miscarried. This they all engaged to do, and entered into writings or covenants to do so, and I made a formal will, disposing of my plantation and effects, in case of my death, making the Captain of the ship that had saved my life, as before, my universal heir, but obliging him to dispose of my effects as I had directed in my will, one half of the produce being to himself, and the other to be shipped to England.

In short, I took all possible caution to preserve my effects and keep up my plantation – had I used half as much prudence to have looked into my own interest, and have made a judgement of what I ought to have done and not to have done, I had certainly never gone away from so prosperous an undertaking, leaving all the probable views of a thriving circumstance, and gone upon a voyage to sea, attended with all its common hazards – to say nothing of the reasons I had to expect particular misfortunes to myself.

But I was hurried on, and obeyed blindly the dictates of my fancy rather than my reason, and accordingly, the ship being fitted out, and the cargo furnished, and all things done as by agreement by my partners in the voyage, I went on board in an evil hour, the first of September, 1659, being the same day eight year* that I went from my father and mother at Hull in order to act the rebel to their authority, and the fool to my own interest.

Our ship was about 120 ton burden, carried six guns and fourteen men, besides the master, his boy and myself; we had on board no large cargo of goods, except of such toys as were fit for our trade with the Negroes, such as beads, bits of glass, shells and odd trifles, especially little looking glasses, knives, scissors, hatchets and the like.

The same day I went on board, we set sail, standing away to the northwards upon our own coast, with design to stretch over for the African coast, when they came about ten or twelve degrees of northern latitude, which it seems was the manner of their course in those days. We had very good weather, only excessive hot, all the way upon our own coast, till we came to the height of Cape St Augustino, from whence keeping further off at sea we lost sight of land, and steered as if we was bound for the isle Fernand de Noronha, holding our course NE by N and leaving those isles on the east. In this course we passed the line in about twelve days time, and were by our last observation in seven degrees twenty-two min. northern latitude, when a violent tornado or hurricane took us quite out of our knowledge; it began from the south-east, came about to the north-west, and then settled into the north-east, from whence it blew in such a terrible manner that for twelve days together we could do nothing but drive and, scudding away before it, let it carry us whither ever fate and the fury of the winds directed; and during these twelve days, I need not say that I expected every day to be swallowed up, nor indeed did any in the ship expect to save their lives.

In this distress, we had, besides the terror of the storm, one of our men died of the calenture, and one man and the boy washed overboard; about the twelfth day, the weather abating a little, the master made an observation as well as he could, and found that he was in about eleven degrees north latitude, but that he was twenty-two degrees of longitude difference west from Cape St Augustino, so that he found he was gotten upon the coast of Guinea, or the north part of Brazil, beyond the river Amazones, towards that of the river Orinoco, commonly called the Great River, and began to consult with me what course he should take, for the ship was leaky and very much disabled, and he was going directly back to the coast of Brazil.

I was positively against that, and, looking over the charts of the sea coast of America with him, we concluded there was no inhabited country for us to have recourse to till we came within the circle of the Caribbee Islands, and therefore resolved to stand away for Barbados, which, by keeping off at sea to avoid the indraught of the bay or gulf of Mexico, we might easily perform, as we hoped, in about fifteen days' sail, whereas we could not possibly make our voyage to the coast of Africa without some assistance, both to our ship and to ourselves.

With this design we changed our course and steered away NW by W in order to reach some of our English islands, where I hoped for relief, but our voyage was otherwise determined, for being in the latitude of twelve deg. eighteen min., a second storm came upon us, which carried us away with the same impetuosity westwards, and drove us so out of the very way of all humane commerce, that had all our lives been saved, as to the sea, we were rather in danger of being devoured by savages than ever returning to our own country.

In this distress, the wind still blowing very hard, one of our men early in the morning cried out, "Land!" and we had no sooner run out of the cabin to look out in hopes of seeing whereabouts in the world we were, but the ship struck upon a sand, and in a moment, her motion being so stopped, the sea broke over her in such a manner that we expected we should all have perished immediately, and we were immediately driven into our close quarters to shelter us from the very foam and spray of the sea.

It is not easy for anyone who has not been in the like condition to describe or conceive the consternation of men in such circumstances; we knew nothing where we were, or upon what land it was we were driven, whether an island or the main, whether inhabited or not inhabited, and as the rage of the wind was still great, though rather less than at first, we could not so much as hope to have the ship hold many minutes without breaking in pieces, unless the winds by a kind of miracle should turn immediately about. In a word, we sat looking upon one another, and expecting death every moment, and every man acting accordingly, as preparing for another world, for there was little or nothing more for us to do in this; that which was our present comfort, and all the comfort we had, was that contrary to our expectation the ship did not break yet, and that the master said the wind began to abate.

Now, though we thought that the wind did a little abate, yet the ship having thus struck upon the sand, and sticking too fast for us to expect her getting off, we were in a dreadful condition indeed, and had nothing to do but to think of saving our lives as well as we could. We had a boat at our stern just before the storm, but she was first staved by dashing against the ship's rudder, and in the next place she broke away, and either sunk or was driven off to sea, so there was no hope from her; we had another boat on board, but how to get her off into the sea was a doubtful thing;

however, there was no room to debate, for we fancied the ship would break in pieces every minute, and some told us she was actually broken already.

In this distress the mate of our vessel lays hold of the boat, and with the help of the rest of the men, they got her slung over the ship's side, and getting all into her, let go, and committed our-selves, being eleven in number, to God's mercy and the wild sea, for though the storm was abated considerably, yet the sea went dreadful high upon the shore, and might well be called *Den wild Zee*, as the Dutch call the sea in a storm.

And now our case was very dismal indeed, for we all saw plainly that the sea went so high that the boat could not live, and that we should be inevitably drowned. As to making sail, we had none, nor, if we had, could we ha' done anything with it: so we worked at the oar towards the land, though with heavy hearts, like men going to execution, for we all knew that when the boat came nearer the shore, she would be dashed in a thousand pieces by the breach of the sea. However, we committed our souls to God in the most earnest manner, and the wind driving us towards the shore, we hastened our destruction with our own hands, pulling as well as we could towards land.

What the shore was, whether rock or sand, whether steep or shoal, we knew not; the only hope that could rationally give us the least shadow of expectation was if we might happen into some bay or gulf, or the mouth of some river, where by great chance we might have run our boat in, or got under the lee of the land and perhaps made smooth water. But there was nothing like this appeared, but as we made nearer and nearer the shore, the land looked more frightful than the sea.

After we had rowed, or rather driven, about a league and a half as we reckoned it, a raging wave, mountain-like, came rolling astern of us, and plainly bade us expect the *coup de grâce*. In a word, it took us with such a fury that it overset the boat at once, and separating us as well from the boat as from one another, gave us not time hardly to say, "Oh God!" for we were all swallowed up in a moment.

Nothing can describe the confusion of thought which I felt when I sunk into the water, for though I swam very well, yet I could not deliver myself from the waves so as to draw breath, till that wave, having driven me, or rather carried me a vast way on towards the shore, and having spent itself, went back, and left me upon the land almost dry, but half-dead with the water I took in. I had so much presence of mind as well as breath left that seeing myself nearer the mainland than I expected, I got upon my feet and endeavoured to make on towards the land as fast as I could, before another wave should return and take me up again. But I soon found it was impossible to avoid it, for I saw the sea come after me as high as a great hill, and as furious as an enemy which I had no means or strength to contend with; my business was to hold my breath, and raise myself upon the water, if I could, and so by swimming to preserve my breathing, and pilot myself towards the shore, if possible, my greatest concern now being that the sea, as it would carry me a great way towards the shore when it came on, might not carry me back again with it when it gave back towards the sea.

The wave that came upon me again buried me at once twenty or thirty foot deep in its own body, and I could feel myself carried with a mighty force and swiftness towards the shore a very great way, but I held my breath and assisted myself to swim still forwards with all my might. I was ready to burst with holding my breath, when, as I felt myself rising up, so to my immediate relief I found my head and hands shoot out above the surface of the water, and though it was not two seconds of time that I could keep myself so, yet it relieved me greatly, gave me breath and new courage. I was covered again with water a good while, but not so long but I held it out, and finding the water had spent itself and began to return, I struck forwards against the return of the waves, and felt ground again with my foot. I stood still a few moments to recover breath, and till the water went from me, and then took to my heels, and ran with what strength I had further towards the shore. But neither would this deliver me from the fury of the sea, which came pouring in after me again, and twice more I was lifted up by the waves and carried forwards as before, the shore being very flat.

The last time of these two had well near been fatal to me, for the sea, having hurried me along as before, landed me, or rather dashed me against a piece of a rock, and that with such force as it left me senseless, and indeed helpless as to my own deliverance; for the blow, taking my side and breast, beat the breath as it were quite out of my body, and had it returned again immediately, I must have been strangled in the water – but I recovered a little before the return of the waves, and seeing I should be covered again with the water, I resolved to hold fast by a piece of the rock, and so to hold my breath, if possible, till the wave went back. Now as the waves were not so high as at first, being nearer land, I held my hold till the wave abated, and then fetched another run, which brought me so near the shore that the next wave, though it went over me, yet did not so swallow me up as to carry me away, and the next run I took, I got to the mainland, where, to my great comfort, I clambered up the cliffs of the shore and sat me down upon the grass, free from danger and quite out of the reach of the water.

I was now landed and safe onshore, and began to look up and thank God that my life was saved in a case wherein there was some

minutes before scarce any room to hope. I believe it is impossible
to express to the life what the ecstasies and transports of the soul
are when it is so saved, as I may say, out of the very grave, and I do
not wonder now at that custom, namely, that when a malefactor
who has the halter about his neck is tied up, and just going to
be turned off, and has a reprieve brought to him – I say, I do not
wonder that they bring a surgeon with it, to let him blood that
very moment they tell him of it, that the surprise may not drive
the animal spirits from the heart, and overwhelm him:

For sudden joys, like griefs, confound at first.*

I walked about on the shore lifting up my hands, and my whole
being, as I may say, wrapped up in the contemplation of my deliverance, making a thousand gestures and motions which I cannot
describe, reflecting upon all my comrades that were drowned,
and that there should not be one soul saved but myself, for, as for
them, I never saw them afterwards, or any sign of them, except
three of their hats, one cap and two shoes that were not fellows.

I cast my eyes to the stranded vessel – when the breach and froth
of the sea being so big I could hardly see it – it lay so far off, and
considered, Lord! – how was it possible I could get onshore?

After I had solaced my mind with the comfortable part of my
condition, I began to look round me to see what kind of place
I was in, and what was next to be done, and I soon found my
comforts abate, and that in a word I had a dreadful deliverance:
for I was wet, had no clothes to shift me, nor anything either to
eat or drink to comfort me; neither did I see any prospect before
me but that of perishing with hunger or being devoured by wild
beasts, and that which was particularly afflicting to me was that
I had no weapon either to hunt and kill any creature for my

sustenance, or to defend myself against any other creature that might desire to kill me for theirs. In a word, I had nothing about me but a knife, a tobacco pipe and a little tobacco in a box – this was all my provision, and this threw me into terrible agonies of mind, that for a while I ran about like a madman. Night coming upon me, I began with a heavy heart to consider what would be my lot if there were any ravenous beasts in that country, seeing at night they always come abroad for their prey.

All the remedy that offered to my thoughts at that time was to get up into a thick bushy tree like a fir, but thorny, which grew near me, and where I resolved to sit all night, and consider the next day what death I should die, for as yet I saw no prospect of life; I walked about a furlong from the shore to see if I could find any fresh water to drink, which I did, to my great joy; and having drunk and put a little tobacco in my mouth to prevent hunger, I went to the tree and, getting up into it, endeavoured to place myself so as that if I should sleep I might not fall; and having cut me a short stick, like a truncheon, for my defence, I took up my lodging; and having been excessively fatigued, I fell fast asleep and slept as comfortably as, I believe, few could have done in my condition, and found myself the most refreshed with it that I think I ever was on such an occasion.

WHEN I WAKED, IT WAS BROAD DAY, the weather clear and the storm abated, so that the sea did not rage and swell as before – but that which surprised me most was that the ship was lifted off in the night from the sand where she lay by the swelling of the tide, and was driven up almost as far as the rock which I first mentioned, where I had been so bruised by the dashing me against it; this being within about a mile from the shore where I was, and the ship seeming to stand upright still, I wished myself on board, that at least I might save some necessary things for my use.

When I came down from my apartment in the tree, I looked about me again, and the first thing I found was the boat, which lay as the wind and the sea had tossed her up upon the land, about two miles on my right hand. I walked as far as I could upon the shore to have got to her, but found a neck or inlet of water between me and the boat, which was about half a mile broad, so I came back for the present, being more intent upon getting at the ship, where I hoped to find something for my present subsistence.

A little after noon I found the sea very calm, and the tide ebbed so far out that I could come within a quarter of a mile of the ship, and here I found a fresh renewing of my grief, for I saw evidently that if we had kept on board we had been all safe – that is to say, we had all got safe onshore, and I had not been so miserable as to be left entirely destitute of all comfort and company, as I now was. This forced tears from my eyes again, but as there was little relief in that, I resolved, if possible, to get to the ship; so I pulled off my clothes, for the weather was hot to extremity, and took the water, but when I came to the ship, my difficulty was still greater to know how to get on board, for as she lay aground and high out of the water, there was nothing within my reach to lay hold of. I swam round her twice, and the second time I spied a small piece of rope, which I wondered I did not see at first, hang down by the fore chains so low as that with great difficulty I got hold of it, and by the help of that rope got up into the forecastle of the ship. Here I found that the ship was bulged,* and had a great deal of water in her hold, but that she lay so on the side of a bank of hard sand, or rather earth, that her stern lay lifted up upon the bank, and her head low almost to the water; by this means all her quarter was free, and all that was in that part was dry; for you may be sure my first work was to search and to see what was spoilt and what was free, and first I found that all the ship's provisions were dry and untouched by the water, and being very well disposed to eat, I went to the bread room and filled my pockets with biscuit, and ate it as I went about other things, for I had no time to lose. I also found some rum in the great cabin, of which I took a large dram, and which I had indeed need enough of to spirit me for what was before me. Now I wanted nothing but a boat to furnish myself with many things which I foresaw would be very necessary to me.

It was in vain to sit still and wish for what was not to be had, and this extremity roused my application. We had several spare yards, and two or three large spars of wood, and a spare topmast or two in the ship; I resolved to fall to work with these, and I flung as many of them overboard as I could manage for their weight, tying every one with a rope that they might not drive away. When this was done I went down the ship's side, and pulling them to me, I tied four of them fast together at both ends as well as I could in the form of a raft, and laying two or three short pieces of plank upon them crossways, I found I could walk upon it very well, but that it was not able to bear any great weight, the pieces being too light; so I went to work, and with the carpenter's saw I cut a spare topmast into three lengths and added them to my raft, with a great deal of labour and pains, but hope of furnishing myself with necessaries encouraged me to go beyond what I should have been able to have done upon another occasion.

My raft was now strong enough to bear any reasonable weight; my next care was what to load it with, and how to preserve what I laid upon it from the surf of the sea, but I was not long considering this. I first laid all the planks or boards upon it that I could get, and having considered well what I most wanted, I first got three of the seamen's chests, which I had broken open and emptied, and lowered them down upon my raft; the first of these I filled with provision, namely, bread, rice, three Dutch cheeses, five pieces of dried goat's flesh, which we lived much upon, and a little remainder of European corn which had been laid by for some fowls which we brought to sea with us, but the fowls were killed. There had been some barley and wheat together, but to my great disappointment, I found afterwards that the rats had eaten or spoilt it all; as for liquors, I found several cases of bottles belonging to our skipper, in which were some cordial waters, and in all about five or six gallons of rack; these I stowed by themselves, there being no need to put them into the chest, nor no room for them. While I was doing this, I found the tide began to flow, though very calm, and I had the mortification to see my coat, shirt and waistcoat, which I had left onshore upon the sand, swim away; as for my breeches, which were only linen and open-kneed, I swam on board in them and my stockings. However, this put me upon rummaging for clothes, of which I found enough, but took no more than I wanted for present use, for I had other things which my eye was more upon, as first tools to work with onshore, and it was after long searching that I found out the carpenter's chest, which was indeed a very useful prize to me, and much more valuable than a ship loading of gold would have been at that time. I got it down to my raft, even whole as it was, without losing time to look into it, for I knew in general what it contained.

My next care was for some ammunition and arms; there were two very good fowling pieces in the great cabin, and two pistols; these I secured first, with some powder horns and a small bag of shot, and two old rusty swords. I knew there were three barrels of powder in the ship, but knew not where our gunner had stowed them – but with much search I found them, two of them dry and good, the third had taken water; those two I got to my raft, with the arms, and now I thought myself pretty well freighted, and began to think how I should get to shore with them, having neither sail, oar or rudder, and the least capful of wind would have overset all my navigation.

I had three encouragements: 1. a smooth, calm sea; 2. the tide rising, and setting in to the shore; 3. what little wind there was blew me towards the land; and thus, having found two or three broken oars belonging to the boat, and besides the tools which were in the chest, I found two saws, an axe and a hammer, and with this cargo I put to sea. For a mile or thereabouts, my raft went very well, only that I found it drive a little distant from the place where I had landed before, by which I perceived that there was some indraught of the water, and consequently I hoped to find some creek or river there which I might make use of as a port to get to land with my cargo.

As I imagined, so it was; there appeared before me a little opening of the land, and I found a strong current of the tide set into it, so I guided my raft as well as I could to keep in the middle of the stream. But here I had like to have suffered a second shipwreck, which, if I had, I think verily would have broke my heart, for knowing nothing of the coast, my raft ran aground at one end of it upon a shoal, and not being aground at the other end, it wanted but a little that all my cargo had slipped off towards that end that was afloat, and so fallen into the water. I did my utmost by setting my back against the chests to keep them in their places, but could not thrust off the raft with all my strength, neither durst I stir from the posture I was in, but holding up the chests with all my might, stood in that manner near half an hour, in which time the rising of the water brought me a little more upon a level, and a little after, the water still rising, my raft floated again, and I thrust her off with the oar I had into the channel, and then driving up higher, I at length found myself in the mouth of a little river, with land on both sides, and a strong current or tide running up. I looked on both sides for a proper place to get to shore, for I was not willing to be driven too high up the river, hoping in time to see some ship at sea, and therefore resolved to place myself as near the coast as I could.

At length I spied a little cove on the right shore of the creek, to which with great pain and difficulty I guided my raft, and at last got so near as that, reaching ground with my oar, I could thrust her directly in, but here I had like to have dipped all my cargo in the sea again, for that shore lying pretty steep, that is to say sloping, there was no place to land but where one end of my float, if it run onshore, would lie so high, and the other sink lower as before, that it would endanger my cargo again. All that I could do was to wait till the tide was at the highest, keeping the raft with my oar like an anchor to hold the side of it fast to the shore, near a flat piece of ground, which I expected the water would flow over – and so it did. As soon as I found water enough, for my raft drew about a foot of water, I thrust her on upon that flat piece of ground, and there fastened or moored her by sticking my two broken oars into the ground, one on one side near one end, and one on the other side near the other end, and thus I lay till the water ebbed away, and left my raft and all my cargo safe onshore.

My next work was to view the country and seek a proper place for my habitation, and where to stow my goods to secure them from whatever might happen. Where I was, I yet knew not, whether on the continent or on an island, whether inhabited or not inhabited, whether in danger of wild beasts or not. There was a hill not above a mile from me, which rose up very steep and high, and which seemed to overtop some other hills, which lay as in a ridge from it northwards; I took out one of the fowling pieces and one of the pistols, and a horn of powder, and thus armed I travelled for discovery up to the top of that hill, where, after I had with great labour and difficulty got to the top, I saw my fate to my great affliction, namely, that I was in an island environed every way with the sea, no land to be seen, except some rocks which lay a great way off, and two small islands less than this, which lay about three leagues to the west.

I found also that the island I was in was barren, and, as I saw good reason to believe, uninhabited except by wild beasts, of whom, however, I saw none; yet I saw abundance of fowls, but knew not their kinds, neither when I killed them could I tell what was fit for food and what not. At my coming back, I shot at a great bird which I saw sitting upon a tree on the side of a great wood. I believe it was the first gun that had been fired there since the creation of the world; I had no sooner fired, but from all the parts of the wood there arose an innumerable number of fowls of many sorts making a confused screaming, and crying every one according to his usual note, but not one of them of any kind that I knew. As for the creature I killed, I took it to be a kind of a hawk, its colour and beak resembling it, but had no talons or claws more than common; its flesh was carrion, and fit for nothing.

Contented with this discovery, I came back to my raft, and fell to work to bring my cargo onshore, which took me up the rest of that day, and what to do with myself at night I knew not, nor indeed where to rest, for I was afraid to lie down on the ground, not knowing but some wild beast might devour me; though, as I afterwards found, there was really no need for those fears.

However, as well as I could, I barricaded myself round with the chests and boards that I had brought onshore, and made a kind of a hut for that night's lodging; as for food, I yet saw not which way to supply myself, except that I had seen two or three creatures like hares run out of the wood where I shot the fowl.

I now began to consider that I might yet get a great many things out of the ship, which would be useful to me, and particularly some of the rigging and sails, and such other things as might come to land, and I resolved to make another voyage on board the vessel, if possible, and as I knew that the first storm that blew must necessarily break her all in pieces, I resolved to set all other things apart, till I got everything out of the ship that I could get. Then I called a council – that is to say, in my thoughts – whether I should take back the raft, but this appeared impracticable, so I resolved to go as before, when the tide was down, and I did so, only that I stripped before I went from my hut, having nothing on but a chequered shirt and a pair of linen drawers, and a pair of pumps on my feet.

I got on board the ship as before, and prepared a second raft, and having had experience of the first, I neither made this so unwieldy, nor loaded it so hard, but yet I brought away several things very useful to me: as first, in the carpenter's stores I found two or three bags full of nails and spikes, a great screw jack, a dozen or two of hatchets, and above all, that most useful thing called a grindstone; all these I secured together, with several things belonging to the gunner, particularly two or three iron crows and two barrels of musket bullets, seven muskets and another fowling piece, with some small quantity of powder more, a large bag full of small shot and a great roll of sheet lead. But this last was so heavy I could not hoist it up to get it over the ship's side.

Besides these things, I took all the men's clothes that I could find, and a spare fore-topsail, a hammock and some bedding, and with this I loaded my second raft, and brought them all safe onshore to my very great comfort.

I was under some apprehensions during my absence from the land that at least my provisions might be devoured onshore, but when I came back, I found no sign of any visitor, only there sat a creature like a wild cat upon one of the chests, which when I came towards it, ran away a little distance and then stood still; she sat very composed and unconcerned, and looked full in my face, as if she had a mind to be acquainted with me. I presented my gun at her, but as she did not understand it, she was perfectly unconcerned at it, nor did she offer to stir away, upon which I tossed her a bit of biscuit – though, by the way, I was not very free of it, for my store was not great. However, I spared her a bit, I say, and she went to it, smelt of it, and ate it, and looked (as pleased) for more, but I thanked her, and could spare no more, so she marched off.

Having got my second cargo onshore – though I was fain to open the barrels of powder and bring them by parcels, for they were too heavy, being large casks – I went to work to make me a little tent with the sail and some poles which I cut for that purpose, and into this tent I brought everything that I knew would spoil, either with rain or sun, and I piled all the empty chests and casks up in a circle round the tent, to fortify it from any sudden attempt, either from man or beast.

When I had done this, I blocked up the door of the tent with some boards within, and an empty chest set up on end without, and spreading one of the beds upon the ground, laying my two pistols just at my head, and my gun at length by me, I went to bed for the first time, and slept very quietly all night, for I was very weary and heavy, for the night before I had slept little, and had laboured very hard all day, as well to fetch all those things from the ship as to get them onshore.

I had the biggest magazine of all kinds now that ever were laid up, I believe, for one man, but I was not satisfied still, for while the ship sat upright in that posture, I thought I ought to get everything out of her that I could; so every day at low water I went on board, and brought away something or other. But particularly the third time I went, I brought away as much of the rigging as I could, as also all the small ropes and rope twine I could get, with a piece of spare canvas, which was to mend the sails upon occasion, and the barrel of wet gunpowder – in a word, I brought away all the sails first and last, only that I was fain to cut them in pieces, and bring as much at a time as I could, for they were no more useful to be sails, but as mere canvas only.

But that which comforted me more still was that at last of all, after I had made five or six such voyages as these, and thought

I had nothing more to expect from the ship that was worth my meddling with – I say, after all this, I found a great hogshead of bread and three large runlets of rum or spirits, and a box of sugar, and a barrel of fine flour. This was surprising to me, because I had given over expecting any more provisions, except what was spoilt by the water; I soon emptied the hogshead of that bread, and wrapped it up parcel by parcel in pieces of the sails, which I cut out – and in a word, I got all this safe onshore also.

The next day I made another voyage, and now having plundered the ship of what was portable and fit to hand out, I began with the cables, and cutting the great cable into pieces, such as I could move, I got two cables and a hawser onshore, with all the ironwork I could get, and having cut down the spritsail yard, and the mizzen yard, and everything I could to make a large raft, I loaded it with all those heavy goods, and came away. But my good luck began now to leave me, for this raft was so unwieldy, and so overloaden, that after I was entered the little cove – where I had landed the rest of my goods, not being able to guide it so handily as I did the other – it overset, and threw me and all my cargo into the water; as for myself it was no great harm, for I was near the shore, but as to my cargo, it was great part of it lost, especially the iron, which I expected would have been of great use to me. However, when the tide was out, I got most of the pieces of the cable ashore, and some of the iron, though with infinite labour, for I was fain to dip for it into the water, a work which fatigued me very much. After this I went every day on board, and brought away what I could get.

I had been now thirteen days onshore, and had been eleven times on board the ship, in which time I had brought away all that one pair of hands could well be supposed capable to bring – though I believe verily, had the calm weather held, I should have brought away the whole ship piece by piece. But preparing the twelfth time to go on board, I found the wind begin to rise – however, at low water I went on board, and though I thought I had rummaged the cabin so effectually as that nothing more could be found, yet I discovered a locker with drawers in it, in one of which I found two or three razors, and one pair of large scissors, with some ten or a dozen of good knives and forks; in another I found about thirty-six pounds value in money, some European coin, some Brazil, some pieces of eight, some gold, some silver.

I smiled to myself at the sight of this money. "O drug!" said I aloud, "what art thou good for? Thou art not worth to me, no, not the taking off of the ground; one of those knives is worth all this heap; I have no manner of use for thee, e'en remain where thou art, and go to the bottom as a creature whose life is not worth saving." However, upon second thoughts, I took it away, and wrapping all this in a piece of canvas, I began to think of making another raft, but while I was preparing this, I found the sky overcast, and the wind began to rise, and in a quarter of an hour it blew a fresh gale from the shore. It presently occurred to me that it was in vain to pretend to make a raft with the wind offshore, and that it was my business to be gone before the tide of flood began, otherwise I might not be able to reach the shore at all. Accordingly I let myself down into the water, and swam across the channel which lay between the ship and the sands, and even that with difficulty enough, partly with the weight of the things I had about me, and partly the roughness of the water, for the wind rose very hastily, and before it was quite high water it blew a storm.

But I was gotten home to my little tent, where I lay with all my wealth about me very secure. It blew very hard all that night, and in the morning, when I looked out, behold, no more ship was to be seen; I was a little surprised, but recovered myself with this satisfactory reflection, namely, that I had lost no time, nor abated no diligence to get everything out of her that could be useful to me, and that indeed there was little left in her that I was able to bring away if I had had more time.

I now gave over any more thoughts of the ship, or of anything out of her, except what might drive onshore from her wreck, as indeed divers pieces of her afterwards did; but those things were of small use to me.

My thoughts were now wholly employed about securing myself against either savages, if any should appear, or wild beasts, if any were in the island, and I had many thoughts of the method how to do this, and what kind of dwelling to make, whether I should make me a cave in the earth, or a tent upon the earth – and in short, I resolved upon both, the manner and description of which it may not be improper to give an account of.

I soon found the place I was in was not for my settlement, particularly because it was upon a low moorish ground near the sea, and I believed would not be wholesome, and more particularly because there was no fresh water near it, so I resolved to find a more healthy and more convenient spot of ground.

I consulted several things in my situation which I found would be proper for me: first, health and fresh water I just now mentioned; secondly, shelter from the heat of the sun; thirdly, security from ravenous creatures, whether men or beasts; fourthly, a view to the sea, that if God sent any ship in sight, I might not lose any advantage for my deliverance, of which I was not willing to banish all my expectation yet.

In search of a place proper for this, I found a little plain on the side of a rising hill, whose front towards this little plain was steep as a house side, so that nothing could come down upon me from the top; on the side of this rock there was a hollow place worn a little way in like the entrance or door of a cave, but there was not really any cave or way into the rock at all.

On the flat of the green, just before this hollow place, I resolved to pitch my tent. This plain was not above a hundred yards broad, and about twice as long, and lay like a green before my door, and at the end of it descended irregularly every way down into the low grounds by the seaside. It was on the NNW side of the hill, so that I was sheltered from the heat every day, till it came to a W and by S sun, or thereabouts, which in those countries is near the setting.

Before I set up my tent, I drew a half-circle before the hollow place, which took in about ten yards in its semi-diameter from the rock, and twenty yards in its diameter, from its beginning and ending.

In this half-circle I pitched two rows of strong stakes, driving them into the ground till they stood very firm like piles, the biggest end being out of the ground about five foot and a half, and sharpened on the top. The two rows did not stand above six inches from one another.

Then I took the pieces of cable which I had cut in the ship, and I laid them in rows one upon another, within the circle between these two rows of stakes up to the top, placing other stakes in the inside, leaning against them, about two foot and a half high, like a spur to a post, and this fence was so strong that neither man or beast could get into it or over it. This cost me a great deal of time and labour, especially to cut the piles in the woods, bring them to the place, and drive them into the earth.

The entrance into this place I made to be not by a door, but by a short ladder to go over the top – which ladder, when I was in, I lifted over after me, and so I was completely fenced in and fortified, as I thought, from all the world, and consequently slept secure in the night, which otherwise I could not have done; though, as it appeared afterwards, there was no need of all this caution from the enemies that I apprehended danger from.

Into this fence or fortress, with infinite labour, I carried all my riches, all my provisions, ammunition and stores – of which you have the account above – and I made me a large tent, which, to preserve me from the rains that in one part of the year are very violent there, I made double – namely, one smaller tent within, and one larger tent above it; and covered the uppermost with a large tarpaulin which I had saved among the sails.

And now I lay no more for a while in the bed which I had brought onshore, but in a hammock, which was indeed a very good one, and belonged to the mate of the ship.

Into this tent I brought all my provisions, and everything that would spoil by the wet, and having thus enclosed all my goods, I made up the entrance, which till now I had left open, and so passed and repassed, as I said, by a short ladder.

When I had done this, I began to work my way into the rock, and bringing all the earth and stones that I dug down out through my tent, I laid 'em up within my fence in the nature of a terrace, that so it raised the ground within about a foot and a half; and thus I made me a cave just behind my tent, which served me like a cellar to my house.

It cost me much labour and many days before all these things were brought to perfection, and therefore I must go back to some other things which took up some of my thoughts. At the same time it happened, after I had laid my scheme for the setting up my tent and making the cave, that a storm of rain falling from a thick dark cloud, a sudden flash of lightning happened, and after that a great clap of thunder, as is naturally the effect of it; I was not so much surprised with the lightning as I was with a thought which darted into my mind as swift as the lightning itself: Oh my powder! My very heart sunk within me when I thought that at one blast all my powder might be destroyed, on which not my defence only, but the providing my food, as I thought, entirely depended. I was nothing near so anxious about my own danger, though had the powder took fire, I had never known who had hurt me.

Such impression did this make upon me, that after the storm was over I laid aside all my works, my building and fortifying, and applied myself to make bags and boxes to separate the powder, and keep it a little and a little in a parcel, in hope that whatever might come, it might not all take fire at once, and to keep it so apart that it should not be possible to make one part fire another. I finished this work in about a fortnight, and I think my powder, which in all was about 240 pounds' weight, was divided in not less than a hundred parcels; as to the barrel that had been wet, I did not apprehend any danger from that, so I placed it in my new cave, which in my fancy I called my kitchen, and the rest I hid up and down in holes among the rocks, so that no wet might come to it, marking very carefully where I laid it.

In the interval of time while this was doing I went out once at least every day with my gun, as well to divert myself as to see if I could kill anything fit for food, and as near as I could to acquaint myself with what the island produced. The first time I went out I presently discovered that there were goats in the island, which was a great satisfaction to me, but then it was attended with this misfortune to me, namely, that they were so shy, so subtle and so swift of foot that it was the difficultest thing in the world to come at them. But I was not discouraged at this, not doubting but I might now and then shoot one, as it soon happened, for after I had found their haunts a little, I laid wait in this manner for them: I observed if they saw me in the valleys, though they were upon the rocks, they would

DANIEL DEFOE

run away as in a terrible fright, but if they were feeding in the
valleys, and I was upon the rocks, they took no notice of me,
from whence I concluded that by the position of their optics
their sight was so directed downwards that they did not readily see objects that were above them; so afterwards I took this
method – I always climbed the rocks first to get above them, and
then had frequently a fair mark. The first shot I made among
these creatures, I killed a she-goat which had a little kid by her
which she gave suck to, which grieved me heartily, but when
the old one fell, the kid stood stock still by her till I came and
took her up, and not only so, but when I carried the old one
with me upon my shoulders, the kid followed me quite to my
enclosure, upon which I laid down the dam, and took the kid in
my arms, and carried it over my pale, in hopes to have it bred
up tame, but it would not eat, so I was forced to kill it and eat
it myself; these two supplied me with flesh a great while, for I
ate sparingly, and saved my provisions (my bread especially) as
much as possibly I could.

Having now fixed my habitation, I found it absolutely necessary to provide a place to make a fire in, and fuel to burn, and
what I did for that, as also how I enlarged my cave, and what
conveniences I made, I shall give a full account of in its place.
But I must first give some little account of myself, and of my
thoughts about living, which it may well be supposed were not
a few.

I had a dismal prospect of my condition, for as I was not
cast away upon that island without being driven, as is said, by
a violent storm quite out of the course of our intended voyage,
and a great way, namely, some hundreds of leagues, out of the
ordinary course of the trade of mankind, I had great reason to
consider it as a determination of Heaven that in this desolate

place and in this desolate manner I should end my life. The tears would run plentifully down my face when I made these reflections, and sometimes I would expostulate with myself why Providence should thus completely ruin its creatures and render them so absolutely miserable, so without help abandoned, so entirely depressed, that it could hardly be rational to be thankful for such a life.

But something always returned swift upon me to check these thoughts and to reprove me, and particularly one day, walking with my gun in my hand by the seaside, I was very pensive upon the subject of my present condition, when reason as it were expostulated with me t'other way thus: Well, you are in a desolate condition, 'tis true, but pray remember, where are the rest of you? Did not you come eleven of you into the boat? Where are the ten? Why were not they saved and you lost? Why were you singled out? Is it better to be here or there? And then I pointed to the sea. All evils are to be considered with the good that is in them, and with what worse attends them.

Then it occurred to me again, how well I was furnished for my subsistence, and what would have been my case if it had not happened, *which was a hundred thousand to one*, that the ship floated from the place where she first struck and was driven so near to the shore that I had time to get all these things out of her. What would have been my case if I had been to have lived in the condition in which I at first came onshore, without necessaries of life, or necessaries to supply and procure them? "Particularly," said I aloud (though to myself), "what should I ha' done without a gun, without ammunition, without any tools to make anything or to work with, without clothes, bedding, a tent or any manner of covering?" and that now I had all these to a sufficient quantity, and was in a fair way to provide myself in such a manner as to live without my gun when my ammunition was spent, so that I had a tolerable view of subsisting without any want as long as I lived, for I considered from the beginning how I would provide for the accidents that might happen, and for the time that was to come, even not only after my ammunition should be spent, but even after my health and strength should decay.

I confess I had not entertained any notion of my ammunition being destroyed at one blast, I mean my powder being blown up by lightning, and this made the thoughts of it so surprising to me when it lightened and thundered, as I observed just now.

And now being to enter into a melancholy relation of a scene of silent life, such perhaps as was never heard of in the world before, I shall take it from its beginning, and continue it in its order. It was, by my account, the 30th of September when, in the manner as above said, I first set foot upon this horrid island, when the sun being, to us, in its autumnal equinox, was almost just over my head, for I reckoned myself by observation to be in the latitude of nine degrees twenty-two minutes north of the line.

After I had been there about ten or twelve days, it came into my thoughts that I should lose my reckoning of time for want of books and pen and ink, and should even forget the sabbath days from the working days, but to prevent this I cut it with my knife upon a large post, in capital letters, and making it into a great cross I set it up on the shore where I first landed: namely, "I came onshore here on the 30th of Sept. 1659." Upon the sides of this square post I cut every day a notch with my knife, and every seventh notch was as long again as the rest, and every first day of the month as long again as that long one, and thus I kept my calendar, or weekly, monthly and yearly reckoning of time.

In the next place we are to observe that among the many things which I brought out of the ship in the several voyages, which, as above mentioned, I made to it, I got several things of less value, but not at all less useful to me, which I omitted setting down before – as in particular, pens, ink and paper, several parcels in the Captain's, mate's, gunner's and carpenter's keeping, three or four compasses, some mathematical instruments, dials, prospectives, charts and books of navigation, all which I huddled together, whether I might want them or no; also I found three very good Bibles which came to me in my cargo from England, and which I had packed up among my things; some Portuguese books also, and among them two or three popish prayer books, and several other books, all which I carefully secured. And I must not forget that we had in the ship a dog and two cats, of whose eminent history I may have occasion to say something in its place, for I carried both the cats with me, and as for the dog, he jumped out of the ship of himself and swam onshore to me the day after I went onshore with my first cargo, and was a trusty servant to me many years. I wanted nothing that he could fetch me, nor any company that he could make up to me, I only wanted to have him talk to me, but that would not do. As I observed before, I found pen, ink and paper, and I husbanded them to the utmost, and I shall show that while my ink lasted, I kept things very exact, but after that was gone I could not, for I could not make any ink by any means that I could devise.

And this put me in mind that I wanted many things, notwithstanding all that I had amassed together, and of these, this of ink was one, as also spade, pickaxe and shovel to dig or remove the earth, needles, pins and thread; as for linen, I soon learnt to want that without much difficulty.

This want of tools made every work I did go on heavily, and it was near a whole year before I had entirely finished my little pale or surrounded habitation. The piles or stakes, which were as heavy as I could well lift, were a long time in cutting and preparing in the woods, and more by far in bringing home, so that I spent sometimes two days in cutting and bringing home one of those posts, and a third day in driving it into the ground, for which purpose I got a heavy piece of wood at first, but at last bethought myself of one of the iron crows, which however, though I found it, yet it made driving those posts or piles very laborious and tedious work.

But what need I ha' been concerned at the tediousness of anything I had to do, seeing I had time enough to do it in? Nor had I any other employment if that had been over, at least that I could foresee, except the ranging the island to seek for food, which I did more or less every day.

I now began to consider seriously my condition, and the circumstances I was reduced to, and I drew up the state of my affairs in writing, not so much to leave them to any that were to come after me – for I was like to have but few heirs – as to deliver my thoughts from daily poring upon them and afflicting my mind, and as my reason began now to master my despondency, I began to comfort myself as well as I could, and to set the good against the evil, that I might have something to distinguish my case from worse, and I stated it very impartially, like debtor and creditor, the comforts I enjoyed against the miseries I suffered, thus:

EVIL	GOOD
I am cast upon a horrible desolate island, void of all hope of recovery.	*But I am alive, and not drowned as all my ship's company was…*
I am singled out and separated, as it were, from all the world, to be miserable.	*But I am singled out too from all the ship's crew to be spared from death, and He that miraculously saved me from death can deliver me from this condition.*
I am divided from mankind, a solitaire, one banished from humane society.	*But I am not starved and perishing on a barren place, affording no sustenance.*
I have not clothes to cover me.	*But I am in a hot climate, where if I had clothes I could hardly wear them.*
I am without any defence or means to resist any violence of man or beast.	*But I am cast on an island where I see no wild beasts to hurt me, as I saw on the coast of Africa – and what if I had been shipwrecked there?*
I have no soul to speak to, or relieve me.	*But God wonderfully sent the ship in near enough to the shore that I have gotten out so many necessary things as will either supply my wants, or enable me to supply my-self even as long as I live.*

Upon the whole, here was an undoubted testimony that there was scarce any condition in the world so miserable, but there was something negative or something positive to be thankful for in it, and let this stand as a direction from the experience of the most miserable of all conditions in this world that we may always find in it something to comfort ourselves from, and to set in the description of good and evil, on the credit side of the accompt.

Having now brought my mind a little to relish my condition, and given over looking out to sea to see if I could spy a ship – I say, giving over these things, I began to apply myself to accommodate my way of living and to make things as easy to me as I could.

I have already described my habitation, which was a tent under the side of a rock surrounded with a strong pale of posts and cables, but I might now rather call it a wall, for I raised a kind of wall up against it of turfs, about two foot thick on the outside, and after some time – I think it was a year and a half – I raised rafters from it leaning to the rock, and thatched or covered it with bows of trees, and such things as I could get to keep out the rain, which I found at some times of the year very violent.

I have already observed how I brought all my goods into this pale, and into the cave which I had made behind me. But I must observe too that at first this was a confused heap of goods, which as they lay in no order, so they took up all my place; I had no room to turn myself, so I set myself to enlarge my cave and works further into the earth – for it was a loose sandy rock which yielded easily to the labour I bestowed on it – and so when I found I was pretty safe as to beasts of prey, I worked sideways to the right hand into the rock, and then turning to the right again, worked quite out and made me a door to come out on the outside of my pale or fortification.

This gave me not only egress and regress – as it were a back way to my tent and to my storehouse – but gave me room to stow my goods.

And now I began to apply myself to make such necessary things as I found I most wanted, particularly a chair and a table, for without these I was not able to enjoy the few comforts I had in the world; I could not write, or eat, or do several things with so much pleasure without a table.

So I went to work – and here I must needs observe that as reason is the substance and original of the mathematics, so by stating and squaring everything by reason, and by making the most rational judgement of things, every man may be in time master of every mechanic art. I had never handled a tool in my life, and yet in time, by labour, application and contrivance, I found at last that I wanted nothing but I could have made it, especially if I had had tools. However, I made abundance of things, even without tools, and some with no more tools than an adze and a hatchet, which perhaps were never made that way before, and that with infinite labour. For example, if I wanted a board, I had no other way but to cut down a tree, set it on an edge before me, and hew it flat on either side with my axe, till I had brought it to be thin as a plank, and then dub it smooth with my adze. It is true, by this method I could make but one board out of a whole tree, but this I had no remedy for but patience, any more than I had for the prodigious deal of time and labour which it took me up to make a plank or board. But my time or labour was little worth, and so it was as well employed one way as another.

However, I made me a table and a chair, as I observed above, in the first place, and this I did out of the short pieces of boards that I brought on my raft from the ship. But when I had wrought out some boards, as above, I made large shelves of the breadth of a foot and a half, one over another, all along one side of my cave, to lay all my tools, nails and ironwork, and in a word, to separate everything at large in their places, that I must come easily at them; I knocked pieces into the wall of the rock to hang my guns and all things that would hang up.

So that had my cave been to be seen, it looked like a general magazine of all necessary things, and I had everything so ready at my hand that it was a great pleasure to me to see all my goods in such order, and especially to find my stock of all necessaries so great.

And now it was when I began to keep a journal of every day's employment, for indeed at first I was in too much hurry, and not only hurry as to labour, but in too much discomposure of mind, and my journal would ha' been full of many dull things. For example, I must have said thus: "Sept. the 30th. After I got to shore and had escaped drowning, instead of being thankful to God for my deliverance, having first vomited with the great quantity of salt water which was gotten into my stomach, and recovering myself a little, I ran about the shore, wringing my hand and beating my head and face, exclaiming at my misery, and crying out I was undone, undone, till, tired and faint, I was forced to lie down on the ground to repose, but durst not sleep for fear of being devoured."

Some days after this, and after I had been on board the ship and got all that I could out of her, yet I could not forbear getting up to the top of a little mountain and looking out to see in hopes of seeing a ship, then fancy at a vast distance I spied a sail, please myself with the hopes of it, and then after looking steadily till I was almost blind, lose it quite, and sit down and weep like a child, and thus increase my misery by my folly.

But having gotten over these things in some measure, and having settled my household stuff and habitation, made me a table and a chair, and all as handsome about me as I could, I began to keep my journal, of which I shall here give you a copy (though in it will be told all these particulars over again) as long as it lasted, for having no more ink I was forced to leave it off.

THE JOURNAL

SEPTEMBER 30TH, 1659. I, poor miserable Robinson Crusoe, being shipwrecked during a dreadful storm in the offing, came onshore on this dismal unfortunate island, which I called the Island of Despair – all the rest of the ship's company being drowned, and myself almost dead.

All the rest of that day I spent in afflicting myself at the dismal circumstances I was brought to – namely, I had neither food, house, clothes, weapon or place to fly to, and in despair of any relief, saw nothing but death before me, either that I should be devoured by wild beasts, murdered by savages, or starved to death for want of food. At the approach of night, I slept in a tree for fear of wild creatures, but slept soundly though it rained all night.

October 1. In the morning, I saw to my great surprise the ship had floated with the high tide, and was driven onshore again much nearer the island, which, as it was some comfort on one hand, for seeing her sit upright, and not broken to pieces, I hoped, if the wind abated, I might get on board, and get some food and necessaries out of her for my relief, so on the other hand it renewed my grief at the loss of my comrades, who I imagined if we had all stayed on board might have saved the ship, or at least that they would not have been all drowned as they were, and that had the men been saved, we might perhaps have built us a boat out of the ruins of the ship, to have carried us to some other part of the world. I spent great part of this day in perplexing myself on these things, but at length seeing the ship almost dry, I went upon the sand as near as I could, and then swam on board; this day also it continued raining, though with no wind at all.

From the 1st of October to the 24th. All these days entirely spent in many several voyages to get all I could out of the ship, which I brought onshore, every tide of flood, upon rafts. Much rain also in these days, though with some intervals of fair weather – but, it seems, this was the rainy season.

Oct. 20. I overset my raft and all the goods I had got upon it, but being in shoal water, and the things being chiefly heavy, I recovered many of them when the tide was out.

Oct. 25. It rained all night and all day, with some gusts of wind, during which time the ship broke in pieces, the wind blowing a little harder than before, and was no more to be seen, except the wreck of her, and that only at low water. I spent this day in covering and securing the goods which I had saved, that the rain might not spoil them.

Oct. 26. I walked about the shore almost all day to find out a place to fix my habitation, greatly concerned to secure myself from an attack in the night, either from wild beasts or men. Towards night I fixed upon a proper place under a rock, and marked out a semicircle for my encampment, which I resolved to strengthen with a work, wall or fortification made of double piles, lined within with cables, and without with turf.

From the 26th to the 30th. I worked very hard in carrying all my goods to my new habitation, though some part of the time it rained exceeding hard.

The 31st. In the morning I went out into the island with my gun to see for some food, and discover the country, when I killed a she-goat, and her kid followed me home, which I afterwards killed also because it would not feed.

November 1. I set up my tent under a rock, and lay there for the first night, making it as large as I could with stakes driven in to swing my hammock upon.

Nov. 2. I set up all my chests and boards, and the pieces of timber which made my rafts, and with them formed a fence round me, a little within the place I had marked out for my fortification.

Nov. 3. I went out with my gun and killed two fowls like ducks, which were very good food. In the afternoon went to work to make me a table.

Nov. 4. This morning I began to order my times of work, of going out with my gun, time of sleep and time of diversion, namely, every morning I walked out with my gun for two or three hours if it did not rain, then employed myself to work till about eleven o'clock, then ate what I had to live on, and from twelve to two I lay down to sleep, the weather being excessive hot, and then in the evening to work again. The working part of this day and of the next were wholly employed in making my table, for I was yet but a very sorry workman, though time and necessity made me a complete natural mechanic soon after, as I believe it would do anyone else.

Nov. 5. This day went abroad with my gun and my dog, and killed a wild cat, her skin pretty soft, but her flesh good for nothing – every creature I killed I took off the skins and preserved them. Coming back by the seashore, I saw many sorts of sea fowls which I did not understand, but was surprised and almost frighted with two or three seals, which, while I was gazing at, not well knowing what they were, got into the sea and escaped me for that time.

Nov. 6. After my morning walk I went to work with my table again, and finished it, though not to my liking; nor was it long before I learnt to mend it.

Nov. 7. Now it began to be settled fair weather. The 7th, 8th, 9th, 10th and part of the 12th (for the 11th was Sunday) I took wholly up to make me a chair, and with much ado brought it to a tolerable shape, but never to please me, and even in the making I pulled it in pieces several times. *Note*: I soon neglected my keeping Sundays, for omitting my mark for them on my post, I forgot which was which.

Nov. 13. This day it rained, which refreshed me exceedingly, and cooled the earth, but it was accompanied with terrible thunder and lightning, which frighted me dreadfully for fear of my powder; as soon as it was over, I resolved to separate my stock of powder into as many little parcels as possible, that it might not be in danger.

Nov. 14, 15, 16. These three days I spent in making little square chests or boxes, which might hold a pound or two pound, at most, of powder, and so putting the powder in, I stowed it in places as secure and remote from one another as possible. On one of these three days I killed a large bird that was good to eat, but I know not what to call it.

Nov. 17. This day I began to dig behind my tent into the rock to make room for my further conveniency. *Note*: Three things I wanted exceedingly for this work, namely, a pickaxe, a shovel, and a wheelbarrow or basket; so I desisted from my work, and began to consider how to supply that want and make me some tools; as for a pickaxe, I made use of the iron crows, which were proper enough, though heavy, but the next thing was a shovel or spade – this was so absolutely necessary, that indeed I could do nothing effectually without it, but what kind of one to make I knew not.

Nov. 18. The next day in searching the woods I found a tree of that wood, or like it, which in the Brazils they call the iron tree, for its exceeding hardness; of this, with great labour and almost spoiling my axe, I cut a piece, and brought it home too with difficulty enough, for it was exceeding heavy.

The excessive hardness of the wood, and having no other way, made me a long while upon this machine, for I worked it effectually by little and little into the form of a shovel or spade, the handle exactly shaped like ours in England, only that the broad part having no iron shod upon it at bottom, it would not last me so long; however, it served well enough for the uses which I had occasion to put it to, but never was a shovel, I believe, made after that fashion, or so long a making.

I was still deficient, for I wanted a basket or a wheelbarrow: a basket I could not make by any means, having no such things as twigs that would bend to make wicker-ware, at least none yet found out, and as to a wheelbarrow, I fancied I could make all but the wheel, but that I had no notion of, neither did I know how to go about it – besides, I had no possible way to make the iron gudgeons for the spindle or axis of the wheel to run in, so I gave it over, and so for carrying away the earth which I dug out of the cave, I made me a thing like a hod, which the labourers carry mortar in when they serve the bricklayers.

This was not so difficult to me as the making the shovel, and yet this, and the shovel, and the attempt which I made in vain to make a wheelbarrow, took me up no less than four days – I mean, always excepting my morning walk with my gun, which I seldom failed, and very seldom failed also bringing home something fit to eat.

Nov. 23. My other work having now stood still because of my making these tools, when they were finished I went on and, working every day, as my strength and time allowed, I spent eighteen days entirely in widening and deepening my cave, that it might hold my goods commodiously.

Note: During all this time, I worked to make this room or cave spacious enough to accommodate me as a warehouse or magazine, a kitchen, a dining room and a cellar; as for my lodging, I kept to the tent, except that sometimes in the wet season of the year it rained so hard that I could not keep myself dry, which caused me afterwards to cover all my place within my pale with long poles in the form of rafters leaning against the rock, and load them with flags and large leaves of trees like a thatch.

December 10th. I began now to think my cave or vault finished, when on a sudden (it seems I had made it too large) a great quantity of earth fell down from the top and one side, so much that in short it frighted me, and not without reason too, for if I had been under it I had never wanted a grave-digger. Upon this disaster I had a great deal of work to do over again, for I had the loose earth to carry out, and, which was of more importance, I had the ceiling to prop up, so that I might be sure no more would come down.

Dec. 11. This day I went to work with it accordingly, and got two shores or posts pitched upright to the top, with two pieces of boards across over each post – this I finished the next day, and setting more posts up with boards, in about a week more I had the roof secured, and the posts, standing in rows, served me for partitions to part of my house.

Dec. 17. From this day to the twentieth I placed shelves, and knocked up nails on the posts to hang everything up that could be hung up, and now I began to be in some order within doors.

Dec. 20. Now I carried everything into the cave, and began to furnish my house, and set up some pieces of boards like a dresser, to order my victuals upon, but boards began to be very scarce with me – also I made me another table.

Dec. 24. Much rain all night and all day; no stirring out.

Dec. 25. Rain all day.

Dec. 26. No rain, and the earth much cooler than before, and pleasanter.

Dec. 27. Killed a young goat, and lamed another so as that I catched it, and led it home in a string; when I had it home, I bound and splintered up its leg, which was broke. NB I took such care of it that it lived, and the leg grew well, and as strong as ever, but by my nursing it so long it grew tame, and fed upon the little green at my door, and would not go away. This was the first time that I entertained a thought of breeding up some tame creatures, that I might have food when my powder and shot was all spent.

Dec. 28, 29, 30. Great heats and no breeze; so that there was no stirring abroad, except in the evening for food; this time I spent in putting all my things in order within doors.

January 1. Very hot still, but I went abroad early and late with my gun, and lay still in the middle of the day. This evening, going further into the valleys which lay towards the centre of the island, I found there was plenty of goats, though exceeding shy and hard to come at; however, I resolved to try, if I could, not bring my dog to hunt them down.

Jan. 2. Accordingly, the next day I went out with my dog, and set him upon the goats, but I was mistaken, for they all faced about upon the dog, and he knew his danger too well, for he would not come near them.

Jan. 3. I began my fence or wall, which, being still jealous of my being attacked by somebody, I resolved to make very thick and strong.

NB *This wall being described before, I purposely omit what was said in the journal; it is sufficient to observe that I was no less*

*time than from the 3rd of January to the 14th of April, working,
finishing and perfecting this wall, though it was no more than
about twenty-four yards in length, being a half-circle from one
place in the rock to another place about eight yards from it, the
door of the cave being in the centre behind it.*

All this time I worked very hard, the rains hindering me many days,
nay, sometimes weeks together, but I thought I should never be
perfectly secure till this wall was finished, and it is scarce credible
what inexpressible labour everything was done with, especially
the bringing piles out of the woods, and driving them into the
ground, for I made them much bigger than I need to have done.

When this wall was finished, and the outside double-fenced
with a turf wall raised up close to it, I persuaded myself that if
any people were to come onshore there, they would not perceive
anything like a habitation, and it was very well I did so, as may
be observed hereafter upon a very remarkable occasion.

During this time I made my rounds in the woods for game every
day when the rain admitted me, and made frequent discoveries in
these walks of something or other to my advantage. Particularly,
I found a kind of wild pigeons, who built not as wood pigeons in
a tree, but rather as house pigeons in the holes of the rocks, and
taking some young ones, I endeavoured to breed them up tame,
and did so, but when they grew older they flew all away, which
perhaps was at first for want of feeding them, for I had nothing to
give them. However, I frequently found their nests, and got their
young ones, which were very good meat.

And now, in the managing my household affairs, I found myself
wanting in many things, which I thought at first it was impossible
for me to make, as indeed as to some of them it was: for instance,
I could never make a cask to be hooped. I had a small runlet or

two, as I observed before, but I could never arrive to the capacity
of making one by them, though I spent many weeks about it. I
could neither put in the heads, or joint the staves so true to one
another as to make them hold water, so I gave that also over.

In the next place, I was at a great loss for candle, so that as
soon as ever it was dark, which was generally by seven o'clock,
I was obliged to go to bed. I remembered the lump of beeswax
with which I made candles in my African adventure, but I had
none of that now. The only remedy I had was that when I had
killed a goat, I saved the tallow, and with a little dish made of
clay, which I baked in the sun, to which I added a wick of some
oakum, I made me a lamp, and this gave me light, though not a
clear steady light like a candle. In the middle of all my labours it
happened that, rummaging my things, I found a little bag, which,
as I hinted before, had been filled with corn for the feeding of
poultry – not for this voyage, but before, as I suppose, when the
ship came from Lisbon. What little remainder of corn had been
in the bag was all devoured with the rats, and I saw nothing in
the bag but husks and dust, and being willing to have the bag for
some other use, I think it was to put powder in, when I divided
it for fear of the lightning, or some such use, I shook the husks
of corn out of it on one side of my fortification under the rock.

It was a little before the great rains, just now mentioned, that
I threw this stuff away, taking no notice of anything, and not so
much as remembering that I had thrown anything there, when
about a month after, or thereabouts, I saw some few stalks of
something green shooting out of the ground, which I fancied might
be some plant I had not seen, but I was surprised and perfectly
astonished, when, after a little longer time, I saw about ten or
twelve ears come out, which were perfect green barley of the same
kind as our European, nay, as our English barley.

It is impossible to express the astonishment and confusion of my thoughts on this occasion. I had hitherto acted upon no religious foundation at all: indeed, I had very few notions of religion in my head, or had entertained any sense of anything that had befallen me, otherwise than as a chance, or, as we lightly say, what pleases God, without so much as enquiring into the end of Providence in these things, or His order in governing events in the world. But after I saw barley grow there, in a climate which I know was not proper for corn, and especially that I knew not how it came there, it startled me strangely, and I began to suggest that God had miraculously caused this grain to grow without any help of seed sown, and that it was so directed purely for my sustenance on that wild miserable place.

This touched my heart a little, and brought tears out of my eyes, and I began to bless myself that such a prodigy of nature should happen upon my account – and this was the more strange to me, because I saw near it still all along by the side of the rock some other straggling stalks, which proved to be stalks of rice, and which I knew, because I had seen it grow in Africa when I was ashore there.

I not only thought these the pure productions of Providence for my support, but not doubting but that there was more in the place, I went all over that part of the island where I had been before, peering in every corner and under every rock to see for more of it, but I could not find any; at last it occurred to my thoughts that I had shook a bag of chickens' meat out in that place, and then the wonder began to cease, and I must confess my religious thankfulness to God's providence began to abate too, upon the discovering that all this was nothing but what was common, though I ought to have been as thankful for so strange and unforeseen providence as if it had been miraculous, for it was really the work of Providence to me that should order or appoint that ten or twelve grains of corn should remain unspoilt (when the rats had destroyed all the rest) as if it had been dropped from heaven – as also that I should throw it out in that particular place, where, it being in the shade of a high rock, it sprung up immediately, whereas if I had thrown it anywhere else at that time, it had been burnt up and destroyed.

I carefully saved the ears of this corn, you may be sure, in their season – which was about the end of June – and laying up every corn, I resolved to sow them all again, hoping in time to have some quantity sufficient to supply me with bread. But it was not till the fourth year that I could allow myself the least grain of this corn to eat, and even then but sparingly, as I shall say afterwards in its order, for I lost all that I sowed the first season by not observing the proper time, for I sowed it just before the dry season, so that it never came up at all, at least not as it would ha' done – of which in its place.

Besides this barley, there was, as above, twenty or thirty stalks of rice, which I preserved with the same care, and whose use was of the same kind or to the same purpose, namely, to make me bread, or rather food, for I found ways to cook it up without baking, though I did that also after some time. But to return to my journal.

I worked excessive hard these three or four months to get my wall done, and the 14th of April I closed it up, contriving to go into it not by a door, but over the wall by a ladder, that there might be no sign in the outside of my habitation.

April 16. I finished the ladder, so I went up with the ladder to the top, and then pulled it up after me, and let it down in the inside. This was a complete enclosure to me, for within I had room enough, and nothing could come at me from without, unless it could first mount my wall.

The very next day after this wall was finished, I had almost had all my labour overthrown at once, and myself killed. The case was thus: as I was busy in the inside of it, behind my tent, just in the entrance into my cave, I was terribly frighted with a most dreadful surprising thing indeed, for all on a sudden I found the earth come crumbling down from the roof of my cave, and from the edge of the hill over my head, and two of the posts I had set up in the cave cracked in a frightful manner. I was heartily scared, but thought nothing of what was really the cause, only thinking that the top of my cave was falling in, as some of it had done before, and for fear I should be buried in it I ran forwards to my ladder, and not thinking myself safe there neither, I got over my wall for fear of the pieces of the hill which I expected might roll down upon me: I was no sooner stepped down upon the firm ground but I plainly saw it was a terrible earthquake, for the ground I stood on shook three times at about eight minutes' distance, with three such shocks as would have overturned the strongest building that could be supposed to have stood on the earth, and a great piece of the top of a rock, which stood about half a mile from me next the sea, fell down with such a terrible noise as I never heard in all my life. I perceived also the very sea was put into violent motion by it, and I believe the shocks were stronger under the water than on the island.

I was so amazed with the thing itself, having never felt the like, or discoursed with anyone that had, that I was like one dead or stupefied, and the motion of the earth made my stomach sick like one that was tossed at sea, but the noise of the falling of the rock awaked me, as it were, and rousing me from the stupefied condition I was in, filled me with horror, and I thought of nothing then but the hill falling upon my tent and all my household goods and burying all at once, and this sunk my very soul within me a second time.

After the third shock was over, and I felt no more for some time, I began to take courage, and yet I had not heart enough to go over my wall again, for fear of being buried alive, but sat still upon the ground, greatly cast down and disconsolate, not knowing what to do. All this while I had not the least serious religious thought, nothing but the common *Lord ha' mercy upon me*, and when it was over that went away too.

While I sat thus I found the air overcast and grow cloudy as if it would rain; soon after that the wind rose by little and little, so that in less than half an hour it blew a most dreadful hurricane. The sea was all on a sudden covered over with foam and froth, the shore was covered with the breach of the water, the trees were torn up by the roots, and a terrible storm it was, and this held about three hours, and then began to abate, and in two hours more it was stark calm, and began to rain very hard.

All this while I sat upon the ground very much terrified and dejected, when on a sudden it came into my thoughts that these winds and rain being the consequences of the earthquake, the earthquake itself was spent and over, and I might venture into my cave again. With this thought my spirits began to revive, and the rain also helping to persuade me, I went in and sat down in my tent, but the rain was so violent that my tent was ready to be beaten down with it, and I was forced to go into my cave, though very much afraid and uneasy for fear it should fall on my head.

This violent rain forced me to a new work, namely, to cut a hole through my new fortification like a sink to let the water go out, which would else have drowned my cave. After I had been in my cave some time, and found still no more shocks of the earthquake follow, I began to be more composed, and now to support my spirits, which indeed wanted it very much, I went to my little store and took a small sup of rum, which, however, I did then and always very sparingly, knowing I could have no more when that was gone.

It continued raining all that night, and great part of the next day, so that I could not stir abroad, but my mind being more composed, I began to think of what I had best do, concluding that if the island was subject to these earthquakes, there would be no living for me in a cave, but I must consider of building me some little hut in an open place which I might surround with a wall as I had done here, and so make myself secure from wild beasts or men, for I concluded if I stayed where I was, I should certainly, one time or other, be buried alive.

With these thoughts I resolved to remove my tent from the place where it stood, which was just under the hanging precipice of the hill, and which, if it should be shaken again, would certainly fall upon my tent. And I spent the next two days, being the 19th and 20th of April, in contriving where and how to remove my habitation.

The fear of being swallowed up alive made me that I never slept in quiet, and yet the apprehensions of lying abroad without any fence was almost equal to it; but still,++ when I looked about and saw how everything was put in order, how pleasantly concealed I was, and how safe from danger, it made me very loath to remove.

In the meantime it occurred to me that it would require a vast deal of time for me to do this, and that I must be contented to run the venture where I was, till I had formed a camp for myself, and had secured it so as to remove to it; so with this resolution I composed myself for a time, and resolved that I would go to work with all speed to build me a wall with piles and cables, etc., in a circle as before, and set my tent up in it when it was finished, but that I would venture to stay where I was till it was finished and fit to remove to. This was the 21st.

April 22. The next morning I began to consider of means to put this resolve in execution, but I was at a great loss about my tools. I had three large axes and abundance of hatchets (for we carried the hatchets for traffic with the Indians), but with much chopping and cutting knotty hard wood, they were all full of notches and dull, and though I had a grindstone, I could not turn it and grind my tools too; this cost me as much thought as a statesman would have bestowed upon a grand point of politics, or a judge upon the life and death of a man. At length I contrived a wheel with a string, to turn it with my foot, that I might have both my hands at liberty. *Note*: I had never seen any such thing in England, or at least not to take notice how it was done, though since I have observed it is very common there – besides that, my grindstone was very large and heavy. This machine cost me a full week's work to bring it to perfection.

April 28, 29. These two whole days I took up in grinding my tools, my machine for turning my grindstone performing very well.

April 30. Having perceived my bread had been low a great while, now I took a survey of it, and reduced myself to one biscuit cake a day, which made my heart very heavy.

May 1. In the morning, looking towards the seaside, the tide being low, I saw something lie on the shore bigger than ordinary, and it looked like a cask; when I came to it, I found a small barrel, and two or three pieces of the wreck of the ship which were driven onshore by the late hurricane and, looking towards the wreck itself, I thought it seemed to lie higher out of the water than it used to do. I examined the barrel which was driven onshore, and soon found it was a barrel of gunpowder, but it had taken water, and the powder was caked as hard as a stone; however, I rolled it further onshore for the present, and went on upon the sands as near as I could to the wreck of the ship to look for more.

WHEN I CAME DOWN TO THE SHIP, I found it strangely removed. The forecastle, which lay before buried in sand, was heaved up at least six foot, and the stern, which was broke to pieces and parted from the rest by the force of the sea soon after I had left rummaging her, was tossed, as it were, up, and cast on one side, and the sand was thrown so high on that side next her stern that whereas there was a great place of water before, so that I could not come within a quarter of a mile of the wreck without swimming, I could now walk quite up to her when the tide was out. I was surprised with this at first, but soon concluded it must be done by the earthquake, and as by this violence the ship was more broken open than formerly, so many things came daily onshore which the sea had loosened, and which the winds and water rolled by degrees to the land.

This wholly diverted my thoughts from the design of removing my habitation, and I busied myself mightily, that day especially, in searching whether I could make any way into the ship, but I found nothing was to be expected of that kind, for that all the inside of the ship was choked up with sand. However, as I had learnt not to despair of anything, I resolved to pull everything to pieces that I could of the ship, concluding that everything I could get from her would be of some use or other to me.

May 3. I began with my saw and cut a piece of beam through, which I thought held some of the upper part or quarterdeck together, and when I had cut it through, I cleared away the sand as well as I could from the side which lay highest, but the tide coming in, I was obliged to give over for that time.

May 4. I went a-fishing, but caught not one fish that I durst eat of, till I was weary of my sport, when just going to leave off, I caught a young dolphin. I had made me a long line of some rope yarn, but I had no hooks, yet I frequently caught fish enough, as much as I cared to eat, all which I dried in the sun, and ate them dry.

May 5. Worked on the wreck, cut another beam asunder, and brought three great fir planks off from the decks, which I tied together, and made swim onshore when the tide of flood came on.

May 6. Worked on the wreck, got several iron bolts out of her, and other pieces of ironwork; worked very hard, and came home very much tired, and had thoughts of giving it over.

May 7. Went to the wreck again, but with an intent not to work, but found the weight of the wreck had broke itself down, the beams being cut, that several pieces of the ship seemed to lie loose, and the inside of the hold lay so open that I could see into it, but almost full of water and sand.

May 8. Went to the wreck, and carried an iron crow to wrench up the deck, which lay now quite clear of the water or sand. I wrenched open two planks, and brought them onshore also with the tide; I left the iron crow in the wreck for next day.

May 9. Went to the wreck, and with the crow made way into the body of the wreck, and felt several casks, and loosened them with the crow, but could not break them up. I felt also a roll of English lead, and could stir it, but it was too heavy to remove.

May 10, 11, 12, 13, 14. Went every day to the wreck, and got a great deal of pieces of timber, and boards, or plank, and two or three hundredweight of iron.

May 15. I carried two hatchets to try if I could not cut a piece off of the roll of lead by placing the edge of one hatchet and driving it with the other, but as it lay about a foot and a half in the water, I could not make any blow to drive the hatchet.

May 16. It had blowed hard in the night, and the wreck appeared more broken by the force of the water; but I stayed so long in the woods to get pigeons for food that the tide prevented me going to the wreck that day.

May 17. I saw some pieces of the wreck blown onshore, at a great distance, near two miles off me, but resolved to see what they were, and found it was a piece of the head, but too heavy for me to bring away.

May 24. Every day to this day I worked on the wreck, and with hard labour I loosened some things so much with the crow that the first blowing tide several casks floated out, and two of the sea-men's chests, but the wind blowing from the shore, nothing came to land that day but pieces of timber and a hogshead which had some Brazil pork in it, but the salt water and the sand had spoilt it.

I continued this work every day to the 15th of June, except the time necessary to get food, which I always appointed, during this part of my employment, to be when the tide was up, that I might be ready when it was ebbed out, and by this time I had gotten timber and plank and ironwork enough to have builded a good boat, if I had known how, and also I got, at several times and in several pieces, near a hundredweight of the sheet lead.

June 16. Going down to the seaside, I found a large tortoise or turtle; this was the first I had seen, which it seems was only my misfortune, not any defect of the place, or scarcity, for had I happened to be on the other side of the island, I might have had hundreds of them every day, as I found afterwards, but perhaps had paid dear enough for them.

June 17. I spent in cooking the turtle; I found in her three score eggs, and her flesh was to me at that time the most savoury and pleasant that ever I tasted in my life, having had no flesh but of goats and fowls since I landed in this horrid place.

June 18. Rained all day, and I stayed within. I thought at this time the rain felt cold, and I was something chilly, which I knew was not usual in that latitude.

June 19. Very ill, and shivering, as if the weather had been cold.

June 20. No rest all night, violent pains in my head, and feverish.

June 21. Very ill, frighted almost to death with the apprehensions of my sad condition – to be sick, and no help – prayed to God for the first time since the storm off of Hull, but scarce knew what I said, or why, my thoughts being all confused.

June 22. A little better, but under dreadful apprehensions of sickness.

June 23. Very bad again, cold and shivering, and then a violent headache.

June 24. Much better.

June 25. An ague very violent; the fit held me seven hours, cold fit and hot, with faint sweats after it.

June 26. Better; and having no victuals to eat, took my gun, but found myself very weak; however, I killed a she-goat, and with much difficulty got it home, and broiled some of it and ate; I would fain have stewed it and made some broth, but had no pot.

June 27. The ague again so violent that I lay abed all day, and neither ate or drank. I was ready to perish for thirst, but so weak I had not strength to stand up, or to get myself any water to drink: prayed to God again, but was light-headed, and when I was not, I was so ignorant that I knew not what to say; only I lay and cried, "Lord look upon me, Lord pity me, Lord have mercy upon me." I suppose I did nothing else for two or three hours, till the fit wearing off, I fell asleep, and did not wake till far in the night. When I waked, I found myself much refreshed, but weak, and exceeding thirsty. However, as I had no water in my whole habitation, I was forced to lie till morning, and went to sleep again. In this second sleep, I had this terrible dream.

I thought that I was sitting on the ground on the outside of my wall, where I sat when the storm blew after the earthquake, and that I saw a man descend from a great black cloud in a bright flame of fire, and light upon the ground. He was all over as bright as a flame, so that I could just bear to look towards him; his countenance was most inexpressibly dreadful, impossible for words to describe; when he stepped upon the ground with his feet, I thought the earth trembled, just as it had done before in the earthquake, and all the air looked, to my apprehension, as if it had been filled with flashes of fire.

He was no sooner landed upon the earth, but he moved forwards towards me, with a long spear or weapon in his hand to kill me, and when he came to a rising ground at some distance, he spoke to me, or I heard a voice so terrible that it is impossible to express the terror of it. All that I can say I understood was this: "Seeing all these things have not brought thee to repentance, now thou shalt die" – at which words I thought he lifted up the spear that was in his hand to kill me.

No one that shall ever read this account will expect that I should be able to describe the horrors of my soul at this terrible vision – I mean that even while it was a dream, I even dreamt of those horrors, nor is it any more possible to describe the impression that remained upon my mind when I awaked and found it was but a dream.

I had – alas! – no divine knowledge; what I had received by the good instruction of my father was then worn out by an uninter-rupted series, for eight years, of seafaring wickedness, and a constant conversation with nothing but such as were like myself: wicked and profane to the last degree. I do not remember that I had in all that time one thought that so much as tended either to looking upwards towards God, or inwards towards a reflection upon my own ways, but a certain stupidity of soul, without desire of good or conscience of evil, had entirely overwhelmed me, and I was all that the most hardened, unthinking, wicked creature among our common sailors can be supposed to be, not having the least sense either of the fear of God in danger, or of thankfulness to God in deliverances.

In the relating what is already past of my story, this will be the more easily believed when I shall add that through all the variety of miseries that had to this day befallen me, I never had so much as one thought of it being the hand of God, or that it was a just punishment for my sin – my rebellious behaviour against my father, or my present sins which were great – or so much as a punishment for the general course of my wicked life. When I was on the desperate expedition on the desert shores of Africa, I never had so much as one thought of what would become of me, or one wish to God to direct me whither I should go, or to keep me from the danger which apparently surrounded me, as well from voracious creatures as cruel savages, but I was merely thought-less of a God or a providence; acted like a mere brute from the principles of nature and by the dictates of common sense only, and indeed hardly that.

When I was delivered and taken up at sea by the Portugal Captain, well used, and dealt justly and honourably with, as well as charitably, I had not the least thankfulness on my thoughts.

When again I was shipwrecked, ruined and in danger of drowning on this island, I was as far from remorse, or looking on it as a judgement; I only said to myself often that I was an unfortunate dog, and born to be always miserable.

It is true, when I got onshore first here, and found all my ship's crew drowned, and myself spared, I was surprised with a kind of ecstasy, and some transports of soul, which, had the grace of God assisted, might have come up to true thankfulness, but it ended where it began, in a mere common flight of joy, or as I may say, being glad I was alive, without the least reflection upon the distinguishing goodness of the hand which had preserved me, and had singled me out to be preserved, when all the rest were destroyed, or an enquiry why Providence had been thus merciful to me – even just the same common sort of joy which seamen generally have after they are got safe ashore from a shipwreck, which they drown all in the next bowl of punch, and forget almost as soon at it is over, and all the rest of my life was like it.

Even when I was afterwards, on due consideration, made sensible of my condition, how I was cast on this dreadful place, out of the reach of humankind, out of all hope of relief or prospect of redemption, as soon as I saw but a prospect of living, and that I should not starve and perish for hunger, all the sense of my affliction wore off, and I begun to be very easy, applied myself to the works proper for my preservation and supply, and was far enough from being afflicted at my condition, as a judgement from Heaven, or as the hand of God against me – there were thoughts which very seldom entered into my head.

The growing up of the corn, as is hinted in my journal, had at first some little influence upon me, and began to affect me with seriousness, as long as I thought it had something miraculous in it, but as soon as ever that part of the thought was removed, all the impression which was raised from it wore off also, as I have noted already.

Even the earthquake, though nothing could be more terrible in its nature, or more immediately directing to the invisible power which alone directs such things, yet no sooner was the first fright over, but the impression it had made went off also. I had no more sense of God or His judgements, much less of the present affliction of my circumstances being from His hand, than if I had been in the most prosperous condition of life.

But now when I began to be sick, and a leisurely view of the miseries of death came to place itself before me, when my spirits began to sink under the burden of a strong distemper, and nature was exhausted with the violence of the fever, conscience, that had slept so long, begun to awake, and I began to reproach myself with my past life, in which I had so evidently, by uncommon wickedness, provoked the justice of God to lay me under uncommon strokes, and to deal with me in so vindictive a manner.

These reflections oppressed me for the second or third day of my distemper, and in the violence, as well of the fever as of the dreadful reproaches of my conscience, extorted some words from me like praying to God, though I cannot say they were either a prayer attended with desires or with hopes; it was rather the voice of mere fright and distress. My thoughts were confused, the convictions great upon my mind, and the horror of dying in such a miserable condition raised vapours into my head with the mere apprehensions, and in these hurries of my soul, I know not what my tongue might express, but it was rather exclamation, such as, "Lord! what a miserable creature am I? If I should be sick, I shall certainly die for want of help, and what will become of me!" Then the tears burst out of my eyes, and I could say no more for a good while.

In this interval, the good advice of my father came to my mind, and presently his prediction which I mentioned at the beginning of this story – namely, that if I did take this foolish step, God would not bless me, and I would have leisure hereafter to reflect upon having neglected His counsel, when there might be none to assist in my recovery. "Now," said I aloud, "my dear father's words are come to pass: God's justice has overtaken me, and I have none to help or hear me. I rejected the voice of Providence, which had mercifully put me in a posture or station of life wherein I might have been happy and easy, but I would neither see it myself, or learn to know the blessing of it from my parents. I left them to mourn over my folly, and now I am left to mourn under the consequences of it. I refused their help and assistance who would have lifted me into the world, and would have made everything easy to me, and now I have difficulties to struggle with, too great even for nature itself to support, and no assistance, no help, no comfort, no advice." Then I cried out, "Lord, be my help, for I am in great distress."

This was the first prayer, if I may call it so, that I had made for many years. But I return to my journal.

June 28. Having been somewhat refreshed with the sleep I had had, and the fit being entirely off, I got up, and though the fright and terror of my dream was very great, yet I considered that the fit of the ague would return again the next day, and now was my time to get something to refresh and support myself when I should be ill; and the first thing I did, I filled a large square case bottle with water, and set it upon my table, in reach of my bed; and to take off the chill or aguish disposition of the water, I put about a quarter of a pint of rum into it, and mixed them together; then I got me a piece of the goat's flesh, and broiled it on the coals, but could eat very little. I walked about, but was very weak, and withal

very sad and heavy-hearted in the sense of my miserable condition, dreading the return of my distemper the next day. At night
I made my supper of three of the turtle's eggs, which I roasted in
the ashes, and ate, as we call it, in the shell, and this was the first
bit of meat I had ever asked God's blessing to, even as I could
remember, in my whole life.

After I had eaten, I tried to walk, but found myself so weak that
I could hardly carry the gun (for I never went out without that),
so I went but a little way, and sat down upon the ground, looking
out upon the sea, which was just before me, and very calm and
smooth. As I sat here, some such thoughts as these occurred to me.

What is this earth and sea of which I have seen so much? Whence
is it produced? And what am I and all the other creatures, wild
and tame, human and brutal? Whence are we?

Sure we are all made by some secret power who formed the earth
and sea, the air and sky – and who is that?

Then it followed most naturally: it is God that has made it all.
Well, but then it came on strangely: if God has made all these things,
He guides and governs them all, and all things that concern them,
for the power that could make all things must certainly have power
to guide and direct them.

If so, nothing can happen in the great circuit of His works either
without His knowledge or appointment.

And if nothing happens without His knowledge, He knows
that I am here, and am in this dreadful condition, and if nothing
happens without His appointment, He has appointed all this to
befall me.

Nothing occurred to my thought to contradict any of these
conclusions, and therefore it rested upon me with the greater
force that it must needs be that God had appointed all this to
befall me; that I was brought into this miserable circumstance by

His direction, He having the sole power, not of me only, but of everything that happened in the world. Immediately it followed:

Why has God done this to me? What have I done to be thus used?

My conscience presently checked me in that enquiry, as if I had blasphemed, and methought it spoke to me like a voice: "WRETCH! dost thou ask what thou hast done? Look back upon a dreadful misspent life, and ask thyself what thou hast *not* done; ask: Why is it that thou wert not long ago destroyed? Why wert thou not drowned in Yarmouth roads? killed in the fight when the ship was taken by the Sallee man-of-war? devoured by the wild beasts on the coast of Africa? or drowned *here*, when all the crew perished but thyself? Dost thou ask, 'What have I done?'"

I was struck dumb with these reflections, as one astonished, and had not a word to say, no, not to answer to myself, but rose up pensive and sad, walked back to my retreat, and went up over my wall, as if I had been going to bed, but my thoughts were sadly disturbed, and I had no inclination to sleep, so I sat down in my chair and lighted my lamp, for it began to be dark. Now as the apprehension of the return of my distemper terrified me very much, it occurred to my thought that the Brazilians take no physic but their tobacco for almost all distempers, and I had a piece of a roll of tobacco in one of the chests which was quite cured, and some also that was green and not quite cured.

I went, directed by Heaven, no doubt, for in this chest I found a cure, both for soul and body. I opened the chest and found what I looked for – namely, the tobacco – and as the few books I had saved lay there too, I took out one of the Bibles which I mentioned before, and which to this time I had not found leisure, or so much as inclination, to look into – I say, I took it out, and brought both that and the tobacco with me to the table.

What use to make of the tobacco I knew not as to my distemper, or whether it was good for it or no, but I tried several experiments with it, as if I was resolved it should hit one way or other. I first took a piece of a leaf, and chewed it in my mouth, which indeed at first almost stupefied my brain, the tobacco being green and strong, and that I had not been much used to it, then I took some and steeped it an hour or two in some rum, and resolved to take a dose of it when I lay down, and lastly, I burnt some upon a pan of coals, and held my nose close over the smoke of it as long as I could bear it, as well for the heat as almost for suffocation.

In the interval of this operation, I took up the Bible and began to read, but my head was too much disturbed with the tobacco to bear reading, at least that time. Only having opened the book casually, the first words that occurred to me were these: *Call on me in the day of trouble, and I will deliver, and thou shalt glorify me.**

The words were very apt to my case, and made some impression upon my thoughts at the time of reading them, though not so much as they did afterwards, for as for being delivered, the word had no sound, as I may say, to me; the thing was so remote, so impossible in my apprehension of things, that I began to say as the children of Israel did, when they were promised flesh to eat: *Can God spread a table in the wilderness?** So I began to say, "Can God Himself deliver me from this place?" and as it was not for many years that any hope appeared, this prevailed very often upon my thoughts, but however, the words made a great impression upon me, and I mused upon them very often. It grew now late, and the tobacco had, as I said, dozed my head so much that I inclined to sleep, so I left my lamp burning in the cave, lest I should want anything in the night, and went to bed, but before I lay down, I did what I never had done in all my life, I knelt down and prayed to God to fulfil the promise to me, that if I called upon Him in the day of trouble, He would deliver me. After my broken and imperfect prayer was over, I drunk the rum in which I had steeped the tobacco, which was so strong and rank of the tobacco that indeed I could scarce get it down. Immediately upon this I went to bed. I found presently it flew up in my head violently, but I fell into a sound sleep, and waked no more till by the sun it must necessarily be near three o'clock in the afternoon the next day – nay, to this hour, I'm partly of the opinion that I slept all the next day and night, and till almost three that day after, for otherwise I knew not how I should lose a day out of my reckoning in the days of the week, as it appeared some years after I had done: for if I had lost it by crossing and recrossing the line, I should have lost more than one day. But certainly I lost a day in my accompt, and never knew which way.

Be that, however, one way or th'other, when I awaked I found myself exceedingly refreshed, and my spirits lively and cheerful. When I got up, I was stronger than I was the day before, and my stomach better, for I was hungry, and in short, I had no fit the next day, but continued much altered for the better: this was the 29th.

The 30th was my well day of course, and I went abroad with my gun, but did not care to travel too far. I killed a sea fowl or two, something like a brand goose, and brought them home, but was not very forward to eat them, so I ate some more of the turtle's eggs, which were very good. This evening I renewed the medicine which I had supposed did me good the day before, namely, the tobacco steeped in rum, only I did not take so much as before, nor did I chew any of the leaf, or hold my head over the smoke; however I was not so well the next day – which was the first of July – as I hoped I should have been, for I had a little spice of the cold fit, but it was not much.

July 2. I renewed the medicine all the three ways, and dozed myself with it as at first – and doubled the quantity which I drank.

July 3. I missed the fit for good and all, though I did not recover my full strength for some weeks after. While I was thus gathering strength, my thoughts ran exceedingly upon this scripture, *I will deliver thee*, and the impossibility of my deliverance lay much upon my mind in bar of my ever expecting it. But as I was discouraging myself with such thoughts, it occurred to my mind that I pored so much upon my deliverance from the main affliction that I disregarded the deliverance I had received, and I was, as it were, made to ask myself such questions as these, namely: Have I not been delivered, and wonderfully too, from sickness? from the most distressed condition that could be, and that was so frightful to me? And what notice had I taken of it? Had I done my part? God had delivered me, but I had not glorified Him – that is to say, I had not owned and been thankful for that as a deliverance, and how could I expect greater deliverance?

This touched my heart very much, and immediately I knelt down and gave God thanks aloud for my recovery from my sickness.

July 4. In the morning I took the Bible, and beginning at the New Testament, I began seriously to read it, and imposed upon myself to read awhile every morning and every night, not tying myself to the number of chapters, but as long as my thoughts should engage me. It was not long after I set seriously to this work but I found my heart more deeply and sincerely affected with the wickedness of my past life. The impression of my dream revived, and the words, *All these things have not brought thee to repentance*, ran seriously in my thought. I was earnestly begging of God to give me repentance, when it happened providentially the very day that, reading the scripture, I came to these words, *He is exalted a Prince and a Saviour, to give repentance, and to give remission.** I threw down the book, and with my heart as well as my hands lifted up to heaven, in a kind of ecstasy of joy,

I cried out aloud, "Jesus, thou son of David, Jesus, thou exalted Prince and Saviour, give me repentance!"

This was the first time that I could say, in the true sense of the words, that I prayed in all my life, for now I prayed with a sense of my condition, and with a true scripture view of hope founded on the encouragement of the word of God, and from this time, I may say, I began to hope that God would hear me.

Now I began to construe the words mentioned above, *Call on me, and I will deliver you*, in a different sense from what I had ever done before – for then I had no notion of anything being called deliverance, but my being delivered from the captivity I was in, for though I was indeed at large in the place, yet the island was certainly a prison to me, and that in the worst sense in the world, but now I learnt to take it in another sense. Now I looked back upon my past life with such horror, and my sins appeared so dreadful that my soul sought nothing of God but deliverance from the load of guilt that bore down all my comfort – as for my solitary life, it was nothing; I did not so much as pray to be delivered from it, or think of it; it was all of no consideration in comparison to this. And I add this part here, to hint to whoever shall read it, that whenever they come to a true sense of things, they will find deliverance from sin a much greater blessing than deliverance from affliction.

But leaving this part, I return to my journal.

My condition began now to be, though not less miserable as to my way of living, yet much easier to my mind, and my thoughts being directed, by a constant reading the scripture and praying to God, to things of a higher nature; I had a great deal of comfort within, which till now I knew nothing of. Also, as my health and strength returned, I bestirred myself to furnish myself with everything that I wanted, and make my way of living as regular as I could.

From the 4th of July to the 14th, I was chiefly employed in walking about with my gun in my hand, a little and a little at a time, as a man that was gathering up his strength after a fit of sickness, for it is hardly to be imagined how low I was, and to what weakness I was reduced. The application which I made use of was perfectly new, and perhaps what had never cured an ague before, neither can I recommend it to anyone to practise by this experiment, and though it did carry off the fit, yet it rather contributed to weakening me, for I had frequent convulsions in my nerves and limbs for some time.

I learnt from it also this in particular, that being abroad in the rainy season was the most pernicious thing to my health that could be, especially in those rains which came attended with storms and hurricanes of wind, for as the rain which came in the dry season was always most accompanied with such storms, so I found that rain was much more dangerous than the rain which fell in September and October.

I HAD BEEN NOW IN THIS UNHAPPY ISLAND above ten months; all possibility of deliverance from this condition seemed to be entirely taken from me, and I firmly believed that no human shape had ever set foot upon that place. Having now secured my habitation, as I thought, fully to my mind, I had a great desire to make a more perfect discovery of the island, and to see what other productions I might find, which I yet knew nothing of.

It was the 15th of July that I began to take a more particular survey of the island itself. I went up the creek first, where, as I hinted, I brought my rafts onshore. I found, after I came about two miles up, that the tide did not flow any higher, and that it was no more than a little brook of running water, and very fresh and good, but this being the dry season, there was hardly any water in some parts of it, at least not enough to run in any stream so as it could be perceived.

On the bank of this brook I found many pleasant savannahs or meadows, plain, smooth and covered with grass, and on the rising parts of them next to the higher grounds, where the water, as it might be supposed, never overflowed, I found a great deal of tobacco, green and growing to a great and very strong stalk; there were divers other plants which I had no notion of, or understanding about, and might perhaps have virtues of their own which I could not find out.

I searched for the cassava root, which the Indians in all that climate make their bread of, but I could find none. I saw large plants of aloes, but did not then understand them. I saw several sugar canes, but wild and, for want of cultivation, imperfect. I contented myself with these discoveries for this time, and came back musing with myself what course I might take to know the virtue and goodness of any of the fruits or plants which I should discover, but could bring it to no conclusion, for, in short, I made so little observation while I was in the Brazils that I knew little of the plants in the field, at least very little that might serve me to any purpose now in my distress.

The next day, the 16th, I went up the same way again, and after going something further than I had gone the day before, I found the brook and the savannahs began to cease, and the country became more woody than before. In this part I found different fruits, and particularly I found melons upon the ground in great abundance, and grapes upon the trees; the vines had spread indeed over the trees, and the clusters of grapes were just now in their prime, very ripe and rich. This was a surprising discovery, and I was exceeding glad of them, but I was warned by my experience to eat sparingly of them, remembering that when I was ashore in Barbary, the eating of grapes killed several of our Englishmen who were slaves there, by throwing them into fluxes and fevers. But I found an excellent use for these grapes, and that was to cure or dry them in the sun, and keep them as dried grapes or raisins are kept, which I thought would be, as indeed they were, as wholesome as agreeable to eat when no grapes might be to be had.

I spent all that evening there, and went not back to my habitation, which, by the way, was the first night, as I might say, I had lain from home. In the night I took my first contrivance, and got up into a tree, where I slept well, and the next morning proceeded upon my discovery, travelling near four miles, as I might judge by the length of the valley, keeping still due north, with a ridge of hills on the south and north side of me.

At the end of this march I came to an opening where the country seemed to descend to the west, and a little spring of fresh water, which issued out of the side of the hill by me, ran the other way – that is, due east – and the country appeared so fresh, so green, so flourishing, everything being in a constant verdure or flourish of spring, that it looked like a planted garden.

I descended a little on the side of that delicious vale, surveying it with a secret kind of pleasure (though mixed with my other afflicting thoughts) to think that this was all my own, that I was king and lord of all this country indefeasibly, and had a right of possession, and if I could convey it, I might have it in inheritance as completely as any lord of a manor in England. I saw here abundance of cocoa trees, orange and lemon and citron trees – but all wild, and very few bearing any fruit, at least not then. However, the green limes that I gathered were not only pleasant to eat, but very wholesome, and I mixed their juice afterwards with water, which made it very wholesome, and very cool and refreshing.

I found now I had business enough to gather and carry home, and I resolved to lay up a store, as well of grapes as limes and lemons, to furnish myself for the wet season, which I knew was approaching.

In order to this, I gathered a great heap of grapes in one place, and a lesser heap in another place, and a great parcel of limes and lemons in another place, and taking a few of each with me, I travelled homewards, and resolved to come again and bring a bag or sack, or what I could make, to carry the rest home.

Accordingly, having spent three days in this journey, I came home – so I must now call my tent and my cave – but before I got thither, the grapes were spoilt, the richness of the fruits and the weight of the juice having broken them and bruised them; they were good for little or nothing – as to the limes, they were good, but I could bring but a few.

The next day, being the 19th, I went back, having made me two small bags to bring home my harvest, but I was surprised when, coming to my heap of grapes – which were so rich and fine when I gathered them – I found them all spread about, trod to pieces, and dragged about, some here, some there, and abundance eaten and devoured. By this I concluded there were some wild creatures thereabouts which had done this, but what they were I knew not.

However, as I found that there was no laying them up on heaps, and no carrying them away in a sack, but that one way they would be destroyed, and the other way they would be crushed with their own weight, I took another course: for I gathered a large quantity of the grapes, and hung them up upon the out branches of the trees, that they might cure and dry in the sun; and as for the limes and lemons, I carried as many back as I could well stand under.

When I came home from this journey, I contemplated with great pleasure the fruitfulness of that valley and the pleasantness of the situation, the security from storms on that side of the water, and the wood, and concluded that I had pitched upon a place to fix my abode, which was by far the worst part of the country. Upon the whole, I began to consider of removing my habitation, and to look out for a place equally safe as where I now was, situate, if possible, in that pleasant, fruitful part of the island.

This thought ran long in my head, and I was exceeding fond of it for some time, the pleasantness of the place tempting me, but when I came to a nearer view of it, and to consider that I was now by the seaside, where it was at least possible that something might happen to my advantage, and by the same ill fate that brought me hither might bring some other unhappy wretches to the same place – and though it was scarce probable that any such thing should ever happen, yet to enclose myself among the hills and woods in the centre of the island was to anticipate my bondage, and to render such an affair not only improbable, but impossible, and that therefore I ought not by any means to remove.

However, I was so enamoured of this place, that I spent much of my time there for the whole remaining part of the month of July, and though upon second thoughts I resolved, as above, not to remove, yet I built me a little kind of a bower, and surrounded it at a distance with a strong fence, being a double hedge, as high as I could reach, well-staked and filled between with brushwood, and here I lay very secure, sometimes two or three nights together, always going over it with a ladder as before, so that I fancied now I had my country house, and my sea-coast house – and this work took me up to the beginning of August.

I had but newly finished my fence, and began to enjoy my labour, but the rains came on, and made me stick close to my first habitation, for though I had made me a tent like the other, with a piece of a sail, and spread it very well, yet I had not the shelter of a hill to keep me from storms, nor a cave behind me to retreat into when the rains were extraordinary.

About the beginning of August, as I said, I had finished my bower, and began to enjoy myself. The third of August, I found the grapes I had hung up were perfectly dried, and indeed were excellent good raisins of the sun, so I began to take them down from the trees, and it was very happy that I did so, for the rains which followed would have spoilt them, and I had lost the best part of my winter food, for I had above two hundred large bunches of them. No sooner had I taken them all down, and carried most of them home to my cave, but it began to rain, and from hence, which was the fourteenth of August, it rained more or less every day till the middle of October, and sometimes so violently that I could not stir out of my cave for several days.

In this season I was much surprised with the increase of my family. I had been concerned for the loss of one of my cats, who ran away from me, or, as I thought, had been dead, and I heard no more tale or tidings of her, till to my astonishment she came home about the end of August with three kittens: this was the more strange to me, because though I had killed a wild cat, as I called it, with my gun, yet I thought it was a quite differing kind from our European cats – yet the young cats were the same kind of house breed like the old one, and both my cats being females, I thought it very strange. But from these three cats, I afterwards came to be so pestered with cats that I was forced to kill them like vermin, or wild beasts, and to drive them from my house as much as possible.

From the fourteenth of August to the twenty-sixth, incessant rain, so that I could not stir, and was now very careful not to be much wet. In this confinement I began to be straitened for food, but venturing out twice, I one day killed a goat, and the last day, which was the twenty-sixth, found a very large tortoise, which was a treat to me, and my food was regulated thus: I ate a bunch of raisins for my breakfast, a piece of the goat's flesh or of the turtle for my dinner – broiled, for to my great misfortune I had no vessel to boil or stew anything – and two or three of the turtle's eggs for my supper.

During this confinement in my cover by the rain, I worked daily two or three hours at enlarging my cave, and by degrees worked it on towards one side, till I came to the outside of the hill, and made a door or way out, which came beyond my fence or wall, and so I came in and out this way, but I was not perfectly easy at lying so open, for as I had managed myself before, I was in a perfect enclosure, whereas now I thought I lay exposed, and open for anything to come in upon me, and yet I could not perceive that there was any living thing to fear, the biggest creature that I had yet seen upon the island being a goat.

September the thirtieth, I was now come to the unhappy anniversary of my landing. I cast up the notches on my post, and found I had been onshore three hundred and sixty-five days. I kept this day as a solemn fast, setting it apart for religious exercise, prostrating myself on the ground with the most serious humiliation, confessing my sins to God, acknowledging His righteous judgements upon me, and praying to Him to have mercy on me through Jesus Christ, and having not tasted the least refreshment for twelve hours, even till the going down of the sun, I then ate a biscuit cake and a bunch of grapes, and went to bed finishing the day as I began it.

I had all this time observed no sabbath day, for as at first I had no sense of religion upon my mind, I had after some time omitted to distinguish the weeks by making a longer notch than ordinary for the sabbath day, and so did not really know what any of the days were, but now having cast up the days, as above, I found I had been there a year – so I divided it into weeks, and set apart every seventh day for a sabbath, though I found at the end of my account I had lost a day or two in my reckoning.

A little after this my ink began to fail me, and so I contented myself to use it more sparingly, and to write down only the most remarkable events of my life, without continuing a daily memo-randum of other things.

The rainy season and the dry season began now to appear regular to me, and I learnt to divide them, so as to provide for them accordingly. But I bought all my experience before I had it, and this, I am going to relate, was one of the most discouraging experiments that I had made at all. I have mentioned that I had saved the few ears of barley and rice – which I had so surprisingly found spring up, as I thought, of themselves, and believe there was about thirty stalks of rice, and about twenty of barley – and now I thought it a proper time to sow it after the rains, the sun being in its southern position, going from me.

Accordingly I dug up a piece of ground as well as I could with my wooden spade, and dividing it into two parts, I sowed my grain, but as I was sowing, it casually occurred to my thoughts that I would not sow it all at first, because I did not know when was the proper time for it; so I sowed about two thirds of the seed, leaving about a handful of each.

It was a great comfort to me afterwards that I did so, for not one grain of that I sowed this time came to anything, for the dry months following, the earth having had no rain after the seed was sown, it had no moisture to assist its growth, and never came up at all till the wet season had come again, and then it grew as if it had been but newly sown.

Finding my first seed did not grow, which I easily imagined was by the drought, I sought for a moister piece of ground to make another trial in, and I dug up a piece of ground near my new bower and sowed the rest of my seed in February, a little before the vernal equinox, and this, having the rainy months of March and April to water it, sprung up very pleasantly, and yielded a very good crop, but having part of the seed left only, and not daring to sow all that I had, I had but a small quantity at last, my whole crop not amounting to above half a peck of each kind.

But by this experiment I was made master of my business, and knew exactly when the proper season was to sow, and that I might expect two seed times and two harvests every year.

While this corn was growing, I made a little discovery which was of use to me afterwards. As soon as the rains were over and the weather began to settle, which was about the month of November, I made a visit up the country to my bower, where though I had not been some months, yet I found all things just as I left them. The circle or double hedge that I had made was not only firm and entire, but the stakes which I had cut out of some trees that grew thereabouts were all shot out and grown with long branches, as much as a willow tree usually shoots the first year after lopping its head. I could not tell what tree to call it, that these stakes were cut from. I was surprised, and yet very well pleased, to see the young trees grow, and I pruned them, and led them up to grow as much alike as I could, and it is scarce credible how beautiful a figure they grew into in three years, so that though the hedge made a circle of about twenty-five yards in diameter, yet the trees, for such I might now call them, soon covered it, and it was a complete shade, sufficient to lodge under all the dry season.

This made me resolve to cut some more stakes, and make me a hedge like this in a semicircle round my wall – I mean that of my first dwelling – which I did, and placing the trees or stakes in a double row, at about eight yards' distance from my first fence, they grew presently, and were at first a fine cover to my habitation, and afterwards served for a defence also, as I shall observe in its order.

I found now that the seasons of the year might generally be divided, not into summer and winter, as in Europe, but into the rainy seasons and the dry seasons, which were generally thus:

Half February March Half April	Rainy, the sun being then on or near the equinox.
Half April May June July Half August	Dry, the sun being then to the north of the line.
Half August September Half October	Rainy, the sun being then come back.
Half October November December January Half February	Dry, the sun being then to the south of the line.

The rainy season sometimes held longer or shorter, as the winds happened to blow, but this was the general observation I made. After I had found by experience the ill consequence of being abroad in the rain, I took care to furnish myself with provisions beforehand, that I might not be obliged to go out, and I sat within doors as much as possible during the wet months.

This time I found much employment (and very suitable also to the time) for I found great occasion for many things which I had no way to furnish myself with, but by hard labour and constant application; particularly, I tried many ways to make myself a basket, but all the twigs I could get for the purpose proved so brittle that they would do nothing. It proved of excellent advantage to me now, that when I was a boy, I used to take great delight in standing at a basket-makers in the town where my father lived, to see them make their wicker-ware, and being, as boys usually are, very officious to help, and a great observer of the manner how they worked those things and sometimes lending a hand, I had by this means full knowledge of the methods of it, that I wanted nothing but the materials, when it came into my mind that the twigs of that tree from whence I cut my stakes that grew might possibly be as tough as the sallows and willows and osiers in England, and I resolved to try.

Accordingly, the next day, I went to my country house, as I called it, and cutting some of the smaller twigs; I found them to my purpose as much as I could desire, whereupon I came the next time prepared with a hatchet to cut down a quantity, which I soon found, for there was great plenty of them. These I set up to dry within my circle or hedge, and when they were fit for use I carried them to my cave, and here during the next season I employed myself in making, as well as I could, a great many baskets, both to carry earth, or to carry or lay up anything as I had occasion – and though I did not finish them very handsomely, yet I made them sufficiently serviceable for my purpose, and thus afterwards I took care never to be without them, and as my wicker-ware decayed, I made more: especially I made strong deep baskets to place my corn in, instead of sacks, when I should come to have any quantity of it.

Having mastered this difficulty, and employed a world of time about it, I bestirred myself to see if possible how to supply two wants. I had no vessels to hold anything that was liquid, except two runlets which were almost full of rum, and some glass bottles, some of the common size, and others which were case bottles

– square, for the holding of waters, spirits, etc. I had not so much as a pot to boil anything, except a great kettle which I saved out of the ship, and which was too big for such use as I desired it, namely, to make broth and stew a bit of meat by itself. The second thing I would fain have had was a tobacco pipe, but it was impossible to make one; however, I found a contrivance for that too at last.

I employed myself in planting my second rows of stakes or piles, and in this wicker working, all the summer or dry season, when another business took me up more time than it could be imagined I could spare.

I MENTIONED BEFORE that I had a great mind to see the whole island, and that I had travelled up the brook and so on to where I built my bower, and where I had an opening quite to the sea on the other side of the island. I now resolved to travel quite cross to the seashore on that side; so taking my gun, a hatchet and my dog, and a larger quantity of powder and shot than usual, with two biscuit cakes and a great bunch of raisins in my pouch for my store, I began my journey. When I had passed the vale where my bower stood as above, I came within view of the sea, to the west, and it being a very clear day, I fairly descried land – whether an island or a continent, I could not tell, but it lay very high, extending from the west to the WSW at a very great distance – by my guess it could not be less than fifteen or twenty leagues off.

I could not tell what part of the world this might be, otherwise than that I knew it must be part of America, and, as I concluded by all my observations, must be near the Spanish dominions, and perhaps was all inhabited by savages, where if I should have landed, I had been in a worse condition than I was now, and therefore I acquiesced in the dispositions of Providence, which I began now to own and to believe ordered everything for the best – I say, I quieted my mind with this, and left off afflicting myself with fruitless wishes of being there.

Besides, after some pause upon this affair, I considered that if this land was the Spanish coast, I should certainly, one time or other, see some vessel pass or repass one way or other; but if not, then it was the savage coast between the Spanish country and Brazils, which are indeed the worst of savages, for they are cannibals, or men-eaters, and fail not to murder and devour all the human bodies that fall into their hands.

With these considerations I walked leisurely forwards, I found that side of the island where I now was much pleasanter than mine, the open or savannah fields sweet, adorned with flowers and grass, and full of very fine woods. I saw abundance of parrots, and fain I would have caught one, if possible, to have kept it to be tame, and taught it to speak to me. I did, after some pains taking, catch a young parrot, for I knocked it down with a stick and, having recovered it, I brought it home, but it was some years before I could make him speak. However, at last I taught him to call me by my name very familiarly. But the accident that followed, though it be a trifle, will be very diverting in its place.

I was exceedingly diverted with this journey. I found in the low grounds hares, as I thought them to be, and foxes, but they differed greatly from all the other kinds I had met with, nor could I satisfy myself to eat them, though I killed several. But I had no need to be venturous, for I had no want of food, and of that which was very good too, especially these three sorts, namely, goats, pigeons and turtle or tortoise, which, added to my grapes, Leadenhall Market* could not have furnished a table better than I, in proportion to the company, and though my case was deplorable enough, yet I had great cause for thankfulness, that I was not driven to any extremities for food, but rather plenty, even to dainties.

I never travelled in this journey above two miles outright in a day or thereabouts, but I took so many turns and returns to see what discoveries I could make that I came weary enough to the place where I resolved to sit down all night, and then I either reposed myself in a tree, or surrounded myself with a row of stakes set upright in the ground, either from one tree to another, or so as no wild creature could come at me without waking me.

As soon as I came to the seashore, I was surprised to see that I had taken up my lot on the worst side of the island, for here indeed the shore was covered with innumerable turtles, whereas on the other side I had found but three in a year and half. Here was also an infinite number of fowls of many kinds, some which I had seen and some which I had not seen before, and many of them very good meat, but such as I knew not the names of, except those called penguins.

I could have shot as many as I pleased, but was very sparing of my powder and shot – and therefore had more mind to kill a she-goat, if I could, which I could better feed on, and though there were many goats here more than on my side the island, yet it was with much more difficulty that I could come near them, the country being flat and even, and they saw me much sooner than when I was on the hill.

I confess this side of the country was much pleasanter than mine, but yet I had not the least inclination to remove, for as I was fixed in my habitation, it became natural to me, and I seemed all the while I was here to be as it were upon a journey, and from home. However, I travelled along the shore of the sea towards the east, I suppose about twelve miles, and then, setting up a great pole upon the shore for a mark, I concluded I would go home again, and that the next journey I took should be on the other side of the island, east from my dwelling, and so round till I came to my post again – of which in its place.

I took another way to come back than that I went, thinking I could easily keep all the island so much in my view that I could not miss finding my first dwelling by viewing the country, but I found myself mistaken, for being come about two or three miles, I found myself descended into a very large valley, but so surrounded with hills, and those hills covered with wood, that I could not see which was my way by any direction but that of the sun, nor even then, unless I knew very well the position of the sun at that time of the day.

It happened to my further misfortune that the weather proved hazy for three or four days while I was in this valley, and not being able to see the sun, I wandered about very uncomfortably, and at last was obliged to find the seaside, look for my post, and come back the same way I went, and then by easy journeys I turned homewards, the weather being exceeding hot, and my gun, ammunition, hatchet and other things very heavy.

In this journey my dog surprised a young kid, and seized upon it, and I, running in to take hold of it, caught it, and saved it alive from the dog. I had a great mind to bring it home if I could, for I had often been musing whether it might not be possible to get a kid or two, and so raise a breed of tame goats, which might supply me when my powder and shot should be all spent.

I made a collar to this little creature and, with a string which I made of some rope yarn which I always carried about me, I led him along, though with some difficulty, till I came to my bower, and there I enclosed him and left him, for I was very impatient to be at home, from whence I had been absent above a month.

I cannot express what a satisfaction it was to me to come into my old hutch and lie down in my hammock bed. This little wandering journey, without settled place of abode, had been so unpleasant to me that my own house, as I called it to myself, was a perfect settlement to me compared to that, and it rendered everything about me so comfortable that I resolved I would never go a great way from it again, while it should be my lot to stay on the island.

I reposed myself here a week to rest and regale myself after my long journey, during which most of the time was taken up in the weighty affair of making a cage for my Poll, who began now to be a mere domestic, and to be mighty well acquainted with me. Then I began to think of the poor kid, which I had penned in within my little circle, and resolved to go and fetch it home, or give it some food; accordingly I went, and found it where I left it, for indeed it could not get out, but was almost starved for want of food. I went and cut bows of trees, and branches of such shrubs as I could find, and threw it over, and having fed it, I tied it as I did before, to lead it away, but it was so tame with being hungry, that I had no need to have tied it, for it followed me like a dog, and as I continually fed it, the creature became so loving, so gentle and so fond, that it became from that time one of my domestics also, and would never leave me afterwards.

The rainy season of the autumnal equinox was now come, and I kept the 30th of September in the same solemn manner as before, being the anniversary of my landing on the island, having now been there two years, and no more prospect of being delivered than the first day I came there. I spent the whole day in humble and thankful acknowledgements of the many wonderful mercies which my solitary condition was attended with, and without which it might have been infinitely more miserable. I gave humble and hearty thanks that God had been pleased to discover to me, even that it was possible I might be more happy in this solitary condition, than I should have been in a liberty of society, and in all the pleasures of the world; that He could fully make up to me the deficiencies of my solitary state, and the want of human society, by His presence and the communications of His grace to my soul, supporting, comforting and encouraging me to depend upon His providence here, and hope for His eternal presence hereafter.

It was now that I began sensibly to feel how much more happy this life I now led was, with all its miserable circumstances, than the wicked, cursed, abominable life I led all the past part of my days, and now I changed both my sorrows and my joys. My very desires altered, my affections changed their gusts, and my delights were perfectly new from what they were at my first coming, or indeed for the two years past.

Before, as I walked about, either on my hunting, or for viewing the country, the anguish of my soul at my condition would break out upon me on a sudden, and my very heart would die within me, to think of the woods, the mountains, the deserts I was in, and how I was a prisoner, locked up with the eternal bars and bolts of the ocean, in an uninhabited wilderness without redemption. In the midst of the greatest composures of my mind, this would break out upon me like a storm, and make me wring my hands and weep like a child. Sometimes it would take me in the middle of my work, and I would immediately sit down and sigh, and look upon the ground for an hour or two together, and this was still worse to me, for if I could burst out into tears, or vent myself by words, it would go off, and the grief having exhausted itself would abate.

But now I began to exercise myself with new thoughts; I daily read the word of God, and applied all the comforts of it to my present state. One morning, being very sad, I opened the Bible upon these words, *I will never, never leave thee, nor forsake thee*;* immediately it occurred that these words were to me; why else should they be directed in such a manner, just at the moment when I was mourning over my condition, as one forsaken of God and man? "Well then," said I, "if God does not forsake me, of what ill consequence can it be, or what matters it, though the world should all forsake me, seeing, on the other hand, if I had all the world, and should lose the favour and blessing of God, there would be no comparison in the loss?"

From this moment I began to conclude in my mind that it was possible for me to be more happy in this forsaken, solitary condition than it was probable I should ever have been in any other particular state in the world, and with this thought I was going to give thanks to God for bringing me to this place.

I know not what it was, but something shocked my mind at that thought, and I durst not speak the words. "How canst thou be such a hypocrite," said I, even audibly, "to pretend to be thankful for a condition, which however thou mayst endeavour to be contented with, thou wouldst rather pray heartily to be delivered from?" So I stopped there, but though I could not say I thanked God for being there, yet I sincerely gave thanks to God for opening my eyes, by whatever afflicting providences, to see the former condition of my life, and to mourn for my wickedness and repent. I never opened the Bible, or shut it, but my very soul within me blessed God for directing my friend in England, without any order of mine, to pack it up among my goods, and for assisting me afterwards to save it out of the wreck of the ship.

Thus, and in this disposition of mind, I began my third year, and though I have not given the reader the trouble of so particular account of my works this year as the first, yet in general it may be observed that I was very seldom idle, but having regularly divided my time, according to the several daily employments that were before me, such as, first, my duty to God and the reading the scriptures, which I constantly set apart some time for thrice every day; secondly, the going abroad with my gun for food, which generally took me up three hours in every morning, when it did not rain; thirdly, the ordering, curing, preserving and cooking what I had killed or catched for my supply. These took up great part of the day; also it is to be considered that the middle of the day, when the sun was in the zenith, the violence of the heat was too great to stir out, so that about four hours in the evening was all the time I could be supposed to work in, with this exception, that sometimes I changed my hours of hunting and working, and went to work in the morning, and abroad with my gun in the afternoon.

To this short time allowed for labour, I desire may be added the exceeding laboriousness of my work; the many hours which, for want of tools, want of help and want of skill, everything I did took up out of my time. For example, I was full two and forty days making me a board for a long shelf which I wanted in my cave, whereas two sawyers, with their tools and a sawpit, would have cut six of them out of the same tree in half a day.

My case was this: it was to be a large tree which was to be cut down, because my board was to be a broad one. This tree I was three days a cutting down, and two more cutting off the bows, and reducing it to a log or piece of timber. With inexpressible hacking and hewing I reduced both sides of it into chips, till it begun to be light enough to move. Then I turned it, and made one side of it smooth and flat as a board from end to end; then turning that side downwards, cut the other side till I brought the plank to be about three inches thick and smooth on both sides. Anyone may judge the labour of my hands in such a piece of work, but labour and patience carried me through that and many other things. I only observe this in particular, to show the reason why so much of my time went away with so little work, namely, that what might be a little to be done with help and tools was a vast labour, and required a prodigious time to do alone and by hand.

But notwithstanding this, with patience and labour I went through many things, and indeed everything that my circumstances made necessary to me to do, as will appear by what follows.

I was now, in the months of November and December, expecting my crop of barley and rice. The ground I had manured or dug up for them was not great, for as I observed, my seed of each was not above the quantity of half a peck, for I had lost one whole crop by sowing in the dry season. But now my crop promised very well, when on a sudden I found I was in danger of losing it all again by enemies of several sorts which it was scarce possible to keep from it, as first the goats and wild creatures which I called hares, who, tasting the sweetness of the blade, lay in it night and day as soon as it came up, and ate it so close that it could get no time to shoot up into stalk.

This I saw no remedy for, but by making an enclosure about it with a hedge, which I did with a great deal of toil, and the more because it required speed. However, as my arable land was but small, suited to my crop, I got it totally well-fenced in about three weeks' time, and shooting some of the creatures in the daytime, I set my dog to guard it in the night, tying him up to a stake at the gate, where he would stand and bark all night long. So in a little time the enemies forsook the place, and the corn grew very strong and well, and began to ripen apace.

But as the beasts ruined me before while my corn was in the blade, so the birds were as likely to ruin me now when it was in the ear, for going along by the place to see how it throve, I saw my little crop surrounded with fowls of I know not how many sorts, who stood as it were watching till I should be gone. I immediately let fly among them (for I always had my gun with me). I had no sooner shot, but there rose up a little cloud of fowls, which I had not seen at all, from among the corn itself.

This touched me sensibly, for I foresaw that in a few days they would devour all my hopes, that I should be starved and never be able to raise a crop at all, and what to do I could not tell. However, I resolved not to lose my corn, if possible, though I should watch it night and day. In the first place, I went among it to see what damage was already done, and found they had spoilt a good deal of it, but that as it was yet too green for them, the loss was not so great but that the remainder was like to be a good crop if it could be saved.

I stayed by it to load my gun, and then coming away, I could easily see the thieves sitting upon all the trees about me as if they only waited till I was gone away, and the event proved it to be so, for as I walked off as if I was gone, I was no sooner out of their sight but they dropped down one by one into the corn again. I was so provoked that I could not have patience to stay till more came on, knowing that every grain that they ate now was, as it might be said, a peck-load to me in the consequence, but coming up to the hedge I fired again, and killed three of them. This was what I wished for, so I took them up, and served them as we serve notorious thieves in England, namely, hanged them in chains for a terror to others. It is impossible to imagine almost that this should have such an effect as it had, for the fowls would not only not come at the corn, but in short they forsook all that part of the island, and I could never see a bird near the place as long as my scarecrows hung there.

This I was very glad of, you may be sure, and about the latter end of December, which was our second harvest of the year, I reaped my crop.

I was sadly put to it for a scythe or a sickle to cut it down, and all I could do was to make one as well as I could out of one of the broadswords or cutlasses which I saved among the arms out of the ship. However, as my first crop was but small, I had no great difficulty to cut it down; in short, I reaped it my way, for I cut nothing off but the ears, and carried it away in a great basket which I had made and so rubbed it out with my hands, and at the end of all my harvesting I found that out of my half-peck of seed I had near two bushels of rice, and above two bushels and half of barley – that is to say, by my guess, for I had no measure at that time.

However, this was a great encouragement to me, and I foresaw that in time it would please God to supply me with bread. And yet here I was perplexed again, for I neither knew how to grind or make meal of my corn, or indeed how to clean it and part it; nor if made into meal, how to make bread of it; and if how to make it, yet I knew not how to bake it. These things being added to my desire of having a good quantity for store, and to secure a constant supply, I resolved not to taste any of this crop, but to preserve it all for seed against the next season, and in the meantime to employ all my study and hours of working to accomplish this great work of providing myself with corn and bread.

It might be truly said that now I worked for my bread; 'tis a little wonderful, and what I believe few people have thought much upon, namely, the strange multitude of little things necessary in the providing, producing, curing, dressing, making and finishing this one article of bread.

I, that was reduced to a mere state of nature, found this to my daily discouragement, and was made more and more sensible of it every hour, even after I had got the first handful of seed corn, which, as I have said, came up unexpectedly, and indeed to a surprise.

First, I had no plough to turn up the earth, no spade or shovel to dig it. Well, this I conquered by making a wooden spade, as I observed before, but this did my work in but a wooden manner, and though it cost me a great many days to make it, yet for want of iron it not only wore out the sooner, but made my work the harder, and made it be performed much worse.

However, this I bore with, and was content to work it out with patience, and bear with the badness of the performance. When the corn was sowed, I had no harrow, but was forced to go over it myself and drag a great heavy bough of a tree over it, to scratch it, as it may be called, rather than rake or harrow it.

When it was growing and grown, I have observed already how many things I wanted to fence it, secure it, mow or reap it, cure and carry it home, thrash, part it from the chaff and save it. Then I wanted a mill to grind it, sieves to dress it, yeast and salt to make it into bread, and an oven to bake it, and yet all these things I did without, as shall be observed; and yet the corn was an inestimable comfort and advantage to me too. All this, as I said, made everything laborious and tedious to me, but that there was no help for, neither was my time so much loss to me, because, as I had divided it, a certain part of it was every day appointed to these works, and as I resolved to use none of the corn for bread till I had a greater quantity by me, I had the next six months to apply myself wholly by labour and invention to furnish myself with utensils proper for the performing all the operations necessary for the making the corn (when I had it) fit for my use.

BUT FIRST, I WAS TO PREPARE more land, for I had now seed enough to sow above an acre of ground. Before I did this, I had a week's work at least to make me a spade, which when it was done was but a sorry one indeed, and very heavy, and required double labour to work with it. However, I went through that, and sowed my seed in two large flat pieces of ground, as near my house as I could find them to my mind, and fenced them in with a good hedge, the stakes of which were all cut of that wood which I had set before, and knew it would grow, so that in one year's time I knew I should have a quick or living hedge that would want but little repair. This work was not so little as to take me up less than three months, because great part of that time was of the wet season, when I could not go abroad.

Within doors – that is when it rained and I could not go out – I found employment on the following occasions, always observing that all the while I was at work I diverted myself with talking to my parrot, and teaching him to speak, and I quickly learnt him to know his own name, and at last to speak it out pretty loud, *POLL*, which was the first word I ever heard spoken in the island by any mouth but my own. This, therefore, was not my work, but an assistant to my work, for now, as I said, I had a great employment upon my hands, as follows: namely, I had long studied, by some means or other, to make myself some earthen vessels, which indeed I wanted sorely, but knew not where to come at them. However, considering the heat of the climate, I did not doubt but if I could find out any such clay, I might botch up some such pot as might, being dried in the sun, be hard enough and strong enough to bear handling, and to hold anything that was dry and required to be kept so, and as this was necessary in the preparing corn, meal, etc., which was the thing I was upon, I resolved to make some as large as I could, and fit only to stand like jars to hold what should be put into them.

It would make the reader pity me, or rather laugh at me, to tell how many awkward ways I took to raise this paste, what odd misshapen ugly things I made, how many of them fell in, and how many fell out, the clay not being stiff enough to bear its own weight; how many cracked by the over-violent heat of the sun, being set out too hastily; and how many fell in pieces with only removing, as well before as after they were dried; and in a word, how, after having laboured hard to find the clay, to dig it, to temper it, to bring it home and work it, I could not make above two large earthen ugly things – I cannot call them jars – in about two months' labour.

However, as the sun baked these two very dry and hard, I lifted them very gently up, and set them down again in two great wicker baskets which I had made on purpose for them that they might not break, and as between the pot and the basket there was a little room to spare, I stuffed it full of the rice and barley straw, and these two pots being to stand always dry, I thought would hold my dry corn, and perhaps the meal, when the corn was bruised.

Though I miscarried so much in my design for large pots, yet I made several smaller things with better success, such as little round pots, flat dishes, pitchers and pipkins, and any things my hand turned to, and the heat of the sun baked them strangely hard.

But all this would not answer my end, which was to get an earthen pot to hold what was liquid, and bear the fire, which none of these could do. It happened after some time, making a pretty large fire for cooking my meat, when I went to put it out after I had done with it, I found a broken piece of one of my earthenware vessels in the fire, burnt as hard as a stone, and red as a tile. I was agreeably surprised to see it, and said to myself that certainly they might be made to burn whole if they would burn broken.

This set me to studying how to order my fire, so as to make it burn me some pots. I had no notion of a kiln, such as the potters burn in, or of glazing them with lead, though I had some lead to do it with, but I placed three large pipkins and two or three pots in a pile one upon another, and placed my firewood all round it with a great heap of embers under them. I plied the fire with fresh fuel round the outside, and upon the top, till I saw the pots in the inside red-hot quite through and observed that they did not crack at all. When I saw them clear red, I let them stand in that heat about five or six hours, till I found one of them, though it did not crack, did melt or run, for the sand which was mixed with the clay melted by the violence of the heat, and would have run into glass if I had gone on, so I slacked my fire gradually till the pots began to abate of the red colour, and watching them all night that I might not let the fire abate too fast, in the morning I had three very good, I will not say handsome, pipkins, and two other earthen pots, as hard-burnt as could be desired, and one of them perfectly glazed with the running of the sand.

After this experiment, I need not say that I wanted no sort of earthenware for my use, but I must needs say, as to the shapes of them, they were very indifferent, as anyone may suppose, when

I had no way of making them but as the children make dirt pies, or as a woman would make pies that never learnt to raise paste.

No joy at a thing of so mean a nature was ever equal to mine, when I found I had made an earthen pot that would bear the fire, and I had hardly patience to stay till they were cold before I set one on the fire again with some water in it, to boil me some meat, which it did admirably well, and with a piece of a kid I made some very good broth, though I wanted oatmeal, and several other ingredients requisite to make it so good as I would have had it been.

My next concern was to get me a stone mortar to stamp or beat some corn in, for as to the mill, there was no thought at arriving to that perfection of art with one pair of hands. To supply this want I was at a great loss, for of all trades in the world I was as perfectly unqualified for a stonecutter as for any whatever – neither had I any tools to go about it with. I spent many a day to find out a great stone big enough to cut hollow and make fit for a mortar, and could find none at all, except what was in the solid rock, and which I had no way to dig or cut out – nor indeed were the rocks in the island of hardness sufficient, but were all of a sandy crumbling stone, which neither would bear the weight of a heavy pestle, nor would break the corn without filling it with sand, so after a great deal of time lost in searching for a stone, I gave it over, and resolved to look out for a great block of hard wood, which I found indeed much easier, and getting one as big as I had strength to stir, I rounded it, and formed it in the outside with my axe and hatchet, and then with the help of fire, and infinite labour, made a hollow place in it, as the Indians in Brazil make their canoes. After this, I made a great heavy pestle or beater, of the wood called the ironwood, and this I prepared and laid by against I had my next crop of corn, when I proposed to myself to grind, or rather pound, my corn into meal to make my bread.

My next difficulty was to make a sieve, or search, to dress my meal, and to part it from the bran and the husk, without which I did not see it possible I could have any bread. This was a most difficult thing, so much as but to think on, for to be sure I had nothing like the necessary thing to make it – I mean fine thin canvas or stuff to search the meal through. And here I was at a full stop for many months, nor did I really know what to do: linen I had none left, but what was mere rags; I had goat's hair, but neither knew I how to weave it or spin it, and had I known how, here was no tools to work it with. All the remedy that I found for this was that at last I did remember I had among the seamen's clothes which were saved out of the ship some neckcloths of calico or muslin, and with some pieces of these I made three small sieves, but proper enough for the work, and thus I made shift for some years – how I did afterwards I shall show in its place.

The baking part was the next thing to be considered, and how I should make bread when I came to have corn. For first I had no yeast: as to that part, as there was no supplying the want, so I did not concern myself much about it, but for an oven, I was indeed in great pain. At length I found out an experiment for that also, which was this: I made some earthen vessels, very broad, but not deep – that is to say, about two foot diameter, and not above nine inches deep – these I burnt in the fire, as I had done the other, and laid them by, and when I wanted to bake, I made a great fire upon my hearth, which I had paved with some square tiles of my own making and burning also – but I should not call them square.

When the firewood was burnt pretty much into embers or live coals, I drew them forwards upon this hearth so as to cover it all over, and there I let them lie till the hearth was very hot; then sweeping away all the embers, I set down my loaf or loaves and, whelming down the earthen pot upon them, drew the embers all round the outside of the pot to keep in and add to the heat, and thus, as well as in the best oven in the world, I baked my barley loaves, and became in little time a mere pastry cook into the bargain, for I made myself several cakes of the rice, and puddings. Indeed I made no pies, neither had I anything to put into them, supposing I had, except the flesh either of fowls or goats.

It need not be wondered at if all these things took me up most part of the third year of my abode here, for it is to be observed that in the intervals of these things, I had my new harvest and husbandry to manage, for I reaped my corn in its season, and carried it home as well as I could, and laid it up in the ear in my large baskets till I had time to rub it out – for I had no floor to thrash it on, or instrument to thrash it with.

And now indeed, my stock of corn increasing, I really wanted to build my barns bigger. I wanted a place to lay it up in, for the increase of the corn now yielded me so much, that I had of the barley about twenty bushels, and of the rice as much, or more, insomuch that now I resolved to begin to use it freely, for my bread had been quite gone a great while. Also I resolved to see what quantity would be sufficient for me a whole year, and to sow but once a year.

Upon the whole, I found that the forty bushels of barley and rice was much more than I could consume in a year, so I resolved to sow just the same quantity every year that I sowed the last, in hopes that such a quantity would fully provide me with bread etc.

All the while these things were doing, you may be sure my thoughts ran many times upon the prospect of land which I had seen from the other side of the island, and I was not without secret wishes that I were onshore there, fancying the seeing the mainland, and in an inhabited country I might find some way or other to convey myself further, and perhaps at last find some means of escape.

But all this while I made no allowance for the dangers of such a condition, and how I might fall into the hands of savages, and perhaps such as I might have reason to think far worse than the lions and tigers of Africa; that if I once came into their power, I should run a hazard more than a thousand to one of being killed, and perhaps of being eaten, for I had heard that the people of the Caribbean coast were cannibals, or man-eaters, and I knew by the latitude that I could not be far off from that shore. That suppose they were not cannibals, yet they might kill me, as many Europeans who had fallen into their hands had been served, even when they had been ten or twenty together; much more I that was but one, and could make little or no defence. All these things, I say, which I ought to have considered well of, and did cast up in my thoughts afterwards, yet took up none of my apprehensions at first, but my head ran mightily upon the thought of getting over to the shore.

Now I wished for my boy Xury, and the longboat with the shoulder-of-mutton sail, with which I sailed above a thousand miles on the coast of Africk, but this was in vain. Then I thought I would go and look at our ship's boat, which, as I have said, was blown up upon the shore a great way in the storm when we were first cast away. She lay almost where she did at first, but not quite, and was turned by the force of the waves and the winds almost bottom upwards, against a high ridge of beachy rough sand, but no water about her as before.

If I had had hands to have refitted her, and to have launched her into the water, the boat would have done well enough, and I might have gone back into the Brazils with her easily enough, but I might have foreseen that I could no more turn her and set her upright upon her bottom than I could remove the island. However, I went to the woods, and cut levers and rollers, and brought them to the boat, resolved to try what I could do, suggesting to myself that if I could but turn her down, I might easily repair the damage she had received, and she would be a very good boat, and I might go to sea in her very easily.

I spared no pains, indeed, in this piece of fruitless toil, and spent, I think, three or four weeks about it. At last finding it impossible to heave it up with my little strength, I fell to digging away the sand to undermine it, and so to make it fall down, setting pieces of wood to thrust and guide it right in the fall.

But when I had done this, I was unable to stir it up again, or to get under it, much less to move it forwards towards the water, so I was forced to give it over, and yet, though I gave over the hopes of the boat, my desire to venture over for the main increased, rather than decreased, as the means for it seemed impossible.

This at length put me upon thinking whether it was not possible to make myself a canoe, or piragua, such as the natives of those climates make, even without tools, or, as I might say, without hands, namely, of the trunk of a great tree. This I not only thought possible, but easy, and pleased myself extremely with the thoughts of making it, and with my having much more convenience for it than any of the Negroes or Indians – but not at all considering the particular inconveniences which I lay under, more than the Indians did, namely, want of hands to move it, when it was made, into the water, a difficulty much harder for me to surmount than all the consequences of want of tools could be to them – for what was it to me, that when I had chosen a vast tree in the woods, I might with much trouble cut it down, if after I might be able with my tools to hew and dub the outside into the proper shape of a boat, and burn or cut out the inside to make it hollow, so to make a boat of it, if, after all this, I must leave it just there where I found it, and was not able to launch it into the water?

One would have thought I could not have had the least reflection upon my mind of my circumstance while I was making this boat, but I should have immediately thought how I should get it into the sea, but my thoughts were so intent upon my voyage over the sea in it that I never once considered how I should get it off the land, and it was really in its own nature more easy for me to guide it over forty-five miles of sea than about forty-five fathom of land, where it lay, to set it afloat in the water.

I went to work upon this boat the most like a fool that ever man did who had any of his senses awake. I pleased myself with the design, without determining whether I was ever able to undertake it – not but that the difficulty of launching my boat came often into my head, but I put a stop to my own enquiries into it, by this foolish answer which I gave myself, "Let's first make it, I'll warrant I'll find some way or other to get it along when 'tis done."

This was a most preposterous method, but the eagerness of my fancy prevailed, and to work I went. I felled a cedar tree; I question much whether Solomon ever had such a one for the building of the temple at Jerusalem. It was five foot ten inches diameter at the lower part next the stump, and four foot eleven inches diameter at the end of twenty two foot, after which it lessened for a while, and then parted into branches. It was not without infinite labour that I felled this tree: I was twenty days hacking and hewing at it at the bottom; I was fourteen more getting the branches and limbs and the vast spreading head of it cut off, which I hacked and hewed through with axe and hatchet, and inexpressible labour. After this, it cost me a month to shape it and dub it to a proportion, and to something like the bottom of a boat, that it might swim upright as it ought to do. It cost me near three months more to clear the inside, and work it out so as to make an exact boat of it. This I did indeed without fire, by mere mallet and chisel, and by the dint of hard labour, till I had brought it to be a very handsome piragua, and big enough to have carried six and twenty men, and consequently big enough to have carried me and all my cargo.

When I had gone through this work, I was extremely delighted with it. The boat was really much bigger than I ever saw a canoe or piragua, that was made of one tree, in my life. Many a weary stroke it had cost, you may be sure, and there remained nothing but to get it into the water, and had I gotten it into the water, I make no question but I should have began the maddest voyage, and the most unlikely to be performed, that ever was undertaken.

But all my devices to get it into the water failed me, though they cost me infinite labour too. It lay about one hundred yards from the water, and not more. But the first inconvenience was, it was uphill towards the creek – well, to take away this discouragement, I resolved to dig into the surface of the earth, and so make a declivity. This I begun, and it cost me a prodigious deal of pains – but who grudges pains that have their deliverance in view? But when this was worked through, and this difficulty managed, it was still much at one, for I could no more stir the canoe than I could the other boat.

Then I measured the distance of ground and resolved to cut a dock or canal to bring the water up to the canoe, seeing I could not bring the canoe down to the water. Well, I began this work, and when I began to enter into it, and calculate how deep it was to be dug, how broad, how the stuff to be thrown out, I found that by the number of hands I had, being none but my own, it must have been ten or twelve years before I should have gone through with it – for the shore lay high, so that at the upper end it must have been at least twenty foot deep – so at length, though with great reluctancy, I gave this attempt over also.

This grieved me heartily, and now I saw, though too late, the folly of beginning a work before we count the cost, and before we judge rightly of our own strength to go through with it.

In the middle of this work, I finished my fourth year in this place, and kept my anniversary with the same devotion, and with as much comfort as ever before, for by a constant study and serious application of the word of God, and by the assistance of His grace, I gained a different knowledge from what I had before. I entertained different notions of things. I looked now upon the world as a thing remote which I had nothing to do with, no expectation from, and indeed no desires about – in a word, I had nothing indeed to do with it, nor was ever like to have – so I thought it looked as we may perhaps look upon it hereafter, namely, as a place I had lived in, but was come out of it, and well might I say, as Father Abraham to Dives, *Between me and thee is a great gulf fixed.**

In the first place, I was removed from all the wickedness of the world here. I had neither *the lust of the flesh, the lust of the eye, or the pride of life.** I had nothing to covet, for I had all that I was now capable of enjoying: I was lord of the whole manor, or if I pleased, I might call myself king or emperor over the whole country which I had possession of. There were no rivals; I had no competitor, none to dispute sovereignty or command with me. I might have raised ship-loadings of corn, but I had no use for it, so I let as little grow as I thought enough for my occasion. I had tortoise or turtles enough, but now and then one was as much as I could put to any use. I had timber enough to have built a fleet of ships. I had grapes enough to have made wine, or to have cured into raisins, to have loaded that fleet when they had been built.

But all I could make use of was all that was valuable. I had enough to eat and to supply my wants, and what was all the rest to me? If I killed more flesh than I could eat, the dog must eat it, or the vermin. If I sowed more corn than I could eat, it must be spoilt. The trees that I cut down were lying to rot on the ground. I could make no more use of them but for fuel, and that I had no occasion for but to dress my food.

In a word, the nature and experience of things dictated to me, upon just reflection, that all the good things of this world are no further good to us than they are for our use, and that whatever we may heap up to give others, we enjoy just as much as we can use and no more. The most covetous griping miser in the world would have been cured of the vice of covetousness if he had been in my case, for I possessed infinitely more than I knew what to do with. I had no room for desire, except it was of things which I had not, and they were but trifles, though indeed of great use to me. I had, as I hinted before, a parcel of money, as well gold as silver, about thirty-six pounds sterling. Alas! There the nasty sorry useless stuff lay: I had no manner of business for it, and I often thought with myself that I would have given a handful of it for a gross of tobacco pipes, or for a hand mill to grind my corn – nay, I would have given it all for a sixpenny worth of turnip and carrot seed out of England, or for a handful of peas and beans, and a bottle of ink. As it was, I had not the least advantage by it, or benefit from it, but there it lay in a drawer, and grew mouldy with the damp of the cave in the wet season, and if I had had the drawer full of diamonds, it had been the same case, and they had been of no manner of value to me, because of no use.

I had now brought my state of life to be much easier in itself than it was at first, and much easier to my mind, as well as to my body. I frequently sat down to my meat with thankfulness, and

admired the hand of God's providence which had thus spread my
table in the wilderness. I learnt to look more upon the bright side
of my condition, and less upon the dark side, and to consider what
I enjoyed, rather than what I wanted, and this gave me sometimes
such secret comforts that I cannot express them – and which I take
notice of here, to put those discontented people in mind of it,
who cannot enjoy comfortably what God has given them because
they see and covet something that He has not given them. All our
discontents about what we want appeared to me to spring from
the want of thankfulness for what we have.

Another reflection was of great use to me, and doubtless would
be so to anyone that should fall into such distress as mine was,
and this was to compare my present condition with what I at first
expected it should be – nay, with what it would certainly have been,
if the good providence of God had not wonderfully ordered the
ship to be cast up nearer to the shore, where I not only could come
at her, but could bring what I got out of her to the shore, for my
relief and comfort; without which I had wanted for tools to work,
weapons for defence or gunpowder and shot for getting my food.

I spent whole hours, I may say whole days, in representing to
myself in the most lively colours how I must have acted if I had
got nothing out of the ship; how I could not have so much as got
any food except fish and turtles, and that as it was long before
I found any of them, I must have perished first; that I should
have lived, if I had not perished, like a mere savage; that if I had
killed a goat or a fowl, by any contrivance, I had no way to flay
or open them, or part the flesh from the skin and the bowels, or
to cut it up, but must gnaw it with my teeth, and pull it with my
claws like a beast.

These reflections made me very sensible of the goodness of
Providence to me, and very thankful for my present condition, with

all its hardships and misfortunes – and this part also I cannot but recommend to the reflection of those who are apt in their misery to say, "Is any affliction like mine!" Let them consider how much worse the cases of some people are, and the case might have been, if Providence had thought fit.

I had another reflection which assisted me also to comfort my mind with hopes, and this was comparing my present condition with what I had deserved, and had therefore reason to expect from the hand of Providence. I had lived a dreadful life, perfectly destitute of the knowledge and fear of God. I had been well instructed by father and mother; neither had they been wanting to me, in their early endeavours, to infuse a religious awe of God into my mind, a sense of my duty, and of what the nature and end of my being required of me. But alas! Falling early into the seafaring life, which of all lives is the most destitute of the fear of God, though His terrors are always before them – I say, falling early into the seafaring life, and into seafaring company, all that little sense of religion which I had entertained was laughed out of me by my messmates, by a hardened despising of dangers, and the views of death, which grew habitual to me by my long absence from all manner of opportunities to converse with anything but what was like myself, or to hear anything that was good or tended towards it.

So void was I of everything that was good, or of the least sense of what I was, or was to be, that in the greatest deliverances I enjoyed, such as my escape from Sallee, my being taken up by the Portuguese master of the ship, my being planted so well in the Brazils, my receiving the cargo from England, and the like, I never had once the word "Thank God" so much as on my mind, or in my mouth; nor in the greatest distress had I so much as a thought to pray to Him, or so much as to say, "Lord have mercy upon me" – no, nor to mention the name of God, unless it was to swear by and blaspheme it.

I had terrible reflections upon my mind for many months, as I have already observed, on the account of my wicked and hardened life past, and when I looked about me and considered what particular providences had attended me since my coming into this place, and how God had dealt bountifully with me; had not only punished me less than my iniquity had deserved, but had so plentifully provided for me; this gave me great hopes that my repentance was accepted, and that God had yet mercy in store for me.

With these reflections I worked my mind up not only to a resignation to the will of God in the present disposition of my circumstances, but even to a sincere thankfulness for my condition, and that I, who was yet a living man, ought not to complain, seeing I had not the due punishment of my sins; that I enjoyed so many mercies which I had no reason to have expected in that place; that I ought never more to repine at my condition, but to rejoice, and to give daily thanks for that daily bread which nothing but a crowd of wonders could have brought. That I ought to consider I had been fed even by miracle, even as great as that of feeding Elijah by ravens* – nay, by a long series of miracles, and that I could hardly have named a place in the unhabitable part of the world where I could have been cast more to my advantage; a place where, as I had no society, which was my affliction on one hand, so I found no ravenous beast, no furious wolves or tigers to threaten my life, no venomous creatures, or poisonous, which I might feed on to my hurt, no savages to murder and devour me.

In a word, as my life was a life of sorrow one way, so it was a life of mercy another, and I wanted nothing to make it a life of comfort, but to be able to make my sense of God's goodness to me, and care over me in this condition, be my daily consolation, and after I did make a just improvement on these things, I went away and was no more sad.

I had now been here so long that many things which I brought onshore for my help were either quite gone or very much wasted and near spent.

My ink, as I observed, had been gone some time, all but a very little, which I eked out with water a little and a little, till it was so pale it scarce left any appearance of black upon the paper. As long as it lasted, I made use of it to minute down the days of the month on which any remarkable thing happened to me. And first by casting up times past, I remember that there was a strange concurrence of days in the various providences which befell me, and which, if I had been superstitiously inclined to observe days as fatal or fortunate, I might have had reason to have looked upon with a great deal of curiosity.

First, I had observed that the same day that I broke away from my father and my friends and ran away to Hull in order to go to sea, the same day afterwards I was taken by the Sallee man-of-war and made a slave.

The same day of the year that I escaped out of the wreck of that ship in Yarmouth roads, that same day year afterwards I made my escape from Sallee in the boat.

The same day of the year I was born on, namely, the 30th of September, that same day I had my life so miraculously saved twenty-six years after, when I was cast onshore in this island, so that my wicked life and my solitary life began both on a day.

The next thing to my ink's being wasted was that of my bread – I mean the biscuit which I brought out of the ship. This I had husbanded to the last degree, allowing myself but one cake of bread a day for above a year, and yet I was quite without bread for near a year before I got any corn of my own, and great reason I had to be thankful that I had any at all, the getting it being, as has been already observed, next to miraculous.

My clothes began to decay too, mightily: as to linen, I had had none a good while, except some chequered shirts which I found in the chests of the other seamen, and which I carefully preserved, because many times I could bear no other clothes on but a shirt, and it was a very great help to me that I had among all the men's clothes of the ship almost three dozen of shirts. There were also several thick watch coats of the seamen's, which were left indeed, but they were too hot to wear, and though it is true that the weather was so violent hot that there was no need of clothes, yet I could not go quite naked – no, though I had been inclined to it, which I was not, nor could not abide the thoughts of it, though I was all alone.

The reason why I could not go quite naked was I could not bear the heat of the sun so well when quite naked as with some clothes on – nay, the very heat frequently blistered my skin – whereas with a shirt on, the air itself made some motion and, whistling under the shirt, was twofold cooler than without it. No more could I ever bring myself to go out in the heat of the sun without a cap or a hat; the heat of the sun, beating with such violence as it does in that place, would give me the headache presently by darting so directly on my head, without a cap or hat on, so that I could not bear it, whereas if I put on my hat, it would presently go away.

Upon these views I began to consider about putting the few rags I had, which I called clothes, into some order. I had worn out all the waistcoats I had, and my business was now to try if I could not make jackets out of the great watch coats which I had by me, and with such other materials as I had, so I set to work a-tailoring, or rather indeed a-botching, for I made most piteous work of it.

However, I made shift to make two or three new waistcoats, which I hoped would serve me a great while – as for breeches or drawers, I made but a very sorry shift indeed, till afterwards.

I have mentioned that I saved the skins of all the creatures that I killed – I mean four-footed ones – and I had hung them up stretched out with sticks in the sun, by which means some of them were so dry and hard that they were fit for little, but others, it seems, were very useful. The first thing I made of these was a great cap for my head, with the hair on the outside to shoot off the rain, and this I performed so well that after this I made me a suit of clothes wholly of these skins – that is to say, a waistcoat and breeches open at knees, and both loose, for they were rather wanting to keep me cool than to keep me warm. I must not omit to acknowledge that they were wretchedly made, for if I was a bad carpenter, I was a worse tailor. However, they were such as I made very good shift with, and when I was abroad, if it happened to rain, the hair of my waistcoat and cap being outermost, I was kept very dry.

After this I spent a great deal of time and pains to make me an umbrella; I was indeed in great want of one, and had a great mind to make one. I had seen them made in the Brazils, where they are very useful in the great heats which are there, and I felt the heats every jot as great here, and greater too, being nearer the equinox. Besides, as I was obliged to be much abroad, it was a most useful thing to me, as well for the rains as the heats. I took a world of pains at it, and was a great while before I could make anything likely to hold – nay, after I thought I had hit the way, I spoilt two or three before I made one to my mind – but at last I made one that answered indifferently well. The main difficulty I found was to make it to let down. I could make it spread, but if it did not let down too, and draw in, it was not portable for me any way but just over my head, which would not do. However, at last, as I said, I made one to answer, and covered it with skins, the hair upwards, so that it cast off the rains like a penthouse, and kept off the sun so effectually that I could walk out in the hottest of the weather with greater advantage than I could before in the coolest, and when I had no need of it, could close it and carry it under my arm.

Thus I lived mighty comfortably, my mind being entirely composed by resigning to the will of God, and throwing myself wholly upon the disposal of His providence. This made my life better than sociable, for when I began to regret the want of conversation, I would ask myself whether thus conversing mutually with my own thoughts, and, as I hope I may say, with even God Himself by ejaculations, was not better than the utmost enjoyment of human society in the world.

I CANNOT SAY THAT AFTER THIS, for five years, any extraordinary thing happened to me, but I lived on in the same course, in the same posture and place, just as before. The chief things I was employed in, besides my yearly labour of planting my barley and rice, and curing my raisins, of both which I always kept up just enough to have sufficient stock of one year's provisions beforehand – I say, besides this yearly labour, and my daily labour of going out with my gun, I had one labour – to make me a canoe, which at last I finished, so that by digging a canal to it of six foot wide and four foot deep, I brought it into the creek, almost half a mile. As for the first, which was so vastly big, as I made it without considering beforehand, as I ought to do, how I should be able to launch it, so, never being able to bring it to the water, or bring the water to it, I was obliged to let it lie where it was as a memorandum to teach me to be wiser next time. Indeed, the next time, though I could not get a tree proper for it, and in a place where I could not get the water to it at any less distance than, as I have said, nearly half a mile, yet as I saw it was practicable at last, I never gave it over, and though I was near two years about it, yet I never grudged my labour, in hopes of having a boat to go off to sea at last.

However, though my little piragua was finished, yet the size of it was not at all answerable to the design which I had in view when I made the first – I mean, of venturing over to the terra firma, where it was above forty miles broad – accordingly, the smallness of my boat assisted to put an end to that design, and now I thought no more of it. But as I had a boat, my next design was to make a tour round the island, for as I had been on the other side in one place, crossing, as I have already described it, over the land, so the discoveries I made in that little journey made me very eager to see other parts of the coast – and now I had a boat, I thought of nothing but sailing round the island.

For this purpose, that I might do everything with discretion and consideration, I fitted up a little mast to my boat, and made a sail to it out of some of the pieces of the ship's sail, which lay in store, and of which I had a great stock by me.

Having fitted my mast and sail, and tried the boat, I found she would sail very well. Then I made little lockers, or boxes, at either end of my boat to put provisions, necessaries, ammunition, etc. into, to be kept dry, either from rain or the spry of the sea, and a little long hollow place I cut in the inside of the boat where I could lay my gun, making a flap to hang down over it to keep it dry.

I fixed my umbrella also in a step at the stern like a mast, to stand over my head and keep the heat of the sun off of me like an awning, and thus I every now and then took a little voyage upon the sea, but never went far out, nor far from the little creek, but at last, being eager to view the circumference of my little kingdom, I resolved upon my tour, and accordingly I victualled my ship for the voyage, putting in two dozen of my loaves (cakes I should rather call them) of barley bread, an earthen pot full of parched rice – a food I ate a great deal of – a little bottle of rum, half a goat, and powder and shot for killing more, and two large watch coats, of those which, as I mentioned before, I had saved out of the seamen's chests – these I took, one to lie upon, and the other to cover me in the night.

It was the sixth of November, in the sixth year of my reign – or my captivity, which you please – that I set out on this voyage, and I found it much longer than I expected, for though the island itself was not very large, yet when I came to the east side of it, I found a great ledge of rocks lie out above two leagues into the sea, some above water, some under it, and beyond that, a shoal of sand, lying dry half a league more, so that I was obliged to go a great way out to sea to double the point.

When first I discovered them, I was going to give over my enterprise, and come back again, not knowing how far it might oblige me to go out to sea, and above all, doubting how I should get back again, so I came to an anchor, for I had made me a kind of an anchor with a piece of a broken grappling which I got out of the ship.

Having secured my boat, I took my gun and went onshore, climbing up a hill, which seemed to overlook that point, where I saw the full extent of it, and resolved to venture.

In my viewing the sea from that hill where I stood, I perceived a strong, and indeed a most furious current, which ran to the east, and even came close to the point, and I took the more notice of it, because I saw there might be some danger; that when I came into it, I might be carried out to sea by the strength of it, and not be able to make the island again, and indeed, had I not gotten first up upon this hill, I believe it would have been so, for there was the same current on the other side the island, only that it set off at a further distance, and I saw there was a strong eddy under the shore, so I had nothing to do but to get out of the first current and I should presently be in an eddy.

I lay here, however, two days, because the wind blowing pretty fresh at ESE – and that being just contrary to the said current – made a great breach of the sea upon the point, so that it was not safe for me to keep too close to the shore for the breach, nor to go too far off because of the stream.

The third day in the morning, the wind having abated overnight, the sea was calm, and I ventured, but I am a warning piece again to all rash and ignorant pilots, for no sooner was I come to the point, when even I was not my boat's length from the shore, but I found myself in a great depth of water, and a current like the sluice of a mill: it carried my boat along with it with such violence that all I could do could not keep her so much as on the edge of it, but I found it hurried me further and further out from the eddy, which was on my left hand. There was no wind stirring to help me, and all I could do with my paddlers signified nothing, and now I began to give myself over for lost, for as the current was on both sides the island, I knew in a few leagues distance they must join again, and then I was irrecoverably gone; nor did I see any possibility of avoiding it, so that I had no prospect before me but of perishing, not by the sea, for that was calm enough, but of starving for hunger. I had indeed found a tortoise on the shore as big almost as I could lift, and had tossed it into the boat, and I had a great jar of fresh water – that is to say, one of my earthen pots – but what was all this to being driven into the vast ocean, where, to be sure, there was no shore, no mainland or island, for a thousand leagues at least?

And now I saw how easy it was for the providence of God to make the most miserable condition mankind could be in, *worse*. Now I looked back upon my desolate solitary island as the most pleasant place in the world, and all the happiness my heart could wish for was to be but there again. I stretched out my hands to it with eager wishes. "O happy desert," said I, "I shall never see thee more. O miserable creature," said I, "whither am I going?" Then I reproached myself with my unthankful temper, and how I had repined at my solitary condition – and now what would I give to be onshore there again! Thus we never see the true state of our condition till it is illustrated to us by its contraries, nor know how to value what we enjoy but by the want of it. It is scarce possible to imagine the consternation I was now in, being driven from my beloved island (for so it appeared to me now to be) into the wide ocean, almost two leagues, and in the utmost despair of ever recovering it again. However, I worked hard, till indeed my strength was almost exhausted, and kept my boat as much to the northwards – that is, towards the side of the current which the eddy lay on – as possibly I could, when about noon, as the sun passed the meridian, I thought I felt a little breeze of wind in my face, springing up from the SSE. This cheered my heart a little, and especially when in about half an hour more it blew a pretty small gentle gale. By this time I was gotten at a frightful distance from the island, and had the least cloud of hazy weather intervened, I had been undone another way too, for I had no compass on board, and should never have known how to have steered towards the island if I had but once lost sight of it, but the weather continuing clear, I applied myself to get up my mast again, and spread my sail, standing away to the north as much as possible, to get out of the current.

Just as I had set my mast and sail and the boat began to stretch away, I saw even by the clearness of the water some alteration of the current was near, for where the current was so strong, the water was foul, but perceiving the water clear, I found the current abate, and presently I found to the east, at about half a mile, a breach of the sea upon some rocks. These rocks I found caused the current to part again, and as the main stress of it ran away more southerly, leaving the rocks to the north-east, so the other returned by the repulse of the rocks, and made a strong eddy, which ran back again to the north-west with a very sharp stream.

They who know what it is to have a reprieve brought to them upon the ladder, or to be rescued from thieves just a going to murder them, or who have been in suchlike extremities, may guess what my present surprise of joy was, and how gladly I put my boat into the stream of this eddy, and the wind also freshening, how gladly I spread my sail to it, running cheerfully before the wind, and with a strong tide or eddy underfoot.

This eddy carried me about a league in my way back again directly towards the island, but about two leagues more to the northwards than the current which carried me away at first, so that when I came near the island, I found myself open to the northern shore of it, that is to say, the other end of the island opposite to that which I went out from.

When I had made something more than a league of way by the help of this current or eddy, I found it was spent and served me no further. However, I found that being between the two great currents – namely, that on the south side, which had hurried me away, and that on the north which lay about a league on the other side – I say, between these two, in the wake of the island, I found the water at least still and running no way, and having still a breeze of wind fair for me, I kept on steering directly for the island, though not making such fresh way as I did before.

About four o'clock in the evening, being then within about a league of the island, I found the point of the rocks which occasioned this disaster, stretching out as is described before to the southwards, and casting off the current more southwardly, had of course made another eddy to the north, and this I found very strong, but not directly setting the way my course lay – which was due west – but almost full north. However, having a fresh gale, I stretched across this eddy slanting north-west, and in about an hour came within about a mile of the shore, where, it being smooth water, I soon got to land.

When I was onshore I fell on my knees and gave God thanks for my deliverance, resolving to lay aside all thoughts of my deliverance by my boat, and refreshing myself with such things as I had, I brought my boat close to the shore in a little cove that I had spied under some trees, and laid me down to sleep, being quite spent with the labour and fatigue of the voyage.

I was now at a great loss which way to get home with my boat. I had run so much hazard and knew too much of the case to think of attempting it by the way I went out, and what might be at the other side (I mean the west side) I knew not, nor had I any mind to run any more ventures. So I only resolved in the morning to make my way westwards along the shore and to see if there was no creek where I might lay up my frigate in safety, so as to have her again if I wanted her. In about three mile or thereabouts, coasting the shore, I came to a very good inlet or bay about a mile over, which narrowed till it came to a very little rivulet or brook, where I found a very convenient harbour for my boat, and where she lay as if she had been in a little dock made on purpose for her. Here I put in, and having stowed my boat very safe, I went onshore to look about me and see where I was.

I soon found I had but a little passed by the place where I had been before, when I travelled on foot to that shore, so taking nothing out of my boat but my gun and my umbrella – for it was exceeding hot – I began my march. The way was comfortable enough after such a voyage as I had been upon, and I reached my old bower in the evening, where I found everything standing as I left it, for I always kept it in good order, being, as I said before, my country house.

I got over the fence, and laid me down in the shade to rest my limbs, for I was very weary, and fell asleep. But judge you, if you can, that read my story, what a surprise I must be in, when I was waked out of my sleep by a voice calling me by my name several times, "Robin, Robin, Robin Crusoe, poor Robin Crusoe, where are you, Robin Crusoe? Where are you? Where have you been?"

I was so dead asleep at first, being fatigued with rowing, or paddling, as it is called, the first part of the day, and with walking the latter part, that I did not wake thoroughly, but dozing between sleeping and waking, thought I dreamt that somebody spoke to me: but as the voice continued to repeat "Robin Crusoe, Robin Crusoe", at last I began to wake more perfectly, and was at first dreadfully frighted, and started up in the utmost consternation. But no sooner were my eyes open, than I saw my Poll sitting on the top of the hedge, and immediately knew that it was he that spoke to me, for just in such bemoaning language I had used to talk to him and teach him, and he had learnt it so perfectly that he would sit upon my finger, and lay his bill close to my face, and cry, "Poor Robin Crusoe, where are you? Where have you been? How came you here?" and such things as I had taught him.

However, even though I knew it was the parrot, and that indeed it could be nobody else, it was a good while before I could compose myself. First, I was amazed how the creature got thither, and then, how he should just keep about the place and nowhere else: but as I was well satisfied it could be nobody but honest Poll, I got it over, and holding out my hand, and calling him by his name, Poll, the sociable creature came to me and sat upon my thumb, as he used to do, and continued talking to me, "Poor Robin Crusoe! And how did I come here? And where had I been?" just as if he had been overjoyed to see me again – and so I carried him home along with me.

I had now had enough of rambling to sea for some time, and had enough to do for many days to sit still and reflect upon the danger I had been in. I would have been very glad to have had my boat again on my side of the island, but I knew not how it was practicable to get it about. As to the east side of the island, which I had gone round, I knew well enough there was no venturing that way – my very heart would shrink, and my very blood run chill, but to think of it – and as to the other side of the island, I did not know how it might be there, but supposing the current ran with the same force against the shore at the east as it passed by it on the other, I might run the same risk of being driven down the stream and carried by the island, as I had been before of being carried away from it. So with these thoughts I contented myself to be without any boat, though it had been the product of so many months' labour to make it, and of so many more to get it unto the sea.

In this government of my temper I remained near a year, lived a very sedate, retired life, as you may well suppose, and my thoughts being very much composed as to my condition, and fully comforted in resigning myself to the dispositions of Providence, I thought I lived really very happily in all things, except that of society.

I improved myself in this time in all the mechanic exercises which my necessities put me upon applying myself to, and I believe could, upon occasion, make a very good carpenter, especially considering how few tools I had.

Besides this, I arrived at an unexpected perfection in my earthenware, and contrived well enough to make them with a wheel, which I found infinitely easier and better, because I made things round and shapable which before were filthy things indeed to look on. But I think I was never more vain of my own performance, or more joyful for anything I found out, than for my being able to make a tobacco pipe. And though it was a very ugly clumsy thing when it was done, and only burnt red like other earthenware, yet as it was hard and firm, and would draw the smoke, I was exceedingly comforted with it, for I had been always used to smoke, and there were pipes in the ship, but I forgot them at first, not knowing that there was tobacco in the island – and afterwards, when I searched the ship again, I could not come at any pipes at all.

In my wicker-ware also I improved much, and made abundance of necessary baskets as well as my invention showed me; though not very handsome, yet they were such as were very handy and convenient for my laying things up in, or fetching things home in. For example, if I killed a goat abroad, I could hang it up in a tree, flay it and dress it, and cut it in pieces and bring it home in a basket; and the like by a turtle: I could cut it up, take out the eggs and a piece or two of the flesh, which was enough for me, and bring them home in a basket, and leave the rest behind me. Also large deep baskets were the receivers for my corn, which I always rubbed out as soon as it was dry and cured, and kept it in great baskets.

I began now to perceive my powder abated considerably, and this was a want which it was impossible for me to supply, and I began seriously to consider what I must do when I should have no more powder, that is to say, how I should do to kill any goat. I had, as is observed, in the third year of my being here kept a young kid, and bred her up tame, and I was in hope of getting a he-goat, but I could not by any means bring it to pass till my kid grew an old goat, and I could never find it in my heart to kill her, till she died at last of mere age.

But being now in the eleventh year of my residence and, as I have said, my ammunition growing low, I set myself to study some art to trap and snare the goats, to see whether I could not catch some of them alive, and particularly I wanted a she-goat great with young.

To this purpose I made snares to hamper them, and I do believe they were more than once taken in them, but my tackle was not good, for I had no wire and I always found them broken and my bait devoured.

At length I resolved to try a pitfall, so I dug several large pits in the earth, in places where I had observed the goats used to feed, and over these pits I placed hurdles, of my own making too, with a great weight upon them, and several times I put ears of barley and dry rice, without setting the trap, and I could easily perceive that the goats had gone in and eaten up the corn, for I could see the mark of their feet. At length I set three traps in one night, and going the next morning, I found them all standing, and yet the bait eaten and gone; this was very discouraging. However, I altered my trap, and, not to trouble you with particulars, going one morning to see my trap, I found in one of them a large old he-goat, and in one of the other three kids, a male and two females.

As to the old one, I knew not what to do with him, he was so fierce I durst not go into the pit to him – that is to say, to go about to bring him away alive, which was what I wanted. I could have killed him, but that was not my business, nor would it answer my end. So I e'en let him out, and he ran away as if he had been frighted out of his wits, but I had forgot then what I learnt afterwards, that hunger will tame a lion. If I had let him stay there three or four days without food, and then have carried him some water to drink and then a little corn, he would have been as tame

as one of the kids, for they are mighty sagacious, tractable creatures where they are well used.

However, for the present I let him go, knowing no better at
that time; then I went to the three kids and, taking them one by
one, I tied them with strings together, and with some difficulty
brought them all home.

It was a good while before they would feed, but throwing them
some sweetcorn, it tempted them and they began to be tame, and
now I found that if I expected to supply myself with goat flesh
when I had no powder or shot left, breeding some up tame was
my only way, when perhaps I might have them about my house
like a flock of sheep.

But then it presently occurred to me that I must keep the tame
from the wild, or else they would always run wild when they grew
up, and the only way for this was to have some enclosed piece
of ground, well-fenced either with hedge or pale, to keep them
in so effectually that those within might not break out, or those
without break in.

This was a great undertaking for one pair of hands, yet as I saw
there was an absolute necessity of doing it, my first piece of work
was to find out a proper piece of ground, namely, where there was
likely to be herbage for them to eat, water for them to drink and
cover to keep them from the sun.

Those who understand such enclosures will think I had very
little contrivance, when I pitched upon a place very proper for
all these, being a plain open piece of meadowland, or savannah
(as our people call it in the western colonies), which had two
or three little drills of fresh water in it and at one end was very
woody – I say, they will smile at my forecast when I shall tell
them I began my enclosing of this piece of ground in such a
manner that my hedge or pale must have been at least two miles

about. Nor was the madness of it so great as to the compass, for if it was ten miles about I was like to have time enough to do it in. But I did not consider that my goats would be as wild in so much compass as if they had had the whole island, and I should have so much room to chase them in that I should never catch them.

My hedge was begun and carried on, I believe, about fifty yards, when this thought occurred to me, so I presently stopped short, and for the first beginning I resolved to enclose a piece of about 150 yards in length and 100 yards in breadth, which as it would maintain as many as I should have in any reasonable time, so as my flock increased I could add more ground to my enclosure.

This was acting with some prudence, and I went to work with courage. I was about three months hedging in the first piece, and till I had done it I tethered the three kids in the best part of it, and used them to feed as near me as possible to make them familiar, and very often I would go and carry them some ears of barley, or a handful of rice, and feed them out of my hand, so that after my enclosure was finished, and I let them loose, they would follow me up and down, bleating after me for a handful of corn.

This answered my end, and in about a year and a half I had a flock of about twelve goats, kids and all, and in two years more I had three and forty, besides several that I took and killed for my food. And after that I enclosed five several pieces of ground to feed them in, with little pens to drive them into, to take them as I wanted, and gates out of one piece of ground into another.

But this was not all, for now I not only had goat's flesh to feed on when I pleased, but milk too, a thing which indeed in my beginning I did not so much as think of, and which, when it came into my thoughts, was really an agreeable surprise. For now I set up my dairy, and had sometimes a gallon or two of milk in a day. And as nature, who gives supplies of food to every creature, dictates even naturally how to make use of it, so I that had never milked a cow, much less a goat, or seen butter or cheese made, very readily and handily, though after a great many essays and miscarriages, made me both butter and cheese at last, and never wanted it afterwards.

How mercifully can our great Creator treat His creatures, even in those conditions in which they seemed to be overwhelmed in destruction! How can He sweeten the bitterest providences, and give us cause to praise Him for dungeons and prisons! What a table was here spread for me in a wilderness, where I saw nothing at first but to perish for hunger!

I T WOULD HAVE MADE A STOIC SMILE to have seen me and my little family sit down to dinner. There was my majesty the prince and lord of the whole island; I had the lives of all my subjects at my absolute command; I could hang, draw, give liberty and take it away, and no rebels among all my subjects.

Then to see how like a king I dined too, all alone, attended by my servants. Poll, as if he had been my favourite, was the only person permitted to talk to me. My dog, who was now grown very old and crazy, and had found no species to multiply his kind upon, sat always at my right hand, and two cats, one on one side the table, and one on the other, expecting now and then a bit from my hand as a mark of special favour.

But these were not the two cats which I brought onshore at first, for they were both of them dead and had been interred near my habitation by my own hand, but, one of them having multiplied by I know not what kind of creature, these were two which I had preserved tame, whereas the rest ran wild in the woods, and became indeed troublesome to me at last, for they would often come into my house, and plunder me too, till at last I was obliged to shoot them, and did kill a great many – at length they left me. With this attendance and in this plentiful manner I lived; neither could I be said to want anything but society, and of that, in some time after this, I was like to have too much.

I was something impatient, as I have observed, to have the use of my boat, though very loath to run any more hazards, and therefore sometimes I sat contriving ways to get her about the island, and at other times I sat myself down contented enough without her. But I had a strange uneasiness in my mind to go down to the point of the island, where, as I have said, in my last ramble, I went up the hill to see how the shore lay and how the current set, that I might see what I had to do. This inclination increased upon me every day, and at length I resolved to travel thither by land, following the edge of the shore. I did so – but had anyone in England been to meet such a man as I was, it must either have frighted them, or raised a great deal of laughter; and as I frequently stood still to look at myself, I could not but smile at the notion of my travelling through Yorkshire with such an equipage, and in such a dress. Be pleased to take a sketch of my figure as follows.

I had a great high shapeless cap, made of a goat's skin, with a flap hanging down behind, as well to keep the sun from me as to shoot the rain off from running into my neck, nothing being so hurtful in these climates as the rain upon the flesh under the clothes.

I had a short jacket of goatskin, the skirts coming down to about the middle of my thighs, and a pair of open-kneed breeches of the same; the breeches were made of the skin of an old he-goat, whose hair hung down such a length on either side that, like pantaloons, it reached to the middle of my legs. Stockings and shoes I had none, but had made me a pair of somethings, I scarce know what to call them, like buskins, to flap over my legs and lace on either side like spatterdashes, but of a most barbarous shape, as indeed were all the rest of my clothes.

I had on a broad belt of goat's skin dried, which I drew together with two thongs of the same, instead of buckles, and in a kind of a frog on either side of this, instead of a sword and a dagger, hung a little saw and a hatchet, one on one side, one on the other. I had another belt not so broad, and fastened in the same manner, which hung over my shoulder, and at the end of it, under my left arm, hung two pouches, both made of goat's skin too – in one of which hung my powder, in the other my shot. At my back I carried my basket, on my shoulder my gun, and over my head a great clumsy ugly goatskin umbrella, but which, after all, was the most necessary thing I had about me next to my gun. As for my face, the colour of it was really not so mulatto-like as one might expect from a man not at all careful of it and living within nine or ten degrees of the equinox. My beard I had once suffered to grow till it was about a quarter of a yard long, but as I had both scissors and razors sufficient, I had cut it pretty short, except what grew on my upper lip, which I had trimmed into a large pair of Mohammedan whiskers, such as I had seen worn by some Turks who I saw at Sallee – for the Moors did not wear such, though the Turks did – of these mustachios or whiskers I will not say they were long enough to hang my hat upon them, but they were of a length and shape monstrous enough, and such as in England would have passed for frightful.

But all this is by the by, for as to my figure, I had so few to observe me that it was of no manner of consequence, so I say no more to that part. In this kind of figure I went my new journey, and was out five or six days. I travelled first along the seashore, directly to the place where I first brought my boat to an anchor, to get up upon the rocks, and having no boat now to take care of, I went over the land a nearer way to the same height that I was upon before, when, looking forwards to the point of the rocks which lay out, and which I was obliged to double with my boat as is said above, I was surprised to see the sea all smooth and quiet, no rippling, no motion, no current any more there than in other places.

I was at a strange loss to understand this, and resolved to spend some time in the observing it to see if nothing from the sets of the tide had occasioned it, but I was presently convinced how it was, namely, that the tide of ebb, setting from the west and joining with the current of waters from some great river on the shore, must be the occasion of this current; and that according as the wind blew more forcibly from the west or from the north, this current came nearer or went further from the shore, for waiting thereabouts till evening, I went up to the rock again, and then the tide of ebb being made, I plainly saw the current again as before, only that it ran further off, being near half a league from the shore – whereas in my case, it set close upon the shore, and hurried me and my canoe along with it, which at another time it would not have done.

This observation convinced me that I had nothing to do but to observe the ebbing and the flowing of the tide, and I might very easily bring my boat about the island again, but when I began to think of putting it in practice, I had such a terror upon my spirit at the remembrance of the danger I had been in that I could not think of it again with any patience – but on the contrary, I took up another resolution which was more safe, though more laborious, and this was that I would build or rather make me another piragua or canoe, and so have one for one side of the island and one for the other.

You are to understand that now I had, as I may call it, two plantations in the island: one my little fortification or tent, with the wall about it under the rock, with the cave behind me – which by this time I had enlarged into several apartments or caves, one within another. One of these, which was the driest and largest, and had a door out beyond my wall or fortification – that is to say, beyond where my wall joined to the rock – was all filled up with the large earthen pots, of which I have given an account, and with fourteen or fifteen great baskets, which would hold five or six bushels each, where I laid up my stores of provision, especially my corn, some in the ear cut off short from the straw, and the other rubbed out with my hand.

As for my wall – made, as before, with long stakes or piles – those piles grew all like trees, and were by this time grown so big, and spread so very much, that there was not the least appearance to anyone's view of any habitation behind them.

Near this dwelling of mine, but a little further within the land, and upon lower ground, lay my two pieces of corn ground, which I kept duly cultivated and sowed, and which duly yielded me their harvest in its season, and whenever I had occasion for more corn, I had more land adjoining as fit as that.

Besides this, I had my country seat, and I had now a tolerable plantation there also: for first, I had my little bower, as I called it, which I kept in repair – that is to say, I kept the hedge which circled it in constantly fitted up to its usual height, the ladder standing always in the inside; I kept the trees – which at first were no more than my stakes, but were now grown very firm and tall – I kept them always so cut that they might spread and grow thick and wild, and make the more agreeable shade, which they did effectually to my mind. In the middle of this I had my tent always standing, being a piece of a sail spread over poles set up for that purpose, and which never wanted any repair or renewing, and under this I had made me a squab or couch with the skins of the creatures I had killed, and with other soft things, and a blanket laid on them, such as belonged to our sea bedding, which I had saved, and a great watch coat to cover me, and here, whenever I had occasion to be absent from my chief seat, I took up my country habitation.

Adjoining to this I had my enclosures for my cattle – that is to say, my goats. And as I had taken an inconceivable deal of pains to fence and enclose this ground, so I was so uneasy to see it kept entire, lest the goats should break through, that I never left off till with infinite labour I had stuck the outside of the hedge so full of small stakes, and so near to one another, that it was rather a pale than a hedge and there was scarce room to put a hand through between them, which afterwards when those stakes grew, as they all did in the next rainy season, made the enclosure strong like a wall; indeed, stronger than any wall.

This will testify for me that I was not idle, and that I spared no pains to bring to pass whatever appeared necessary for my comfortable support, for I considered the keeping up a breed of tame creatures thus at my hand would be a living magazine of flesh, milk, butter and cheese for me as long as I lived in the place, if it were to be forty years, and that keeping them in my reach depended entirely upon my perfecting my enclosures to such a degree that I might be sure of keeping them together, which by this method indeed I so effectually secured that, when these little stakes began to grow, I had planted them so very thick I was forced to pull some of them up again.

In this place also I had my grapes growing, which I principally depended on for my winter store of raisins, and which I never failed to preserve very carefully as the best and most agreeable dainty of my whole diet, and indeed they were not agreeable only, but physical, wholesome, nourishing and refreshing to the last degree.

As this was also about halfway between my other habitation and the place where I had laid up my boat, I generally stayed and lay here in my way thither, for I used frequently to visit my boat, and I kept all things about or belonging to her in very good order. Sometimes I went out in her to divert myself, but no more hazardous voyages would I go, nor scarce ever above a stone's cast or two from the shore, I was so apprehensive of being hurried out of my knowledge again by the currents or winds, or any other accident. But now I come to a new scene of my life.

It happened one day about noon: going towards my boat, I was exceedingly surprised with the print of a man's naked foot on the shore, which was very plain to be seen in the sand. I stood like one thunderstruck, or as if I had seen an apparition; I listened, I looked round me, I could hear nothing, nor see anything; I went up to a rising ground to look further; I went up the shore and down the shore, but it was all one – I could see no other impression but that one. I went to it again to see if there were any more, and to observe if it might not be my fancy, but there was no room for that, for there was exactly the very print of a foot, toes, heel and every part of a foot – how it came thither I knew not, nor could in the least imagine. But after innumerable fluttering thoughts, like a man perfectly confused and out of myself, I came home to my fortification, not feeling, as we say, the ground I went on, but terrified to the last degree, looking behind me at every two or three steps, mistaking every bush and tree, and fancying every stump at a distance to be a man; nor is it possible to describe how many various shapes affrighted imagination represented things to me in, how many wild ideas were found every moment in my fancy, and what strange unaccountable whimsies came into my thoughts by the way.

When I came to my castle, for so I think I called it ever after this, I fled into it like one pursued; whether I went over by the ladder as first contrived, or went in at the hole in the rock which I called a door, I cannot remember – no, nor could I remember the next morning, for never frighted hare fled to cover, or fox to earth, with more terror of mind than I to this retreat.

I slept none that night; the further I was from the occasion of my fright, the greater my apprehensions were, which is something contrary to the nature of such things, and especially to the usual practice of all creatures in fear: but I was so embarrassed with my own frightful ideas of the thing that I formed nothing but dismal imaginations to myself, even though I was now a great way off of it. Sometimes I fancied it must be the Devil, and reason joined in with me upon this supposition, for how should any other thing in human shape come into the place? Where was the vessel that brought them? What marks was there of any other footsteps? And how was it possible a man should come there? But then to think that Satan should take human shape upon him in such a place where there could be no manner of occasion for it but to leave the print of his foot behind him, and that even for no purpose too, for he could not be sure I should see it. This was an amusement the other way; I considered that the Devil might have found out abundance of other ways to have terrified me than this of the single print of a foot; that as I lived quite on the other side of the island, he would never have been so simple to leave a mark in a place where 'twas ten thousand to one whether I should ever see it or not, and in the sand too, which the first surge of the sea upon a high wind would have defaced entirely. All this seemed inconsistent with the thing itself, and with all the notions we usually entertain of the subtlety of the Devil.

Abundance of such things as these assisted to argue me out of all apprehensions of its being the Devil, and I presently concluded then that it must be some more dangerous creature, namely, that it must be some of the savages of the mainland over against me, who had wandered out to sea in their canoes and, either driven by the currents or by contrary winds, had made the island, and had been onshore, but were gone away again to sea, being as loath, perhaps, to have stayed in this desolate island as I would have been to have had them.

While these reflections were rolling upon my mind, I was very thankful in my thoughts that I was so happy as not to be thereabouts at that time, or that they did not see my boat, by which they would have concluded that some inhabitants had been in the place and perhaps have searched further for me. Then terrible thoughts racked my imagination about their having found my boat and that there were people here, and that if so, I should certainly have them come again in greater numbers and devour me; that if it should happen so that they should not find me, yet they would find my enclosure, destroy all my corn, carry away all my flock of tame goats, and I should perish at last for mere want.

Thus my fear banished all my religious hope; all that former confidence in God, which was founded upon such wonderful experience as I had had of His goodness, now vanished, as if He that had fed me by miracle hitherto could not preserve by His power the provision which He had made for me by His goodness. I reproached myself with my easiness, that would not sow any more corn one year than would just serve me till the next season, as if no accident could intervene to prevent my enjoying the crop that was upon the ground, and this I thought so just a reproof that I resolved for the future to have two or three years' corn beforehand, so that whatever might come, I might not perish for want of bread.

How strange a chequer work of providence is the life of man! And by what secret differing springs are the affections hurried about as differing circumstances present! Today we love what tomorrow we hate; today we seek what tomorrow we shun; today we desire what tomorrow we fear, nay, even tremble at the apprehensions of. This was exemplified in me at this time in the most lively manner imaginable, for I whose only affliction was that I seemed banished from human society, that I was alone, circumscribed by the boundless ocean, cut off from mankind and condemned to what I called silent life; that I was as one who Heaven thought not worthy to be numbered among the living, or to appear among the rest of His creatures; that to have seen one of my own species would have seemed to me a raising from death to life, and the greatest blessing that Heaven itself, next to the supreme blessing of salvation, could bestow – I say, that I should now tremble at the very apprehensions of seeing a man, and was ready to sink into the ground at but the shadow or silent appearance of a man's having set his foot in the island.

Such is the uneven state of human life, and it afforded me a great many curious speculations afterwards, when I had a little recovered my first surprise. I considered that this was the station of life the infinitely wise and good providence of God had determined for me; that as I could not foresee what the ends of divine wisdom might be in all this, so I was not to dispute His sovereignty, who, as I was His creature, had an undoubted right by creation to govern and dispose of me absolutely as He thought fit, and who, as I was a creature who had offended Him, had likewise a judicial right to condemn me to what punishment He thought fit; and that it was my part to submit to bear His indignation because I had sinned against Him.

I then reflected that God – who was not only righteous but omnipotent – as He had thought fit thus to punish and afflict me, so He was able to deliver me; that if He did not think fit to do it, 'twas my unquestioned duty to resign myself absolutely and entirely to His will; and on the other hand, it was my duty also to hope in Him, pray to Him and quietly to attend the dictates and directions of His daily providence.

These thoughts took me up many hours, days – nay, I may say weeks and months – and one particular effect of my cogitations on this occasion I cannot omit: namely, one morning early, lying in my bed, and filled with thought about my danger from the appearance of savages, I found it discomposed me very much, upon which those words of the scripture came into my thoughts: *Call upon me in the day of trouble, and I will deliver, and thou shalt glorify me.**

Upon this, rising cheerfully out of my bed, my heart was not only comforted, but I was guided and encouraged to pray earnestly to God for deliverance. When I had done praying, I took up my Bible, and opening it to read, the first words that presented to me were, *Wait on the Lord, and be of good cheer, and he shall strengthen thy heart; wait, I say, on the Lord.** It is impossible to express the comfort this gave me. In answer I thankfully laid down the book, and was no more sad, at least not on that occasion.

In the middle of these cogitations, apprehensions and reflections, it came into my thought one day that all this might be a mere chimera of my own, and that this foot might be the print of my own foot when I came onshore from my boat. This cheered me up a little too, and I began to persuade myself it was all a delusion; that it was nothing else but my own foot, and why might not I come that way from the boat, as well as I was going that way to the boat? Again I considered also that I could by no means tell for certain where I had trod and where I had not, and that if at last this was only the print of my own foot, I had played the part of those fools who strive to make stories of spectres and apparitions, and then are frighted at them more than anybody.

Now I began to take courage, and to peep abroad again, for I had not stirred out of my castle for three days and nights, so that I began to starve for provision, for I had little or nothing within doors but some barley cakes and water. Then I knew that my goats wanted to be milked too, which usually was my evening diversion, and the poor creatures were in great pain and inconvenience for want of it, and indeed, it almost spoilt some of them, and almost dried up their milk.

Heartening myself therefore with the belief that this was nothing but the print of one of my own feet, and so I might be truly said to start at my own shadow, I began to go abroad again, and went to my country house to milk my flock, but to see with what fear I went forwards, how often I looked behind me, how I was ready every now and then to lay down my basket and run for my life, it would have made anyone have thought I was haunted with an evil conscience, or that I had been lately most terribly frighted, and so indeed I had.

However, as I went down thus two or three days, and having seen nothing, I began to be a little bolder and to think there was really nothing in it but my own imagination, but I could not persuade myself fully of this till I should go down to the shore again, and see this print of a foot, and measure it by my own, and see if there was any similitude or fitness, that I might be assured it was my own foot. But when I came to the place, *first*, it appeared evidently to me that when I laid up my boat I could not possibly be onshore anywhere thereabouts; *secondly*, when I came to measure the mark with my own foot, I found my foot not so large by a great deal. Both these things filled my head with new imaginations, and gave me the vapours again to the highest degree, so that I shook with cold, like one in an ague, and I went home again filled with the belief that some man or men had been onshore there – or in short, that the island was inhabited, and I might be surprised before I was aware – and what course to take for my security I knew not.

Oh what ridiculous resolution men take when possessed with fear! It deprives them of the use of those means which reason offers for their relief. The first thing I proposed to myself was to throw down my enclosures and turn all my tame cattle wild into the woods, that the enemy might not find them, and then frequent the island in prospect of the same, or the like booty; then to the simple thing of digging up my two cornfields, that they might not find such a grain there, and still be prompted to frequent the island; then to demolish my bower and tent, that they might not see any vestiges of habitation, and be prompted to look further in order to find out the persons inhabiting.

These were the subject of the first night's cogitation after I was come home again, while the apprehensions which had so overrun my mind were fresh upon me and my head was full of vapours, as above. Thus fear of danger is ten thousand times more terrifying than danger itself when apparent to the eyes, and we find the burden of anxiety greater by much than the evil which we are anxious about – and, which was worse than all this, I had not that relief in this trouble from the resignation I used to practise that I hoped to have. I looked, I thought, like Saul, who complained not only that the Philistines were upon him, but that God had forsaken him,* for I did not now take due ways to compose my mind by crying to God in my distress and resting upon His providence, as I had done before, for my defence and deliverance – which if I had done, I had at least been more cheerfully supported under this new surprise, and perhaps carried through it with more resolution.

This confusion of my thoughts kept me waking all night, but in the morning I fell asleep, and having, by the amusement of my mind, been as it were tired, and my spirits exhausted, I slept very soundly, and waked much better composed than I had ever been before, and now I began to think sedately, and upon the utmost debate with myself, I concluded that this island, which was so exceeding pleasant, fruitful and no further from the mainland than as I had seen, was not so entirely abandoned as I might imagine; that although there were no stated inhabitants who lived on the spot, yet that there might sometimes come boats off from the shore, who either with design, or perhaps never but when they were driven by crosswinds, might come to this place.

That I had lived here fifteen years now, and had not met with the least shadow or figure of any people yet, and that if at any time they should be driven here, it was probable they went away again as soon as ever they could, seeing they had never thought fit to fix there upon any occasion to this time.

That the most I could suggest any danger from was from any such casual accidental landing of straggling people from the main, who, as it was likely if they were driven hither, were here against their wills, so they made no stay here, but went off again with all possible speed, seldom staying one night onshore, lest they should not have the help of the tides and daylight back again; and that therefore I had nothing to do but to consider of some safe retreat, in case I should see any savages land upon the spot.

Now I began sorely to repent that I had dug my cave so large as to bring a door through again, which door, as I said, came out beyond where my fortification joined to the rock. Upon maturely considering this therefore, I resolved to draw me a second fortification, in the same manner of a semicircle, at a distance from my wall just where I had planted a double row of trees about twelve years before, of which I made mention. These trees having been planted so thick before, they wanted but a few piles to be driven between them that they should be thicker and stronger, and my wall would be soon finished.

So that I had now a double wall, and my outer wall was thickened with pieces of timber, old cables and everything I could think of to make it strong, having in it seven little holes about as big as I might put my arm out at. In the inside of this, I thickened my wall to above ten foot thick, with continual bringing earth out of my cave and laying it at the foot of the wall and walking upon it, and through the seven holes I contrived to plant the muskets – of which I took notice that I got seven onshore out of the ship – these, I say, I planted like my cannon, and fitted them into frames that held them like a carriage, that so I could fire all the seven guns in two minutes' time. This wall I was many a weary month a finishing, and yet never thought myself safe till it was done.

When this was done, I stuck all the ground without my wall, for a great way every way, as full with stakes or sticks of the osier-like wood, which I found so apt to grow, as they could well stand, insomuch that I believe I might set in near twenty thousand of them, leaving a pretty large space between them and my wall, that I might have room to see an enemy, and they might have no shelter from the young trees if they attempted to approach my outer wall.

Thus in two years' time I had a thick grove, and in five or six years' time I had a wood before my dwelling, growing so monstrous thick and strong that it was indeed perfectly impassable, and no men of what kind soever would ever imagine that there was anything beyond it, much less a habitation. As for the way which I proposed to myself to go in and out – for I left no avenue – it was setting two ladders, one to a part of the rock which was low and then broke in, and left room to place another ladder upon that, so when the two ladders were taken down, no man living could come down to me without mischieving himself – and if they had come down they were still on the outside of my outer wall.

Thus I took all the measures human prudence could suggest for my own preservation, and it will be seen at length that they were not altogether without just reason, though I foresaw nothing at that time more than my mere fear suggested to me.

WHILE THIS WAS DOING, I was not altogether careless of my other affairs, for I had a great concern upon me for my little herd of goats. They were not only a present supply to me upon every occasion, and began to be sufficient to me without the expense of powder and shot, but also without the fatigue of hunting after the wild ones, and I was loath to lose the advantage of them, and to have them all to nurse up over again.

To this purpose, after long consideration, I could think of but two ways to preserve them; one was to find another convenient place to dig a cave underground, and to drive them into it every night; and the other was to enclose two or three little bits of land remote from one another and as much concealed as I could, where I might keep about half a dozen young goats in each place – so that if any disaster happened to the flock in general, I might be able to raise them again with little trouble and time, and this, though it would require a great deal of time and labour, I thought was the most rational design.

Accordingly I spent some time to find out the most retired parts of the island, and I pitched upon one which was as private indeed as my heart could wish for; it was a little damp piece of ground in the middle of the hollow and thick woods, where, as is observed, I almost lost myself once before endeavouring to come back that way from the eastern part of the island. Here I found a clear piece of land near three acres, so surrounded with woods that it was almost an enclosure by nature; at least it did not want near so much labour to make it so as the other pieces of ground I had worked so hard at.

I immediately went to work with this piece of ground, and in less than a month's time I had so fenced it round that my flock or herd – call it which you please – who were not so wild now as at first they might be supposed to be, were well enough secured in it. So, without any further delay, I removed ten young she-goats and two he-goats to this piece, and when they were there, I continued to perfect the fence till I had made it as secure as the other, which, however, I did at more leisure, and it took me up more time by a great deal.

All this labour I was at the expense of purely from my apprehensions on the account of the print of a man's foot which I had seen, for as yet I never saw any human creature come near the island, and I had now lived two years under these uneasinesses, which indeed made my life much less comfortable than it was before, as may well be imagined by any who know what it is to live in the constant snare of the fear of man. And this I must observe with grief too, that the discomposure of my mind had too great impressions also upon the religious part of my thoughts, for the dread and terror of falling into the hands of savages and cannibals lay so upon my spirits that I seldom found myself in a due temper for application to my Maker, at least not with the sedate calmness and resignation of soul which I was wont to do. I rather prayed to God as under great affliction and pressure of mind, surrounded with danger, and in expectation every night of being murdered and devoured before morning, and I must testify from my experience that a temper of peace, thankfulness, love and affection is much more the proper frame for prayer than that of terror and discomposure, and that under the dread of mischief impending, a man is no more fit for a comforting performance of the duty of praying to God than he is for repentance on a sickbed – for these discomposures affect the mind as the others do the body, and the discomposure of the mind must necessarily be as great a disability as that of the body, and much greater, praying to God being properly an act of the mind, not of the body.

But to go on. After I had thus secured one part of my little living stock, I went about the whole island, searching for another private place to make such another deposit, when, wandering more to the west point of the island than I had ever gone yet, and looking out to sea, I thought I saw a boat upon the sea at a great distance. I had found a prospective glass or two in one of the seamen's chests, which I saved out of our ship, but I had it not about me, and this was so remote that I could not tell what to make of it though I looked at it till my eyes were not able to hold to look any longer. Whether it was a boat or not, I do not know, but as I descended from the hill, I could see no more of it, so I gave it over; only I resolved to go no more out without a prospective glass in my pocket.

When I was come down the hill to the end of the island, where indeed I had never been before, I was presently convinced that the seeing the print of a man's foot was not such a strange thing in the island as I imagined, and but that it was a special providence that I was cast upon the side of the island where the savages never came, I should easily have known that nothing was more frequent than for the canoes from the main, when they happened to be a little too far out at sea, to shoot over to that side of the island for harbour; likewise as they often met and fought in their canoes, the victors, having taken any prisoners, would bring them over to this shore, where, according to their dreadful customs, being all cannibals, they would kill and eat them – of which hereafter.

When I was come down the hill to the shore, as I said above, being the SW point of the island, I was perfectly confounded and amazed – nor is it possible for me to express the horror of my mind at seeing the shore spread with skulls, hands, feet and other bones of human bodies, and particularly I observed a place where there had been a fire made, and a circle dug in the earth like a cockpit, where it is supposed the savage wretches had sat down to their inhuman feastings upon the bodies of their fellow creatures.

I was so astonished with the sight of these things that I entertained no notions of any danger to myself from it for a long while; all my apprehensions were buried in the thoughts of such a pitch of inhuman, hellish brutality and the horror of the degeneracy of human nature, which, though I had heard of often, yet I never had so near a view of before – in short, I turned away my face from the horrid spectacle. My stomach grew sick, and I was just at the point of fainting, when nature discharged the disorder from my stomach and, having vomited with an uncommon violence, I was a little relieved, but could not bear to stay in the place a moment, so I got me up the hill again with all the speed I could, and walked on towards my own habitation.

When I came a little out of that part of the island, I stood still awhile as amazed, and then recovering myself, I looked up with the utmost affection of my soul and, with a flood of tears in my eyes, gave God thanks that had cast my first lot in a part of the world where I was distinguished from such dreadful creatures as these, and that, though I had esteemed my present condition very miserable, had yet given me so many comforts in it that I had still more to give thanks for than to complain of – and this above all, that I had even in this miserable condition been comforted with the knowledge of Himself, and the hope of His blessing, which was a felicity more than sufficiently equivalent to all the misery which I had suffered, or could suffer.

In this frame of thankfulness, I went home to my castle, and began to be much easier now as to the safety of my circumstances than ever I was before, for I observed that these wretches never came to this island in search of what they could get – perhaps not seeking, not wanting or not expecting anything here, and having often, no doubt, been up in the covered woody part of it without finding anything to their purpose. I knew I had been here now almost eighteen years, and never saw the least footsteps of human creature there before, and I might be here eighteen more, as entirely concealed as I was now, if I did not discover myself to them, which I had no manner of occasion to do – it being my only business to keep myself entirely concealed where I was, unless I found a better sort of creatures than cannibals to make myself known to.

Yet I entertained such an abhorrence of the savage wretches that I have been speaking of, and of the wretched inhuman custom of their devouring and eating one another up, that I continued pensive and sad, and kept close within my own circle for almost two years after this. When I say my own circle, I mean by it my three plantations – namely, my castle, my country seat which I called my bower, and my enclosure in the woods; nor did I look after this for any other use than as an enclosure for my goats, for the aversion which Nature gave me to these hellish wretches was such that I was as fearful of seeing them as of seeing the Devil himself; nor did I so much as go to look after my boat in all this time, but began rather to think of making me another, for I could not think of ever making any more attempts to bring the other boat round the island to me, lest I should meet with some of these creatures at sea, in which if I had happened to have fallen into their hands, I knew what would have been my lot.

Time, however, and the satisfaction I had that I was in no danger of being discovered by these people, began to wear off my uneasiness about them, and I began to live just in the same composed manner as before, only with this difference, that I used more caution, and kept my eyes more about me than I did before, lest I should happen to be seen by any of them, and particularly, I was more cautious of firing my gun, lest any of them being on the island should happen to hear of it – and it was therefore a very good providence to me that I had furnished myself with a tame breed of goats, that I needed not hunt any more about the woods, or shoot at them, and if I did catch any of them after this, it was by traps and snares, as I had done before, so that for two years after this, I believe I never fired my gun once off, though I never went out without it. And, which was more, as I had saved three pistols out of the ship, I always carried them out with me, or at least two of them, sticking them in my goatskin belt. Also I furbished up one of the great cutlasses that I had out of the ship, and made me a belt to put it on also, so that I was now a most formidable fellow to look at when I went abroad, if you add to the former description of myself the particular of two pistols and a great broadsword hanging at my side in a belt, but without a scabbard.

Things going on thus, as I have said, for some time, I seemed, excepting these cautions, to be reduced to my former calm, sedate way of living. All these things tended to show me more and more how far my condition was from being miserable compared to some others – nay, to many other particulars of life, which it might have pleased God to have made my lot. It put me upon reflecting how little repining there would be among mankind at any condition of life, if people would rather compare their condition with those that are worse, in order to be thankful, than be always comparing them with those which are better, to assist their murmurings and complainings.

As in my present condition there were not really many things which I wanted, so indeed I thought that the frights I had been in about these savage wretches and the concern I had been in for my own preservation had taken off the edge of my invention for my own conveniences, and I had dropped a good design, which I had once bent my thoughts too much upon, and that was to try if I could not make some of my barley into malt, and then try to brew myself some beer. This was really a whimsical thought, and I reproved myself often for the simplicity of it, for I presently saw there would be the want of several things necessary to the making my beer that it would be impossible for me to supply; as first, casks to preserve it in, which was a thing that, as I have observed already, I could never compass, no, though I spent not many days, but weeks, nay, months in attempting it, but to no purpose. In the next place, I had no hops to make it keep, no yeast to make it work, no copper or kettle to make it boil, and yet all these things notwithstanding, I verily believe, had not these things intervened – I mean the frights and terrors I was in about the savages – I had undertaken it, and perhaps brought it to pass too, for I seldom gave anything over without accomplishing it when I once had it in my head enough to begin it.

But my invention now ran quite another way, for night and day I could think of nothing but how I might destroy some of these monsters in their cruel bloody entertainment, and, if possible, save the victim they should bring hither to destroy. It would take up a larger volume than this whole work is intended to be to set down all the contrivances I hatched, or rather brooded upon in my thought, for the destroying these creatures, or at least frightening them so as to prevent their coming hither any more, but all was abortive, nothing could be possible to take effect, unless I was to be there to do it myself – and what could one man do among them, when perhaps there might be twenty or thirty of them together, with their darts, or their bows and arrows with which they could shoot as true to a mark as I could with my gun?

Sometimes I contrived to dig a hole under the place where they made their fire, and put in five or six pounds of gunpowder, which when they kindled their fire would consequently take fire, and blow up all that was near it, but as in the first place I should be very loath to waste so much powder upon them – my store being now within the quantity of one barrel – so neither could I be sure of its going off at any certain time when it might surprise them, and at best, that it would do little more than just blow the fire about their ears and fright them, but not sufficient to make them forsake the place, so I laid it aside and then proposed that I would place myself in ambush in some convenient place, with my three guns all double-loaded, and in the middle of their bloody ceremony let fly at them, when I should be sure to kill or wound perhaps two or three at every shoot, and then falling in upon them with my three pistols and my sword, I made no doubt but that if there was twenty I should kill them all. This fancy pleased my thoughts for some weeks, and I was so full of it that I often dreamt of it, and sometimes that I was just going to let fly at them in my sleep.

I went so far with it in my imagination that I employed myself several days to find out proper places to put myself in ambuscade, as I said, to watch for them, and I went frequently to the place itself, which was now grown more familiar to me, and especially while my mind was thus filled with thoughts of revenge and of a bloody putting twenty or thirty of them to the sword, as I may call it, the horror I had at the place, and at the signals of the barbarous wretches devouring one another, abated my malice.

Well, at length I found a place in the side of the hill where I was satisfied I might securely wait till I saw any of their boats coming, and might then, even before they would be ready to come onshore, convey myself unseen into thickets of trees, in one of which there was a hollow large enough to conceal me entirely, and where I might sit and observe all their bloody doings, and take my full aim at their heads when they were so close together as that it would be next to impossible that I should miss my shoot, or that I could fail wounding three or four of them at the first shoot.

In this place then I resolved to fix my design, and accordingly I prepared two muskets and my ordinary fowling piece. The two muskets I loaded with a brace of slugs each, and four or five smaller bullets about the size of pistol bullets, and the fowling piece I loaded with near a handful of swan shot of the largest size. I also loaded my pistols with about four bullets each, and in this posture, well-provided with ammunition for a second and third charge, I prepared myself for my expedition.

After I had thus laid the scheme of my design, and in my imagination put it in practice, I continually made my tour every morning up to the top of the hill – which was from my castle, as I called it, about three miles or more – to see if I could observe any boats upon the sea coming near the island, or standing over towards it, but I began to tire of this hard duty, after I had for two or three months constantly kept my watch, but came always back without any discovery, there having not in all that time been the least appearance, not only on or near the shore, but not on the whole ocean, so far as my eyes or glasses could reach every way.

As long as I kept up my daily tour to the hill to look out, so long also I kept up the vigour of my design, and my spirits seemed to be all the while in a suitable form for so outrageous an execution as the killing twenty or thirty naked savages, for an offence which I had not at all entered into a discussion of in my thoughts, any further than my passions were at first fired by the horror I conceived at the unnatural custom of that people of the country, who it seems had been suffered by Providence, in His wide disposition of the world, to have no other guide than that of their own abominable and vitiated passions, and consequently were left, and perhaps had been so for some ages, to act such horrid things, and receive such dreadful customs, as nothing but Nature entirely abandoned of Heaven, and acted by some hellish degeneracy, could have run them into. But now, when, as I have said, I began to be weary of the fruitless excursion, which I had made so long, and so far, every morning in vain, so my opinion of the action itself began to alter, and I began with cooler and calmer thoughts to consider what it was I was going to engage in; what authority or call I had to pretend to be judge and executioner upon these men as criminals, whom Heaven had thought fit for so many ages to suffer unpunished, to go on, and to be, as it were, the executioners of His judgements one upon another; how far these people were offenders against me, and what right I had to engage in the quarrel of that blood which they shed promiscuously one upon another. I debated this very often with myself thus: how do I know what God Himself judges in this particular case? It is certain these people either do not commit this as a crime; it is not against their own consciences reproving, or their light reproaching them. They do not know it be an offence, and then commit it in defiance of divine justice, as we do in almost all the sins we commit. They think it no more a crime to kill a captive taken in war than we do to kill an ox; nor to eat human flesh than we do to eat mutton.

When I had considered this a little, it followed necessarily that I was certainly in the wrong in it; that these people were not murderers in the sense that I had before condemned them in my thoughts, any more than those Christians were murderers who often put to death the prisoners taken in battle – or more frequently, upon many occasions, put whole troops of men to the sword, without giving quarter, though they threw down their arms and submitted.

In the next place it occurred to me that albeit the usage they thus gave one another was thus brutish and inhumane, yet it was really nothing to me: these people had done me no injury. That if they attempted me, or I saw it necessary for my immediate preservation to fall upon them, something might be said for it, but that as I was yet out of their power, and they had really no knowledge of me – and consequently no design upon me – and therefore it could not be just for me to fall upon them. That this would justify the conduct of the Spaniards in all their barbarities practised in America, where they destroyed millions of these people, who, however they were idolaters and barbarians, and had several bloody and barbarious rites in their customs, such as sacrificing human bodies to their idols, were yet, as to the Spaniards, very innocent people; and that the rooting them out of the country is spoken of with the utmost abhorrence and detestation by even the Spaniards themselves at this time, and by all other Christian nations of Europe, as a mere butchery, a bloody and unnatural piece of cruelty, unjustifiable either to God or man, and such, as for which the very name of a Spaniard is reckoned to be frightful and terrible to all people of humanity, or of Christian compassion – as if the kingdom of Spain were particularly eminent for the product of a race of men who were without principles of tenderness, or the common bowels of pity to the miserable, which is reckoned to be a mark of generous temper in the mind.

These considerations really put me to a pause, and to a kind of a full stop, and I began by little and little to be off of my design, and to conclude I had taken wrong measures in my resolutions to attack the savages; that it was not my business to meddle with them unless they first attacked me, and this it was my business if possible to prevent, but that if I were discovered and attacked, then I knew my duty.

On the other hand, I argued with myself that this really was the way not to deliver myself, but entirely to ruin and destroy myself, for unless I was sure to kill everyone that not only should be onshore at that time, but that should ever come onshore afterwards, if but one of them escaped to tell their country people what had happened, they would come over again by thousands to revenge the death of their fellows, and I should only bring upon myself a certain destruction, which at present I had no manner of occasion for.

Upon the whole I concluded that neither in principle or in policy I ought one way or other to concern myself in this affair. That my business was by all possible means to conceal myself from them, and not to leave the least signal to them to guess by that there were any living creatures upon the island – I mean of human shape.

Religion joined in with this prudential, and I was convinced now many ways that I was perfectly out of my duty when I was laying all my bloody schemes for the destruction of innocent creatures – I mean innocent as to me. As to the crimes they were guilty of towards one another, I had nothing to do with them; they were national, and I ought to leave them to the justice of God, who is the Governor of nations, and knows how by national punishments to make a just retribution for national offences, and to bring public judgements upon those who offend in a public manner by such ways as best pleases Him.

This appeared so clear to me now that nothing was a greater satisfaction to me than that I had not been suffered to do a thing which I now saw so much reason to believe would have been no less a sin than that of wilful murder, if I had committed it, and I gave most humble thanks on my knees to God that had thus delivered me from blood guiltiness, beseeching Him to grant me the protection of His providence, that I might not fall into the hands of the barbarians, or that I might not lay my hands upon them unless I had a more clear call from Heaven to do it, in defence of my own life.

In this disposition I continued for near a year after this, and so far was I from desiring an occasion for falling upon these wretches that in all that time I never once went up the hill to see whether there were any of them in sight, or to know whether any of them had been onshore there or not, that I might not be tempted to renew any of my contrivances against them, or be provoked by any advantage which might present itself to fall upon them; only this I did: I went and removed my boat, which I had on the other side the island, and carried it down to the east end of the whole island, where I ran it into a little cove which I found under some high rocks, and where I knew, by reason of the currents, the savages durst not, at least would not come with their boats, upon any account whatsoever.

With my boat I carried away everything that I had left there belonging to her, though not necessary for the bare going thither – namely, a mast and sail which I had made for her, and a thing like an anchor, but indeed which could not be called either anchor or grappling – however, it was the best I could make of its kind. All this I removed, that there might not be the least shadow of any discovery, or any appearance of any boat or of any human habitation upon the island.

Besides this, I kept myself, as I said, more retired than ever, and seldom went from my cell, other than upon my constant employment, namely, to milk my she-goats, and manage my little flock in the wood, which, as it was quite on the other part of the island, was quite out of danger, for certain it is that these savage people who sometimes haunted this island never came with any thoughts of finding anything here, and consequently never wandered off from the coast, and I doubt not but they might have been several times onshore after my apprehensions of them had made me cautious, as well as before – and indeed, I looked back with some horror upon the thoughts of what my condition would have been if I had chopped upon* them and been discovered before that, when naked and unarmed, except with one gun – and that loaden often only with small shot – I walked everywhere peeping and peeping about the island to see what I could get. What a surprise should I have been in, if when I discovered the print of a man's foot, I had instead of that seen fifteen or twenty savages, and found them pursuing me, and by the swiftness of their running, no possibility of my escaping them.

The thoughts of this sometimes sunk my very soul within me, and distressed my mind so much that I could not soon recover it, to think what I should have done, and how I not only should not have been able to resist them, but even should not have had presence of mind enough to do what I might have done – much less what now after so much consideration and preparation I might be able to do. Indeed, after serious thinking of these things, I should be very melancholy, and sometimes it would last a great while, but I resolved it at last all into thankfulness to that Providence which had delivered me from so many unseen dangers, and had kept me from those mischiefs which I could no way have been the agent in delivering myself from, because I had not the least notion of any such thing depending, or the least supposition of it being possible.

This renewed a contemplation which often had come to my thoughts in former time, when first I began to see the merciful dispositions of Heaven in the dangers we run through in this life: how wonderfully we are delivered when we know nothing of it; how when we are in a quandary, as we call it, a doubt or hesitation whether to go this way or that way, a secret hint shall direct us this way, when we intended to go that way – nay, when sense, our own inclination, and perhaps business has called to go the other way, yet a strange impression upon the mind, from we know not what springs, and by we know not what power, shall overrule us to go this way, and it shall afterwards appear that had we gone that way which we should have gone, and even to our imagination ought to have gone, we should have been ruined and lost. Upon these and many like reflections, I afterwards made it a certain rule with me that whenever I found those secret hints or pressings of my mind to doing or not doing anything that presented, or to going this way or that way, I never failed to obey the secret dictate, though I knew no other reason for it than that such a pressure or such a hint hung upon my mind. I could give many examples of the success of this conduct in the course of my life, but more especially in the latter part of my inhabiting this unhappy island, besides many occasions which it is very likely I might have taken notice of, if I had seen with the same eyes then that I saw with now. But 'tis never too late to be wise, and I cannot but advise all considering men, whose lives are attended with such extraordinary incidents as mine, or even though not so extraordinary, not to slight such secret intimations of providence, let them come from what invisible intelligence they will – that I shall not discuss, and perhaps cannot account for – but certainly they are a proof of the converse of spirits, and the secret communication between those embodied and those unembodied, and such a proof as can never be withstood. Of which I shall have occasion to give some very remarkable instances in the remainder of my solitary residence in this dismal place.

I believe the reader of this will not think it strange if I confess that these anxieties, these constant dangers I lived in and the concern that was now upon me put an end to all invention, and to all the contrivances that I had laid for my future accommodations and conveniences. I had the care of my safety more now upon my hands than that of my food. I cared not to drive a nail or chop a stick of wood now, for fear the noise I should make should be heard; much less would I fire a gun, for the same reason, and above all, I was intolerably uneasy at making any fire, lest the smoke which is visible at a great distance in the day should betray me, and for this reason I removed that part of my business which required fire, such as burning of pots and pipes, etc., into my new apartment in the woods, where, after I had been some time, I found, to my unspeakable consolation, a mere natural cave in the earth, which went in a vast way, and where, I dare say, no savage, had he been at the mouth of it, would be so hardy as to venture in, nor indeed would any man else but one who, like me, wanted nothing so much as a safe retreat.

The mouth of this hollow was at the bottom of a great rock, where by mere accident (I would say, if I did not see abundant reason to ascribe all such things now to providence) I was cutting down some thick branches of trees to make charcoal, and before I go on, I must observe the reason of my making this charcoal, which was thus:

I was afraid of making a smoke about my habitation, as I said before, and yet I could not live there without baking my bread, cooking my meat, etc., so I contrived to burn some wood here, as I had seen done in England, under turf, till it became chark, or dry coal, and then putting the fire out, I preserved the coal to carry home and perform the other services for which fire was wanting without danger of smoke.

But this is by the by. While I was cutting down some wood here, I perceived that behind a very thick branch of low brush-wood, or underwood, there was a kind of hollow place; I was curious to look into it, and getting with difficulty into the mouth of it, I found it was pretty large – that is to say, sufficient for me to stand upright in it, and perhaps another with me – but I must confess to you, I made more haste out than I did in when looking further into the place, and which was perfectly dark, I saw two broad shining eyes of some creature, whether devil or man I knew not, which twinkled like two stars, the dim light from the cave's mouth shining directly in and making the reflection.

However, after some pause, I recovered myself, and began to call myself a thousand fools and tell myself that he that was afraid to see the Devil was not fit to live twenty years in an island all alone, and that I durst to believe there was nothing in this cave that was more frightful than myself. Upon this, plucking up my courage, I took up a great firebrand, and in I rushed again, with the stick flaming in my hand. I had not gone three steps in, but I was almost as much frighted as I was before, for I heard a very loud sigh, like that of a man in some pain, and it was followed by a broken noise, as if words half-expressed, and then a deep sigh again. I stepped back, and was indeed struck with such a surprise that it put me into a cold sweat, and if I had had a hat on my head, I will not answer for it that my hair might not have lifted it off. But still plucking up my spirits as well as I could, and encouraging myself a little with considering that the power and presence of God was everywhere and was able to protect me, upon this I stepped forwards again, and by the light of the firebrand, holding it up a little over my head, I saw lying on the ground a most monstrous frightful old he-goat, just making his will, as we say, and gasping for life, and dying indeed of mere old age.

I stirred him a little to see if I could get him out, and he essayed to get up, but was not able to raise himself, and I thought with myself he might even lie there, for if he had frighted me so, he would certainly fright any of the savages, if any of them should be so hardy as to come in there while he had any life in him.

I was now recovered from my surprise and began to look round me, when I found the cave was but very small — that is to say, it might be about twelve foot over — but in no manner of shape, either round or square, no hands having ever been employed in making it but those of mere Nature. I observed also that there was a place at the further side of it that went in further, but was so low that it required me to creep upon my hands and knees to go into it, and whither I went I knew not; so having no candle, I gave it over for some time, but resolved to come again the next day, provided with candles and a tinderbox, which I had made of the lock of one of the muskets, with some wildfire in the pan.

Accordingly, the next day I came provided with six large candles of my own making, for I made very good candles now of goat's tallow, and going into this low place, I was obliged to creep upon all fours, as I have said, almost ten yard — which, by the way, I thought was a venture bold enough, considering that I knew not how far it might go, nor what was beyond it. When I was got through the strait, I found the roof rose higher up, I believe near twenty foot, but never was such a glorious sight seen in the island, I dare say, as it was to look round the sides and roof of this vault or cave; the walls reflected 100,000 lights to me from my two candles – what it was in the rock, whether diamonds, or any other precious stones, or gold – which I rather supposed it to be – I knew not.

The place I was in was a most delightful cavity or grotto of its kind, as could be expected, though perfectly dark; the floor was dry and level, and had a sort of small loose gravel upon it, so that there was no nauseous or venomous creature to be seen, neither was there any damp or wet on the sides or roof. The only difficulty in it was the entrance, which, however, as it was a place of security, and such a retreat as I wanted, I thought that was a convenience, so that I was really rejoiced at the discovery, and resolved without any delay to bring some of those things which I was most anxious about to this place; particularly, I resolved to bring hither my magazine of powder, and all my spare arms, namely, two fowling pieces – for I had three in all – and three muskets – for of them I had eight in all – so I kept at my castle only five, which stood ready-mounted like pieces of cannon on my outmost fence and were ready also to take out upon any expedition.

Upon this occasion of removing my ammunition, I took occasion to open the barrel of powder which I took up out of the sea, and which had been wet, and I found that the water had penetrated about three or four inches into the powder on every side, which, caking and growing hard, had preserved the inside like a kernel in a shell, so that I had near sixty pounds of very good powder in the centre of the cask, and this was an agreeable discovery to me at that time, so I carried all away thither, never keeping above two or three pounds of powder with me in my castle, for fear of a surprise of any kind – I also carried thither all the lead I had left for bullets.

I fancied myself now like one of the ancient giants which are said to live in caves and holes in the rocks, where none could come at them, for I persuaded myself while I was here if five hundred savages were to hunt me, they could never find me out – or if they did, they would not venture to attack me here.

The old goat who I found expiring died in the mouth of the cave the next day after I made this discovery, and I found it much easier to dig a great hole there, and throw him in and cover him with earth, than to drag him out, so I interred him there, to prevent the offence to my nose.

I WAS NOW IN MY TWENTY-THIRD YEAR of residence in this island, and was so naturalized to the place, and to the manner of living, that could I have but enjoyed the certainty that no savages would come to the place to disturb me, I could have been content to have capitulated for spending the rest of my time there, even to the last moment, till I had laid me down and died, like the old goat in the cave. I had also arrived to some little diversions and amusements, which made the time pass more pleasantly with me a great deal than it did before: as first, I had taught my Poll, as I noted before, to speak, and he did it so familiarly and talked so articulately and plain that it was very pleasant to me, and he lived with me no less than six and twenty years – how long he might live afterwards, I know not, though I know they have a notion in the Brazils that they live a hundred years. Perhaps poor Poll may be alive there still, calling after poor Robin Crusoe to this day. I wish no Englishman the ill luck to come there and hear him, but if he did, he would certainly believe it was the Devil. My dog was a very pleasant and loving companion to me for no less than sixteen years of my time, and then died of mere old age. As for my cats, they multiplied, as I have observed, to that degree that I was obliged to shoot several of them at first, to keep them from devouring me and all I had, but at length, when the two old ones

I had brought with me were gone, and after some time continually driving them from me, and letting them have no provision with me, they all ran wild into the woods, except two or three favourites, which I kept tame, and whose young, when they had any, I always drowned – and these were part of my family. Besides these, I always kept two or three household kids about me, who I taught to feed out of my hand, and I had two more parrots which talked pretty well, and would all call Robin Crusoe – but none like my first, nor indeed did I take the pains with any of them that I had done with him. I had also several tame sea fowls, whose names I know not, who I caught upon the shore, and cut their wings, and the little stakes which I had planted before my castle wall being now grown up to a good thick grove, these fowls all lived among these low trees, and bred there, which was very agreeable to me, so that, as I said above, I began to be very well contented with the life I led, if it might but have been secured from the dread of the savages.

But it was otherwise directed, and it may not be amiss for all people who shall meet with my story to make this just observation from it – namely, how frequently, in the course of our lives, the evil which in itself we seek most to shun, and which when we are fallen into it the most dreadful to us, is oftentimes the very means or door of our deliverance, by which alone we can be raised again from the affliction we are fallen into. I could give many examples of this in the course of my unaccountable life, but in nothing was it more particularly remarkable than in the circumstances of my last years of solitary residence in this island.

It was now the month of December, as I said above, in my twenty-third year, and this being the southern solstice – for winter I cannot call it – was the particular time of my harvest, and required my being pretty much abroad in the fields, when, going out pretty early in the morning, even before it was thorough daylight, I was surprised with seeing a light of some fire upon the shore, at a distance from me of about two mile towards the end of the island, where I had observed some savages had been as before, but not on the other side; but to my great affliction, it was on my side of the island.

I was indeed terribly surprised at the sight, and stopped short within my grove, not daring to go out lest I might be surprised, and yet I had no more peace within from the apprehensions I had that if these savages, in rambling over the island, should find my corn standing or cut, or any of my works and improvements, they would immediately conclude that there were people in the place, and would then never give over till they had found me out. In this extremity I went back directly to my castle, pulled up the ladder after me, and made all things without look as wild and natural as I could.

Then I prepared myself within, putting myself in a posture of defence; I loaded all my cannon, as I called them – that is to say, my muskets which were mounted upon my new fortification, and all my pistols, and resolved to defend myself to the last gasp, not forgetting seriously to commend myself to the divine protection, and earnestly to pray to God to deliver me out of the hands of the barbarians, and in this posture I continued about two hours, but began to be mighty impatient for intelligence abroad, for I had no spies to send out.

After sitting awhile longer, and musing what I should do in this case, I was not able to bear sitting in ignorance any longer, so setting up my ladder to the side of the hill where there was a flat place, as I observed before, and then pulling the ladder up after me, I set it up again and mounted to the top of the hill and, pulling out my prospective glass, which I had taken on purpose, I laid me down flat on my belly on the ground, and began to look for the place. I presently found there was no less than nine naked savages, sitting round a small fire they had made – not to warm them, for they had no need of that, the weather being extreme hot, but, as I supposed, to dress some of their barbarous diet of human flesh, which they had brought with them, whether alive or dead I could not know.

They had two canoes with them, which they had haled up upon the shore, and as it was then tide of ebb, they seemed to me to wait for the return of the flood to go away again. It is not easy to imagine what confusion this sight put me into, especially seeing them come on my side the island, and so near me too, but when I observed their coming must always be with the current of the ebb, I began afterwards to be more sedate in my mind, being satisfied that I might go abroad with safety all the time of the tide of flood, if they were not onshore before – and having made this observation, I went abroad about my harvest work with the more composure.

As I expected, so it proved, for as soon as the tide made to the westwards, I saw them all take boat, and row (or paddle as we call it) all away. I should have observed that for an hour and more before they went off, they went to dancing, and I could easily discern their postures and gestures by my glasses: I could not perceive, by my nicest observation, but that they were stark naked, and had not the least covering upon them, but whether they were men or women, that I could not distinguish.

As soon as I saw them shipped and gone, I took two guns upon my shoulders, and two pistols at my girdle and my great sword by my side, without a scabbard, and with all the speed I was able to make, I went away to the hill where I had discovered the first appearance of all, and as soon as I got thither, which was not less than two hours (for I could not go apace, being so loaden with arms as I was), I perceived there had been three canoes more of savages on that place – and looking out further, I saw they were all at sea together, making over for the main.

This was a dreadful sight to me, especially when going down to the shore, I could see the marks of horror which the dismal work they had been about had left behind it, namely, the blood, the bones and part of the flesh of human bodies eaten and devoured by those wretches with merriment and sport. I was so filled with indignation at the sight that I began now to premeditate the destruction of the next that I saw there, let them be who or how many soever.

It seemed evident to me that the visits which they thus make to this island are not very frequent, for it was above fifteen months before any more of them came onshore there again – that is to say, I neither saw them, or any footsteps or signals of them, in all that time – for as to the rainy seasons, then they are sure not to come abroad, at least not so far. Yet all this while I lived uncomfortably, by reason of the constant apprehensions I was in of their coming upon me by surprise – from whence I observe that the expectation of evil is more bitter than the suffering, especially if there is no room to shake off that expectation or those apprehensions.

During all this time I was in the murdering humour, and took up most of my hours, which should have been better employed in contriving how to circumvent and fall upon them the very next time I should see them, especially if they should be divided, as they were the last time, into two parties; nor did I consider at all that if I killed one party, suppose ten or a dozen, I was still the next day, or week, or month, to kill another, and so another, even ad infinitum, till I should be at length no less a murderer than they were in being man-eaters – and perhaps much more so.

I spent my days now in great perplexity and anxiety of mind, expecting that I should one day or other fall into the hands of these merciless creatures, and if I did at any time venture abroad, it was not without looking round me with the greatest care and caution imaginable. And now I found, to my great comfort, how happy it was that I provided for a tame flock or herd of goats, for I durst not upon any account fire my gun, especially near that side of the island where they usually came, lest I should alarm the savages, and if they had fled from me now, I was sure to have them come back again, with perhaps two or three hundred canoes with them, in a few days, and then I knew what to expect.

However, I wore out a year and three months more before I ever saw any more of the savages, and then I found them again, as I shall soon observe. It is true, they might have been there once or twice, but either they made no stay, or at least I did not hear them – but in the month of May, as near as I could calculate, and in my four and twentieth year, I had a very strange encounter with them, of which in its place.

The perturbation of my mind during this fifteen or sixteen months' interval was very great. I slept unquiet, dreamt always frightful dreams, and often started out of my sleep in the night; in the day, great troubles overwhelmed my mind, and in the night I dreamt often of killing the savages, and of the reasons why I might justify the doing of it – but to waive all this for a while. It was in the middle of May, on the sixteenth day I, think, as well as my poor wooden calendar would reckon – for I marked all upon the post still – I say, it was the sixteenth of May, that it blew a very great storm of wind all day, with a great deal of lightning and thunder, and a very foul night it was after it. I know not what was the particular occasion of it, but as I was reading in the Bible and taken up with very serious thoughts about my present condition, I was surprised with a noise of a gun, as I thought, fired at sea.

This was to be sure a surprise of a quite different nature from any I had met with before, for the notions this put into my thoughts were quite of another kind. I started up in the greatest haste imaginable, and in a trice clapped my ladder to the middle place of the rock, and pulled it after me, and, mounting it the second time, got to the top of the hill the very moment that a flash of fire bid me listen for a second gun, which accordingly in about half a minute I heard, and by the sound knew that it was from that part of the sea where I was driven down the current in my boat.

I immediately considered that this must be some ship in distress, and that they had some comrade, or some other ship in company, and fired these guns for signals of distress, and to obtain help. I had this presence of mind at that minute as to think that though I could not help them, it may be they might help me, so I brought together all the dry wood I could get at hand, and making a good handsome pile, I set it on fire upon the hill; the wood was dry and blazed freely, and though the wind blew very hard, yet it burned fairly out, that I was certain, if there was any such thing as a ship, they must needs see it, and no doubt they did, for as soon as ever my fire blazed up, I heard another gun, and after that several others, all from the same quarter. I plied my fire all night long till day broke, and when it was broad day, and the air cleared up, I saw something at a great distance at sea, full east of the island, whether a sail or a hull I could not distinguish, no, not with my glasses, the distance was so great, and the weather still something hazy also – at least it was so out at sea.

I looked frequently at it all that day, and soon perceived that it did not move, so I presently concluded that it was a ship at an anchor, and being eager, you may be sure, to be satisfied, I took my gun in my hand, and ran towards the south side of the island to the rocks where I had formerly been carried away with the current, and getting up there, the weather by this time being perfectly clear, I could plainly see, to my great sorrow, the wreck of a ship cast away in the night upon those concealed rocks which I found when I was out in my boat, and which rocks, as they checked the violence of the stream and made a kind of counter-stream or eddy, were the occasion of my recovering from the most desperate hopeless condition that ever I had been in in all my life.

Thus what is one man's safety is another man's destruction, for it seems these men, whoever they were, being out of their knowledge and the rocks being wholly underwater, had been driven upon them in the night, the wind blowing hard at E and ENE. Had they seen the island, as I must necessarily suppose they did not, they must, as I thought, have endeavoured to have saved themselves onshore by the help of their boat, but their firing of guns for help, especially when they saw, as I imagined, my fire, filled me with many thoughts. First, I imagined that upon seeing my light, they might have put themselves into their boat and have endeavoured to make the shore, but that the sea going very high, they might have been cast away; other times I imagined they might have lost their boat before, as might be the case many ways, as particularly by the breaking of the sea upon their ship, which many times obliges men to stave or take in pieces their boat, and sometimes to throw it overboard with their own hands; other times I imagined they had some other ship or ships in company, who, upon the signals of distress they had made, had taken them up and carried them off; other whiles I fancied they were all gone off to sea in their boat, and being hurried away by the current that I had been formerly in, were carried out into the great ocean, where there was nothing but misery and perishing, and that perhaps they might by this time think of starving, and of being in a condition to eat one another.

As all these were but conjectures at best, so in the condition I was in I could do no more than look upon the misery of the poor men and pity them, which had still this good effect on my side that it gave me more and more cause to give thanks to God who had so happily and comfortably provided for me in my desolate condition, and that of two ships' companies who were now cast away upon this part of the world, not one life should be spared but mine. I learnt here again to observe that it is very rare that the providence of God casts us into any condition of life so low, or to any misery so great, but we may see something or other to be thankful for, and may see others in worse circumstances than our own.

Such, certainly, was the case of these men, of whom I could not so much as see room to suppose any of them were saved; nothing could make it rational so much as to wish or expect that they did not all perish there, except the possibility only of their being taken up by another ship in company, and this was but mere possibility indeed, for I saw not the least signal or appearance of any such thing.

I cannot explain by any possible energy of words what a strange longing or hankering of desires I felt in my soul upon this sight, breaking out sometimes thus: "Oh that there had been but one or two – nay, or but one soul saved out of this ship, to have escaped to me, that I might but have had one companion, one fellow creature to have spoken to me, and to have conversed with!" In all the time of my solitary life, I never felt so earnest, so strong a desire after the society of my fellow creatures, or so deep a regret at the want of it.

There are some secret moving springs in the affections, which when they are set a-going by some object in view, or be it some object, though not in view, yet rendered present to the mind by the power of imagination, that motion carries out the soul by its impetuosity to such violent eager embracings of the object that the absence of it is insupportable.

Such were these earnest wishings that but one man had been saved! "Oh that it had been but one!" I believe I repeated the words "Oh that it had been but one!" a thousand times, and the desires were so moved by it that when I spoke the words my hands would clinch together, and my fingers press the palms of my hands, that if I had had any soft thing in my hand, it would have crushed it involuntarily, and my teeth in my head would strike together and set against one another so strong that for some time I could not part them again.

Let the naturalists explain these things, and the reason and manner of them; all I can say to them is to describe the fact, which was even surprising to me when I found it, though I knew not from what it should proceed. It was doubtless the effect of ardent wishes, and of strong ideas formed in my mind, realizing the comfort which the conversation of one of my fellow Christians would have been to me.

But it was not to be – either their fate or mine, or both, forbid it – for till the last year of my being on this island, I never knew whether any were saved out of that ship or no, and had only the affliction, some days after, to see the corpse of a drowned boy come onshore, at the end of the island which was next the shipwreck. He had on no clothes but a seaman's waistcoat, a pair of open-kneed linen drawers and a blue linen shirt, but nothing to direct me so much as to guess what nation he was of. He had nothing in his pocket but two pieces of eight, and a tobacco pipe – that last was to me of ten times more value than the first.

It was now calm, and I had a great mind to venture out in my boat to this wreck, not doubting but I might find something on board that might be useful to me, but that did not altogether press me so much as the possibility that there might yet be some living creature on board whose life I might not only save, but might, by saving that life, comfort my own to the last degree. And this thought clung so to my heart that I could not be quiet, night or day, but I must venture out in my boat on board this wreck, and committing the rest to God's providence, I thought the impression was so strong upon my mind that it could not be resisted, that it must come from some invisible direction, and that I should be wanting to myself if I did not go.

Under the power of this impression, I hastened back to my castle, prepared everything for my voyage, took a quantity of bread, a great pot for fresh water, a compass to steer by, a bottle of rum – for I had still a great deal of that left – a basket full of raisins; and thus loading myself with everything necessary, I went down to my boat, got the water out of her and got her afloat, loaded all my cargo in her, and then went home again for more. My second cargo was a great bag full of rice, the umbrella to set up over my head for shade, another large pot full of fresh water, and about two dozen of my small loaves or barley cakes, more than before, with a bottle of goat's milk and a cheese; all which, with great labour and sweat, I brought to my boat, and, praying to God to direct my voyage, I put out, and rowing or paddling the canoe along the shore, I came at last to the utmost point of the island on that side, namely, NE. And now I was to launch out into the ocean, and either to venture, or not to venture. I looked on the rapid currents which ran constantly on both sides of the island at a distance, and which were very terrible to me, from the remembrance of the hazard I had been in before, and my heart began to fail me, for I foresaw that if I was driven into either of those currents, I should be carried a vast way out to sea, and perhaps out of my reach, or sight, of the island again, and that then, as my boat was but small, if any little gale of wind should rise, I should be inevitably lost.

These thoughts so oppressed my mind that I began to give over my enterprise, and having haled my boat into a little creek on the shore, I stepped out and sat me down upon a little rising bit of ground, very pensive and anxious, between fear and desire about my voyage, when, as I was musing, I could perceive that the tide was turned, and the flood come on, upon which my going was for so many hours impracticable. Upon this, presently it occurred to me that I should go up to the highest piece of ground I could find, and observe, if I could, how the sets of the tide or currents lay when the flood came in, that I might judge whether, if I was driven one way out, I might not expect to be driven another way home, with the same rapidness of the currents. This thought was no sooner in my head but I cast my eye upon a little hill which sufficiently overlooked the sea both ways, and from whence I had a clear view of the currents or sets of the tide, and which way I was to guide myself in my return. Here I found that as the current of the ebb set out close by the south point of the island, so the current of the flood set in close by the shore of the north side, and that I had nothing to do but to keep to the north of the island in my return, and I should do well enough.

Encouraged with this observation, I resolved the next morning to set out with the first of the tide, and reposing myself for the night in the canoe, under the great watch coat I mentioned, I launched out. I made first a little out to sea full north, till I began to feel the benefit of the current, which set eastwards, and which carried me at a great rate, and yet did not so hurry me as the southern side current had done before, and so as to take from me all government of the boat, but having a strong steerage with my paddle, I went at a great rate directly for the wreck, and in less than two hours I came up to it.

It was a dismal sight to look at: the ship, which by its building was Spanish, stuck fast, jammed in between two rocks; all the stern and quarter of her was beaten to pieces with the sea, and as her forecastle, which stuck in the rocks, had run on with great violence, her mainmast and foremast were brought by the board, that is to say, broken short off, but her boltsprit was sound and the head and bow appeared firm. When I came close to her, a dog appeared upon her, who, seeing me coming, yelped and cried, and as soon as I called him, jumped into the sea to come to me, and I took him into the boat, but found him almost dead from hunger and thirst. I gave him a cake of my bread, and he ate it like a ravenous wolf that had been starving a fortnight in the snow. I then gave the poor creature some fresh water, with which, if I would have let him, he would have burst himself.

After this I went on board, but the first sight I met with was two men drowned in the cook room or forecastle of the ship, with their arms fast about one another. I concluded, as is indeed probable, that when the ship struck, it being in a storm, the sea broke so high and continually over her that the men were not able to bear it, and were strangled with the constant rushing in of the water, as much as if they had been underwater. Besides the dog, there was nothing left in the ship that had life, nor any goods that I could see but what were spoilt by the water. There were some casks of liquor, whether wine or brandy I knew not, which lay lower in the hold, and which, the water being ebbed out, I could see – but they were too big to meddle with. I saw several chests which I believed belonged to some of the seamen, and I got two of them into the boat, without examining what was in them.

Had the stern of the ship been fixed and the forepart broken off, I am persuaded I might have made a good voyage, for by what I found in these two chests, I had room to suppose the ship had a great deal of wealth on board, and if I may guess by the course she steered, she must have been bound from the Buenos Aires, or the Rio de la Plata, in the south part of America, beyond the Brazils, to the Havana in the Gulf of Mexico, and so perhaps to Spain. She had no doubt a great treasure in her, but of no use at the time to anybody, and what became of the rest of her people, I then knew not.

I found, besides these chests, a little cask full of liquor, of about twenty gallons, which I got into my boat with much difficulty. There were several muskets in a cabin, and a great powder horn with about four pounds of powder in it; as for the muskets, I had no occasion for them, so I left them, but took the powder horn. I took a fire shovel and tongs, which I wanted extremely, as also two little brass kettles, a copper pot to make chocolate, and a gridiron, and with this cargo, and the dog, I came away, the tide beginning to make home again, and the same evening, about an hour within night, reached the island again, weary and fatigued to the last degree.

I reposed that night in the boat, and in the morning I resolved to harbour what I had gotten in my new cave, not to carry it home to my castle. After refreshing myself, I got all my cargo onshore, and began to examine the particulars. The cask of liquor I found to be a kind of rum, but not such as we had at the Brazils – and in a word, not at all good – but when I came to open the chests, I found several things of great use to me: for example, I found in one a fine case of bottles of an extraordinary kind, and filled with cordial waters, fine and very good; the bottles held about three pints each, and were tipped with silver. I found two pots of very good succades or sweetmeats, so fastened also on top that the salt water had not hurt them, and two more of the same, which the water had spoilt. I found some very good shirts, which were very welcome to me, and about a dozen and half of linen white handkerchiefs and coloured neckcloths – the former were also very welcome, being exceeding refreshing to wipe my face in a hot day. Besides this, when I came to the till in the chest, I found there three great bags of pieces of eight, which held about eleven hundred pieces in all, and in one of them, wrapped up in a paper, six doubloons of gold, and some small bars or wedges of gold; I suppose they might all weigh near a pound.

The other chest I found had some clothes in it, but of little value, but by the circumstances it must have belonged to the gunner's mate, though there was no powder in it but about two pounds of fine glazed powder, in three small flasks – kept, I suppose, for charging their fowling pieces on occasion. Upon the whole, I got very little by this voyage that was of any use to me, for as to the money, I had no manner of occasion for it: 'twas to me as the dirt under my feet, and I would have given it all for three or four pair of English shoes and stockings, which were things I greatly wanted, but had not had on my feet now for many years. I had indeed gotten two pair of shoes now, which I took off of the feet of the two drowned men who I saw in the wreck, and I found two pair more in one of the chests, which were very welcome to me, but they were not like our English shoes, either for ease or service, being rather what we call pumps than shoes. I found in this seaman's chest about fifty pieces of eight in rials, but no gold – I suppose this belonged to a poorer man than the other, which seemed to belong to some officer.

Well, however, I lugged this money home to my cave, and laid it up, as I had done that before which I brought from our own ship, but it was great pity, as I said, that the other part of this ship had not come to my share, for I am satisfied I might have loaded my canoe several times over with money, which, if I had ever escaped to England, would have lain here safe enough, till I might have come again and fetched it.

Having now brought all my things onshore, and secured them, I went back to my boat, and rowed or paddled her along the shore to her old harbour, where I laid her up, and made the best of my way to my old habitation, where I found everything safe and quiet, so I began to repose myself, live after my old fashion and take care of my family affairs. And for a while, I lived easy enough, only that I was more vigilant than I used to be, looked out oftener, and did not go abroad so much; and if at any time I did stir with any freedom, it was always to the east part of the island, where I was pretty well satisfied the savages never came, and where I could go without so many precautions, and such a load of arms and ammunition as I always carried with me if I went the other way.

I lived in this condition near two years more, but my unlucky head, that was always to let me know it was born to make my body miserable, was all this two years filled with projects and designs – how, if it were possible, I might get away from this island, for sometimes I was for making another voyage to the wreck, though my reason told me that there was nothing left there worth the hazard of my voyage; sometimes for a ramble one way, sometimes another, and I believe verily, if I had had the boat that I went from Sallee in, I should have ventured to sea, bound anywhere, I knew not whither.

I have been in all my circumstances a memento to those who are touched with the general plague of mankind, whence, for ought I know, one half of their miseries flow – I mean that of not being satisfied with the station wherein God and Nature has placed them – for not to look back upon my primitive condition, and the excellent advice of my father – the opposition to which was, as I may call it, my original sin – my subsequent mistakes of the same kind had been the means of my coming into this miserable condition, for had that Providence, which so happily had seated me at the Brazils as a planter, blessed me with confined desires, and I could have been contented to have gone on gradually, I might have been by this time (I mean, in the time of my being in this island) one of the most considerable planters in the Brazils. Nay, I am persuaded that by the improvements I had made in that little time I lived there, and the increase I should probably have made if I had stayed, I might have been worth a hundred thousand moidores – and what business had I to leave a settled fortune, a well-stocked plantation, improving and increasing, to turn supercargo to Guinea, to fetch Negroes, when patience and time would have so increased our stock at home that we could have bought them at our own door, from those whose business it was to fetch them? And though it had cost us something more, yet the difference of that price was by no means worth saving at so great a hazard.

But as this is ordinarily the fate of young heads, so reflection upon the folly of it is as ordinarily the exercise of more years, or of the dear-bought experience of time – and so it was with me now – and yet so deep had the mistake taken root in my temper that I could not satisfy myself in my station, but was continually poring upon the means and possibility of my escape from this place – and that I may with the greater pleasure to the reader bring on the remaining part of my story, it may not be improper to give some account of my first conceptions on the subject of this foolish scheme for my escape, and how, and upon what foundation I acted.

I am now to be supposed retired into my castle, after my late voyage to the wreck, my frigate laid up and secured underwater as usual, and my condition restored to what it was before. I had more wealth indeed than I had before, but was not at all the richer, for I had no more use for it than the Indians of Peru had before the Spaniards came there.

It was one of the nights in the rainy season in March, the four and twentieth year of my first setting foot in this island of solitariness; I was lying in my bed, or hammock, awake, very well in health, had no pain, no distemper, no uneasiness of body – no, nor any uneasiness of mind more than ordinary – but could by no means close my eyes, that is, so as to sleep – no, not a wink all night long, otherwise than as follows:

It is as impossible as needless to set down the innumerable crowd of thoughts that whirled through that great thoroughfare of the brain, the memory, in this night's time: I ran over the whole history of my life in miniature, or by abridgement, as I may call it, to my coming to this island, and also of the part of my life since I came to this island. In my reflections upon the state of my case since I came onshore on this island, I was comparing the happy posture of my affairs in the first years of my habitation here, compared to the life of anxiety, fear and care which I had lived in ever since I had seen the print of a foot in the sand – not that I did not believe the savages had frequented the island even all the while, and might have been several hundreds of them at times onshore there, but I had never known it, and was incapable of any apprehensions about it; my satisfaction was perfect, though my danger was the same, and I was as happy in not knowing my danger, as if I had never really been exposed to it. This furnished my thoughts with many very profitable reflections, and particularly this one: how infinitely good that Providence is which has provided in its government of mankind such narrow bounds to his sight and knowledge of things, and though he walks in the midst of so many thousand dangers, the sight of which, if discovered to him, would distract his mind and sink his spirits, he is kept serene and calm by having the events of things hid from his eyes, and knowing nothing of the dangers which surround him.

After these thoughts had for some time entertained me, I came to reflect seriously upon the real danger I had been in for so many years, in this very island, and how I had walked about in the greatest security, and with all possible tranquillity, even when perhaps nothing but a brow of a hill, a great tree or the casual approach of night had been between me and the worst kind of destruction, namely, that of falling into the hands of cannibals and savages, who would have seized on me with the same view as I did of a goat or a turtle, and have thought it no more a crime to kill and devour me than I did of a pigeon or a curlew. I would unjustly slander myself if I should say I was not sincerely thankful to my great Preserver, to whose singular protection I acknowledged, with great humility, that all these unknown deliverances were due, and without which I must inevitably have fallen into their merciless hands.

When these thoughts were over, my head was for some time taken up in considering the nature of these wretched creatures – I mean the savages – and how it came to pass in the world that the wise Governor of all things should give up any of His creatures to such inhumanity, nay, to something so much below even brutality itself as to devour its own kind, but as this ended in some (at that time fruitless) speculations, it occurred to me to enquire what part of the world these wretches lived in; how far off the coast was from whence they came; what they ventured over so far from home for; what kind of boats they had; and why I might not order myself and my business so that I might be as able to go over thither as they were to come to me.

I never so much as troubled myself to consider what I should do with myself when I came thither, what would become of me if I fell into the hands of the savages, or how I should escape from them, if they attempted me – no, nor so much as how it was possible for me to reach the coast, and not to be attempted by some or other of them, without any possibility of delivering myself – and if I should not fall into their hands, what I should do for provision, or whither I should bend my course. None of these thoughts, I say, so much as came in my way, but my mind was wholly bent upon the notion of passing over in my boat to the mainland. I looked back upon my present condition as the most miserable that could possibly be, that I was not able to throw myself into anything but death that could be called worse; that if I reached the shore of the main, I might perhaps meet with relief, or I might coast along, as I did on the shore of Africk, till I came to some inhabited country, and where I might find some relief; and after all, perhaps I might fall in with some Christian ship that might take me in, and if the worse came to the worst, I could but die, which would put an end to all these miseries at once. Pray note, all this was the fruit of a disturbed mind, an impatient temper, made as it were desperate by the long continuance of my troubles and the disappointments I had met in the wreck I had been on board of, and where I had been so near the obtaining what I so earnestly longed for – namely, somebody to speak to, and to learn some knowledge from, of the place where I was, and of the probable means of my deliverance – I say, I was agitated wholly by these thoughts. All my calm of mind in my resignation to providence, and waiting the issue of the dispositions of Heaven, seemed to be suspended, and I had, as it were, no power to turn my thoughts to anything but to the project of a voyage to the main, which came upon me with such force, and such an impetuosity of desire, that it was not to be resisted.

When this had agitated my thoughts for two hours or more, with such violence that it set my very blood into a ferment, and my pulse beat as high as if I had been in a fever merely with the extraordinary fervour of my mind about it, Nature, as if I had been fatigued and exhausted with the very thought of it, threw me into a sound sleep; one would have thought I should have dreamt of it, but I did not, nor of anything relating to it, but I dreamt that as I was going out in the morning as usual from my castle, I saw upon the shore two canoes and eleven savages coming to land, and that they brought with them another savage, who they were going to kill, in order to eat him; when on a sudden, the savage that they were going to kill jumped away and ran for his life, and I thought, in my sleep, that he came running into my little thick grove before my fortification to hide himself; and that I, seeing him alone, and not perceiving that the other sought him that way, showed myself to him and, smiling upon him, encouraged him; that he knelt down to me, seeming to pray me to assist him, upon which I showed my ladder, made him go up, and carried him into my cave, and he became my servant; and that as soon as I had gotten this man, I said to myself, "Now I may certainly venture to the mainland, for this fellow will serve me as a pilot, and will tell me what to do and whether to go for provisions; and whether not to go for fear of being devoured, what places to venture into and what to escape." I waked with this thought, and was under such inexpressible impressions of joy at the prospect of my escape in my dream, that the disappointments which I felt upon coming to myself and finding it was no more than a dream were equally extravagant the other way, and threw me into a very great dejection of spirit.

Upon this, however, I made this conclusion: that my only way to go about an attempt for an escape was, if possible, to get a savage into my possession, and if possible, it should be one of their prisoners, whom they had condemned to be eaten, and should bring thither to kill. But these thoughts still were attended with this difficulty, that it was impossible to effect this without attacking a whole caravan of them, and killing them all – and this was not only a very desperate attempt, and might miscarry – but on the other hand, I had greatly scrupled the lawfulness of it to me, and my heart trembled at the thoughts of shedding so much blood, though it was for my deliverance. I need not repeat the arguments which occurred to me against this, they being the same mentioned before, but though I had other reasons to offer now – namely, that those men were enemies to my life and would devour me if they could; that it was self-preservation in the highest degree, to deliver myself from this death of a life, and was acting in my own defence as much as if they were actually assaulting me, and the like – I say, though these things argued for it, yet the thoughts of shedding human blood for my deliverance were very terrible to me, and such as I could by no means reconcile myself to a great while.

However, at last, after many secret disputes with myself, and after great perplexities about it – for all these arguments one way and another struggled in my head a long time – the eager prevailing desire of deliverance at length mastered all the rest, and I resolved, if possible, to get one of those savages into my hands, cost what it would. My next thing then was to contrive how to do it, and this indeed was very difficult to resolve on. But as I could pitch upon no probable means for it, so I resolved to put myself upon the watch – to see them when they came onshore, and leave the rest to the event, taking such measures as the opportunity should present, let be what would be.

With these resolutions in my thoughts, I set myself upon the scout as often as possible, and indeed so often till I was heartily tired of it, for it was above a year and a half that I waited, and for a great part of that time went out to the west end, and to the south-west corner of the island, almost every day, to see for canoes, but none appeared. This was very discouraging, and began to trouble me much, though I cannot say that it did in this case as it had done some time before that – namely, wear off the edge of my desire to the thing. But the longer it seemed to be delayed, the more eager I was for it – in a word, I was not at first so careful to shun the sight of these savages, and avoid being seen by them, as I was now eager to be upon them.

Besides, I fancied myself able to manage one, nay, two or three savages, if I had them, so as to make them entirely slaves to me, to do whatever I should direct them, and to prevent their being able at any time to do me any hurt. It was a great while that I pleased myself with this affair, but nothing still presented; all my fancies and schemes came to nothing, for no savages came near me for a great while.

About a year and a half after I had entertained these notions, and, by long musing, had as it were resolved them all into nothing, for want of an occasion to put them in execution, I was surprised one morning early with seeing no less than five canoes all onshore together on my side the island, and the people who belonged to them all landed, and out of my sight. The number of them broke all my measures, for seeing so many, and knowing that they always came four or six, or sometimes more, in a boat, I could not tell what to think of it, or how to take my measures to attack twenty or thirty men single-handed, so I lay still in my castle, perplexed and discomforted; however, I put myself into all the same postures for an attack that I had formerly provided, and was just ready for action, if anything had presented. Having waited a good while, listening to hear if they made any noise, at length, being very impatient, I set my guns at the foot of my ladder, and clambered up to the top of the hill, by my two stages as usual – standing so, however, that my head did not appear above the hill, so that they could not perceive me by any means. Here I observed, by the help of my prospective glass, that they were no less than thirty in number, that they had a fire kindled, that they had had meat dressed. How they cooked it, that I knew not, or what it was, but they were all dancing in I know not how many barbarous gestures and figures, their own way, round the fire.

While I was thus looking on them, I perceived by my prospective two miserable wretches dragged from the boats, where it seems they were laid by, and were now brought out for the slaughter. I perceived one of them immediately fell, being knocked down, I suppose, with a club or wooden sword, for that was their way, and two or three others were at work immediately cutting him open for their cookery, while the other victim was left standing by himself till they should be ready for him. In that very moment, this poor wretch seeing himself a little at liberty, Nature inspired him with hopes of life, and he started away from them, and ran with incredible swiftness along the sands directly towards me – I mean, towards that part of the coast where my habitation was.

I was dreadfully frighted (that I must acknowledge) when I perceived him to run my way, and especially when, as I thought, I saw him pursued by the whole body, and now I expected that part of my dream was coming to pass, and that he would certainly take shelter in my grove, but I could not depend by any means upon my dream for the rest of it – namely, that the other savages would not pursue him thither, and find him there. However, I kept my station, and my spirits began to recover when I found that there was not above three men that followed him, and still more was I encouraged when I found that he outstripped them exceedingly in running, and gained ground of them, so that if he could but hold it for half an hour, I saw easily he would fairly get away from them all.

There was between them and my castle the creek which I mentioned often at the first part of my story, when I landed my cargoes out of the ship, and this I saw plainly: he must necessarily swim over, or the poor wretch would be taken there. But when the savage escaping came thither, he made nothing of it, though the tide was then up, but plunging in, swam through in about thirty strokes or thereabouts, landed, and ran on with exceeding strength and swiftness. When the three persons came to the creek, I found that two of them could swim, but the third could not, and that, standing on the other side, he looked at the other, but went no further, and soon after went softly back again, which, as it happened, was very well for him in the main.

I observed that the two who swam were yet more than twice as long swimming over the creek as the fellow was that fled from them. It came now very warmly upon my thoughts, and indeed irresistibly, that now was my time to get me a servant, and perhaps a companion or assistant, and that I was called plainly by Providence to save this poor creature's life. I immediately ran down the ladders with all possible expedition, fetched my two guns – for they were both but at the foot of the ladders, as I observed above – and getting up again with the same haste to

225

the top of the hill, I crossed towards the sea and, having a very short cut, and all downhill, clapped myself in the way between the pursuers and the pursued, hallooing aloud to him that fled, who, looking back, was at first perhaps as much frighted at me as at them. But I beckoned with my hand to him to come back, and in the meantime, I slowly advanced towards the two that followed; then rushing at once upon the foremost, I knocked him down with the stock of my piece. I was loath to fire, because I would not have the rest hear, though at that distance it would not have been easily heard, and being out of sight of the smoke too, they would not have easily known what to make of it. Having knocked this fellow down, the other who pursued with him stopped, as if he had been frighted, and I advanced apace towards him, but as I came nearer, I perceived presently he had a bow and arrow, and was fitting it to shoot at me, so I was then necessitated to shoot at him first, which I did, and killed him at the first shoot. The poor savage who fled, but had stopped, though he saw both his enemies fallen and killed, as he thought, yet was so frighted with the fire and noise of my piece, that he stood stock still, and neither came forwards or went backwards, though he seemed rather inclined to fly still than to come on. I hallooed again to him, and made signs to come forwards, which he easily understood, and came a little way, then stopped again, and then a little further, and stopped again, and I could then perceive that he stood trembling, as if he had been taken prisoner, and had just been to be killed, as his two enemies were. I beckoned him again to come to me, and gave him all the signs of encouragement that I could think of, and he came nearer and nearer, kneeling down every ten or twelve steps in token of acknowledgement for my saving his life. I smiled at him, and looked pleasantly, and beckoned to him to come still nearer; at length he came close to me, and then he knelt down again, kissed the ground, and laid his head upon the ground and, taking me by the foot, set my foot upon his head. This, it seems, was in token of swearing to be my slave for ever; I took him up, and made much of him, and encouraged him all I could. But there was more work to do yet, for I perceived the savage who I knocked down was not killed, but stunned with the blow, and began to come to himself. So I pointed to him, and showing him the savage, that he was not dead, upon this he spoke some words to me, and though I could not understand them, yet I thought they were pleasant to hear, for they were the first sound of a man's voice that I had heard, my own excepted, for above twenty-five years. But there was no time for such reflections now; the savage who was knocked down recovered himself so far as to sit up upon the ground, and I perceived that my savage began to be afraid, but when I saw that, I presented my other piece at the man, as if I would shoot him. Upon this, my savage, for so I call him now, made a motion to me to lend him my sword, which hung naked in a belt by my side, so I did: he no sooner had it, but he runs to his enemy, and at one blow cut off his head as cleverly, no executioner in Germany could have done it sooner or better – which I thought very strange, for one who I had reason to believe never saw a sword in his life before, except their own wooden swords. However, it seems, as I learnt afterwards, they make their wooden swords so sharp, so heavy, and the wood is so hard, that they will cut off heads even with them, ay and arms, and that at one blow too. When he had done this, he comes laughing to me in sign of triumph, and brought me the sword again and, with abundance of gestures which I did not understand, laid it down with the head of the savage that he had killed, just before me.

But that which astonished him most was to know how I had killed the other Indian so far off; so pointing to him, he made signs to me to let him go to him, so I bade him go as well as I could; when he came to him, he stood like one amazed, looking at him, turned him first on one side, then on t'other, looked at the wound the bullet had made, which it seems was just in his breast, where it had made a hole, and no great quantity of blood had followed, but he had bled inwardly, for he was quite dead. He took up his bow and arrows, and came back, so I turned to go away, and beckoned to him to follow me, making signs to him that more might come after them.

Upon this he signed to me that he should bury them with sand, that they might not be seen by the rest if they followed, and so I made signs again to him to do so. He fell to work, and in an instant he had scraped a hole in the sand with his hands big enough to bury the first in, and then dragged him into it, and covered him, and did so also by the other – I believe he had buried them both in a quarter of an hour – then calling him away, I carried him not to my castle, but quite away to my cave on the further part of the island, so I did not let my dream come to pass in that part, namely, that he came into my grove for shelter.

Here I gave him bread and a bunch of raisins to eat, and a draught of water, which I found he was indeed in great distress for by his running, and having refreshed him, I made signs for him to go lie down and sleep, pointing to a place where I had laid a great parcel of rice straw and a blanket upon it, which I used to sleep upon myself sometimes. So the poor creature laid down, and went to sleep.

He was a comely, handsome fellow, perfectly well-made, with straight strong limbs, not too large, tall and well-shaped and, as I reckon, about twenty-six years of age. He had a very good countenance, not a fierce and surly aspect, but seemed to have something very manly in his face, and yet he had all the sweetness and softness of a European in his countenance too, especially when he smiled. His hair was long and black, not curled like wool; his forehead very high and large, and a great vivacity and sparkling sharpness in his eyes. The colour of his skin was not quite black, but very tawny, and yet not of an ugly yellow nauseous tawny as the Brazilians and Virginians, and other natives of America are, but of a bright kind of a dun olive colour that had in it something very agreeable, though not very easy to describe. His face was round and plump; his nose small, not flat like the Negroes, a very good mouth, thin lips, and his fine teeth well-set and white as ivory. After he had slumbered, rather than slept, about half an hour, he waked again, and comes out of the cave to me, for I had been milking my goats, which I had in the enclosure just by. When he espied me, he came running to me, laying himself down again upon the ground with all the possible signs of a humble thankful disposition, making a many antic gestures to show it. At last he lays his head flat upon the ground close to my foot, and sets my other foot upon his head as he had done before, and after this made all the signs to me of subjection, servitude and submission imaginable, to let me know how he would serve me as long as he lived. I understood him in many things, and let him know I was very well pleased with him. In a little time I began to speak to him, and teach him to speak to me, and first, I made him know his name should be Friday, which was the day I saved his life – I called him so for the memory of the time – I likewise taught him to say Master, and then let him know that was to be my name; I likewise taught him to say yes and no, and to know the meaning of them. I gave him some milk in an earthen pot, and let him see me drink it before him, and sop my bread in it, and I gave him a cake of bread to do the like, which he quickly complied with, and made signs that it was very good for him.

I kept there with him all that night, but as soon as it was day, I beckoned to him to come with me, and let him know I would give him some clothes, at which he seemed very glad, for he was stark naked. As we went by the place where he had buried the two men, he pointed exactly to the place, and showed me the marks that he had made to find them again, making signs to me that we should dig them up again and eat them. At this I appeared very angry, expressed my abhorrence of it, made as if I would vomit at the thoughts of it, and beckoned with my hand to him to come away, which he did immediately, with great submission. I then led him up to the top of the hill to see if his enemies were gone, and pulling out my glass, I looked, and saw plainly the place where they had been, but no appearance of them, or of their canoes, so that it was plain they were gone and had left their two comrades behind them, without any search after them.

But I was not content with this discovery – but having now more courage, and consequently more curiosity, I took my man Friday with me, giving him the sword in his hand, with the bow and arrows at his back, which I found he could use very dexterously, making him carry one gun for me, and I two for myself, and away we marched to the place where these creatures had been, for I had a mind now to get some fuller intelligence of them. When I came to the place, my very blood ran chill in my veins and my heart sunk within me at the horror of the spectacle: indeed it was a dreadful sight, at least it was so to me, though Friday made nothing of it. The place was covered with human bones, the ground dyed with their blood, great pieces of flesh left here and there, half-eaten, mangled and scorched – and in short, all the tokens of the triumphant feast they had been making there after a victory over their enemies. I saw three skulls, five hands and the bones of three or four legs and feet, and abundance of other parts of the bodies, and Friday, by his signs, made me understand that they brought over four prisoners to feast upon; that three of them were eaten up, and that he, pointing to himself, was the fourth; that there had been a great battle between them and their next king, whose subjects it seems he had been one of; and that they had taken a great number of prisoners, all which were carried to several places by those that had taken them in the fight, in order to feast upon them, as was done here by these wretches upon those they brought hither.

I caused Friday to gather all the skulls, bones, flesh and whatever remained, and lay them together on a heap and make a great fire upon it, and burned them all to ashes: I found Friday had still a hankering stomach after some of the flesh, and was still a cannibal in his nature, but I discovered so much abhorrence at the very thoughts of it, and at the least appearance of it, that he durst not discover it, for I had by some means let him know that I would kill him if he offered it.

When we had done this, we came back to our castle, and there I fell to work for my man Friday, and first of all I gave him a pair of linen drawers, which I had out of the poor gunner's chest I mentioned, and which I found in the wreck – and which with a little alteration fitted him very well – then I made him a jerkin of goat's skin, as well as my skill would allow – and I was now grown a tolerable good tailor – and I gave him a cap, which I had made of a hareskin, very convenient, and fashionable enough: and thus he was clothed for the present, tolerably well, and was mighty well pleased to see himself almost as well-clothed as his master. It is true, he went awkwardly in these things at first – wearing the drawers was very awkward to him, and the sleeves of the waistcoat galled his shoulders and the inside of his arms – but a little easing them where he complained they hurt him, and using himself to them, at length he took to them very well.

The next day after I came home to my hutch with him, I began to consider where I should lodge him, and that I might do well for him, and yet be perfectly easy myself, I made a little tent for him in the vacant place between my two fortifications, in the inside of the last and in the outside of the first. And as there was a door or entrance there into my cave, I made a formal framed door case, and a door to it of boards, and set it up in the passage a little within the entrance, and causing the door to open on the inside, I barred it up in the night, taking in my ladders too, so that Friday could no way come at me in the inside of my inner-most wall without making so much noise in getting over that it must needs waken me, for my first wall had now a complete roof over it of long poles, covering all my tent, and leaning up to the side of the hill, which was again laid cross with smaller sticks instead of laths, and then thatched over a great thickness with the rice straw, which was strong like reeds. And at the hole or place which was left to go in or out by the ladder, I had placed a kind of trapdoor, which if it had been attempted on the outside, would not have opened at all, but would have fallen down and made a great noise – and as to weapons, I took them all in to my side every night.

But I needed none of all this precaution, for never man had a more faithful, loving, sincere servant than Friday was to me, without passions, sullenness or designs, perfectly obliged and engaged. His very affections were tied to me like those of a child to a father, and I dare say he would have sacrificed his life for the saving mine upon any occasion whatsoever – the many testimonies he gave me of this put it out of doubt, and soon convinced me that I needed to use no precautions as to my safety on his account.

This frequently gave me occasion to observe, and that with wonder, that however it had pleased God in His providence, and in the government of the works of His hand, to take from so great a part of the world of His creatures the best uses to which their faculties and the powers of their souls are adapted, yet that He has bestowed upon them the same powers, the same reason, the same affections, the same sentiments of kindness and obligation, the same passions and resentments of wrongs, the same sense of gratitude, sincerity, fidelity and all the capacities of doing good and receiving good that He has given to us; and that when He pleases to offer to them occasions of exerting these, they are as ready, nay, more ready to apply them to the right uses for which they were bestowed, than we are – and this made me very melancholy sometimes, in reflecting as the several occasions presented, how mean a use we make of all these, even though we have these powers enlightened by the great lamp of instruction, the spirit of God and by the knowledge of His word added to our understanding; and why it has pleased God to hide the like saving knowledge from so many millions of souls, who, if I might judge by this poor savage, would make a much better use of it than we did.

From hence, I sometimes was led too far to invade the sovereignty of Providence, and as it were arraign the justice of so arbitrary a disposition of things that should hide that light from some and reveal it to others, and yet expect a like duty from both. But I shut it up, and checked my thoughts with this conclusion: (1st) that we did not know by what light and law these should be condemned, but that as God was necessarily, and by the nature of His being, infinitely holy and just, so it could not be but that if these creatures were all sentenced to absence from Himself, it was on account of sinning against that light which, as the Scripture says, was a law to themselves, and by such rules as their consciences would acknowledge to be just, though the foundation was not discovered to us; and (2nd) that still as we are all the clay in the hand of the potter, no vessel could say to Him, "Why hast Thou formed me thus?"

But to return to my new companion: I was greatly delighted with him, and made it my business to teach him everything that was proper to make him useful, handy and helpful – but especially to make him speak, and understand me when I spake, and he was the aptest scholar that ever was, and particularly was so merry, so constantly diligent, and so pleased when he could but understand me or make me understand him, that it was very pleasant to me to talk to him, and now my life began to be so easy that I began to say to myself that could I but have been safe from more savages, I cared not if I was never to remove from the place while I lived.

A FTER I HAD BEEN TWO OR THREE DAYS returned to my castle, I thought that, in order to bring Friday off from his horrid way of feeding and from the relish of a cannibal's stomach, I ought to let him taste other flesh, so I took him out with me one morning to the woods. I went indeed intending to kill a kid out of my own flock, and bring him home and dress it, but as I was going, I saw a she-goat lying down in the shade, and two young kids sitting by her. I catched hold of Friday. "Hold," said I, "stand still," and made signs to him not to stir; immediately I presented my piece, shot and killed one of the kids. The poor creature, who had at a distance seen me kill the savage his enemy, but did not know or could imagine how it was done, was sensibly surprised, trembled and shook, and looked so amazed that I thought he would have sunk down. He did not see the kid I shot at, or perceive I had killed it, but ripped up his waistcoat to feel if he was not wounded, and as I found, presently thought I was resolved to kill him, for he came and knelt down to me, and embracing my knees, said a great many things I did not understand, but I could easily see that the meaning was to pray me not to kill him.

I soon found a way to convince him that I would do him no harm and, taking him up by the hand, laughed at him, and pointed to the kid which I had killed, beckoned to him to run and fetch it

– which he did – and while he was wondering and looking to see how the creature was killed, I loaded my gun again, and by and by I saw a great fowl like a hawk sit upon a tree within shot. So to let Friday understand a little what I would do, I called him to me again, pointed at the fowl – which was indeed a parrot, though I thought it had been a hawk – I say, pointing to the parrot, and to my gun, and to the ground under the parrot, to let him see I would make it fall, I made him understand that I would shoot and kill that bird. According I fired and bade him look, and immediately he saw the parrot fall, he stood like one frighted again, notwithstanding all I had said to him, and I found he was the more amazed because he did not see me put anything into the gun, but thought that there must be some wonderful fund of death and destruction in that thing, able to kill man, beast, bird or anything near or far off, and the astonishment this created in him was such as could not wear off for a long time, and I believe, if I would have let him, he would have worshipped me and my gun. As for the gun itself, he would not so much as touch it for several days after, but would speak to it, and talk to it, as if it had answered him, when he was by himself – which, as I afterwards learnt of him, was to desire it not to kill him.

Well, after his astonishment was a little over at this, I pointed to him to run and fetch the bird I had shot, which he did, but stayed some time, for the parrot, not being quite dead, was fluttered away a good way off from the place where she fell. However, he found her, took her up, and brought her to me, and as I had perceived his ignorance about the gun before, I took this advantage to charge the gun again, and not let him see me do it, that I might be ready for any other mark that might present. But nothing more offered at that time, so I brought home the kid, and the same evening I took the skin off, and cut it out as well as I could and, having a pot for that purpose, I boiled or stewed some of the flesh, and made some very good broth and, after I had begun to eat some, I gave some to my man, who seemed very glad of it, and liked it very well, but that which was strangest to him was to see me eat salt with it. He made a sign to me that salt was not good to eat and, putting a little into his own mouth, he seemed to nauseate it, and would spit and sputter at it, washing his mouth with fresh water after it; on the other hand, I took some meat in my mouth without salt, and I pretended to spit and sputter for want of salt, as fast as he had done at the salt, but it would not do, he would never care for salt with his meat or in his broth – at least not a great while, and then but a very little.

Having thus fed him with boiled meat and broth, I was resolved to feast him the next day with roasting a piece of the kid; this I did by hanging it before the fire on a string, as I had seen many people do in England, setting two poles up, one on each side of the fire, and one cross on the top, and tying the string to the cross-stick, letting the meat turn continually. This Friday admired very much, but when he came to taste the flesh, he took so many ways to tell me how well he liked it that I could not but understand him – and at last he told me he would never eat man's flesh any more, which I was very glad to hear.

The next day I set him to work to beating some corn out, and sifting it in the manner I used to do, as I observed before, and he soon understood how to do it as well as I, especially after he had seen what the meaning of it was, and that it was to make bread of, for after that I let him see me make my bread, and bake it too, and in a little time Friday was able to do all the work for me as well as I could do it myself.

I began now to consider that, having two mouths to feed instead of one, I must provide more ground for my harvest, and plant a larger quantity of corn than I used to do, so I marked out a larger piece of land, and began the fence in the same manner as before, in which Friday not only worked very willingly and very hard, but did it very cheerfully, and I told him what it was for; that it was for corn to make more bread, because he was now with me, and that I might have enough for him and myself too. He appeared very sensible of that part, and let me know that he thought I had much more labour upon me on his account than I had for myself, and that he would work the harder for me if I would tell him what to do.

This was the pleasantest year of all the life I led in this place. Friday began to talk pretty well, and understand the names of almost everything I had occasion to call for, and of every place I had to send him to, and talked a great deal to me, so that, in short, I began now to have some use for my tongue again, which indeed I had very little occasion for before – that is to say, about speech – besides the pleasures of talking to him, I had a singular satisfaction in the fellow himself; his simple, unfeigned honesty appeared to me more and more every day, and I began really to love the creature – and on his side, I believe he loved me more than it was possible for him ever to love anything before.

I had a mind once to try if he had any hankering inclination to his own country again, and having learnt him English so well that he could answer me almost any questions, I asked him whether the nation that he belonged to never conquered in battle, at which he smiled, and said, "Yes, yes, we always fight the better" – that is, he meant always get the better in fight – and so we began the following discourse: "You always fight the better," said I, "how came you to be taken prisoner then, Friday?"

FRIDAY: My nation beat much, for all that.

MASTER: How beat? If your nation beat them, how came you to be taken?

FRIDAY: They more many than my nation in the place where me was; they take one, two, three and me; my nation over-beat them in the yonder place, where me no was; there my nation take one, two, great thousand.

MASTER: But why did not your side recover you from the hands of your enemies then?

FRIDAY: They run one, two, three and me, and make go in the canoe; my nation have no canoe that time.

MASTER: Well, Friday, and what does your nation do with the men they take, do they carry them away and eat them, as these did?

FRIDAY: Yes, my nation eat mans too, eat all up.

MASTER: Where do they carry them?

FRIDAY: Go to other place where they think.

MASTER: Do they come hither?

FRIDAY: Yes, yes, they come hither; come other else place.

MASTER: Have you been here with them?

FRIDAY: Yes, I been here. [*points to the* NW *side of the island, which, it seems, was their side.*]

By this I understood that my man Friday had formerly been among the savages who used to come onshore on the further part of the island, on the same man-eating occasions that he was now brought for, and some time after, when I took the courage to carry him to that side, being the same I formerly mentioned, he presently knew the place, and told me he was there once when they ate up twenty men, two women and one child. He could not tell twenty in English, but he numbered them by laying so many stones on a row, and pointing to me to tell them over.

I have told this passage because it introduces what follows; that after I had had this discourse with him I asked him how far it was from our island to the shore, and whether the canoes were not often lost. He told me there was no danger, no canoes ever lost, but that after a little way out to the sea there was a current and wind, always one way in the morning, the other in the afternoon.

This I understood to be no more than the sets of the tide, as going out or coming in, but I afterwards understood it was occasioned by the great draught and reflux of the mighty river Orinoco – in the mouth or the gulf of which river, as I found afterwards, our island lay – and this land which I perceived to the W and NW was the great island Trinidad, on the north point of the mouth of the river. I asked Friday a thousand questions about the country, the inhabitants, the sea, the coast and what nations were near; he told me all he knew with the greatest openness imaginable. I asked him the name of the several nations of his sort of people, but could get no other name than Caribs, from whence I easily understood that these were the Caribbees, which our maps place on the part of America which reaches from the mouth of the river Orinoco to Guiana, and onwards to St Martha. He told me that up a great way beyond the moon – that was, beyond the setting of the moon, which must be W. from their country – there dwelt white bearded men like me, and pointed to my great whiskers, which I mentioned before; and that they had killed "much mans", that was his word – by all which I understood he meant the Spaniards, whose cruelties in America had been spread over the whole countries, and was remembered by all the nations from father to son.

I enquired if he could tell me how I might come from this island, and get among those white men; he told me, yes, yes, I might go "in two canoe". I could not understand what he meant, or make him describe to me what he meant by "two canoe", till at last, with great difficulty, I found he meant it must be in a large great boat, as big as two canoes.

This part of Friday's discourse began to relish with me very well, and from this time I entertained some hopes that one time or other I might find an opportunity to make my escape from this place, and that this poor savage might be a means to help me to do it.

During the long time that Friday had now been with me, and that he began to speak to me and understand me, I was not wanting to lay a foundation of religious knowledge in his mind – particularly I asked him one time who made him. The poor creature did not understand me at all, but thought I had asked him who was his father, but I took it by another handle, and asked him who made the sea, the ground we walked on, and the hills and woods; he told me it was one old Benamuckee, that lived beyond all. He could describe nothing of this great person, but that he was very old – much older, he said, than the sea or the land, than the moon or the stars. I asked him then if this old person had made all things, why did not all things worship him: he looked very grave, and with a perfect look of innocence said, "All things do say O to him." I asked him if the people who die in his country went away anywhere. He said, yes, they all went to Benamuckee; then I asked him whether these they ate up went thither too. He said yes.

From these things I began to instruct him in the knowledge of the true God. I told him that the great Maker of all things lived up there, pointing up towards heaven; that He governs the world by the same power and providence by which He had made it; that He was omnipotent, could do everything for us, give everything to us, take everything from us – and thus, by degrees, I opened his eyes. He listened with great attention, and received with pleasure the notion of Jesus Christ being sent to redeem us, and of the manner of making our prayers to God, and His being able to hear us, even into heaven. He told me one day that if our God could hear us up beyond the sun, He must needs be a greater god than their Benamuckee, who lived but a little way off, and yet could not hear till they went up to the great mountains where he dwelt to speak to him. I asked him if ever he went thither to speak to him; he said no, they never went that were young men; none went thither but the old men, who he called their *oowocakee* – that is, as I made him explain it to me, their religious, or clergy – and that they went to say O (so he called saying prayers) and then came back, and told them what Benamuckee said. By this, I observed that there is priestcraft even amongst the most blinded ignorant pagans in the world, and the policy of making a secret religion, in order to preserve the veneration of the people to the clergy, is not only to be found in the Roman, but perhaps among all religions in the world, even among the most brutish and barbarous savages.

I endeavoured to clear up this fraud to my man Friday, and told him that the pretence of their old men going up the mountains to say O to their god Benamuckee was a cheat, and their bringing word from thence what he said was much more so; that if they met with any answer, or spake with anyone there, it must be with an evil spirit. And then I entered into a long discourse with him about the Devil, the original of him, his rebellion against God, his enmity to man, the reason of it, his setting himself up the dark parts of the world to be worshipped instead of God, and as God; and the many stratagems he made use of to delude mankind to his ruin; how he had a secret access to our passions and to our affections, to adapt his snares to our inclinations, as to cause us even to be our own tempters, and to run upon our destruction by our own choice.

I found it was not so easy to imprint right notions in his mind about the Devil as it was about the being of a God. Nature assisted all my arguments to evidence to him even the necessity of a great First Cause and overruling governing Power, a secret directing Providence, and of the equity and justice of paying homage to Him that made us, and the like. But there appeared nothing of all this in the notion of an evil spirit; of his original, his being, his nature and above all of his inclination to do evil, and to draw us in to do so too, and the poor creature puzzled me once in such a manner, by a question merely natural and innocent, that I scarce knew what to say to him. I had been talking a great deal to him of the power of God, His omnipotence, His dreadful nature to sin, His being a consuming fire to the workers of iniquity; how, as He had made us all, He could destroy us and all the world in a moment, and he listened with great seriousness to me all the while.

After this, I had been telling him how the Devil was God's enemy in the hearts of men, and used all his malice and skill to defeat the good designs of Providence, and to ruin the kingdom of Christ in the world, and the like. "Well," says Friday, "but you say God is so strong, so great; is He not much strong, much might as the Devil?" "Yes, yes," says I, "Friday, God is stronger than the Devil, God is above the Devil, and therefore we pray to God to tread him down under our feet, and enable us to resist his temptations and quench his fiery darts." "But," says he again, "if God much strong, much might as the Devil, why God no kill the Devil, so make him no more do wicked?"

I was strangely surprised at his question, and after all, though I was now an old man, yet I was but a young doctor, and ill enough qualified for a casuist, or a solver of difficulties, and at first I could not tell what to say, so I pretended not to hear him, and asked him what he said. But he was too earnest for an answer to forget his question; so that he repeated it in the very same broken words, as above. By this time I had recovered myself a little, and I said, "God will at last punish him severely; he is reserved for the judgement, and is to be cast into the bottomless pit to dwell with everlasting fire." This did not satisfy Friday, but he returns upon me, repeating my words, "*Reserve, at last*, me no understand, but why not kill the Devil now, not kill great ago?" "You may as well ask me," said I, "why God does not kill you and I when we do wicked things here that offend Him. We are preserved to repent and be pardoned." He muses awhile at this. "Well, well," says he, mighty affectionately, "that well; so you, I, Devil, all wicked, all preserve, repent, God pardon all." Here I was run down again by him to the last degree, and it was a testimony to me how the mere notions of nature, though they will guide reasonable creatures to the knowledge of a God, and of a worship or homage due to the supreme Being, of God as the consequence of our nature, yet nothing but divine revelation can form the knowledge of Jesus Christ, and of a redemption purchased for us, of a Mediator of the new covenant, and of an Intercessor at the footstool of God's throne – I say, nothing but a revelation from heaven can form these in the soul, and that therefore the gospel of our Lord and Saviour Jesus Christ, I mean, the word of God, and the spirit of God promised for the guide and sanctifier of His people, are the absolutely necessary instructors of the souls of men in the saving knowledge of God and the means of salvation.

I therefore diverted the present discourse between me and my man, rising up hastily, as upon some sudden occasion of going out; then sending him for something a good way off, I seriously prayed to God that He would enable me to instruct savingly this poor savage, assisting by His spirit the heart of the poor ignorant creature to receive the light of the knowledge of God in Christ, reconciling him to Himself, and would guide me to speak so to him from the word of God as his conscience might be convinced, his eyes opened and his soul saved. When he came again to me, I entered into a long discourse with him upon the subject of the redemption of man by the Saviour of the world, and of the doctrine of the gospel preached from heaven, namely, of repentance towards God, and faith in our blessed Lord Jesus. I then explained to him, as well as I could, why our blessed Redeemer took not on Him the nature of angels, but the seed of Abraham, and how for that reason the fallen angels had no share in the redemption; that he came only to the lost sheep of the house of Israel, and the like.

I had, God knows, more sincerity than knowledge, in all the methods I took for this poor creature's instruction, and must acknowledge what I believe all that act upon the same principle will find, that in laying things open to him, I really informed and instructed myself in many things that either I did not know, or had not fully considered before, but which occurred naturally to my mind upon my searching into them for the information of this poor savage, and I had more affection in my inquiry after things upon this occasion than ever I felt before, so that whether this poor wild wretch was the better for me or no, I had great reason to be thankful that ever he came to me. My grief sat lighter upon me, my habitation grew comfortable to me beyond measure, and when I reflected that in this solitary life which I had been confined to I had not only been moved myself to look up to heaven, and to seek to the hand that had brought me there, but was now to be made an instrument under Providence to save the life, and, for ought I knew, the soul of a poor savage, and bring him to the true knowledge of religion, and of the Christian doctrine, that he might know Christ Jesus, to know whom is life eternal – I say, when I reflected upon all these things, a secret joy ran through every part of my soul, and I frequently rejoiced that ever I was brought to this place, which I had so often thought the most dreadful of all afflictions that could possibly have befallen me.

In this thankful frame I continued all the remainder of my time, and the conversation which employed the hours between Friday and I was such as made the three years which we lived there together perfectly and completely happy, if any such thing as complete happiness can be formed in a sublunary state. The savage was now a good Christian, a much better than I, though I have reason to hope, and bless God for it, that we were equally penitent, and comforted restored penitents; we had here the word of God to read, and no further off from His spirit to instruct than if we had been in England.

I always applied myself in reading the Scripture, to let him know, as well as I could, the meaning of what I read, and he again, by his serious inquiries and questionings, made me, as I said before, a much better scholar in the Scripture knowledge than I should ever have been by my own private mere reading. Another thing I cannot refrain from observing here also from experience, in this retired part of my life: namely, how infinite and inexpressible a blessing it is that the knowledge of God, and of the doctrine of salvation by Christ Jesus, is so plainly laid down in the word of God, so easy to be received and understood that, as the bare reading the Scripture made me capable of understanding enough of my duty to carry me directly on to the great work of sincere repentance for my sins, and laying hold of a Saviour for life and salvation, to a stated reformation in practice, and obedience to all God's commands, and this without any teacher or instructor – I mean, human – so the same plain instruction sufficiently served to the enlightening this savage creature, and bringing him to be such a Christian as I have known few equal to him in my life.

As to all the disputes, wranglings, strife and contention which has happened in the world about religion, whether niceties in doctrines, or schemes of church government, they were all perfectly useless to us – as for ought I can yet see, they have been to all the rest of the world. We had the sure guide to heaven, namely, the word of God, and we had, blessed be God, comfortable views of the spirit of God teaching and instructing us by His word, leading us into all truth, and making us both willing and obedient to the instruction of His word, and I cannot see the least use that the greatest knowledge of the disputed points in religion which have made such confusions in the world would have been to us, if we could have obtained it – but I must go on with the historical part of things, and take every part in its order.

After Friday and I became more intimately acquainted, and that he could understand almost all I said to him, and speak fluently – though in broken English – to me, I acquainted him with my own story, or at least so much of it as related to my coming into the place, how I had lived there, and how long. I let him into the mystery, for such it was to him, of gunpowder and bullet, and taught him how to shoot; I gave him a knife, which he was wonderfully delighted with, and I made him a belt, with a frog hanging to it, such as in England we wear hangers in, and in the frog, instead of a hanger, I gave him a hatchet, which was not only as good a weapon in some cases, but much more useful upon other occasions.

I described to him the country of Europe, and particularly England, which I came from; how we lived, how we worshipped God, how we behaved to one another and how we traded in ships to all parts of the world. I gave him an account of the wreck which I had been on board of, and showed him as near as I could the place where she lay, but she was all beaten in pieces before, and gone.

I showed him the ruins of our boat, which we lost when we escaped, and which I could not stir with my whole strength then, but was now fallen almost to pieces. Upon seeing this boat, Friday stood musing a great while, and said nothing. I asked him what it was he studied upon; at last says he, "Me see such boat like come to place at my nation."

I did not understand him a good while, but at last, when I had examined further into it, I understood by him that a boat – such as that had been – came onshore upon the country where he lived – that is, as he explained it, was driven thither by stress of weather. I presently imagined that some European ship must have been cast away upon their coast, and the boat might get loose and drive ashore, but was so dull that I never once thought of men making escape from a wreck thither, much less whence they might come, so I only enquired after a description of the boat.

Friday described the boat to me well enough, but brought me better to understand him when he added with some warmth, "We save the white mans from drown." Then I presently asked him if there was any white mans, as he called them, in the boat. "Yes," he said, "the boat full white mans." I asked him how many; he told upon his fingers seventeen. I asked him then what become of them; he told me, "They live, they dwell at my nation."

This put new thoughts into my head, for I presently imagined that these might be the men belonging to the ship that was cast away in sight of my island, as I now call it, and who, after the ship was struck on the rock, and they saw her inevitably lost, had saved themselves in their boat, and were landed upon that wild shore among the savages.

Upon this, I enquired of him more critically what was become of them. He assured me they lived still there; that they had been there about four years; that the savages let them alone, and gave them victuals to live. I asked him how it came to pass they did not kill them and eat them. He said, "No, they make brother with them" – that is, as I understood him, a truce – and then he added, "They no eat mans but when makes the war fight" – that is to say, they never eat any men but such as come to fight with them, and are taken in battle.

It was after this some considerable time that, being upon the top of the hill, at the east side of the island – from whence, as I have said, I had in a clear day discovered the main or continent of America – Friday, the weather being very serene, looks very earnestly towards the mainland, and in a kind of surprise, falls a jumping and dancing, and calls out to me, for I was at some distance from him. I asked him what was the matter. "Oh joy!" says he. "Oh glad! There see my country, there my nation!"

I observed an extraordinary sense of pleasure appeared in his face, and his eyes sparkled, and his countenance discovered a strange eagerness, as if he had a mind to be in his own country again, and this observation of mine put a great many thoughts into me, which made me at first not so easy about my new man Friday as I was before – and I made no doubt but that if Friday could get back to his own nation again, he would not only forget all his religion, but all his obligation to me, and would be forward enough to give his countrymen an account of me, and come back perhaps with a hundred or two of them, and make a feast upon me, at which he might be as merry as he used to be with those of his enemies when they were taken in war.

But I wronged the poor honest creature very much, for which I was very sorry afterwards. However, as my jealousy increased, and held me some weeks, I was a little more circumspect, and not so familiar and kind to him as before, in which I was certainly in the wrong too, the honest grateful creature having no thought about it, but what consisted with the best principles, both as a religious Christian and as a grateful friend, as appeared afterwards to my full satisfaction.

While my jealousy of him lasted, you may be sure I was every day pumping him to see if he would discover any of the new thoughts which I suspected were in him, but I found everything he said was so honest and so innocent that I could find nothing to nourish my suspicion, and in spite of all my uneasiness he made me at last entirely his own again, nor did he in the least perceive that I was uneasy, and therefore I could not suspect him of deceit.

One day, walking up the same hill, but the weather being hazy at sea, so that we could not see the continent, I called to him and said, "Friday, do not you wish yourself in your own country, your own nation?" "Yes," he said, "he be much oh glad to be at his own nation." "What would you do there?" said I, "would you turn wild again, eat men's flesh again, and be a savage as you were before?" He looked full of concern, and shaking his head said, "No, no, Friday tell them to live good, tell them to pray God, tell them to eat cornbread, cattle flesh, milk, no eat man again." "Why then," said I to him, "they will kill you." He looked grave at that, and then said, "No, they no kill me, they willing love learn." He meant by this, they would be willing to learn. He added, they learnt much of the bearded mans that came in the boat. Then I asked him if he would go back to them. He smiled at that, and told me he could not swim so far. I told him I would make a canoe for him. He told me he would go, if I would go with him. "I go?" says I. "Why, they will eat me if I come there." "No, no," says he, "me make they no eat you; me make they much love you." He meant he would tell them how I had killed his enemies and saved his life, and so he would make them love me; then he told me as well as he could how kind they were to seventeen white men, or bearded men, as he called them, who came onshore there in distress.

From this time I confess I had a mind to venture over and see if I could possibly join with these bearded men, who I made no doubt were Spaniards or Portuguese, not doubting but if I could we might find some method to escape from thence – being upon the continent, and a good company together – better than I could from an island forty miles off the shore, and alone without help. So after some days I took Friday to work again, by way of discourse, and told him I would give him a boat to go back to his nation, and accordingly I carried him to my frigate which lay on the other side of the island and, having cleared it of water, for I always kept it sunk in the water, I brought it out, showed it him, and we both went into it.

I found he was a most dextrous fellow at managing it, would make it go almost as swift and fast again as I could, so when he was in, I said to him, "Well, now, Friday, shall we go to your nation?" He looked very dull at my saying so, which it seems was because he thought the boat too small to go so far. I told him then I had a bigger, so the next day I went to the place where the first boat lay which I had made, but which I could not get into water. He said that was big enough, but then as I had taken no care of it, and it had lain two or three and twenty years there, the sun had split and dried it, that it was in a manner rotten. Friday told me such a boat would do very well, and would carry "much enough vittle, drink, bread" – that was his way of talking.

U PON THE WHOLE, I was by this time so fixed upon my
design of going over with him to the continent that I told
him we would go and make one as big as that, and he should go
home in it. He answered not one word, but looked very grave
and sad. I asked him what was the matter with him. He asked me
again thus, "Why you angry mad with Friday, what me done?" I
asked him what he meant; I told him I was not angry with him
at all. "No angry! No angry!" says he, repeating the words several times, "Why send Friday home away to my nation?" "Why,"
says I, "Friday, did you not say you wished you were there?"
"Yes, yes," says he, "wish be both there, no wish Friday there,
no master there." In a word, he would not think of going there
without me. "I go there! Friday," says I, "what shall I do there?"
He turned very quick upon me at this: "You do great deal much
good," says he, "you teach wild mans be good sober tame mans;
you tell them know God, pray God, and live new life." "Alas!
Friday," says I, "thou knowest not what thou sayest, I am but an
ignorant man myself." "Yes, yes," says he, "you teachee me good,
you teachee them good." "No, no, Friday," says I, "you shall go
without me, leave me here to live by myself, as I did before." He
looked confused again at that word, and running to one of the
hatchets which he used to wear, he takes it up hastily, comes and

gives it me. "What must I do with this?" says I to him. "You take, kill Friday," says he. "What must I kill you for?" said I again. He returns very quick, "What you send Friday away for? Take, kill Friday, no send Friday away?" This he spoke so earnestly that I saw tears stand in his eyes. In a word, I so plainly discovered the utmost affection in him to me, and a firm resolution in him, that I told him then, and often after, that I would never send him away from me if he was willing to stay with me.

Upon the whole, as I found by all his discourse a settled affection to me, and that nothing should part him from me, so I found all the foundation of his desire to go to his own country was laid in his ardent affection to the people, and his hopes of my doing them good; a thing which as I had no notion of myself, so I had not the least thought or intention or desire of undertaking it. But still I found a strong inclination to my attempting an escape as above, founded on the supposition gathered from the discourse – namely, that there were seventeen bearded men there, and therefore, without any more delay, I went to work with Friday to find out a great tree proper to fell, and make a large piragua or canoe to undertake the voyage. There were trees enough in the island to have built a little fleet, not of piraguas and canoes, but even of good large vessels. But the main thing I looked at was to get one so near the water that we might launch it when it was made, to avoid the mistake I committed at first.

At last Friday pitched upon a tree, for I found he knew much better than I what kind of wood was fittest for it, nor can I tell to this day what wood to call the tree we cut down, except that it was very like the tree we call fustic, or between that and the Nicaragua wood, for it was much the same colour and smell. Friday was for burning the hollow or cavity of this tree out to make it for a boat. But I showed him how rather to cut it out with tools, which, after

I had showed him how to use, he did very handily, and in about a month's hard labour we finished it, and made it very handsome, especially when with our axes, which I showed him how to handle, we cut and hewed the outside into the true shape of a boat. After this, however, it cost us near a fortnight's time to get her along as it were inch by inch upon great rollers into the water. But when she was in, she would have carried twenty men with great ease.

When she was in the water, and though she was so big, it amazed me to see with what dexterity and how swift my man Friday would manage her, turn her and paddle her along, so I asked him if he would, and if we might venture over in her. "Yes," he said, "he venture over in her very well, though great blow wind." However, I had a further design that he knew nothing of, and that was to make a mast and sail and to fit her with an anchor and cable. As to a mast, that was easy enough to get, so I pitched upon a straight young cedar tree which I found near the place, and which there was great plenty of in the island, and I set Friday to work to cut it down, and gave him directions how to shape and order it. But as to the sail, that was my particular care; I knew I had old sails, or rather pieces of old sails enough, but as I had had them now six and twenty years by me, and had not been very careful to preserve them, not imagining that I should ever have this kind of use for them, I did not doubt but they were all rotten – and indeed most of them were so. However, I found two pieces which appeared pretty good, and with these I went to work, and with a great deal of pains and awkward tedious stitching (you may be sure) for want of needles, I at length made a three-cornered ugly thing, like what we call in England a shoulder-of-mutton sail, to go with a boom at bottom, and a little short sprit at the top, such as usually our ships' longboats sail with, and such as I best knew how to manage, because it was such a one as I had to the boat in which I made my escape from Barbary, as related in the first part of my story.

I was near two months performing this last work, namely, rigging and fitting my mast and sails, for I finished them very complete, making a small stay, and a sail or foresail to it, to assist if we should turn to windwards, and which was more than all, I fixed a rudder to the stern of her to steer with. And though I was but a bungling shipwright, yet as I knew the usefulness, and even necessity of such a thing, I applied myself with so much pains to do it that at last I brought it to pass – though considering the many dull contrivances I had for it that failed, I think it cost me almost as much labour as making the boat.

After all this was done too, I had my man Friday to teach as to what belonged to the navigation of my boat, for though he knew very well how to paddle a canoe, he knew nothing what belonged to a sail and a rudder, and was the most amazed when he saw me work the boat to and again in the sea by the rudder, and how the sail gybed, and filled this way or that way as the course we sailed changed – I say, when he saw this, he stood like one astonished and amazed. However, with a little use, I made all these things familiar to him, and he became an expert sailor, except that as to the compass – I could make him understand very little of that. On the other hand, as there was very little cloudy weather, and seldom or never any fogs in those parts, there was the less occasion for a compass, seeing the stars were always to be seen by night, and the shore by day, except in the rainy seasons, and then nobody cared to stir abroad, either by land or sea.

I was now entered on the seven and twentieth year of my captivity in this place – though the last three years that I had this creature with me ought rather to be left out of the account, my habitation being quite of another kind than in all the rest of the time. I kept the anniversary of my landing there with the same thankfulness to God for His mercies as at first, and if I had such cause of acknowledgement at first, I had much more so now, having such additional testimonies of the care of Providence over me, and the great hopes I had of being effectually and speedily delivered, for I had an invincible impression upon my thoughts that my deliverance was at hand, and that I should not be another year in this place. However, I went on with my husbandry, digging, planting, fencing, as usual; I gathered and cured my grapes, and did every necessary thing as before.

The rainy season was in the meantime upon me, when I kept more within doors than at other times. So I had stowed our new vessel as secure as we could, bringing her up into the creek – where, as I said, in the beginning I landed my rafts from the ship – and haling her up to the shore at high water mark, I made my man Friday dig a little dock, just big enough to hold her, and just deep enough to give her water enough to fleet in; and then when the tide was out, we made a strong dam cross the end of it, to keep the water out, and so she lay dry, as to the tide from the sea, and to keep the rain off we laid a great many boughs of trees, so thick that she was as well thatched as a house – and thus we waited for the month of November and December, in which I designed to make my adventure.

When the settled season began to come in, as the thought of my design returned with the fair weather, I was preparing daily for the voyage, and the first thing I did was to lay by a certain quantity of provisions, being the stores for our voyage, and intended, in a week or a fortnight's time, to open the dock and launch out our boat. I was busy one morning upon something of this kind, when I called to Friday, and bid him go to the seashore and see if he could find a turtle or tortoise, a thing which we generally got once a week, for the sake of the eggs as well as the flesh. Friday had not been long gone, when he came running back, and flew over my outer wall, or fence, like one that felt not the ground or the steps he set his feet on, and before I had time to speak to him, he cries out to me, "Oh master! Oh master! Oh sorrow! Oh bad!" "What's the matter, Friday?" says I. "Oh yonder, there," says he, "one, two, three canoe! One, two, three!" By his way of speaking, I concluded there were six, but on inquiry I found it was but three. "Well, Friday," says I, "do not be frighted," so I heartened him up as well as I could. However, I saw the poor fellow was most terribly scared, for nothing ran in his head but that they were come to look for him, and would cut him in pieces and eat him, and the poor fellow trembled so, that I scarce knew what to do with him. I comforted him as well as I could, and told him I was in as much danger as he, and that they would eat me as well as him. "But," says I, "Friday, we must resolve to fight them – can you fight, Friday?" "Me shoot," says he, "but there come many great number." "No matter for that," said I again, "our guns will fright them that we do not kill," so I asked him whether if I resolved to defend him, he would defend me, and stand by me, and do just as I bid him. He said, "Me die, when you bid die, master," so I went and fetched a good dram of rum, and gave him, for I had been so good a husband of my rum that I had a great deal left. When he drank it, I made him take the two fowling pieces, which we always carried, and load them with large swan shot, as big as small pistol bullets; then I took four muskets, and loaded them with two slugs and five small bullets each, and my two pistols I loaded with a brace of bullets each. I hung my great sword as usual naked by my side, and gave Friday his hatchet.

When I had thus prepared myself, I took my prospective glass and went up to the side of the hill to see what I could discover, and I found quickly, by my glass, that there were one and twenty savages, three prisoners and three canoes, and that their whole business seemed to be the triumphant banquet upon these three human bodies (a barbarous feast indeed), but nothing more than as I had observed was usual with them.

I observed also that they were landed not where they had done when Friday made his escape, but nearer to my creek, where the shore was low, and where a thick wood came close almost down to the sea. This, with the abhorrence of the inhuman errand these wretches came about, filled me with such indignation that I came down again to Friday, and told him I was resolved to go down to them and kill them all, and asked him if he would stand by me. He was now gotten over his fright and, his spirits being a little raised with the dram I had given him, he was very cheerful, and told me, as before, he would die when I bid die.

In this fit of fury, I took first and divided the arms which I had charged, as before, between us; I gave Friday one pistol to stick in his girdle, and three guns upon his shoulder, and I took one pistol and the other three myself, and in this posture we marched out. I took a small bottle of rum in my pocket, and gave Friday a large bag, with more powder and bullet – and as to orders, I charged him to keep close behind me, and not to stir, or shoot, or do anything till I bid him, and in the meantime, not to speak a word. In this posture I fetched a compass to my right hand of near a mile, as well to get over the creek as to get into the wood, so that I might come within shoot of them before I should be discovered, which I had seen by my glass it was easy to do.

While I was making this march, my former thoughts returning, I began to abate my resolution – I do not mean that I entertained any fear of their number, for as they were naked, unarmed wretches 'tis certain I was superior to them, nay, though I had been alone – but it occurred to my thoughts what call, what occasion, much less what necessity I was in to go and dip my hands in blood, to attack people who had neither done or intended me any wrong, who as to me were innocent, and whose barbarous customs were their own disaster, being in them a token indeed of God's having left them, with the other nations of that part of the world, to such stupidity, and to such inhuman courses, but did not call me to take upon me to be a judge of their actions, much less an executioner of His justice; that whenever He thought fit, He would take the cause into His own hands, and by national vengeance punish them as a people for national crimes; but that in the meantime, it was none of my business; that it was true, Friday might justify it, because he was a declared enemy, and in a state of war with those very particular people, and it was lawful for him to attack them, but I could not say the same with respect to me. These things were so warmly pressed upon my thoughts, all the way as I went, that I resolved I would only go and place myself near them, that I might observe their barbarous feast, and that I would act then as God should direct, but that unless something offered that was more a call to me than yet I knew of, I would not meddle with them.

With this resolution I entered the wood, and with all possible wariness and silence, Friday following close at my heels, I marched till I came to the skirt of the wood, on the side which was next to them – only that one corner of the wood lay between me and them – here I called softly to Friday and, showing him a great tree, which was just at the corner of the wood, I bade him go to the tree and bring me word if he could see there plainly what they were doing. He did so, and came immediately back to me, and told me they might be plainly viewed there; that they were all about their fire, eating the flesh of one of their prisoners; and that another lay bound upon the sand, a little from them, which he said they would kill next, and which fired all the very soul within me. He told me it was not one of their nation, but one of the bearded men who he had told me of, that came to their country in the boat. I was filled with horror at the very naming the white bearded man and, going to the tree, I saw plainly by my glass a white man who lay upon the beach of the sea, with his hands and his feet tied, with flags, or things like rushes, and that he was a European, and had clothes on.

There was another tree, and a little thicket beyond it, about fifty yards nearer to them than the place where I was, which by going a little way about, I saw I might come at undiscovered, and that then I should be within half-shot of them. So I withheld my passion, though I was indeed enraged to the highest degree, and going back about twenty paces, I got behind some bushes, which held all the way till I came to the other tree, and then I came to a little rising ground, which gave me a full view of them, at the distance of about eighty yards.

I had now not a moment to lose, for nineteen of the dreadful wretches sat upon the ground, all close huddled together, and had just sent the other two to butcher the poor Christian, and bring him perhaps limb by limb to their fire, and they were stooped down to untie the bands at his feet. I turned to Friday. "Now, Friday," said I, "do as I bid thee"; Friday said he would. "Then, Friday," says I, "do exactly as you see me do, fail in nothing"; so I set down one of the muskets and the fowling piece upon the ground, and Friday did the like by his, and with the other musket I took my aim at the savages, bidding him do the like; then asking him if he was ready, he said yes. "Then fire at them," said I, and the same moment I fired also.

Friday took his aim so much better than I, that on the side that he shot, he killed two of them and wounded three more, and on my side, I killed one and wounded two. They were, you may be sure, in a dreadful consternation, and all of them who were not hurt jumped up upon their feet, but did not immediately know which way to run, or which way to look – for they knew not from whence their destruction came. Friday kept his eyes close upon me, that as I had bid him, he might observe what I did; so as soon as the first shot was made, I threw down the piece, and took up the fowling piece, and Friday did the like; he sees me cock and present, he did the same again. "Are you ready, Friday?" said I; "Yes," says he; "Let fly then," says I, "in the name of God," and with that I fired again among the amazed wretches, and so did Friday, and as our pieces were now loaden with what I called swan shot, or small pistol bullets, we found only two drop, but so many were wounded that they ran about yelling and screaming like mad creatures, all bloody and miserably wounded, most of them, whereof three more fell quickly after, though not quite dead.

"Now, Friday," says I, laying down the discharged pieces, and taking up the musket which was yet loaden, "follow me," says I; which he did, with a great deal of courage, upon which I rushed out of the wood, and showed myself and Friday close at my foot. As soon as I perceived they saw me, I shouted as loud as I could, and bade Friday do so too, and running as fast as I could – which by the way, was not very fast, being loaden with arms as I was – I made directly towards the poor victim, who was, as I said, lying upon the beach or shore, between the place where they sat and the sea. The two butchers who were just going to work with him had left him at the surprise of our first fire, and fled in a terrible fright to the seaside, and had jumped into a canoe, and three more of the rest made the same way. I turned to Friday, and bid him step forwards and fire at them; he understood me immediately and, running about forty yards to be near them, he shot at them, and I thought he had killed them all, for I see them all fall of a heap into the boat, though I saw two of them up again quickly: however, he killed two of them, and wounded the third, so that he lay down in the bottom of the boat as if he had been dead.

While my man Friday fired at them, I pulled out my knife, and cut the flags that bound the poor victim, and loosing his hands and feet, I lifted him up, and asked him in the Portuguese tongue what he was. He answered in Latin, "Christianus," but was so weak and faint that he could scarce stand or speak; I took my bottle out of my pocket, and gave it him, making signs that he should drink, which he did, and I gave him a piece of bread, which he ate. Then I asked him what countryman he was, and he said, "Espagnole", and being a little recovered, let me know by all the signs he could possibly make how much he was in my debt for his deliverance. "Señor," said I, with as much Spanish as I could make up, "we will talk afterwards, but we must fight now – if you have any strength left, take this pistol and sword, and lay about you." He took them very thankfully, and no sooner had he the arms in his hands, but as if they had put new vigour into him, he flew upon his murderers like a fury, and had cut two of them in pieces in an instant – for the truth is, as the whole was a surprise to them, so the poor creatures were so much frighted with the noise of our pieces that they fell down for mere amazement and fear, and had no more power to attempt their own escape than their flesh had to resist our shot, and that was the case of those five that Friday shot at in the boat, for as three of them fell with the hurt they received, so the other two fell with the fright.

I kept my piece in my hand still, without firing, being willing to keep my charge ready, because I had given the Spaniard my pistol and sword. So I called to Friday and bade him run up to the tree from whence we first fired, and fetch the arms which lay there that had been discharged, which he did with great swiftness, and then, giving him my musket, I sat down myself to load all the rest again, and bade them come to me when they wanted. While I was loading these pieces, there happened a fierce engagement between the Spaniard and one of the savages, who made at him with one of their great wooden swords, the same weapon that was to have killed him before, if I had not prevented it. The Spaniard, who was as bold and as brave as could be imagined, though weak, had fought this Indian a good while, and had cut him two great wounds on his head, but the savage being a stout lusty fellow, closing in with him, had thrown him down (being faint) and was wringing my sword out of his hand, when the Spaniard, though undermost, wisely quitting the sword, drew the pistol from his girdle, shot the savage through the body, and killed him upon the spot, before I, who was running to help him, could come near him.

Friday, being now left to his liberty, pursued the flying wretches with no weapon in his hand but his hatchet, and with that he dispatched those three who, as I said before, were wounded at first and fallen, and all the rest he could come up with, and the Spaniard coming to me for a gun, I gave him one of the fowling pieces, with which he pursued two of the savages, and wounded them both, but as he was not able to run, they both got from him into the wood, where Friday pursued them, and killed one of them, but the other was too nimble for him, and though he was wounded, yet had plunged himself into the sea, and swam with all his might off to those who were left in the canoe – which three in the canoe, with one wounded, who we know not whether he died or no, were all that escaped our hands of one and twenty. The account of the rest is as follows:

3 killed at our first shot from the tree.
2 killed at the next shot.
2 killed by Friday in the boat.
2 killed by ditto, of those at first wounded.
1 killed by ditto, in the wood.
3 killed by the Spaniard.
4 killed, being found dropped here and there of their wounds, or killed by Friday in his chase of them.
4 escaped in the boat, whereof one wounded if not dead.
—
21 in all.

Those that were in the canoe worked hard to get out of gunshot, and though Friday made two or three shot at them, I did not find that he hit any of them. Friday would fain have had me took one of their canoes and pursued them, and indeed I was very anxious about their escape, lest carrying the news home to their people, they should come back perhaps with two or three hundred of their canoes and devour us by mere multitude. So I consented to pursue them by sea and, running to one of their canoes, I jumped in, and bade Friday follow me, but when I was in the canoe, I was surprised to find another poor creature lie there alive, bound hand and foot, as the Spaniard was, for the slaughter, and almost dead with fear, not knowing what the matter was, for he had not been able to look up over the side of the boat, he was tied so hard, neck and heels, and had been tied so long that he had really but little life in him.

I immediately cut the twisted flags or rushes which they had bound him with, and would have helped him up, but he could not stand or speak, but groaned most piteously, believing, it seems, still that he was only unbound in order to be killed.

When Friday came to him, I bade him speak to him and tell him of his deliverance and, pulling out my bottle, made him give the poor wretch a dram, which, with the news of his being delivered, revived him, and he sat up in the boat. But when Friday came to hear him speak and look in his face, it would have moved anyone to tears to have seen how Friday kissed him, embraced him, hugged him, cried, laughed, hollowed, jumped about, danced, sung, and then cried again, wrung his hands, beat his own face and head, and then sung and jumped about again like a distracted creature. It was a good while before I could make him speak to me, or tell me what was the matter, but when he came a little to himself, he told me that it was his father.

It is not easy for me to express how it moved me to see what ecstasy and filial affection had worked in this poor savage at the sight of his father and of his being delivered from death, nor indeed can I describe half the extravagancies of his affection after this, for he went into the boat and out of the boat a great many times. When he went in to him, he would sit down by him, open his breast and hold his father's head close to his bosom, half an hour together, to nourish it; then he took his arms and ankles, which were numbed and stiff with the binding, and chafed and rubbed them with his hands, and I, perceiving what the case was, gave him some rum out of my bottle to rub them with, which did them a great deal of good.

This action put an end to our pursuit of the canoe with the other savages, who were now gotten almost out of sight, and it was happy for us that we did not, for it blew so hard within two hours after, and before they could be gotten a quarter of their way, and continued blowing so hard all night – and that from the north-west, which was against them – that I could not suppose their boat could live, or that they ever reached to their own coast.

But to return to Friday, he was so busy about his father that I could not find in my heart to take him off for some time, but after I thought he could leave him a little, I called him to me, and he came jumping and laughing, and pleased to the highest extreme; then I asked him if he had given his father any bread. He shook his head, and said, "None: ugly dog eat all up self," so I gave him a cake of bread out of a little pouch I carried on purpose – I also gave him a dram for himself, but he would not taste it, but carried it to his father. I had in my pocket also two or three bunches of my raisins, so I gave him a handful of them for his father. He had no sooner given his father these raisins, but I saw him come out of the boat, and run away, as if he had been bewitched. He ran at such a rate – for he was the swiftest fellow of his foot that ever I saw – I say, he ran at such a rate that he was out of sight, as it were, in an instant, and though I called, and hallooed too, after him, it was all one: away he went, and in a quarter of an hour I saw him come back again, though not so fast as he went, and as he came nearer, I found his pace was slacker because he had something in his hand.

When he came up to me, I found he had been quite home for an earthen jug or pot to bring his father some fresh water, and that he had got two more cakes or loaves of bread: the bread he gave me, but the water he carried to his father – however, as I was very thirsty too, I took a little sup of it. This water revived his father more than all the rum or spirits I had given him, for he was just fainting with thirst.

When his father had drank, I called to him to know if there was any water left; he said yes, and I bade him give it to the poor Spaniard, who was in as much want of it as his father, and I sent one of the cakes that Friday brought to the Spaniard too, who was indeed very weak, and was reposing himself upon a green place under the shade of a tree, and whose limbs were also very stiff, and very much swelled with the rude bandage he had been tied with. When I saw that upon Friday's coming to him with the water, he sat up and drank, and took the bread, and began to eat, I went to him and gave him a handful of raisins; he looked up in my face with all the tokens of gratitude and thankfulness that could appear in any countenance. But he was so weak, notwithstanding he had so exerted himself in the fight, that he could not stand up upon his feet; he tried to do it two or three times, but was really not able, his ankles were so swelled and so painful to him, so I bade him sit still, and caused Friday to rub his ankles and bathe them with rum, as he had done his father's.

I observed the poor affectionate creature every two minutes – or perhaps less – all the while he was here, turned his head about to see if his father was in the same place and posture as he left him sitting, and at last he found he was not to be seen, at which he started up and, without speaking a word, flew with that swiftness to him that one could scarce perceive his feet to touch the ground as he went. But when he came, he only found he had laid himself down to ease his limbs, so Friday came back to me presently, and I then spoke to the Spaniard to let Friday help him up if he could, and lead him to the boat, and then he should carry him to our dwelling, where I would take care of him. But Friday, a lusty strong fellow, took the Spaniard quite up upon his back, and carried him away to the boat, and set him down softly upon the side or gunnel of the canoe, with his feet in the inside of it, and then lifted him quite in, and set him close to his father, and presently stepping out again, launched the boat off, and paddled it along the shore faster than I could walk, though the wind blew pretty hard too. So he brought them both safe into our creek, and leaving them in the boat, runs away to fetch the other canoe. As he passed me, I spoke to him, and asked him whither he went; he told me, "Go fetch more boat," so away he went like the wind. For sure never man or horse ran like him, and he had the other canoe in the creek, almost as soon as I got to it by land. So he wafted me over, and then went to help our new guests out of the boat, which he did, but they were neither of them able to walk, so that poor Friday knew not what to do.

To remedy this, I went to work in my thought, and calling to Friday to bid them sit down on the bank while he came to me, I soon made a kind of hand barrow to lay them on, and Friday and I carried them up both together upon it between us. But when we got them to the outside of our wall or fortification, we were at a worse loss than before, for it was impossible to get them over, and I was resolved not to break it down: so I set to work again, and Friday and I, in about two hours' time, made a very handsome tent, covered with old sails, and above that with boughs of trees, being in the space without our outward fence, and between that and the grove of young wood which I had planted: and here we made them two beds of such things as I had – namely, of good rice straw, with blankets laid upon it to lie on, and another to cover them on each bed.

My island was now peopled, and I thought myself very rich in subjects, and it was a merry reflection which I frequently made, how like a king I looked. First of all, the whole country was my own mere property, so that I had an undoubted right of dominion. Secondly, my people were perfectly subjected: I was absolute lord and lawgiver; they all owed their lives to me, and were ready to lay down their lives, if there had been occasion of it, for me. It was remarkable too – we had but three subjects, and they were of three different religions. My man Friday was a Protestant, his father was a pagan and a cannibal, and the Spaniard was a

Papist – however, I allowed liberty of conscience throughout my dominions. But this is by the way.

As soon as I had secured my two weak rescued prisoners and given them shelter and a place to rest them upon, I began to think of making some provision for them. And the first thing I did, I ordered Friday to take a yearling goat, betwixt a kid and a goat, out of my particular flock to be killed, when I cut off the hinder quarter and, chopping it into small pieces, I set Friday to work to boiling and stewing, and made them a very good dish, I assure you, of flesh and broth, having put some barley and rice also into the broth, and as I cooked it without doors, for I made no fire within my inner wall, so I carried it all into the new tent and, having set a table there for them, I sat down and ate my own dinner also with them, and, as well as I could, cheered them and encouraged them – Friday being my interpreter, especially to his father, and indeed to the Spaniard too, for the Spaniard spoke the language of the savages pretty well.

After we had dined, or rather supped, I ordered Friday to take one of the canoes, and go and fetch our muskets and other fire-arms, which for want of time we had left upon the place of battle, and the next day I ordered him to go and bury the dead bodies of the savages, which lay open to the sun, and would presently be offensive, and I also ordered him to bury the horrid remains of their barbarous feast, which I knew were pretty much, and which I could not think of doing myself – nay, I could not bear to see them, if I went that way – all which he punctually performed, and defaced the very appearance of the savages being there, so that when I went again, I could scarce know where it was, otherwise than by the corner of the wood pointing to the place.

I then began to enter into a little conversation with my two new subjects, and first I set Friday to enquire of his father what he thought of the escape of the savages in that canoe, and whether we might expect a return of them with a power too great for us to resist. His first opinion was that the savages in the boat never could live out the storm which blew that night they went off, but must of necessity be drowned or driven south to those other shores, where they were as sure to be devoured as they were to be drowned if they were cast away; but as to what they would do if they came safe onshore, he said he knew not, but it was his opinion that they were so dreadfully frighted with the manner of their being attacked, the noise and the fire, that he believed they would tell their people they were all killed by thunder and lightning, not by the hand of man, and that the two which appeared – namely, Friday and me – were two heavenly spirits or furies come down to destroy them, and not men with weapons. This he said he knew, because he heard them all cry out so in their language to one another, for it was impossible to them to conceive that a man could dart fire, and speak thunder, and kill at a distance without lifting up the hand, as was done now. And this old savage was in the right, for, as I understood since by other hands, the savages never attempted to go over to the island afterwards; they were so terrified with the accounts given by those four men (for it seems they did escape the sea), that they believed whoever went to that enchanted island would be destroyed with fire from the gods.

This however I knew not, and therefore was under continual apprehensions for a good while, and kept always upon my guard, me and all my army, for as we were now four of us, I would have ventured upon a hundred of them fairly in the open field at any time.

I N A LITTLE TIME, HOWEVER, no more canoes appearing, the fear of their coming wore off, and I began to take my former thoughts of a voyage to the main into consideration, being likewise assured by Friday's father that I might depend upon good usage from their nation on his account if I would go.

But my thoughts were a little suspended when I had a serious discourse with the Spaniard, and when I understood that there were sixteen more of his countrymen and Portuguese, who, having been cast away, and made their escape to that side, lived there at peace indeed with the savages, but were very sore put to it for necessaries, and indeed for life. I asked him all the particulars of their voyage, and found they were a Spanish ship bound from the Rio de la Plata to the Havana, being directed to leave their loading there, which was chiefly hides and silver, and to bring back what European goods they could meet with there; that they had five Portuguese seamen on board, who they took out of another wreck; that five of their own men were drowned when the first ship was lost, and that these escaped through infinite dangers and hazards, and arrived almost starved on the cannibal coast, where they expected to have been devoured every moment.

He told me they had some arms with them, but they were perfectly useless, for that they had neither powder or ball, the washing of the sea having spoilt all their powder but a little, which they used at their first landing to provide themselves some food.

I asked him what he thought would become of them there, and if they had formed no design of making any escape. He said they had many consultations about it, but that having neither vessel, or tools to build one, or provisions of any kind, their councils always ended in tears and despair.

I asked him how he thought they would receive a proposal from me which might tend towards an escape, and whether, if they were all here, it might not be done. I told him with freedom, I feared mostly their treachery and ill usage of me, if I put my life in their hands, for that gratitude was no inherent virtue in the nature of man, nor did men always square their dealings by the obligations they had received, so much as they did by the advantages they expected. I told him it would be very hard that I should be the instrument of their deliverance, and that they should afterwards make me their prisoner in New Spain, where an Englishman was certain to be made a sacrifice, what necessity or what accident soever brought him thither, and that I had rather be delivered up to the savages, and be devoured alive, than fall into the merciless claws of the priests and be carried into the Inquisition. I added that otherwise I was persuaded, if they were all here, we might, with so many hands, build a barque large enough to carry us all away, either to the Brazils southwards, or to the islands or Spanish coast northwards, but that if in requital they should, when I had put weapons into their hands, carry me by force among their own people, I might be ill used for my kindness to them, and make my case worse than it was before.

He answered with a great deal of candour and ingenuity that their condition was so miserable, and they were so sensible of it, that he believed they would abhor the thought of using any man unkindly that should contribute to their deliverance, and that, if I pleased, he would go to them with the old man, and discourse with them about it, and return again, and bring me their answer; that he would make conditions with them upon their solemn oath, that they should be absolutely under my leading, as their commander and captain, and that they should swear upon the holy sacraments and the Gospel to be true to me, and to go to such Christian country as that I should agree to, and no other, and to be directed wholly and absolutely by my orders till they were landed safely in such country as I intended, and that he would bring a contract from under their hands for that purpose.

Then he told me he would first swear to me himself that he would never stir from me as long as he lived till I gave him orders, and that he would take my side to the last drop of his blood, if there should happen the least breach of faith among his countrymen.

He told me they were all of them very civil, honest men, and they were under the greatest distress imaginable, having neither weapons or clothes, nor any food, but at the mercy and discretion of the savages, out of all hopes of ever returning to their own country, and that he was sure, if I would undertake their relief, they would live and die by me.

Upon these assurances, I resolved to venture to relieve them, if possible, and to send the old savage and this Spaniard over to them to treat. But when we had gotten all things in a readiness to go, the Spaniard himself started an objection which had so much prudence in it on one hand, and so much sincerity on the other hand, that I could not but be very well satisfied in it, and by his advice put off the deliverance of his comrades for at least half a year. The case was thus:

He had been with us now about a month, during which time I had let him see in what manner I had provided, with the assistance of Providence, for my support, and he saw evidently what stock of corn and rice I had laid up, which as it was more than sufficient for myself, so it was not sufficient, at least without good husbandry, for my family, now it was increased to number four – but much less would it be sufficient, if his countrymen – who were, as he said, fourteen still alive – should come over. And least of all should it be sufficient to victual our vessel, if we should build one, for a voyage to any of the Christian colonies of America. So he told me, he thought it would be more advisable to let him and the two others dig and cultivate some more land, as much as I could spare seed to sow, and that we should wait another harvest, that we might have a supply of corn for his countrymen when they should come, for want might be a temptation to them to disagree, or not to think themselves delivered otherwise than out of one difficulty into another. "You know," says he, "the children of Israel, though they rejoiced at first for their being delivered out of Egypt, yet rebelled even against God Himself that delivered them, when they came to want bread in the wilderness."

His caution was so seasonable, and his advice so good, that I could not but be very well pleased with his proposal, as well as I was satisfied with his fidelity. So we fell to digging all four of us, as well as the wooden tools we were furnished with permitted, and in about a month's time, by the end of which it was seed time, we had gotten as much land cured and trimmed up as we sowed twenty-two bushels of barley on, and sixteen jars of rice, which was in short all the seed we had to spare, nor indeed did we leave ourselves barley sufficient for our own food, for the six months that we had to expect our crop – that is to say, reckoning from the time we set our seed aside for sowing, for it is not to be supposed it is six months in the ground in that country.

Having now society enough, and our number being sufficient to put us out of fear of the savages, if they had come, unless their number had been very great, we went freely all over the island, wherever we found occasion, and as here we had our escape or deliverance upon our thoughts, it was impossible, at least for me, to have the means of it out of mine. To this purpose, I marked out several trees which I thought fit for our work, and I set Friday and his father to cutting them down, and then I caused the Spaniard, to whom I imparted my thought on that affair, to oversee and direct their work. I showed them with what indefatigable pains I had hewed a large tree into single planks, and I caused them to do the like, till they had made about a dozen large planks of good oak, near two foot broad, thirty-five foot long, and from two inches to four inches thick – what prodigious labour it took up, anyone may imagine.

At the same time, I contrived to increase my little flock of tame goats as much as I could, and to this purpose, I made Friday and the Spaniard go out one day, and myself with Friday the next day, for we took our turns, and by this means we got about twenty young kids to breed up with the rest, for whenever we shot the dam, we saved the kids, and added them to our flock. But above all, the season for curing the grapes coming on, I caused such a prodigious quantity to be hung up in the sun that I believe, had we been at Alicant, where the raisins of the sun are cured, we could have filled sixty or eighty barrels, and these with our bread was a great part of our food, and very good living too, I assure you, for it is an exceeding nourishing food.

It was now harvest, and our crop in good order; it was not the most plentiful increase I had seen in the island, but, however, it was enough to answer our end, for from our twenty-two bushels of barley we brought in and thrashed out above 220 bushels, and the like in proportion of the rice, which was store enough for our food to the next harvest, though all the sixteen Spaniards had been onshore with me – or if we had been ready for a voyage, it would very plentifully have victualled our ship to have carried us to any part of the world – that is to say, of America.

When we had thus housed and secured our magazine of corn, we fell to work to make more wicker work, namely, great baskets in which we kept it, and the Spaniard was very handy and dextrous at this part, and often blamed me that I did not make some things for defence of this kind of work – but I saw no need of it.

And now having a full supply of food for all the guests I expected, I gave the Spaniard leave to go over to the main to see what he could do with those he had left behind him there. I gave him a strict charge in writing not to bring any man with him who would not first swear in the presence of himself and of the old savage that he would no way injure, fight with or attack the person he should find in the island – who was so kind to send for them in order to their deliverance – but that they would stand by and defend him against all such attempts, and wherever they went, would be entirely under and subjected to his commands, and that this should be put in writing, and signed with their hands. How we were to have this done, when I knew they had neither pen or ink, that indeed was a question which we never asked.

Under these instructions, the Spaniard and the old savage, the father of Friday, went away in one of the canoes, which they might be said to come in, or rather were brought in, when they came as prisoners to be devoured by the savages.

I gave each of them a musket with a firelock on it, and about eight charges of powder and ball, charging them to be very good husbands of both, and not to use either of them but upon urgent occasion.

This was a cheerful work, being the first measures used by me in view of my deliverance for now twenty-seven years and some days. I gave them provisions of bread and of dried grapes, sufficient for themselves for many days, and sufficient for all their countrymen for about eight days' time, and wishing them a good voyage, I see them go, agreeing with them about a signal they should hang out at their return, by which I should know them again when they came back, at a distance, before they came onshore.

They went away with a fair gale on the day that the moon was at full by my account, in the month of October – but as for an exact reckoning of days, after I had once lost it, I could never recover it again, nor had I kept even the number of years so punctually as to be sure that I was right, though as it proved, when I afterwards examined my account, I found I had kept a true reckoning of years.

It was no less than eight days I had waited for them, when a strange and unforeseen accident intervened, of which the like has not perhaps been heard of in history. I was fast asleep in my hutch one morning, when my man Friday came running in to me, and called aloud, "Master, master, they are come, they are come."

I jumped up and, regardless of danger, I went out, as soon as I could get my clothes on, through my little grove, which, by the way, was by this time grown to be a very thick wood – I say, regardless of danger, I went without my arms, which was not my custom to do, but I was surprised when, turning my eyes to the sea, I presently saw a boat at about a league and a half's distance, standing in for the shore, with a shoulder-of-mutton sail, as they call it, and the wind blowing pretty fair to bring them in – also I observed presently that they did not come from that side which the shore lay on, but from the southernmost end of the island. Upon this I called Friday in, and bid him lie close, for these were not the people we looked for, and that we might not know yet whether they were friends or enemies.

In the next place, I went in to fetch my prospective glass, to see what I could make of them, and having taken the ladder out, I climbed up to the top of the hill, as I used to do when I was apprehensive of anything, and to take my view the plainer without being discovered.

I had scarce set my foot on the hill when my eye plainly discovered a ship lying at an anchor, at about two leagues and a half's distance from me south-south-east, but not above a league and a half from the shore. By my observation it appeared plainly to be an English ship, and the boat appeared to be an English longboat.

I cannot express the confusion I was in, though the joy of seeing a ship, and one who I had reason to believe was manned by my own countrymen, and consequently friends, was such as I cannot describe, but yet I had some secret doubts hung about me – I cannot tell from whence they came – bidding me keep upon my guard. In the first place, it occurred to me to consider what business an English ship could have in that part of the world, since it was not the way to or from any part of the world where the English had any traffic, and I knew there had been no storms to drive them in there, as in distress, and that if they were English really, it was most probable that they were here upon no good design, and that I had better continue as I was, than fall into the hands of thieves and murderers.

Let no man despise the secret hints and notices of danger which sometimes are given him when he may think there is no possibility of its being real. That such hints and notices are given us, I believe few that have made any observations of things can deny; that they are certain discoveries of an invisible world, and a converse of spirits, we cannot doubt, and if the tendency of them seems to be to warn us of danger, why should we not suppose they are from some friendly agent – whether supreme or inferior and subordinate is not the question – and that they are given for our good?

The present question abundantly confirms me in the justice of this reasoning, for had I not been made cautious by this secret admonition, come it from whence it will, I had been undone inevitably, and in a far worse condition than before, as you will see presently.

I had not kept myself long in this posture, but I saw the boat draw near the shore as if they looked for a creek to thrust in at for the convenience of landing; however, as they did not come quite far enough, they did not see the little inlet where I formerly landed my rafts, but ran their boat onshore upon the beach, at about half a mile from me, which was very happy for me, for otherwise they would have landed just, as I may say, at my door, and would soon have beaten me out of my castle, and perhaps have plundered me of all I had.

When they were onshore I was fully satisfied that they were Englishmen, at least most of them – one or two I thought were Dutch, but it did not prove so. There were in all eleven men, whereof three of them I found were unarmed, and, as I thought, bound, and when the first four or five of them were jumped onshore, they took those three out of the boat as prisoners. One of the three I could perceive using the most passionate gestures of entreaty, affliction and despair, even to a kind of extravagance; the other two I could perceive lifted up their hands sometimes, and appeared concerned indeed, but not to such a degree as the first.

I was perfectly confounded at the sight, and knew not what the meaning of it should be. Friday called out to me in English, as well as he could, "Oh master! You see Englishmans eat prisoner as well as savage mans." "Why," says I, "Friday, do you think they are a going to eat them then?" "Yes," says Friday, "they will eat them." "No, no," says I, "Friday, I am afraid they will murder them indeed, but you may be sure they will not eat them."

All this while I had no thought of what the matter really was, but stood trembling with the horror of the sight, expecting every moment when the three prisoners should be killed – nay, once I saw one of the villains lift up his arm with a great cutlass, as the seamen call it, or sword, to strike one of the poor men, and I expected to see him fall every moment, at which all the blood in my body seemed to run chill in my veins.

I wished heartily now for my Spaniard, and the savage that was gone with him, or that I had any way to have come undiscovered within shot of them, that I might have rescued the three men, for I saw no firearms they had among them, but it fell out to my mind another way.

After I had observed the outrageous usage of the three men by the insolent seamen, I observed the fellows run scattering about the land, as if they wanted to see the country. I observed that the three other men had liberty to go also where they pleased, but they sat down all three upon the ground, very pensive, and looked like men in despair.

This put me in mind of the first time when I came onshore and began to look about me; how I gave myself over for lost; how wildly I looked round me; what dreadful apprehensions I had; and how I lodged in the tree all night for fear of being devoured by wild beasts.

As I knew nothing that night of the supply I was to receive by the providential driving of the ship nearer the land by the storms and tide, by which I have since been so long nourished and supported, so these three poor desolate men knew nothing how certain of deliverance and supply they were, how near it was to them, and how effectually and really they were in a condition of safety, at the same time that they thought themselves lost, and their case desperate.

So little do we see before us in the world, and so much reason have we to depend cheerfully upon the great Maker of the world, that He does not leave his creatures so absolutely destitute, but that in the worst circumstances they have always something to be thankful for, and sometimes are nearer their deliverance than they imagine – nay, are even brought to their deliverance by the means by which they seem to be brought to their destruction.

It was just at the top of high water when these people came onshore, and while partly they stood parleying with the prisoners they brought, and partly while they rambled about to see what kind of a place they were in, they had carelessly stayed till the tide was spent and the water was ebbed considerably away, leaving their boat aground.

They had left two men in the boat, who, as I found afterwards, having drank a little too much brandy, fell asleep; however, one of them, waking sooner than the other, and finding the boat too fast aground for him to stir it, hallooed for the rest who were straggling about, upon which they all soon came to the boat, but it was past all their strength to launch her, the boat being very heavy, and the shore on that side being a soft oozy sand, almost like a quicksand.

In this condition, like true seamen who are perhaps the least of all mankind given to forethought, they gave it over, and away they strolled about the country again, and I heard one of them say aloud to another, calling them off from the boat, "Why, let her alone, Jack, can't ye, she will float next tide," by which I was fully confirmed in the main enquiry of what countrymen they were.

All this while I kept myself very close, not once daring to stir out of my castle any further than to my place of observation near the top of the hill, and very glad I was, to think how well it was fortified. I knew it was no less than ten hours before the boat could be on float again, and by that time it would be dark, and I might be at more liberty to see their motions, and to hear their discourse, if they had any.

In the meantime, I fitted myself up for a battle, as before, though with more caution, knowing I had to do with another kind of enemy than I had at first. I ordered Friday also, who I had made an excellent marksman with his gun, to load himself with arms; I took myself two fowling pieces, and gave him three muskets. My figure indeed was very fierce; I had my formidable goatskin coat on, with the great cap I have mentioned, a naked sword by my side, two pistols in my belt, and a gun upon each shoulder.

It was my design, as I said above, not to have made any attempt till it was dark – but about two o'clock, being the heat of the day, I found that in short they were all gone straggling into the woods and, as I thought, were laid down to sleep. The three poor distressed men, too anxious for their condition to get any sleep, were however set down under the shelter of a great tree, at about a quarter of a mile from me and, as I thought, out of sight of any of the rest.

Upon this, I resolved to discover myself to them, and learn something of their condition. Immediately I marched in the figure as above, my man Friday at a good distance behind me, as formidable for his arms as I, but not making quite so staring a spectre-like figure as I did.

I came as near them undiscovered as I could, and then, before any of them saw me, I called aloud to them in Spanish, "What are ye, gentlemen?"

They started up at the noise, but were ten times more confounded when they saw me, and the uncouth figure that I made. They made no answer at all, but I thought I perceived them just going to fly from me, when I spoke to them in English: "Gentlemen," said I, "do not be surprised at me; perhaps you may have a friend near you when you did not expect it." "He must be sent directly from heaven then," said one of them very gravely to me, and pulling off his hat at the same time to me, "for our condition is past the help of man." "All help is from heaven, sir," said I. "But can you put a stranger in the way how to help you, for you seem to me to be in some great distress? I saw you when you landed, and when you seemed to make applications to the brutes that came with you, I saw one of them lift up his sword to kill you."

The poor man, with tears running down his face, and trembling, looking like one astonished, returned, "Am I talking to god or man? Is it a real man, or an angel?" "Be in no fear about that, sir," said I, "if God had sent an angel to relieve you, he would have come better clothed, and armed after another manner than you see me in. Pray lay aside your fears, I am a man, an Englishman, and disposed to assist you, you see; I have one servant only; we have arms and ammunition – tell us freely, can we serve you? What is your case?"

"Our case," said he, "sir, is too long to tell you, while our murderers are so near, but in short, sir, I was commander of that ship, my men have mutinied against me; they have been hardly prevailed on not to murder me, and at last have set me onshore in this desolate place, with these two men with me – one my mate, the other a passenger – where we expected to perish, believing the place to be uninhabited, and know not yet what to think of it."

"Where are those brutes, your enemies?" said I. "Do you know where they are gone?" "There they lie, sir," said he, pointing to a thicket of trees, "my heart trembles for fear they have seen us, and heard you speak; if they have, they will certainly murder us all."

"Have they any firearms?" said I. He answered they had only two pieces, and one which they left in the boat. "Well then," said I, "leave the rest to me; I see they are all asleep: it is an easy thing to kill them all – but shall we rather take them prisoners?" He told me there were two desperate villains among them that it was scarce safe to show any mercy to, but if they were secured, he believed all the rest would return to their duty. I asked him which they were. He told me he could not at that distance describe them, but he would obey my orders in anything I would direct. "Well," says I, "let us retreat out of their view or hearing, lest they awake, and we will resolve further." So they willingly went back with me, till the woods covered us from them.

"Look you, sir," said I, "if I venture upon your deliverance, are you willing to make two conditions with me?" He anticipated my proposals by telling me that both he and the ship, if recovered, should be wholly directed and commanded by me in everything, and if the ship was not recovered, he would live and die with me in what part of the world soever I would send him, and the two other men said the same.

"Well," says I, "my conditions are but two. 1. That while you stay on this island with me, you will not pretend to any authority here, and if I put arms into your hands, you will upon all occasions give them up to me, and do no prejudice to me or mine upon this island, and in the meantime be governed by my orders.

"2. That if the ship is or may be recovered, you will carry me and my man to England passage free."

He gave me all the assurances that the invention and faith of man could devise that he would comply with these most reasonable demands, and besides would owe his life to me, and acknowledge it upon all occasions as long as he lived.

"Well then," said I, "here are three muskets for you, with powder and ball; tell me next what you think is proper to be done." He showed all the testimony of his gratitude that he was able, but offered to be wholly guided by me. I told him I thought it was hard venturing anything, but the best method I could think of was to fire upon them at once, as they lay, and if any was not killed at the first volley, and offered to submit, we might save them, and so put it wholly upon God's providence to direct the shot.

He said very modestly that he was loath to kill them, if he could help it, but that those two were incorrigible villains, and had been the authors of all the mutiny in the ship, and if they escaped, we should be undone still, for they would go on board and bring the whole ship's company, and destroy us all. "Well then," says I, "necessity legitimates my advice, for it is the only way to save our lives." However, seeing him still cautious of shedding blood, I told him they should go themselves, and manage as they found convenient.

In the middle of this discourse, we heard some of them awake, and soon after we saw two of them on their feet. I asked him if either of them were of the men who he had said were the heads of the mutiny. He said no. "Well then," said I, "you may let them escape, and Providence seems to have wakened them on purpose to save themselves. Now," says I, "if the rest escape you, it is your fault."

Animated with this, he took the musket I had given him in his hand and a pistol in his belt, and his two comrades with him, with each man a piece in his hand. The two men who were with him, going first, made some noise, at which one of the seamen who was awake turned about and, seeing them coming, cried out to the rest, but it was too late then, for the moment he cried out, they fired – I mean the two men, the Captain wisely reserving his own piece. They had so well aimed their shot at the men they knew, that one of them was killed on the spot, and the other very much wounded, but not being dead, he started up upon his feet, and called eagerly for help to the other, but the Captain, stepping to him, told him 'twas too late to cry for help, he should call upon God to forgive his villainy, and with that word knocked him down with the stock of his musket, so that he never spoke more. There were three more in the company, and one of them was also slightly wounded. By this time I was come, and when they saw their danger, and that it was in vain to resist, they begged for mercy. The Captain told them he would spare their lives, if they would give him any assurance of their abhorrence of the treachery they had been guilty of, and would swear to be faithful to him in recovering the ship, and afterwards in carrying her back to Jamaica, from whence they came. They gave him all the protestations of their sincerity that could be desired, and he was willing to believe them, and spare their lives, which I was not against, only that I obliged him to keep them bound hand and foot while they were upon the island.

While this was doing, I sent Friday with the Captain's mate to the boat, with orders to secure her and bring away the oars and sail, which they did, and by and by, three straggling men that were (happily for them) parted from the rest came back upon hearing the guns fired, and, seeing their Captain, who before was their prisoner, now their conqueror, they submitted to be bound also – and so our victory was complete.

It now remained that the Captain and I should enquire into one another's circumstances. I began first, and told him my whole history, which he heard with an attention even to amazement – and particularly at the wonderful manner of my being furnished with provisions and ammunition – and indeed, as my story is a whole collection of wonders, it affected him deeply, but when he reflected from thence upon himself, and how I seemed to have been preserved there on purpose to save his life, the tears ran down his face, and he could not speak a word more.

After this communication was at an end, I carried him and his two men into my apartment, leading them in just where I came out – namely, at the top of the house, where I refreshed them with such provisions as I had, and showed them all the contrivances I had made during my long, long inhabiting that place.

All I showed them, all I said to them, was perfectly amazing, but above all, the Captain admired my fortification, and how perfectly I had concealed my retreat with a grove of trees, which having been now planted near twenty years, and the trees growing much faster than in England, was become a little wood, and so thick that it was unpassable in any part of it but at that one side where I had reserved my little winding passage into it. I told him this was my castle and my residence, but that I had a seat in the country, as most princes have, whither I could retreat upon occasion, and I would show him that too another time, but at present our business was to consider how to recover the ship. He agreed with me as to that, but told me he was perfectly at a loss what measures to take, for that there were still six and twenty hands on board, who, having entered into a cursed conspiracy by which they had all forfeited their lives to the law, would be hardened in it now by desperation, and would carry it on, knowing that if they were reduced, they should be brought to the gallows as soon as they came to England, or to any of the English colonies, and that therefore there would be no attacking them with so small a number as we were.

I mused for some time upon what he had said, and found it was a very rational conclusion, and that therefore something was to be resolved on very speedily, as well to draw the men on board into some snare for their surprise, as to prevent their landing upon us and destroying us. Upon this it presently occurred to me that in a little while the ship's crew, wondering what was become of their comrades and of the boat, would certainly come onshore in their other boat to see for them, and that then perhaps they might come armed, and be too strong for us; this he allowed was rational.

Upon this, I told him the first thing we had to do was to stave the boat which lay upon the beach, so that they might not carry her off, and taking everything out of her, leave her so far useless as not to be fit to swim; accordingly we went on board, took the arms which were left on board out of her, and whatever else we found there, which was a bottle of brandy and another of rum, a few biscuit cakes, a horn of powder and a great lump of sugar in a piece of canvas – the sugar was five or six pounds – all which was very welcome to me, especially the brandy and sugar, of which I had had none left for many years.

When we had carried all these things onshore (the oars, mast, sail and rudder of the boat were carried away before, as above) we knocked a great hole in her bottom, that if they had come strong enough to master us, yet they could not carry off the boat.

Indeed, it was not much in my thoughts that we could be able to recover the ship, but my view was that if they went away without the boat, I did not much question to make her fit again, to carry us away to the Leeward Islands, and call upon our friends, the Spaniards, in my way, for I had them still in my thoughts.

W HILE WE WERE THUS PREPARING our designs, and had first by main strength heaved the boat up upon the beach, so high that the tide would not fleet her off at high water mark – and besides, had broke a hole in her bottom too big to be quickly stopped, and were sat down musing what we should do – we heard the ship fire a gun, and saw her make a waft with her ancient, as a signal for the boat to come on board – but no boat stirred, and they fired several times, making other signals for the boat.

At last, when all their signals and firing proved fruitless, and they found the boat did not stir, we saw them, by the help of my glasses, hoist another boat out, and row towards the shore, and we found as they approached that there was no less than ten men in her, and that they had firearms with them.

As the ship lay almost two leagues from the shore, we had a full view of them as they came, and a plain sight of the men, even of their faces, because the tide having set them a little to the east of the other boat, they rowed up under shore, to come to the same place where the other had landed, and where the boat lay.

By this means, I say, we had a full view of them, and the Captain knew the persons and characters of all the men in the boat, of whom he said that there were three very honest fellows, who he was sure were led into this conspiracy by the rest, being overpowered and frighted.

But that as for the boatswain, who it seems was the chief officer among them, and all the rest, they were as outrageous as any of the ship's crew, and were no doubt made desperate in their new enterprise, and terribly apprehensive he was that they would be too powerful for us.

I smiled at him, and told him that men in our circumstances were past the operation of fear; that seeing almost every condition that could be was better than that which we were supposed to be in, we ought to expect that the consequence, whether death or life, would be sure to be a deliverance. I asked him what he thought of the circumstances of my life, and whether a deliverance were not worth venturing for. "And where, sir," said I, "is your belief of my being preserved here on purpose to save your life, which elevated you a little while ago? For my part," said I, "there seems to be but one thing amiss in all the prospect of it." "What's that?" says he. "Why," said I, "'tis that as you say, there are three or four honest fellows among them, which should be spared; had they been all of the wicked part of the crew, I should have thought God's providence had singled them out to deliver them into your hands, for depend upon it, every man of them that comes ashore are our own, and shall die or live as they behave to us."

As I spoke this with a raised voice and cheerful countenance, I found it greatly encouraged him, so we set vigorously to our business. We had, upon the first appearance of the boat's coming from the ship, considered of separating our prisoners, and had indeed secured them effectually.

Two of them, of whom the Captain was less assured than ordinary, I sent with Friday and one of the three (delivered men) to my cave, where they were remote enough, and out of danger of being heard or discovered, or of finding their way out of the woods, if they could have delivered themselves. Here they left them bound, but gave them provisions, and promised them, if they continued there quietly, to give them their liberty in a day or two, but that if they attempted their escape, they should be put to death without mercy. They promised faithfully to bear their confinement with patience, and were very thankful that they had such good usage as to have provisions and a light left them, for Friday gave them candles (such as we made ourselves) for their comfort, and they did not know but that he stood sentinel over them at the entrance.

The other prisoners had better usage: two of them were kept pinioned indeed, because the Captain was not free to trust them, but the other two were taken into my service upon their Captain's recommendation, and upon their solemnly engaging to live and die with us – so with them and the three honest men, we were seven men, well-armed, and I made no doubt we should be able to deal well enough with the ten that were a coming, considering that the Captain had said there were three or four honest men among them also.

As soon as they got to the place where their other boat lay, they ran their boat into the beach, and came all onshore, haling the boat up after them, which I was glad to see, for I was afraid they would rather have left the boat at an anchor some distance from the shore with some hands in her to guard her, and so we should not be able to seize the boat.

Being onshore, the first thing they did, they ran all to their other boat, and it was easy to see that they were under a great surprise to find her stripped, as above, of all that was in her, and a great hole in her bottom.

After they had mused awhile upon this, they set up two or three great shouts, hallooing with all their might to try if they could make their companions hear, but all was to no purpose. Then they came all close in a ring, and fired a volley of their small arms, which indeed we heard, and the echoes made the woods ring, but it was all one: those in the cave we were sure could not hear, and those in our keeping, though they heard it well enough, yet durst give no answer to them.

They were so astonished at the surprise of this that, as they told us afterwards, they resolved to go all on board again to their ship, and let them know that the men were all murdered, and the longboat staved; accordingly they immediately launched their boat again, and got all of them on board.

The Captain was terribly amazed and even confounded at this, believing they would go on board the ship again and set sail, giving their comrades for lost, and so he should still lose the ship, which he was in hopes we should have recovered, but he was quickly as much frighted the other way.

They had not been long put off with the boat, but we perceived them all coming onshore again, but with this new measure in their conduct, which it seems they consulted together upon, namely, to leave three men in the boat, and the rest to go onshore, and go up into the country to look for their fellows.

This was a great disappointment to us, for now we were at a loss what to do, for our seizing those seven men onshore would be no advantage to us if we let the boat escape, because they would then row away to the ship, and then the rest of them would be sure to weigh and set sail, and so our recovering the ship would be lost.

However, we had no remedy but to wait and see what the issue of things might present. The seven men came onshore, and the three who remained in the boat put her off to a good distance from the shore, and came to an anchor to wait for them, so it was impossible for us to come at them in the boat.

Those that came onshore kept close together, marching towards the top of the little hill under which my habitation lay, and we could see them plainly, though they could not perceive us. We could have been very glad they would have come nearer to us, so that we might have fired at them, or that they would have gone further off, that we might have come abroad.

But when they were come to the brow of the hill, where they could see a great way into the valleys and woods which lay towards the north-east part and where the island lay lowest, they shouted and hallooed till they were weary and, not caring it seems to venture far from the shore, nor far from one another, they sat down together under a tree, to consider of it. Had they thought fit to have gone to sleep there, as the other party of them had done, they had done the job for us, but they were too full of apprehensions of danger to venture to go to sleep, though they could not tell what the danger was they had to fear neither.

The Captain made a very just proposal to me, upon this consultation of theirs, namely, that perhaps they would all fire a volley again to endeavour to make their fellows hear, and that we should all sally upon them just at the juncture when their pieces were all discharged, and they would certainly yield, and we should have them without bloodshed. I liked the proposal, provided it was done while we were near enough to come up to them, before they could load their pieces again.

But this event did not happen, and we lay still a long time, very irresolute what course to take; at length I told them there would be nothing to be done, in my opinion, till night, and then if they did not return to the boat, perhaps we might find a way to get between them and the shore, and so might use some stratagem with them in the boat to get them onshore.

We waited a great while, though very impatient for their removing, and were very uneasy when, after long consultations, we saw them start all up and march down towards the sea. It seems they had such dreadful apprehensions upon them of the danger of the place that they resolved to go on board the ship again, give their companions over for lost, and so go on with their intended voyage with the ship.

As soon as I perceived them go towards the shore, I imagined it to be as it really was, that they had given over their search, and were for going back again, and the Captain, as soon as I told him my thoughts, was ready to sink at the apprehensions of it, but I presently thought of a stratagem to fetch them back again, and which answered my end to a tittle.

I ordered Friday and the Captain's mate to go over the little creek westwards, towards the place where the savages came onshore when Friday was rescued, and as soon as they came to a little rising ground, at about half a mile distance, I bade them halloo as loud as they could, and wait till they found the seamen heard them; that as soon as ever they heard the seamen answer them, they should return it again, and then, keeping out of sight, take a round, always answering when the other hallooed, to draw them as far into the island and among the woods as possible, and then wheel about again to me, by such ways as I directed them.

They were just going into the boat, when Friday and the mate hallooed, and they presently heard them, and answering, ran along the shore westwards, towards the voice they heard, when they were presently stopped by the creek, where the water being up, they could not get over, and called for the boat to come up and set them over, as indeed I expected.

When they had set themselves over, I observed that the boat being gone a good way into the creek and, as it were, in a harbour within the land, they took one of the three men out of her to go along with them, and left only two in the boat, having fastened her to the stump of a little tree on the shore.

This was what I wished for, and immediately leaving Friday and the Captain's mate to their business, I took the rest with me and, crossing the creek out of their sight, we surprised the two men before they were aware, one of them lying onshore, and the other being in the boat; the fellow onshore was between sleeping and waking, and going to start up; the Captain, who was foremost, ran in upon him and knocked him down, and then called out to him in the boat to yield, or he was a dead man.

There needed very few arguments to persuade a single man to yield when he saw five men upon him and his comrade knocked down; besides, this was, it seems, one of the three who were not so hearty in the mutiny as the rest of the crew, and therefore was easily persuaded not only to yield, but afterwards to join very sincerely with us.

In the meantime, Friday and the Captain's mate so well managed their business with the rest that they drew them by hallooing and answering from one hill to another, and from one wood to another, till they not only heartily tired them, but left them where they were very sure they could not reach back to the boat before it was dark – and indeed they were heartily tired themselves also by the time they came back to us.

We had nothing now to do but to watch for them in the dark, and to fall upon them, so as to make sure work with them.

It was several hours after Friday came back to me before they came back to their boat, and we could hear the foremost of them, long before they came quite up, calling to those behind to come along, and could also hear them answer and complain how lame and tired they were, and not able to come any faster, which was very welcome news to us.

At length they came up to the boat, but 'tis impossible to express their confusion when they found the boat fast aground in the creek, the tide ebbed out, and their two men gone. We could hear them call to one another in a most lamentable manner, telling one another they were gotten into an enchanted island; that either there were inhabitants in it, and they should all be murdered, or else there were devils and spirits in it, and they should be all carried away and devoured.

They hallooed again, and called their two comrades by their names a great many times, but no answer. After some time, we could see them, by the little light there was, run about wringing their hands like men in despair, and that sometimes they would go and sit down in the boat to rest themselves, then come ashore again, and walk about again, and so over the same thing again.

My men would fain have me give them leave to fall upon them at once in the dark, but I was willing to take them at some advantage, so to spare them, and kill as few of them as I could, and especially I was unwilling to hazard the killing any of our men, knowing the others were very well armed. I resolved to wait to see if they did not separate, and therefore to make sure of them, I drew my ambuscade nearer, and ordered Friday and the Captain to creep upon their hands and feet as close to the ground as they could that they might not be discovered, and get as near them as they could possibly, before they offered to fire.

They had not been long in that posture, but that the boatswain, who was the principal ringleader of the mutiny, and had now shown himself the most dejected and dispirited of all the rest, came walking towards them with two more of their crew; the Captain was so eager, as having this principal rogue so much in his power, that he could hardly have patience to let him come so near as to be sure of him, for they only heard his tongue before, but when they came nearer, the Captain and Friday, starting up on their feet, let fly at them.

The boatswain was killed upon the spot, the next man was shot into the body and fell just by him, though he did not die till an hour or two after, and the third ran for it.

At the noise of the fire, I immediately advanced with my whole army, which was now eight men, namely, myself, *generalissimo*, Friday my lieutenant general, the Captain and his two men, and the three prisoners of war who we had trusted with arms.

We came upon them indeed in the dark, so that they could not see our number, and I made the man we had left in the boat, who was now one of us, call to them by name, to try if I could bring them to a parley, and so might perhaps reduce them to terms which fell out just as we desired – for indeed it was easy to think, as their condition then was, they would be very willing to capitulate – so he calls out as loud as he could to one of them, "Tom Smith, Tom Smith!" Tom Smith answered immediately, "Who's that – Robinson?" for it seems he knew his voice. T'other answered, "Ay, ay, for God's sake, Tom Smith, throw down your arms and yield, or you are all dead men this moment."

"Who must we yield to? Where are they?" says Smith again. "Here they are," says he, "here's our Captain, and fifty men with him, have been hunting you this two hours; the boatswain is killed, Will Frye is wounded, and I am a prisoner, and if you do not yield, you are all lost."

"Will they give us quarter then," says Tom Smith, "and we will yield?" "I'll go and ask, if you promise to yield," says Robinson, so he asked the Captain, and the Captain then calls himself out, "You, Smith, you know my voice, if you lay down your arms immediately and submit, you shall have your lives all but Will Atkins."

Upon this, Will Atkins cried out, "For God's sake, Captain, give me quarter, what have I done? They have been all as bad as I" – which, by the way, was not true neither, for it seems this Will Atkins was the first man that laid hold of the Captain, when they first mutinied, and used him barbarously, in tying his hands and giving him injurious language. However, the Captain told him he must lay down his arms at discretion, and trust to the Governor's mercy, by which he meant me, for they all called me governor.

In a word, they all laid down their arms, and begged their lives, and I sent the man that had parleyed with them, and two more, who bound them all, and then my great army of fifty men – which, particularly with those three, were all but eight – came up and seized upon them all, and upon their boat, only that I kept myself and one more out of sight, for reasons of state.

Our next work was to repair the boat and think of seizing the ship, and as for the Captain, now he had leisure to parley with them, he expostulated with them upon the villainy of their practices with him, and at length upon the further wickedness of their design, and how certainly it must bring them to misery and distress in the end, and perhaps to the gallows.

They all appeared very penitent, and begged hard for their lives; as for that, he told them, they were none of his prisoners, but the commander's of the island; that they thought they had set him onshore in a barren, uninhabited island, but it had pleased God so to direct them that the island was inhabited, and that the Governor was an Englishman; that he might hang them all there, if he pleased, but as he had given them all quarter, he supposed he would send them to England to be dealt with there as justice required, except Atkins, who he was commanded by the Governor to advise to prepare for death, for that he would be hanged in the morning.

Though this was all a fiction of his own, yet it had its desired effect; Atkins fell upon his knees to beg the Captain to intercede with the Governor for his life, and all the rest begged of him, for God's sake, that they might not be sent to England.

It now occurred to me that the time of our deliverance was come, and that it would be a most easy thing to bring these fellows in to be hearty in getting possession of the ship, so I retired in the dark from them, that they might not see what kind of a governor they had, and called the Captain to me; when I called, as at a good distance, one of the men was ordered to speak again, and say to the Captain, "Captain, the commander calls for you," and presently the Captain replied, "Tell his Excellency I am just a coming." This more perfectly amused them, and they all believed that the commander was just by with his fifty men.

Upon the Captain's coming to me, I told him my project for seizing the ship, which he liked of wonderfully well, and resolved to put it in execution the next morning.

But in order to execute it with more art, and secure of success, I told him we must divide the prisoners, and that he should go and take Atkins and two more of the worst of them, and send them pinioned to the cave where the others lay: this was committed to Friday and the two men who came onshore with the Captain.

They conveyed them to the cave, as to a prison, and it was indeed a dismal place, especially to men in their condition.

The other I ordered to my bower, as I called it, of which I have given a full description, and as it was fenced in, and they pinioned, the place was secure enough, considering they were upon their behaviour.

To these in the morning I sent the Captain, who was to enter into a parley with them, in a word to try them, and tell me whether he thought they might be trusted or no to go on board and surprise the ship. He talked to them of the injury done him; of the condition they were brought to, and that though the Governor had given them quarter for their lives as to the present action, yet that if they were sent to England, they would all be hanged in chains, to be sure, but that if they would join in so just an attempt as to recover the ship, he would have the Governor's engagement for their pardon.

Anyone may guess how readily such a proposal would be accepted by men in their condition; they fell down on their knees to the Captain, and promised with the deepest imprecations that they would be faithful to him to the last drop, and that they should owe their lives to him, and would go with him all over the world, that they would own him for a father to them as long as they lived.

"Well," says the Captain, "I must go and tell the Governor what you say, and see what I can do to bring him to consent to it." So he brought me an account of the temper he found them in, and that he verily believed they would be faithful.

However, that we might be very secure, I told him he should go back again, and choose out those five and tell them they might see that he did not want men, that he would take out those five to be his assistants, and that the Governor would keep the other two, and the three that were sent prisoners to the castle (my cave), as hostages for the fidelity of those five, and that if they proved unfaithful in the execution, the five hostages should be hanged in chains alive upon the shore.

This looked severe, and convinced them that the Governor was in earnest; however, they had no way left them but to accept it, and it was now the business of the prisoners, as much as of the Captain, to persuade the other five to do their duty.

Our strength was now thus ordered for the expedition: 1. The Captain, his mate, and passenger. 2. Then the two prisoners of the first gang, to whom, having their characters from the Captain, I had given their liberty and trusted them with arms. 3. The other two whom I had kept till now in my bower, pinioned, but upon the Captain's motion, had now released. 4. These five released at last – so that they were twelve in all, besides five we kept prisoners in the cave, for hostages.

I asked the Captain if he was willing to venture with these hands on board the ship, for as for me and my man Friday, I did not think it was proper for us to stir, having seven men left behind, and it was employment enough for us to keep them asunder and supply them with victuals.

As to the five in the cave, I resolved to keep them fast, but Friday went in twice a day to them to supply them with necessaries, and I made the other two carry provisions to a certain distance, where Friday was to take it.

When I showed myself to the two hostages, it was with the Captain, who told them I was the person the Governor had ordered to look after them, and that it was the Governor's pleasure they should not stir anywhere but by my direction; that if they did, they should be fetched into the castle, and be laid in irons – so that as we never suffered them to see me as governor, so I now appeared as another person, and spoke of the Governor, the garrison, the castle and the like, upon all occasions.

The Captain now had no difficulty before him but to furnish his two boats, stop the breach of one, and man them. He made his passenger captain of one, with four other men, and himself, his mate and five more went in the other, and they contrived their business very well, for they came up to the ship about midnight. As soon as they came within call of the ship, he made Robinson hail them, and tell them they had brought off the men and the boat, but that it was a long time before they had found them, and the like, holding them in a chat till they came to the ship's side, when the Captain and the mate, entering first with their arms, immediately knocked down the second mate and carpenter with the butt end of their muskets, being very faithfully seconded by their men. They secured all the rest that were upon the main and quarter decks, and began to fasten the hatches, to keep them down that were below, when the other boat and their men, entering at the fore chains, secured the forecastle of the ship, and the scuttle which went down into the cook room, making three men they found there prisoners.

When this was done, and all safe upon deck, the Captain ordered the mate with three men to break into the roundhouse where the new rebel Captain lay, and having taken the alarm was gotten up, and with two men and a boy had gotten firearms in their hands, and when the mate with a crow split open the door, the new Captain and his men fired boldly among them, and wounded the mate with a musket ball, which broke his arm, and wounded two more of the men, but killed nobody.

The mate, calling for help, rushed however into the roundhouse, wounded as he was, and with his pistol shot the new Captain through the head, the bullet entering at his mouth, and came out again behind one of his ears, so that he never spoke a word, upon which the rest yielded, and the ship was taken effectually, without any more lives lost.

As soon as the ship was thus secured, the Captain ordered seven guns to be fired, which was the signal agreed upon with me to give me notice of his success, which you may be sure I was very glad to hear, having sat watching upon the shore for it till near two of the clock in the morning.

Having thus heard the signal plainly, I laid me down, and it having been a day of great fatigue to me, I slept very sound, till I was something surprised with the noise of a gun, and presently starting up, I heard a man call me by the name of Governor, Governor, and presently I knew the Captain's voice, when, climbing up to the top of the hill, there he stood, and pointing to the ship, he embraced me in his arms, "My dear friend and deliverer," says he, "there's your ship — for she is all yours, and so are we, and all that belong to her." I cast my eyes to the ship, and there she rode, within little more than half a mile of the shore, for they had weighed her anchor as soon as they were masters of her, and, the weather being fair, had brought her to an anchor just against the mouth of the little creek, and the tide being up, the Captain had brought the pinnace in near the place where I had first landed my rafts, and so landed just at my door.

I was at first ready to sink down with the surprise. For I saw my deliverance indeed visibly put into my hands, all things easy, and a large ship just ready to carry me away whither I pleased to go. At first, for some time, I was not able to answer him one word, but as he had taken me in his arms, I held fast by him, or I should have fallen to the ground.

He perceived the surprise, and immediately pulls a bottle out of his pocket, and gave me a dram of cordial, which he had brought on purpose for me; after I had drank it, I sat down upon the ground, and though it brought me to myself, yet it was a good while before I could speak a word to him.

All this while the poor man was in as great an ecstasy as I, only not under any surprise as I was, and he said a thousand kind tender things to me to compose me and bring me to myself, but such was the flood of joy in my breast, that it put all my spirits into confusion; at last it broke out into tears and, in a little while after, I recovered my speech.

Then I took my turn, and embraced him as my deliverer, and we rejoiced together. I told him I looked upon him as a man sent from heaven to deliver me, and that the whole transaction seemed to be a chain of wonders; that such things as these were the testimonies we had of a secret hand of Providence governing the world, and an evidence that the eyes of an infinite power could search into the remotest corner of the world, and send help to the miserable whenever He pleased.

I forgot not to lift up my heart in thankfulness to Heaven, and what heart could forbear to bless Him, who had not only in a miraculous manner provided for one in such a wilderness, and in such a desolate condition, but from whom every deliverance must always be acknowledged to proceed.

When we had talked awhile, the Captain told me he had brought me some little refreshment such as the ship afforded, and such as the wretches that had been so long his master had not plundered him of. Upon this he called aloud to the boat, and bid his men bring the things ashore that were for the Governor, and indeed it was a present, as if I had been one not that was to be carried away along with them, but as if I had been to dwell upon the island still, and they were to go without me.

First, he had brought me a case of bottles full of excellent cordial waters, six large bottles of Madeira wine – the bottles held two quarts apiece – two pounds of excellent good tobacco, twelve good pieces of the ship's beef, and six pieces of pork, with a bag of peas, and about a hundredweight of biscuit.

He brought me also a box of sugar, a box of flour, a bag full of lemons and two bottles of lime juice, and abundance of other things. But besides these, and what was a thousand times more useful to me, he brought me six clean new shirts, six very good neckcloths, two pair of gloves, one pair of shoes, a hat and one pair of stockings, and a very good suit of clothes of his own, which had been worn but very little – in a word, he clothed me from head to foot.

It was a very kind and agreeable present, as anyone may imagine to one in my circumstances, but never was anything in the world of that kind so unpleasant, awkward and uneasy, as it was to me to wear such clothes at their first putting on.

After these ceremonies passed, and after all his good things were brought into my little apartment, we began to consult what was to be done with the prisoners we had, for it was worth considering whether we might venture to take them away with us or no, especially two of them who we knew to be incorrigible and refractory to the last degree, and the Captain said he knew they were such rogues that there was no obliging them, and if he did carry them away, it must be done in irons, as malefactors to be delivered over to justice at the first English colony he could come at – and I found that the Captain himself was very anxious about it.

Upon this, I told him that if he desired it, I durst undertake to bring the two men he spoke of to make it their own request that he should leave them upon the island. "I should be very glad of that," says the Captain, "with all my heart."

"Well," says I, "I will send for them up, and talk with them for you." So I caused Friday and the two hostages – for they were now discharged, their comrades having performed their promise – I say, I caused them to go to the cave, and bring up the five men pinioned, as they were, to the bower, and keep them there till I came.

After some time, I came thither dressed in my new habit, and now I was called governor again. Being all met, and the Captain with me, I caused the men to be brought before me, and I told them I had had a full account of their villainous behaviour to the Captain, and how they had run away with the ship, and were preparing to commit further robberies, but that Providence had ensnared them in their own ways, and that they were fallen into the pit which they had digged for others.

I let them know that by my direction the ship had been seized, that she lay now in the road, and they might see by and by that their new Captain had received the reward of his villainy, for that they might see him hanging at the yardarm.

That as to them, I wanted to know what they had to say, why I should not execute them as pirates taken in the fact, as by my commission they could not doubt I had authority to do.

One of them answered in the name of the rest that they had nothing to say but this: that when they were taken, the Captain promised them their lives, and they humbly implored my mercy, but I told them I knew not what mercy to show them, for as for myself, I had resolved to quit the island with all my men, and had taken passage with the Captain to go for England. And as for the Captain, he could not carry them to England, other than as prisoners in irons to be tried for mutiny and running away with the ship – the consequence of which, they must needs know, would be the gallows – so that I could not tell what was best for them unless they had a mind to take their fate in the island; if they desired that, I did not care, as I had liberty to leave it, I had some inclination to give them their lives if they thought they could shift onshore.

They seemed very thankful for it, said they would much rather venture to stay there than to be carried to England to be hanged, so I left it on that issue.

However, the Captain seemed to make some difficulty of it, as if he durst not leave them there. Upon this I seemed a little

angry with the Captain, and told him that they were my prisoners, not his, and that seeing I had offered them so much favour,
I would be as good as my word; and that if he did not think
fit to consent to it, I would set them at liberty as I found them;
and if he did not like it, he might take them again if he could
catch them.

Upon this they appeared very thankful, and I accordingly set
them at liberty, and bade them retire into the woods to the place
whence they came, as I would leave them some firearms, some
ammunition and some directions how they should live very well,
if they thought fit.

Upon this I prepared to go on board the ship, but told the
Captain that I would stay that night to prepare my things, and
desired him to go on board in the meantime, and keep all right
in the ship, and send the boat onshore the next day for me –
ordering him in the meantime to cause the new Captain who
was killed to be hanged at the yardarm, that these men might
see him.

When the Captain was gone, I sent for the men up to me to
my apartment, and entered seriously into discourse with them
of their circumstances. I told them I thought they had made a
right choice; that if the Captain carried them away, they would
certainly be hanged. I showed them the new Captain hanging
at the yardarm of the ship, and told them they had nothing less
to expect.

When they had all declared their willingness to stay, I then
told them I would let them into the story of my living there, and
put them into the way of making it easy to them. Accordingly
I gave them the whole history of the place, and of my coming
to it, showed them my fortifications, the way I made my bread,
planted my corn, cured my grapes – and in a word, all that was

necessary to make them easy. I told them the story also of the sixteen Spaniards that were to be expected, for whom I left a letter, and made them promise to treat them in common with themselves.

I left them my firearms, namely, five muskets, three fowling pieces and three swords. I had above a barrel and half of powder left, for after the first year or two, I used but little, and wasted none. I gave them a description of the way I managed the goats, and directions to milk and fatten them, and to make both butter and cheese.

In a word, I gave them every part of my own story, and I told them I would prevail with the Captain to leave them two barrels of gunpowder more, and some garden seeds, which I told them I would have been very glad of; also I gave them the bag of peas which the Captain had brought me to eat, and bade them be sure to sow and increase them.

HAVING DONE ALL THIS, I left them the next day, and went on board the ship: we prepared immediately to sail, but did not weigh that night. The next morning early, two of the five men came swimming to the ship's side and, making a most lamentable complaint of the other three, begged to be taken into the ship, for God's sake, for they should be murdered, and begged the Captain to take them on board, though he hanged them immediately.

Upon this the Captain pretended to have no power without me, but after some difficulty, and after their solemn promises of amendment, they were taken on board, and were some time after soundly whipped and pickled, after which they proved very honest and quiet fellows.

Some time after this, the boat was ordered onshore, the tide being up, with the things promised to the men, to which the Captain at my intercession caused their chests and clothes to be added, which they took, and were very thankful for. I also encouraged them by telling them that if it lay in my way to send any vessel to take them in, I would not forget them.

When I took leave of this island, I carried on board for relics the great goat's-skin cap I had made, my umbrella and my parrot; also I forgot not to take the money I formerly mentioned, which had laid by me so long useless that it was grown rusty or tarnished, and could hardly pass for silver till it had been a little rubbed and handled, as also the money I found in the wreck of the Spanish ship.

And thus I left the island, the nineteenth of December as I found by the ship's account, in the year 1686, after I had been upon it eight-and-twenty years, two months and nineteen days, being delivered from this second captivity the same day of the month that I first made my escape in the barca longa, from among the Moors of Sallee.

In this vessel, after a long voyage, I arrived in England, the eleventh of June, in the year 1687, having been thirty-and-five years absent.

When I came to England, I was as perfect a stranger to all the world, as if I had never been known there. My benefactor and faithful steward, who I had left in trust with my money, was alive, but had had great misfortunes in the world, was become a widow the second time, and very low in the world. I made her easy as to what she owed me, assuring her I would give her no trouble, but on the contrary, in gratitude for her former care and faithfulness to me, relieved her as my little stock would afford, which at that time would indeed allow me to do but little for her; but I assured her I would never forget her former kindness to me, nor did I forget her, when I had sufficient to help her, as shall be observed in its place.

I went down afterwards into Yorkshire, but my father was dead, and my mother, and all the family extinct, except that I found two sisters, and two of the children of one of my brothers, and as I had been long ago given over for dead, there had been no provision made for me, so that in a word, I found nothing to relieve or assist me, and that little money I had would not do much for me as to settling in the world.

I met with one piece of gratitude indeed, which I did not expect, and this was that the master of the ship, who I had so happily delivered, and by the same means saved the ship and cargo, having given a very handsome account to the owners of the manner how I had saved the lives of the men, and the ship, they invited me to meet them and some other merchants concerned, and altogether made me a very handsome compliment upon the subject, and a present of almost two hundred pounds sterling.

But after making several reflections upon the circumstances of my life, and how little way this would go towards settling me in the world, I resolved to go to Lisbon, and see if I might not come by some information of the state of my plantation in the Brazils, and of what was become of my partner, who I had reason to suppose had some years now given me over for dead.

With this view I took shipping for Lisbon, where I arrived in April following; my man Friday accompanying me very honestly in all these ramblings, and proving a most faithful servant upon all occasions.

When I came to Lisbon I found out by inquiry, and to my particular satisfaction, my old friend the Captain of the ship, who first took me up at sea, off the shore of Africk. He was now grown old, and had left off the sea, having put his son, who was far from a young man, into his ship, and who still used the Brazil trade. The old man did not know me, and indeed, I hardly knew him, but I soon brought him to my remembrance, and as soon brought myself to his remembrance, when I told him who I was.

After some passionate expressions of the old acquaintance, I enquired, you may be sure, after my plantation and my partner. The old man told me he had not been in the Brazils for about nine years, but that he could assure me that when he came away my partner was living, but the trustees, who I had joined with

him to take cognizance of my part, were both dead; that however, he believed that I would have a very good account of the
improvement of the plantation, for that upon the general belief
of my being cast away and drowned, my trustees had given in
the account of the produce of my part of the plantation to the
procurator fiscal, who had appropriated it, in case I never came
to claim it – one third to the king, and two thirds to the monastery of St Augustine, to be expended for the benefit of the poor,
and for the conversion of the Indians to the Catholic faith – but
that if I appeared, or anyone for me, to claim the inheritance,
it should be restored – only that the improvement, or annual
production, being distributed to charitable uses, could not be
restored. But he assured me that the steward of the king's revenue
(from lands) and the proviedor, or steward of the monastery, had
taken great care all along that the incumbent, that is to say my
partner, gave every year a faithful account of the produce, of
which they received duly my moiety.

I asked him if he knew to what height of improvement he had
brought the plantation, and whether he thought it might be
worth looking after – or whether on my going thither I should
meet with no obstruction to my possessing my just right in
the moiety.

He told me he could not tell exactly to what degree the plantation was improved – but this he knew, that my partner was grown
exceeding rich upon the enjoying but one half of it, and that to
the best of his remembrance, he had heard that the king's third
of my part, which was, it seems, granted away to some other
monastery or religious house, amounted to above two hundred
moidores a year; that as to my being restored to a quiet possession
of it, there was no question to be made of that, my partner being
alive to witness my title, and my name being also enrolled in the

register of the country. Also, he told me that the survivors of my two trustees were very fair, honest people, and very wealthy, and he believed I would not only have their assistance for putting me in possession, but would find a very considerable sum of money in their hands for my account – being the produce of the farm while their fathers held the trust, and before it was given up as above, which, as he remembered, was for about twelve years.

I showed myself a little concerned and uneasy at this account, and enquired of the old Captain how it came to pass that the trustees should thus dispose my effects, when he knew that I had made my will, and had made him, the Portuguese Captain, my universal heir, etc.

He told me that was true, but as there was no proof of my being dead, he could not act as executor until some certain account should come of my death, and that besides, he was not willing to intermeddle with a thing so remote; that it was true he had registered my will, and put in his claim; and could he have given any account of my being dead or alive, he would have acted by procuration, and taken possession of the *ingenio* – so they called the sugar house – and had given his son, who was now at the Brazils, order to do it.

"But," says the old man, "I have one piece of news to tell you, which perhaps may not be so acceptable to you as the rest, and that is that, believing you were lost, and all the world believing so also, your partner and trustees did offer to accompt to me in your name, for six or eight of the first years of profits, which I received, but there being at that time," says he, "great disbursements for increasing the works, building an *ingenio*, and buying slaves, it did not amount to near so much as afterwards it produced – however," says the old man, "I shall give you a true account of what I have received in all, and how I have disposed of it."

After a few days' further conference with this ancient friend, he brought me an account of the six first years' income of my plantation, signed by my partner and the merchant trustees, being always delivered in goods – namely, tobacco in roll and sugar in chests, besides rum, molasses, etc., which is the consequence of a sugar work, and I found by this account that every year the income considerably increased. But as above, the disbursement being large, the sum at first was small. However, the old man let me see that he was debtor to me 470 moidores of gold, besides sixty chests of sugar, and fifteen double rolls of tobacco, which were lost in his ship – he having been shipwrecked coming home to Lisbon about eleven years after my leaving the place.

The good man then began to complain of his misfortunes, and how he had been obliged to make use of my money to recover his losses, and buy him a share in a new ship. "However, my old friend," says he, "you shall not want a supply in your necessity; and as soon as my son returns, you shall be fully satisfied."

Upon this, he pulls out an old pouch, and gives me 160 Portugal moidores in gold, and giving me the writing of his title to the ship, which his son was gone to the Brazils in, of which he was a quarter part owner, and his son another, he puts them both into my hands for security of the rest.

I was too much moved with the honesty and kindness of the poor man to be able to bear this, and remembering what he had done for me, how he had taken me up at sea, and how generously he had used me on all occasions, and particularly how sincere a friend he was now to me, I could hardly refrain weeping at what he said to me. Therefore, first I asked him if his circumstances admitted him to spare so much money at that time, and if it would not straiten him. He told me, he could not say but it might straiten him a little, but however it was my money, and I might want it more than he.

Everything the good man said was full of affection, and I could hardly refrain from tears while he spoke. In short, I took 100 of the moidores, and called for a pen and ink to give him a receipt for them; then I returned him the rest, and told him if ever I had possession of the plantation, I would return the other to him also, as indeed I afterwards did, and that as to the bill of sale of his part in his son's ship, I would not take it by any means; but that if I wanted the money, I found he was honest enough to pay me; and if I did not, but came to receive what he gave me reason to expect, I would never have a penny more from him.

When this was passed, the old man began to ask me if he should put me into a method to make my claim to my plantation. I told him I thought to go over to it myself. He said I might do so if I pleased; but that if I did not, there were ways enough to secure my right, and immediately to appropriate the profits to my use; and as there were ships in the river of Lisbon, just ready to go away to Brazil, he made me enter my name in a public register, with his affidavit, affirming upon oath that I was alive, and that I was the same person who took up the land for the planting the said plantation at first.

This being regularly attested by a notary, and a procuration affixed, he directed me to send it, with a letter of his writing, to a merchant of his acquaintance at the place, and then proposed my staying with him till an account came of the return.

Never anything was more honourable than the proceedings upon this procuration; for in less than seven months I received a large packet from the survivors of my trustees the merchants, for whose account I went to sea, in which were the following particular letters and papers enclosed.

First, there was the account current of the produce of my farm or plantation, from the year when their fathers had balanced with my old Portugal Captain, being for six years; the balance appeared to be 1,174 moidores in my favour.

Secondly, there was the account of four years more while they kept the effects in their hands, before the government claimed the administration, as being the effects of a person not to be found, which they called civil death; and the balance of this, the value of the plantation increasing, amounted to 38,892 crusados, which made 3,241 moidores.

Thirdly, there was the prior of the Augustins' account, who had received the profits for above fourteen years; but not being to account for what was disposed to the hospital, very honestly declared he had 872 moidores not distributed, when he acknowledged to my account; as to the king's part, that refunded nothing.

There was a letter of my partner's, congratulating me very affectionately upon my being alive, giving me an account how the estate was improved, and what it produced a year, with a particular of the number of squares or acres that it contained; how planted, how many slaves there were upon it; and making two and twenty crosses for blessings, told me he had said so many Ave Marias to thank the blessed Virgin that I was alive; inviting me very passionately to come over and take possession of my own; and in the meantime to give him orders to whom he should deliver my effects, if I did not come myself; concluding with a hearty tender of his friendship, and that of his family, and sent me, as a present, seven fine leopards' skins, which he had it seems received from Africa, by some other ship which he had sent thither, and who it seems had made a better voyage than I. He sent me also five chests of excellent sweetmeats, and a hundred pieces of gold uncoined, not quite so large as moidores.

By the same fleet, my two merchant trustees shipped me 1,200 chests of sugar, 800 rolls of tobacco, and the rest of the whole accompt in gold.

I might well say, now indeed, that the latter end of Job was better than the beginning.* It is impossible to express here the flutterings of my very heart, when I looked over these letters, and especially when I found all my wealth about me; for as the Brazil ships come all in fleets, the same ships which brought my letters brought my goods; and the effects were safe in the river before the letters came to my hand. In a word, I turned pale, and grew sick; and had not the old man run and fetched me a cordial, I believe the sudden surprise of joy had overset nature, and I had died upon the spot.

Nay after that, I continued very ill, and was so some hours, till a physician being sent for, and something of the real cause of my illness being known, he ordered me to be let blood; after which I had relief, and grew well: but I verily believe, if it had not been eased by a vent given in that manner to the spirits, I should have died.

I was now master, all on a sudden, of above 5,000*l.* sterling in money, and had an estate, as I might well call it, in the Brazils, of above a thousand pounds a year, as sure as an estate of lands in England: and, in a word, I was in a condition which I scarce knew how to understand, or how to compose myself for the enjoyment of it.

The first thing I did was to recompense my original benefactor, my good old Captain, who had been first charitable to me in my distress, kind to me in my beginning, and honest to me at the end. I showed him all that was sent me; I told him that, next to the providence of Heaven, which disposes all things, it was owing to him; and that it now lay on me to reward him, which I would do a hundredfold. So I first returned to him the hundred moidores I had received of him, then I sent for a notary, and caused him to draw up a general release or discharge for the 470 moidores, which he had acknowledged he owed me, in the fullest and firmest manner possible; after which, I caused a procuration to be drawn, empowering him to be my receiver of the annual profits of my plantation, and appointing my partner to accompt to him, and make the returns by the usual fleets to him in my name; and a clause in the end, being a grant of 100 moidores a year to him, during his life, out of the effects, and fifty moidores a year to his son after him, for his life: and thus I requited my old man.

I was now to consider which way to steer my course next, and what to do with the estate that Providence had thus put into my hands; and indeed, I had more care upon my head now than I had in my silent state of life in the island, where I wanted nothing but what I had, and had nothing but what I wanted: whereas I had now a great charge upon me, and my business was how to secure it. I had ne'er a cave now to hide my money in, or a place where it might lie without lock or key, till it grew mouldy and tarnished before anybody would meddle with it: on the contrary, I knew not where to put it, or who to trust with it. My old patron, the Captain, indeed was honest, and that was the only refuge I had.

In the next place, my interest in the Brazils seemed to summon me thither; but now I could not tell how to think of going thither, till I had settled my affairs, and left my effects in some safe hands behind me. At first I thought of my old friend the widow, who I knew was honest and would be just to me, but then she was in years, and but poor, and, for ought I knew, might be in debt; so that in a word, I had no way but to go back to England myself, and take my effects with me.

It was some months, however, before I resolved upon this; and therefore, as I had rewarded the old Captain fully, and to his satisfaction, who had been my former benefactor, so I began to think of my poor widow, whose husband had been my first benefactor, and she, whilst it was in her power, my faithful steward and instructor. So the first thing I did, I got a merchant in Lisbon to write to his correspondent in London, not only to pay a bill, but to go find her out, and carry her in money a hundred pounds from me, and to talk with her, and comfort her in her poverty, by telling her she should, if I lived, have a further supply. At the same time, I sent my two sisters in the country each of them a hundred pounds, they being, though not in want, yet not in very good circumstances; one having been married and left a widow, and the other having a husband not so kind to her as he should be.

But among all my relations or acquaintances, I could not yet pitch upon one to whom I durst commit the gross of my stock, that I might go away to the Brazils, and leave things safe behind me; and this greatly perplexed me.

I had once a mind to have gone to the Brazils, and have settled myself there; for I was, as it were, naturalized to the place; but I had some little scruple in my mind about religion, which insensibly drew me back, of which I shall say more presently. However, it was not religion that kept me from going there for the present; and as I had made no scruple of being openly of the religion of the country, all the while I was among them, so neither did I yet; only that now and then, having of late thought more of it than formerly, when I began to think of living and dying among them, I began to regret my having professed myself a Papist, and thought it might not be the best religion to die with.

But, as I have said, this was not the main thing that kept me from going to the Brazils, but that really I did not know with whom to leave my effects behind me; so I resolved at last to go to England with it, where, if I arrived, I concluded I should make some acquaintance or find some relations that would be faithful to me; and according I prepared to go for England with all my wealth.

In order to prepare things for my going home, I first – the Brazil fleet being just going away – resolved to give answers suitable to the just and faithful account of things I had from thence; and first, to the prior of St Augustine, I wrote a letter full of thanks for their just dealings, and the offer of the 872 moidores which was indisposed of, which I desired might be given, 500 to the monastery and 372 to the poor, as the prior should direct, desiring the good padre's prayers for me, and the like.

I wrote next a letter of thanks to my two trustees, with all the acknowledgement that so much justice and honesty called for; as for sending them any present, they were far above having any occasion of it.

Lastly, I wrote to my partner, acknowledging his industry in the improving the plantation, and his integrity in increasing the stock of the works, giving him instructions for his future government of my part, according to the powers I had left with my old patron, to whom I desired him to send whatever became due to me, till he should hear from me more particularly; assuring him that it was my intention not only to come to him, but to settle myself there for the remainder of my life. To this, I added a very handsome present of some Italian silks for his wife and two daughters – for such the Captain's son informed me he had – with two pieces of fine English broad cloth, the best I could get in Lisbon, five pieces of black baize and some Flanders lace of a good value.

Having thus settled my affairs, sold my cargo, and turned all my effects into good bills of exchange, my next difficulty was which way to go to England. I had been accustomed enough to the sea, and yet

I had a strange aversion to going to England by sea at that time; and though I could give no reason for it, yet the difficulty increased upon me so much, that though I had once shipped my baggage in order to go, yet I altered my mind, and that not once, but two or three times.

It is true, I had been very unfortunate by sea, and this might be some of the reason; but let no man slight the strong impulses of his own thoughts in cases of such moment. Two of the ships which I had singled out to go in, I mean, more particularly singled out than any other – that is to say, so as in one of them to put my things on board, and in the other to have agreed with the Captain; I say, two of these ships miscarried – namely, one was taken by the Algerines, and the other was cast away on the Start near Torbay, and all the people drowned except three; so that in either of those vessels I had been made miserable; and in which most, it was hard to say.

Having been thus harassed in my thoughts, my old pilot, to whom I communicated everything, pressed me earnestly not to go by sea, but either to go by land to the Groyne, and cross over the Bay of Biscay to Rochelle, from whence it was but an easy and safe journey by land to Paris, and so to Calais and Dover; or to go up to Madrid, and so all the way by land through France.

In a word, I was so prepossessed against my going by sea at all, except from Calais to Dover, that I resolved to travel all the way by land; which, as I was not in haste, and did not value the charge, was by much the pleasanter way; and to make it more so, my old Captain brought an English gentleman, the son of a merchant in Lisbon, who was willing to travel with me: after which, we picked up two more English merchants also, and two young Portuguese gentlemen, the last going to Paris only; so that we were in all six of us, and five servants; the two merchants and the two Portuguese contenting themselves with one servant between two, to save the charge; and as for me, I got an English sailor to travel with me as a servant, besides my man Friday, who was too much a stranger to be capable of supplying the place of a servant on the road.

In this manner I set out from Lisbon; and our company being all very well mounted and armed, we made a little troop, whereof they did me the honour to call me captain, as well because I was the oldest man, as because I had two servants, and indeed was the original of the whole journey.

As I have troubled you with none of my sea journals, so I shall trouble you now with none of my land journal: but some adventures that happened to us in this tedious and difficult journey I must not omit.

When we came to Madrid, we, being all of us strangers to Spain, were willing to stay some time to see the court of Spain, and to see what was worth observing; but it being the latter part of the summer, we hastened away, and set out from Madrid about the middle of October: but when we came to the edge of Navarre, we were alarmed at several towns on the way, with an account that so much snow has fallen on the French side of the mountains, that several travellers were obliged to come back to Pampeluna, after having attempted, at an extreme hazard, to pass on.

When we came to Pampeluna itself, we found it so indeed; and to me that had been always used to a hot climate, and indeed to countries where we could scarce bear any clothes on, the cold was insufferable; nor indeed was it more painful than it was surprising, to come but ten days before out of the Old Castile, where the weather was not only warm but very hot, and immediately to feel a wind from the Pyrenean mountains, so very keen, so severely cold, as to be intolerable, and to endanger benumbing and perishing of our fingers and toes.

Poor Friday was really frighted when he saw the mountains all covered with snow, and felt cold weather, which he had never seen or felt before in his life.

To mend the matter, when we came to Pampeluna, it continued snowing with so much violence, and so long, that the people said winter was come before its time, and the roads which were difficult before were now quite impassable: for in a word, the snow lay in some places too thick for us to travel; and being not hard frozen, as is the case in northern countries, there was no going without being in danger of being buried alive every step. We stayed no less than twenty days at Pampeluna; when (seeing the winter coming on, and no likelihood of its being better; for it was the severest winter all over Europe that had been known in the memory of man) I proposed that we should all go away to Fonterabia, and there take shipping for Bordeaux, which was a very little voyage.

But while we were considering this, there came in four French gentlemen who, having been stopped on the French side of the passes, as we were on the Spanish, had found out a guide who, traversing the country near the head of Languedoc, had brought them over the mountains by such ways that they were not much incommoded with the snow; and where they met with snow in any quantity, they said it was frozen hard enough to bear them and their horses.

We sent for this guide, who told us he would undertake to carry us the same way with no hazard from the snow, provided we were armed sufficiently to protect ourselves from wild beasts; for he said, upon these great snows, it was frequent for some wolves to show themselves at the foot of the mountains, being made ravenous for want of food, the ground being covered with snow. We told him we were well enough prepared for such creatures as they were, if he would ensure us from a kind of two-legged wolves, which we were told we were in most danger from, especially on the French side of the mountains.

He satisfied us there was no danger of that kind in the way that we were to go; so we readily agreed to follow him, as did also twelve other gentlemen, with their servants, some French, some Spanish; who, as I said, had attempted to go, and were obliged to come back again.

Accordingly, we all set out from Pampeluna, with our guide, on the fifteenth of November; and indeed, I was surprised, when instead of going forwards, he came directly back with us on the same road that we came from Madrid, about twenty miles; when, having passed two rivers, and come into the plain country, we found ourselves in a warm climate again, where the country was pleasant, and no snow to be seen; but, on a sudden, turning to his left, he approached the mountains another way; and though it is true the hills and precipices looked dreadful, yet he made so many tours, such meanders, and led us by such winding ways, that we insensibly passed the height of the mountains without being much encumbered with the snow; and all on a sudden he showed us the pleasant and fruitful provinces of Languedoc and Gascony, all green and flourishing, though at a great distance, and we had some rough way to pass yet.

We were a little uneasy, however, when we found it snowed one whole day and a night, so fast that we could not travel; but he bid us be easy – we should soon be past it all. We found, indeed, that we began to descend every day, and to come more north than before; and so depending upon our guide, we went on.

It was about two hours before night when, our guide being something before us, and not just in sight, out rushed three monstrous wolves, and after them a bear, out of a hollow way, adjoining to a thick wood; two of the wolves flew upon the guide, and had he been half a mile before us, he had been devoured indeed, before we could have helped him. One of them fastened upon his horse, and the other attacked the man with that violence, that he had not time, or not presence of mind enough, to draw his pistol, but hollowed and cried out to us most lustily; my man Friday being next me, I bid him ride up and see what was the matter; as soon as Friday came in sight of the man, he hollowed as loud as t'other, "Oh master! Oh master!" but like a bold fellow, rode directly up to the poor man, and with his pistol shot the wolf that attacked him into the head.

It was happy for the poor man that it was my man Friday; for he, having been used to that kind of creatures in his country, had no fear upon him, but went close up to him, and shot him as above; whereas any of us would have fired at a further distance, and have perhaps either missed the wolf, or endangered shooting the man.

But it was enough to have terrified a bolder man than I, and indeed it alarmed all our company, when with the noise of Friday's pistol, we heard on both sides the dismalest howling of wolves, and the noise redoubled by the echo of the mountains, that it was to us as if there had been a prodigious multitude of them; and perhaps indeed there was not such a few, as that we had no cause of apprehensions.

However, as Friday had killed this wolf, the other, that had fastened upon the horse, left him immediately, and fled, having happily fastened upon his head, where the bosses of the bridle had stuck in his teeth, so that he had not done him much hurt. The man indeed was most hurt; for the raging creature had bit him twice, once on the arm, and the other time a little above his knee; and he was just as it were tumbling down by the disorder of his horse, when Friday came up and shot the wolf.

It is easy to suppose that at the noise of Friday's pistol, we all mended our pace, and rid up as fast as the way (which was very difficult) would give us leave, to see what was the matter; as soon as we came clear of the trees, which blinded us before, we saw clearly what had been the case, and how Friday had disengaged the poor guide; though we did not presently discern what kind of creature it was he had killed.

B UT NEVER WAS A FIGHT MANAGED so hardily, and in such a surprising manner, as that which followed between Friday and the bear, which gave us all (though at first we were surprised and afraid for him) the greatest diversion imaginable. As the bear is a heavy, clumsy creature, and does not gallop as the wolf does, who is swift and light, so he has two particular qualities, which generally are the rule of his actions. First, as to men, who are not his proper prey; I say, not his proper prey, because though I cannot say what excessive hunger might do, which was now their case, the ground being all covered with snow; but as to men, he does not usually attempt them, unless they first attack him: on the contrary, if you meet him in the woods, if you don't meddle with him, he won't meddle with you; but then you must take care to be very civil to him, and give him the road; for he is a very nice gentleman, he won't go a step out of his way for a prince; nay, if you are really afraid, your best way is to look another way, and keep going on; for sometimes if you stop, and stand still, and look steadily at him, he takes it for an affront; but if you throw or toss anything at him, and it hits him, though it were but a bit of a stick as big as your finger, he takes it for an affront, and sets all his other business aside to pursue his revenge; for he will have satisfaction in point of honour; that is his first quality. The next is that, if he be once affronted, he will never leave you, night or day, till he has his revenge; but follows at a good round rate, till he overtakes you.

My man Friday had delivered our guide, and when we came up to him he was helping him off from his horse; for the man was both hurt and frighted, and indeed the last more than the first; when on the sudden we spied the bear come out of the wood, and a vast monstrous one it was, the biggest by far that ever I saw. We were all a little surprised when we saw him; but when Friday saw him, it was easy to see joy and courage in the fellow's countenance. "Oh! Oh! Oh!" says Friday three times, pointing to him; "Oh master! You give me te leave! Me shakee te hand with him: me make you good laugh."

I was surprised to see the fellow so pleased. "You fool you," says I, "he will eat you up." "Eatee me up! Eatee me up!" says Friday, twice over again. "Me eatee him up: me make you good laugh: you all stay here, me show you good laugh"; so down he sits, and gets his boots off in a moment, and put on a pair of pumps, as we call the flat shoes they wear, and which he had in his pocket, gives my other servant his horse, and with his gun away he flew swift like the wind.

The bear was walking softly on, and offered to meddle with nobody, till Friday, coming pretty near, calls to him, as if the bear could understand him; "Hark ye, hark ye," says Friday, "me speakee with you." We followed at a distance; for now being come down on the Gascogne side of the mountains, we were entered a vast great forest, where the country was plain, and pretty open, though many trees in it scattered here and there.

Friday, who had, as we say, the heels of the bear, came up with him quickly, and takes up a great stone, and throws at him, and hit him just on the head; but did him no more harm than if he had thrown it against a wall; but it answered Friday's end; for the rogue was so void of fear that he did it purely to make the bear follow him, and show us some "laugh" as he called it.

As soon as the bear felt the stone and saw him, he turns about and comes after him, taking devilish long strides, and shuffling along at a strange rate, so as would have put a horse to a middling gallop; away runs Friday, and takes his course as if he run towards us for help; so we all resolved to fire at once upon the bear and deliver my man; though I was angry at him heartily for bringing the bear back upon us, when he was going about his own business another way; and especially I was angry that he had turned the bear upon us, and then run away; and I called out, "You dog," said I, "is this your making us laugh? Come away, and take your horse, that we may shoot the creature." He hears me, and cries out, "No shoot, no shoot, stand still, you get much laugh." And, as the nimble creature ran two foot for the beast's one, he turned on a sudden on one side of us and, seeing a great oak tree fit for his purpose, he beckoned to us to follow and, doubling his pace, he gets nimbly up the tree, laying his gun down upon the ground, at about five or six yards from the bottom of the tree.

The bear soon came to the tree, and we followed at a distance; the first thing he did, he stopped at the gun, smelt to it, but let it lie, and up he scrambles into the tree, climbing like a cat, though so monstrously heavy. I was amazed at the folly, as I thought it, of my man, and could not for my life see anything to laugh at yet, till seeing the bear get up the tree, we all rode nearer to him.

When we came to the tree, there was Friday got out to the small end of a large limb of the tree, and the bear got about halfway to him; as soon as the bear got out to that part where the limb of the tree was weaker, "Ha," says he to us, "now you see me teachee the bear dance"; so he falls a jumping and shaking the bough, at which the bear began to totter, but stood still, and begun to look behind him, to see how he should get back; then indeed we did laugh heartily. But Friday had not done with him by a great deal; when he sees him stand still he calls out to him again, as if he had supposed the bear could speak English, "What, you no come further? Pray you come further"; so he left jumping and shaking the bough; and the bear, just as if he had understood what he said, did come a little further, then he fell a-jumping again, and the bear stopped again.

We thought now was a good time to knock him on the head, and I called to Friday to stand still, and we would shoot the bear; but he cried out earnestly, "Oh pray! Oh pray! No shoot, me shoot, by and then" – he would have said "by and by". However, to shorten the story, Friday danced so much, and the bear stood so ticklish, that we had laughing enough indeed, but still could not imagine what the fellow would do; for first we thought he depended upon shaking the bear off; and we found the bear was too cunning for that too; for he would not go out far enough to be thrown down, but clings fast with his great broad claws and feet, so that we could not imagine what would be the end of it, and where the jest would be at last.

But Friday put us out of doubt quickly; for seeing the bear cling fast to the bough, and that he would not be persuaded to come any further, "Well, well," says Friday, "you no come further, me go, me go; you no come to me, me go come to you"; and upon this, he goes out to the smaller end of the bough, where it would bend with his weight, and gently let himself down by it, sliding down the bough, till he came near enough to jump down on his feet, and away he runs to his gun, takes it up, and stands still.

"Well," said I to him, "Friday, what will you do now? Why don't you shoot him?" "No shoot," says Friday, "no yet, me shoot now, me no kill; me stay, give you one more laugh"; and indeed so he did, as you will see presently; for when the bear see his enemy gone, he comes back from the bough where he stood; but did it mighty leisurely, looking behind him every step, and coming backwards, till he got into the body of the tree; then with the same hinder end foremost, he came down the tree, grasping it with his claws, and moving one foot at a time, very leisurely; at this juncture, and just before he could set his hind feet upon the ground, Friday stepped up close to him, clapped the muzzle of his piece into his ear, and shot him dead as a stone.

Then the rogue turned about, to see if we did not laugh, and when he saw we were pleased by our looks, he falls a-laughing himself very loud. "So we kill bear in my country," says Friday. "So you kill them," says I, "why, you have no guns." "No," says he, "no gun, but shoot great much long arrow."

This was indeed a good diversion to us; but we were still in a wild place, and our guide very much hurt, and what to do we hardly knew; the howling of wolves run much in my head; and indeed, except the noise I once heard on the shore of Africa, of which I have said something already, I never heard anything that filled me with so much horror.

These things, and the approach of night, called us off, or else, as Friday would have had us, we should certainly have taken the skin of this monstrous creature off, which was worth saving; but we had three leagues to go, and our guide hastened us, so we left him, and went forwards on our journey.

The ground was still covered with snow, though not so deep and dangerous as on the mountains, and the ravenous creatures, as we heard afterwards, were come down into the forest and plain country, pressed by hunger to seek for food; and had done a great deal of mischief in the villages, where they surprised the country people, killed a great many of their sheep and horses, and some people too.

We had one dangerous place to pass, which our guide told us, if there were any more wolves in the country, we should find them there; and this was in a small plain, surrounded with woods on every side, and a long narrow defile or lane, which we were to pass to get through the wood, and then we should come to the village where we were to lodge.

It was within half an hour of sunset when we entered the first wood; and a little after sunset when we came into the plain. We met with nothing in the first wood, except that in a little plain within the wood, which was not above two furlongs over, we saw five great wolves cross the road, full speed one after another, as if they had been in chase of some prey, and had it in view; they took no notice of us, and were gone and out of our sight in a few moments.

Upon this our guide, who, by the way, was a wretched faint-hearted fellow, bid us keep in a ready posture; for he believed there were more wolves a-coming.

We kept our arms ready, and our eyes about us, but we saw no more wolves, till we came through that wood, which was near half a league, and entered the plain; as soon as we came into the plain we had occasion enough to look about us. The first object we met with was a dead horse; that is to say, a poor horse which the wolves had killed, and at least a dozen of them at work; we could not say eating of him, but picking of his bones rather; for they had eaten up all the flesh before.

We did not think fit to disturb them at their feast, neither did they take much notice of us: Friday would have let fly at them, but I would not suffer him by any means; for I found we were like to have more business upon our hands than we were aware of. We were not gone half over the plain, but we began to hear the wolves howl in the wood on our left in a frightful manner, and presently after we saw about a hundred coming on directly towards us, all in a body, and most of them in a line, as regularly as an army drawn up by experienced officers. I scarce knew in what manner to receive them; but found to draw ourselves in a close line was the only way: so we formed in a moment. But that we might not have too much interval, I ordered that only every other man should fire, and that the others who had not fired should stand ready to give them a second volley immediately, if they continued to advance upon us, and that then those who had fired at first should not pretend to load their fusees again, but stand ready with every one a pistol; for we were all armed with a fusee and a pair of pistols each man; so we were by this method able to fire six volleys, half of us at a time; however, at present we had no necessity; for upon firing the first volley, the enemy made a full stop, being terrified as well with the noise as with the fire; four of them, being shot into the head, dropped; several others were wounded, and went bleeding off, as we could see by the snow. I found they stopped, but did not immediately retreat; whereupon, remembering that I had been told that the fiercest creatures were terrified at the voice of a man, I caused all our company to hollow as loud as we could; and I found the notion not altogether mistaken; for upon our shout, they began to retire and turn about; then I ordered a second volley to be fired in their rear, which put them to the gallop, and away they went to the woods.

This gave us leisure to charge our pieces again, and that we might lose no time, we kept going; but we had but little more than loaded our fusees, and put ourselves into a readiness, when we heard a terrible noise in the same wood, on our left, only that it was further onwards the same way we were to go.

The night was coming on, and the light began to be dusky, which made it worse on our side; but the noise increasing, we could easily perceive that it was the howling and yelling of those hellish creatures; and on a sudden, we perceived two or three troops of wolves, one on our left, one behind us and one on our front; so that we seemed to be surrounded with 'em; however, as they did not fall upon us, we kept our way forwards, as fast as we could make our horses go, which, the way being very rough, was only a good large trot; and in this manner we came in view of the entrance of a wood, through which we were to pass, at the further side of the plain; but we were greatly surprised when, coming nearer the lane or pass, we saw a confused number of wolves standing just at the entrance.

On a sudden, at another opening of the wood, we heard the noise of a gun; and looking that way, out rushed a horse, with a saddle and a bridle on him, flying like the wind, and sixteen or seventeen wolves after him, full speed; indeed, the horse had the heels of them; but as we supposed that he could not hold it at that rate, we doubted not but they would get up with him at last, and no question but they did.

But here we had a most horrible sight; for riding up to the entrance where the horse came out, we found the carcass of another horse, and of two men, devoured by the ravenous creatures, and one of the men was no doubt the same who we heard fired the gun; for there lay a gun just by him, fired off; but as to the man, his head and the upper part of his body was eaten up.

This filled us with horror, and we knew not what course to take, but the creatures resolved us soon; for they gathered about us presently, in hopes of prey; and I verily believe there were three hundred of them. It happened very much to our advantage that, at the entrance into the wood, but a little way from it, there lay some large timber trees, which had been cut down the summer before, and I suppose lay there for carriage; I drew my little troop in among those trees and, placing ourselves in a line behind one long tree, I advised them all to light, and keeping that tree before us for a breastwork, to stand in a triangle, or three fronts, enclosing our horses in the centre.

We did so, and it was well we did; for never was a more furious charge than the creatures made upon us in the place; they came on us with a growling kind of noise (and mounted the piece of timber, which, as I said, was our breastwork) as if they were only rushing upon their prey; and this fury of theirs, it seems, was principally occasioned by their seeing our horses behind us, which was the prey they aimed at: I ordered our men to fire, as before, every other man; and they took their aim so sure, that indeed they killed several of the wolves at the first volley; but there was a necessity to keep a continual firing; for they came on like devils – those behind pushing on those before.

When we had fired our second volley of our fusees, we thought they stopped a little, and I hoped they would have gone off; but it was but a moment; for others came forwards again; so we fired two volleys of our pistols, and I believe in these four firings we had killed seventeen or eighteen of them, and lamed twice as many; yet they came on again.

I was loath to spend our last shot too hastily; so I called my servant – not my man Friday, for he was better employed; for with the greatest dexterity imaginable, he had charged my fusee and his own, while we were engaged – but as I said, I called my other man and, giving him a horn of powder, I had him lay a train all along the piece of timber, and let it be a large train; he did so, and had but just time to get away, when the wolves came up to it, and some were got up upon it; when I, snapping an uncharged pistol close to the powder, set it on fire; those that were upon the timber were scorched with it, and six or seven of them fell, or rather jumped in among us, with the force and fright of the fire; we dispatched these in an instant, and the rest were so frighted with the light, which the night, for it was now very dark, made more terrible, that they drew back a little.

Upon which I ordered our last pistol to be fired off in one volley, and after that we gave a shout; upon this, the wolves turned tail, and we sallied immediately upon near twenty lame ones, who we found struggling on the ground, and fell a-cutting them with our swords, which answered our expectation; for the crying and howling they made was better understood by their fellows, so that they all fled and left us.

We had, first and last, killed about three score of them; and had it been daylight, we had killed many more. The field of battle being thus cleared, we made forwards again; for we had still near a league to go. We heard the ravenous creatures howl and yell in the woods as we went, several times; and sometimes we fancied we saw some of them, but the snow dazzling our eyes, we were not certain; so, in about an hour more, we came to the town where we were to lodge, which we found in a terrible fright, and all in arms; for it seems that the night before, the wolves and some bears had broke into the village in the night, and put them in a terrible fright; and they were obliged to keep guard night and day, but especially in the night, to preserve their cattle, and indeed their people.

The next morning, our guide was so ill – and his limbs swelled with the rankling of his two wounds – that he could go no further; so we were obliged to take a new guide there, and go to Toulouse, where we found a warm climate, a fruitful pleasant country, and no snow, no wolves, or anything like them; but when we told our story at Toulouse, they told us it was nothing but what was ordinary in the great forest at the foot of the mountains, especially when the snow lay on the ground: but they enquired much what kind of a guide we had gotten, that would venture to bring us that way in such a severe season; and told us it was very much we were not all devoured. When we told them how we placed ourselves, and the horses in the middle, they blamed us exceedingly, and told us it was fifty to one but we had been all destroyed; for it was the sight of the horses which made the wolves so furious, seeing their prey; and that at other times they are really afraid of a gun; but the being excessive hungry, and raging on that account, the eagerness to come at the horses had made them senseless of danger; and that if we had not by the continued fire, and at last by the stratagem of the train of powder, mastered them, it had been great odds but that we had been torn to pieces; whereas had we been content to have sat still on horseback, and fired as horsemen, they would not have taken the horses for so much their own, when men were on their backs, as otherwise; and withal they told us, that at last, if we had stood altogether, and left our horses, they would have been so eager to have devoured them, that we might have come off safe, especially having our firearms in our hands, and being so many in number.

For my part, I was never so sensible of danger in my life; for seeing above three hundred devils come roaring and open-mouthed to devour us, and having nothing to shelter us, or retreat to, I gave myself over for lost; and as it was, I believe I shall never care to cross those mountains again; I think I would much rather go a thousand leagues by sea, though I were sure to meet with a storm once a week.

I have nothing uncommon to take notice of in my passage through France; nothing but what other travellers have given an account of, with much more advantage than I can. I travelled from Toulouse to Paris, and without any considerable stay, came to Calais, and landed safe at Dover, the fourteenth of January, after having had a severely cold season to travel in.

I was now come to the centre of my travels, and had in a little time all my new discovered estate safe about me, the bills of exchange which I brought with me having been very currently paid.

My principal guide and privy counsellor was my good ancient widow, who, in gratitude for the money I had sent her, thought no pains too much, or care too great, to employ for me; and I trusted her so entirely with everything, that I was perfectly easy as to the security of my effects; and indeed, I was very happy from my beginning, and now to the end, in the unspotted integrity of this good gentlewoman.

And now I began to think of leaving my effects with this woman, and setting out for Lisbon, and so to the Brazils; but now another scruple came in my way, and that was religion; for as I had entertained some doubts about the Roman religion, even while I was abroad, especially in my state of solitude; so I knew there was no going to the Brazils for me, much less going to settle there, unless I resolved to embrace the Roman Catholic religion without any reserve; unless, on the other hand, I resolved to be a sacrifice to my principles, be a martyr for religion, and die in the Inquisition; so I resolved to stay at home, and if I could find means for it, to dispose of my plantation.

To this purpose, I wrote to my old friend at Lisbon, who in return gave me notice that he could easily dispose of it there: but that if I thought fit to give him leave to offer it in my name to the two merchants, the survivors of my trustees, who lived in the Brazils, who must fully understand the value of it, who lived just upon the spot, and who I knew were very rich; so that he believed they would be fond of buying it; he did not doubt, but I should make four or 5,000 pieces of eight the more of it.

Accordingly I agreed, gave him order to offer it to them, and he did so; and in about eight months more, the ship being then returned, he sent me account that they had accepted the offer, and had remitted 33,000 pieces of eight to a correspondent of theirs at Lisbon to pay for it.

In return I signed the instrument of sale in the form which they sent from Lisbon, and sent it to my old man, who sent me bills of exchange for 32,800 pieces of eight for the estate; reserving the payment of 100 moidores a year to him, the old man, during his life, and fifty moidores afterwards to his son for his life, which I had promised them, which the plantation was to make good as a rent charge. And thus I have given the first part of a life of fortune and adventure, a life of Providence's chequer-work, and of a variety which the world will seldom be able to show the like of: beginning foolishly, but closing much more happily than any part of it ever gave me leave so much as to hope for.

Anyone would think that in this state of complicated good fortune I was past running any more hazards; and so indeed I had been, if other circumstances had concurred; but I was inured to a wandering life, had no family, not many relations, nor, however rich, had I contracted much acquaintance; and though I had sold my estate in the Brazils, yet I could not keep the country out of my head, and had a great mind to be upon the wing again; especially I could not resist the strong inclination I had to see my island, and to know if the poor Spaniards were in being there, and how the rogues I left there had used them.

My true friend, the widow, earnestly dissuaded me from it, and so far prevailed with me, that for almost seven years she prevented my running abroad; during which time I took my two nephews, the children of one of my brothers, into my care. The eldest, having something of his own, I bred up as a gentleman, and gave him a settlement of some addition to his estate, after my decease; the other I put out to a Captain of a ship; and after five years, finding him a sensible, bold, enterprising young fellow, I put him into a good ship, and sent him to sea: and this young fellow afterwards drew me in, as old as I was, to further adventures myself.

In the meantime I in part settled myself here; for first of all I married, and that not either to my disadvantage or dissatisfaction, and had three children, two sons and one daughter: but my wife dying, and my nephew coming home with good success from a voyage to Spain, my inclination to go abroad, and his importunity, prevailed and engaged me to go in his ship as a private trader to the East Indies. This was in the year 1694.

In this voyage I visited my new colony in the island, saw my successors the Spaniards, had the whole story of their lives, and of the villains I left there; how at first they insulted the poor Spaniards, how they afterwards agreed, disagreed, united, separated, and how at last the Spaniards were obliged to use violence with them, how they were subjected to the Spaniards, how honestly the Spaniards used them; a history, if it were entered into, as full of variety and wonderful accidents as my own part; particularly also as to their battles with the Caribbeans, who landed several times upon the island, and as to the improvement they made upon the island itself, and how five of them made an attempt upon the mainland, and brought away eleven men and five women prisoners, by which, at my coming, I found about twenty young children on the island.

Here I stayed about twenty days, left them supplies of all necessary things, and particularly of arms, powder, shot, clothes, tools, and two workmen, which I brought from England with me – namely, a carpenter and a smith.

Besides this, I shared the island into parts with 'em, reserved to myself the property of the whole, but gave them such parts respectively as they agreed on; and having settled all things with them, and engaged them not to leave the place, I left them there.

From thence I touched at the Brazils, from whence I sent a barque, which I bought there, with more people to the island, and in it, besides other supplies, I sent seven women, being such as I found proper for service, or for wives to such as would take them. As to the Englishmen, I promised them to send them some women from England, with a good cargo of necessaries, if they would apply themselves to planting, which I afterwards performed. And the fellows proved very honest and diligent after they were mastered and had their properties set apart for them. I sent them also from the Brazils five cows, three of them being big with calf, some sheep and some hogs, which, when I came again, were considerably increased.

But all these things, with an account how 300 Caribbees came and invaded them, and ruined their plantations, and how they fought with that whole number twice, and were at first defeated, and three of them killed; but at last a storm destroying their enemies canoes, they famished or destroyed almost all the rest, and renewed and recovered the possession of their plantation, and still lived upon the island; all these things, with some very surprising incidents in some new adventures of my own, for ten years more, I may perhaps give a further account of hereafter.

Note on the Text

The text is based on the first edition of 1719, incorporating the alterations made in the successive reprints of that year. Spelling and punctuation have been modernized, standardized and made consistent throughout.

Notes

p. 3, *Bremen*: A city in north-west Germany.

p. 4, *propension of nature tending directly*: By this, Crusoe means an instinctive tendency pushing him towards something.

p. 4, *the wise man... neither poverty or riches*: See Proverbs 30:8.

p. 11, *We had not... hard*: Crusoe explains that they should have attempted to use the tide to carry them upriver as soon as they arrived, but the wind prevented them from doing so.

p. 11, *ship rid forecastle... bitter end*: The boat turned with the tide, some water sloshed onboard and the crew worried the anchor had come loose; an additional anchor was dropped, the ropes of which were stretched taut with the strength of the tide.

p. 12, *at all adventures*: At great hazard.

p. 15, *an emblem of... fatted calf*: The Parable of the Prodigal Son. See Luke 15:11–32.

p. 16, *Jonah... Tarshish*: See Jonah 1:3–15.

p. 20, *from the latitude... line itself*: very close to the Equator – and therefore very hot.

p. 20, *a Turkish rover of Sallee*: Sallee, or Salé as it is now known, is a Moroccan port, which used to be notorious as a pirates' den.

p. 43, *I should have my equal... the stock*: The offer is that, in return for his services, Crusoe would be given an equal share of the slaves brought back, but wouldn't have to make any investment, as the others would.

p. 45, *the same day eight year*: The same day, eight years on, from the date he ran away from home.

p. 51, *For sudden joys, like griefs, confound at first*: A line from 'Wild's Humble Thanks for His Majesties Gracious Declaration for Liberty of Conscience, March 15, 1672' (1672) by Robert Wild (1609–79).

p. 54, *the ship was bulged*: Had its bilge breached.

p. 103, *Call on me... glorify me*: See Psalm 50:15.

p. 103, *Can God... the wilderness?*: See Psalm 78:19.

p. 105, *He is exalted... give remission*: See Acts 5:31.

p. 121, *Leadenhall Market*: A historic market on the eastern edge of the City of London, which was famous for its fresh produce.

p. 125, *I will never, never leave thee, nor forsake thee*: See Joshua 1:5

p. 142, *Between me and thee is a great gulf fixed*: See Luke 16:26.

p. 142, *the lust... the pride of life*: See 1 John 2:16.

p. 146, *feeding Elijah by ravens*: See 1 Kings 17:4–6.

p. 175, *Call upon me... glorify me*: See Psalms 50:15.

p. 175, *Wait... on the Lord*: See Psalms 27:14

p. 177, *Saul... forsaken him*: See 1 Samuel 28:15.

p. 194, *chopped upon*: Chanced upon.

p. 317, *that the latter end of Job was better than the beginning*: See Job 42:12. This mirrors Job's reward – Crusoe's tale ends with his becoming rich.

EXTRA MATERIAL
FOR YOUNG READERS

THE WRITER

No one knows exactly when Daniel Defoe was born, but it was roughly in the year 1660, in London. We don't know very much about his early years, either, but his father was a merchant who sold tallow – fat from cows and sheep that was processed so that it could be made into candles and other goods. London for young Daniel must have been both exciting and scary, teeming with people and dangers. When he was only about five (in 1665), the Great Plague hit the city, killing 100,000 people; the next year came the Great Fire, which burned down a third of all the houses.

But Daniel survived, and went on to study at a school called a "dissenting academy". Dissenters were people who did not agree with the teachings of the Anglican Church, or Church of England, which was the official state church, and so were not allowed to study at Anglican schools or universities such as Oxford and Cambridge. All the same, the Newington Green academy that Daniel went to was excellent – perhaps even better than the traditional schools, because it taught a wide range of subjects in English rather than Latin.

After leaving school, Defoe led an extremely busy life. He became a businessman, trading in a variety of goods; he started writing political pamphlets, and he even became a volunteer soldier to support the "Glorious Revolution" of 1688 – this was when the English Parliament decided that England no longer wanted a

Catholic king, and summoned William and Mary, from the Dutch royal family, to rule instead. They became King William III and Queen Mary II of England.

After a few years as a businessman, it was clear that Daniel Defoe had lost a lot of money. He went bankrupt in 1692 with huge debts to pay. This could have crippled some men for life, but not Defoe. He picked himself up again and was soon back in business, this time running a tile and brickworks in Tilbury, Essex (not far from London). Not only that: he kept writing. He wrote about many political subjects; he criticized the bankruptcy laws, defended the king and expressed his opinions on how society could be improved.

In the course of all this, Defoe became close to King William himself. When the king died in 1702, it was bad news for him, because the new Queen Anne was an Anglican, and opposed to his religious views. He landed himself in trouble by writing a provocative pamphlet, and was sentenced to being "pilloried". The pillory was a wooden structure that secured the prisoner's head and hands, usually somewhere very public like a marketplace, so that people could laugh and throw rotten vegetables at them. According to legend, however, many people agreed with what Defoe had written, so they threw flowers at him instead; he even wrote a poem about it, called *A Hymn to the Pillory*. After all that, however, he still had to spend time in prison.

By 1703, he was free again. His brickworks business had collapsed in the meantime, but he bounced back once more from his tough experiences. When a terrible storm hit in November 1703, killing thousands of people, he collected people's memories in a book called *The Storm*. He was soon back in political circles, too, and in 1706 he was sent by the English government to be a spy in Scotland. At the time, Scotland was a separate country, but discussions were going on about a union with England. It was Defoe's job to find out what Scottish people really thought – a dangerous thing to do, because many in Scotland were violently opposed to the union. Defoe wrote a great deal about it all – as he did about everything – and published *The History of the Union of Great Britain* in 1709.

By now, Defoe had more or less given up his business activities; and as he grew older, he started thinking about other sorts of writing. When his first novel, *Robinson Crusoe*, appeared in 1719, he was almost sixty years old. But he didn't stop there. It's thought that he wrote over 500 different pamphlets, books or other works in his lifetime.

Daniel Defoe died on 24th April 1731 and was buried in Islington, London. Despite having led such a hectic life, he had also been married from his early twenties; his wife gave birth to eight children.

THE BOOK

Real life, and events of the times, seem likely to be at the heart of Daniel Defoe's inspiration for *Robinson Crusoe*. In those days, the only way to travel from England was by boat. There were many shipwrecks, and some stories of survival, too. One of the best-known during Defoe's lifetime was of a Scottish man named Alexander Selkirk. In 1704, convinced that the ship he was travelling on was unsafe, he asked to be left on a remote island off the coast of Chile, in South America (and he was right – the ship was wrecked shortly afterwards). Although Selkirk regretted his decision at first, he soon adapted to life on the island. Many of the things described in *Robinson Crusoe* were features of his life – finding goats and fruit to live off, making clothes from goatskins, reading the Bible and using his wits to make tools. Selkirk survived on the island for over four years before being rescued in early 1709. Over the next few years, his story became famous, so it's probable that Daniel Defoe made use of it.

Some people claim that *Robinson Crusoe* was the first novel ever to have been written in English. But was it? There are so many different definitions of the novel that it can be argued in many ways. The big difference between this book and earlier stories is that it gives a realistic account of what happens to the main character: there is nothing magical or mythical about it, which is why it represents a new kind of writing. This was pointed out by a literary critic, Ian Watt, in a book called *The Rise of the Novel* that was published in 1957, and many have agreed with him since.

Having lived such an eventful life, adventure writing suited Daniel Defoe very well. He may not have experienced a shipwreck himself, but he had certainly pushed himself to the limit, and had bounced back from many misfortunes and failures – bankruptcy and even being sent to prison. He had also witnessed terrible events such as the Great Plague, the Great Fire of London and the Great Storm of 1703 (thanks to his efforts to record the storm, he is also thought of as one of the first journalists).

Defoe continued to write novels after the publication of *Robinson Crusoe*, and completed another eight. However, none of the others have proved quite so enduring or significant. *Moll Flanders* – a story about a woman criminal – comes closest. *Robinson Crusoe*, however, even led to a whole new kind of book, called a "Robinsonade". Robinsonades were survival stories that showed their characters triumphing over their difficult circumstances by using their wits and learning how to master both their new environment and any other characters they met (such as the cannibals in Defoe's story).

In addition to this, *Robinson Crusoe* has been retold or adapted countless times – in other novels, plays and comics, on television and in films – and the text has been studied for generations. Many theories have been put forward about its significance and what it shows us about society in Daniel Defoe's times. Many have looked back at Robinson Crusoe himself as being a typical British colonialist: tough, independent, resourceful, but with a belief that he is master and has the right to dominate everyone he meets.

CHARACTERS

Robinson Crusoe

Robinson Crusoe could lead a successful, happy life by staying at home in England and developing a career, which is what his father wants him to do. But he won't listen: he's stubborn. He longs to go off to sea. His passion for the sea, and for adventure, is so strong that he still seeks it out even when things go wrong; he is shipwrecked, and then enslaved, but none of this puts him off further adventures. Even when he has a successful plantation in Brazil, he can't resist the pull of the sea – and this time, he ends up a castaway.

Once he is on the island, the reader begins to see all sorts of other qualities in him: he is very resourceful, patient and determined. He thinks up ingenious solutions to the difficulties he encounters, and also faces his own fears. It is hard not to admire the way he adapts to his new life and slowly accepts his situation. He changes his attitude and regrets ignoring his father; he rediscovers faith in God.

Later, when Friday is living with him, we see another side to his character. He believes he is superior to Friday, and teaches him to call him "Master"; he sees himself as a sort of king, who owns the island and governs everyone who lands there. Many people have interpreted this as an example of the British attitude that led to the creation of the British Empire in the centuries that followed. Robinson also shows himself to be cold and ruthless at times, and to kill when necessary for his own survival.

Friday

In many ways, Friday is the polar opposite of Robinson Crusoe. Of course, he comes from a very different culture, but his personality is different, too. Friday is loving, warm and impulsive. Given that Robinson has saved his life, it is perhaps not surprising that he is loyal, but his loyalty goes particularly deep: when Robinson gives him the option of returning to his own people, he says he would rather die. Friday is intelligent, quick to learn everything he is taught; he also asks Robinson very logical, insightful questions about his religion, and why he should abandon his own beliefs. He is much younger than Robinson, strong and fit, and proves himself to be extremely capable. We also discover that he is mischievous and fun-loving when, on their journey to England, he plays a trick on a bear.

Robinson Crusoe's father

Robinson Crusoe's father is a sensible, unadventurous man, who broods over the early part of the book with his gloomy predictions about his son's life. He does everything in his power to dissuade Robinson from going to sea.

The English captain and wife

Robinson Crusoe's second sea voyage happens thanks to a kind captain, who takes him on board his ship as a companion and helps him to invest a little money in the voyage. Robinson Crusoe does very well out of it, turning £40 to £300, all thanks to the captain's generosity. When the captain dies not long afterwards, Robinson leaves £200 in the care of the captain's widow, who he knows to be an honest woman. She sends half the money to him when he needs it in Brazil, and looks after the rest faithfully for him until his return from the island. At the end of the story, Robinson rewards her for her honesty and kindness.

Pirate captain of Sallee

The captain of the Turkish ship that takes Robinson Crusoe prisoner treats him well and makes him his personal slave at his house in Sallee (a town in north Africa). He turns out to be very trusting, and gives Robinson responsibility for a well-equipped fishing boat – which he uses to escape.

Xury

A young slave boy who is forced to go with Robinson when he escapes from Sallee to drift down the African coast. Xury is loyal, but has little choice in the matter, as his life depends on it. He shows himself to be useful, but Robinson does not see him as an equal human being: he sells him to the Portuguese captain once they are rescued.

The Portuguese captain

After the escape from Sallee, it is a Portuguese ship that picks up Robinson Crusoe and Xury. The Portuguese captain, like the English one, is very kind to Robinson: he buys his boat, his animal skins and the boy Xury, who is treated as a possession like everything else. The captain also arranges for Robinson's money to be delivered to him in Brazil, which allows Robinson to equip his plantation and start a new life. Later, once Robinson has escaped the island, he is reunited with the Portuguese captain and discovers that he has faithfully protected his profits from the plantation. This enables Robinson to become a rich man.

The Spaniard and Friday's father
These two are rescued from cannibals by Robinson Crusoe and Friday. They are hugely grateful, and immediately become loyal "subjects" to Crusoe. Other than the deep love that we see between Friday and his father, we discover little about these two as individuals; instead, they serve to demonstrate Crusoe's domineering attitude towards everyone he encounters on "his" island.

Captain of the rescue ship
Even though he is a ship's captain, this man is first of all made prisoner by a mutiny of his own sailors. When he is rescued by Robinson and Friday, he is very grateful. As a result, he is only too glad to do as Robinson says.

REAL-LIFE SURVIVAL STORIES

If you were stranded on an island, up a mountain or in a desert, would you survive, as Robinson Crusoe did? He was a fictional character, but there are plenty of amazing true accounts of people who have survived against the odds – even in quite recent times.

Poon Lim
Poon Lim was born in China. By the time he was in his early twenties, he was working on board the British merchant ship SS *Ben Lomond*. On this particular journey, the ship was travelling slowly north from Cape Town to New York in November 1942, when the Second World War was still raging. The SS *Ben Lomond* was

spotted by a German U-boat (a military submarine), which fired two torpedoes into it. The ship sank almost immediately, and the whole crew drowned – apart from one man. That man was Poon Lim.

When Poon Lim realized the ship was sinking, he grabbed a life jacket and jumped overboard. It saved his life, because the ship pulled down the rest of the crew with it. He managed to stay afloat for two hours until he found one of the ship's life rafts; inside, he found some drinking water, biscuits, some sugar and chocolate, and a few other objects, including a flashlight. At first, he lived on the biscuits and water, rationing them carefully and hoping that he'd soon be rescued. But the days went past and he didn't see any other ships. So he made a hook out of a wire that was in the flashlight and began to fish. He also collected rainwater in a lifejacket. He had just enough food and water to keep him going, but realized that he needed to keep up his strength by swimming regularly, too – making sure he was attached to the boat first.

The weeks drifted by. One ship passed, but seemed to ignore him, and a plane seemed to see him too. But still no one came. After over four months at sea, Poon Lim noticed that the colour of the water had changed – it was lighter, not like the deep blue of the ocean. He was near land, at last. Soon afterwards, some fisherman found him and took him to shore – he had reached Brazil. In total, he had survived for 133 days. This is still the world record for survival at sea in a life raft.

The Andes survivors

At about 3.30 in the afternoon of 13th October 1972, the pilot of an Air Force plane from Uruguay began to descend towards Chile, with 44 other people on board. Unable to see through the clouds, he thought they had already crossed the treacherous Andes mountains. But he had made a terrible mistake. They were still far from their destination and the plane crashed, high up among the rocks and snow.

At first it seemed that only five people had been killed; but others were badly injured, and some were missing – thrown out of the plane when it crashed. Everyone was badly shaken and shocked. Over the next few days, the reality began to sink in. Without any proper medical care, the injured passengers began to die, one by one. They were stranded up a high mountainside with just a few snacks, like some chocolate bars and wine. At least there was plenty of clean snow, which they could melt to make water; but soon everyone was desperately hungry and weak.

The survivors discussed what to do. They guessed, correctly, there would be a big hunt for the missing plane; but in fact, the searchers were looking in the wrong places – and anyway, the white plane was hard to see against the white snow. Days ticked by. They had to eat *something* – but what? They hunted the wreckage of the plane for anything at all. Nothing. Apart from one thing...

Their fellow passengers who had been killed lay well preserved in the cold snow. The truth slowly dawned: they would have to survive by eating their flesh. It was a terrible decision to have to make, but in the end it was a simple choice: eat the bodies or die. One by one everyone gave in, and began to eat.

Days turned into weeks. Still no rescue. An avalanche killed eight more of the survivors; now there were just seventeen left. The only solution was for some of them to climb down the mountain, with no idea where they were, how long it would take, or whether they had enough strength to manage it. But eventually, 69 days after the crash, two of them made it down the mountain and contacted the outside world. Three days later, the rest were rescued. Thanks to the bodies of the other passengers, sixteen people survived.

Henno Martin and Hermann Korn

It was 1940, and the Second World War was spreading. Even in Namibia, southern Africa, its effects could be felt. Namibia had once been a German colony, but now the new South African government was locking Germans away in internment camps. Two German friends, Henno and Hermann, knew that they wanted nothing to do with the war – but they didn't want to be locked up, either. Their solution? They packed up their old lorry with as many provisions as they could manage and disappeared into the Namib Desert to hide.

Like any desert, the Namib is very, very dry, with little vegetation. The pair drove to a remote canyon and began their new life with no idea how long the war – or their provisions – would last. The canyon had a waterhole, but to survive they would have to hone their hunting skills. They had guns, but they were not really suitable for hunting, as they discovered when they tried to kill a wild bull. They had to use their wits, tracking animals down and devising new ways to kill and trap them.

They managed like this for over two years – but a diet of meat (and even then, not enough of it) began to take its toll. They were permanently hungry, and Hermann began to get sick from lack of vitamins. Reluctantly, they decided to return to civilization. When they did, their story was so amazing that they weren't locked up by the government after all.

Tom Neale

Tom Neale's experiences were closer to those of Robinson Crusoe than any of the other survivors listed here, because he managed to live alone on an island in the Pacific Ocean for many years. But there is one big difference – he *chose* to live there! He was born in New Zealand in 1902, spent some time in the Navy and then spent many years working on or around the Pacific islands. One day, someone told him about an island called Suwarrow, which had been uninhabited ever since the Second World War. Suwarrow captured Tom's imagination, and he decided that it was the place where he wanted to live.

It was a long time before his dream became possible. Eventually, in 1952, a ship dropped him there with as many provisions as he could gather, and his solitary life began. He found pigs and chickens there, left over from the war; the pigs were a nuisance, so he killed them, but he found the chickens very useful. He also had cats, like Robinson Crusoe, and found plenty of fruit to add to his diet. Although he returned to the mainland several times, Tom was Suwarrow's only resident for a total of sixteen years.

TEST YOURSELF

Do you have your wits about you, like Robinson Crusoe and Friday? Or are you all at sea? Try this quiz to find out. Answers are overleaf.

1. When Turkish pirates attack the ship carrying Robinson Crusoe to Guinea, he is:
   A) Forced to drink bilge water
   B) Taken to Sallee to become a slave
   C) Kept in chains at the bottom of a ship
   D) Asked to marry the captain's daughter

2. When making his escape from Sallee, Robinson Crusoe has to get rid of the captain's accomplice on the boat. Does he:
   A) Shoot him
   B) Sneakily leave Sallee without him
   C) Push him overboard and tell him to swim for shore
   D) Feed him poisonous fish

3. How does Crusoe discover that other humans may be on his island?
   A) He sees a footprint in the sand
   B) Someone has eaten his breakfast
   C) All his goats start bleating
   D) He hears someone singing

4. Robinson Crusoe manages to make himself clothes with:
   A) Woven reeds
   B) Goatskins
   C) Vine leaves
   D) Seaweed

5. The character Poll is:
   A) The English captain's widow
   B) Xury's sister
   C) A parrot
   D) Crusoe's favourite goat

6. Robinson Crusoe reads a book regularly on his island. Is it:
   A) The complete works of Shakespeare
   B) *Moll Flanders*
   C) The Qur'an
   D The Bible

7. Later on, Robinson Crusoe discovers that his island lay not far from the mouth of a great river. Which river was it?
   A) The Orinoco
   B) The Thames
   C) The Amazon
   D) The Nile

8. On their journey back to England, Robinson Crusoe and his companions have to fight off hordes of which creature?
   A) Hyenas
   B) Wolves
   C) Vultures
   D) Mosquitoes

ANSWERS

1—B
2—C
3—A
4—B
5—C
6—D
7—A
8—B

SCORES

1 to 3 correct: There's no rescue in sight. **4 to 6 correct:** Not bad: have a turtle's egg for tea. **7 to 8 correct:** Well done! You're master of the desert island.

Glossary

abatement	Lessening; calming.
abortive	Failing.
abroad	Far. Not necessarily to a foreign land – used similarly to "going out".
abundance	Large amount.
accompt	Account.
acquiesce	Unprotestingly, reluctantly accepting something.
ad infinitum	Infinitely; Latin: "to infinity".
adventure	Sometimes used to refer to a sum of money.
adze	A tool, much like an axe, used for cutting or shaping large bits of wood.
ague	Illness involving fever, usually malaria.
allurement	Mysterious attractiveness.
ambuscade	Ambush; position from which to launch an ambush.
ancient	Flag. See also *antient*.
antic	Bizarre.
antient	Flag. Archaic form of *ensign*. See also *ancient*.
apace	Quickly.
application	Hard work, with full concentration.
arable	Suitable for growing crops.
arraign	Bring to account.
astern	At the rear end of a ship.
asunder	Apart.
athwart	To the side of.
baize	A type of coarse, woollen cloth.

barbarous	Primitive; uncivilized.
barque	A sailing ship.
barricade	A protective fence of upright wooden posts.
beseech	Beg.
bilges	The lowest internal area of a ship's structure.
blood	Used to suggest what we might call "a rush of blood to the head" – an act of impulse.
boatswain	The officer on a ship in charge of crew and equipment.
boltsprit	The large pole which sticks out at the front of a ship, to which the *foremast* is tethered.
bondage	Bound; being unable to escape.
boom	The crossbar on a mast, to which sails are attached.
bower	A pleasant spot under a tree; a summer house.
bows	The front end of a ship.
breastwork	A temporary defence.
broadside	The firing of cannons from one side of a ship. Also, the side of a boat or ship.
broadsword	A wide-bladed sword, intended for cutting rather than thrusting.
broiled	Cooked by direct exposure to heat.
bushel	A unit of volume: approximately 36.5 litres.
buskins	Knee-high boots.
calenture	Feverish delirium.
candour	Honesty.
carrion	Decaying flesh.
chequer work	Patchwork; a whole made up of many smaller and contrasting parts.
chimera	Fire-breathing monster.
circumvent	Avoid; outwit.

citron	A citrus fruit that resembles a lemon.
cogitations	Thoughts.
cognizance	Knowledge.
colliers	Ships used for carrying coal.
comely	Attractive; nice to look at.
commodiously	Comfortably; conveniently.
compass	Accomplish.
concurrence	Happening at the same time.
consequence	Future.
contrary (wind)	Wind blowing opposite to the direction of travel.
contrivance	A big effort, or use of skill. Also, a makeshift object.
counsel	Advice.
coup de grâce	The final, fatal blow or shot to a wounded person or animal.
covenant	An agreement; a legally binding contract.
crazy	Infirm.
credible	Believable.
crusados	Coins – approx. 20 crusados to the *moidore* by Crusoe's calculations.
cutlass	A short sword with a curved blade.
cut masts	Take down the masts and lie them on deck.
dainty	Delicacy.
dam	Mother of an animal.
declivity	A downward slope.
decree	An official command.
degeneracy	Existing in a state of immorality.
deliverance	Being set free; escape.
descried	Caught sight of.
design	Plan.
desolation	A state of severe loneliness or destruction.

despondency	A state of utter disinterest, low spirits and hopelessness.
destitute	Poor; lacking.
dextrous	Skilled.
dictates	Orders which must be obeyed.
diligence	Care; effort.
discomposed	Disturbed.
disconsolate	Unhappy.
dispatched	Left out; sent away.
disposition	Arrangement of one thing in relation to another. Also, the way things turn out.
distemper	Illness or disease.
divers	Several; varying types of.
diverting	Distracting; amusing.
dominions	Territory under someone's control.
dram	A small drink of spirits.
drawers	Underwear.
drills	Holes; wells.
ducats	A gold coin, used in most European currencies.
durst	Dared.
eddy	A circular movement of water – a whirlpool.
egress	Entrance. See also *regress*.
elopement	Escape.
endeavour	Try hard.
enmity	Hostility.
ensign	Flag.
equinox	The date – twice a year – when the day and night are the same length.
equipage	Equipment.
essayed	Attempted.
exhort	Strongly encourage.

expostulate	Express disapproval.
extant	In existence.
fain	Obliged. Also, rather; would have liked to.
felicity	Happiness.
Flanders	A region of the *Low Countries*.
Flanders lace	An intricate lace from *Flanders*.
fleet	Move.
flux	Diarrhoea, usually caused by dysentery (an intestinal infection).
forbear	Restrain an impulse to do something; refrain.
forecastle	The front end of the space below deck on a ship; often where the crew's living quarters are.
fore chains	Chains attached to the fore, or the front, of a ship.
foremast	The mast of a ship closest to the *bows*.
foremast man	A common sailor.
forsook	Left; abandoned.
fortification	Castle; fort.
founder	Fill with water and sink.
fowling	Shooting birds.
fowling pieces	Light guns used for shooting birds.
freighted	Laden with goods.
freshwater sailor	Someone used to sailing inland, not on the sea.
frigate	A light boat – fast, built for rowing. Also, a warship.
frog	The loop on a belt on which a sword can be hung.
furbish	Renovate; clean up.
furlong	Unit of length – about an eighth of a mile.
fusees	Muskets.
fustic	A tropical tree from America, from which dye is obtained.
garrison	A group of troops attached to a specific location.

generalissimo	The chief commander of the army.
girdle	Belt.
gout	A disease that affects the joints, producing arthritic symptoms. Often associated with drinking alcohol to excess.
grindstone	A round stone that is used to sharpen tools.
ground tackle	All the equipment used to fasten a ship to the ground.
gunner	The person in charge of weapons on the ship.
gybe	Move direction (in the case of an entire ship) or swing across (in the case of a sail or *boom*) due to the wind.
hale	Haul.
halter	A rope tied around the head or neck – used for tethering.
handmaids	Female servants.
hanger	A short sword, which is worn on a belt.
harrow	A heavy piece of metal equipment with "teeth", which is dragged over ploughed land.
hatchet	A small axe.
hawser	A thick rope used to moor a ship.
hod	An open, V-shaped container, usually on a pole, used by builders to transport materials.
hogshead	A large cask.
hold	The downstairs compartment of a boat in which cargo is stored.
hollow	To shout in order to get someone's attention.
homage	A public show of respect.
hooped	Bound with hoops, like a barrel.
hundredweight	A unit of weight, approximately fifty kilograms.
husbanded	Used economically, sparingly.

husbandry	Farming; the care of crops and animals.
idolaters	Worshippers of idols – figures considered to be fake gods.
impetuosity	The quickness and carelessness with which something is carried out.
importunities	Annoying and persistent demands or requests.
inclination	Tendency or desire to do something.
incommoded	Inconvenienced.
incongruous	Out of keeping with its surroundings.
indefatigable	Tireless.
indefeasibly	Unarguably.
Indians	Native Americans – a term which is no longer used.
indraught	Inward current.
industry	Hard work.
iniquity	Immoral behaviour.
injurious	Harmful.
inlet	A small arm of water.
Inquisition	The Spanish Inquisition tribunal run by the Catholic Church and famous for using torture to procure confessions.
intercede	Intervene on someone's behalf.
inured	Accustomed.
in years	Old.
iron crows	Crowbars.
juncture	Point in time.
l.	Pounds – equivalent to the modern £ symbol.
lamed	Made unable to walk.
league	Unit of length – about three miles.
lee shore	The shore lying downwind of a ship.
leewards	Downwind.

liberty	Freedom.
light	Descend; get off.
line	The equator.
loath	Reluctant.
Low Countries	An area now divided between present-day northern France, Belgium, Luxembourg and the Netherlands.
made shift	Made do.
magazine	Store.
mainsheet	The rope used to pull up or down the mainsail.
malefactor	Someone who commits a crime.
man-of-war	An armed sailing ship.
mate	Second in command on a ship.
meanders	Winding routes.
messmate	Someone with whom one shares a cabin.
mizzen	The front, shorter mast of the ship; the sail attached to this mast.
Mohammedan	Another word for Muslim – now considered offensive.
moidores	Portuguese gold coins – one coin was worth about twenty-seven shillings.
moiety	Share; part.
Moors	Muslims from north-west Africa.
Morisco	A *Moor* in Spain.
mortification	Embarrassment; shame.
mulatto	A person with one black and one white parent. Now considered offensive.
NB	Abbreviation of the Latin *Nota bene*: "mark well".
norward	Northward.
notary	Someone authorized to perform some legal duties – such as writing contracts.

oakum	Loose fibre made by untwisting old ropes.
officious	Overly enthusiastic in offering help.
omnipotent	All-powerful.
osiers	Willow trees that grow in wet habitats.
pale	Fence; boundary.
pantaloons	Baggy trousers, drawn in at the ankle.
Papist	See *popish*.
peck	A unit of volume – approximately nine litres.
pendants	A flag that tapers.
penitence	The act of feeling sorry, or apologizing, for doing wrong.
penthouse	A shelter with a sloping roof.
pernicious	Damaging; unhealthy.
perplexed	Confounded; puzzled.
prospective (glass)	Telescope.
physic	Drugs.
physical	Medicinal.
pickled	This refers to the pouring of salt or vinegar onto wounds after a flogging in order to inflict more pain.
pile	A heavy stake.
pinioned	Tied up.
pinnace	A small boat, with sails and oars, which is kept on a larger ship.
pipkin	A small earthenware pot or pan.
piragua	A canoe made from a single tree trunk – long and narrow.
popish	Roman Catholic.
poring	Studying.
powder chests	Improvised bombs: wooden boxes fixed to the deck of a ship, containing gunpowder,

stones, old nails, etc. – used against boarding enemies.

powder horn	A horn – cow, ox – used for storing gunpowder.
procuration	A document that gives someone the authority to act on someone else's behalf.
prodigious	Impressive; large.
prophetic	Accurately predicting the future.
prosperous	Rich.
prostrating	Lying on the ground, face down.
Providence	God or nature's protective care.
prudence	Shrewdness, cautiousness.
quart	A unit of volume – just over a litre in capacity.
quarter	Sometimes used to refer to the side of a ship.
rack	A type of distilled spirits.
regress	Exit. See also *egress*.
repined	Expressed or felt discontent.
reproach	Express disapproval or disappointment.
requital	The returning of a favour.
requited	See *requital*.
rials	Small, silver Spanish coins.
rid	Obsolete past-tense form of verb "ride".
roundhouse	The cabin on the deck of a sailing ship.
runlet	A small stream.
sabbath	A day of religious observance – for Christians, this refers to Sundays – when, traditionally, no work is done.
sagacious	Having keen judgement.
sallied	Charged.
sallows	Also known as pussy willows – low-growing, shrubby willows.
sawyer	Someone who saws timber for a living.

scarce	Barely.
screw jack	A device used for raising heavy objects – operated with a screw.
sea-room	Space (at sea) in which a boat can be manoeuvred easily.
seat	Country house; estate.
sedate	Calm, unhurried.
sequel	Something that takes place after an earlier event.
shipwright	Someone who crafts ships.
shoal	Shallow; sandbank.
shoulder-of-mutton sail	An almost-triangular sail.
similitude	Similarity.
skipper	Captain.
slugs	Bullets; long, round pieces of metal.
solitaire	Someone who lives away from civilization; a recluse.
spatterdash	Leggings worn over trousers to keep them clean – often used when horse riding.
splintered up	Having splints attached (to a limb), in order that it might heal.
spritsail	A small sail attached diagonally to the mast.
squab	A thick cushion.
squall	Sudden gust of wind; brief storm.
staved	Broken; smashed inwards.
steerage	The back of a ship, which historically housed the steering wheel and where the cheapest accommodation could be found.
stern	The very back of a ship.
strait	A narrow passage.
straitened	Inadequate; lacking.

subsistence	The act of supporting oneself – usually barely enough to survive.
succades	Preserved fruit – either candied or in syrup.
supercargo	The owner's representative onboard a ship – responsible for overseeing the cargo – and its sale.
swan shot	A large dose of gunpowder.
thither	Towards that place.
tided	Used the tide to carry a boat along its current.
topmast	The upper bit of mast, which carries the sails.
tractable	Easily controlled.
traffic	Dealings.
twist	Crotch.
veneration	Great respect for something.
verily	Certainly.
vicissitudes	Unwelcome changes in fortune.
victuals	Food.
vigilant	Attentive, unwavering.
vivacity	Liveliness.
voracious	Hungry; in need of much food.
waive	Postpone; refrain from using or doing something.
weigh	See *weigh anchor* – used to mean "leave".
weigh anchor	Raise the anchor.
withal	In addition.
without	Outside.
wrought	Made, with great physical effort.
yard	A long, thin length of wood, used to stretch a sail.
yardarm	The farthest reaches of the outside of a ship.
yearling	An animal that is a year old.
zenith	Most powerful; highest point.

OTHER TITLES IN OUR ALMA CLASSICS
ILLUSTRATED CHILDREN'S LIST

———————

The Little Prince, by Antoine de Saint-Exupéry

The Selfish Giant and Other Stories, by Oscar Wilde

Dracula, by Bram Stoker

The Hound of the Baskervilles, by Arthur Conan Doyle

The Adventures of Pipì the Pink Monkey, by Carlo Collodi

The Complete Peter Pan, by J.M. Barrie

Arsène Lupin vs Sherlock Holmes, by Maurice Leblanc

Robinson Crusoe, by Daniel Defoe

Treasure Island, by Robert Louis Stevenson

Belle and Sebastian, by Cécile Aubry

www.almaclassics.com

§ BARE-ARSED BANDITTI §

BARE–ARSED BANDITTI

THE MEN OF THE '45

MAGGIE CRAIG

MAINSTREAM
PUBLISHING

EDINBURGH AND LONDON

First published in Great Britain in 2009 by
MAINSTREAM PUBLISHING COMPANY
(EDINBURGH) LTD
7 Albany Street
Edinburgh EH1 3UG

ISBN 9781845967024

A catalogue record for this book is available
from the British Library

Typeset in Bembo

3 5 7 9 10 8 6 4 2

Penguin Random House is committed to a sustainable future for
our business, our readers and our planet. This book is made from
Forest Stewardship Council® certified paper.

MIX
Paper from
responsible sources
FSC® C018179

Printed and bound in Great Britain by Clays Ltd, St Ives plc

This one's with much love for Alexander, who wanted
a book about the men, and whose keen intelligence,
sense of humour and unique way of looking at the world
brings so much laughter and nonsense into all our lives.

ACKNOWLEDGEMENTS

I should like to thank the following institutions and individuals who have helped me in my research for this book and the sourcing of illustrations to accompany the text: the National Archives of Scotland at Register House, Edinburgh, in particular the very knowledgeable and helpful Patrick Watt and his colleagues in the Historical Search Room; the National Library of Scotland, in particular Rare Books and Manuscripts; Inverness Library; Aberdeenshire Libraries and Information Service; author and classical scholar David Wishart, who most kindly translated two Latin poems for me; Her Majesty Queen Elizabeth II for permission to quote from letters in the Cumberland Papers regarding Major James Lockhart; Elspeth Morrison of the Incorporation of Goldsmiths of the City of Edinburgh; Colonel Dick Mason, Curator, Royal Scots Regimental Museum, Edinburgh Castle; Iain Milne of the Royal College of Physicians of Edinburgh; Mike Craig and Caroline Craig, Photographic Unit, Aberdeen University Library; Eileen Murison, photographer, McManus Galleries and Museum, Dundee; Sarah Jeffcot of the National Galleries of Scotland; Laura Yeoman, Archivist, Group Archives, The Royal Bank of Scotland Group; and Kate Holyoak, Picture Library Assistant, the Royal Collection, St James's Palace, London.

I should also like to thank all at Mainstream, in particular Editorial Coordinator Graeme Blaikie, and for their meticulous editing and fantastic cover design respectively, Karyn Millar and Kate McLelland.

My sincere thanks go to author, colleague and friend Maggie Kingsley and her family – James F. Gray, Nancy and Christina Gray – for giving me inside information on how the Panners felt and still feel about the Battle of Prestonpans.

I'd like to thank all my writing friends for their quick wits, generosity of spirit and lots of laughs along the way.

Finally, I want to express my love and thanks to the wonderful Tamise Totterdell, who's always there when I need her, and just for being herself, which is quite something; and to Will, as usual, for everything he quietly does – especially this time. Fools to the left of us, jokers to the right.

CONTENTS

PREFACE

When I first published this book's companion volume, *Damn' Rebel Bitches: The Women of the '45*, I became used to men I met at talks and events taking a step back from me and asking nervously if what I had researched and written was 'a feminist book'. My answer to that question was the same then as it is now. It's a book about people. So is this one.

The Jacobite Rising of 1745 convulsed Scotland. While hostilities were raging many men and women simply wanted it all to be over. Many others, often with huge regret and after enormous soul-searching, saw armed conflict as the only way to achieve their political aims.

In *Damn' Rebel Bitches* – a book to which I gave a working title of *Not Flora MacDonald* – I wrote about the women who helped and supported the fighting men. With all due respect to Flora, I felt passionately that the contribution of so many other women had been ignored. They had been written out of history.

I went searching for them in libraries, archives and record offices the length and breadth of Britain and beyond. They were there all right, jumping out at me from original lists, letters, documents and contemporary newspaper reports. So were their men.

I did much research at the Public Record Office in London, then in its former home in Chancery Lane. It was charmingly Dickensian in style and atmosphere, with latter-day Bob Cratchits perched on high wooden stools peering over their specs at you to ensure you were treating the paper and parchment entrusted to you with due care.

It was in Chancery Lane that I read the transcript of the trial of Captain Andrew Wood of Glasgow, whose story is told in Chapter 30 of *Bare-Arsed Banditti: The Men of the '45*. He was interrogated beforehand, those questions and answers also recorded. Facing almost certain death on the gallows, he did nothing to try to save himself from that fate, obstinately refusing to cooperate with his captors. The one who questioned him noted several times that 'he refuses to answer further'.

Andrew Wood's comrade-in-arms, Captain Donald MacDonald, was asked during his interrogation to confirm his name. 'If you want to know my name,' the 25 year old replied, 'you may go ask my mother.' The heart-stopping defiance rang out at me across the centuries which separated us.

Yet men such as these have also been written out of history. If they are mentioned at all, they are depicted as gallant but misguided fools. In *Bare-Arsed Banditti* I have done my best to give them a voice, too. I hope they come across as real, living, breathing people who made choices and decisions which made sense to them in the context of their age and time.

The events and wider historical context of the '45 will be familiar to many readers. Those who are new to the subject might like to have some background.

Scotland and England waged war with one another for centuries. As an independent sovereign state, the ancient kingdom of Scotland always resisted England's attempts to conquer it. England found its northern neighbours troublesome both in their own right and because of Scotland's long-standing alliance with France, that country and England being equally long-standing rivals in an ongoing European power struggle.

More peaceful ways of resolving the conflict between Scotland and England were tried, for instance intermarriage between the royal houses of both countries. The resulting family relationships meant that when Elizabeth I of England died childless in 1603, the only possible successor was James VI of Scotland. He then also became James I of England, bringing the Scottish House of Stuart to the British throne and ushering in the Jacobean age. This term applies also to the style of the period in architecture, furniture, fashion and literature, and derives from *Jacobus,* Latin for James, the name of many of the Stuart kings.

James VI and I was succeeded by his son Charles I, whose arguments with Parliament led to civil war and his own execution. His son Charles II, restored to the throne in 1660 after the death of Oliver Cromwell, was a popular monarch. Father of several illegitimate children but no legal heirs, Charles II was succeeded by his brother, James.

King James VII and II was a devout Catholic, making him unpopular with many of his overwhelmingly Protestant subjects. Like his father, Charles I, he adhered to the doctrine of the divine right of kings, believing his position to be God-given. His reluctance to rule with Parliament as a constitutional monarch proved an even more insurmountable obstacle to his continuing to wear the British crown.

In 1688, in what became known to its supporters as the Glorious Revolution, James was deposed and forced to go into exile in Europe with his wife, Mary of Modena, and their young son, also James. The throne was offered to the deposed king's daughter Mary and her husband, the Protestant William of Orange. When they died without issue, Mary's sister, Anne, succeeded, ruling from 1702 to 1714. The last Stuart to wear the British crown married a Danish prince and endured 17 pregnancies. Many of these ended in miscarriage or stillbirth. None of her children survived her.

At this point Anne's younger half-brother – King James VIII and III to his supporters, and the Old Pretender to his opponents – might have been invited back. However, James could not bring himself to renounce his Catholic faith or his inherited belief in the divine right of kings. A German cousin, safely Protestant and willing to reign with Parliament, was offered the throne instead. The Elector of Hanover became George I and founder of what became today's House of Windsor.

There were several attempts made to win the throne back for the Stuarts, most significantly in 1715 and 1745. The Stuart Cause was given added impetus when, in 1707, during the reign of Queen Anne, the parliaments of England and Scotland united, putting an end to Scotland's status as an ancient and independent European country.

There was huge opposition to this move within Scotland, with rioting in the streets and impassioned speeches within the Scottish Parliament. However, Scotland's economy was in a bad way after the ill-fated Darien expedition, an attempt to found a Scottish colony in Central America, and some members of that Parliament saw the Union with England as the only way to secure Scotland's future prosperity.

Self-interest also played its part, with English bribes to other members of the Scottish Parliament ensuring they voted in favour of the Treaty of Union. On the day it came into force, the bells of St Giles', the High Kirk of Edinburgh, played a tune called 'Why am I so Sad on my Wedding Day?'

This mourning for the loss of nationhood was hugely significant in attracting men and women to what was now known as the Jacobite Cause. While some Scots did well out of Scotland becoming North Britain, as pro-Unionists were keen to call it, others felt themselves over-taxed, over-governed and under-represented. The Stuarts being the old Scottish royal house, there was also a deep-seated personal loyalty to them. This was especially so in the Highlands and, although by no means exclusively, among Episcopalians and Catholics.

The '15 ended inconclusively at the Battle of Sheriffmuir, leaving 'German Geordie' once more safe on his throne. However, discontent continued to simmer, boiling over most notably in Glasgow's Malt Tax riots and Edinburgh's Porteous Riot.

This discontent found a focus in the Jacobite Cause. In the 1740s, that Cause found a leader in Prince Charles Edward Stuart, the

Bonnie Prince Charlie of legend and song. My aim in writing this book has been to shine the spotlight on some of the lesser known but fascinating men who rallied to his Standard, playing their part in the dramatic events which unfolded in Scotland and England in 1745–6: the Year of the Prince.

Where they speak in their own words, I have, whenever possible, retained their eighteenth-century spelling, punctuation and frequent use of capital letters. This was correct at the time for nouns, as it still is today in the German language, but some people went a bit overboard, using capitals on other words, too, as the fancy took them. It can look wonderfully eccentric to modern eyes, and I think it gives a real flavour of the times. The only alteration I have made is to change the eighteenth-century *f* to a modern *s*. When it comes to names which can be spelled in more than one way, especially Highland names, I've done my best to be consistent. This is not always so easy when original documents, letters and even the owners of the names themselves sometimes moved between one version and the other.

I apologize to speakers of the 'language of the Garden of Eden' for not quoting the original Gaelic version of poems but only the English translations, albeit very fine ones.

In the hope of producing a flowing and readable narrative, I have chosen to use neither footnotes nor endnotes, a decision I also made when I wrote *Damn' Rebel Bitches*. My sources are cited within the text or are listed in my bibliography.

Throughout the book, I have alternated between 'Rebellion' and 'Rising', usually dependent on whether I am writing from the perspective of the Jacobites or their adversaries: and sometimes, as a proud daughter of Red Clydeside, I've used 'Rebellion' and 'Rebel' simply because I love the defiance inherent in the words.

The Rebellion of 1745 may have ended in failure. The spirit of the men who fought in it – and the women who stood beside them – lives on.

1

THE YEAR OF THE PRINCE: HIGH SUMMER AT HIGH BRIDGE

TWELVE MEN AND A PIPER

John Sweetenham was an English Redcoat officer '& a piece of an Ingenier', a captain in Guise's Regiment. On 14 August 1745, he was travelling from Ruthven Barracks near Kingussie to Fort William, his mission to inspect and repair the fortifications there. This was the first Government response to the news that Prince Charles Edward Stuart had landed in Scotland. Charles's mission was to reclaim his birthright, place the crown of Great Britain on his father's head and put the Stuart dynasty back on the throne.

Those charged with the task of stopping him were putting their faith in what they called the Chain, the string of forts garrisoned by the British Army which lay along the Great Glen: Fort William, Fort Augustus and Fort George. At that time, Fort George was in Inverness itself. The one we know today, which lies on the coast between Inverness and Nairn, was built after the '45 and as a direct consequence of it.

The hope was that Charles could be confined to the north-west Highlands. That strategy was unlikely to succeed without remedial work being done on the long-neglected forts which made up the

Chain. Captain Sweetenham was not, however, destined to be the engineer carrying out and supervising that work. In a succinct but evocative description, he was 'surpriz'd at an inn' by a party commanded by Donald MacDonell of Tirnadris.

Tirnadris and his men took Sweetenham's sword and made him their prisoner – and, with this act of overt rebellion, the '45 began. Two days later, Tirnadris was at it again. Following in Sweetenham's footsteps, two companies of the Royal Scots were marching from Fort Augustus to reinforce the garrison at Fort William. From the Jacobite point of view, this they could not be allowed to do.

At High Bridge, a mile or two south-west of modern-day Spean Bridge, the Redcoats were ambushed. This first skirmish of the '45 has become a classic tale of a handful of wily Highlanders defeating a much larger military force. Tirnadris had only a dozen men and a piper at his disposal and there were 60 Royal Scots.

Outnumbered five to one though they were, Donald MacDonell and his men leapt about from rock to rock, raining sniper fire down on the hapless Redcoats from every possible direction. As they darted through the trees above the Spean, they held their belted plaids out wide, which also helped give the impression that their numbers were much greater than they were.

The Royal Scots didn't stand a chance. Most of them were raw recruits recently raised in Ireland, where the regiment had been stationed. They were not used to the terrain of the Highlands nor the fighting techniques of the Highlanders. They panicked, turned and fled, MacDonell and his men in hot pursuit.

In a cross between a rout and a running battle, they chased them for seven or eight miles, all the way up the hill on which the Commando Memorial now stands and back to Loch Lochy. Two were killed and several, including Captain John Scott of Scotstarvet in Fife, were wounded.

At Glenfintaig, he and his fellow captain, James Thomson, gamely tried to rally their men, forming the classic hollow square. When, however, reinforcements arrived for the Highlanders in the shape of a party of Camerons and another led by Tirnadris's chief, MacDonald of Keppoch, Captain Scott realized the game was up and surrendered.

It was here that the Jacobites – not yet officially an army but clearly feeling themselves to be under starter's orders – began as they were to go on, by showing mercy to their defeated foes. Captain Scott was carried to Cameron of Lochiel's home at Achnacarry and treated more as an honoured guest than an enemy, his wounds dressed by Lady Lochiel.

Meanwhile, Captain Sweetenham was being taken west. On 19 August 1745, three days after the engagement at High Bridge, he witnessed the Raising of the Standard at Glenfinnan. He later reported how the clansmen cheered and threw their bonnets up into the air, so many of them they looked like a cloud.

The novelist D. K. Broster took inspiration from the true stories of Captains Sweetenham and Scott in the creation of her fictional Captain Keith Wyndham. His unlikely friendship with the Highland Jacobite Ewen Cameron of Ardroy, an imagined kinsman of Lochiel's, is told in *The Flight of the Heron*, the romantic tale par excellence of the Jacobite Rising of 1745.

Despite the cheers and those blue bonnets tossed high into the air, Charles Edward Stuart was taking a huge gamble when he raised his Standard at Glenfinnan. He had landed in Scotland with 1,800 swords 'such as are fit for the highlanders' and several cases of pistols but only a few companions, the romantically named Seven Men of Moidart. (Actually, there were more than seven, but that number obviously had a ring to it.)

Despite the magic number, romance was not enough, even for committed Jacobites. They wanted to know where the previously promised well-armed French troops were, believing that without them the Rising had little chance of succeeding. In a famous exchange, one of the first Scottish Jacobites to meet the Prince, Alexander MacDonald of Boisdale, told him to 'Go home, sir.' Charles Edward Stuart's reply has gone down in history. 'I am come home,' he said.

He gave Cameron of Lochiel an equally telling response when, dismayed by the lack of those French troops, the chief of the Camerons expressed his reluctance to commit himself and his clan to the enterprise. If that was how Lochiel felt, then he would have to stay at home and read of the fate of his Prince in the newspapers. Like many others in the tumultuous year which was to follow, Donald Cameron found himself unable to resist that plea.

Others did say no. The chiefs of the MacLeods and MacDonalds of Skye were among the most significant of those, their refusal a crushing disappointment for the Prince. It was not simply the extra soldiers they would have brought to the Jacobite Army which mattered but also the influence the decisions of such powerful men would have on others who were trying to decide which way to jump. The consequences of failure were well understood by everyone.

Captain Sweetenham was well treated by the Jacobites, one of whom described him as 'the most polite among the few English officers who were at all sociable'. They released him two days after Glenfinnan on his parole of honour not to fight them or contribute in any way to the measures being taken against them, this restriction to apply for a year and a day. Not all the Redcoat officers who gave such an undertaking during the '45 kept their promise. Sweetenham did.

What the Jacobites kept was his sword, saddle and horse. Captain Scott's fine gelding had also been one of the first spoils of war. Although the Prince gave orders that Sweetenham was to be given two horses in exchange for his – it, too, must have been a handsome steed – this was forgotten about. Presumably the English officer decided not to contest the issue, preferring while the going was good to get the hell out of Dodge.

On his long walk back to Ruthven Barracks, he met several parties of well-armed Highlanders on their way to join the newly raised Jacobite Amy. He estimated he passed about 100 men in all. He spoke with several of them, so he must have had a safe conduct from his erstwhile captors to compensate for his now highly politically incorrect vivid scarlet coat.

Those erstwhile captors were not far behind him, although he was well away from Ruthven by the time they got there on 30 August 1745, 11 days after the Raising of the Standard. This outpost of the British Army, perched on a steep-sided man-made grassy motte on the opposite side of the modern-day A9 from Kingussie, was being held for King George by Sergeant Terry Molloy of Lee's 55th Foot.

The sergeant had all of sixteen men to help him hold back the newly formed Jacobite Army, and four of them were invalids. To say that the London Government, their representatives in Edinburgh and the British Army's commanders in Scotland were woefully unprepared for the Jacobite emergency would be putting it mildly.

It was a full month after the Prince's arrival in Scotland, the day after Glenfinnan, before General Sir John Cope left Stirling to march north with a Government army. Six days later, he reached Dalwhinnie, 'where the great Road divides into two; that on the Right, leading to *Inverness*, and that on the Left, passing over a remarkable Mountain, call'd the Corriarrick, goes to *Fort-Augustus*'.

Cope and Captain Sweetenham passed one another on the road, meeting at Dalnacardoch, halfway between Blair Atholl and the Drumochter Pass. Sweetenham gave Cope valuable first-hand information, confirming the reality of the Rebellion and the determination of the Rebels. He reported that they had plenty of 'Firelocks, Broad-Swords, Pistols and Cutlasses', and that they were planning to head Cope and his men off at the pass: the Corrieyairack, that is. Confirmation of this came from Duncan Forbes of Culloden, Lord President of the Court of Session in Edinburgh and a supremely loyal supporter of the London Government, who was then at his home near Inverness. Cope immediately feared an ambush.

Not only was the route through the pass 'of so very sharp an Ascent, that the Road traverses the whole Breadth of the Hill seventeen times before it arrives at the Top ... the *Highlanders*, from their Knowledge of the Country, their natural Agility, and their Attachment to Ambushes and Skirmishes, would, in this Situation, have indulged their Genius, and would, doubtless, have proved most formidable Opponents'.

The general opted instead to lead his troops, depleted by desertions on the march north, to Inverness. In doing so, he left the road wide open for the Jacobites to march south to the Lowlands without having to fire a shot or draw a sword.

Delaying to make absolutely sure Cope was heading for Inverness, a 300-strong detachment of Jacobites on the hunt for arms and supplies called past Ruthven Barracks. In a conversation shouted over the parapet, they suggested to Sergeant Molloy that he surrender the little fortress to them.

Molloy was one of the many Irishmen in the British Army. He was, however, no raw recruit. The Jacobites informed him that if he put up no resistance they would allow him and his men to leave with their 'bag and baggage'. He told them he was 'too old a Soldier to surrender a Garrison of such strength, without bloody noses'.

The response to that was a threat to storm the barracks and hang him and every man in his garrison. Molloy told them to come on if they were hard enough – which they did. Unfortunately, there was not a ladder to be found anywhere nearby which would enable them to scale this complex of high-walled buildings set, as Colonel John O'Sullivan of the Prince's army put it, 'upon a sugre loaf'.

An attempt to burn their way in using an empty barrel 'prepared with combustible matters' also failed, Molloy employing the obvious method to put paid to that. On his parapet some way above, he simply poured water on it and extinguished the flames. This comic opera turned to tragedy when shots were exchanged and the Jacobites took their first casualties of the war. Three men were killed and four wounded.

Molloy lost one man. As he wrote to Sir John Cope the next day, this soldier was 'shot through the Head, by foolishly holding his Head too high over the Parapet, contrary to Orders'. So now we know why it's a bad idea to stick your head above the parapet – although some of us keep doing it, all the same.

Colonel O'Sullivan, one of the Seven Men of Moidart, ordered the withdrawal, regretting the attack on the barracks had ever been attempted. Nevertheless, it had, as blood had now been spilled on both sides. The deadly game had begun.

John William O'Sullivan was in his mid-forties in 1745. An Irishman who had sold his family's ancestral acres in Munster because the law would not allow him to keep them unless he renounced his Catholic faith, he was originally destined for the priesthood. Realizing he was more suited to soldiering, he saw action with the French Army in Corsica, Italy and Germany well before he became Adjutant General of the Jacobite Army.

A good organizer, O'Sullivan was dismayed in the days after Glenfinnan by how unwilling the Highlanders were to be corralled into companies along the military lines he thought necessary to form an efficient fighting force. In his later report to Prince Charles's father, James, he always refers to himself in the third person and shortens his name to Sullivan.

The spelling of the eighteenth century could be diabolically and hilariously bad. When it came to the mangling of the English language, O'Sullivan too was no slouch:

> The Prince staid at Glenfeenen to deliver armes & amunition to the men, to give time to Clenranold to raise all his men & to give some form to 'em, wch they wanted, for all was confused. Sullivan, who was the only officer there, or the only one yt acted, was charged with this; his propossition was to form into compagnies, to set fifty men, a Captn, Lt & four sergents, to each Compagny, but yt cou'd not be followed, they must go by tribes; such a chife of a tribe had sixty men, another thirty, another twenty, more or lesse: they wou'd not mix nor seperat, & wou'd have double officers, yt is two Captns, & two Lts, to each Compagny, strong or weak. That was useless ...

Yet this army of tribal warriors, gathering its strength in one of the most remote parts of the British Isles, its ranks soon to be swelled by

Scotsmen and a few Englishmen from very different backgrounds, was to sweep south almost to London and come within a hair's breadth of tipping a king off his throne.

The stories of the men who played their part in this bold and dangerous adventure intertwine, as they must, with those of the men who were doing their damnedest to stop them. Some adversaries were more worthy than others.

2

THE PRINCE, THE PROVOST & THE GLASGOW SHOPKEEPERS' MILITIA: ANDREW COCHRANE

TWO THOUSAND BROADSWORDS, AT REASONABLE RATES

It was the high summer of 1745, and Provost Andrew Cochrane of Glasgow was a worried man. Rumours were flying that the young man known to his friends as Prince Charles Edward Stuart, and to his enemies as the Pretender's Son, had landed in the Highlands.

The Pretended Prince – as his opponents also contemptuously called him – was not going to march south on his own. Even without the thousands of French troops who featured so terrifyingly in the rumours, he would certainly be at the head of a body of ferocious Highlanders, all armed to the teeth and ready for action – and Glasgow was a sitting target.

A busy port full of warehouses, textile mills, workshops and wealthy merchants, the city had nailed its colours to the Hanoverian mast, its growing prosperity dependent on the political union with England. That union had given Glasgow access to England's colonies, opening up a mutually profitable trade with North America and the West Indies. By the 1770s, half of all the tobacco being exported from Virginia and North Carolina was being landed at quaysides on the Clyde.

Long before that, the tobacco ships were being sent back across the Atlantic laden with the goods the then colonists needed and which the city had geared itself up to manufacture. Sugar cane from the West Indies and the product from its subsequent refining also became hugely important to the economy of the west of Scotland.

Daniel Defoe, author of *Robinson Crusoe* and a Government spy, toured Scotland before, during and after the Union of 1707. Writing after the event, he said that 'the rabble of Glasgow made the most formidable attempt to prevent it, yet now they know better'. In other words, Glaswegians knew which side their bread was buttered. The Jacobite rallying cry of 'Prosperity to Scotland – and no Union!' cut very little ice here.

The Glasgow merchants, as Defoe also noted, traded with more than just the Americas. Their ships sailed to the Mediterranean, too, and far beyond it. The graceful vessel which rides the globe on top of the Merchants' House in the modern city's George Square is a model of the *Bonnie Nancy*. She belonged to Mr Glassford, one of the most famous of the Tobacco Lords and reluctant host to Bonnie Prince Charlie during the latter's unwelcome visit to Glasgow at the end of 1745. The real *Bonnie Nancy* went missing, presumed sunk, on a voyage to China.

When Provost Cochrane, Mr Glassford and their other friends prominent in the Virginia trade enjoyed their Glasgow punch – not, of course, to be confused with a Glasgow kiss – the toast before they drank their concoction of rum, water, sugar, lemons and limes was, 'The trade of Glasgow and the outward bound!'

When the '45 broke out, Glasgow's prosperity became a liability. Not only had the city's pro-Union stance made it, in Provost Cochrane's own words, 'obnoxious to the rebels', it was also filled with everything an advancing army needed: food, clothes, shoes and well-off citizens on whom taxes could be levied.

Glasgow was also completely undefended. Unlike Edinburgh,

it had no city wall. Nor, unlike both Edinburgh and Stirling, did it have a castle-fortress into which a garrison might withdraw and regroup. Nobody was more aware of these disadvantages than Andrew Cochrane.

He was in his early fifties in 1745, serving his third term in office. Born in Ayr in 1693, he had moved to Glasgow at the age of 30 and married Janet Murdoch. She was, in turn, a daughter, a sister and a wife to three successive Lord Provosts of Glasgow.

Cochrane had the opportunity to discuss his fears of a march on Glasgow by a Jacobite Army when the city's youthful Member of Parliament dined with him and other members of the Town Council at the end of July 1745, only a few days after Charles Edward Stuart had landed on the Scottish mainland.

Jack Campbell of Mamore was, after his father – Major General John Campbell of Mamore – heir to the Duke of Argyle. Travelling with his powerful relative to Inveraray, where the duke was building a fine new castle, Jack, just 22 years old at the time, wrote that the Glasgow magistrates 'were all extremely civil'. They were, he thought, also appreciative of how much the duke had done for them since Jack's election to serve as their MP the year before. His elevation to political office was not unconnected to his being the heir to one of the most powerful men in Scotland.

Andrew Cochrane's ability to remain civil to the lords and lairds who ran Scotland on behalf of the London Government was to be sorely tested over the months of turmoil which followed. So were his nerves.

Despite the city's lack of defences, Glasgow did have a military garrison. However, one of the first responses to the growing emergency – on 12 August 1745 – was to order those troops off to Stirling, a place of much greater strategic importance in military terms. A week later, a letter arrived from the Marquis of Tweeddale, then Secretary of State for Scotland. He was writing from London, where he spent much of his time, and he wanted to let Glasgow know:

that the Lords Justices had received intelligence that the
Pretender's son was already landed, or intending to land
in Scotland, and desiring them to exert there care and
vigilance on this occasion, and to use such precautions
as they judge necessary for preserving the publick peace
within there bounds.

At this point presumably Glasgow collectively rolled its eyes
heavenwards and asked to be told something it didn't know. Walking
a political tightrope as they were, Cochrane and the magistrates
sent a polite reply the same day telling the Secretary of State they
would do everything necessary 'for preserving the publick peace'
and assuring him that 'our inhabitants were all firmly attached to
his Majesty'.

It was to be the first of many such protestations of Glasgow's loyalty
to the House of Hanover. They pepper Cochrane's letters. Reading
them now, even allowing for the highly deferential tone the class
structure of the time obliged him to adopt, it can feel as though the
good provost was protesting a little too much.

As elsewhere in Lowland Scotland, there were those in Glasgow
who supported the Jacobites. Cochrane did his utmost to conceal this
and for entirely understandable reasons. If he was to protect Glasgow's
prosperity and its citizens' livelihoods, he had a difficult course to steer
through the rocks and reefs in which he found himself in 1745–6.

Given the source of Glasgow's wealth, he could not afford to sit
on the fence. Having then committed himself to what he had to
hope would be the winning side, he also had to assure its various
representatives that Glasgow's loyalty to the political status quo was
total. If the Rebellion ended in failure for the Jacobites, nobody was
in any doubt that there would be reprisals.

With the magistrates, Cochrane formed an emergency committee
of the 'principal inhabitants' of the city. The situation they faced was
daunting, the boulders in their path rolled there as often by their
friends as their enemies. The committee's first action was to take a

quick census, establishing there were around 500 able-bodied men who could form a citizens' militia.

Despite Glasgow's subsequent reputation for fighting men, the volunteers of the summer of 1745 were not used to wielding swords and guns. There weren't too many weapons available anyway, such as were to hand in a bad state of repair. A small detachment of dragoons under a Lieutenant Chisholm had remained in Glasgow. Now Chisholm told the provost he had orders to take himself and his men to Dumbarton Castle forthwith. On 4 September 1745, with the Jacobite Army having entered Perth the previous day, Cochrane wrote a frantic letter to General Guest, the Government military commander based at Edinburgh Castle, pleading for the dragoons to stay. He was particularly worried about John MacGregor of Glengyle, 'by whom we are threatened, or any stragling party'. Glengyle was the colonel of a regiment in the Jacobite Army which included two of the infamous Rob Roy's sons, and stragglers were always considered dangerous, ill-disciplined and on the hunt for booty.

The answer which came back was that no soldiers could be spared to help defend Glasgow. Nor could any arms and ammunition be supplied for distribution to the citizens' militia. Lord Justice Clerk Andrew Fletcher wrote to Cochrane from Edinburgh on 10 September 1745, while the Jacobite Army was still at Perth. He admitted things were in a sorry state 'owing to our not taking the alarm soon enough, and forming a proper and timeous scheme for putting the nation in a posture of defence'. He tried to reassure Cochrane that the 'Highland host' was not so numerous as previously thought and some of them were not even armed. The trouble was, lots of towns were asking for help. He would, however, try to put Glasgow to the top of the list for 'firelocks and ammunition'.

The next day, the Lord Advocate, Robert Craigie, wrote to Cochrane in reply to a letter from the provost. He too offered words of comfort:

and I assure you I sincerely sympathize with the city of
Glasgow. That they should be under apprehensions that
the fruits of their industry, as well as their persons and
their families, may be exposed to the insults of a rabble of
Highlanders, I am sorry to use the expression, assembled
under the conduct of gentlemen of no fortunes, and, I
think, of no principles, as they act under the direction
of a Popish Pretender and his son, under the influence
of France and Rome.

This was very much the party line but of little practical help to
Cochrane. Adding insult to injury, the Lord Advocate went on to
advise the provost that the 'friends of the government' should be on
their guard:

in this view, the inhabitants of this place are associating
themselves under the direction of the Magistrates to
defend the rebels, I hope you'll forgive me in suggesting
that its the proper course for Glasgow to follow.

This must have infuriated Cochrane, whose fellow citizens had been
getting themselves organized to do exactly that for the previous month.
Still offering soothing words, Robert Craigie wrote that he thought
many of the estimated 1,800 Highlanders at Perth were poorly armed
and 'either very old or young'.

So that's all right, then. Although an army of nearly 2,000
occupying Perth still sounds pretty alarming, however decrepit at one
end of the scale and not yet needing to shave at the other its soldiers
might have been. Lord Justice Clerk Andrew Fletcher did at least seem
embarrassed about the situation:

I am sorry I have no power to be usefull to Glasgow.
Those who differ from me, I am bound to believe they
act according to the best of their judgment. I pray God
may avert the evils we are threatened with. I would not

have you to permitt copies of my letter, or show it to
any but a few.

Despite being part of the Hanoverian establishment himself, clearly
Fletcher didn't want to be seen to be critical of it, either. At around
the very time he was assuring Andrew Cochrane that he was his most
obedient and humble servant, on the afternoon of 14 September 1745,
two officers of the Jacobite Army rode into Glasgow. They had a letter
to deliver and it was signed 'Charles P. R.'

> I need not inform you of my being come hither nor of
> my view in coming. That is already sufficiently known;
> All those who love their country and the true interest of
> Britain ought to wish for my success and do what they
> can to promote it. It would be a needless repetition to tell
> you that all the priviledges of your Town are included in
> my Declaration, And what I have promised I will never
> Depart from. I hope this is your way of thinking And
> therefore Expect your Compliance with my Demands.
> A Sum of money besides what is due to the
> Government not exceeding fifteen thousand pounds
> Sterling and whatever arms can be found in your City is
> at present what I require. The terms offered you are very
> reasonable and what I promise to make good I chuse to
> make these demands, but if not comply'd with I shall
> take other measures; and you must be answerable for the
> consequences.

The threat is scarcely veiled, and that 'at present what I require' cannot
have done much for Andrew Cochrane's stress levels. He himself wrote
of 'infinite disorder and confusion' in Glasgow – in other words,
blind panic. When his committee of magistrates and principal citizens
made the decision to negotiate with the Jacobites, the bulk of whom
were now at Falkirk, he knew this was going to be seen by many on
the Government side as both cowardice and treason. We don't talk

to terrorists. He also knew that not negotiating might lead to the plundering and sacking of Glasgow he so feared. The provost took the difficult decision to send a deputation to Falkirk in the hope of opening those negotiations with the Jacobite high command.

At the same time, Cochrane did his level best to explain the town's decision to 'truckle to a pretended prince and rebels', once again forced to bend over backwards to affirm loyalty to the Government and the House of Hanover. The letters to and from the Lord Advocate, the Duke of Argyle and the Secretary of State for Scotland flew backwards and forwards with a speed and frequency one might envy today, all the more amazing in a country in such uproar as central Scotland was by this stage.

Although the deputation of magistrates turned back at Kilsyth, persuaded the Jacobite Army was not now heading for Glasgow, Cochrane remained to be convinced. Other reports led him to believe that the city was 'expecting every moment a visit from the Highlanders; unable to resist, and absolutely at there mercy'. Naturally, Glasgow would remain loyal to the Government 'whatever our fate or misfortunes may be'.

Presumably Cochrane gave three small cheers when the Lord Advocate at last sent a warrant from the king to 'our trusty and wellbeloved the Provost, Magistrates and Town council of our City of Glasgow'. It graciously permitted its 'good subjects in that part of our kingdom of Great Britain called Scotland' to 'raise, assemble and arm such men as they shall judge necessary'.

As for supplying some of those arms – well, Robert Craigie did have a warrant for this, to go to General Guest at Edinburgh Castle, but this was impracticable now. The Lord Advocate also thought it inadvisable to send this second warrant with his letter, in case it should be intercepted by the Jacobites. If they thought Glasgow had a decent arsenal, they would be much more likely to pay the city that dreaded visit.

Again, this was all less than useless to Cochrane, especially when he received a further demand from Charles Edward Stuart. It was sent from the Palace of Holyroodhouse, four days after the Jacobite victory over Government forces under Sir John Cope at the Battle of Prestonpans on 21 September 1745.

> Seeing it has pleased God to grant us a compleat victory over all our enemys in Scotland, and as the present expedition we are now engaged in does not permitt us to visit the town of Glasgow, we have thought proper to intimate to you of the Town Council and University, that, whereas the exigency of the times do not permitt us to leave the publick money as should be done in time of peace, we are obliged to have recourse to you for a loan of fifteen thousand pounds sterling, which we hereby oblige ourselves to pay back so soon as the nation shall be in a state of tranquillity.

Charles promised his goodwill and protection for Glasgow and her university if his demands were 'chearfully and readily comply'd with by Munday first'. Helpfully, he also wrote: 'And furthermore, we are willing, in part of this sum, to accept of two thousand broadswords, at reasonable rates.'

This remarkable missive was delivered by John Hay of Restalrig, one of Charles Edward Stuart's private secretaries, who rode into Glasgow with an escort. Although he was an abrasive man, he did listen to representations from a meeting attended by what Provost Cochrane called 'our whole inhabitants', who managed to reduce the demand to £5,500, mostly in money but partly in goods.

The provost's justification for coming up with this ransom was the threat of violence from the Rebel army, whose members 'consisting of many thousands and daily increasing, were within a day and a half's march of us'. As if that weren't enough, MacGregor of Glengyle was 'in the town and suburbs' with some of his clansmen.

Cochrane sent this justification to the Duke of Argyle after the Government defeat at Prestonpans, reaffirming Glasgow's continuing loyalty to King George. He followed it up with another letter one week later. Lamenting the defeat and the Rebels' occupation of Edinburgh, he didn't neglect to mention that 'His Majesty's friends are without arms'.

> There is an absolute interruption of business; our manufactures at a stand, for want of sales and cash to pay there servants, and an intire stop to payments; the rebels harassing the burrows, distressing the collectors of the publick revenues, and endeavouring forcibly to get all the money they can, without regard to the merchant's drawbacks or laws of the revenue.

In that 'harassing the burrows', it must be regretfully assumed that Cochrane meant the villages and communities on Glasgow's outskirts, not that even Scotland's rabbit population was in danger from the wicked Jacobites. Although, given that an army marches on its stomach, it probably was.

Less than a month later, the beleaguered provost was fielding demands coming at him from the other side. These were first made by Major General John Campbell of Mamore, young Jack's father, writing from Somerset House in London on 25 October 1745 to say he was being sent north to take military command of the west of Scotland and the Highlands. An army also marches on its feet:

> as I flatter myselfe that my good friends in Glasgow will in every shape assist me in the publick service, I take this opportunity of beging you will be so good as to inquire if in your town there are any Highland shoo-makers who can make broges. I shall want about one thousand pairs, to be made immediatly; and as soon as any tolerable quantety are gott ready, you will order the contractor to send them by parcels to Dumbarton castle, where they will be secure till I shall have occasion for them. As I apprehend it to be one branch of your trade to the West Indies furnishing shoos, I need give

you no particular directions for contracting and fixing
a pattern, &c.

Andrew Cochrane must have been tempted to howl an exasperated
'Gie us a break, pal', and maybe he did. For public consumption, he
wrote to the Duke of Argyle to tell him how Glasgow had celebrated
King George's birthday on 30 October. This was despite another visit
from the Jacobites in the shape of a raiding party with drawn swords
who swept into town demanding horses and money, 'the Rebels
carrying matters with as high a hand as ever'.

Gallus Glasgow thumbed its nose at them, ringing its bells and lighting
its bonfires. The great and the good, including 'the Earl of Selkirk, several
persons of distinction, the principal inhabitants and gentlemen of the
colledge', proceeded to the town hall to drink numerous loyal toasts,
including one, of course, to the Duke of Argyle himself.

It's easy to imagine Cochrane, wig off and dressing gown on, asking
Janet over the breakfast table the next morning if she thought he had
laid it on thick enough. It would appear that he hadn't. In November
1745, he wrote to Patrick Crawford, a Member of Parliament in
London, bitterly expressing the view that Glasgow had suffered so
much because of its loyalty to the Government but was still getting
no thanks for it:

> our country robbed, plundered and harassed, by the rebel
> partys, and has got such a blow as it will not recover during
> my life. At same time we are represented as disaffected to
> his Majesty's government, when sure I am he has no such
> faithful subjects in his dominions as this place and adjacent
> countys. The rebels have been masters of Scotland for six
> weeks, yet not one man from this place has joined them,
> nor I believe six men from the neighbouring shires.

In denying that even one man from Glasgow had joined the Rebels,
the provost was being a little economical with the truth. He was still

having to be very careful about what he said. By this time, however, with Glasgow's trade and business at a standstill and 4,000 barrels of tobacco lying unloaded on the Clyde, he was finding it harder to conceal his anger and irritation, at least from someone he obviously trusted.

Patrick Crawford, not the MP for Glasgow but possibly a Glasgow man, seems to have been sounding out opinion about how the emergency had been dealt with. The provost was very clear in his own mind what the Government had done wrong, and it was almost everything.

The threat posed by the Jacobite Army hadn't been taken seriously enough, allowing them to quickly advance south. Sir John Cope had made the mistake of heading off too rapidly for the north instead of waiting at Stirling for more troops. The Rebellion could have been nipped in the bud if only the well-affected (those who were loyal to the Government as opposed to those who were disaffected to it) had been trusted with the arms and the authority to 'guard the passes' and defend their own towns and communities. He asked Crawford not to tell anyone his views:

> I desire not to be interested in any inquiry concerning
> my superiors' conduct. I have had great care and fatigue,
> and would not go through such another scene for a
> great deal of money: God grant it were all over.

The provost went on doggedly making requests for arms, asking if he should send carts to collect them. He finally got the weapons at the end of November, and the 500-strong Glasgow Militia and 150 men from Paisley were knocked into some kind of shape. They were promptly marched off to defend Stirling, leaving Glasgow in a worse situation than it had been before.

Demonstrating a fine grasp of dramatic timing, the Jacobite Army chose Christmas Day 1745 to march into Glasgow. For Andrew Cochrane, it was very far from being over. His nightmare was only just beginning.

3

SOLDIER, POET & JACOBITE SPY: JOHN ROY STUART

WHEN YOUNG CHARLES COMES OVER, THERE WILL BE BLOOD AND BLOWS

The '45 did not explode out of nowhere. It had been brewing for years – but for the 'Protestant Wind', we might have known it as the '44. In February and March of that year, two violent storms blew up in the English Channel and wreaked havoc on a fleet of French warships gathered off Dunkirk. Poised to invade England in support of the restoration of the Stuarts to the throne of Great Britain, the fearsome weather rendered them useless. The invasion was called off – or at least postponed.

Previous attempts to restore the Stuarts had all failed and by the mid-1740s lay 30 years in the past. For many, the Jacobite Cause was yesterday's news, the House of Hanover and the Union between Scotland and England too well established to think of upsetting an arrangement which seemed to work well enough. On the other hand, dedicated Jacobites took strength in 1720 from the birth of Charles Edward Stuart.

As Charles and his younger brother Henry grew to manhood, the hopes of those people grew along with them. The reports were encouraging. Charles was fit and handsome, brave and bold, more than willing to fulfil his destiny. As the abortive attempt of 1744 showed, the French might be persuaded to help him achieve it.

There were Jacobites in many parts of Britain. They included powerful and influential men such as the Duke of Beaufort in England and Sir Watkin Williams Wynn in Wales. Many in the north of England had strong Jacobite sympathies, most especially in Northumberland. Oxford was considered a nest of Jacobites, and how many covert supporters of the Stuarts there were in London was anyone's guess.

Old loyalties to the House of Stuart remained strong, particularly, of course, in Scotland. A few highly placed Scottish Jacobites formed themselves into the Association or Concert of Gentlemen. They included the Duke of Perth, Lord Lovat and Donald Cameron of Lochiel. John Murray of Broughton, who was to become Charles Edward Stuart's secretary during the '45 and subsequently a notorious traitor to the Jacobite Cause, carried their coded letters backwards and forwards to the Jacobite court in exile in Rome.

In the years of plotting which culminated in the '45, there were many other messengers travelling secretly between Rome, France, England and Scotland. One of them was a man called John Roy Stuart.

John Roy is the quintessential romantic Jacobite: a warrior poet, dashing lover and cultured Highland gentleman. Iain Ruadh Stiùbhart in his native Gaelic, he was born in 1700 at Knock of Kincardine in Badenoch, not far from present-day Coylumbridge. The towering Cairngorms were the backdrop to his childhood.

His family traced its descent from Alexander Stewart, the much-famed and much-feared Wolf of Badenoch, and through him claimed kinship with the Royal Stewarts. Accounts of John Roy's life and adventures spell his surname in both variations, although he seems always to have used *Stuart*.

Perhaps he did so to emphasize his connection with the royal house. Or perhaps it was simpler for a man who spent a large part of his life in France. It is traditionally said to have been Mary, Queen of Scots, who invented the *Stuart* spelling. Spending most of her childhood and young womanhood at the French court, she adapted the name to be more easily pronounced by speakers of a language which did not include the letter *w*.

As was typical of many Highland gentlemen of his period, John Roy Stuart's impressive family tree did not go hand in hand with having any money. This may be why he sought employment in the British Army, serving as a quartermaster with the Scots Greys. The experience was to stand him in good stead in 1745.

When, however, he was refused a commission in the Black Watch, he resigned. Whether his rejection had anything to do with his Jacobite sympathies or whether it helped strengthen them is not clear. It does seem to be at this point, though, when he was in his early to mid-thirties, that he became a Jacobite secret agent.

While still in the British Army and serving in Scotland, he got into trouble for a certain lack of enthusiasm in pursuing a suspected Jacobite and ended up in Inverness Gaol. Lord Lovat, the Old Fox, a master of the esoteric art of fence-sitting, was Sheriff of Inverness at the time – and somehow John Roy managed to escape from prison. The two men spent the next six weeks together at Lovat's home, Castle Downie.

That they had a whale of a time there emerged at Lovat's trial for treason in 1746, when his luck and ability to serve two masters at last ran out. Proving his Jacobite sympathies, evidence was given that during those six weeks he and John Roy Stuart 'diverted themselves composing "burlesque" verse, that when young Charles comes over, there will be blood and blows'. Sadly, none of these Gaelic ditties have survived.

In addition to being a Jacobite spy, a poet, a cultured man, the master of several languages and having a fine head of red hair into the bargain, John Roy seems to have been something of a dandy. The Jacobites of 1745 were well aware of how important it was to dress to impress, and John Roy knew better than anybody that a man clad in shabby clothes did not inspire confidence.

Already on a monthly allowance from the Stuart court in exile, in 1744 he wrote to James Edgar, secretary to the king in exile, asking for a few more livres to enable him to buy 'cloaths & a little linen'. He was ashamed to go out in what he was wearing, believing that 'a tolerable Clean apportment & Cloaths are necessar to keep one from falling into contempt'.

He must have got the money from somewhere to smarten up his appearance. 'Cross-examined at the bar of the House of Commons' during Lord Lovat's trial, cattle-drover John Gray of Rogart in Sutherland was asked if he had ever seen John Roy Stuart with the Rebels and what he had been wearing. It was a standard question, tartan and any other form of Highland dress being taken as the badge of a Jacobite.

Gray's reply is guaranteed to raise a smile in the modern reader: 'He goes always very gay. Sometimes he had Highland cloaths, and other times long cloaths on.' Long clothes were, of course, full-skirted frockcoats and greatcoats, as opposed to the shorter jackets worn over the kilt.

Intriguingly, the officer serving under the Duke of Cumberland who confirms the colour of John Roy's hair gives us another detail of his appearance, referring to 'that officer with the red hair and the little hand'. Whether this was a deformity he was born with or the result of a wound, it did not prevent him from being a formidable fighter.

In May 1745, he fought for the French against the British at the Battle of Fontenoy in what is now Belgium. Astonishingly, he paid a visit to the British camp the night before the battle, spending an hour or so with a friend from Strathspey. If they came face to face the next day, did they give one another a wry smile, step sideways and fight someone else?

Like other men involved in the '45, John Roy could have faced an even worse dilemma but seems to have been spared it. He had an illegitimate son called Charles Stewart, who fought in Lord Loudoun's Regiment. Father and son may therefore have lined up on opposite sides to one another at the Battle of Prestonpans, but there is no record of any encounter between them there.

A month after Fontenoy, John Roy sailed from Holland to Scotland, leaving behind in Boulogne in France his wife, Sarah Hall, and their young daughter, asking that the exiled king should arrange for them to be looked after should anything happen to him. He landed quietly in East Lothian: a more discreet return home than disembarking at Leith, the busy and bustling port for Edinburgh.

He joined the Prince at Blair Atholl at the end of August. Charles was then on his way south after the Raising of the Standard at Glenfinnan. He knew John Roy well from his visit to Rome and trusted him implicitly. No time was wasted in sending him north with letters for Lord Lovat at Castle Downie.

What John Roy had been up to in the two months before then is not known. It's logical to assume that he visited family and friends, of whom he had many. Since he brought back from Europe letters from prominent people pledging aid to the Jacobite Cause, it's also logical to assume that he was doing his silver-tongued best to persuade them, and anyone else who would listen to him, that they should declare their support for the Prince. The man had a way with words.

Sometimes that got him into trouble. The English translation of his 'Oran a' Bhranndaih', or 'Song to Brandy', paints a vivid picture:

> A thousand curses on the folly!
> Woe to him who would drink brandy!
> It fills us with wind and boastfulness
> And there will be much said of it.
> That's just what happened to me.
> In this glen I took to drinking.
> Temptation led me on
> And it struck me on the head.
>
> Woe to him who would go seeking
> Friendship, payment or pledge

Among some of the women of Kincardine!
I am ashamed to speak of them.
In particular, when I make love to them,
However sweet their words might be,
They would rather have a chance
To adjust my guts with a knife.

In 1746, after it all went wrong, John Roy Stuart was to pen some of the saddest verses imaginable. Mourning the deaths of his friends, the treachery and cruelty of his enemies, and the ravaging of the Highlands by an English army, they are melancholy laments for everything that has been lost.

In the summer of 1745, there was no thought of any of that. The time had come at last, and the endless waiting was over. The longed-for Stuart prince was here, and the pent-up frustrations of the past 30 years could explode into action.

Stepping out of the shadows of Jacobite espionage, John Roy Stuart was in the thick of it. With him were thousands of Scotsmen who were tired of rule from far-off London and the unfair taxes and restrictions which went with it – and they were all spoiling for a fight.

4

A SCHOLAR & A GENTLEMAN: ALEXANDER FORBES, LORD PITSLIGO

MARCH, GENTLEMEN

While Provost Cochrane in Glasgow was anxiously gathering scraps of information about the movements and intentions of Charles Edward Stuart and the Jacobite Army in the summer of 1745, a man of mature years at the other end of the country was doing much the same, albeit in a rather more eager frame of mind.

He was Alexander, 4th Lord Forbes of Pitsligo. His home at Pitsligo Castle, now an impressive ruin, stands on the hill above the old fishertown of Rosehearty in Buchan. It lies a few miles west of Fraserburgh on Scotland's north-east shoulder, where the Moray Firth gives way to the North Sea.

Alexander Forbes inherited his title and Pitsligo Castle – along with the estate's debts – at an early age, although, like many young Scotsmen, he completed his education in France, spending several years there. He became friends with François Fénelon, one of the greatest thinkers of his age. Fénelon advocated a mystical Christianity that appealed strongly to Alexander Forbes, the study and discussion of religion and philosophy to become a lifelong passion.

The French cleric also believed Christians should not shut themselves away from the world but had a duty to be involved in it. This philosophy took a liberal approach to education and politics, and believed in criticizing the state when it acted oppressively towards its citizens. It was a lesson Alexander Forbes learned well.

Returning home in 1700 at the age of 22, he immediately took his seat in the Scottish Parliament and was an active member of it. A boy of ten when the Stuarts were deposed from the British throne, he remained a committed Jacobite throughout his long life.

He was also a vehement opponent of Scotland's political union with England. In 1706, during the dying days of the old Scottish Parliament, he spoke out strongly against the proposal. When the majority of his fellow Members of Parliament chose – many persuaded by English bribes – to vote an independent Scotland out of existence, Alexander Forbes, not yet 30 years old, retired to Buchan.

He did not, however, retire from life. Burdened with debt though his estate was, the young Lord Pitsligo quickly won the affection of his tenants through his care and consideration for them. Although he was deeply spiritual, his Christianity was also of a very practical bent, and he hated unfairness and unkindness with a passion. Some described him as a saint. He would have laughed at that, being a convivial man who enjoyed good food, good wine and good conversation. He was an early supporter of education for girls and counted many women among his friends and numerous correspondents, both at home and across Europe.

His peaceful and sociable life at Pitsligo Castle with his first wife, Rebecca Norton, and their son, John, the Master of Pitsligo, was brutally shattered in 1715, when Charles Edward Stuart's father – James VIII to his friends, the Old Pretender to his enemies – landed at Peterhead, down the coast from Fraserburgh.

Following the Jacobite Standard raised by his cousin, the Earl of Mar, Lord Pitsligo, by now in his late thirties, picked up his sword, mounted his horse and went out for the Cause, fighting at the inconclusive

Battle of Sheriffmuir. When the Rising of 1715 guttered out, he was forced, like many other Jacobites, to spend several years in exile in Europe. By about 1720, when things had calmed down, he was able to slip quietly home.

The middle years of his life were spent studying literature and religion. In 1730, he published a book of essays on moral and philosophical questions. It's a wide-ranging work that includes a discussion on why we find it funny when someone falls over: 'What shall we make of that readiness to laugh, when one slips a foot and tumbles over? We are even afraid he is hurt, and yet cannot refrain from laughing.'

In 1745, when the call to arms came again, he was 67 years old and not in robust health, being a chronic asthmatic. Nobody would have blamed him if he'd stayed at home and let younger men rally to the Standard. Yet his loyalty to the Stuart Cause was unswerving. 'Did you ever know me absent at the second day of a wedding?' he asked well-meaning friends who remonstrated with him. He'd been out in the '15; it was his duty to go out this time, too.

Always ready to laugh at himself, he was amused when the young son of a friend brought a stool to help him mount his horse when leaving the house. Smiling down at the boy, he said, 'My little fellow, this is the severest reproof I have yet met with, for presuming to go on such an expedition.'

Yet go he did. The two hundred 'gentleman and their servants' of Pitsligo's Horse provided one of the Jacobite Army's seven cavalry regiments. Lord Pitsligo's son, John, the Master of Pitsligo, did not ride with them. This may have been because he did not share his father's politics. Or, like many Scottish families at the time, they may have been hedging their bets.

After the failure of the '45 Rising, Lord Pitsligo was one of the many Jacobite leaders declared an attainted Rebel, stripped of his title and property, his estate forfeit to the crown. His son took legal action to try to win some of this back, instructing his lawyer so soon after the event it might be thought he was poised to do so.

If father and son did agree that only one of them should go out for the Prince, it might seem odd that John Forbes was happy to allow his father to put his life on the line rather than the other way around. Then again, maybe he was not at all happy about it; his father might have insisted this was how it had to be.

This makes sense in the context of Lord Pitsligo's strength and nobility of character, and his devotion to the Stuarts. In the context of the '45, it is also noticeable how many of those Jacobites who were prepared to stand up and be counted were at opposite ends of the age spectrum.

The commitment of those in their twenties might be attributed to youthful passion and idealism. Their seniors, such as Lord Pitsligo, Gordon of Glenbucket and others, might have felt they had spent too many years compromising their principles. This was their last chance to go out and fight for them.

The value of Alexander Forbes to the Prince in terms of moral authority was incalculable. When he and his regiment joined the Jacobite Army at Duddingston near Edinburgh at the beginning of October 1745, a contemporary observer said it was as though religion, virtue and justice had just ridden into the camp, all embodied in the slight figure of Lord Pitsligo.

His decision to come out for the Prince persuaded many other Scots to do likewise, particularly his friends and neighbours in the north-east. Angus supplied Lord and Lady Ogilvy and the Forfarshire Regiment. Aberdeenshire and Banffshire provided not only Pitsligo's Horse but also regiments under Gordon of Glenbucket, Lord Lewis Gordon, James Moir of Stoneywood, Francis Farquharson of Monaltrie and James Farquharson of Balmoral. Despite the name, John Roy Stuart's Edinburgh Regiment also included many men from Aberdeenshire and Banffshire. After a lifetime spent researching through contemporary letters and lists, Jacobite historians Alistair and Henrietta Tayler estimated that around 20 per cent of the Jacobite Army's fighting men came from the north-east of Scotland.

Old loyalties and old religion had a lot to do with this. Although the persecuted Catholic Church clung on tenaciously in a few isolated pockets of Upper Banffshire, the beleaguered Episcopalian Church had a much larger membership in the area. All over Scotland, it was not the Roman Catholics but these Protestant believers who were most closely intertwined with the Jacobites and the Stuart Cause.

Before Pitsligo's Horse left its assembly point in Aberdeen, Alexander Forbes, 4th Lord Pitsligo, took off his hat and raised his face for a moment to the sky. 'Lord,' he said, 'Thou knowest that our cause is just. March, gentlemen.'

All over Scotland in the late summer and early autumn of 1745, thousands of men were doing exactly that.

5

Johnnie Cope & the Barking Dogs of Tranent

For Shame, Gentlemen, behave like Britons!
For Shame, Gentlemen, don't let us be
beat by a Set of Banditti!

Condemned by a song: that's what happened to Johnnie Cope. The Battle of Prestonpans was barely over before the taunting, triumphant words were written:

> Cope sent a challenge frae Dunbar
> Saying, Charlie, meet ye an' ye daur:
> An' I'll learn ye the art o' war
> Gin ye'll meet me in the mornin'.

> When Charlie looked the letter upon
> He drew his sword the scabbard from:
> Come, follow me, my merry, merry men
> An' we'll meet Johnnie Cope in the mornin'.

> When Johnnie Cope he heard o' this
> He thocht tae himsel' that it wouldna be amiss,

For tae saddle his horse in readiness
Tae flee awa' in the mornin'.

When Johnnie Cope tae Dunbar came
They speired at him, 'Where's a' your men?'
'The de'il confound me gin I ken
For I left them a' in the mornin'.

Hey, Johnnie Cope, are ye waukin' yet?
Or are your drums a-beatin' yet?
If I were waukin', I wad wait
Tae gang tae the coals in the mornin'.

That's it, then: he was a bad commander, ill-prepared and taken by surprise. Worse still, he was a coward who saved his own skin, leaving his men in the lurch and to their fate. When a breathless Cope and his panting horse reached Dunbar, one smirking local remarked that he didna ken wha had won the battle but he kent fine wha had won the race.

Cope's bad press started early, so much so that after the emergency was over, a public enquiry was held into his conduct during it. He had already been found guilty at the court of public opinion, as the preface to the published report of the board of enquiry makes clear:

> From the Beginning of the Rebellion, and the first
> Motion of the King's Troops in *Scotland*, it was generally
> believed, that Sir *John Cope* had acted with less Vigilance
> than he ought to have done: and all the Advantages of
> the Rebels, previous to the Battle of *Preston-pans*, were,
> by the Publick, imputed to his Mismangement;

Examine the evidence, however, and it's not long before the word *scapegoat* springs to mind.

General Sir John Cope was a career soldier who found the time at certain periods in his life also to be a Member of Parliament. He actively sought high office in the British Army and achieved it. When the '45 broke out, he was commander-in-chief of King George II's forces in 'that part of Great Britain called Scotland'.

Duncan Forbes of Culloden was Lord President of the Court of Session in Edinburgh and the prime mover in Scotland of opposition to Charles Edward Stuart and the Jacobites. Forbes was the first to set the alarm bells ringing, firing off letters to everyone who needed to know about the rumours flying around the Highlands that the Prince had landed on the west coast. Many of the recipients of those letters dismissed the threat. Cope was one of the few who took it seriously.

The rumours were soon confirmed. On 13 August 1745, Cope received a letter from Alexander Campbell, the deputy governor of Fort William. Campbell was sorry to be able to assure the general that 'Part of the *French* Fleet, design'd for invading this Country, is arrived in *Moidart*' and that 'The Pretender's eldest Son is along with them, and has been a-shore a-shooting on the Hills.'

Cope was already making his preparations, having instructed the officers of the dragoons under his command to recall their regiments' horses from summer pasture and be ready for immediate action. He wrote to the commanders of the forts which made up the Chain, asking them to be vigilant and gather every piece of information they could on the Jacobite Army's movements.

It was Cope who realized the Rebellion might be nipped in the bud if Charles and his men could be kept on the wrong side of the Great Glen. Well aware of the importance of psychology in warfare, he believed, too, that the most effective way of stopping other clans and individuals that might be contemplating joining the Prince would be to present them with a resounding show of strength from the Government.

He knew this was not going to be easy. Many of the Government troops stationed in Scotland were untested in the field. There were not too many of them either, the experienced soldiers off fighting

Britain's wars on the Continent. Despite this, pinning his hopes on taking the war to the enemy, Cope marched into the Highlands – and came seriously unstuck.

He was leading his 1,500 dragoons and foot soldiers into bandit country, each and every step of man and horse taking them farther away from civilization. Even without a Jacobite Army heading towards them, this was hostile territory. So he took the sensible precaution of stationing his two companies of the Black Watch – then a young Highland regiment in the British Army – in the rear. That way they could keep an eye on the crests of the hills which rose on either side of the road and give warning of any imminent ambushes. It was not Cope's fault that most of these 200 men deserted before he reached Dalwhinnie.

A captain in Lord Loudoun's Regiment in the Government army, Ewan Macpherson of Cluny met Cope at Dalwhinnie and was ordered to return the next day with his company. As Lieutenant Colonel Whitefoord, with Cope on the journey north and one of his witnesses at the board of enquiry, rather plaintively put it: 'but he never came.' From the Redcoat point of view, Cluny had gone over to the Dark Side.

Feeding the expeditionary force once they had crossed the Highland line was a major problem. The general had done his best to prepare for this:

> I gave the utmost application to every one thing for bringing the troops from their respective quarters to Stirling, and for proving what was absolutely necessary for their march through the Highland: the ovens at Leith, Stirling and Perth, were kept at work day and night, Sunday not excepted, to provide Biscuit, which was no other way to be got. I contracted with proper persons for horses, to carry a small train of four field-pieces, and four cohorns, (the country horses being too small for that service) and with a butcher, to carry some cattle along with the army, to kill upon the march.

He needed bread as well as biscuit for his army. Knowing he would be lucky to find it once he left the towns of the Lowlands (and, intriguingly, finding it worthy of note that one of the bakers was Jewish), he set them to work on that too. 'Notwithstanding whereof, we were obliged to halt a whole day at Crieff, waiting for a hundred horse load of it, which was not quite ready when we marched from Stirling.'

Impatient though he was to get moving, Cope had to wait before leaving Edinburgh because he needed money with which 'to subsist the troops; I knew there was none to be got in the country we were to march into'. It was a fortnight before he received the necessary letters of credit from London which could be presented to the banks in Edinburgh. These came from the Marquis of Tweeddale, Secretary of State for Scotland, who helpfully also offered some advice:

> I have laid it before the Lords Justices, who entirely approve of your conduct . . . And their Lordships are of Opinion, that how soon you receive Information, that any Number of the Disaffected are gathered together, you should immediately attack them.
>
> A little Vigour shown in the Beginning, may prevent their coming to a Head . . . It is impossible at this Distance to give any particular Directions; your Judgment and Conduct will enable you, to make the best of the Circumstances that may occur.

Which all sounds remarkably like 'you're on your own, pal'. Cope must indeed have felt very much on his own when he met up with Captain Sweetenham on the road north and discovered that the delay in leaving Edinburgh had allowed the Jacobites to take control of the Corrieyairack Pass, barring his way to Fort Augustus.

Many of the Black Watch had by this time deserted and cantered off on mounts belonging to the British Army. Other horses had been rustled by the locals during the night, while their riders slept. There being 'no such thing as enclosures to keep them in', the sentries posted to guard them could do very little if a horse wandered off to graze and kept right on going.

With not enough horses to carry it, much of the precious bread had to be left by the road. Adding to Cope's woes, his hopes that the clans which supported the Government would join him on his march northwards had also been comprehensively dashed.

It's no wonder he and his senior officers decided at their council of war held at Dalwhinnie on 26 August that they should head north to the relative safety of Inverness. Turning around and going back the way they had come was not an option. They knew now, from Captain Sweetenham, that the Jacobites were armed, dangerous and on the march. The possibility of a party of them heading over the hills and ambushing Cope and his men before they reached Stirling could not be ruled out.

By the time Cope marched his men from Inverness to Aberdeen, the Jacobite Army had the upper hand. Well on its way south and thinking ahead, 'the Rebels had carried all the Boats on the Tay to the south side of that river.' So Cope shipped his men out of Aberdeen, although he had to endure yet another delay while they waited for a favourable wind.

On 17 September, the day the general arrived off Dunbar, a messenger came on-board his ship to tell him the Jacobites had taken Edinburgh earlier that morning. This they did by the simple expedient of walking in through the Netherbow Port when it was opened to allow a carriage to come out.

That Scotland's capital was now in the hands of the Rebels was a military disaster and a huge personal embarrassment for Cope. He'd been chasing them around Scotland for a month and had failed to even get in their way. Resolving to do so now, he chose the place where he would offer them battle with great care.

This was a flat plain between the Firth of Forth at Prestonpans and the rising ground to the south of it, on the ridge of which stood the mining village of Tranent, as it still does. In Cope's considered opinion, there was not 'in the whole of the ground between

Edinburgh and Dunbar, a better spot for both horse and foot to act upon'.

Although the Jacobites commanded the higher ground behind and to the west of Tranent, he considered that this advantage would be negated by the marsh which lay between them and his army. There was, he thought, no way they could approach him unseen and catch him unawares.

His choice of ground was giving the Prince's army a headache and not only because of the boggy ground. The area around Prestonpans and Tranent being one of the cradles of the Industrial Revolution, this was not a smooth and unblemished grassy field. There were open coal pits, the stone dykes which bounded farmland, and the Waggonway, one of the first railway tracks in the world. Long before the invention of the steam engine, horses pulled the trucks of coal along the iron rails. None of these obstacles was going to be easy to fight over.

On the other hand, this worked both ways, affording the Jacobites protection from Cope's cavalry. Land broken by these 'hollow roads, coal pits and enclosures' was no good for horses either. These difficulties led to much manoeuvring by both sides before they lined up to face one another in the early morning mist on Thursday, 21 September. At times it reads like an elaborate dance.

One of its passes and promenades involved the Jacobites occupying the kirkyard at Tranent and firing down on the Government army. Its gunners returned cannon fire, inflicting some casualties, and the Jacobites withdrew.

'About an hour before sunset', Cope spotted a large group of Jacobites marching down Falside Hill. Assuming an attack was imminent, he edged his men around so they weren't at right angles to their approaching enemies but facing them. Once again, a dancing image springs to mind. The Redcoats sound like a troupe of old-fashioned high-kicking chorus girls smoothly changing position – except, of course, that the soldiers' manoeuvre was carried out with deadly intent.

Now front-on to the enemy, they could let loose a full and

murderous volley of musket shot and cannon fire at the Jacobite Army. When they saw what the Government troops were up to, however, they once more withdrew.

The jockeying for position did not cease as night fell. Both armies sent out patrols which criss-crossed the area, each side trying to find out what the other was up to. Cope later recalled that 'two platoons were posted on our right, in the road that leads by Colonel Gardiner's house'.

This country road, which runs down from Birsley Brae, now crosses over the busy traffic lanes of the A1 and down into the new car park at Prestonpans railway station. Generations of Panners knew it as the 'Copie Stanes'. However, since modern-day Prestonpans decided the battle should be better commemorated – under the evocative slogan of 'Victory, Hope, Ambition' – it's now being referred to by its Sunday name of 'Johnnie Cope's Road'.

In none of the accounts of the Battle of Prestonpans, and the busy days before and after it, is much, if anything, recorded about what the locals were thinking, doing or feeling while all hell broke loose around them. In the case of the coal miners, the disturbances might have been going on above them, too. The popular view in Prestonpans and Tranent has always been that people kept their heads down and hoped and prayed it would soon be over.

Trying to let it all sweep over you cannot have been easy with all these patrols creeping through the September night. One group of Jacobites attracted the attention of some highly sensitive ears, as General Cope recalled at the board of enquiry:

> About nine of the Clock that Night, all the Dogs in the Village of *Tranent* began to bark with the utmost Fury, which, it was believed, was occasioned by the Motions of the Rebels. Upon which I visited some of the most advanced Guards and Centries, and found all very alert; but could see or hear nothing but the barking of the Dogs, which ceased about half an Hour past ten; in

which Time the Rebels had removed from the West to
the East Side of *Tranent*.

So the dogs of Tranent barked for a good 90 minutes – which cannot
have done much for anyone's nerves. Meanwhile, the Jacobite colonels
and captains were burning the midnight oil, wondering how they
might deal with the obstacle posed by the marshy ground lying
between them and the enemy. When a local man called Robert
Anderson offered to lead them safely through the bog by the paths
he knew because he often went wild-fowling there, they jumped at
the chance.

Setting off behind him at four o'clock on the morning of Thursday,
21 September, the Jacobite Army took about one hour to negotiate
the marsh. Colonel O'Sullivan was uneasy about that:

> for we cou'd not come to them but by two defiles
> between Morrasses and ponds, where two men cou'd
> hardly go together; if they had only fifty men at each of
> those passes, or let half of us passe, & fall upon us before
> we cou'd be formed, why all was over.

He needn't have worried. Despite the patrols, and although Cope and
his men 'lay upon our Arms all Night', the Government soldiers at
first thought the approaching Jacobites were nothing more than a
row of bushes, becoming visible as night slowly gave way to day. Then
those bushes raised their muskets and took aim.

It was the horses of the Government troops which suffered first,
shot in the head and neck. The dragoons who rode the horses – many
men and mounts alike new to the horror of battle – stared in terror
from the bleeding animals to the ferocity of what was now bearing
down on them out of the morning mist.

Tartan-clad warriors. Blood-curdling war-cries. Swinging, glinting
broadswords. And an even more vicious weapon.

Short of swords, Captain Malcolm MacGregor of the Jacobite Army had looked around for what was available locally and come up with scythes. Sharpened and lashed to poles seven or eight feet long, they were wielded to bloody and horrific effect.

The horses were now deliberately targeted. James Johnstone, a well-off young man from Edinburgh and one of the gentlemen volunteers in the Prince's army, later described how the Highlanders rushed towards the enemy:

> They had been frequently enjoined to aim at the noses of the horses with their swords, without minding the riders, as the natural movement of a horse, wounded in the face, is to wheel round, and a few horses wounded in that manner are sufficient to throw a whole squadron into such disorder that it is impossible afterwards to rally it. They followed this advice most implicitly, and the English cavalry were instantly thrown into confusion.
>
> Macgregor's company did great execution with their scythes. They cut the legs of the horses in two, and their riders through the middle of their bodies.

The Rebels kept on coming, causing ever more panic in the Government ranks on the receiving end of this horror. All sense even of self-preservation gone, many of the Redcoat foot soldiers came up against stone dykes in a human log-jam, and were shot there. As James Johnstone put it:

> The panic-terror of the English surpassed all imagination. They threw down their arms that they might run with more speed, thus depriving themselves by their fears of the only means of arresting the vengeance of the Highlanders. Of so many men in a condition, from their numbers, to preserve order in their retreat, not one thought of defending himself. Terror had taken entire possession of their minds. I saw a young Highlander, about fourteen years of age, scarcely formed, who was

presented to the Prince as a prodigy, having killed, it was said, fourteen of the enemy. The Prince asked him if this was true. 'I do not know,' replied he, 'if I killed them, but I brought fourteen soldiers to the ground with my sword.' Another Highlander brought ten soldiers to the Prince, whom he had made prisoners, driving them before him like a flock of sheep.

There is no sense of triumphalism in James Johnstone's description of what happened at Prestonpans, rather a shocked realization that this 'terrible carnage' was what war actually was, even if this was less like a battle than a massacre: 'The field of battle presented a spectacle of horror, being covered with heads, legs, arms and mutilated bodies: for the killed all fell by the sword.' And those gleaming, bloody scythes.

The man who had turned ploughshares into swords died in the battle. Yet even as Malcolm MacGregor lay bleeding on the ground, his body pierced 'through and through' by musket balls, he urged his men to fight on.

Horses whinnying in pain and fear, blood pouring down their long faces from the wounds they had sustained, men screaming in agony, the only thought in their heads to get away from flailing blades and flying bullets, it's hard to see how General Cope could have stemmed this tide of panic-stricken humanity. The evidence he gave to the board of enquiry is that he and his officers did their best:

> The Motion of the Rebels was so very rapid, that the whole Line was broken in a very few Minutes. The Pannick seiz'd the Foot also, and they ran away, notwithstanding all the Endeavours used by their Officers to prevent it. All possible Methods were taken to bring them back from the first Instant they began to run. I endeavour'd all I could to rally them, but to no Purpose. When they could not be brought to their Ground again, it was try'd to get them into a Body for

their own Safety; when that would not do, Endeavours were used to get them to load again in Hopes that they would then be brought to make a Stand; but that was likewise ineffectual. By this Time the Rebels were mixed with them. The Foot dispersed and shifted for themselves all over the Country.

A swift council of war came to the decision that the only thing for it was to retreat.

Johnnie Cope left his coach behind. It had been waiting for him close by the battlefield and contained some of his home comforts. Drinking chocolate being a rare treat in Scotland at this time, the Jacobites who triumphantly seized the general's coach tried to take the brown powder they found inside it as snuff.

What Cope also left behind on the battlefield was his reputation. Up until then, the threat posed by the Prince and his army had been seen as minor, a little local difficulty, easy to quash, not a problem, happening in distant North Britain, so who gave a damn? Not any more. The defeat of a British Army by a bunch of bare-arsed banditti sent out shock waves which ran all the way down to London.

As the preface to the published report of the enquiry put it: 'The Defeat at Preston-pans was attended by such a Train of Mischiefs . . .' Once the crisis was over, in that grand old British tradition, they looked around for someone to blame and thought they had found him in General Sir John Cope.

The board of enquiry was held at 'the Great Room at the Horse-Guards', their deliberations open to the public. This 'examination into the Conduct, Behaviour, and Proceedings' of Sir John Cope also called Colonel Peregrine Lascelles and Brigadier General Thomas Fowke, two of the commanders who served under Cope, to answer for their own conduct.

It began on Monday, 1 September 1746 and lasted for several days. There were five members and the board was chaired by Field Marshal George Wade. He was very well acquainted with the lie of the land that was being discussed. As General Wade, he had directed the great road-building programme which began in the 1720s with the aim of making it easier for Government forces to move quickly around the Highlands and thus more easily control them and their troublesome inhabitants.

'If you had seen these roads before they were made, you would lift up your hands and bless General Wade.' Among the first to bless him were the troublesome inhabitants. In a delicious and satisfying irony, the Jacobite Army found his roads extremely useful when it came to moving themselves and their equipment around.

The witnesses called included Captain Sweetenham, who told the board members what he had told General Cope about the strength of the Jacobites in terms of men and weapons. Lord President Duncan Forbes also gave evidence, confirming that he had warned Cope about the danger waiting for him should he try to lead his men through the Corrieyairack Pass.

David Bruce, who had been 'a voluntary Spectator in the Field of Battle, in which he arrived just at Day-Break, and kept in the Rear of the left of the King's troops till they were routed', gave evidence that he had seen 'no Misconduct or Misbehaviour in the General, or any of the Officers'. After the battle, in what may well be a masterpiece of understatement, David Bruce then simply 'went on to Edinburgh'.

Cope himself gave chapter and verse on the difficulties he had experienced which had led to his delay in heading north and consequent failure to intercept the Jacobite Army before it calmly walked down to the Lowlands. Other witnesses confirmed these difficulties, especially when it came to the problem of the bread to feed the troops.

Every aspect of what had happened on the march north, the return to Dunbar and at the Battle of Prestonpans was enquired into, Cope asked to justify every decision he had taken. This he comprehensively did. Deeply wounded by the allegations of incompetence, he left no stone unturned when it came to preparing his defence.

As well as the witnesses who spoke for him, he also brought with him reports of letters of support from officers who had served with him and under him. A dozen junior officers who had fought at Prestonpans – captains, lieutenants and cornets – spoke up in person for Cope, Lascelles and Fowke.

> They say, they saw Sir *John Cope* from their different Posts, ride along in the Front of the Line, just before the Attack began; giving Orders as he went along, speaking to the Men, and encouraging them: And after the Troops had broke, they saw him endeavouring to rally them again; and particularly Captain *Forester* says, He saw Sir *John* ride in among the Men when they were broke, and try to rally them: And Captain *Pointz* also says, that when the Foot began to break after the first Fire, Sir *John Cope* call'd out to them, *For Shame, Gentlemen, behave like Britons, give them another Fire, and you'll make them run.* And Lieutenant Greenwell also says, that after the Foot have given one Fire, they faced to the Right about, and Sir *John Cope* immediately rode up and called to them to halt, saying, *For Shame, Gentlemen, don't let us be beat by such a Set of Banditti!*

It's pretty convincing stuff. It certainly convinced the board of enquiry, whose members decided that Cope, Lascelles and Fowke had no case to answer, saying specifically of Cope that 'he used all possible Diligence and Expedition before, and in his March to Dalwhinny, considering the Difficulties and Disappointments he met with.' When it came to Prestonpans, the board's considered opinion was:

> That he did his Duty as an officer, both before, at, and after the Action. And that his Personal Behaviour was without Reproach.
>
> And that the Misfortune, on the Day of Action, was owing to the shameful Behaviour of the Private Men;

and not to any Misconduct or Misbehaviour of Sir *John Cope*, or any of the Officers under his Command.

So General Sir John Cope was completely exonerated, with not a stain or blemish on his character or professional integrity – but it's the Johnnie Cope of the song who's remembered.

6

SANDY THE STUDENT &
THE EDINBURGH VOLUNTEERS:
DR ALEXANDER CARLYLE

HE HAD ONLY FOUR BOTTLES OF BURGUNDY,
WHICH IF WE DID NOT ACCEPT OF, HE WOULD BE
OBLIGED TO GIVE TO THE HIGHLANDERS

Alexander Carlyle was a son of the manse. Following in his father's footsteps, he became minister of the same church, serving his parishioners at St Michael's kirk in Inveresk, right behind Musselburgh, for 55 years. He and his wife are buried to the left of the church's front door. A luminary of the Church of Scotland, he was so esteemed for his intellect and Old Testament-prophet good looks that he was nicknamed 'Jupiter' Carlyle.

In the summer of 1745, he was young Sandy Carlyle, 23 years old, impulsive, passionate and with a lively interest in the opposite sex. After studying at Edinburgh University, he spent a year at Glasgow. Like many a student before and since, he paid as much attention to his social life as to his studies, throwing himself into what he called 'college theatricals'.

He and his friends wanted to put on the tragedy of *Cato*, written by Joseph Addison earlier in the eighteenth century. The play was both popular and influential, and its central message of an individual standing up to the tyranny of the state in the cause of personal liberty found a huge resonance in what became the United States. The famous battle-cry which rang around St John's Church in Richmond, Virginia, in the run-up to the American War of Independence, of 'Give me liberty or give me death!' is said to have been inspired by Joseph Addison's play.

While Sandy Carlyle was at Glasgow University, he attended lectures by Professor Francis Hutcheson. The economist Adam Smith, who had been at Glasgow a few years before Carlyle, described this gifted professor, born in Ulster to a Scottish father, as 'the never to be forgotten Hutcheson'. He lectured not only to the students but to the people of Glasgow, throwing open the doors of his lecture theatre on Sunday evenings at six o'clock to anyone who cared to attend. Sandy Carlyle remembered that he used no notes, walking backwards and forwards as he spoke.

One of the fathers of the Scottish Enlightenment, Hutcheson believed in religious tolerance and political liberty, and that men and women were basically good, contradicting the prevalent religious view of humankind as miserable sinners. He also believed people should see themselves as citizens and not subjects of the state. If you lived under a tyrannical regime, you should not only be expected to rebel but consider it your duty to do so. These ideas, too, were to have a profound influence on the American revolutionaries.

Alexander Carlyle was a man of huge intellect. As young Sandy Carlyle, he and his friends were also interested in *Cato* for rather less elevated reasons than its noble message of freedom:

> McLean and I allotted the parts: I was to be Cato; he was Marcus; our friend Sellar, Juba; a Mr. Lesly was to do Lucius; an English student of the name of Seddon was to be Styphax; and Robin Bogle, Sempronius. Miss Campbell was our Marcia, and Miss Wood, Lucia; I have

forgot our Portius. We rehearsed it twice, but never acted it. Though we never acted our play, we attained one of our chief purposes, which was, to become more intimate with the ladies.

The plan being for him to go on to study at 'some foreign Protestant university', Sandy spent June and July of 1745 preaching as a probationer in Haddington, and in August went on holiday to Dumfriesshire. He was to stay with some friends from Glasgow at Moffat, a fashionable resort where those and such as those went to drink the whey from goat's milk, believing this to be good for their health. When he got there, he found the place in uproar at the news that Charles Edward Stuart had landed in the north, gathered together an army of Highlanders and was even now descending on the Lowlands. The enemy would soon be at the gates of Edinburgh.

Hurrying back home, Sandy enlisted with friends from Edinburgh University in a volunteer corps which was christened the College Company. On the very day he joined it, 14 September 1745, he had 'arms put into my hands'. How Provost Cochrane would have envied the student soldiers. Whether they knew what to do with their guns was another matter, although they did receive some rudimentary training.

Sandy Carlyle was not the only person to make the observation that two-thirds of the male population of Edinburgh was anti-Jacobite, while two-thirds of the female variety were for the Prince and his Cause. He also observed that some people, particularly Edinburgh's Provost Stewart and his friends, showed a distinct lack of enthusiasm for defending the city. The suspicion was rife that they were hoping the Jacobites would find a way in but without their overt help.

The raw recruits of the College Company, on the other hand, declared themselves happy to 'expose our lives in defence of the capital of Scotland, and the security of our country's laws and liberties'. On the morning of Sunday, 15 September, they were marched up to the Lawnmarket.

While some women wept at the sight of these fresh-faced young intellectuals ready and willing to do their bit, the Edinburgh mob expressed its derision in various ways. A group of ladies at a row of windows overlooking the street laughed and made fun of the volunteers. They drew back and hurriedly closed the windows when the students threatened to fire warning shots into the rooms – on a mere two or three hours' training, no wonder.

While the students were eating the bread, cheese, ale and brandy supplied by the friendlier local publicans, Sandy Carlyle was found by his 15-year-old brother William, who had been anxiously searching for him. He took William aside and 'endeavoured to abate his fears'. The Volunteers weren't going to be in any great danger, he told the boy, their march out of the city designed only to make the Highlanders delay their approach.

Unfortunately, Sandy then asked William to look after his money for him. William burst into tears, saying his brother really must be going into danger if he was willing to part with his cash. Sandy redoubled his efforts to comfort the boy, and the two brothers arranged a meeting place for nine o'clock that night.

Other people were worried about the College Company, too, a group of ministers addressing them with a plea that they should not march out to meet the Rebels. They were 'the flower of the youth of Edinburgh, and the hope of the next generation'. Their loss would be irreparable, and didn't they think they should stay inside the city which would otherwise be defenceless? That suggestion allowed youthful ardour an honourable method of withdrawal, and, after another hour or so milling about the Grassmarket, the Volunteers were marched back to the College.

That evening a few of them – 'twelve or thirteen of the most intimate friends' – had a late supper at Mrs Turnbull's, whose tavern stood next to the Tron church in the High Street. Spirits were high and fiery, proposals for marching off and offering their services to Sir John Cope as soon as he landed being put forward. Sandy Carlyle later wrote that it was difficult to put any counter-arguments without being damned as cowardly or a secret Jacobite, but he gathered courage from noticing that one or two other students weren't too enthusiastic about this mad proposal either.

The dozen or so young men then took their turn on nightwatch, guarding the Trinity Hospital in Leith Wynd, 'one of the weakest parts of the city'. This forerunner of Leith Walk began just outside the Netherbow Port, its Edinburgh end now lost under modern-day Jeffrey Street.

The students had a boring night. They had nothing to do but respond 'all's well' every half an hour, using a variation on MacDonell of Tirnadris's ploy at High Bridge in the hope that any approaching Jacobites would think Edinburgh was a lot better defended than it was.

At one o'clock, the little brigade was visited by Provost Stewart and his guard. To a man, the students were now convinced he actively wanted the city to fall into Jacobite hands, and they were thoroughly ashamed of him. 'Did you not see how pale the traitor looked, when he found us so vigilant?' asked one of Sandy Carlyle's friends after Stewart had left them to it. To which Sandy offered the practical reply that he thought it was just the light from the lantern that had made the provost look so pale.

The friend who made the comment was John Home. Born in Leith in 1722, the son of the town clerk, he too was to become a minister but is better known as a playwright, his most famous work being *Douglas*. This is the play which was so well received at its first performance that it famously prompted an enraptured member of the audience to shout out from the stalls, 'Whaur's your Willie Shakespeare noo?'

When the student volunteers came off duty the following morning, Sandy Carlyle returned to his lodgings and tried to get some sleep. It was too noisy outside, and he himself was too agitated, so he went out again at midday. It was Monday, 16 September, and it was to be a chaotic day for Edinburgh. The place was in uproar, arguments raging as to how to best defend the city, whether it should even be defended. If, as seemed likely, the Jacobites were going to take it anyway, why risk bloodshed in a futile attempt to save it?

The professional soldiers – two companies of dragoons – were little help. At about four o'clock that afternoon, they were seen hurrying away from Coltbridge, just on the city side of Corstorphine, towards Leith. On horseback, they clattered along what was then known as the Long Dykes and is now George Street in the New Town. This ignominious retreat swiftly became known as the Canter of Coltbridge.

With the professional soldiers having run away, the four companies of Volunteers once more rendezvoused in the Grassmarket. A free and frank exchange of views between two young men over what should be done grew heated. Hands went to weapons, each on the point of attacking the other, 'one with his musket and bayonet, and the other with his small sword', until their friends separated them. Tempers were running high.

Just then, a man on horseback rode past the Volunteers, calling out to them that the Highlanders were at the gates of the city and were 16,000 strong. The man 'did not stop to be examined, but rode off at the gallop'. At the same time, the provost was convening a public meeting whose mood was very much in favour of surrendering the city to Prince Charles and his army. The Volunteers were stood down. They took their weapons up to General Guest's garrison in the castle to prevent them from falling into the hands of the Jacobites.

Sandy and William Carlyle met up as they had previously arranged at a house near the Netherbow Port, but the gate was locked. It was eight o'clock at night before the brothers were able to squeeze through the large crowd assembled around it, some wanting in and some wanting out of the city. Then Sandy and William walked through Holyrood Park, where they met hardly anyone. There they chose to head for home along the coast, 'rather than the road through the whins', which was too 'dark and solitary' on a moonless night.

Walking slowly because they were both so tired, they eventually reached Lucky Vint's Courtyard – a tavern at the western end of Prestonpans – where they met a group of Government officers. After the Canter of Coltbridge, unconvinced that Leith was safe, these officers had moved further out.

Although Sandy assured them that Edinburgh was not yet in the hands of the Highlanders, the dragoons remained very panicky. As the Carlyle brothers headed through town towards their home at Inveresk, the soldiers began to move untidily and in a state of some confusion 'on the road that leads by the back of the gardens to Port Seaton, Aberlady and North Berwick, all the way by the shore'.

Scornful of their unreasoning fear, Sandy Carlyle told them the Highlanders had 'neither wings nor horses'. Nor were they invisible, able to suddenly appear out of nowhere in front of the dragoons. His robust common sense did not help one iota. When one of the dragoons guided his horse off to the side of the road so that it might find some grass to graze on, both man and animal fell into a coal shaft.

They fell with an enormous clatter, the noise robbing the dragoon's comrades of what little courage they had left. They bolted, in their haste dropping many of their weapons onto the road. The next morning, Sandy and a friend organized the gathering up and safe-keeping of these until they could be delivered to General Cope's army. He does not tell us whether the unfortunate dragoon and his horse made it back up out of the coal shaft; probably not, as the man's broadsword was later shown off by someone else as their booty from the battlefield.

At noon the next day, Tuesday, 17 September, Sandy Carlyle learned that Edinburgh had fallen to the Jacobites and that Cope was due to land at Dunbar later that afternoon or evening. He and a couple of friends resolved to head there to offer their services, delaying only for some dinner at the Carlyle home, the manse at Inveresk. They washed down their meal with a bowl of whisky punch: as you do.

While they were finishing it, a neighbour arrived. He invited the young men to join him for a 'small collation' at his house with his sister and himself. The would-be volunteers to Cope's army demurred. The afternoon was wearing on, and they had already eaten. The neighbour insisted. He had four bottles of burgundy. If they didn't help him drink the wine, he would have to give it to the Highlanders.

Since they obviously could not let that happen, Sandy and his friends repaired to the neighbour's house, where they ate apples, pears and biscuits, drank a bottle of claret to 'wash away the taste of the whisky punch' and then fell upon the 'excellent' burgundy. A mere one hour later, they considered themselves fit to take to the road. By this time it was five o'clock in the afternoon.

With a brief stop at Maggie Johnstone's pub, a mile or two to the north of Haddington, 'for some beer or porter to refresh us after our walk', they pressed on. At ten o'clock that evening, two of the party decided it might be a good idea to look for a bed for the night. Sandy and one of his friends went on to Dunbar, where Cope was setting up his camp. They were refused admittance.

It took them until two in the morning to find somewhere to sleep, waking up the occupants of the manse at Linton. Thinking they might be 'marauders from the camp', the minister kept them standing at his door for an hour before he could be persuaded to let them in. After only a couple of hours' sleep, they in their turn were abruptly roused from their slumbers by their friends who'd taken to their beds at ten o'clock the previous night. It sounds as though they were revoltingly bright-eyed and bushy-tailed.

At two o'clock that afternoon, Wednesday, 18 September, Sandy took his dinner with Government commander and family friend Colonel James Gardiner at his home, Bankton House at Prestonpans. The colonel's spirits were low, but the conversational shortfall was supplied by a young relative of his, Cornet Kerr, who teased Carlyle about his hunt for a bed the night before. He advised the civilian that an experienced soldier always took up the first half-decent quarters he found. Kerr thought the battle that they all knew could not be far away would be an assured victory – 'if God were on our side'.

Between then and that 'approaching event', Sandy met up with several of his comrades from the Edinburgh Volunteers, their ardour for offering their services to Cope undimmed. He had the chance to talk with a Redcoat officer and was astonished by the man's ignorance of 'the state of the country and of the character of the Highlanders'.

He also observed, with the pomposity of youth, that it seemed to him 'very imprudent to allow all the common people to converse with the soldiers on their march as they pleased, by which means their panic was kept up, and perhaps their principles corrupted'. As he put it, most of the common people in East Lothian and perhaps two-thirds of the gentry had 'no aversion to the family of Stuart'. If their religion could have been secured, they would have been very glad to see them on the throne again.

Later that day, around 25 of the student volunteers gathered together at an inn in Haddington. Their determination to throw themselves at the enemy was to be thwarted yet again when they received a message via a Captain Drummond that General Cope thought they would be more use to him if they reconnoitred the roads round about, going out in pairs. This they did, at eight in the evening and again at midnight. It was so quiet that Sandy Carlyle and his companion ended up having supper at Sandy's parents' house, with nothing to report.

By the time they got back to Haddington, all the beds were taken, and they had to sleep on benches and chairs in the kitchen. To their disgust, they later discovered that 'several Volunteers had single beds to themselves, a part of which we might have occupied'. It was quite usual at the time for men travelling together to share a bed at an inn.

Two of their fellow volunteers had rather more to worry about. Having been out on patrol all night, they were captured after daylight had broken by a party of Jacobite cavalry, who spotted them through an open window sitting in Crystal's Inn in Musselburgh enjoying a breakfast of white wine and oysters. It's hard not to see the College Company as a bunch of well-educated, well-bred, well-fed and well-lubricated young gentlemen having an awfully big adventure.

John Roy Stuart, the senior officer among the Jacobites who took the oyster-eaters prisoner, threatened to have them hanged. Hardened and experienced soldier though he was, this seems a tad out of character. Perhaps he too thought they were were well-off boys playing at soldiers and wanted to put the fear of God into them, sending them scurrying back home to the safety of their parents' houses.

Cope lined his men up later that day in a field whose crop of corn had been harvested only the night before and which was bare except for one solitary thorn tree. Sandy Carlyle spent most of that same day at the top of his father's church steeple in Inveresk, observing the movements of the Jacobite Army. He came down only to mount his horse and ride off to inform Colonel Gardiner and Cope's aide-de-camp of what he had seen.

When the fight which had been brewing for several nerve-jangling days finally erupted very early the following morning, Sandy Carlyle was asleep. Woken by the first cannon shot, he threw on his clothes, spoke hurriedly with his parents and headed for the field. By the time he got there, it was all over.

He estimated it could only have lasted ten to fifteen minutes. Lord Elcho, fighting on the Jacobite side, concurred. When he and Sandy stumbled upon one another, Elcho demanded to know where he could find a public house. This was probably because he was scouting out somewhere for the wounded to be taken rather than because he was desperate for a drink. The young student 'answered him meekly, not doubting but that, if I had displeased him with my tone, his reply would have been with a pistol bullet'.

Sandy then saw some Government soldiers running as fast as they could away from the field. 'Many had their coats turned as prisoners but were still trying to reach the town in hopes of escaping.' Many of these Redcoats voluntarily became turncoats, joining the Jacobite Army. Tradition has it that Alan Breck Stewart, immortalized by Robert Louis Stevenson in *Kidnapped*, was one of them.

By this stage, in the immediate aftermath of the battle, young Mr Carlyle seems to have been acting as tour guide, directing the Duke of Perth to the house which someone else in the Jacobite Army had designated the field hospital for wounded Government officers.

He was impressed by the duke's tone of 'victorious clemency' but highly critical of the tears and howling of the women camp followers. Crying over their wounded and dying men, their distress apparently 'suppressed manhood and created despondency'. Presumably they should have pulled themselves together, come to terms with their loss, drawn a line under their grief and stopped making such a terrible fuss.

Horrified by the bloodshed, Mr Carlyle senior was growing ever more worried about his elder son's safety. If the Rebels came to the manse and realized Sandy had been one of the pro-Government Edinburgh Volunteers, they might decide to take their revenge. With a farewell to Mrs Carlyle and the younger children, father and son rode out on horseback along the sands. At Port Seton, forced to come back up onto the road, they witnessed a Highlander shooting another man. Deeply shaken, they returned home.

To his credit, Sandy Carlyle then offered to help the surgeons treating the wounded Government officers, which soon had him out and about among the Jacobites, searching for a lost medicine chest. In the meantime, the Duke of Perth had ordered a guard to be assigned to the Carlyles. Whether this was to keep an eye on them or protect them is not entirely clear.

On the Sunday evening after the battle, a Jacobite officer by the name of Brydone, very young and very polite, managed to resist Mrs Carlyle's 'faint invitation to supper' but was persuaded to return for breakfast the following morning at nine o'clock. Mr Carlyle senior said prayers before they ate.

> We knelt down, when Brydone turning awkwardly, his broadsword swept off the table a china plate with a roll of butter on it. Prayer being ended, the good lady did not forget her plate, but, taking it up whole, she said, smiling, and with a curtsey, 'Captain Brydone, this is a good omen, and I trust our cause will be as safe in the end from your army as my plate has been from the sweep of your sword.' The young man bowed, and sat down to breakfast and ate heartily; but I afterwards thought that the bad success of his sword and my mother's application had made him thoughtful, as Highlanders are very superstitious.

Over the next couple of days, Sandy Carlyle tried to convince Brydone that the Rebellion had to end in failure. It may have worked. Brydone left the Jacobite Army shortly before the Battle of Falkirk the following January, and his name does not appear in any lists of prisoners.

Sandy Carlyle stayed at home for the next week and then, proceeding with his plans to complete his divinity studies in Holland, went to Edinburgh to buy some things he needed for his journey. The Prince had issued a proclamation to say he would pardon every member of the Edinburgh Volunteers who went to Holyroodhouse to 'pay their court to him'.

Sandy described Charles Edward Stuart as 'a good-looking man, of about five feet ten inches; his hair was dark red, and his eyes black. His features were regular, his visage long, much sunburnt and freckled, and his countenance thoughtful and melancholy.'

Sandy himself sailed from Newcastle to Rotterdam on Monday, 14 October. The following spring he returned home via Harwich, spending a few weeks in London on the way. He was still there in April when the news arrived of the defeat of the Jacobites at Culloden. With a new friend, writer Tobias Smollett, they were sitting in the British Coffee House in Charing Cross, a well-known meeting place for Scots in London, when the news came through. They walked home with their swords in their hands. The mob was out in force and 'London all over was in a perfect uproar of joy'.

Smollett warned Sandy Carlyle not to open his mouth. If the mob found out by his accent that he was a Scotsman, they might 'become insolent'.

In September 1745, it was Edinburgh that was in an uproar of joy. Out at Prestonpans, there was nothing but shock and grief.

7

HERO IN A RED COAT:
THE GALLANT COLONEL GARDINER

WE HAVE AN ETERNITY TO SPEND TOGETHER

If popular opinion dismissed Cope as a bungler, those who opposed the Jacobites found a hero in Colonel James Gardiner, whose estate at Bankton has now been swallowed up by Prestonpans. Born near Linlithgow and educated at the grammar school there, he was a career soldier. This was despite the best efforts of his mother and aunt, who had each sacrificed a husband to Britain's wars in Continental Europe waged under the leadership of the Duke of Marlborough. Mrs Gardiner had lost her eldest son, too, killed on his 16th birthday at the Siege of Namur in 1692.

Despite – or perhaps because of – the deaths of his father and brother, James Gardiner was determined to join the army. He showed early signs of a warlike spirit, fighting his first duel at the age of eight and bearing forever afterwards a scar on his right cheek to prove it. This story becomes more believable after learning that by the age of 14 he had been in the military for several years.

Five years later, when he was 19 years old, he was 'of a party of the forlorn hope' at the Battle of Ramillies, dispatched on a desperate bid to capture the churchyard there from the French. He was shot in the mouth, the bullet passing through his neck to come out to the left of his spine. Left for dead throughout a bitterly cold night, the next morning the young man found a French soldier standing over him with the point of his sword on his chest, ready to administer the *coup de grâce*. A Franciscan friar who was with the swordsman implored him to show mercy: 'Do not kill that poor child.'

James Gardiner was nursed back to health at a nearby convent. He spent several months there, and the sisters grew very fond of him, as he did of them, although he resisted their attempts to convince him he should convert to Catholicism in gratitude for his miraculous escape from death.

It was common at this time for Protestants to believe the worst of nuns and priests, who were frequently lampooned as licentious hypocrites and often featured in pornography. Strong in the Protestant faith though he later became, James Gardiner retained a lifelong respect for the women who had cared for him, often stating that everything he had seen while he had been inside the convent's walls had been conducted with 'the utmost decency and decorum'.

Much to the distress of his mother and aunt, at this stage in his life he himself was a stranger to those virtues and not much interested in religion of any variety. Notoriously foul-mouthed even for a soldier, he was by his own admission also far too fond of casual sexual encounters. He later spoke to a friend of 'that sin I was so strongly addicted to, that I thought nothing but shooting me through the head could have cured me of it'.

Being made aide-de-camp and master of the horse to the Earl of Stair when that gentleman was appointed British Ambassador to the French court in 1714 gave James Gardiner many opportunities to exercise his addiction. He spent much of his twenties in Paris, indulging himself to the full. Never much of a drinker, he was, however, always so sunny-tempered and pleasant that he earned himself the nickname of 'the Happy Rake'.

One evening in Paris in 1719, with an hour to kill before a rendezvous with his current lover, a married woman, Gardiner picked up a book his mother or aunt had 'slipped into his portmanteau' – presumably while he wasn't looking. As he read *The Christian Soldier, or Heaven Taken By Storm* by Thomas Watson, something very strange happened. Twenty years later he told the tale to his friend and biographer, the Reverend Philip Doddridge.

The author of several books and more than 50 hymns, including 'Oh God of Bethel' and the original version of 'Oh Happy Day', which was to become a huge gospel hit 250 years after it was first written, Doddridge described his friend's experience:

> He thought he saw an unusual blaze of light fall on the book while he was reading, which he at first imagined might happen by some accident in the candle. But, lifting up his eyes, he apprehended, to his extreme amazement, that there was before him, as it were suspended in the air, a visible representation of the Lord Jesus Christ upon the cross, surrounded on all sides with a glory, and was impressed as if a voice, or something equivalent to a voice, had come to him to this effect, (for he was not confident as to the very words) 'Oh, sinner! Did I suffer this for thee, and these are the returns?'

This being the eighteenth century and the Age of Reason, even Doddridge, the man of the cloth, felt bound to ask James Gardiner if he hadn't dreamt he had seen Christ. Gardiner was adamant that he had been awake. The vision didn't last long, but it changed his life, sending him off on a voyage of spiritual discovery and a determination to change his ways. He did not keep his assignation with the married woman, and the casual affairs stopped.

This story is only very slightly spoiled by Alexander Carlyle later pouring cold water on some of the details:

> Dr. Doddridge has marred this story, either through mistake, or through a desire to make Gardiner's conversion

more supernatural, for he says that his appointment was
at midnight, and introduces some sort of meteor or blaze
of light, that alarmed the new convert. But this was not
the case; for I have heard Gardiner tell the story at least
three or four times . . .

According to the version Sandy Carlyle got from the horse's mouth –
the colonel liked telling this story – the assignation was at midday, not
midnight. The lady's husband was either a surgeon or an apothecary
and had 'shown some sign of jealousy, and they chose a time of day
when he was necessarily employed abroad in his business'.

At whatever time of day Gardiner experienced his religious
conversion, his friends soon thought he had gone 'stark mad'. He
met their ridicule with good humour, a quality he retained after he
found religion. His Christian belief was a joyous one, his God one
of forgiveness, although he could display the irritating zeal of the
reformed sinner. Even the Reverend Doddridge remarked how his
friend could work religion into every conversation.

It's easy to visualize his junior officers stifling a groan as he bore
down on them with yet another jolly sermon on his lips. His mother,
too, may have smiled ruefully when her son advised her in a letter not
to entertain guests on a Sunday. His concern was that she couldn't be
sure all of them were Christians, whose conversation would give due
reverence to the Sabbath.

On the plus side, he always practised what he preached. In a
sometimes brutal age, he was notable for concerning himself with the
welfare of his officers, his men and the regiment's horses. He made
charitable donations to the poor whenever he could afford to and
was courteous to his fellow man and woman whatever station they
occupied in life. Nor did he set much store on the accumulation of
wealth, saying, 'I know the rich are only stewards for the poor, and
must give an account of every penny; therefore, the less I have, the
more easy will it be to give an account of it.'

He was an early advocate of the swear box, seeking to eradicate in his officers' speech, as he had done in his own, what Doddridge called 'that horrid language which is so peculiar a disgrace to our soldiery, and so absurdly common on such occasions of extreme danger'. While the Reverend's views might lead us to suspect that he himself had never been in a situation of extreme danger, Gardiner had. The money he raised by imposing a fine for every curse went into a fund to provide care and comfort for soldiers who were wounded or fell ill.

It's impossible not to warm to a man who said his wife's only real fault was 'that she valued and loved him more than he deserved'. She was Lady Frances Erskine, daughter of the Earl of Buchan, and she bore him thirteen children, eight of whom did not survive to adulthood. Each death was a tragedy, but the bereft parents took strength from the conviction so incomprehensible to those who cannot share it, accepting the loss of their children as the will of God. Religion occupied as important a place in Lady Frances's life as it did in her husband's.

He was a faithful correspondent whenever his military duties took him away from home. Some of his letters to 'my dearest Fany' can be read today in the National Archives of Scotland in Edinburgh. In one, he tells her that he has dined with Mrs Doddridge; in another he writes of hearing the Reverend Doddridge preach. Almost invariably, the colonel signed off to 'my dearest sweetest Jewel Fany' and sent 'my Love to my children and service to all friends'.

In the summer of 1745, James Gardiner was 57 years old and not in the best of health, the rigours of a military life beginning to take their toll. He remained in command of the 13th Dragoons, one of only two regiments stationed in Scotland at the outbreak of hostilities, and was outspoken in his condemnation of the inadequacy of Scotland's and Britain's defences. As he saw the perilous state of affairs, 'a few thousands might have a fair chance for marching from Edinburgh to London uncontrolled, and throw the whole Kingdom into an astonishment.'

This prediction, based on his knowledge of how many people in Scotland were dissatisfied with the Union with England and disaffected to the London Government, demonstrates that he remained as aware and astute as he always had been. Perhaps because of his failing health, his good humour was beginning to desert him, leaving him morose and gripped by forebodings of doom. He condemned the citizens of Edinburgh for 'spending their times in balls, assemblies, and other gay amusements':

> I am greatly surprised that the people of Edinburgh should be employed in such foolish diversions, when our situation is at present more melancholy than ever I saw it in my life. But there is one thing which I am very sure of, and that comforts me, viz., that it shall go well with the righteous, come what will.

He wrote those words at the end of July 1745, while at Scarborough in an effort to improve his health. On his return, the 13th Dragoons were called to Stirling and then ordered to Dunbar to meet General Cope.

When James Gardiner said his farewells at Stirling Castle to his wife and eldest daughter, Mrs Gardiner broke down, sobbing out her fear that she might be going to lose him. Her husband had invariably comforted her before by reminding her how Providence had always taken care of him. This time he told her not to fear a separation from him because 'We have an eternity to spend together.' Several people who talked with the colonel in the days before the battle recalled that, like his wife, Gardiner seemed to have a sense of foreboding, a premonition of his own death. Sandy Carlyle described him as being 'grave, but serene and resigned', the colonel's religious faith giving him the strength to meet his fate.

Considering his own bravery, Gardiner must have been horribly ashamed that the dragoons under his command had taken part in the infamous Canter of Coltbridge, leaving Edinburgh defenceless against the approaching Jacobites. Walking with Sandy Carlyle in the garden of the manse at Dunbar on Thursday, 19 September, two days before the Battle of Prestonpans, the colonel expressed himself with his customary forcefulness when the young student raised the subject:

> I said, that to be sure they had made a very hasty retreat, 'a foul flight,' said he, 'Sandie and they have not recovered from their panic, and I'll tell you in confidence that I have not above ten men in my regiment whom I am certain will follow me. But we must give them battle now, and God's will be done!'

James Gardiner spent the evening of Friday, 20 September trying to persuade Cope and other senior officers to immediately mount an attack on the enemy, rather than wait for the Jacobite Army to make the first move. He also recommended that the Government cannon be placed in the middle of the line, as far away from the horses as possible. Like too many of the men, they were untested in battle, and he feared the animals would panic at the sound of the big guns. Much to Gardiner's dismay, neither suggestion was taken up. Robert Douglas was a fellow student of Alexander Carlyle's and, like him, one of the pro-Government Edinburgh Volunteers:

> He observed Colonel Gardiner in discourse with several officers on the evening before the engagement, at which time, it was afterwards reported, he gave his advice to attack the rebels, and when it was overruled, he afterwards saw the colonel walk by himself in a very pensive manner.

Gardiner stayed out in the newly harvested cornfield near his house overnight, wrapping himself in his cloak and snatching a few hours' sleep. In the early hours of the morning, he told three of his servants to go home, keeping back only his faithful man-servant John Foster.

When the Jacobite Army attacked at daybreak, almost all of James Gardiner's dragoons turned and fled, only about 15 of them standing their ground. Citing as his authority John Foster's eyewitness account, Doddridge says Colonel Gardiner was shot twice but stayed on his horse, dismissing his injuries as flesh wounds.

When he saw a group of foot soldiers fighting on despite having lost their officer, he cried out, 'Those brave fellows will be cut to pieces for want of a commander,' and rode up to them, shouting, 'Fire on, my lads, and fear nothing.'

As he said the words, he was struck a powerful, swinging blow from a Highlander wielding a scythe. The long curving blade slashed a deep cut in his right arm; Gardiner dropped his sword and was dragged off his horse. Once on the ground, he was struck again, this time on the back of his head. In the chaos, confusion and gun smoke, John Foster could not tell whether the blow had come from a broadsword or a Lochaber-axe, both of which were being used by the Jacobites.

A Jacobite called John MacNaughton, quartermaster of the Perthshire Horse, was later accused at his trial in Carlisle of having struck the fatal blow, although he denied it. Another account attributes it to Samuel Cameron of Kilmallie in Lochaber. He accepted responsibility but maintained until the end of his days that he had acted in self-defence as Gardiner and his horse bore down on him. The animal survived to be ridden by Prince Charles when he entered Derby.

Lying mortally wounded on the ground, the colonel urged John Foster to 'Take care of *yourself*!' When Foster returned to the battlefield almost two hours later, James Gardiner had been robbed of his watch, outer clothes and boots but was still breathing. According to Doddridge, Foster lifted him into a cart and took him to the kirk at Tranent where he died in the minister's bed at eleven o'clock that morning.

Colonel O'Sullivan of the Prince's staff offers an alternative ending to the story. He says that Gardiner died on the mattress of his own bed, which his servants had brought out into the garden of Bankton House. Since it was being used as a field hospital for Jacobite officers, this story sounds as plausible as the other.

Wherever he breathed his last, Colonel Gardiner was buried in the kirk at Tranent on Tuesday, 24 September. Many attended the funeral despite the continued presence of the Jacobite Army in the neighbourhood. It was said that they, too, mourned his death.

The two gunshot wounds and the cuts to his head are not in doubt. General Cope mentions them in his evidence to the board of enquiry, stating he got the information not only from John Foster but also from the minister at Tranent and the surgeon who attended the colonel. Unwell as Gardiner already was, some have questioned how he could have been able to carry on after being shot. Perhaps the adrenalin was flowing along with the blood.

What is also in absolutely no doubt is his courage. James Gardiner went down fighting. The moment of his fall was immortalized by Sir Walter Scott in *Waverley* and captured by William Allan in his painting of the Battle of Prestonpans. The man who was a survivor of so many of Europe's battlefields was cut down no distance from his own front door.

He was killed close by the thorn tree which was the only thing growing in the harvested cornfield. For years afterwards, it was shown to visitors as the place where Colonel Gardiner was struck the fatal blow.

His home, Bankton House, has now been converted into flats. Ten miles south of Edinburgh, and sandwiched between the A1 and the railway line, its bright ochre harling makes it unmissable. His monument stands in front of it, very close to Prestonpans railway station.

A tall and imposing obelisk, it's a hero's memorial. Four magnificently doleful stone lions guard it. They pay eternal tribute to this gallant Scotsman: a husband, father and soldier who, till his dying breath, did his duty as he saw it to God and his country.

8

THE YEAR OF THE PRINCE:
TRIUMPHANT AUTUMN
AT HOLYROODHOUSE

THEY WERE REALLY VASTLY CIVIL

Charles Edward Stuart would not permit bonfires to be lit or church bells to be rung to mark the victory at Prestonpans. Those who had died or been horribly wounded there had been his father's subjects as much as the men who had fought under his own Standard. Nobody was to be seen exulting in their suffering. He had delayed before leaving the battlefield, visiting the injured on both sides and giving orders that the dead were to be given decent burial. Colonel O'Sullivan described what the Prince said immediately after the battle when urged to rest:

> They then propos'd him to refraish & repose himself, yt
> he had great need of it; 'no' says he, with a tender hart
> & in a most feeling way, 'I cant rest until I see my own
> poor men taken care of, & the other wounded too, for
> they are the Kings Subjets as well we, & it's none of their
> fault if they are led on blindly,' upon sch he immediately
> sent orders, to the neighboring villedges, upon peine of

military execution yt houses & every thing necessary shou'd be provided for the wounded & yt the inhabitants shou'd come with speads & other instruments, to bury the Dead. He spoak to the Chirurgens, first to dress the highlanders, & afterwards to neglect nothing for the others; he neigher wou'd eat or drink until he saw people set about this.

O'Sullivan was partisan, writing his account for the Prince's father and therefore keen to paint his young master in the best possible light, but plenty of other eyewitnesses confirm Charles's concern for the living and regret for the dead.

It was the shell-shocked locals who did the dirty work, of course. Did the sights and sounds and smells of that cornfield's second, bloody harvest of butchered men and horses haunt their dreams and give them waking nightmares forever afterwards?

For the next six weeks, the Prince divided his time between the Jacobite camp at Duddingston and the Palace of Holyroodhouse at the foot of Edinburgh's Royal Mile. When he first arrived there, he was ceremonially escorted into the home of his ancestors by James Hepburn of Keith, a man whose devotion to the Stuart Cause went back to the Rising of 1715.

Four days before Prestonpans, Charles's father had been proclaimed James VIII and III at the Mercat Cross, up the High Street from Holyroodhouse, close by St Giles' Cathedral and the old Parliament House. A huge crowd listened, watched and cheered. As if by magic, all those in Edinburgh who had been against the Jacobites seemed to have faded away.

However, one man who never made a secret of his politics was Duncan Forbes of Culloden. He was still at his Highland home near Inverness and would not be returning to Edinburgh anytime soon. He was, as ever, well informed, as his description of Edinburgh in September and October 1745 demonstrates:

All Jacobites, how prudent soever, became mad; all
doubtful people became Jacobites; and all bankrupts
became heroes and talked of nothing but hereditary
rights and victories; and what was more grievous to
men of gallantry, and if you will believe me, much more
mischievous to the public, all the fine ladies, except
one or two, became passionately fond of the young
Adventurer and used all their arts and industry for him
in the most intemperate manner.

Less than a week after he took up residence at Holyroodhouse, in a
magnificent piece of cheek, the Prince issued a warrant for Duncan
Forbes' arrest. From 'Charles, Prince of Wales, and Regent of Scotland, England, France, and Ireland, and the Dominions thereunto
belonging', it empowered James Fraser of Foyers to 'seize upon the
person of the above-named Duncan Forbes', apprehend him and 'to
carry him prisoner to us at Edinburgh, or where we shall happen to
be for the time'.

Meanwhile, in Edinburgh, the stunning success of the Jacobite
campaign so far was being celebrated. Balls were held at Holyroodhouse,
the Long Gallery glorious with men in tartan, velvet and lace, and
women in billowing silks and satins, tartan sashes and white roses.
Inspired by the white rosebushes at Fassefern, the home of Cameron
of Lochiel's brother, this had been adopted as the Jacobite badge. The
Prince did not dance, telling his officers he was happy to see them
enjoying themselves but that he had other things on his mind.

So did his officers, of course. Enjoyable in themselves, the dancing
and flirting were also an important part of Jacobite PR. They gave
receptions and organized balls wherever they were. However, more
practical measures also had to be taken. That 'where we shall happen
to be for the time' indicates that Edinburgh was not to be the Jacobites'
final destination. Whether they were to head south or not, supplies
were needed: weapons, food, clothes and – as always – shoes, money
to pay for the supplies and money to pay the men.

The Jacobite Army prided itself on paying for what it took, both because this was the honourable thing to do and because not doing so was a sure way to antagonize people: not a good move for a Prince hoping to win hearts and minds.

On the other hand, if antagonism towards him and the Jacobite Cause was already there, a heaven-sent opportunity presented itself to show the haughtier Whigs and friends of the Government who were the masters now. The cocky young Jacobite officers who came up against Lady Jane Nimmo at Red Braes Castle near Polwarth in the Scottish Borders tried it – but found themselves facing a formidable adversary.

Lady Jane's husband was the Collector of Excise in Edinburgh and had volunteered to serve with the Government forces. With him away as the Jacobites drew closer to the city, she retreated with her three young daughters and one female servant to the safety of her childhood home. Red Braes was the seat of her brother, the Earl of Marchmont, an MP who spent much of his time in London. When Red Braes turned out not to be so safe after all, Lady Jane kept her brother up to date in a series of letters.

On 30 September 1745, she told him she now knew she 'must expect a visit from the Highlanders 150 of them being sent to Duns to Levy Cess'. This was one of the Jacobites' neater tricks. They were not highwaymen demanding your money or your life; they were collecting taxes due to the lawful Government. Charles Edward Stuart was now the Prince Regent, ruling Scotland as the representative of his father, King James VIII.

Lady Jane was understandably worried by the imminent arrival of these armed tax collectors: 'as we have not heard how they have behaved in other places I know not what to expect.' She did know they would be looking for guns and horses, and also feared Red Braes' neighbours 'would be our greatest Enemys, as it happen'd at the Last Rebellion'. One of her major concerns was that the Jacobite soldiers might destroy Red Braes' painting of the late king. It was far too big for her to be able to hide it.

Despite her natural trepidation, Lady Jane was a woman of courage and character. She'd been brought up that way by her aunt, Lady Grisell Baillie, the estimable lady whose household account books paint a fascinating picture of domestic life in early eighteenth-century Scotland.

Lady Jane's letters to her brother are a mixture of reports of what was going on at Red Braes, requests to be remembered to his wife and children, and snippets of news she has been able to gather about their mutual friends and acquaintances who were fighting the Jacobites. There was, for instance, nothing definite about James Sandilands. She had heard he'd been taken prisoner by the Rebels but did not know whether or not he had been wounded.

The dreaded visit of the Jacobites to Red Braes came on Wednesday, 9 October 1745 when:

> after it was dark bounces in at the Door Some highland Gentlemen with 3 pistols each the first thing they did was to clap a Pistol to Laubrechts breast and demanded Horses and arms. John Hunter mean while rode off with all the Horses. My three daughters had Courage enough to step down Stairs and receive them, Six Gentlemen came up with the Girls after they had Placed Centinels at all the doors and Glengary had drawn up his men upon the Green, they search'd all the House and my Daughters carried the Lights before 'em and kept them as far from the King's Picture as Possible. However they were really vastly Civil and would not go into the Bedchambers.

In between taking Lord Marchmont's horses off to a safe hiding place, the useful John Hunter had 'provided Spirits from Duns for the Common Fellows', but he had nothing suitable for the officers. 'They were extremely Cold and Hungery So he was obliged to produce 6 Bottles of Your Lops. Canary with good will Lest they should have taken it all at once.'

Guided through the house by the Nimmo girls, Lieutenant Robert Grahame of Garvock and his party found 91 old firelocks. A Mr Carre – who, given the joys of Scottish pronunciation, may well have been a Mr Kerr – pronounced them not worth the effort of carrying away, after which the young officers repaired to the fire in the dining room. Despite Lady Jane's reference to Glengarry and his regiment, Robert Grahame was actually an officer in the Perthshire Squadron. Like all cavalry regiments, it had a good conceit of itself, as obviously did he.

For the next two hours, the unwelcome visitors sat round the fire with Jane Nimmo's daughters, eating bread, drinking Lord Marchmont's wine and laughing themselves silly at Johnnie Cope and his headlong flight from the field at Prestonpans.

Lady Jane disapproved of them making fun of Cope and referring to him in such a familiar way, but softened a little when they brought apples out of their pockets and presented them with a flourish to her girls. Just as the Jacobite raiding party arrived, she had received a letter telling her that her husband, the pro-Government volunteer, had 'fallen ill upon the road'.

'In too great distress to mind or care what they did,' she was proud of her daughters for how they coped. 'I believe the children killed them with courtesy,' she wrote.

Politeness all round, then. When Lieutenant Grahame later decided – after a word in his ear from one of those malicious neighbours – that Lady Jane had made a fool of him by hiding the horses, the civility slipped. Brusque letters were exchanged. The 91 firelocks might be old and fairly useless, but he was determined she would send them to him. She was equally determined she would not. She won.

Throughout the Jacobite occupation of Edinburgh, the Castle remained in Government hands under the command of General Guest. In retaliation for being blockaded, he had his gunners terrorize the people living in the Lawnmarket by firing a few cannonballs down the hill. One of them lodged in the gable end of a house at the foot of the modern esplanade and is still there to this day.

Alexander Carlyle and his friends had made sure the guns of the Edinburgh Volunteers had been taken back to the Castle before the Jacobite Army entered Edinburgh. The reserves of Edinburgh's banks had also been stored there for safe keeping, and the banks themselves had closed their doors.

Much of the money which was being collected – including what Provost Cochrane in Glasgow, gritting his teeth, had been forced to hand over after the visit from John Hay – was in Royal Bank of Scotland notes. The Bank of Scotland had been smart enough to withdraw as many of its notes from circulation as it could while the Jacobite Army was heading for Edinburgh.

Disappointingly, the Prince did not relish the thought of taking Scottish banknotes to London and having a stimulating fight over their being accepted as legal tender. He wanted coin, hard cash. His secretary, John Murray of Broughton, therefore called on John Campbell, the cashier of the Royal Bank of Scotland, demanding he exchange the notes for coin. If he did not supply this within 48 hours, 'the estates and effects of the directors and managers should be distressed for the same'.

Campbell said he could not do it. The coin was all in Edinburgh Castle. Well, go and ask for it, said Murray of Broughton. General Guest won't let us in, replied John Campbell. Besides which, the troops in the Castle were still lobbing cannonballs down the High Street.

For their part, the Camerons blockading the Castle were firing their muskets at anyone approaching it. Some of the people on the receiving end of these potshots were taking butter and eggs in for General Guest. This was in deference to his great age and delicate stomach. Although this kindness had been agreed by senior Jacobite officers, nobody seemed to have told the foot soldiers.

Understandably reluctant to be caught in the crossfire, John Campbell 'bespoke a pott of Coffee at Muirhead's' and discussed the situation with the directors of the Royal Bank. None of them wanted their property 'distressed'. This time, a letter to General Guest resulted in their request to enter the Castle being granted. They did so waving

a white flag all the way, as well they might. Hostilities did not cease
while they were in there, as John Campbell related in his diary:

> During our continuance in the Castle which was from
> about 9 'till near three a clock . . . one Watson a soldier
> was so courageous as to go down over the Castle wall
> upon a rope, fire upon the Gardner's house, kill some of
> the volunteers there, carried off a firelock or two from
> them, sett the house in fire, returned with these firelocks
> by his rope into the Castle, where he was received with
> loud huzzas for his valour.
>
> On his return the garrison was preparing for a sally,
> but as the men were a-drawing up we got liberty from
> General Guest to go out again and Captain Robert
> Mirry escorted us to the gate, where I again raised my
> white flagg, and with my friends returned to town in
> safety, landed at my house from whence we adjourned
> to dine at Mrs Clerks' vintner.

Before he ate, John Campbell exchanged the bags of gold coin for the
banknotes, the total sum handed over being £3,076. In his fascinating
introduction to the copy of the banker's diary published by the Royal
Bank of Scotland in 1995 to commemorate the 250th anniversary of
the '45, John Sibbald Gibson argues convincingly that it was this money
which financed the Jacobite invasion of England.

He further suggests that John Campbell was by no means reluctant to
help provide it. The Edinburgh banker was also a Highland gentleman.
In a pretty unequivocal demonstration of where his sympathies lay, he
chose, during the period of the tartan ban which followed the failure
of the Rising, to have himself painted in full Highland dress.

That's not all. In his portrait, John Campbell stands next to a bag
of coins and some paper money, an indication of his profession as a
banker. His political convictions as a Jacobite may be inferred not
only from his Highland dress but also from other objects depicted in
the painting. The tartan ban went hand-in-hand with a disarming of

the Highlands, the ownership of weapons becoming illegal. Yet John Campbell is armed with a dirk and a broadsword, and the butt of a Doune pistol and a musket are clearly visible on the table beside him.

It is very clear, too, where the sympathies of Charles Leslie, the editor and publisher of the *Edinburgh Evening Courant*, lay. While the Jacobites occupied Edinburgh, he had to walk down to Holyroodhouse to submit his copy for approval before it was printed, 'having,' as he sarcastically wrote, 'meritoriously incurred their Displeasure by some Paragraphs'.

Quietly seething, Leslie vented his wrath at this censorship by composing a neatly written memorandum in which he named Jacobite collaborators in Edinburgh. Chief amongst these was Provost Archibald Stewart.

Citing the housekeeper at Holyroodhouse as his back-up for the story, Leslie alleged that the provost had given orders for rooms to be got ready for the Young Pretender the day *before* the Jacobites took Edinburgh, when, in theory, nobody knew when or if they would succeed in their efforts. Leslie thought the 'Scandalous Surrender' of Scotland's capital also owed much to the make-up of the so-called meeting where it had been decided not to offer any resistance to the Jacobite Army.

The well-affected citizens being away trying to prevent Edinburgh's fall at the time the meeting was held, the people who had voted for surrender had been 'Smuglers, some Nonjurant Merchants, Common tradesmen and even Street Cadies, Chairmen and the lowest of Ale house keepers'.

Out in the streets, people of a higher social class – Leslie named George Gordon Junior of Gordonbank – had been observed and heard pushing 'the mean People to go and make a Noice'.

It seems likely that this is the same Charles Leslie who later vented his spleen by denouncing people to the English Attorney General, almost certainly the people he mentions in his memorandum. The Attorney General dismissed his evidence, writing that what he had received:

purports to be a List delivered by one Charles Leslie, and there is no evidence transmitted to us against one of the Persons contained in it, Except that of Mr Leslie himself, which from his own account in the List seems to be plain against them.

If the editor of the *Edinburgh Evening Courant* could – more or less – spell, another Edinburgh man implacably opposed to the Jacobites quite gloriously could not.

Patrick Crichton was a saddler and ironmonger in the Canongate, and Laird of Woodhouselee, just outside Edinburgh. *The Woodhouselee Manuscript* is his journal of what went on while the Jacobite Army occupied Scotland's capital.

Forced like Lady Jane Nimmo to admit that some of the 'highland banditti' were 'very civil', he thought others were complete 'hillskipers, scownderalls and poltrowns'. Crichton, too, believed that Provost Stewart was a traitor, and he reserved special venom for the wife of the Prince's secretary and long-time Jacobite plotter, John Murray of Broughton. Directly involved in requisitioning horses and raising money for the Jacobite Army, the beautiful Margaret Murray was the daughter of a good Whig, which only made it all the more disgusting that she had so far gone 'into the spirit of the gang'.

Yet perhaps the worst thing about this 'Polish Italian prince with the oddest crue Britain cowld produce', who had come 'all with plaids, bagpips and bairbuttocks', was that they set 'caterpillars' to guard the gates of Edinburgh. Presumably the Laird of Woodhouselee meant caterans – thieves and freebooters, and a common insult thrown at Highlanders – but it's a lovely image.

In those heady six weeks in Edinburgh in the autumn of 1745, the Jacobites could afford to ignore the mutterers. Everything was going their way, their success thus far quite astounding – and they revelled in it.

John Roy Stuart commissioned artist Allan Ramsay to paint a portrait of Prince Charles. The Palace of Holyroodhouse glittered with the light of hundreds of candles. Highland chiefs and their wives, Lowland lairds and their ladies, and the breathlessly excited young women of Edinburgh danced under the brown-eyed gaze of a Stuart prince and the portraits of his ancestors. For the first time in almost a century and a half, Scotland had a royal court again.

Fortune had favoured the brave. There was every reason to believe it would continue to do so.

9

THE YOUNG ADVENTURER: CHARLES EDWARD STUART

GOD IS NOT ON THE SIDE OF THE BIG BATTALIONS, BUT THE BEST SHOTS

As well as prizing skill over sheer force of numbers, Voltaire also said that history is a pack of tricks we play upon the past. Nowhere is this more evident than in the millions of words and libraries of books which have been written about the '45 and the personality and character of the man who led it.

Charles was for a long time portrayed as the Bonnie Prince, the young adventurer celebrated in song and legend, but he can also be seen as the selfish and ruthlessly self-centred user of other people and their loyalty to his family and Scotland, a historical irrelevance. It's certainly easy to read him in an almost entirely negative way. There is plenty of damning evidence.

Take the impulsive nature of the attempt itself. He travelled to Scotland with only a handful of men, without any real help from the French or realistic hopes that such help would be forthcoming. For as long as he possibly could, he concealed that fact from the men and women who risked their lives, homes and families' futures for him.

Take his belief in the divine right of kings, the idea that he and his family had been chosen by God to rule Britain. Or his inability to realize that while some of his supporters were equally convinced of this doctrine, it did not mean the monarch or his son could behave like tyrants. For Scots in particular, the divine right had to go hand-in-hand with the acceptance that the kings and queens of Scotland had always ruled only with the consent of the people.

This is why we speak of Mary, Queen of *Scots* and not Mary, Queen of *Scotland*. This is why the Scottish unicorn, symbol of Scottish royalty, wears a heavy chain around its neck. The monarch's powers are restricted, dependent on the people allowing their ruler to exercise them. Scotland belongs to the Scots, not to any government or ruler.

In theory, Charles Edward Stuart was at pains to emphasize that his vote on the council he held at Holyroodhouse at nine o'clock every morning was just another vote. In practice, his unwillingness to listen to any advice unless it was what he wanted to hear was obvious and sometimes overt. He had more than once to be reminded that free-born Britons could not be treated like slaves.

To be fair, the Prince was not helped by disagreements and personal antipathies between his commanders. The most damaging of these was between Colonel O'Sullivan and Lord George Murray, the latter having joined the Prince at Perth and become his commander-in-chief.

O'Sullivan and Sir John Macdonald, another of the Seven Men of Moidart and a senior cavalry officer in the Jacobite Army, both tell in their accounts of the '45 a curious story about Lord George, whose family seat was at Blair Atholl, north of Pitlochry. A Macdonald woman and a Cameron man came to see Sir John at Perth, the former explaining they were there 'on purpose to warn H. R. H. that Lord George was one of his greatest enemies'.

The story was that Lord George had, a little while before, gathered together some of the Atholl men, telling them they were going to join the Prince. Later, however, he told them they would be joining Cope's army instead. The Macdonald woman said she had known Lord George 'for many years as a scoundrel' and begged Sir John to pass on the story 'because she was convinced, as were many others also, that this man would betray us and would cause the ruin of the party and of his fellow Scots'.

Other people had a quite different view of Lord George, considering him to be an honourable, if short-tempered, man and a gifted military commander. James Johnstone, one of the gentlemen volunteers to the Jacobite Army, was a big fan:

> Had Prince Charles slept during the whole of the expedition, and allowed Lord George to act for him, there is every reason for supposing he would have found the crown of Great Britain on his head when he awoke.

Johnstone was clear also as to what the Prince should have done after Prestonpans, which had made him 'the entire master of Scotland, where the only English troops which remained were the garrisons of the castles of Edinburgh and Stirling'. Since Charles was now Regent of Scotland on behalf of his father, King James, he ought to have concentrated on hanging on to one country rather than trying immediately to conquer another:

> His chief object ought to have been to endeavour, by every possible means, to secure himself in the government of his ancient kingdom, and to defend himself against the English armies (which would not fail to be sent against him) without attempting, for the present, to extend his views to England. This was the advice which every one gave the Prince and, if he had followed it, he might still perhaps have been in possession of that kingdom. He was strongly advised to dissolve and annul the union between Scotland and England, made during the usurpation of Queen Anne by a cabal of a few Scots peers, whom the English court had gained over to its interests by force of gold,

contrary to the general wish of the Scottish nation, all ranks of which, down to the lowest peasant, have ever held this act in abhorrence. Such a step would have given infinite pleasure to all Scotland, and the sole consideration of being freed from the English yoke would have induced the Scots to declare themselves generally in his favour.

John Roy Stuart was another vociferous supporter of the opinion that, first and foremost, Scotland should be secured and held fast. He thought the decision to invade England was the first of many mistakes and that it was madness to leave Scotland without having captured the strategically crucial fortresses of Edinburgh and Stirling castles.

If it had been up to John Roy, James Johnstone and the many other Jacobites – perhaps the majority – who were of the same opinion, Charles would have proclaimed his father king of Scots, revoked the Treaty of Union, called a parliament in Edinburgh and taken full control of Scotland. Wondering what might have happened if these views had prevailed leads inevitably to one of the most tantalizing 'what ifs?' of history.

John Roy Stuart was the only colonel in the Jacobite Army not invited to attend Charles's daily council meetings at Holyroodhouse. This is curious, as he and the Prince had known one another for at least ten years and were good friends. If John Roy was a Catholic, as the evidence strongly suggests, this may have had something to do with his exclusion.

The Prince and at least some of his closest advisers were well aware of how delicate the religious issue was. A Catholic himself, Colonel O'Sullivan thought it advisable that Charles should not be seen to be surrounding himself with Catholics. On the other hand, John Roy himself believed his exclusion resulted from his vehement opposition to the invasion of England.

When the council first discussed this plan, most of its members, especially the clan chiefs, were initially hostile to it. However, the

Prince's determination meant that when the vote was taken, half the council members reluctantly agreed with him, and the proposal was carried. John Roy's vote would have made the difference. Before the vote, so might his persuasive tongue.

Charles wanted London. That he used his faithful Scots, much against their better judgement, in a vain attempt to get there and in an equally vain attempt to inspire the English Jacobites to rise en masse is, for many, another reason to condemn him. After the Battle of Falkirk in January 1746, when the Highland chiefs and his other commanders insisted, against his will, that the Jacobite Army had to retreat to Inverness, the Prince wrote an angry letter to Lord George Murray:

> When I came to Scotland, I knew well enough what I was to expect from my Ennemies, but I little foresaw what I meet with from my Friends. I came vested with all the Authority the King could give me, one chief part of which is the Command of the Armies, and now I am required to give this up to fifteen persons, who may afterwards depute five or seven of their own number to exercise it, for fear, if they were six or eight, that I might myself pretend to ye casting vote.
>
> I am often hit in the teeth that this is an Army of Volontiers, consisting of Gentlemen of Rank and fortune, and who came into it merely upon motives of Duty and Honours; what one wou'd expect from such an Army is more zeal, more resolution, and more good manners than in those that fight merely for pay. Everyone knew before he engaged in the cause what he was to expect in case it miscarried, and shou'd have staid at home if cou'd not face death in any shape.

The ingratitude is monumental. Yet, to quote Joseph Addison, the author of *Cato*: 'Much might be said on both sides.'

To come to Scotland with only a handful of companions in the hope that thousands would rise in his support must have taken enormous courage, determination and self-belief. For a young man in his mid-twenties, it must also have taken guts to argue his case with men old enough to be his father and grandfather.

Maybe staying in Edinburgh and securing Scotland was not an option. Shocked by their defeat at Prestonpans, the Government had finally been galvanized into action. The next army sent against the Jacobites would not be made up of terrified raw recruits but of battle-hardened veterans. They were already being shipped back from the war in Europe. Would England have accepted Scotland reclaiming her independence without a fight?

The Jacobites had to seize the initiative. Marching into England did that. It was the wrong time of year to launch such a move, of course, when autumn would soon be giving way to winter. Then again, expect the unexpected. Be bold. It was in keeping with the whole attempt and with the Prince's character and personality.

There was another crucial consideration. French interest in supporting Charles's campaign was quite naturally bound up with what would be best for France. They wanted England distracted from the wars in Europe and preferably removed altogether from the scene. They had been ready to send an invasion fleet across the Channel in 1744, when the Protestant Wind blew up, and were poised to do the same again in 1745.

The embarkation of the fleet was planned for Christmas, and Voltaire himself had written a manifesto in support of a Stuart restoration. He was a great admirer of Charles Edward Stuart and of the British. He saw Charles as a prince who could inspire the British people to do great things. On the great philosopher's recommendation, the French had sent an unofficial ambassador to the Jacobites: Alexandre Boyer, the Marquis d'Eguilles. When he landed at Montrose in October 1745, it was taken as a promise of French support.

Winning back the crown of Britain for his family was what Charles had been raised for. This was his destiny. He had grown up in the knowledge and belief that he was the Prince of Wales, his younger brother Henry the Duke of York, their parents the King and Queen of the Kingdoms of Great Britain and Ireland and all the dominions pertaining thereto. His father had failed to make those phantom titles a reality. Now it was Charles's turn.

His mother, the Polish princess Clementina Sobieska, died when he was 15, leaving him, his brother and his father bereft and distraught. This was despite James and Clementina's marriage having always been a difficult one, and Clementina herself a rather distant and ethereal figure, inclined to retreat into prayer and fasting.

Writing to his 'Dear Papa', the six-year-old Charles promised that 'I will be very dutiful to dear Mamma, and not jump too near her.' It's rather sad to think of a boisterous and energetic young boy having to promise not to be a boy for fear of disturbing his languid mother.

Charles's father was affectionate towards his jumping boy and his younger brother, Henry. James took great care over their education, although he despaired of his elder son's lack of interest in book-learning and his terrible spelling – but, hey, this was the eighteenth century.

Balancing the books was Charles's gift for languages. While still very young, he mastered English, French and Italian, all in daily usage at his home, the Jacobite court in exile at the Palazzo Muti in Rome. Almost as soon as he made landfall in Scotland in 1745, he made it his business to learn some Gaelic.

He was tall, strong and physically fit, enjoying sport and exercise for their own sake as well as because he was quite consciously in training for the time when he would lead the military campaign to reclaim his father's kingdom. He was a good shot. He also played golf and the violin and, by all accounts, did both rather well. Despite spending much of his life in a state of financial embarrassment, he was a good tipper, too.

He had the common touch, to the extent that he often comes across as being happier in the company of ordinary people than those of a more elevated social class. With them, he could be prickly and haughty. With boatmen, maidservants and his 'brave Highlanders', he seemed more able to relax.

While he was on the run in the Hebrides, often wet, hungry and in deadly danger, his behaviour was impeccable. He ate what food could be got without complaint, and, while sometimes understandably depressed, he did his best to keep everyone else's spirits up. The famous Stuart charm was an enormously powerful weapon. It could sweep the most unlikely people off their feet.

Assembling at Dalkeith, the Jacobite Army began its march south on 3 November 1745. Six days later, they reached Carlisle. It was so foggy that, as O'Sullivan put it, a man could hardly see his horse's ears. When the mist lifted, the guns of Carlisle Castle fired at the Jacobites, who were gathered outside the gates of the city demanding entry. They withdrew and sent a local man in with a letter from the Prince.

In it, Charles called on the citizens of Carlisle to surrender. Surely both sides had no wish to spill English blood? Although some within the doughty border fortress were ready and willing to hold out, this proved as effective an argument as it had been at Edinburgh. Six days later again, the Jacobites found themselves masters of Carlisle.

Stories which had grown arms and legs in the telling were spreading rapidly through the towns and villages in England, their citizens terrified they might be on the route of the advancing Scottish army. Concentrating on the exotic mountain men, the peddlers of propaganda – who included Henry Fielding, author, satirist and co-founder of the Bow Street Runners – had told these now panic-stricken people that the bare-arsed banditti burnt, raped and murdered wherever they went. They were cannibals, too, known to be particularly partial to babies and children.

Colonel O'Sullivan noted that wherever they went in England they seldom saw any children. It soon emerged that worried parents had hidden them away for safety. Cameron of Lochiel had to reassure one woman he was not going to eat her children before she dared bring them out from the cupboard where she had concealed them. The Prince allayed the fears of another terrified mother:

The prince lodged this night in a Quaquers house; being in his room with Sr Thomas & Locheil they heard something groning under the Bed, they cal'd for the woman of the house & asked what yt may be. The poor woman began to cry & begged the prince to spear yt child, yt it was the only one she had of seven; the child was drawn from under the bed. Yu never saw a woman in yt condition; she thought the child wou'd be set upon the Spit, as there was not much to eat in the house, but Sr Thomas, who spoak their language very well, appaissed her, & rassured her, so she told him the whole story.

The other Quaquers hearing this, came to see the Prince, being at supper, & knowing yt the Beer of the house was not of the best, they brought him some of theirs; an Old man goes out & brings him two bottles of his, sets them before the Prince & tells him "thou'l find this better." The Prince drinks it, find it very good, & thanks him most gratiously; the Old man lifts up his hand, as if he was to have given him his blessing – "Thou are not a man, but an angel," with tears in his eyes.

This story is a beautiful illustration of how strong Charles's personal charisma must have been. This kindly member of the Society of Friends was clearly dazzled by him.

Charles was a handsome man, too. Anyone who doubts this should take a look at Maurice Quentin de la Tour's 1748 painting of him, which now hangs in the Scottish National Portrait Gallery in Edinburgh. The man with the warm brown eyes who gazes back out at you when you stand in front of it is attractive, masculine and confident.

Curiously, many modern Scots do their utmost to deny this, denigrating Charles and his physical appearance whenever his name is mentioned. The underlying message of these snide remarks seems to be that he was hopeless in every way and that we Scots must therefore have been hopeless to have followed him. This says rather more about our national crisis of self-confidence and self-esteem than it does about Charles Edward Stuart.

That he knew how to inspire men and women is something else which cannot be denied. The New Spalding Club was a group of gentleman scholars active in Aberdeen during the 1890s. In their *Historical Papers Relating To The Jacobite Period 1699–1750,* editor James Allardyce juxtaposed two speeches. One is what General Sir John Cope said when he addressed the Government army shortly before the Battle of Prestonpans:

> Gentlemen, you are just now to engage with a parcel of rabble; a parcel of brutes, being a small number of Scots Highlanders. You can expect no booty from such a poor despicable pack. I have authority to declare, that you shall have eight full hours liberty to plunder and pillage the city of Edinburgh, Leith, and suburbs, (the places which harboured and succoured them) at your discretion with impunity.

And here is what Charles said to his men:

> The Prince being clothed in a plain Highland habit, docked his blue bonnet, drew his sword, threw away the scabbard, and said, 'Gentlemen, follow me, by the assistance of God, I will, this day, make you a free and happy people.'

James Allardyce made no editorial comment. He didn't need to.
Which one would you rather follow?

10

Home by Christmas: The Family Men

All the Lads are in Top Spirits

As might be expected, men on the campaign trail were anxious to hear the news from home and took every opportunity offered to let their families and friends know how they were getting on. As might also be expected, both sides were concerned the other should not worry too much.

Many of the letters sent to and from Jacobite soldiers did not reach the intended recipients. A postman's job – the man very likely to be a boy – during the '45 could be a hazardous one. Knowledge being power, both sides went in for a little tampering with the mail. John Murray of Broughton, the Prince's secretary, gave precise instructions on how to do this. The man he sent to lie in wait for the postie was to tie him up, slap his horse on the rump so it would bolt a few miles down the road, and make off with the bag of letters.

Mail being intercepted made life difficult for both sides. Young Jack Campbell of Mamore wrote to his father from Inveraray on 16 October 1745. There had, he explained, been no point in writing earlier 'as all communication from this country has been interrupted for some time':

> As the rebels are still at Edinburg we have no accounts
> that can be depended on of what is doing there or in
> England, for as their affairs are in a very bad situation they
> take great pains to hinder any true account to be sent,
> especially to the Highlands. On the contrary we are daily
> entertained here with the most extravagant lyes that ever
> were heard of. There is not a day passes but we are told
> of some foreign troops being landed to their assistance,
> and tho there is not the least truth in these reports the
> common people believe it firmly throughout all the
> Highlands ... certainly it is a most unhappy thing that the
> misbehaviour of a few should have given the Government
> so bad an opinion in General of all Scotland ...

Telling his father that 'there has been a party of fifty men headed by
a madman plundering the country and raising contributions for six
weeks past in and about Dunbartonshire', Jack signed himself 'your
most obedient Son and Servant'.

One little cache of intercepted mail is hidden away in a brown
cardboard box at the Public Record Office in London. It contains letters
written by Jacobite soldiers camped at Moffat while they were on their
way south on the march into England. The letters and the man carrying
them fell into Government hands when he was riding north.

The phrase 'in top spirits' crops up so often in this collection it
suggests one of the letter writers offered it to the others as a way of
reassuring the folks back home. It's in this bundle of emotion and
longing we find the letter of a 60-year-old sergeant in Glengarry's
Regiment to his lover, asking after her children and telling her how
much he misses her. Duncan McGillis did not make it back to Scotland,
so it's all the more poignant that Margaret McDonnell, barmaid at the
barracks at Fort Augustus, never received his letter.

The information in those letters which were safely received had to
be passed on to other family members. Katherine Hepburn was the
daughter of James Hepburn of Keith, the man who had ceremoniously

escorted the Prince into Holyroodhouse. Katie was still in Edinburgh
a week and more after the Jacobites had left and was anxious to tell
her aunt in Aberdeen, her father's sister, the latest news:

> Papa writes us they had crossed Tweed, was all in great
> health and spirits. They were to be in Carlisle on Saturday
> night where the whole Army are to join, as it hs been
> divided in two different parts, because the Country they
> went through could not provide Meat and Lodging for
> such a number of men.

The proud daughter and dutiful niece ended her letter on a note of
resignation:

> P. S. I hear all the letters are kept up at the Post Office
> three or four weeks or they be delivered. As they cant
> read all the Letters they only open the ones to the most
> suspected persons, and in case there should be any
> information in the others they dont deliver them till it
> cant be of no use. So I suppose it will be about Christmas
> till this comes to your hand. Adiue, My Sisters join me
> in their Duty to Grandmama and you.

Three days after Katie Hepburn wrote those words to her aunt in
Aberdeen, the Reverend Robert Lyon, chaplain to Ogilvy's Regiment,
wrote to his sister Cecelia in Perth, telling her that he was with the
main body of the Jacobites at Brampton outside Carlisle and 'All as yet
goes well, and all your friends and acquaintances are in good health
and in full spirits.'

The Post Office throughout the British Isles was well established by
the middle of the eighteenth century, but Katie Hepburn believed its
postmasters and -mistresses would not undertake to deliver letters sent
to and from the Jacobite Army while it was on the move. Robert Lyon
offered Cecelia one way of keeping in touch with him.

P. S. If you meet with any Body going to the Army write me your news and direct it to me in Lord Ogilvy's Regiment and it will come to hand.

Another phrase crops up in the letters sent and never received from Moffat. Angus MacDonnell was just one of those who told his wife that if the English Jacobites rose he might not even have to draw his sword. He added that in any case he would definitely be home for Christmas – which makes you wonder if all soldiers in all wars have kept their spirits up by thinking that.

Duncan Forbes of Culloden was a prolific letter writer. In his position as Lord President of the Court of Session in Edinburgh, many of these were official, sending and passing on reports to military men and politicians, but there were personal letters, too. On 25 October 1745, he wrote more in sorrow than in anger to the Laird of Pitcalnie. The Laird's son Malcolm, the Lord President's great-nephew, had gone over to the Jacobites. He had been serving in the Government army when he did so, with Lord Loudoun's Regiment, so it's possible he was one of those who changed sides at Prestonpans.

Knowing his impetuous young relative was likely to be hanged for desertion if caught, Forbes saw his defection as an unmitigated disaster:

> I NEVER was more astonish'd, & but seldom more afflicted, in my life, than I was when I heard of the madness of your son. I cannot conceive of what magick he has been prevail'd on to forfeit utterly his own honours; in a signall manner to affront & dishonour me, whom you made answerable for him; to risk a halter, which, if he do not succeed, must be his doom, without any other tryall than that of a court martial; & to break the heart of an indulgent father, as you are: which, I am perswaded, must be ths case, unless he reclaim'd; the villains who seduced him, profiting of his tender years &

want of experience, tho' I hope I am a Christian, I never
will forgive; tho' him I will, if he return quickly to his
duty, without committing further folly.

He wrote to young Malcolm, too, asking him to come and see him,
and assuring him he would not try to forcibly stop him returning to
the Jacobite Army. Signing himself 'your affectionate Uncle', he also
wrote: 'I need not tell you that I wish you well.'

Many of the men who wrote letters in 1745–6 and ached so much
for home, hearth and family never did come home again. They left a
legacy in their words of love, care and longing:

> Oh a month's rest at home would be a blessing.

> Donald Ram desires his father-in-law to hire a lad for
> his wife and he desires that his wife would sell the black
> cow but if she can't get a good price for her, let her kill
> her and be eaten in the house.

> Give my kind service to all friends and neighbours.

> All the lads are well.

> I shall not sleep easy until I see you and the Bairns.

Duncan McGillis, who was never to see his lover, Margaret, or Scotland
again, wrote the most poignant words of all: 'Nothing ails me but the
wanting of you.'

11

BONNIE PRINCE CHARLIE MEETS SIR OSWALD MOSLEY: THE MANCHESTER REGIMENT

FAREWELL, MANCHESTER, THO' MY HEART FOR YOU STILL BEATS,
NE'ER AGAIN WILL I SWAGGER DOWN YOUR STREETS

Although he was not in favour of the march into England, James Johnstone did his duty throughout it. Johnstone was now in command of a company within the Duke of Perth's Regiment, whose ranks had been swelled by the considerable number of Government soldiers who deserted to the Jacobites at Prestonpans. Sergeant Thomas Dickson was one of them.

James Johnstone described him as 'a young Scotsman, as brave and intrepid as a lion, and very much attached to my interest'. At Preston on the way south, Dickson offered to go on ahead to Manchester to beat up for recruits.

Johnstone said no, rebuking Dickson 'for entertaining so wild and extravagant a project, which exposed him to the danger of being taken and hanged'. The sergeant went anyway, riding through the night from Preston to Manchester with his mistress and the Regiment's drummer. Johnstone was uneasy rather than angry, although he was irritated that Dickson had carried off his blunderbuss and his portmanteau, presumably leaving his captain without a clean shirt or his razor.

Although surrounded by a hostile mob when he first told the drummer to start beating up, the power of Dickson's considerable personality brought him out on top. The blunderbuss came in useful, too. Swinging round in a continuous circle, the sergeant kept it trained on the crowd. At the same time, he roared like the lion to which Johnstone had compared him, yelling out bloodcurdling threats. If anyone attacked him, his girlfriend or the drummer, he would blow their bloody brains out.

Taking their cue from him, some of Manchester's Jacobites – of whom there were many – found their courage. As they stepped forward, the balance of the crowd shifted in favour of Sergeant Dickson and his unorthodox recruiting party, and the Jacobite Manchester Regiment was born.

Dickson brought Johnstone back a list of one hundred and eighty recruits, his captain 'agreeably surprised to find that the whole amount of his expenses did not exceed three guineas'. Everyone had a good laugh at Manchester's expense, declaring that the city had been taken for the Jacobites by a sergeant, a drummer and a whore.

Although dismissed both then and now as riff-raff and rabble, unemployed and workshy labourers with time on their hands and nothing better to do than seize the chance of making mischief, the Manchester Regiment included many men whose commitment to the Stuart Cause ran deep.

The Regiment's colonel was Francis Townley, who came from a devoutly Catholic and passionately Jacobite Lancashire family. He was a professional soldier, having served in the French Army, earning his spurs during the War of the Polish Succession.

While several of the senior officers and many of the rank and file of the Manchester Regiment were Catholics, the majority of the officers were Protestants. These included brothers Robert, Thomas and Charles Deacon, who were the sons of the non-juring Anglican Bishop of Manchester. Non-jurors were clergymen who maintained their loyalty to the House of Stuart and refused to take the oath of allegiance to George II.

When the main body of the Jacobite Army arrived in Manchester, the supporters of King George and the political status quo retreated into their homes, just as they had in Edinburgh. The Manchester Jacobites had a field day. As in Edinburgh, young women were strongly attracted to the Cause. One of them was Elizabeth Byrom, who wrote it all up in her diary.

'Beppy' to her friends and family, she went out on the street with hundreds of other Mancunians to hear King James proclaimed the rightful king. That night she sat up late with her aunt, stitching blue-and-white St Andrew's crosses. The next day was 30 November, and there were celebrations in honour of Scotland's patron saint and the Scottish visitors. The Manchester Regiment was also officially constituted.

Gazing in admiration at the Prince as he rode through the streets of Manchester, Beppy declared it a 'noble sight'. Wearing her white gown, the colour of choice for a Jacobite lady, she was introduced to him that evening, kissing his hand. After that, she and her friends drank so many toasts to Charles and his father that she got tipsy.

Beppy's father, John Byrom, was a complex and interesting man. He invented a system of shorthand, a useful tool for a man who spent much of his life embroiled in plots and intrigues, and the clandestine correspondence which went along with them. One of these was a sexual adventure: he was for several years the lover of Queen Caroline, wife of George II.

Byrom also composed a famous Jacobite toast – one suitable for those who wanted to hint at where their allegiance lay:

> God bless the King! God bless the Faith's Defender!
> God bless – no harm in blessing – the Pretender!
> Who that Pretender is, and who that King –
> God bless us all – is quite another thing!

In *The Queen's Chameleon,* Byrom's biographer, Joy Hancox, tells a fascinating story which suggests that Charles Edward Stuart's visit to Manchester in 1745 was not his first. The tale comes from the memoirs of one of several men who bore the title and name Sir Oswald Mosley, the first name being a traditional one in that family.

These memoirs were published in 1849 and refer back to a woman, 84 years old in 1815, whose father had been the landlord of Manchester's Bull's Head inn. In his time, the tavern was a favourite watering-hole for the local Jacobites. In the summer of 1744, when his daughter was a girl of 13, she remembered a handsome young gentleman riding in on several occasions from Ancoats Hall, where he was staying with Sir Oswald Mosley.

The handsome young gentleman was interested in the London newspapers, which he read with great concentration. On one occasion, he asked the landlord's daughter to bring him a basin of water and a towel to wash the newsprint off his hands. When she came to take the basin and towel away, he gave her half a crown. The generous tip made a big impression on her.

In November 1745, she was standing at the tavern door watching the Jacobite Army march into Manchester. The Prince passed by – and she recognized the handsome young man who had been so avid a reader of the newspapers the year before.

It's a good story, given extra credence by the evidence of Thomas Coppack, the Anglican chaplain to the Manchester Regiment. When he and other members of the newly formed regiment sat drinking at the Bull's Head at the end of November 1745, they were joined by young Oswald Mosley, son of the house of Ancoats Hall. Had he come to visit a friend as well as show his support? The Prince is known to have made at least one incognito visit to England during his life. It's entirely possible that he made more.

Support for the Jacobites in Manchester was about a lot more than drinking yourself silly through innumerable loyal toasts to the Stuarts. Many in the city could be counted among those who, as people said then, were disaffected to the Government and the House of Hanover.

Manchester had its own issues. It was growing rapidly, as was its textile industry, yet felt itself sidelined and distanced from those who held the reins of power in London.

Hand-in-hand with this went the powerful Jacobite convictions of the officers of the Manchester Regiment. Like many of their Scottish counterparts, their devotion to the Stuarts was inextricably bound up with their religious beliefs. Yet coupled with this almost mystical strand of their political philosophy was straightforward distaste that Old England was now being ruled by a bloody foreigner.

Some people thought Charles Edward Stuart was a bloody foreigner too, of course, seeing little to choose between a usurping German and a half-Italian and half-Polish adventurer. The officers of the Manchester Regiment did not see Charles that way. They believed he was their best and perhaps last hope of protecting and safeguarding hard-won English liberties.

This interesting point of view, that Charles could deliver national and personal freedom, was shared by many of his Scottish supporters. It goes against the grain of the traditional historical view. As with the Scottish Jacobites, and pointing to the association of the English Jacobites with the Tory party, such thinking has dismissed Jacobite political thought as reactionary and right wing.

According to this analysis, the Rising of 1745 and the attempt to restore the Stuarts was the last gasp of the old world. Jacobitism had to be stamped on and stamped out, as Scotland had to stay inextricably bound into the Union with England. Only then could Great Britain steam ahead into the sunlit uplands of the modern age.

Some strands of the Jacobite movement were undoubtedly reactionary, belonging much more to the old world than the new, not least the absolute authority many Highland chiefs wielded over their clansmen and -women. Yet, as the only available opportunity at that time for achieving a groundbreaking political change, the Jacobite movement was a focus for the discontent felt by people of many different backgrounds and with many different aspirations.

The eighteenth century was a fascinating period of transition between the old and the new. In Scotland, the seeds of the Enlightenment were beginning to sprout. Throughout the British Isles, the Industrial Revolution was poised to roar into action, transforming the cities and the countryside. In agriculture, new methods of working on and profiting from the land were being introduced.

In terms of social class, these changes exacerbated old tensions as well as introducing new ones but, after a long and tortuous struggle, led to the democracy and personal freedoms we enjoy today. In their belief that Charles Edward Stuart could deliver such political and personal liberty, it could be argued that the officers of the Manchester Regiment were the forerunners of the political Radicals which the cotton mills and factories of Manchester and Lancashire were later to produce in such abundance.

Apart from the unemployed riff-raff jibe, the private men of the Manchester Regiment have also been dismissed as 'Irish immigrant rabble'. This is an interesting insult. There are many people of Irish descent in Manchester, descendants of those who left their homeland in search of the work to be found in the city's many textile mills. Although this industry took off from the 1760s onwards, the real influx of Irish people happened in the nineteeth century, before, during and after the potato famine.

How many Irishmen and -women there were in the Manchester of 1745 is therefore debatable. It would seem racism and anti-Catholicism were at work, the latter being, of course, a particularly powerful bogeyman in Protestant England at this time. It would seem, too, that these twin prejudices of race and religion have continued to colour attitudes towards the Manchester Regiment. A read-through of its officers' and men's names does not in fact turn up many Irishmen. Instead, we find Henry Bibby, a weaver from Wigan; James Braithwaite, a saddler from Penrith; Thomas Ogden, a weaver from Manchester; and Thomas Warrington, a chair-maker from Macclesfield. James Sparkes, a framework knitter from Derby, joined the Manchester Regiment when the Jacobites occupied his home town. He was later hanged at York.

❖ ❖ ❖

The Jacobites' march into England had seemed unstoppable. In some places, such as Manchester, the welcome accorded to the Prince and his men had been wildly enthusiastic. Yet even the Manchester Regiment did not supply anything like the number of recruits hoped for. At Derby, after heated debate and bitter argument, this lack of support led to the decision to abandon the march on London. The Manchester Regiment turned round and trudged north with everyone else. Although some of these new recruits deserted along the way, around 120 were left behind at Carlisle when Charles and the rest of the Jacobite Army crossed back into Scotland.

The Prince has often been criticized for leaving them to their fate in order to satisfy his vanity by hanging onto one of England's mightiest fortresses. Some argue, however, that Colonel Townley preferred to stay in Carlisle rather than cross into Scotland.

Many of his men were unwilling to leave their native country for the uncertainty of what might await them in Scotland. A handful of them did, including John Daniel, the gentleman volunteer from Lancashire, although he too was reluctant to cross the border, as he later wrote: 'Every thing being now in readiness, we began our march, in order (alas! As it happened) to bid adieu to old England for ever!'

There were also Scotsmen in the short-lived Jacobite garrison at Carlisle. A fair number came from John Roy Stewart's Edinburgh Regiment, although many of them actually belonged to Perthshire and Banffshire.

With no real hope of defending Carlisle against artillery brought in from Whitehaven, the Jacobite garrison surrendered to the Duke of Cumberland on 30 December 1745. The treatment meted out to them was chilling in its cruelty.

The officers were sent to London, while the 300 or so other ranks, including some women and children who had followed the Jacobite Army into England, were locked up in a gloomy dungeon within Carlisle Castle. They were kept there for several freezing January days, shackled and without food, drink or light. There is a stone on one wall of this vault which still today has an unusual shape. The story is that moisture collected there and the prisoners took turns to lick it in an attempt to assuage their thirst.

Subsequently transferred to other prisons, we do not know how many men of the Manchester Regiment died as a result of this maltreatment. Of those who survived, many were among the 1,000 prisoners, again including some women and children, who were transported to the West Indies to work as indentured servants in the plantations there.

More than half the officers of the Manchester Regiment were executed. Eighteen of them, including the chaplain, Thomas Coppack, and seven of the Regiment's eight sergeants, went to the gallows. There was a strong feeling that punishment was even more severe for them because they were Englishmen and so seen as greater traitors than the Scottish Jacobites.

Bishop Deacon lost all three of his sons. Robert died of illness as a prisoner at Carlisle, Thomas was hanged and Charles was transported to the West Indies, dying soon after he got there.

John Daniel and James Bradshaw are the only two members of the Manchester Regiment known to have fought at Culloden. John Daniel escaped; Jem Bradshaw was taken. He was hung, drawn and quartered on Kennington Common in November 1746. Six other members of the Manchester Regiment, including Colonel Townley, Thomas Sydall, Adjutant of the Regiment, Thomas Deacon and Jem Dawson, were executed there in July of the same year. An old, sad story says that Jem Dawson's sweetheart was there and died of a broken heart moments after she witnessed his death.

William Harrison Ainsworth was a nineteenth-century Manchester lawyer who turned to writing, producing 39 novels, all heavily based on historical fact. One of them was *The Manchester Rebels*. In it, he tells the tale of the deaths of Jem Dawson and his sweetheart, and has Colonel Townley mount the ladder to the scaffold with a straight back and a scornful smile.

Ainsworth also has Thomas Deacon, with his dying breath, cry out 'God save King James III!' When Thomas Sydall hears the executioner remark, as he puts the noose over his head, that he is trembling, Sydall indignantly denies it: 'I recoil from thy hateful touch – that is all.' And to prove that his courage was unshaken, he took a pinch of snuff.

The heads of Colonel Townley and Jem Dawson were displayed on Temple Bar in London. Those of Jem Bradshaw and Thomas Deacon were sent to Manchester to be displayed on the Exchange there as both an act of gloating revenge and a vicious warning.

It is recorded that Bishop Deacon went there and stared for a long time at the heads. When a sympathetic bystander asked why he did not weep, he said because he did not mourn for his son, who had died the death of a martyr. Then the bishop took off his hat and bowed to both heads, and every time he passed Manchester's Exchange thereafter, he did the same.

12

THE YEAR OF THE PRINCE:
BLACK FRIDAY AT DERBY

WITHIN THREE DAYS' MARCH OF THE CAPITAL

B oost for morale though the new regiment was, the numbers
were a mere drop in the ocean. Colonel O'Sullivan had been
hoping for one thousand five hundred volunteers from Manchester,
ten times more than actually did enlist. He believed that many English
people wanted to see a restoration of the Stuarts but feared to commit
themselves – especially without the back-up of those conspicuously
absent French troops.

Sir John Macdonald felt that appeals should be made to the many
Catholics in Lancashire, via letters sent to their priests. He suggested
this to Sir Thomas Sheridan, another of the Seven Men of Moidart
and former tutor to Prince Charles. Sheridan would have none of it,
unwilling for the Prince and his army to have 'anything to do with
Roman Catholic priests'. Macdonald considered this attitude foolish
in the extreme:

> Catholics should not hide their feelings – or what those
> feelings should be. Namely that the Protestant religion
> should remain the dominant one in England, since it

was established by acts of Parliament, while at the same time the Catholic religion should have full liberty as in England Presbyterians and other nonconformists have likewise.

Macdonald believed openness and honesty would be the best way to counteract the anti-Catholic propaganda which 'filled the newspapers' about the Prince and the Jacobites. It was stupid to try to pretend they had nothing to do with Catholics when the army had 'nearly as many of them as of Protestants'. Given that many people even now try to maintain that this was a Catholic army, this is an interesting statistic.

That the propaganda had much impact on those Protestants who might otherwise have rallied to the Prince's Standard seems unlikely. Not exactly appealing to deep thinkers, the pamphlets, prints and broadsides which were the tabloid press of their day attacked the Jacobites by evoking the spectre of rule from Rome by a despotic Pope whose shock troops would be sinister priests. Jesuits were the favourite bogeymen.

Although the burnings of 400 Protestant martyrs during the reign of Mary Tudor might have still been vivid in the public imagination, those horrors had happened almost 200 years before. That was then and this was now. Added to which, many eighteenth-century Englishmen and -women retained a romantic and sentimental attachment to the Stuarts. After all, one of the most popular kings ever to sit upon the British throne had been a Stuart.

Charles II might have famously remarked that Presbyterianism was no religion for a gentleman. Unlike his brother James, who succeeded him and lost the throne, Charles had been smart enough and cynical enough not to embrace the Catholic religion. He was fondly remembered in the 1740s, as he still is today, as the Merry Monarch, the encourager of arts, industry and science, hero of the Great Fire of London, legendary lover of women and friend to all men. As a future politician might have said, Charles II truly was the People's King.

His great-nephew had inherited all of his charm and seemed as promising in other respects. Except when he rode officially into a town or city, during most of the invasion of England the Prince walked on foot at the head of his men, putting in the same effort as they did and presumably having the blisters to prove it. The London mob – as volatile, unpredictable, brutally sentimental and potentially influential as that of any eighteenth-century city – might well have taken him to their hearts.

By and large the Hanoverians were not an attractive bunch, either in their looks or their personalities. The Stuarts were much sexier: physically attractive, exciting, a little bit louche and at the same time touched by God. John Daniel, the gentleman volunteer to the Manchester Regiment, summed it up beautifully:

> The first time I saw this loyal army was betwixt Lancaster and Garstang: the brave Prince marching on foot at their head like a Cyrus or a Trojan Hero, drawing admiration and love from all those who beheld him, raising their long-dejected hearts, and solacing their minds with the happy prospect of another Golden Age. Struck with this charming sight and seeming invitation '*Leave your nets and follow me,*' I felt a paternal ardour pervade my veins, and having before my eyes the admonition '*Serve God and then your King,*' I immediately became one of his followers.

Yet there was a big difference between looking back longingly to Good King Charles's golden days or wiping away a tear at the sight of the 'golden-haired laddie' – the schmaltz had started even then – and committing yourself to the Stuart Cause. Those who enlisted in the Jacobite Army were risking their lives, their livelihoods and their families' futures. This was not like deciding which way to vote at the next election.

As in Scotland, there may have been Stuart sympathizers who simply felt the House of Hanover was too well established to be unseated. Or that it was not worth the blood which would have to be shed to do it.

Despite the failure of the English Jacobites to rise, by the time the Prince's army reached Derby on 4 December, morale was high and the men were ready for action. James Johnstone watched them crowding into cutlers' shops 'quarrelling about who should be the first to sharpen and give a proper edge to his sword'.

Derby did not supply many recruits either, but the welcome given to the Jacobites was remarkably cordial. They seem to have earned this by demonstrating their famous civility. They might requisition your horses or ask if you could spare 'a brace or two of good pistols', but they did it with a disarming smile and never entered any ladies' bedchambers uninvited.

Of course, if you knew they were coming, and even if your absent master was suspected of having Jacobite sympathies – or maybe because he did – you might hide the best horses, as was done at Kedleston, the home of Sir Nathaniel Curzon. A Dr Mather wrote to Curzon's son to tell him what happened:

> You will guess how the stables were furnish'd when I tell you what they took, viz., the two old brown mares, Miss Glanville, and out of the Coach Horse Stable, Old Bully. (There were a set left in the latter, tho' the best of them were put out of the way and others put in their stead, as was done with the rest, expecting a visit.) They went away with these saddled and bridled, and the Pistols, and that was all. They wou'd drink very little, and gave so little disturbance that my Lady and half the family knew not of their having been in the House till Morning.

The news that the advancing Jacobite Army was in Derby, only 120 miles away, sent London into a spiral of panic. Shops and theatres closed, and there was a run on the Bank of England. Cunning as foxes, its directors and cashiers worked out a strategy to stem the flow of outgoing funds. First, they planted their own agents in the crowd of clamouring customers. When these agents presented their notes and demanded coin in return, they were paid in sixpences so the transaction would take as long as possible. They then went out one door and back in the other, elbowed their way to the front and presented more notes, preventing the genuine customers from removing any money from the bank.

Government troops were being mobilized to defend the capital, but if Hogarth's *March to Finchley* is to be believed, they were strolling rather than marching, dallying with their doxies all the way. As many among the civilian population still felt a tug of loyalty towards Charles Edward Stuart as the Prince of the old royal house, so did many in the military. Rumours abounded of Jacobite sympathies among Government officers – and they and the men under their command were in a position to take action. Had they done so, the balance of power might well have tipped in favour of Charles Edward Stuart and the Jacobites. Many on both sides believed these soldiers might rather have gone over to the Prince than fight under the command of his cousin several times removed, the Duke of Cumberland. Called back from the ongoing conflict in Continental Europe, King George's son was now in charge of the war against the Jacobites.

Well-off Londoners were packing up and hiding their valuables. There was a rumour that King George himself had two yachts stowed with treasures waiting at Tower Quay, ready at a moment's notice to carry him and the Royal Family to the safety of Holland. The Duke of Newcastle, principal Secretary of State, shut himself away in his house, considering his options.

Yet on the very day Newcastle was perhaps wondering if he should spend more time with his family, the Jacobites were marching back to Scotland, having taken the agonizing decision to turn around. A council of war was called on the morning of Thursday, 5 December, meeting in Derby's Exeter House. All the colonels were present this time, including John Roy Stuart, and the atmosphere was tense.

Lord George Murray spoke first, calling it as he saw it, as he always did. The English Jacobites had not risen, nor the Welsh under Sir

Watkin Williams Wynn, as had been hoped for. The French had sent no troops to help take London. Thousands of Government troops now stood ready to defend the city, in two or perhaps even three separate armies. If the Prince's army was to give all of them battle, Jacobite casualties were likely to be heavy.

The Scots were far from home. They would undoubtedly suffer more losses on a hurried and forced retreat; it would be far better to make an organized and disciplined withdrawal now. In Lord George's opinion, this was the only sensible option.

There was a long silence. Then the Prince spoke, beginning to discuss the order in which the regiments of the army would line up the following day for the march south. Lord George interrupted, angrily reminding him no decision had yet been made that they were going to march south.

The Prince turned to the other members of his council. The Duke of Perth and Jacobite Colonel Ranald MacDonald of Clanranald, son of the chief of that title and himself known as Young Clanranald, agreed with him. The others agreed with Lord George. Lords Elcho and Ogilvy were particularly warm in their support for the retreat. Charles brought out what he thought was his trump card, the news that Lord John Drummond, brother of the Duke of Perth, had landed in Montrose with a regiment of Scots and Irishmen in the French service. To Lord George, that was another reason for going home. They could rendezvous with Lord John's Regiment and make a stand in Scotland.

Charles lost his temper. Lord Elcho said that the Prince used 'very Abusive Language' against him, Lord George and Lord Ogilvy, accusing them of betraying him. The Prince argued passionately that if they could only get to London, he would be welcomed with open arms. The English and the Welsh Jacobites would rise en masse, and on this great wave of popular support the Stuarts would be restored to the throne. Men such as the Duke of Newcastle would declare their support and other influential figures would follow.

When pressed, Charles admitted to his war council that he had no promises of support from any Jacobites south of the border or west of

Offa's Dyke. The council members were horrified, and the meeting broke up in acrimony.

Lobbying through the day by the Prince did not bring many round to his way of thinking. A second meeting of the council called that evening started with Lord George assuming the retreat had been decided and outlining his plans for it to be executed as efficiently as possible. If they had to fight a Government army on the way, so be it, but the focus would be on getting back to Scotland as quickly as possible. The powerful clan chiefs agreed with him.

Forced to accept the decision, Charles was nevertheless devastated by it, saying 'I shall summon no more Councils, since I am accountable to nobody for my actions but to God and my father, and therefore I shall no longer ask or accept advice.' Colonel O'Sullivan summed up the Prince's feelings:

> but a Young Prince, yt sees himself within three days, or at utmost four days, march of the Capital, where if he was once arrived, wou'd in all appearance restor the King, cou'd not relish the word of retrait, & really he wou'd not hear yt word from the beginning, he had an avertion to the word it self, but finding every body almost of yt opinion was oblidged to consent. I never saw any body so concerned as he was for this disapointmet, nor never saw him take any thing after so much to heart as he did it.

Dr Robert Mather added some more snippets of information, when he wrote to Sir Nathaniel Curzon's son about the horses and pistols being taken:

> They listed Sparkes, the fishing-tackle-man at Derby, but sent him back from Ashburn as too great a rogue to keep with them. He fell to plundering at Bradley, so He will probably be hanged.

Which is exactly what happened to the unfortunate Mr Sparkes, who as well as being the 'fishing-tackle-man' also apparently moonlighted as a framework knitter. Dr Mather had another story about Miss Glanville, the old brown mare he had mentioned earlier in his letter. When the Jacobite Army marched out of Derby, the horse was seen 'dancing among them with a Highlander on her back', who cried in delight that this one was going to 'gollope, gollope, this will gollope!' Did her new rider know she was called Miss Glanville, or did he give her a new name?

Although some stragglers from the Jacobite Army were 'killed by the country people', the retreat was carried out swiftly and efficiently, despite the terrible weather, frequent bombardments of torrential rain and freezing sleet. The men in charge of the baggage train had a particularly hard time, bumping carts along rough and rutted roads.

Although it was the Jacobites who now feared ambushes, these did not materialize. Sir John Macdonald was relieved but surprised by this:

> It seems that the English army is not acquainted with what is called guerrilla warfare. We only saw some of their militia on horseback on the hill tops watching our march and being very careful to keep out of shot, even by a single soldier.

They were, however, being pursued, the Duke of Cumberland by now hot on their heels. John Roy Stuart and his Edinburgh Regiment formed the rearguard, protecting the baggage train and scooping up any stragglers. As Cumberland caught up with them, several skirmishes and running battles ensued.

At some point in the various melees, at or near Lowther Hall, a few miles north of Shap Fell, John Roy lost his servant, his targe and one of his pair of Doune pistols. What became of the servant is not known, but the shield and pistol can be seen today in Aberdeen's Marischal Museum.

The fighting culminated in what was to become the last military engagement fought on English, as opposed to British, soil. Now officially relegated to the status of a skirmish, locally they still prefer to call it the Battle of Clifton Moor. It was fought on a dark winter's afternoon along narrow country lanes lined with hedges, not ideal terrain for either side. The Edinburgh Regiment provided back-up to the soldiers fighting under Lord George Murray, the Jacobite commander-in-chief. The Appin Stewarts, Angus MacDonell of Glengarry and Cluny Macpherson and their men were also in the thick of the fight, which lasted for about half an hour.

The Jacobites lost 12 men and inflicted casualties of about 50 dead and wounded on their opponents, mainly troopers from Bland's Regiment. Although the Jacobites then retreated, both sides claimed Clifton as a victory.

Angus MacDonell of Glengarry did not live long to celebrate it. Despite surviving Clifton and, a month later, the Battle of Falkirk, he was accidentally shot in the streets of Falkirk shortly after that battle by a Highland soldier cleaning his gun.

Inconclusive it might have been, but the engagement at Clifton and the disinclination of Cumberland to follow them into a snowy Scotland gave the Jacobite Army the breathing space it needed to head north, cross the border and get back home.

After brief sojourns at Dumfries and Hamilton, the next stop on the itinerary was Glasgow.

13

THE PRINCE, THE PROVOST & THE TWELVE THOUSAND SHIRTS

OUR VERY LADYS HAD NOT THE CURIOSITY TO GO NEAR HIM

Andrew Cochrane must have watched the advance guard of the Jacobite Army ride into Glasgow on Christmas Day 1745 with real trepidation. When the emergency had begun, his concern had been that Glasgow was full of essential supplies, an irresistible sitting target for an army on the march.

After the comings and goings of the past autumn, with the demands for money and goods, there was now a history of mutual and bitter antagonism between the city and the Jacobites. Once again, it was John Hay who played the heavy. After it was all over, Cochrane wrote again to MP Patrick Crawford in London:

> On the 25th December, about one forenoon, arrived
> the vanguard of the Highland army, and with them John
> Hay, late a writer, now a minister, kinsman to a certain
> great man, who had undertaken to be our scourge and
> persecutor. He came to the clerk's chamber, where the
> Magistrates and some of the principal inhabitants were,
> and made us a long harangue on our late rebellion and

appearance in arms, by marching a battalion to Stirling, and concluded that his H---ness was resolved to make us an example of his just severity, to strike a terror into other places. We did all we could, consistent with our duty, to soften him, and applied to some of the chiefs who arrived that night with a column of the army.

Frustrated by Glasgow's continuing defiance of him and by how it had continued to 'show too much Zelle to the Government', Charles threatened to sack the city. He would let his army loose to plunger and pillage as they pleased. This was not the Bonnie Prince's finest hour.

It was Donald Cameron of Lochiel who stayed his hand. Lochiel had close family and business connections with Glasgow. In 1743, he had placed an order for a large quantity of tartan cloth with one of the town's weavers, helping fuel the rumours of an impending Rising. Everything a clan chief should be and often was not, Lochiel was a humane man who cared deeply for his clansmen and -women, and felt responsible for their well-being. They, in return, looked up to him. Now he showed that care and concern for the people of Glasgow.

It's a strongly held tradition in Glasgow that, in gratitude for Lochiel having saved the city from being sacked, the bells of the Tolbooth at Glasgow Cross should ring out whenever he or any of his descendants came to town. This tradition has been observed in modern times.

Although Lochiel had prevented a violent sacking of the city, a peaceful plundering was to take place instead. According to Provost Cochrane, the men who billeted themselves in pubs and private houses did not pay for their accommodation. This was unusual for the 'we pay our way' Jacobite Army.

Cochrane might have been trying to paint them all in as bad a light as possible, or he might have been telling the truth. After the long walk home, they may have felt they were entitled to be fed and watered, and provided with clean sheets and a soft bed free, gratis and for nothing in this city which had stood so stubbornly against them.

They were certainly in no mood to be crossed, as the next demand made on Provost Cochrane showed. The unwelcome visitors wanted 6,000 cloth jackets, 12,000 linen shirts, 6,000 pairs of shoes, 6,000 blue bonnets and 6,000 pairs of tartan stockings, plus a sum of money which the provost does not specify.

Presumably pausing only to reel back, strike their foreheads with the backs of their hands and ask incredulously *how* many shirts, Glasgow scrabbled around trying to gather together as much as they could of the Jacobites' list of demands. Angry though they were, the citizens of Glasgow were terrified that if they didn't show willing the sacking would be back on the agenda.

Having put the fear of God into the Glaswegians and got what he wanted from them, the Prince now switched to a charm offensive. It did not go down well. Or did it? Falling over backwards, as usual, to prove Glasgow's loyalty to King George after the scary men in tartan were safely away Cochrane wrote to everyone he could think of, maintaining that not even 'the meanest inhabitant' had accorded Charles Edward Stuart the slightest amount of respect, or even taken an interest in him:

> Our very ladys had not the curiosity to go near him, and declined going to a ball held by his chiefs. Very few were at the windows when he made his appearance, and such as were declared him not handsome. This no doubt fretted.

Once more, the good provost seems to be protesting too much. Despite their resentment at the demands made of them, Glaswegians have always enjoyed a good show, and a good show was what the Prince and his men put on for them. It was all great street theatre.

Despite Cochrane's denials, a few members of the Jacobite Army were Glaswegians. One of them was Andrew Wood, described as both a shoemaker and a gentleman. He had been with the Prince in England, a member of John Roy Stuart's Edinburgh Regiment. He probably found that hard to live down when he got home.

Charles personally presented Andrew Wood with his captain's commission, probably at the Shawfield Mansion on the Trongate, where he had taken up residence. This beautiful building was the home of Mr Glassford, one of the foremost of Glasgow's Tobacco Lords. A plaque at the foot of what used to be his garden and is now Glassford Street marks where his house once stood.

Provost Cochrane's denial that any local ladies went to that 'ball held by his chiefs' is also suspect. Another strong local tradition has it that they did, naming one in particular. She was Clementine Walkinshaw, who was to become Charles's long-term mistress and the mother of his only acknowledged child.

Distracted though he might have been by dallying with Clemmie, Charles took particular care to dress with great elegance while he was in Glasgow, and to make sure the locals saw him and his army. Sharp as tacks, more than one eagle-eyed Glaswegian spotted that when the Prince put on a show of strength by reviewing his troops on Glasgow Green, the men marched down one street and up another in order to appear a larger force than they actually were.

There's another account from an anonymous eyewitness of how Glasgow reacted to the invasion of the 'Hieland raggymuffins':

> Like other young people, I was extremely anxious to see Prince Charles, and for that purpose stationed myself in the Trongate, where it was reported he would pass. He was holding a muster of his troops in the Green; and when it was over, he passed on horseback at the head of his men, on his way to his head-quarters. I managed to get so near him that I could have touched him with my hand; and the impression which his appearance made upon my mind shall never fade from it as long as I live. He had a princely aspect; and its interest was much deepened by the dejection that appeared in his pale countenance and downcast eye. He evidently wanted confidence in his own cause, and seemed to have a

melancholy foreboding of that disastrous issue which
ruined the hopes of his family forever.

The Jacobite Army left Glasgow on 3 January 1746, taking a printing
press and two magistrates as hostages to ensure the city's future good
behaviour. Within a week, Provost Cochrane was fielding demands
coming from the Government side.

Jack Campbell, Glasgow's MP, future 5th Duke of Argyle and now
serving the Government as the dashing Colonel Jack of the Argyle
Militia, wrote from Dumbarton to ask that the 40 kettles he wanted be
a little bigger than the sample Cochrane had sent him. If the knapsacks
he had ordered weren't 'made of calves' skin such as soldiers always
have', Cochrane was to proceed no further with them. The young
Colonel Jack at least finished his letter with 'I am sorry to give you so
much trouble.'

Glasgow's sacrifice was soon to be counted in more than kettles,
shirts and bonnets. In the middle of January 1746, the Glasgow
Regiment lined up at Falkirk to face the Jacobites in battle.

14

REPORTER IN RHYME: DOUGAL GRAHAM, THE BELLMAN OF GLASGOW

FIRST THEN, I HAVE AN ITCH FOR SCRIBBLING

Many men wrote about their experiences during the '45, in letters home, journals, succinct official reports, longer narratives and books. Many expressed themselves in verse, pouring out into poetry the emotions aroused by armed and bloody combat and the experience of being a fugitive hunted down like a wild animal in your own country. Only one wrote a complete *History of the Rebellion* in rhyming couplets.

Dougal Graham was that soldier – or was he? He claimed in the preface to his book to have been an eyewitness to most of the 'Movements of the Armies, from the Rebels first crossing the Ford of Frew to their final defeat at Culloden'. This has led many writers to assume he was a volunteer in the Jacobite Army.

His name does not appear in the records of the Jacobite Army to be found in *No Quarter Given: The Muster Roll of Prince Charles Edward Stuart's Army, 1745–46*, but this proves very little, as omissions are inevitable. Nor would the muster roll of any Jacobite regiment include the camp followers who went on the march into England, such as wives and children, prostitutes and traders in other commodities who saw a potentially lucrative business opportunity.

In 1745, Dougal Graham was 21 and working as a chapman, a pedlar who went around the country selling ribbons, pins, shoe-laces and cheaply produced books known as 'chapbooks'. In size, these were more like booklets or pamphlets. It was from the chapman that ordinary people bought romances, tales of the heroes and heroines of old – the life of William Wallace was a perennial favourite – sermons, almanacs, broadsides, the prophecies of Peden, Cargill and Thomas the Rhymer, and poems. Criss-crossing Scotland as these travelling salesmen did, they also brought news and gossip about what was happening in the here and now.

The interesting conclusion which can be drawn from this is that enough working-class Scots could read to make the sale of chapbooks worthwhile. Those who had the skill might also have read them aloud to their families and neighbours. There was clearly a thirst throughout Scotland for news, information and thrilling tales of romance and adventure. Nothing new there, then.

Sometimes people terrified themselves by what they read. A group of women in Port Glasgow were thrown into terrible distress after reading a book bought from a pedlar of the prophecies of Peden. One of these foretold that the people of Scotland would suffer untold woes in the year 1744 and that the Clyde would run red with blood. A year out because of the Protestant Wind, perhaps? And if the Clyde itself did not run red, burns, pools and wells at Prestonpans, Falkirk and Culloden famously did.

It seems likely that when the Rebellion started, Dougal Graham saw an opportunity to make both money and his name by carrying on his existing profession and keeping his eyes and ears open. A Victorian historian of Glasgow wrote of 'an old man who knew Dougal well, that he was only a follower of the army, and carried a pack with small wares'. Dougal Graham could have set off, perhaps on horseback, with his pedlar's pack, which he could replenish out of his takings along the way. It would have been an ideal occupation for a man like Dougal, a smooth-talking salesman with a keen interest in his fellow man and woman, and the world about him.

He certainly did his research. He cannot have been present at every incident of which he writes, but all the well-known stories of the events of 1745–6 feature in his *History*. He also got his book out into the marketplace as quickly as any contemporary reporter's account of a modern war, as an advert in the *Glasgow Courant* of 29 September 1746 demonstrates:

> That there is to be sold by James Duncan, Printer in Glasgow, in the Saltmercat, the 2nd shop below Gibson's Wynd, a Book Intitled, A full, particular, and true Account of the late Rebellion in the Year 1745 and 1746 beginning with the Pretender's Embarking for Scotland, and then an Account of every Battle, Siege, and Skirmish that has happened in either Scotland or England.

This book and his subsequent writings were to bring Dougal fame and fortune, or at least a comfortable living. He became one of the characters of Glasgow and a successful businessman, surmounting humble beginnings and physical deformity to do so. He was born in 1724 in what was then the village of Raploch (now part of Stirling) and may have grown up, as a brief nineteenth-century biography of him puts it, in 'the quaint village of Campsie'.

In the parlance of his own times, Dougal Graham was 'humphie backit'. In addition to the hunchback, he had a growth on his chest and never grew taller than five feet. His brain, however, was razor-sharp. Intelligent and quick-thinking, he was a dab hand at the repartee and a master of the witty one-liner – and he knew how to market his work.

The advert he placed in the *Glasgow Courant* in September 1746 ends with a proud boast: 'The like has not been done in Scotland since

the days of Sir David Lindsay.' He evokes the name of the author of
Ane Satyre of the Thrie Estaitis for exactly the same purpose as a modern
publisher asking an established writer to endorse a new writer's work.

The *Courant* advert informs eager readers that the book costs
fourpence but discreetly suggests there may be a bulk discount for
booksellers and packmen if they go directly to the printer or Dougal
Graham himself. This implies he was already enough of a 'kent' face
for everyone to know where to find him. If he wasn't already living in
Glasgow before he went off on his adventure with the Jacobites, as he
seems not to have been, he may have gone there to buy the chapbooks
he hawked around Stirlingshire.

Although the evidence suggests that his *History of the Rebellion* sold
thousands of copies, no first edition of it has survived. Chapbooks were
not made to last. In 1752, he published a second edition, describing
himself as 'Dougal Graham, merchant'. He had by now become the
publisher and printer of his own works. Like a modern author writing
straight onto a computer, he composed directly onto the printing
press, 'at once spinning thought into typography', without first writing
his verses by hand.

By this time he was living in Glasgow and had become the city's
unofficial Poet Laureate, recording current events in his trademark
rhyme, although he also wrote prose. George Caldwell, a publisher and
bookseller in Paisley, was always keen to get hold of Dougal's works to
offer to his customers:

> A' his books took weel, they were level to the meanest
> capacity, and had plenty o' coarse jokes to season them.
> I never kent a history of Dougal's that stuck in the
> sale yet.

The Scottish literati of the time looked down on him, of course, as
their modern counterparts still do on any writer who tells a rattling
good yarn, writes something readers want to read and is appreciated
by ordinary people. One reviewer dipped his quill in vinegar: 'This

is a sorry performance.' Dougal got his revenge in sales. *History of the Rebellion* went to three editions in his lifetime and at least eight after his death.

He has been much appreciated by scholars and historians ever since. One of them was Mr McVean, 'the antiquarian bibliophile of the High Street'. Another was Sir Walter Scott, who found the *History of the Rebellion* fascinating, especially in the details it records which are not to be found in other accounts of the '45. Robert Burns was also a fan of Dougal's work, particularly its often bawdy humour.

Despite his success, Dougal Graham had no great conceit of himself. One of his other books, *John Cheap, the Chapman,* is thought to be autobiographical. If it is, the picture he paints of himself is most definitely warts and all:

> John Cheap, the chapman, was a very comical short thick
> fellow, with a broad face and a long nose; both lame
> and lazy, and something lecherous among the lasses; he
> chused rather to sit idle than work at any time, as he was
> a hater of hard labour. He got the name of John Cheap
> the chapman, by his selling twenty needles for a penny,
> and twa leather laces for a farthing.

The titles of some of his later publications would now be considered very politically incorrect. Take *The Comical Sayings of Paddy from Cork, with his Coat button'd behind.* Or, in the splendidly long-winded style of eighteenth-century titles, *Grannie McNab's Lecture in the Society of Clashing Wives, Glasgow, on Witless Mithers and Dandy Daughters, who bring them up to hoodwink the men, and deceive them with their braw dresses, when they can neither wash a sark, mak' parritch, or gang to the well.*

Throughout his life, Dougal responded in writing to current events, as when road tolls were first introduced to Scotland in the mid-1760s. 'Turnimspike' was a song designed to be sung to the tune of 'Clout the Cauldron' – whatever that was. Dr Charles Mackay, a student of Dougal's works, has left us an eloquent commentary:

Turnimspike, or Turnspike, is ludicrously descriptive of
the agonies of a real Highlander at the introduction of
toll gates, and other paraphernalia of modern civilisation,
into the remote mountain fastness of his native land.
Long after the suppression of the Rebellion, great
consternation was excited in Ross-shire, by the fact
that a sheriff's officer had actually served a writ in Tain.
'Lord, preserve us!' said a Highlandman to his neighbour,
'What'll come next? The law has reached Tain.'

Dougal's works also received the ultimate accolade of being among
those most frequently shoplifted. A bookseller by the name of
Motherwell complained bitterly about this:

> There are a number of infamous creatures, who acquire
> large libraries of curious things, by borrowing books
> they never mean to return, and some not unfrequently
> slide a volume into their pocket, at the very moment you
> are fool enough to busy yourself in showing them some
> nice typographic gem or bibliographic rarity. These
> dishonest and heartless villains, ought to be cut above
> the breath whenever they cross the threshold. They
> deserve no more courtesy than was of old vouchsafed to
> witches, under bond and indenture to the Devil.

Dougal Graham himself was regarded as an infamous creature by some
in his own time. When he applied for the post of Glasgow bellman,
they objected on the grounds of his involvement with the Jacobites.
The appointment was in the gift of the Glasgow magistrates and,
following Provost Cochrane's gallant efforts – no Jacobites in Glasgow,
sir – they were not keen on the connection.

Mr Caldwell, the Paisley bookseller, offered an explanation of how
Dougal Graham got the job he wanted, maintaining that the would-be
bellman told the magistrates he had been pressed into Charles Edward
Stuart's service. This excuse rather contradicts another one Dougal

made, that at the time of the outbreak of the '45, as Caldwell was later to put it, 'he was naething mair than a hafflins callant that scarcely kent his left hand frae his richt, or a B frae a bull's fit.'

Be that as it may, Dougal Graham got the job as 'skellat' bellman. The unusual word simply means that he gave out the news of the day, while the 'mort' bellman announced who had died. In his official uniform of tricorne hat, long red coat, blue breeches, white stockings and buckled shoes, Dougal walked around Glasgow ringing his bell and giving out useful information. He might let everyone know there were caller herring freshly landed at the Broomielaw this morning, or list the departure times of the stagecoaches which regularly left the Black Bull and the Saracen's Head inns. His bell tolled closing time at these and other hostelries, too. The bellman also searched for 'wander'd weans' whose distraught mothers had been unable to find them. He was popular with children – at only five feet tall, he wasn't much bigger than many of them – and there was usually a crowd of them around him when he rang his bell.

He died in 1779, when he was in his mid-fifties, but the memories and tales of his wit lived on for many years afterwards, as did his chapbook stories and his *History of the Rebellion*. It's a highly detailed and comprehensive study of what happened in 1745–6, and it begins by giving the historical background:

> In the year se'enteen hundred and forty one,
> An imperious and bloody war began,
> Amongst kings and queens in Germanie,
> Who should the Roman Emperor be.
> French and Prussians did jointly go,
> The Hungarian queen to ovethro';
> But British, Hanoverians, and Dutch,
> Espous'd her cause, and that too much.
> From year to year, the flame it grew,
> Till armies to the field they drew.
> At Dettingen and Fontenoy,

Did many thousand lives destroy.
And then the French, they form'd a plan,
To animate our Highland clan,
By sending the Pretender's son
To claim Great Britain as his own;
Which drew the British forces back,
And made the German war to slack.

Beautifully summed up, and it scans not too badly either. Not all of his poetry does, and some of his rhymes are less successful than others:

His MANIFESTOES, also spread,
Which for the Scots, great favour had;
How that the Union, he'd dissolve,
And the tax from Malt, Salt and Coal:

What's interesting is that he confirms many of the less well-known stories of the Rising, including, for example, the tale of 'Swethenham of Guise's foot' being released on parole. Did a clansman in MacDonald of Keppoch's Regiment tell the funny little pedlar that tale one night around the campfire on the march into England?

Dougal also tells stories which other people don't. There's one about bands of robbers 'in tartan dress'd from top to toe' going around demanding horses and money from people, which recalls Colonel Jack Campbell of the Argyle Militia's letter to his father telling him that a 'madman' and his gang had been stravaiging about Dunbartonshire demanding money with menaces. The Prince's men got the blame for such raids, but, according to Dougal, these were opportunist thieves rather than soldiers of the Jacobite Army. Dougal mourned the death of Colonel James Gardiner as a good Christian and a good soldier, and his description of the run-up to Prestonpans has a certain poetic charm, followed though it is by a grim eighteenth-century pun:

Then tidings came in from Dunbar,
Of Gen'ral Cope's arrival there
But twenty miles from Ed'nburgh east,
Which made them all take arms in haste.
On the east side of Arthur's seat,
They rendezvouz'd both small and great,
And call'd a council what to do;
For ten miles east they had a view
Of all the coast to Aberlady,
And so for battle made all ready.

Although they did for quarters cry,
The vulgar clans made this reply,
'Quarters! You curst soldiers, mad,
It is o'er soon to go to bed.'

He mentions, too, a prediction made by Thomas the Rhymer, that one day the area around Prestonpans would be the site of a terrible battle fought in the early morning, as indeed it was. According to Dougal, both Merlin and the Venerable Bede had also predicted this.

His words describing the exhausted Jacobite Army marching into Glasgow paint a picture as vivid as it is humane:

Their count'nance fierce as a wild bear
Out o'er their eyes hang down their hair,
Their very thighs red tanned quite;
But yet as nimble as they'd been white;
Their beards were turned black and brown,
The like was ne'er seen in that town,
Some of them did barefooted run,
Minded no mire nor stony groun';
But when shav'n, drest and cloth'd again
They turn'd to be like other men.

149

The Battle of Falkirk brings us back to 'Brave col'nel JACK, being then a boy, His warlike genious did employ'. Dougal also covers the Prince's wanderings after Culloden in some detail, including the part played in his rescue by Flora MacDonald, and the hangings of the Jacobites in the aftermath of the Rising. Since these reprisals happened between September and November 1746, they cannot have formed part of the first edition of *History of the Rebellion,* which had only been published in September of that year.

It seems unlikely that Dougal Graham was present at those executions which took place in London. He makes an easy but basic mistake when writing about them, having them take place at Kensington. In fact they were carried out south of the Thames, at *Kennington.* Might he, though, have actually attended the executions at Carlisle in person? The distance from Glasgow is only 100 miles and he already knew the way – and he writes of them with real horror:

> Of these poor souls at Carlisle,
> Whose execution was so vile,
> A wooden stage they did erect,
> And first, half strangl'd by the neck,
> A fire upon the stage was born,
> Their hearts out of their breasts were torn
> The privy part unspared was,
> Cut off, and dash'd into their face,
> Then expanded into the fire;
> But such a sight I'll ne'er desire,
> Some beholders swooned away,
> Others stood mute, had nought to say,
> And some of a more brutish nature,
> Did shout *Huzza,* to seal the matter,
> Some a mourning, turn'd about
> A praying for their souls, no doubt
> Some curs'd the butcher, Haxam Willie,
> Who without remorse used his *gullie,*

And for the same a pension got,
Thus butchering the *Rebel Scot*.

After that, it's no surprise that Dougal issued the following warnings
to his fellow countrymen:

My dear Scots-men, a warning take
Superior pow'rs not to forsake,
Mind the Apostle's words, of law and love,
Saying, *All power is giv'n from above*.
'Tis by will of heav'n kings do reign,
The chain of Fate's not rul'd by men.
Every thing must serve its time,
And so have kings of Stewart's line.

And those who trust in France or Spain,
Are fools if e'er they do't again:
Witness poor Charlie and the Scots,
What have they got but bloody throats?

On the alleged treachery of Lord George Murray, he writes wisely,
too, of human nature:

For there is never a Battle lost, but the Commander gets
the Blame, and when one is won, the Commander gets
all the Praise, as if the Soldiers had done nothing; And
it is further observed, after the loss of a Battle it is the
cry of the Public and the run-away Soldiers, WE ARE
SOLD, WE ARE SOLD.

Because Dougal published his first edition of *History of the Rebellion*
so quickly, he had to be careful what he said. Showing overt sympathy
for the Jacobite soldiers and criticizing the Government troops could
have had him arrested for sedition. By the time he published the
third edition, in 1774, he could be more frank. As he wrote in his

preface, Charles's Cause was now well and truly lost, and the Duke of Cumberland had 'gone to the house of Silence'. Therefore Dougal Graham could write of the cruelty of the Redcoats in the aftermath of Culloden and the consequent suffering of so many Highlanders, men, women and children, who'd had nothing to do with the Rebellion.

In the third edition, he also emphasized that he had done his research, including reading what the celebrated Monsieur Voltaire had written about the attempt of 1745, which may have helped Dougal set the historical scene and place the Rising in its European context. Of course, he himself had an advantage over Voltaire in that he had his own eyewitness observations to rely on. He had written his *History* for the ordinary man and woman in the street and for himself, to satisfy his 'itch for scribbling', and now offered this 'brat of his brain' to the public – and the public loved it.

15

WITH GOD ON OUR SIDE:
PISKIES, PAPISTS & PRESBYTERIANS

BY THE ASSISTANCE OF GOD, I WILL, THIS DAY,
MAKE YOU A FREE AND HAPPY PEOPLE

Both sides in the '45 believed, of course, that God was on their side. The loyal oath sworn by the men of the Duke of Perth's Regiment went like this:

> I solemnly promise and swear In the Presence of Almighty God That I shall faithfully and diligently serve James the Eighth King of Scotland England France and Ireland against all his Enemies foreign or domestick And shall not desert or leave his service without leave asked and given of my officer. And hereby pass from all former alledgeance given by me to George Elector of Hannover. So help me God.

As every regiment in the Jacobite Army had its surgeon, so it also had its chaplain, who was given captain's status. Some regiments had more than one, an interesting indicator of the varied religious make-up of the men who followed Charles Edward Stuart.

Cameron of Lochiel's Regiment had three padres: the Reverend John Cameron of Fort William for the Presbyterians, the Reverend Duncan Cameron of Fortingall for the Episcopalians and Father Alexander Cameron, a Jesuit, for the Catholics. Alexander Cameron was also Cameron of Lochiel's brother.

When Alexander had first converted to Catholicism, it came as quite a shock to his Presbyterian family. It was an even bigger shock when he became a priest, and a Jesuit at that: Christ's shock troops. Father Cameron himself was happy to admit that in his youth he had been a bit 'wilde'.

At the time, and sometimes even today, the '45 was presented as a Protestant–Catholic struggle. The unlikely assertion is made that if Charles Edward Stuart had been successful, Britain would now be a Catholic country. Charles was indeed a Roman Catholic, raised in a Catholic country by devoutly Catholic parents. His father, James, put his faith before regaining his lost crown. At various points in his life, most specifically when Queen Anne died in 1714, it's very possible that if he had been prepared to renounce the Catholic religion, the Stuarts would have found themselves back on the throne. However, James could never bring himself to follow the example of the pragmatic and Protestant Henri of Navarre, who declared Paris to be worth a Mass and so became king of France.

Charles was not nearly so devout a Catholic as his parents. Lord Elcho famously said that his religion was 'to seek'. In 1750, the Prince even made a secret visit to London where, in the church of St Mary's in the Strand, he was received into the Protestant Church of England. Although he later returned to the Catholic Church, he was beside himself with rage and grief when his brother Henry became a Cardinal, believing the Stuart Cause's identification with Catholicism had contributed hugely to the failure of the '45. With Henry now a Prince of the Roman Catholic Church, Charles saw his chances of ever becoming Prince of Wales vanishing into the mist.

Charles's willingness to convert in 1750 begs the question as to why he did not do so in 1745 or before. The answer is that converting at that time would have had negative as well as positive effects on his Cause. He was hoping for support from France, a Catholic country. His father would have been both furious and heartbroken if his son had left the Catholic Church, and, at that time, James was a very powerful figure in his son's life. Charles's Catholic supporters in Britain, some of them men and women of high social status and potential influence, might also have turned against him.

There is another important point. Full of youthful idealism, the Prince may have thought his often-repeated guarantees of religious freedom for all would be enough to reassure those Protestants who worried about restoring a Catholic monarch. In his relaxed attitude to religion, he was light years ahead of the monarch and the government he sought to overturn.

Roman Catholics in eighteenth-century Britain were treated as worse than second-class citizens. They were seen as the enemy within, owing their primary allegiance not so much to God as to an Italian Pope, French priests and Spanish Jesuits. In 1701, the Act of Settlement made it impossible for the king or queen of Great Britain to be a Catholic or marry a Catholic. This law remains on the statute books today.

Even before that, in 1700, the Scottish Parliament had passed stringent laws which not only allowed the authorities to arrest any man suspected of being a priest, but also made it illegal for individual Catholics to attend Catholic church services. They were also banned from inheriting or even renting land and property, and were required to send their children to Protestant schools.

Being thrawn Scots as well as Catholics, they found ways around these laws. In country areas in particular, most Protestants and Catholics managed to rub along together without too much friction. Be that as it may, the priests who rode around Scotland – incognito, in ordinary clothes and never to be addressed as 'Father' for fear of giving the game away – were running enormous personal risks. If found or reported to have been saying Mass, or celebrating marriages, baptisms and funerals according to Catholic rites, they could be banished. If they returned to Britain, they could, in theory, be sentenced to death.

Their flock made up only a very small part of the Scottish population, between 2 and 3 per cent, and was widely scattered into the bargain. This was long before the waves of migrations of Irish Catholics to Glasgow and the west of Scotland. At the time of the '45, Scotland's Catholics were to be found keeping their heads down in the Borders, Galloway, the western Highlands and Islands, the central Highlands and upland Aberdeenshire and Banffshire.

Many of their descendants have discreetly kept the faith into our own times. In particular, the ornate Catholic churches and beautiful little chapels of north-east Scotland can take non-Catholic Scots by surprise. One of the most moving relics of the days of persecution is the seminary at Scalan, in the breathtakingly lovely and still remote Braes of Glenlivet. They trained what were called 'heather priests' there. After Culloden, the Redcoat garrison at nearby Corgarff Castle burned the place down. It was later rebuilt and is now permanently open to visitors of all faiths or none who choose to make the pilgrimage.

There is no doubt that Catholics in both Scotland and England had high hopes of what the restoration of the Stuarts would mean for them, or of how closely their faith intertwined with their politics. Looked at in the wider context, however, the Catholics were only one group among many who found in the Jacobite Cause a focus for their discontent with the status quo.

The church most strongly associated with the Jacobites was the Episcopalian. You could hardly be the latter without being the former. Because so many of them had remained faithful to the Stuarts, they refused to take the loyalty oath to the Hanoverian succession. This made them non-jurors, and, like the Anglican non-jurors in England, they too were persecuted.

Throughout the '45, Episcopalian meeting houses were ransacked and wrecked by Redcoat soldiers. Considering that the Episcopalians and the established Church of England were so close together in terms of doctrine and style of worship, this is more than a little ironic. Given how much the Episcopalians suffered because of their loyalty to the House of Stuart, it's also rather sad that their church is so often in Scotland today referred to as the English church.

The Church of Scotland, on the other hand, was as closely bound up with what was then called the Protestant Succession as the Episcopalians were with the Stuart Cause. Some Presbyterian ministers even took to the battlefield on the Government side, most notably at the Battle of Falkirk. Many more thundered fire and brimstone sermons from their pulpits at Jacobites, Catholics and Episcopalians. Charles Edward Stuart was a 'Pope-bred princeling' who had 'suck'd in malice with his milk' and stood at the head of 'banditti, thieves, robbers' and 'ragged ruffians of the north and savage mountaineers'.

Church of England clergymen spat out this vitriol, too. Some published their interminably long sermons as pamphlets, so that their dire warnings of the dangers posed by these malevolent Catholics might reach a wider audience than their own congregations. Consciously or not, the perceived external danger posed by the Jacobites was a great way of keeping people in line. Sitting round the campfire might at times be uncomfortably hot, but there were goblins and demons circling out there in the darkness, waiting to pounce.

The Duke of Cumberland issued a proclamation soon after Culloden telling lurking Jacobites that they should surrender themselves and their weapons to their nearest Church of Scotland minister. Yet despite keeping an inquisitive eye on their Jacobite neighbours before, during and after the event, many Presbyterian ministers refused to supply lists of those either well-affected or disaffected in their neighbourhood. Many, to their eternal credit, hid Jacobite fugitives and helped them to escape. Among those were the Reverend Lumsden and his wife, of Towie in Aberdeenshire.

When Charles Gordon of Blelack and his friend Jonathan Forbes managed to make it to Towie, the Lumsdens hid them for some time in the attic of the manse. Comments were made about the amount of food the household was going through. Mrs Lumsden blithely blamed it on the two pigs she was fattening for market. When the maids complained of seeing shadows in the night, she terrified them with tales of ghosts.

Another Charles Gordon, skulking near his home at Terpersie near Alford, was flushed out by a Redcoat patrol. They frogmarched him to the local minister and demanded he confirm Gordon's identity. The minister declined to cooperate. The soldiers then took him to his own home. His small children came rushing out, happily shouting 'Daddy! Daddy!', and thus unwittingly sealed their father's fate.

When it was all over, many Catholic priests were arrested and some were treated very brutally, although only one man of the cloth was tried for treason and hanged. The Reverend Robert Lyon was, of course, an Episcopalian.

16

BARDS & BROADSWORDS:
THE BATTLE OF FALKIRK

DOWN THEY CHARGE, UNHESITATING,
SWORDS EAGER HEADS TO SEVER

In a telling illustration of the interesting times through which they lived, two of Scotland's greatest Gaelic poets fought on opposite sides during the '45. In their mother tongue – the language of the Garden of Eden – they were Alasdair MacMhaighstir Alasdair and Donnchadh Ban Mac an t-Saoir. The English versions of their names are Alexander MacDonald and Duncan Ban MacIntyre, respectively.

Alexander MacDonald was in his mid-forties in 1745. A Clanranald MacDonald and cousin to the famous Flora, he was one of the first people to greet Charles Edward Stuart when he landed on the Scottish mainland on the shores of Loch nan Uamh in July 1745. So as to draw no undue attention to himself, the Prince was dressed very plainly that day. Unaware to whom he was speaking, it took one of Alexander MacDonald's clansmen to give him a black look before 'he began to suspect he was using too much freedom with one above his own rank'.

Charles obviously didn't mind the familiarity. He appointed Alexander MacDonald his Gaelic tutor and gave him the first military commission that he issued during the campaign. MacDonald served throughout the campaign as a captain in Clanranald's Regiment.

He was writing political verse well before Charles arrived. His 'Oran Do'n Phrionnsa' ('A Song to the Prince') celebrates that longed-for event. Translated into English by John Lorne Campbell, it reads:

> O, hi ri ri, he is coming,
> O, hi ri ri, our exiled King,
> Let us take our arms and clothing,
> And the flowing tartan plaid.

> Joyful I am, he is coming,
> Son of our rightful exiled King,
> A mighty form which becomes armour,
> The broad-sword and the bossy shield.

> He is coming o'er the ocean
> Of stature tall, and fairest face,
> A happy rider of the war-horse,
> Moving lightly in the charge.

MacDonald wrote many more songs in the same vein: joyous, lively and bloodthirsty. In 'Oran Nuadh' (or 'New Song'), he called for genuine commitment, not mere gestures:

> Let slashing, clashing blades of steel
> Answer skirl of chanters;
> When you've set the headlong rout,
> Far and wide re-echo
> Whistling blows, which smite to sever
> Bodies clean asunder;
> To flight they'll take in panic-spate,
> And ne-er again turn on you.
> There's many a man who'd drink the health
> Of our rightful ruler,

Provost Andrew Cochrane
of Glasgow. (Author's collection)

Contemporary map of the Battle of Prestonpans from
the *Gentleman's Magazine* of 1745. (Author's collection)

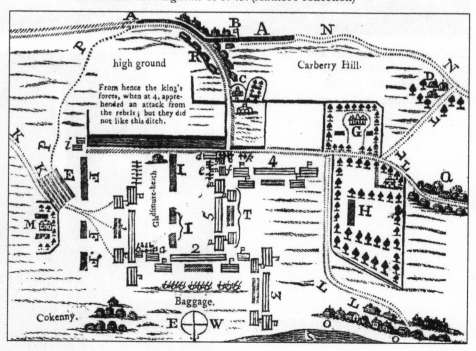

high ground

From hence the king's
forces, when at 4, appre-
hended an attack from
the rebels; but they did
not like this ditch.

Carberry Hill.

Gladsmuir-heath

Baggage.

Cokenny.

E · W

S

Reverend Alexander Carlyle.
(© The MacBean Collection,
Aberdeen University Library)

'The Battle of Prestonpans and
the Death of Colonel Gardiner'.
(© The MacBean collection,
Aberdeen University Library)

Colonel Gardiner's Monument and
Bankton House. (W.R. Totterdell)

John Campbell, cashier of
The Royal Bank of Scotland.
(Reproduced by kind permission
of The Royal Bank of Scotland
Group © 2008)

Bonnie Prince Charlie entering
the ballroom at Holyrood House,
with Cameron of Lochiel to his
right and Lord Pitsligo to his left.
(The Royal Collection © 2008,
Her Majesty Queen Elizabeth II)

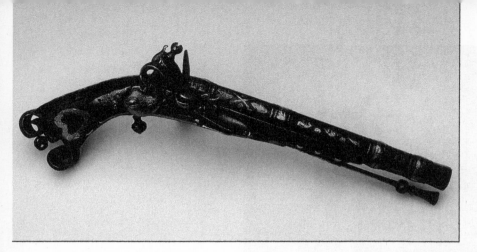

John Roy Stuart's flintlock Doune pistol.
(© University of Aberdeen)

Dougal Graham, Skellat Bellman of Glasgow.
(Courtesy of Aberdeenshire Libraries
and Information Service)

Sir Stuart Threipland's medicine chest.
(Royal College of Physicians of Edinburgh)

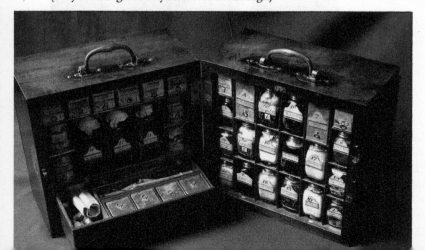

'Colonel Jack', John Cambell of Mamore, later 56th Duke of Argyle. (Author's collection)

Angus Banner. (Dundee Art Galleries and Museums)

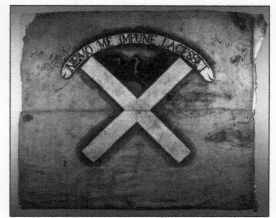

'Rebell Gratitude', a contemporary print showing the death of Captain Grossett. (Courtesy of the Trustees of the National Library of Scotland)

REBELL GRATITUDE,

Of a Representation of the Treachery and Barbarity of two Rebell Officers, at the Battle of Culloden, who had their Lives Generously given them by the Earl of Ancram, (Who had a considerable Command that Day) and by Captain Grosett Engineer & Aid De Camp to the General. The One attempted to shoar His Lordship behind his back with a Pistol, which He had kept concealed & which luckily only Flashd in the Pan. The Other Shot Captain Grosett Dead with his own Pistol, which happened Accidentally to fall from him as he was on Horseback, under pretence of restoring the same to the Captain. These Rebell received the first reward of their Perfidy, by being immediately cut to pieces by the Kings Troops. And it is Generally believed that this their Ingratitude and Treachery greatly heightned the Slaughter that was that Day made of their Party. —— Captain Grossett left behind him a Distressed Widow, with Six young Children.

This Battle was fought the 16 of April 1746. Publishd According to Act of Parliament Jan.y 14 1747.

Ranald MacDonald.
(© The MacBean Collection,
Aberdeen University Library)

Duncan Forbes of Culloden, Lord
President of the Court of Session.
(Author's collection)

Execution of MacDonnell of Tirnadris and other
Jacobite prisoners at Carlisle. (Author's collection)

Francis Farquharson of Monaltrie.
(Courtesy of the Trustees of the
National Library of Scotland)

Captain Andrew Wood's Halfpenny.
(In a private Scottish collection)

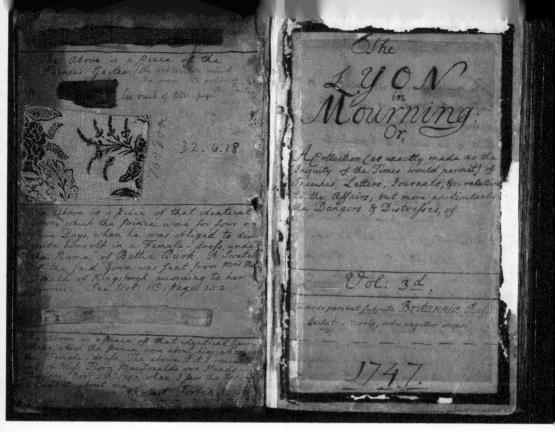

Frontispiece of *The Lyon in Mourning*, Vol. 3.
(Courtesy of the Trustees of the National Library of Scotland)

The Culloden Memorial. (Author's photograph)

> Smashing his wineglass on the hearth,
> Cursing the usurper;
> But honour now lives more in deeds
> Than drinking toasts unnumbered,
> A gill of blood shed on the moor
> Excels wine drunk in gallons.

There were plenty of 'whistling blows' at the Battle of Falkirk, a subject which also exercised Duncan Ban MacIntyre's pen. He went there as part of the Argyle Militia, persuaded to stand in for his landlord in return for a cash payment and the loan of that reluctant gentleman's broadsword. When MacIntyre came home after the militia had been disbanded and claimed his fee, it was refused on the grounds that he had lost the sword.

Never annoy someone who has a way with words. Inspired to get his revenge by writing his first song, Duncan Ban complains of having had no leadership at the battle and declares: 'Ne'er again shall I go forward, / To the Whiggish King's assistance.' He has a go at his landlord, too – and his rotten sword.

> Mighty iron with small edge to it,
> That describes the sword completely,
> It was pliant, starting, notchy,
> And its neck was curved and crooked;
> I was bruised on my thigh-side
> After carrying it while marching,
> Heavy as a pile of alder,
> Woe to him who asked 'twere lucky.

Despite the unlucky sword, and unlike many on the Government side, Duncan Ban MacIntyre had the good fortune to survive the Battle of Falkirk.

The lead-up to the Jacobite victory at Falkirk was unpromising. After they left Glasgow on 3 January 1746, the Jacobite Army spent a few fruitless weeks trying to capture Stirling Castle. Given that this fortress sits on a sheer volcanic rock high above a flat plain – that's why they built it there – the enterprise was more or less doomed to failure.

Nor did it help that the engineer in charge of the operation was spectacularly incompetent. James Johnstone was one of many who offered a sarcastic summing-up of this Frenchman of Scottish extraction. A Chevalier of the Order of St Louis, no less, his name was Mirabelle de Gordon:

> It was supposed that a French engineer, of a certain age and decorated with an order, must necessarily be a person of experience, talents, and capacity; but it was unfortunately discovered, when too late, that his knowledge as an engineer was extremely limited, and that he was totally destitute of judgment, discernment and common sense. His figure being as whimsical as his mind, the Highlanders, instead of Monsieur Mirabelle, called him always Mr Admirable.

The stalemate at Stirling did the Jacobite Army's morale no good. Men were beginning to desert, sloping off home when nobody was looking. Edinburgh was once more in Government hands and thousands of troops were marching north to defend it, making the logical assumption that the Jacobites would try to recapture the Scottish capital. To prevent this, the Duke of Cumberland had called on the services of the ruthless general known as Hangman Hawley. Notorious for meting out harsh punishment to deserters from his regiment and soldiers under his command who had been found guilty of other breaches of military discipline, until he came north of the border it was his own men he strung up.

Determined to take the fight to the enemy and end the siege of Stirling Castle, Hawley marched out of Edinburgh. The Jacobites marched to meet him, which they did at Falkirk. As at Prestonpans, both sides did a considerable amount of manoeuvring before it all began. Alerted at three o'clock on the morning of 17 January that the enemy's drums were beating, Sir John Macdonald described what happened next:

> It was decided to march on the enemy, Lord George at the head of the Highlanders on the heights leaving the high road to Edinburgh on the left and came to a halt with his right resting on a small wall on a heather moor opposite the town of Falkirk and on his left the enemy's camp, who were quietly remaining in their camp until they saw us on the moors. Then they moved towards the town of Falkirk, and came towards us, crossing a ditch between the two armies, their cavalry on the left in front of the infantry. The cavalry rode up the slope in good order ready to charge our right, then composed of Macdonalds who waited for them, kneeling on one knee till they were within pistol shot, then firing their volley, attacked the cavalry sword in hand, and it fled by the right across our front line, receiving the whole of its fire. This charge took place before our second line was formed. Suddenly the Highlanders of the front line attacked and beat the enemy. (I could not well see this manoeuvre on account of the inequalities of the land.) At the same time our second line, consisting of Lowlanders, smitten apparently with terror took to flight. I therefore quitted the cavalry which would not listen to orders, to go and rally a large body of our people going off on the right. I met Sulivan and together we managed to halt them and bring them back.

The manoeuvre which Sir John could not see because of the lie of the land was vividly described, as ever, by James Johnstone:

The Highlanders . . . discharged their muskets the moment the cavalry halted and killed about eighty men, each of them having aimed at a rider. The commander of this body of cavalry, who had advanced some paces before his men, was of the number. The cavalry closing their ranks, which were opened by our discharge, put spurs to their horses and rushing upon the Highlanders at a hard trot, breaking their ranks, throwing down everything before them and tramping the Highlanders under the feet of their horses. The most singular and extraordinary combat immediately followed.

Horribly, this 'singular and extraordinary combat' involved the Highlanders knifing the horses in the belly with their dirks before grabbing at the animals' riders, pulling them down by their clothes and stabbing them, too.

Because of this, Falkirk is notable as one of the few battles where infantry attacked cavalry rather than the other way around. Johnstone believed this ferocity was what defeated the Government forces, although he acknowledged that the high wind and heavy rain in which the battle was fought also had something to do with it.

In a grim foreshadowing of Culloden, where the men of the Jacobite Army had sleet driving into their faces, at Falkirk it was the Government soldiers who were face-on to the wind and rain. The pans of their musket also became waterlogged. Although they tried to adjust their position to compensate for the direction of the stormy weather, the Jacobites adjusted theirs in return.

Trying to determine what was going on, two opposing commanders moved forward and found themselves no distance apart. Each recognized the other, perhaps because they had both served in the British Army or perhaps because they'd had an encounter with one another at Prestonpans. One was John Roy Stuart. The Government officer rejoiced in the name of Shugborough Whitney. Sadly for him, he was not destined to rejoice in anything for very much longer.

'Ha!' called Whitney, 'Are you there? We shall soon be up with you!'

John Roy growled back in return: 'You shall be welcome when you come, and by God, you shall have a warm reception!'

A few moments later, Whitney was dead. Whether John Roy struck the fatal blow is not recorded.

Falkirk was a messy battle, both sides ending up with their ranks in complete confusion. In the driving rain and descending darkness, Donald MacDonell of Tirnadris, the hero of High Bridge, found himself captured by a group of Government officers who had failed to persuade their men to remain on the battlefield and were debating what to do next. As at Prestonpans, many of the soldiers under their command had simply turned and run. These included the soldiers of an English Redcoat regiment led by Scotsman and Highlander Sir Robert Munro, who abandoned their colonel to his fate. His brother Duncan was also killed.

In the midst of this horror of violence and storm, the men of the Glasgow and Paisley militias *did* stand their ground. At least 19 of the Glasgow men died, while a dozen of the militia men were wounded and a dozen more taken prisoner. These figures would have been higher but for the compassion of Andrew Wood of the Jacobite Army, the young shoemaker who had recently received his captain's commission from the Prince. He saw several of his friends and neighbours safely through the Jacobite lines and on their way home to Glasgow.

As darkness fell on the sodden battlefield, the confusion grew worse. It was quite some time before the Jacobite Army realized it had, in fact, won, the Government troops having abandoned the field. At about half past seven that evening, the Prince's army walked into Falkirk as the victors. It was the second defeat the Jacobite Army had inflicted on Government troops, and the humiliation was not to be forgotten.

A few days after the battle, Dr William Leechman, a professor at Glasgow University, sent a very polite letter to Lord Pitsligo asking him to intervene on behalf of four young men who had been taken prisoner at Falkirk: two Church of Scotland ministers and two divinity students. They had, Leechman wrote, only been spectators and had taken no part in the fighting. Acknowledging that they should have had more sense, the professor asked Lord Pitsligo if he could help return them safely to their friends and their congregations. In a P. S., Leechman passed on Mrs Leechman's 'most respectful Compliments to your Lordship'. They also asked to be remembered to 'our agreeable Guest and friend Mr Forbes', so if he and Lord Pitsligo had been billeted upon them while the Jacobite Army was in Glasgow over Christmas and New Year, relations must have been cordial. Given what we know of Lord Pitsligo's character, it's very possible that he backed up Cameron of Lochiel when he persuaded the Prince not to sack Glasgow.

Someone was, however, telling lies. At least one of the young ministers had not gone to Falkirk merely to watch the battle as a spectator. He had raised a militia from his parishioners at Beith and ridden at the head of it. Although they were stood down at Glasgow, the Reverend went on to Falkirk with every intention of fighting there on the Government side.

Lord Pitsligo's reply to the professor has been lost. He may well have been prepared to help the young ministers, but at least one of them released himself, escaping from his Jacobite gaolers after they locked him up in Doune Castle, north of Stirling. He was there with John Home, Alexander Carlyle's friend and fellow volunteer to Edinburgh's College Company, who had also gone to Falkirk as a volunteer to the Government forces. The young minister, only 23 at the time, was John Wotherspoon (also spelled Witherspoon). He was later to become one of the founding fathers of Princeton University and a signatory of the American Declaration of Independence.

Lord Pitsligo certainly responded to a request for help from another minister, the Reverend James Robb of Kilsyth. The clergyman was diplomatically away from home when 'my house had the Honour of such a Lodger for a night'. However, he used the connection of Lord

Pitsligo having stayed under his roof to plead for one of his parishioners, who had been taken prisoner by the Jacobites because they wrongly believed him to have stolen one of their horses. Alexander Forester was a Kilsyth man who 'kept the best public house upon the road and is known to several of your people who have a kindness for him'. Lord Pitsligo wrote back to say he would do what he could.

Despite their victory at Falkirk, the Jacobites decided to retreat north. It was the Highland chiefs who insisted on this, and their decision was questioned then as it continues to be questioned now. They argued that their men would go home whether they were given permission to or not and that it made sense to secure Inverness and make a stand on their own home ground.

To many, the failure to capitalize on the victory at Falkirk and retake Edinburgh remains one of those inexplicable Jacobite mistakes. James Johnstone always maintained the Government did not win the war so much as the Jacobites lost it.

Always preferring to travel light, the Jacobites abandoned much of the contents of the baggage train at Falkirk, including most of those shirts, jackets and stockings Glasgow had been forced to come up with. For the sake of his blood pressure, we have to hope Andrew Cochrane never found out.

Although the Prince ordered that Shugborough Whitney and the Munro brothers should be brought into Falkirk and buried in the graveyard, the rest of the dead were shown no such respect. The lashing rain which accompanied the battle was still pouring down 24 hours later when James Johnstone was dispatched with a sergeant – he does not tell us whether this was the redoubtable Thomas Dickson – and 20 men from the town back up the hill to the battlefield, with orders to bury the bodies and gather up the cannons which the Government troops had left behind in their haste and confusion.

It was another miserable night, windy as well as wet, and it was soon to become more unpleasant still, for man and beast alike:

The sergeant carried a lantern, but the light was soon extinguished, and by that accident we immediately lost our way and wandered a long time at the foot of the hill among heaps of dead bodies, which their whiteness rendered visible notwithstanding the obscurity of a very dark night. To add to the disagreeableness of our situation from the horror of this scene, the wind and rain were full in our faces. I even remarked a trembling and strong agitation in my horse, which constantly shook when it was forced to put its feet on the heaps of dead bodies and climb over them. However, after we had wandered a long time amongst these bodies, we at length found the cannon.

Along with Alexander MacDonald and Duncan Ban McIntyre, there was – at least – a third poet and songwriter at Falkirk. Ferocious in battle, John Roy Stuart could write ferocious words, too, but also those expressing the deepest of regrets. He was thinking of Culloden when he wrote of 'the white bodies that lie out on yonder hillsides', but he could as easily have been describing Falkirk.

The memory of still and silent white bodies haunted the imaginations of many men, as the reaction of his horse to the dead of Falkirk on that rain-swept night was to haunt James Johnstone for the rest of his long life.

17

LANCETS, SCALPELS & GOLF BALLS: THE MEDICAL MEN

COULD I BUT GET MY INSTRUMENTS . . .

The muster roll lists 14 men who were officially attached to their individual regiments in the Jacobite Army in the role of either surgeon or physician, and other sources greatly increase that number. Lord Pitsligo, for example, took along his own doctor, John Cruickshank of Fraserburgh. How Dr Cruickshank's other patients coped during his long absence on the campaign trail is not recorded, although we can probably guess they did not do so uncomplainingly.

The most famous Jacobite doctor was Archibald Cameron, brother to Cameron of Lochiel. Both sides in the conflict benefited from Dr Archie's medical skills, kindness and compassion. These were deployed right from the start of the hostilities. He treated the wounds of the Royal Scots who were so terrifyingly attacked at High Bridge by the 12 men and a piper under MacDonell of Tirnadris.

Captain John Scott of Scotstarvet was impressed, not having expected to be cared for at all by the wild mountain men. It was great PR for the Jacobites, especially when Captain Scott's own side, metaphorically speaking, shot itself in the foot by refusing to send out its own surgeons to tend to the Government soldiers wounded in the ambush.

The medicine of the time was not as primitive as might be thought. Although we might now grimace at the thought of expecting a child with a cold to sleep with a dead dormouse on his or her chest, many plant-based remedies well known in the eighteenth century still exist today, either in their herbal form or transformed into modern drugs. For example, a cure for headache was to prepare an infusion of willow bark, the original basis for aspirin. Inoculation against smallpox was well known and widely practised, especially in the Highlands.

There were travelling charlatans talking up their own somewhat dubious pills and potions, and the term 'quack' was in common use. In country areas especially, many people doctored themselves and their families. Good housewives would have a comprehensive medicine chest, as would many Church of Scotland ministers, ministering to their flocks' bodies as well as their souls.

There was a class distinction between surgeons and physicians, as some of the latter may think there still is. The physicians saw themselves as superior to mere sawbones. This may be why one medic in the Jacobite Army described himself as a 'gentleman surgeon'.

Surgery was pretty basic, largely due to the lack of any effective and predictable anaesthesia. This was a century before Sir James Young Simpson's wife came back into her dining room in Queen Street in Edinburgh's New Town, thinking it was time the gentlemen joined the ladies, and found her husband and his friends under the table. They weren't drunk but knocked out by chloroform, acting as their own guinea pigs to see how it would work.

Some operations were routinely performed. Trepanning was a procedure in which a hole was drilled into the skull to relieve pressure on the brain. Arms and legs too badly injured in accidents to be saved and which were threatening to turn gangrenous were amputated. Kidney and gallstones were excised. Mastectomies because of breast cancer were performed; later in the eighteenth century, the novelist Fanny Burney was one of those who endured such a procedure. All of these operations were carried out while the patient was fully conscious. Surgeons therefore had to be quick both in making cuts and in making decisions. Two doctors on the Government side at Prestonpans took one of those quick decisions, surrendering themselves so as to be able to help their injured comrades.

Too late for the battle but finding 23 wounded Government officers in a house near his own, these were the men Sandy Carlyle volunteered to help in whatever way he could. He knew one of them, Alexander Cunningham, 'afterwards the most eminent surgeon in Dublin', and surgeon to Ligonier's Dragoons during the '45. Unfortunately, neither Cunningham nor his colleague William Trotter, surgeon to Hamilton's Dragoons, had their medicine chests or their instruments. Those had been in the baggage train, which was now either somewhere on the battlefield or in the hands of the Jacobite Army.

Cunningham indicated one young Redcoat officer called Captain Blake. Slumped unconscious in an armchair, to Sandy Carlyle he looked to be on the point of death. On the chest of drawers next to him lay part of Blake's skull, 'two fingers' breadth and an inch and a half long'. Horrified, Sandy cried out that there was surely no hope for the man. Cunningham contradicted him, saying: 'The brain is not affected, nor any vital part: he has youth and a fine constitution on his side; and could I but get my instruments, there would be no fear of him.'

Volunteering to go and look for the missing medicine chests and instruments, Sandy was given a guard by the Jacobite Captain Stewart, a man who was 'good-looking, grave, and of polished manners'. The guard took him to Cameron of Lochiel. He, too, was courteous, ordering a soldier to help the student in his search. Although it was fruitless, by the time Sandy Carlyle returned, Cunningham and Trotter had been supplied with instruments by a local surgeon. All the casualties had their wounds dressed, and 'Captain Blake's head was trepanned, and he was laid in bed.'

Amazingly, Blake was up and dressed a few days later, well enough to invite Sandy to have a glass of wine with him. After expressing his surprise – 'Captain Blake, are you allowed to drink wine?' – the two young men 'drank out the bottle of claret'.

More than 50 years later, seeing Blake's name and address in a letter to a newspaper, Carlyle wrote to him. Blake wrote back, extending an invitation to his home in George Street, Westminster, 'where he hoped we would uncork a bottle with more pleasure than we had done in 1745, but to come soon, for he was verging on eighty-one'.

There is a second and wonderfully gruesome postscript to this story. When the *Gentleman's Magazine* subsequently noted the death of Captain Blake's daughter, it recorded that she had always worn a distinctive necklace. Set all round with diamonds, what hung from its chain was the piece of her father's skull hacked away from the rest of it at Prestonpans. *Souvenir de la guerre.*

Some doctors and medical students came out from Edinburgh to help tend the wounded at Prestonpans, too. One of the latter was Alexander Wood, just 20 years old at the time, and tall and lanky. In later life, he was to become Lang Sandy Wood, held in high esteem by his patients and his colleagues. He is allegedly the first man in Edinburgh ever to use an umbrella, the sensation of the 1780s.

One of the qualified doctors who went out to Prestonpans was Alexander Monro, the first generation of a medical dynasty. He, his son and his grandson, all named Alexander, dominated medical teaching at Edinburgh University for 150 years. They were known successively as Monro *primus, secundus* and *tertius.*

In September 1745 the concern of the first Alexander Monro was to get the wounded taken to the new Royal Infirmary, which had opened its doors only a few years before. It was a state-of-the-art facility, if still not quite finished. One of its very modern touches was a staircase wide enough to allow patients to be carried to the upstairs wards in sedan chairs.

Although a friend of the Government and supporter of the political status quo, Alexander Monro, like Charles Edward Stuart, made no distinction between Jacobite and Redcoat wounded. Many Jacobite soldiers also shared these feelings. They could fight as viciously as wild dogs, but once the battle was won they were more likely to take prisoners than finish off their defeated adversaries. Written evidence of this can be found in *The Lockhart Papers*. This collection of the extensive correspondence of Jacobite agent Sir George Lockhart also includes this eyewitness account of Prestonpans and its aftermath:

> I observed some of our private men run to Port Seton for ale and other liquors to support the wounded. And as one proof for all, in my own particular observation I saw a Highlander supporting a poor wounded soldier by the arms 'till he should ease nature and afterwards carry him on his back into a house and left him sixpence at parting. In all which we followed not only the dictates of humanity but the orders of our Prince in all.

In contrast, when the Jacobites left Edinburgh, and the garrison in the Castle sallied forth to retake it, some Redcoats are said to have rampaged through the wards of the new Royal Infirmary tormenting Jacobite soldiers recovering from wounds sustained at Prestonpans.

It comes as a surprise to learn from the doctors who, over the years, have naturally taken an interest in their Jacobite counterparts that the men who were wounded at Prestonpans were less likely to have suffered serious injuries if they had been on the business end of a broadsword, which were well known for inflicting wide but not deep cuts. Although these bled profusely, they usually left the internal organs unscathed. It was the sharpened scythes and Lochaber-axes which had sliced off heads and arms and legs that did the real damage. Serving your time in the army or navy was a traditional training ground for surgeons, giving them intensive experience of a wide variety of wounds. Dealing with the wounded of Prestonpans must have proved a steep learning curve.

Another of the well-known doctors on the Jacobite side was John Rattray, whom the *Oxford Dictionary of National Biography* describes as a 'golfer and physician'. The order in which these twin passions are placed is not insignificant. Born at Craighall Castle, Blairgowrie, he was the son of the Episcopalian Bishop of Dunkeld. Rattray's second wife was Mary Lockhart of Carnwath, who had two brothers fighting in the Jacobite Army. John Rattray played golf – rather a lot, it would appear – at Leith Links, and was prominent in the Company of Gentlemen Golfers, which drew up the first-ever rules of golf. In 1744, Rattray won the first-ever Open, making him 'captain of the goff', his trophy a silver club. He was unable to defend his title the following year due to the little local difficulty of what some people sarcastically referred to as the 'scuffle' at Prestonpans.

Asked to lend his medical skills to the Cause, Rattray came out to the battlefield with George Lauder, another surgeon. Both men subsequently accompanied the Jacobite Army into England and back north to Inverness, Rattray becoming on the way one of the Prince's two personal medical advisers.

The Prince's other adviser was Dr Stuart Threipland of Fingask, later Sir Stuart Threipland. His younger brother David, briefly a member of a Jacobite cavalry regiment, was killed at Prestonpans. Although he spent some time in exile in France after Culloden, Dr Threipland later returned to Edinburgh, had a successful medical practice and became a leading light of the medical establishment. Throughout the '45, he travelled with a medicine chest which it is believed the Prince gave him. It is today one of the treasures of the Royal College of Physicians of Edinburgh.

George Lauder later stated that he and Rattray had been kidnapped by the Jacobites after Prestonpans and pressed into service as army surgeons. When he made this statement, however, he was trying to get them both out of trouble, so it should be taken with a large pinch of salt.

There is no ambivalence in his description of the Herculean task which he and Rattray faced at Prestonpans. One thousand Government officers and men were prisoners, and many of those had sustained horrific and multiple wounds. There was Captain Poyntz, 'who had one very dangerous wound in his hand and five in his head'. Lieutenant Disney 'had his hand cutt of with a Sword and a shot in his shoulder, and must have dyed with loss of Blood in a very short time without assistance'.

A young Mr Bishop, whose father, Captain Bishop, had been killed in the battle, had 14 wounds. Lauder operated on him, dressed his wounds, gave him medicines – as he did to many others – without any hope of being paid for them. He 'even found him Lodgings, Nurses and Money for his Subsistence, he being an orphan destitute of Friends and Money'.

On the day of the battle and in the days which followed it, Lauder, Rattray and their six student apprentices treated three hundred men, operating when necessary, dressing wounds and amputating limbs which could not be saved. They were assisted by Hugh Hunter, who was the surgeon to Lord Loudoun's Regiment in the Government army.

They were also visited in Edinburgh by another paroled Government officer. He was Colonel Halkett of Lee's Regiment, and, after expressing his thanks for the care being taken of his men, he asked for a favour: could Lauder come with him to their camp, about seven miles from Edinburgh, where the young surgeon of Lee's Regiment was facing an agonizing dilemma?

There were three or four men whom he thought needed amputations, but he felt he did not have the experience necessary to make that irrevocable decision. He also doubted his ability to perform the operations. Lauder went out to see the young surgeon and the soldiers under his care, decided that the amputations were not required, brought the men into Edinburgh and saw that they were taken care of until they recovered from their wounds.

At the Battle of Falkirk, Lauder showed the same care and compassion, looking after Captain Fitzgerald and Captain Halley of the Redcoat Munro's Regiment. Not only did he treat their wounds, he also insisted that, for the sake of their health, they must not be taken along with the Jacobite Army as prisoners on its retreat north, effectively winning the Redcoat officers their liberty.

Cameron of Lochiel sustained a minor wound at Falkirk, a musket ball hitting his heel. As his brother Archie was helping him, he too received an injury. Elsewhere on the wind-lashed battlefield, two other brothers were in a similar situation. The Cameron brothers made it safely away. The Munro brothers did not.

Dr Duncan Munro was another Edinburgh surgeon and another supporter of King George, as was his brother. Sir Robert Munro of Foulis was a soldier in command of one of the English regiments which fought at Falkirk. Duncan had gone along to be on hand if his brother were to be wounded.

Their fears were not unfounded. When his men broke and ran, leaving their colonel to his fate, Sir Robert was viciously attacked by six Highlanders at once. Over 60 and famously fat, it seems likely that they recognized him and immediately targeted him as a fellow Highlander fighting, as they saw it, on the wrong side. Robert and Duncan Munro were cousins of Duncan Forbes of Culloden. Robert's son Harry wrote a couple of days later to let the Lord President know what had happened:

> I think it my duty to acquaint your Lop of the deplorable situation I am in. The Engagt. Between the King's troops and Highlanders on Thursday last, w'in a mile of Falkirk, proves to me a series of woe! There both my dear father & uncle Obsdale wer slain! The last, your Lop knows, had no particular business to go to the Action; but, out of a most tender love & concern for his Brother, cou'd not be dissuaded from attending him, to give assistance if need required.
>
> My father, after being deserted, was attacked by six of Locheal's Regt, & and for some time defended himself with his half Pike. Two of the six, I'm inform'd, he kill'd; a seventh, coming up, fired a Pistol into my father's Groin; upon wch falling, the Highlander wh his sword gave him two strokes in the face, one over the Eyes & another on the mouth, wch instantly ended a brave Man.
>
> The same Highlander fired another Pistol into my uncle's breast, & wh his Sword terribly slashed him . . . My father's Corpse was honourably interred in the Church-

yd of Falkirk by direction of the E. Of Cromertie & the McDonalds, all the Chieffs attended his funerals.

Despite being buried with respect in the kirkyard in Falkirk, their deaths, especially that of the unarmed non-combatant Dr Munro, were considered by the opponents of the Jacobites as a war crime and an atrocity.

A few doctors and physicians died in captivity. Others were captured and condemned but then acquitted. Whether their status as healers helped secure their release is not clear. James Stratton of Berwickshire was captured while acting as surgeon to the short-lived Jacobite garrison at Carlisle. One of those medical men who was acquitted, at his trial it was said that although he had not carried arms, he was as a surgeon 'a party to levying war'.

Dr Archibald Cameron, Cameron of Lochiel's brother, escaped capture after Culloden but was betrayed on a covert trip back to Scotland. In 1753, he was tried and hanged in London for his part in, as he wrote, 'what they term *Rebellion*'. Imprisoned in the Tower of London, he complained that he was not allowed pen, ink or paper, 'not even the use of a knife with which I might cut a poor blunted pencil that had escaped the diligence of my searchers'. He wrote with the blunt pencil anyway, on a few scraps of paper, anxious to set the record straight before he died, and gave what he had written to his devoted wife, Jean. Interestingly, he confirms the speculation about his brother having saved Glasgow from being plundered by the Jacobite Army, giving himself some credit, too:

> My brother and I did service to the town of Glasgow, of which the principal gentry in the neighbourhood were then, and are to this day, very sensible, if they durst own the truth. But that might be construed as disaffection to a Government founded on and supported by lies and falsehood.

He immediately goes on to say that he saved Kirkintilloch from a similar fate, his brother's men being 'justly incensed against it for the inhuman murder of two of Lady Lochiel's servants', a story which does not seem to be recorded elsewhere.

Dr Archie's devotion to his Prince was undimmed. Charles remained affable, courteous and courageous. As one of his aides-de-camp, the doctor declared that the allegation of an order issued to the Jacobite Army the day before Culloden to give no quarter to their enemies was a 'most unjust and horrid calumny' put about 'by the rebels under the command of the inhuman son of the Elector of Hanover, which served as an excuse for the unparalleled butchery committed by his orders in cold blood after the unhappy affair of Culloden'.

The day before his execution, Archie Cameron wrote to his eldest son. It's a letter filled with love and a father's last words of advice, enjoining the boy to serve God, his King, his Prince and his country, and to care always for his mother, brothers and sister. His pencil was so blunt he had to break off in the middle of sending his 'love and dying benediction to my children, affection to my brother's children, best wishes to all my friends, and hearty compliments to all my good acquaintance and ...' That's where the letter finishes.

He had no money to leave his son, but he sent him his steel shoe-buckles along with a verbal message that even if he'd had gold buckles he would not have sent them, for he had worn the steel ones while he was skulking with the Prince: 'For as steel is hard and of small value, it therefore an emblem of constancy and disinterestedness.'

Archie Cameron was hung, drawn and quartered at Tyburn, which occupied the site at the end of Oxford Street where Marble Arch now stands.

The doctor was the last martyr to the Jacobite Cause.

18

GENTLEMEN, TAKE NO NOTICE! ROBERT STEWART OF GLENLIVET

HE ACKNOWLEDGED THAT HE WAS BEGINNING TO FEEL 'A LITTLE WEAK'

While the bulk of the Jacobite Army marched into England at the end of 1745, other detachments of it had held onto northeast Scotland. Despite the heavy snows of the winter of 1745–6, the Jacobite line in Aberdeenshire was a shifting one.

With a few notable exceptions, such as James Moir of Stoneywood, who came out for the Prince, by and large Aberdeen was for the Government and Aberdeenshire was for the Jacobites. At the end of September 1745, it had been John Hamilton, factor to the Duke of Gordon in Huntly, who marched into Aberdeen and proclaimed King James VIII and III the rightful king. When the Provost of Aberdeen declined to drink James's health, John Hamilton threw the glass of claret he was proffering in the provost's face. One of those left behind in England to garrison Carlisle three months later, he was to pay dearly for his moment of triumph.

Out in Aberdeenshire, Jacobite sentiment was strong. Many of the country people were Episcopalian, a good number were Catholic and the farmers bitterly resented the Malt Tax. Imposed by the London

Government after the Union, it was a perennial source of discontent throughout Scotland. The fishing villages around the Buchan coast were considered to be Jacobite to a man – and woman.

A letter from a Government spy complains bitterly about women spreading information useful to the rebels. If a troop of soldiers came into Strathbogie – present-day Huntly – at six o'clock at night, writes the anonymous correspondent, the Jacobites in Peterhead would know about it by eight o'clock the following morning. The Aberdeenshire women were well organized. When a piece of news was received, each would pass it on to two friends who would head off in different directions to spread it further. Clearly exasperated, the spy mentions 'Barbara Strachan, the Jackobite, post mistres off Buchan', whose job made it easy for her to traverse the countryside passing on information: 'Thers not one place of it all she travels not once a-week, when business is throng.'

Not everyone in Aberdeenshire was well-inclined towards the Jacobites. Cosmo, the 3rd Duke of Gordon, declared himself for the Government, but his attitude was highly ambivalent. It's hard to resist the conclusion that, like Lord Lovat, he was sitting firmly if uncomfortably on the fence, waiting to see which way the wind would blow. His brother Lord Charles Gordon was actively involved on the Government side, while their younger brother Lord Lewis Gordon threw his lot in with the Prince:

> O, send Lewie Gordon hame,
> And the lad I daurna name!
> Though his back be at the wa',
> Here's to him that's far awa'!

Unfortunately, reality falls sadly short of the romantic image of the dashing young Lord Lewie, just 20 years old at the outbreak of hostilities. Being Jacobite in sentiment could be a long way from being prepared to take the huge risks involved in leaving your family and going for a soldier. Lord Lewie was incensed, and not a little embarrassed, by the difficulties he encountered while raising his regiment.

Any hopes ordinary men might have had of keeping their heads down until it was all over were shattered by his recruitment tactics. He himself wrote, chillingly, 'We have been obliged to use great threatenings', and, indeed, 'Come with me or I'll burn your cornfield' must have been a powerfully persuasive threat to a farmer struggling to make a living and feed his family. It's one still remembered with a shudder by some descendants of those farmers today.

At the end of December 1745, Lord Loudoun, commander of the Government troops in the north of Scotland, sent a force west and south from their base in Inverness in an attempt to retake Aberdeen, Aberdeenshire and Banffshire. The MacLeods, led by their chief, who had declined to support the Prince, marched through Cullen, Banff and Oldmeldrum. A detachment of pro-Government Munros, Grants and Mackenzies came by Keith and Strathbogie, successfully forcing the two Jacobite garrisons there to retreat to Aberdeen.

Led by Captain George Munro of Culcairn, a professional soldier, Lord Loudoun's troops met up with the MacLeods at Inverurie. The surrounding countryside being largely Jacobite, Culcairn was scared of losing men if he sent out patrols. His knowledge of Jacobite movements was therefore non-existent.

To add to his woes, Lord Loudoun had seriously underestimated the strength of the Jacobite garrison in Aberdeen. Over a thousand men marched out of the city at nine o'clock on the morning of Monday, 23 December. One column, commanded by Gordon of Avochie, approached Inverurie along the King's High Road through Kintore and another led by Lord Lewie Gordon crossed the Don to make a flanking movement, approaching the town from the east.

It was a high-risk strategy. Both Jacobite detachments might have to ford a river in full view of the enemy – Lord Lewie and his men the Urie, and Gordon of Avochie the Don. It was always a vulnerable position in which to put yourself. If this pincer movement were to work, surprise and timing would be crucial.

Jacobite organization was magnificent. Patrols and scouts were everywhere, ensuring that the enemy remained unaware of the approaching danger. At Kintore, the minister was arrested and houses along the main road were occupied to prevent any word being sent to Inverurie.

MacLeod of MacLeod and Munro of Culcairn were taken completely by surprise when the shout went up that a large Jacobite force was advancing down the hill from Keith Hall, behind Inverurie. MacLeod and Culcairn were positioned just outside the town, slightly to the north and west of the small but steep man-made hill known as the Bass of Inverurie, halfway between the Urie and the Don. Only now did they realize that their enemies were approaching the fords of both rivers.

While the Redcoats tried, fruitlessly, to decide which ford to attack, Lord Lewie's French adviser, Major Cuthbert, took the initiative. With a group of chosen men, he waded through the icy waters of the Urie and took up a position in the shelter of the Bass and the nearby churchyard. It was four o'clock on a winter's afternoon, and daylight was fading fast. Accurate shooting was difficult.

Gordon of Avochie and around 60 of his men came across the Don and joined up with Lord Lewie and Major Cuthbert. The two Jacobite detachments then advanced, shooting as they went. Their enemies were forced to retreat. They went right through Inverurie, Old Rayne and Huntly, not stopping to rest till they had crossed the Spey. The engagement had lasted less than 20 minutes, and Aberdeenshire and Banffshire were once more in Jacobite hands.

A little less than two months later, after the Prince's army had taken the fateful decision at Falkirk to head for Inverness, the Jacobites chose to leave Aberdeen. They did so just as the weather began to close in again. John Daniel, the gentleman volunteer from Lancashire, gives us a graphic description of how bad conditions were:

> When we marched out of Aberdeen, it blew, snowed, hailed, and froze to such a degree, that few Pictures ever represented Winter, with all its icicles about it, better

than many of us did that day; for here men were covered with icicles hanging at their eyebrows and beards; and an entire coldness seizing all their limbs, it may be wondered at how so many could bear up against the storm, a severe contrary wind driving snow and little cutting hail bitterly down upon our faces, in such a manner that it was impossible to see ten yards before us. And very easy it now was to lose our companions; the road being bad and leading over large commons, and the paths being immediately filled up with drifted snow.

Anyone who knows the A96 Aberdeen to Inverness road and the Glens o' Foudland – still to be dreaded in a warm car in snowy winters today – will immediately get the picture.

John Daniel and his horse made it through because he remembered he had a bottle of spirits in his riding-coat pocket. He drank some, and it warmed him up just fine. On the point of finishing it off, he thought of 'my poor horse, which seemed to be in as bad a situation as myself, being one of a delicate and tender breed'. He knew his mount 'could drink beer', so he poured some of the spirits into his hat, diluted it with a handful of snow, and presented it to the beast. It did them both the world of good.

As the Prince and his men drew nearer to Inverness, Lord Loudoun retreated north to Dornoch, and Lord President Duncan Forbes took himself off to Skye. Old Fort George, on the hill by the river Ness where Inverness Castle now stands, was besieged by the Jacobites and fell. A Frenchman helping to blow the castle up afterwards was clearly of the school of Mr Admirable, the incompetent engineer who had failed to help the Jacobites capture Stirling Castle. The Frenchman at Inverness, wondering why a charge had not gone off, bent over it at exactly the wrong moment, and went with it to kingdom come. Although the trip up into the air and back down to earth gave his dog a gammy leg for ever afterwards, it survived the explosion.

Fort Augustus was also besieged and also fell, while Fort William withstood a siege which lasted weeks and was not taken. The redoubtable Sergeant Molloy was, however, persuaded to surrender Ruthven Barracks. He did so with considerable dignity and only after he had negotiated and been guaranteed humane treatment for his men.

At Moy Hall, the home of the equally redoubtable 'Colonel' Anne Mackintosh, yet another variation on the famous 12-men-and-a-piper trick saved Prince Charles from a much larger Government force led by Lord Loudoun, again trying and failing to get the better of the Jacobites.

Meanwhile, Lord Pitsligo was acting as Jacobite Governor of Elgin in Morayshire, trying, as he always did, to be fair to everybody. As the Prince's army was by now running short of just about everything, horses, carts and oatmeal were being requisitioned from wherever they could be found:

> There are fifteen horses more sent from this place today
> . . . which is such a burden upon this Country that a
> great many of the Farmers will be incapacitated from
> tilling their ground and their familys consequently
> reduced to Beggary. I'm sure it was allways the Prince's
> intention (since hardships must be) that none should
> suffer beyond their proportion.

When Cullen House on the Moray coast was plundered by the Jacobites, Lord Pitsligo was mortified. The troop of soldiers sent there was supposed only to bring in some supplies from the estate but decided to take revenge on the house's owner, the Earl of Findlater, who was most definitely a friend of the Government. They rampaged through the house, stealing what they could easily carry away and wrecking what they couldn't. Mirrors were smashed, feather cushions and mattresses were ripped open, their contents strewn on the floor, and all the dust and feathers were mixed up with 'jelly and marmalade and honey and wet and all sorts of nastiness'.

Worried that the entire Jacobite Army would get a bad name or that there might be revenge attacks on the homes of the Prince's supporters, Lord Pitsligo wrote to Sir Thomas Sheridan, one of Charles's closest advisers:

> As this unlucky affair will make a noise over all the world, I would humbly suggest that the Prince should testify his dislike of such proceedings in some publick Declaration. I have this moment spoke with a Servant of Lord Findlater's who tells the dammages are far beyond what I imagine, for there is hardly a bit of Glass left in the windows.

Sheridan wrote back the next day to say that of course the Prince 'is concern'd at any damage done in a country which he came not to oppress but set free', but that unfortunate things happen in war.

The Duke of Cumberland and his army arrived in Aberdeen on 27 February 1746, ten days after the Jacobites had left it. The hostile weather shut them in there for six weeks. Cumberland stayed in the Guest Row, in the building behind present-day Union Street now known as Provost Skene's House. He and his men used their time in Aberdeen well, practising a new bayonet drill.

This involved ignoring the enemy soldier standing straight in front of you and instead thrusting your bayonet diagonally at the man standing to his left. He would be holding his targe in his left hand and have his sword arm upraised, thus leaving the right-hand side of his body unprotected.

The technique required absolute trust in your comrades, whom you had to hope and pray were covering your own vulnerable left side. Rehearsed over and over again in Aberdeen, this new drill was to have devastating consequences for the Jacobites at Culloden, although perhaps as much because it fostered trust among the Redcoats as for its effectiveness.

When the snow began to ease off towards the middle of March

1746, the Duke of Cumberland sent out a scouting party. In response, the Jacobites in Strathbogie thought it wiser to retreat to the place which the Hanoverian General Bland spelled 'Forcoborse'. Following his quarry to Fochabers was likely to be more successful with some local help. Captain Alexander Campbell, leading 70 of his own men and 30 riders of Kingston's Light Horse, found the assistant minister at Cairnie Kirk, halfway between Huntly and Keith, more than willing to act as a scout.

The minister, who was also a Campbell, suggested hiding the troop of soldiers along the Cairnie burn, 'that being a very hollow burn with a good deal of planting in it' – which it still is today. If the minister came back pursued by Jacobites, the Campbells and the cavalrymen would be in an ideal position to mount an ambush.

The Reverend Campbell found no immediate sign of the Jacobite Army, allowing the Government troops to advance to Keith. They entered the town in the early morning of 19 March, waking up the inhabitants by breaking windows and looting shops. It did not take the Jacobites long to get wind of what had happened. It's more than likely that someone, furious at the plundering, slipped quietly out of Keith that misty morning and headed for Fochabers.

Later that day, the Jacobites decided to send a party of about 50 men back to Keith. Most of them were from John Roy Stewart's Edinburgh Regiment, which included quite a few Banffshire men, perhaps newly raised from the local area. The officer in charge of the expedition was Captain Robert Stewart of Glenlivet, a man who was very much on home territory. Accompanied by a small troop of cavalry, they marched openly towards Keith. A few miles before they reached the town, however, they veered off to the east, crossed the Isla and skirted the town in a wide arc. All of this was designed to make it look as though they had come in from the direction of Huntly and thus were not foes but friends.

Midnight was striking as they approached the town – and their ruse was successful. On being challenged by the Campbell sentry, Robert Stewart answered without hesitation: 'We're friends, Campbells.' The sentry, greatly relieved, approached them with a broad smile and told them he was glad to see them. He was sure the enemy was close at hand.

He was immediately seized, flung to the ground and held there. 'Make a sound,' he was told, 'and you'll get a dirk through your heart.' Captain Stewart led his men to the churchyard, where the main body of the Campbell militia was encamped. Forty-five years before, the infamous James Macpherson, who went so rantingly to his death after playing a tune on his fiddle below the gallows tree in Banff, had been captured here in Keith kirkyard.

The shooting started, the Campbells returning fire vigorously from the windows of the old kirk. 'Yield, or die!' yelled Robert Stewart. A few minutes later, twisting round to check the positions of his men, he was struck by a musket ball. It passed right through him, entering his left shoulder and coming out at the right.

Dismayed, his men lowered their weapons. 'Gentlemen,' Captain Stewart said briskly, 'take no notice!' The shooting went on for about half an hour before the Campbells surrendered. The skirmish at Keith, however, was not yet over.

The Jacobite cavalry had surrounded the town, a much smaller place then than it is now, and was fighting a desperate action against the dragoons of Kingston's Horse. Fearing they were about to be overpowered, Jacobite Major Nicholas Glasgow sent an urgent plea for help to the kirkyard.

Ignoring his wound, which was bleeding profusely, Robert Stewart immediately led some of his party down the street. There was a short, sharp engagement which ended disastrously for the Redcoats, with nine of them killed and the rest captured, along with their thirty horses.

Stewart lined the prisoners up two abreast, with his own men guarding them on either side, and prepared to march them back to Fochabers. Only then did he acknowledge that he was beginning to feel 'a little weak'. His wound may well have saved his life, as it prevented him from being at Culloden.

Some of the Campbells managed to escape and hide down by the Auld Brig of Keith. Next to it there is an enormous stone slab which even today could conceal a dozen men. Under the stone, there is a large cavity which is said to lead to caves which run backwards under the old toll-road, the present-day A96. The spot was always known afterwards as the Campbells' Hole.

The front line had been redefined yet again, but General Bland was philosophical, saying, 'I hope we shall soon have our revenge with interest.'

Culloden was less than a month away.

19

THE YEAR OF THE PRINCE: BITTER SPRING

OUR MEN ATTACKED WITH ALL THE FURY IMAGINABLE

As Jacobite Governor of Elgin, Lord Pitsligo had to field bad-tempered demands for safe conducts from people at whose tables he had probably dined and to whom he was very possibly related. Anne, Lady Innes, wrote to him nine days before Culloden demanding to know why she was being refused a pass to go to Aberdeen. Her health was such that she felt the need to 'retire from amidst these unhappie Confusions'. Since she was prepared to give him her oath that she would not tell the Government commanders anything about the Jacobite forces, she could not understand why Lord Pitsligo would not permit her to travel. He answered her frankly but in his usual gentlemanly fashion:

> To deal openly with your Ladyship, I did hear you had declared your intention of going to Aberdeen, which would not be permitted in any army, and accordingly I thought it was required of me to hinder your journey. But now that you are pleased to assure me in the most binding terms that you are to give no Intelligence, I

shall no longer oppose it. This, I reckon, will serve for a
Pass the length of Speyside, my Commission extending
no farther . . .

The next day, Lord Pitsligo received a letter from Lord John
Drummond, telling him the Duke of Cumberland had spent the
previous night at Oldmeldrum. Had he perhaps been aware when he
granted Lady Innes her pass that it might all too soon not be worth
the paper it was written on?

Two days later, he was sent word from Fochabers that he and
the men stationed at Elgin had to be ready to move at 'a moment's
warning' – which, indeed, they did, decamping that very same day
through Forres and on to Nairn.

The Duke of Cumberland was right behind them. He and his
'vermine of Red Quites' crossed the Spey unopposed. Why the
Jacobites did not attempt to prevent them from doing so has often
been debated. There were plans to guard the fords, but they came
to nothing, perhaps because the river was very low. If it was easy to
cross, then the soldiers could come over quickly in large groups and
would not be in the vulnerable position they would have occupied
had the river been high and flowing fast. Cumberland recorded that
he 'only lost one Dragoon and 4 women drowned'.

The duke was relaxed enough to rest his men at Garmouth
overnight before marching on to Nairn. As the Government army
came in at one end of the town, the Jacobite rearguard were leaving
it at the other. Cumberland stayed in Nairn, and his army set up
camp.

The Prince had made his base at Culloden House, just outside
Inverness. In his choice of headquarters, there must have been an
element of getting his own back on the Lord President, Duncan
Forbes of Culloden, who had done so much to organize the effort
against him. Orders issued by Charles to all his officers 'civil and
military' are worded in a somewhat ambivalent way:

> These are requiring you to protect and defend the House
> of Colloden and furniture from any insults or violence
> that may be done by any person or persons, except such
> Orders as are issued by us. Given at Inverness, 28ᵗʰ Feb.
> 1746. By His Highness's Command.

It seems Charles reserved the right to 'insult' Culloden House if he saw fit.

The two armies were now only twelve miles apart. All that remained was to choose a time and a place. It was Colonel O'Sullivan who selected the ground, a piece of high moorland up the hill from Culloden House. One of the things he liked about it was the moor road which ran through it and is still there today, albeit now covered over. Battles were usually fought on or near a road: it made it easier to run the cannons in.

Lord George did not like the ground at all, not so much because it was very marshy in places as because it was flat and featureless, and he thought it would allow the Government troops to use their cannons to 'anoy the Highlanders prodigiously before they could possibly make an attack'. His opinion was shared by many in the Jacobite Army. This may be why Lord George's suggestion of a night march and surprise attack on Cumberland's camp at Nairn was, at first, greeted with enthusiasm. The Prince's army had, after all, most successfully surprised the Government army at Prestonpans.

The Jacobite Army set off at seven o'clock in the evening of Tuesday, 15 April, leaving fires burning in their own camp so the ships in the Royal Navy flotilla which had just dropped anchor out in the Moray Firth would suspect nothing. The night march ended in failure in the small hours of the following morning. It was dark and wet and men kept getting lost in the woods, the army not making the progress it had to if it was to reach Nairn before daybreak.

After a series of furious arguments between Charles and his colonels, the attempt was abandoned. All it had achieved was to exhaust men who were already weary and hungry. The Prince himself rode into Inverness when he returned from the night march to see what provisions could be got, but in the twenty-four hours before the battle was finally fought, most of the rank and file had been issued with a ration of one biscuit and some not even that.

Later that morning, on Wednesday, 16 April 1746, the Marquis d'Eguilles, French Ambassador to the Jacobites, asked if he might speak with Charles in private. When they were alone together, d'Eguilles threw himself at the Prince's feet and begged him not to give battle that day. Half the men had gone off to Inverness in search of something more to eat than that one biscuit. The Marquis suggested they retreat to Inverness, get the men fed and rested, and take Cumberland on the next day. When d'Eguilles found he could not change the Prince's mind, he returned to his own lodgings in Inverness to burn his papers.

No formal council of war was held at Culloden House, but opinions were expressed. Lord George, MacDonald of Keppoch and Cameron of Lochiel liked neither the chosen ground nor the idea of giving battle when the men were so tired and hungry, but the Prince was determined. The choice was soon taken out of everyone's hands.

A man who had fallen asleep in the woods on the way back from Nairn and been abruptly roused from his slumbers rushed in with the news that the Duke of Cumberland and his army were approaching and had been sighted a mere four miles away. Duncan Forbes' household staff, obeying the laws of Highland hospitality even under these most difficult of circumstances, were about to serve the Prince and his officers a midday meal – a roast side of lamb and two chickens. Charles had angrily rejected the food, as Colonel O'Sullivan reported:

> 'Eat,' says the Prince, 'I can neither eat nor rest while my poor peoples are starving,' & imediatly gave orders to get meat of one kind or other for the men, who were in great need of it. All hands were at work to distribute among them proportionably what there was, liberty given to kill Cows, wch the Prince wou'd give bills for;

necessity has no law, on those occasions, but poor people
they had not time to dresse their Victuals.

Charles flung himself out of Culloden House into the chilly April
day, ordering the bagpipes to play so the men lying asleep in the
surrounding fields would hear the call to arms. Riders were sent to
Inverness to gather up anyone who might be there. James Johnstone
was one of them.

After the failure of the night march, he had gone back to his
lodgings, the only thought in his head to get some sleep. He was out
of luck. When he 'had already one leg in the bed', he heard 'the drum
beat to arms and the trumpets of the picket of Fitzjames sounding the
call to boot and saddle'.

Meanwhile, the Prince had ridden up onto the moor and was
moving among the men beginning to line up there. He reminded
them of their great victories at Prestonpans and Falkirk. Telling them
they had the same swords now as they did then, he asked one man to
hand him up his blade. 'I'll answer this will cut off some heads & arms
today,' Charles said before returning it to its owner. 'Go on my Lads,
the day will be ours & we'll want for nothing after.' He himself was
carrying a pair of silver-mounted pistols and a leather targe decorated
with a silver head of Medusa.

John Daniel, the gentleman volunteer from Lancashire, estimated
when he watched the Redcoats advance 'like a deep sullen river' that
there were around 11,000 of them to 4,000 Jacobites. The National
Trust for Scotland in their visitor centre at the battlefield quotes the
numbers at 7,500 and 5,500 respectively, but other authorities dispute
those figures, putting the Government army at 9,000 and the Jacobite
at 5,000.

John Daniel was proud to be carrying 'a curious fine standard',
which he had acquired at Falkirk from Colonel Gardiner's leaderless
dragoons. Its motto read, '*Britons, strike home!*' He clearly found this
entirely appropriate. After all, apart from a handful of Hessians on the
Government side and the French and Franco-Scots on the Jacobite

side, the men lining up across the moor road in both armies were indeed Britons.

As he approached the Jacobite lines, the Duke of Cumberland briefly stopped his own troops and made a short speech, addressing them as 'Gentlemen and Fellow-Soldiers':

> I have but little Time to address myself to you; but I think proper to acquaint you, That you are instantly to engage in the Defence of your King and Country, your Religion, your Liberties, and Properties; and thro' the Justice of your Cause, I make no Doubt of leading you on to certain Victory. Stand but firm, and your Enemies will soon fly before you.

The Government soldiers did stand firm, and, because of where they chose to do so, they moved the fight forward from where the Jacobites wanted it to be. This deprived them of what had been seen as the protection of the stone dykes on either side of their line. These enclosed the fields belonging to Duncan Forbes' estate.

The epicentre of the battle has long been thought to be around the cairn which now commemorates it. Recent investigation by Dr Tony Pollard and his team from Glasgow University's Centre for Battlefield Archaeology and the physical evidence they found moves it closer towards the modern visitor centre, on the rise above the dip of the Well of the Dead. This is where the fighting was at its most intense.

The battle started shortly after one o'clock with an exchange of artillery fire. Some people described as 'gentlemen from Inverness' had come out to view the event as spectators, reportedly even carrying picnic baskets with them. It wasn't an ideal day for eating out of doors: bitterly cold with wintry showers. In any case, when a few cannonballs thudded into the ground in front of the would-be voyeurs of death and injury, they beat a hasty retreat.

Although it was the Jacobites who opened fire, the Government artillery was far superior. Among it were two batteries of three coehorn mortars apiece. Lighter than other cannons, they could be lifted and repositioned to deadly effect as a battle developed. They also fired up and over, so could be placed behind troops who would keep their gunners safe from attack.

Terrible damage was done to the Jacobite front line as the men there stood waiting for the order to advance. It never came. Lachlan MacLachlan, a young aide-de-camp to the Prince, had his head taken off by a cannonball on his way to deliver it.

As the Jacobites had edged forward and come through and beyond the dykes which should have protected both flanks of their army, their front line had stretched out and opened up. There were shouts of 'Close up! Close up!' John Roy Stuart's Edinburgh Regiment, initially stationed in the second line, moved forward to help plug the gaps.

Unable to bear the punishing bombardment any longer, the right wing of the Jacobite Army surged forward and charged. They were led from the centre of the front line by Alexander MacGillivray of Dunmaglass at the head of the Clan Chattan regiment that his cousin, Anne, Lady Mackintosh, now famously known as 'Colonel' Anne, had raised. The Camerons, Stewarts of Appin, Frasers and the Atholl Regiment were also heading across the field, as was Francis Farquharson of Monaltrie and the men of Braemar and Deeside.

As they ran forward through artillery fire, swirling smoke and sleety rain, they swerved to the right, probably to avoid boggy ground and find firmer footing beside the moor road, which also curved to the right. This made it difficult for the men of the Atholl Regiment to fire their muskets, for fear of hitting friends rather than foes.

Those who were not felled by gun and artillery fire and made it to the Government front line flung themselves in a great mass against the regiments on its left wing, inflicting heavy casualties on the men of Barrell's Regiment. One who survived described the horror of it:

> It was dreadful to see the enemies' swords circling in
> the air, as they were raised from the strokes! And no less

> to see the officers of the army, some cutting with their swords, others pushing with the spontoons, the sergeants running their halberds into the throats of the enemy, while the soldiers mutually defended each other, and pierced the heart of his opponent, ramming their fixed bayonets up to the socket.

Cameron of Lochiel was drawing his sword from his scabbard to attack Barrell's when he was hit by grapeshot in both ankles. Two of his faithful clansmen carried him out of danger.

To the right of Barrell's Regiment stood the men of Sir Robert Munro's Regiment, who had broken at Falkirk. At Culloden, they stood their ground, but the force and fury of the Highland charge was so great the Jacobites succeeded in pushing through them to the Government second line. At this point, the Jacobites found they had been outflanked. From their right, they were being shot at by the men of James Wolfe's Regiment, which had been moved forward and around from the Government second line for that purpose.

Although it may be questionable how effective the much-practised bayonet drill could be in such a melee, General Huske was heard to bark out an order to 'Give 'em the bayonet!' Surrounded and trapped, it's estimated that 700 Jacobites were killed in a few minutes by the guns and bayonets of the Government soldiers.

Many had been shot down before they reached the Government front line. Clan Chattan was slaughtered. Alexander MacGillivray of Dunmaglass fell, never to rise again, by the Well of the Dead. Those who survived retreated back across the field.

Back there, another outflanking manoeuvre was being put into action. The Campbells of the Argyle Militia had been ordered to demolish the stone dykes of the Culwhiniac enclosure on the right wing of the Jacobite Army to allow mounted dragoons to ride through them. It was the Campbells who emerged from them first, rushing out to attack the fleeing clansmen.

They were unaware that they were also taking on the experienced marksmen and French Army officers of the Royal Ecossais, the troops who had landed at Montrose in November 1745 under the command of Lord John Drummond. They rode to the rescue of the Jacobite foot soldiers, covering them and allowing many to get away in safety. Again, archaeological investigation of skulls found on the battlefield shows that several of the Campbells coming through the breach in the stone dykes were shot between the eyes. Colonel Jack Campbell of the Argyle Militia wrote to his father from Inverness that night:

> I have just time to informe you that we have gain'd a compleat victory over the rebels. The main body of my corps was order'd as a guard for the baggage by which means I had no oppertunity of seeing the affair distinctly and must therefore differ writing particularly till another oppertunity. Part of our men were engag'd and behav'd incomparably well amongst whom Ballimore was kill'd and Achnaba dangerously wounded.

The death of Colin Campbell of Ballimore had been foreseen a few days before by a 'half-witted' Campbell clansmen who was reputed to have the second sight. 'What,' he asked, 'can be the reason that my captain has a stream of blood running down his brow?' Ballimore is said to have heard of his question and laughed it off.

A handful of heroes from John Gordon of Avochie's Strathbogie Battalion, men from Huntly, Banff and Fochabers and the countryside in between, did not leave the field but stayed where they were, firing from behind a dyke to cover the retreat of others. They were set upon by the Redcoats and 'killed to a man'.

Over on the left wing of the Jacobite Army, the fight was also raging. James Johnstone was there, momentarily stunned when his friend Donald MacDonald of Scotus fell dead beside him. Clan chief MacDonald of Keppoch died, too, the spot now marked by a small memorial stone.

The Irish Picquets, professional soldiers from the Irish Brigade of the French Army, covered the retreat of Keppoch's fleeing clansmen and lost 100 of their own men in the process. A group of Jacobite gunners stayed at their post behind another of the stone walls enclosing the Lord President's fields. Four cannons and three coehorn mortars were moved in to attack and annihilate them.

Although James Johnstone tells a story of a troop of Government cavalry clearing a path to allow a group of Highlanders to leave the field, other horsemen cantered after fugitives and cut them down. Kingston's Horse took their revenge for being humiliated at Keith, their General Humphrey Bland later commended by Cumberland for having 'made a great slaughter'.

Realizing victory was theirs, the Redcoat infantry advanced across the field, killing many of the wounded Jacobites where they lay. One of the Government soldiers later described himself and his comrades as looking 'like so many butchers', their white gaiters stained red from the blood they were splashing over each other.

One who escaped their attention was Ranald MacDonald of Belfinlay. Not long after the battle had ended, he saw a coach with ladies in it. As it passed, the coachman 'made a lick at me with his whip as if I had been a dog'. One of the women in the coach was the Countess of Findlater, whose house at Cullen had been plundered by the party of Jacobites of whom Lord Pitsligo had been so ashamed. Thanks to the humanity of a Captain Hamilton in the Government army, Belfinlay lived to tell the tale – but before Hamilton rescued him, the young man lay all night in agony on the freezing field.

Satisfied with what had been achieved within the space of an hour, the Duke of Cumberland sat down to eat a late lunch on the large boulder which now stands at the crossroads just east of the battlefield. He had observed much of the action from there, and it has been known ever since as the Cumberland Stone. Some of us will remember being encouraged by our fathers and mothers to spit on it.

Some people now work very hard to convince themselves and the rest of us that at Culloden, more Scots fought for Cumberland than

for Charles Edward Stuart. This remarkable idea does not stand up to
scrutiny or, indeed, five minutes' concentrated thought.

The current party line is that the '45 was not the last battle between
Scotland and England – Auld Enemy 1, Auld Caledonia 0 – but the
final act of a Scottish – and British – civil war. In which case, it would
be interesting to know where the Englishmen in the Jacobite Army
were. Apart from the Manchester Regiment and, at Culloden, John
Daniel, Jem Bradshaw and – perhaps – some of the deserters from
Prestonpans, they're not there.

Curiously, many who advance this point of view are latter-day
Jacobites, their sympathies entirely with the Prince and his men.
They usually also assert that the Scots in the Government army were
Lowlanders. Undaunted by the facts, this neat theory presents the '45 as
a struggle between noble, doomed Highlanders and quisling Lowlanders
failing to support the Stuart Cause in favour of kowtowing to English
masters for the sake of the main chance and advancement within an
ever-more powerful Great Britain. According to this scenario, the souls
of the Highlanders rose above such cynical materialism.

The argument that more Scots fought on the Government side
than on the Jacobite stems from the presence of Scottish regiments
within the Government army. Of the twenty-two regiments that the
Duke of Cumberland commanded on the day, four were Scottish: the
Scots Fusiliers, Lord Mark Kerr's 11th Dragoons, the Royal Scots and
the Campbell Argyle Militia, led by Colonel Jack. (Although led by a
Scotsman, Munro's Regiment on the Government side, still bearing
the name of Sir Robert, who had died at Falkirk, was an English one.
As was often the custom in those days, it was known by the name of
its colonel. Three months on, and with the British Army at full stretch,
his successor as their commander had not yet been appointed.)

Despite its name, the Royal Scots may not have contained as many
Scotsmen as might be thought. Wedded though we are now to the
concept that a regiment recruits from a specific geographical area,
this was not the case in the eighteenth century. Regiments beat up
for recruits wherever they were stationed. The evidence of Colonel

Gardiner's letters to his wife shows that he and his nominally Scottish regiment, for example, were stationed at various times in different towns in various parts of England. Furthermore, in the period before Culloden, the Royal Scots had been on an extended tour of duty in Ireland. Colonel Dick Mason, curator of the Royal Scots Regimental Museum in Edinburgh Castle, believes that in the mid-1740s there were probably many Irishmen within the regiment's ranks. At this time, of course, Ireland, both north and south, was ruled over by the British monarch.

Cumberland had other Scotsmen under his command, largely officers serving with English regiments, although this cuts both ways. It's an unscientific form of analysis, but it does seem unlikely that Captain Norton Knatchbull of the Scots Fusiliers was one of the Kirkintilloch Knatchbulls; likewise Lieutenant Guildford Killigrew of Lord Mark Kerr's 11th Dragoons.

All the Redcoat officers – English, Scottish, Irish or Welsh – were at Culloden because they were professional soldiers and it was their duty to be there. The political opinions they held privately were another matter. There were rumours that several of them – and not only the Scottish officers – were secretly more inclined towards the House of Stuart than the House of Hanover. Even the aged General Guest at Edinburgh Castle had been suspected of having Jacobite tendencies.

In this connection, Cumberland's decision to initially set Colonel Jack Campbell of Mamore and his Campbell clansmen to guard the baggage train, well behind the Government lines, is interesting. The duke may have felt that a locally raised militia would not be as effective in a full-scale battle as a regiment of regular soldiers. Or, given that he never really trusted Scots, he may not have wanted to run the risk that the Campbell clansmen would be tempted to go over to the other side. Despite traditional clan enmities, there were a good many Campbells within the ranks of the Jacobite Army.

With the exception of the Irish Picquets and the Franco-Scots, that 5,000-strong army was overwhelmingly Scottish. If we do the sums for the four Scottish regiments within the 9,000-strong Government army – albeit having to assume the numbers in each were similar – we come up with a figure of 1,350 Scots: around 15 per cent of the total. We then have to make another assumption, although it seems a fair one: that the Scottish officers in English regiments were more than balanced out by the Irish private men in the Royal Scots. With around 5,000 Scotsmen in the Jacobite Army, then, and 1,350 on the Government side, the arithmetic of the claim that more Scots fought against Charles Edward Stuart than for him simply does not add up.

The neat theory that the '45 in general and Culloden in particular was a struggle between noble, doomed Highlanders and Englishmen aided and abetted by quisling Lowlanders also does not hold water for two reasons: first, substantial numbers of Highlanders weighed in on the Government side, and second, there were numerous Jacobite supporters in the Lowlands and elsewhere.

The forces ranged against the Jacobites included the men in Lord Loudoun's Regiment, the Black Watch and the Independent Highland Companies. (These local militia were first raised to police the Highlands shortly after the Stewarts were deposed back in 1688. Duncan Forbes of Culloden and Lord Loudoun did much to encourage their activities in support of the Government during the '45.) The chiefs of the MacLeods and the MacDonalds of Skye, who had declined to support the Prince, both commanded their own pro-Government companies. There were Munros and Grants who supported the Government side, too, carrying out policing actions and assisting in the hunt for Charles Edward Stuart and other prominent Jacobites after Culloden. Again, the private politics of the men may well have been anti-Government and pro-Jacobite, as in the case of Gaelic bard Duncan Ban MacIntyre. When it came to hunting the Prince and those other fugitives, many in these militias showed, as Sir Alexander MacDonald of Sleat put it, that they 'felt a certain delicacy' about fighting or persecuting their own relatives and friends. Then again, there were others who used their positions in the militias to settle scores arising from inter-clan rivalries, grudges and disputes.

On the other side of the conflict, there were Jacobites to be found outwith the Highlands, notably in the Orkney Islands and scattered throughout southern Scotland. These were not only the gentlemen volunteers. Although they more than did their bit, they were not a huge group in terms of numbers, as the men of Angus, Aberdeenshire and Banffshire were. Geographically, much of this area might be in the north of Scotland but culturally it is and was Lowland. Indeed, the Jacobite Army referred to this 20 per cent of their fighting men as the 'Lowland Regiments'. As historian Henrietta Tayler put it: 'It takes a real Scot to know that Aberdeen is Lowland!'

In the reprisals which were soon to be taken against the Jacobites and the communities from which they came, Aberdeenshire, Angus and Banffshire were not excluded. A proclamation was read in churches throughout Aberdeenshire: 'Wherever arms of any kind are found, the house, and all houses belonging to the proprietor, shall be immediately burnt to ashes.' And if any arms were discovered underground, 'the adjacent houses and fields shall be immediately laid waste and destroyed'.

These threats were carried out in many places. Despite that, the year after Culloden, a Government spy filed a report to his political masters, saying, 'Tho' the people of Aberdeenshire are all quiet at home', they were 'as much disposed to rebellion as ever'.

All that was yet to come. Having finished his lunch, Cumberland moved on to the next task. Out on the moor, at least 2,000 men lay dead. Estimates put the Government fatalities at 50, although, again, there is some debate about this. The estimates of 1,500 Jacobite dead are considered more reliable.

At four o'clock that afternoon, the duke led his victorious army into Inverness.

20

That Old Woman Who Spoke to Me of Humanity: Duncan Forbes of Culloden

When this affair blows over, as I hope it soon will . . .

D r John Rattray, the Edinburgh surgeon who had treated the wounded after Prestonpans and subsequently marched with the Jacobites as one of the Prince's two personal physicians, had been on the abortive march to Nairn. Exhausted after its abandonment, he went back to Inverness and threw himself 'upon the top of a bed'.

He woke up only after the Battle of Culloden had started. Hurrying towards the sound of gunfire, he met Sir John Macdonald, one of the Seven Men of Moidart. Reining in his horse, Sir John issued an impassioned warning:

> For God's sake, Mr Rattray, go not, for they are hewing down all before them, and are giving no quarters, and it is not possible you can be safe. You had therefore best return with me to Inverness, for as I am a French officer I have nothing to fear, and I am to give myself up as their prisoner. And as you attended the army only as a

surgeon, you have as little to fear, and therefore you may deliver yourself up with me.

Sir John was wrong: Rattray had a great deal to fear. Standing in the streets of Inverness, he was passed by a Redcoat officer he knew, Lord Cathcart. Cathcart looked at him and shook his head, saying, 'Mr Rattray, I am sorry to see you there; I am afraid it will go hard with you.'

The Government officers who followed Cathcart into Inverness thought so, too, and they were much more hostile. 'Damn' you, Sir,' one of them said, 'we know who you are, the Pretender's physician. If anyone hang, you shall.'

Rattray and his colleague Lauder both ended up being flung into the Old High Church of Inverness, on the site now occupied by Leakey's Bookshop, crammed in with other Jacobite prisoners. It's from here we get the chilling story that 'all their instruments and everything that could be useful to the wounded were carefully taken from them'. The two surgeons were distraught, surrounded by injured men who gazed at them with pleading eyes and begged for help, but able to do very little for them.

Jem Bradshaw of the Manchester Regiment, who had fought at Culloden under Lord Elcho, confirmed this story in the speech he gave from the scaffold before his execution:

> I was put into one of the Scotch kirks together with a great number of wounded prisoners who were stript naked and then left to die of their wounds without the least assistance; and tho' we had a surgeon of our own, a prisoner in the same place, yet he was not permitted to dress their wounds, but his instruments were taken from him on purpose to prevent it; and in consequence of this many expired in the utmost agonies.

Bradshaw also used his dying speech to passionately deny the claim that the barbarities of Government troops in the aftermath of Culloden were in response to a Jacobite order to show them no mercy. He called it a 'wicked malicious lie, raised by the friends of usurpation in hopes of an excuse for the cruelties committed in Scotland, which were many more and greater than I have time to describe'.

It's impossible not to compare the mercy the Jacobites showed to their enemies with the heartless cruelty meted out to them after Culloden. Those among them who had a French commission were treated very differently. The Marquis d'Eguilles wrote home to his 'cher papa': 'Nous sommes prisoniers de guerre, mais traités à l'angloise [sic], c'est-à-dire, très-bien. La ville d'Inverness est notre prison.'

There was as yet no Geneva Convention, but there was an understanding that prisoners of war should be treated in a humane way. The French and Franco-Scottish prisoners were allowed to move about Inverness, and the wounded among them, as the Marquis wrote to the French Foreign Office, were being treated by Monsieur Barret, a French surgeon.

The Duke of Cumberland went so far as to give d'Eguilles 1,000 guineas for the subsistence of the Frenchmen. The Marquis also noted that the duke's secretary, Sir Everard Falkener – the Frenchman impressed to find they had a mutual friend in Voltaire – was treating the French officers with great politeness. The Marquis d'Eguilles was relieved that he and his compatriots were being treated well, or, as he had put it, 'in the English way'. The English way was to be entirely different when it came to those regarded as Scottish Rebels. They were to be treated as less than human. It took great courage to run the gauntlet of the English soldiers who were 'hewing down all before them', let alone think of trying to help any wounded men left alive on the battlefield. Yet three women did.

Anne Leith, a young widow from Aberdeenshire, went out to Culloden with her friend Mrs Stonor and a maid known only as 'Eppy' on the very afternoon of the battle. With their baskets full of bandages, the three women did what they could for wounded and dying Jacobites. In the days and weeks which followed, Anne Leith went round the cellars and churches and makeshift prisons in Inverness with more bandages and as much bread as she could buy. She got herself arrested but kept on doing it. A few brave souls in Inverness matched her courage.

One was the Provost of the Highland burgh, John Fraser, and his predecessor in that office, John Hossack. When they ventured to suggest to Hangman Hawley and General Huske that the treatment of the defeated might be more humane, they were evicted. One of Hawley's officers kicked John Hossack downstairs and out into the street.

Another who spoke up for humanity was Duncan Forbes of Culloden, Lord President of the Court of Session and friend, par excellence, of the British Government and the British state. In 1745 he was a widower of 57, a fond and affectionate father to his only son, and desperately worried about Scotland. Convinced that the country's future progress and development would be best served by remaining in the Union with England, he also passionately believed that prosperity would bring Scotland lasting peace.

A lawyer to trade, his position as Lord President of the Court of Session gave him power and authority far beyond the legal sphere. The Secretary of State for Scotland at the time was the Marquis of Tweeddale. His Edinburgh home was in Tweeddale Court at the foot of the Canongate, but he spent much of his time in London, leaving the day-to-day administration of Scotland in the hands of the Lord President and other senior legal officers and members of the nobility.

Duncan Forbes also divided his time between two homes, his elegant mansion on his estate at Culloden and his Edinburgh home at Musselburgh. He had a good intelligence service wherever he was, dispatching discreet people who listened more than they spoke to bring the news back to him. After the debacle of what might have become the '44, when the Protestant Wind wrecked the French ships waiting to sail to Scotland, he was well aware of the renewed rumours circulating at the beginning of 1745, that Charles Edward Stuart was planning a landing in Scotland.

The Rebellion of 1715 had touched Duncan Forbes both professionally and personally. Despite being a rising young lawyer, he had rejected the request to conduct the prosecutions of those found guilty of treason afterwards. He was a humane man and also believed the rigorous punishments he was likely to be involved in handing down would be counterproductive. In this, as in so many other things, he was to be proved right.

By the time of the '15, he was already a young widower and a single parent, his wife Mary Rose of Kilravock having died within a year or two of their marriage. They were childhood sweethearts and a large stone still to be seen and sat on in Culloden Woods is traditionally said to be where he proposed to her.

When Mary died, Duncan's mother stepped into the breach. Mary Innes was a strong-minded woman who loved her family dearly. Sadly, she died when Duncan's son was only six or seven. His father wrote to a female friend: 'Tomorrow my aged mother will be buried. If you saw my little destitute brat, you'd at once love and pity him.'

The funeral of Mary Innes did not go entirely according to plan. In an age of heroic claret drinkers, Duncan Forbes and his brother John more than earned their place. Receiving family and friends at Culloden House that morning, so much wine was drunk it was only when the mourners arrived at the kirkyard that they realized they'd left the coffin and the much-lamented Mary Innes back at the house.

The same woman friend to whom Duncan Forbes wrote about his son's grief at losing his grandmother was concerned that he drank too much. Reminding him that in a flirtatious moment he had once told her he was all hers, she told him to take better care of her property. A few days before his 'justly honoured' mother's death, he told his friend she hadn't quite got it right:

> I never said more than that I was as much thine as I was
> my own, thus thou canst not pretend to more than one
> half of me, and I do assure you that as I have been no
> more than half drunk since I saw thee, I took a special

care that my own half of myself should be drunk while
yours remained in perfect sobriety.

For Duncan Forbes, a different kind of liquid refreshment posed
huge dangers. This was a 'vile drug' and a 'contemptible beverage'
– and it was tea that he had in his sights. Although his spluttering
condemnation of this innocuous drink sounds comical to modern
ears, there was a serious side to his complaint. There was a tax on
tea, unless, of course, you bought it from one of the free-trading
gentlemen who dropped anchor in secluded coves all round the
Scottish coast. Huge amounts of revenue were being lost.

The Lord President was concerned that people should pay their
taxes because the money was needed to help foster trade and industry.
He was directly involved with the project which, in 1729, invited 21
French weavers to come to Edinburgh to teach the locals how to make
cambric. Where those weavers once lived and worked and handed on
their skills is now Picardy Place in Edinburgh's New Town.

Picture, then, his horror when his dream of a productive, prosperous
and peaceful Scotland was shattered by the arrival of Charles Edward
Stuart. Using his many contacts, Forbes had done his utmost in the
run-up to the '45, when everyone knew something was afoot, to
persuade people not to throw in their lot with the Jacobites. Lord
George Murray, the commander of Prince Charles's army, was one of
them. The Lord President and Lord Lovat were also friends.

Duncan Forbes was equally active once battle commenced. Working
in Inverness with Lord Loudoun, he helped raise and organize the
pro-Government militias. Despite his stern and sincere disapproval of
those who supported the Prince, after the defeat at Culloden he was
deeply concerned by the maltreatment of the prisoners.

In this, he was out of step with the Duke of Cumberland, Hangman
Hawley and many among the British Army's senior command. 'That
old woman who spoke to me of humanity' is how Cumberland
described him. When Forbes continued to remonstrate, mentioning
'the laws of the country', Cumberland's reply was blunt: 'The Laws

of the Country, my Lord? I'll make a brigade give laws, by God!'

This interchange is reported in *The Lyon in Mourning,* the unashamedly Jacobite compilation of evidence put together by another member of the Forbes clan, Episcopalian Bishop Robert Forbes. There is no record of a family relationship between him and the Lord President.

The Bishop repeats a conversation he had with 'an honest Whig' who said the cruelties perpetrated by the Redcoats under Cumberland and others would be the best recruiting sergeant the supporters of the House of Stuart would ever have. Whether this honest Whig really existed or was a device for Bishop Forbes to tell his tale might be open to doubt. What is clear is the respect felt by Bishop Forbes and many other Jacobites for Duncan Forbes of Culloden, who got very little reward from his own side for the huge effort he put in to maintain the status quo.

Apart from begging the Duke of Cumberland to show mercy to the defeated Jacobites, Duncan Forbes asked for only one personal favour for a personal friend. The Lord President loved his golf, so much so he would even play when there was snow lying on the links at Musselburgh. At the same time as Dr John Rattray was the captain of the Company of Gentlemen Golfers, Duncan Forbes was the secretary. Forbes asked Cumberland to free his golfing friend. When Rattray said he wasn't leaving Inverness without his colleague George Lauder, Forbes asked Cumberland to let him go, too. Although the two of them were arrested again once they returned to Edinburgh, and subsequently taken to London and held prisoner there, they were released for good six months later.

Duncan Forbes did not live long after the Battle of Culloden, dying at the beginning of December 1747. It is deeply ironic that the name of his home has become synonymous with the barbarous cruelty towards his fellow Highlanders which so distressed this humane man.

Like Colonel Gardiner of Prestonpans, his death was mourned as much by his enemies as by his friends. Friend and foe alike said they knew what Duncan Forbes had died of: a broken heart.

21

YOU HAVE KILLED YOUR PRINCE: RODERICK MACKENZIE

HE CHOSE TO DIE WITH SWORD IN HAND

Inverness was a terrible place to be in the vicious days which followed Culloden. One description of the horror comes from a young Scotsman called David Calder, who was a gentleman volunteer with the Government army, serving under Lord Loudoun. Loudoun and his men had not made it to Culloden. Fearing that his father, Benjamin, might have heard otherwise, David wrote to him from Inverness a week after the battle to reassure him that his son was safe and well. David Calder also told his father that he was 'heartily sorry for the Gentlemen of our Country that has been so foolish as to Concern in this unluckie rebellion'. Quietly but clearly distressed, the young man also commented on the treatment being meted out by the victors to the vanquished: 'Nothing is seen amongst us but continuell processions of prisoners and wounded, all meeting houses destroyed, dead bodies exposed to dogs and ravens, none allowed to burry them.'

One of the first things Cumberland did was to root out the deserters from the Government forces who had gone over to the Jacobites at Prestonpans and elsewhere. This was summary justice at its most brutal. Gibbets were erected in the streets of Inverness, and 36 men were hanged. One of them was Malcolm Forbes of Pitcalnie, the great-nephew of Duncan Forbes. The Lord President's prediction that the young man would find himself a halter had been all too accurate.

As Malcolm Forbes swung from the gibbet, an English officer thrust his sword into the body, declaring that 'all his countrymen were traitors and rebels like himself' – and a Scottish Redcoat officer took extreme exception to what he had just said. This man drew his sword and demanded satisfaction for the insult to his country. At this point, the dispute flared up to include everyone else around them. James Johnstone heard the story while he was on the run after Culloden:

> whilst they fought, all the officers took part in the quarrel and swords were drawn in every direction. At the same time, the soldiers, of their own accord, beat to arms and drew up along the streets, the Scots on one side and the English on the other, beginning a very warm combat with fixed bayonets.

Only when someone sent for the Duke of Cumberland to smooth the ruffled feathers of the Scotsmen under his command did this Scottish–English conflict stop.

In the following days and weeks, the hundreds of Jacobite prisoners crammed into the gaol, the High Kirk and every other lockable space in Inverness were shipped south. The officers and a few of the private soldiers were to be tried for treason. Many more of the latter were to be transported to the West Indies to work as indentured servants. This was to be the fate of almost 1,000 Scots, including around 50 of the women and children who had followed the Jacobite Army into England and not made it back.

Cumberland was quite clear in his own mind that Jacobite prisoners must not be left in Scottish prisons or tried in Scotland. His fear was that their fellow countrymen would be too lenient with them. As

Duncan Forbes of Culloden and Provosts Fraser and Hossack had learned, 'leniency' was not a word in the duke's own vocabulary.

This 'horrid and unnatural Scotch Rebellion' had to be stamped on with all the force at his command. There was a war going on in Europe and he wanted to get back to it, although it would be a handsome feather in his cap if he could capture Charles Edward Stuart before he left North Britain and its troublesome inhabitants. Government patrols fanned out across the Highlands and Islands, looking everywhere for Charles. They called it the 'summer's hunting'.

Roderick Mackenzie – Rorie to his friends and family – had been in the Jacobite cavalry, serving in the elite Lifeguards under Lords Elcho and Balmerino. In his mid-twenties, he was tall, blond and handsome. The same age and physical build as the Prince, he bore a slight facial resemblance, too.

Skulking in Glenmoriston after Culloden, Rorie Mackenzie came face to face with a troop of Redcoats. Faced with a hellish choice, he raised his sword and fought, preferring a quick death to imprisonment, trial, almost certain condemnation and the prolonged and brutal agony of being hung, drawn and quartered.

Outnumbered as Rorie Mackenzie was, the outcome was inevitable. Yet he snatched one triumph from the jaws of death. With his dying breath he called out an impassioned reproach to the Government soldiers who had ended his life: 'You have killed your Prince!'

Standing looking down at the dead body, the Government soldiers could not be sure if they had or not. None of them had ever seen the Prince. What they did know was that there was a £30,000 reward on Charles Edward Stuart's head – and they took that literally. They buried Roderick Mackenzie's body near where he had fallen, but they cut off his head first, put it in a bag and carried it to Fort Augustus.

Alexander MacDonald of Kingsburgh was a prisoner there at the time, accused of having given succour to the enemy by helping the Prince as he fled from the Western Isles to Skye. A Redcoat officer came to him and asked if he would recognize the head of the Young Pretender if he saw it. Kingsburgh replied that he would, adding –

with a nervous joke – as long as it was still attached to Charles's body. The officer then asked if he would recognize it if it wasn't attached. Did an uncomfortable pause then ensue, both men finding it difficult to meet the other's eyes?

When Kingsburgh told the English officer he doubted he would recognize the head without the body, the man went away and no more was said. The nightmarish story does not end there. The head was pickled in spirits to preserve it and taken to London, in the hope that some imprisoned Jacobite might be persuaded or coerced into identifying it. To whom it was presented for such identification is not recorded. Imagining the possible scenarios sends a shiver down the spine, as does wondering what eventually happened to this now gruesome relic.

This story seems always to have been well known in the Glenmoriston area, one of the many tales handed down from one generation to the next in the tradition of the Highlands. Despite that, Bishop Robert Forbes, compiler of *The Lyon in Mourning*, was still unsuccessfully trying to get the exact details 13 years after that death and hideous decapitation in Glenmoriston. The Bishop was told by one of his correspondents that Roderick Mackenzie's mother and sisters were still living in Edinburgh, but no letter to or from them appears in the *Lyon,* his collection of accounts and eyewitness reports of the events of 1745–6.

Versions of the story set down in writing much later state that Roderick Mackenzie had been a student at Edinburgh University and that his father was a goldsmith. The Incorporation of Goldsmiths of the City of Edinburgh does have a record of a Roderick Mackenzie in 1726. The Roderick Mackenzie of the Glenmoriston story is described in the muster roll of the Jacobite Army as a 'Timber merchant. Fisherow'– which could be the famous Fisherrow in Musselburgh.

James Johnstone tells the story in his memoirs, with evident admiration for Roderick Mackenzie's bravery and quick wits. As two young Edinburgh gentlemen in the Prince's army, it's very likely that they knew one another. Johnstone does not say whether he heard the story while he was on the run after Culloden or whether he was told it many years later. Judging by Bishop Forbes' requests for information, it does appear to have been doing the rounds. There is at least one contemporary written source. Dougal Graham, the Glasgow Bellman, told the story of Roderick Mackenzie's death like this:

> Rod'rick MacKenzie, a merchant-man,
> At Ed'nburgh town had join'd the Clan,
> Had in the expedition been,
> And at this time durst not be seen,
> Being sculking in Glen-Morriston,
> Him the soldiers lighted on,
> Near about the Prince's age and size,
> Genteely drest, in no disguise.
> In every feature, for's very face,
> Might well be taken in any case,
> And lest he'd like a dog be hang'd,
> He chose to die with sword in hand,
> And round him like a mad-man struck,
> Vowing alive he'd ne'er be took:
> Deep wounds he got, and wounds he gave,
> At last a shot he did receive,
> And as he fell, them to convince,
> Cry'd, Ah! Alas! *You've kill'd your Prince:*
> *You murderers and bloody crew*
> *You had no orders this to do.*

It goes on in the same vein for another 20 lines, ending with a couplet which stands comparison with the work of the late, great William Topaz McGonagall himself:

> And ere that he was really dead,
> They forthwith did cut off his head.

When the road through Glenmoriston was widened ten years ago, great care was taken to preserve and then move the cairn which was erected there in Rorie Mackenzie's memory. On the other side of the road, steps lead down from a lay-by to his grave, which is well marked. Many today still make the pilgrimage to visit both it and the cairn.

It may not only be wishful thinking on the part of latter-day Jacobites to believe that Roderick Mackenzie's gallantry in his last seconds of life were not in vain. For a time, the search for the Prince did relax. Then it started up again with a vengeance.

22

THE QUIET MAN:
NEIL MACEACHAINN

THE WORST PRETENDER HE'D EVER SEEN

Neil MacEachainn was by Charles Edward Stuart's side during much of his wandering through the Hebrides in the weeks and months after Culloden. Neil himself had not been in what he called 'the misfortunate battle of Culloden' or otherwise involved with the Jacobite Army, but he met up with the Prince and his companions when they came in a rowing boat on a wild night from Arisaig to Roshinish near Benbecula.

The local schoolmaster, Neil was a well-educated man. He had studied at the Scots College in Douai near Paris, although this does not necessarily mean that he was destined for the priesthood. Catholic Scots, barred from studying at any of the universities in their homeland or England, sometimes used this route to access higher education.

The young dominie often called himself Neil MacDonald, the MacEachainns being a sept of the Clanranald branch of that clan. It could be useful, too, in these dangerous times to have a *nom de guerre* or two up your sleeve. As far as the British Government was concerned, helping the Prince after the defeat made you as guilty of 'levying war against the King's Most Excellent Majesty' as any soldier in the Jacobite Army.

Neil MacEachainn may have chosen to risk his life for Charles Edward Stuart when he had not chosen to join his army simply because chance gave him the opportunity to help. Many people sheltered and helped other fugitives to escape. Even people unconvinced by the Cause baulked at handing over their fellow countrymen to the rigours of English justice.

The suggestion has been made that Neil MacEachainn might have been a French agent. The French were certainly very keen to get the Prince out of Scotland, as they eventually did. Whether he was working for the French or not, Neil did play a pivotal role in Charles's escape over the sea to Skye with Flora MacDonald. Neil liked to portray himself as a simple country boy, but he was a lot more than that.

He provided the Prince with a hiding place at Corradale in South Uist, where Charles stayed in safety for almost a month. Neil's admiration for the Prince shines through the account he wrote of the time he spent with him. He praises Charles's 'top spirits' and his confidence that the Cause was not yet lost. It would seem that, in this, Charles was taking comfort from another kind of spirit:

> It was wonderful how he preserved his health all the time
> . . . He took care to warm his stomach every morning
> with a hearty bumper of brandy, of which he always
> drank a vast deal; for he was seen to drink a whole bottle
> of a day, without being in the least concerned.

The Prince loved to sit on a convenient stone in front of the house in Corradale with his face turned up to the sun. When Neil suggested he might be in danger of giving himself a headache, Charles cheerfully told him to mind his own business. He knew what was good for him, and 'the sun did him all the good in the world'.

Given the defeat at Culloden and its associated horrors, it's perhaps not surprising that Neil describes Charles as being up in the clouds at one moment and down in the dumps the next. He improved his mood by dancing, whistling a reel to himself for accompaniment. It must have been quite something to watch 'the lad who was born to be King' whirling and birling in the sunshine outside a wee cottage in the Outer Isles.

One day Charles amused himself by taking potshots at a school of whales which swam in close to the beach. Convinced he had killed one of them, he ordered Neil, a strong swimmer, to strip and go and haul the whale ashore. Neil himself seems to have been an early conservationist, or perhaps he was just kind-hearted. Referring to himself in the third person, he writes: 'Neil, in obedience to his orders and to humour him, began to strip very slowly till he saw the whale which had received no hurt out of sight.'

Initially imagining every ship he saw was a French vessel come to rescue him, Charles soon began to despair of that ever happening. Somehow he was going to have to find a ship to take him away from Scotland. Neil was dispatched to ask Alexander MacDonald of Boisdale if he would help. Boisdale was the man who told Charles when he first landed to 'Go home, sir.' He might now have thought himself justified in saying 'I told you so', but he agreed to come and see him.

Boisdale found Charles and some others still sleeping it off, 'very much disordered by the foregoing night's carouse'. His Prince's fondness for the bottle was clearly beginning to bother Neil MacEachainn, but Boisdale joined in, and 'he and the other gentlemen were very busie and very hearty taking their bottle'.

The news that hundreds of members of the pro-Government Skye Militia had landed on Barra and were soon to be reinforced by hundreds more under the dreaded Captain Fergusson gave the drinkers a sharp reality check. Boisdale was the first to come to his senses, realizing the Prince had to be moved. As he was trying to arrange that, he was arrested. He was taken to London and kept prisoner there for the next year but then released.

Two ladies stepped into the breach: Boisdale's wife and Lady Clanranald, whom everyone called Lady Clan. Although her husband was ostensibly a friend of the Government, he helped, too. So, despite being a captain in the Skye Militia, did one Hugh MacDonald, and he had a stepdaughter called Flora.

Charles went personally to ask for Flora's help, taking with him Felix O'Neil, a young man of Irish extraction, born in Rome, and who had served in both the French and Spanish armies before joining the Prince. Neil MacEachainn went along, too. He and Flora were related and knew one another well. Although terrified by the very idea of what was being suggested to her, Flora allowed herself to be persuaded. The plan was for the Prince to disguise himself as Flora's maidservant, supposedly an Irish girl named 'Betty Burke'. Her stepfather would give her a travel pass for two women, who, because of their gender, would be less likely to arouse suspicion, and they would cross the Minch to Skye.

When the Prince wanted to secrete a pair of pistols under his dress, Flora demurred, asking how it would look if they were searched and a maidservant was found to be carrying weapons. Charles replied – and maybe we can allow him a twinkle in his bonnie brown eyes as he said it – that if anyone searched him so closely as to find pistols, the game would certainly be up.

Appalled by how bad the Prince was at playing the part of a woman, still taking manly strides in his petticoats, Neil said he was the worst 'pretender' he'd ever seen. He went with him and Flora to Skye, and, like Flora, said his farewells at Portree.

Except that for Neil it was only *au revoir*. Almost three months later, he was one of the Jacobite fugitives who accompanied the Prince back to the safety of France. He spent the rest of his life there, serving as a soldier in the regiment in the French Army commanded by Jacobite exile Lord Ogilvy. Neil had a son who became one of Napoleon's generals, a marshal of France and the Duke of Tarentum. The good ship *L'Heureux – The Happy* – put in at Loch nan Uamh near Arisaig and left on 20 September with several of the clan chiefs and gentlemen who had been involved in the Rising on-board. One of the passengers in this illustrious company was Neil MacEachainn.

Simple country boy? Aye, that'll be right.

23

ODE TO HIS WOUNDED FOOT: DONALD ROY MACDONALD

NO LONGER DO I HUNT, OR JUMP, OR SWIM, NOR CARE TO TOUCH THE SWELLING BREASTS OF GIRLS

Donald Roy MacDonald was a volunteer to the Jacobite Army, a captain in MacDonald of Clanranald's Regiment. He was in his late thirties at the time of the '45, six feet tall, strong and vigorous. The MacDonalds who had come out for the Prince did their utmost to persuade their fellow clansmen to follow suit, and Donald Roy was their messenger.

As the Jacobites retreated north after the Battle of Falkirk in January 1746, Donald Roy was sent with a letter to Sir Alexander MacDonald, signed by all the Highland chiefs, imploring him to join them with every man he could muster. Donald Roy reached Skye and handed over the letter on the very same day that Sir Alexander received another letter from Lord Loudoun, Duncan Forbes of Culloden and the Laird of MacLeod, asking him to form his clansmen into a militia and join in on the Government side.

Sir Alexander gave Donald Roy a letter to take back to his clan chief, MacDonald of Keppoch. He did not know what was in it until he delivered it, when Keppoch told him its contents:

> Seeing I look upon your affairs as in a desperate way I
> will not join you; but then I assure you I will as little rise
> against you. If any misfortune shall happen to yourself I
> desire you may leave your son, Ranald, to my care, etc.

Sir Alexander had tried to persuade Donald Roy not to go back to the Jacobite Army, saying he did not like the idea of him being killed by one of 'his own blood relations'. Several of his cousins were serving under Lord Loudoun.

Donald Roy was not to be dissuaded. Heading for the ferry back to the mainland, he met a very close blood relation indeed: his brother Hugh MacDonald of Baleshare, captain in the local militia and Flora MacDonald's stepfather into the bargain. The MacDonald brothers spent three days together, eating, drinking and making merry at the expense of King George. Donald Roy kept his white cockade in his blue bonnet and many in the Skye Militia happily toasted the Prince's Cause.

At Culloden, Donald Roy saw MacDonald of Keppoch fall wounded to the ground, not once but twice. The second time, Keppoch looked at Donald Roy and said, 'O God, have mercy upon me. Donald, do the best for yourself, for I am gone.'

Donald Roy did as he was bid but was shot as he was leaving the field, the bullet going through the sole of his left foot and out at the top of it, taking his shoe with it. He walked five miles barefoot, his wound bleeding all the way. He did not dare to stop until he got to Bunchrew, two miles beyond Inverness. He got a horse there and rode on for another eight miles, heading doggedly for Skye, although he could not put his injured foot in the stirrup because it had swollen so much. By sheer luck, he met up the next day with William Balfour, surgeon to MacGregor's Regiment.

The young man 'dressed the foot by only putting some dry tow upon the hole beneath and the hole above and rolling a bandage above all'. That was all the medical attention Donald Roy's foot got until he reached Skye one week later, where he went to stay with John MacLean, a surgeon who lived in Trotternish.

MacLean dressed the wound, which had now become infected, giving off 'such a stink that one could scarce enter the room where he was'. Two months later, Donald Roy was still lodging at the surgeon's house and about to become involved in the plot to keep Charles Edward Stuart out of harm's way after he came over to Skye with Flora MacDonald and Neil MacEachainn.

There were plans for the Prince to lie low on an island off the coast from Trotternish. Donald Roy's brother, Hugh, was involved in this, and he asked him to help by keeping a look-out and going across to the tiny island to deliver some supplies to Charles. The Prince was short of everything, especially shirts. He was also very keen to have the latest newspapers, which Lady Margaret MacDonald was already sending to him as often as she could.

Baleshare gave his brother an instruction to which Jacobite plotters were well used: burn this letter. Donald Roy was to make sure any incriminating missives, most especially any which came from the Prince, were to be read carefully and then immediately flung into the fire.

When Donald Roy gave a letter to Lady Margaret from Charles thanking her for sending him the newspapers, she was upset at the thought of destroying such a precious souvenir of the Prince. She did burn it later, though, when the unpleasant Captain Fergusson and his men came to her house looking for him.

Lady Margaret had six of her husband's best shirts washed and told the maid who did the laundry they were for Donald Roy, who had lost all his with his baggage at Culloden. There had to be an excuse for Donald Roy to go out to the little island, so he told the man he asked to row him over that he wanted 'to divert himself some time at fishing'. When the boatman told Donald Roy the fishing was fine where he was, Donald Roy had to admit what he was really up to, drawing his dirk and asking the man to swear by 'the Holy Iron' that he would never breathe a word to anyone. The oath was taken and kept.

Lady Margaret MacDonald then had a boat sent out to the little island on the pretext of gathering shells to make lime, Donald Roy going along to supervise and also taking some fishing lines with him, in keeping with the cover story. He also had the six shirts and twenty guineas for the Prince – but found he was on a fool's errand.

The Prince was not on the island, nor on a small flat rock near it, where Donald Roy suspected a couple of men could hide. Despite his bad foot, he scrambled onto the rock from the rowing boat and climbed to the top of it. It, too, was empty.

A few days later, a letter from Lady Margaret asked him to come to her home at Monkstadt. Donald Roy borrowed the horse belonging to his landlord the surgeon, and set out. He found Lady Margaret with Alexander MacDonald of Kingsburgh, and very agitated. Kingsburgh was Lady Margaret's factor, and his son Allan was later to become Flora MacDonald's husband.

The Prince had only just got to Skye and had landed no distance from her house. Lieutenant MacLeod of the Militia was currently in the dining room of the house with Flora MacDonald, and the Prince was still in the rowing boat disguised – not very convincingly – as a woman. Even worse, Lieutenant MacLeod had a troop of men under his command with orders to investigate every boat they saw.

Lady Margaret, Donald Roy and MacDonald of Kingsburgh discussed what to do but 'all choices were bad'. Then Donald Roy had a brainwave. The coast was being closely watched, so why not send the Prince overland to Portree, 14 miles away? Kingsburgh asked if Donald Roy would go down to the shore and communicate the plan to Charles. As Donald Roy 'had been in the scrape', the Prince was more likely to take advice from him. Donald Roy demurred, saying that 'as the Prince he was sure would make a monstrous appearance in women's cloaths', it would look suspicious if he was seen talking to him. He suggested that Flora should go instead.

While this agonized discussion was going on, Charles Edward Stuart was sitting on a rock gazing out to sea, wearing his flowery frock and 'patiently waiting his fate'. Kingsburgh took a bottle of wine and some bread down to the shore, and Donald Roy went off in search of the laird's son known as young Raasay, who was currently staying near Portree. The island from which young Raasay took his name, just across the water from the north-east coast of Skye, had already been harried by Government troops. They had done their work well, burning every house and hut on it. Since there was now no reason for the Redcoats to return there, it seemed, at least temporarily, to be likely to provide a safe refuge for the Prince. The MacLeods of Raasay had provided a small regiment to the Jacobite Army. Given their support for the Cause and the destruction done to their island home, they were only too willing to help Charles escape.

Charles and Neil MacEachainn walked overland to Portree on a night of wind and rain and were met there by Donald Roy, who had arrived on horseback. The Prince was soaked through, and at the inn which is now the Royal Hotel he changed into a clean shirt and dry clothes, and sat down to a dinner of butter, cheese, bread and roasted fish with Neil, Donald Roy and Flora, who had gone there by 'taking a different road'. The three men drank from a bottle of whisky they bought from the landlord.

Being in a public place was making Donald Roy nervous. Anyone might walk in. He thought Charles should move on as soon as possible. Charles wanted to stay the night, understandably reluctant to go back out into the torrential rain. He wanted to smoke a pipe, too.

When the landlord weighed some tobacco and asked for fourpence halfpenny for it, the Prince gave the man sixpence and told him to keep the change. Donald Roy insisted the Prince keep it because 'in his present situation he would find bawbees very useful to him'. Amused, Charles slid the coins into his purse.

He then set about trying to persuade Donald Roy to come with him on the next leg of his journey. Donald Roy begged him not to even think of it. The wound in his foot was still open, making it difficult for him to walk. If he undertook any sort of a journey, he would have to do it on horseback, and if the search parties saw two riders they would undoubtedly come up and question them.

The Prince countered by saying he always felt safe when he had a MacDonald with him. The Stuart charm strikes again. Donald Roy was, however, still on his guard. He would join him later. He stopped Charles from paying over the odds for their meal, again worried that too big a tip would make the landlord suspicious.

The Prince said goodbye to Flora MacDonald, paying back to her a half-crown he had borrowed, kissing her hand and telling her, 'For all that has happened I hope, Madam, we shall meet in St James' yet.' Then he took his leave of Neil MacEachainn. Neil, Donald Roy and Flora spent that night in Portree.

Donald Roy saw Charles to his rendezvous with the next safe pair of hands. Attached to his belt, the Prince had what was left in the whisky bottle, a bottle of brandy, the clean shirts and a cold, cooked chicken. Donald Roy spotted the landlord looking very closely at Charles as they went out of the inn and deliberately turned the wrong way. They went round in a big circle to get back to the quayside, where Charles stepped into the boat which was to take him to Raasay.

It was now the early morning of Tuesday, 1 July, and Donald Roy returned to the inn and slept as best he could in the short Highland night. The next morning, the landlord was curious as to who the fair-haired young man had been. Donald Roy told him he was a comrade-in-arms from the Jacobite Army, to which the landlord replied that he had wondered if he might be Prince Charles in disguise, 'for that he had something about him that looked very noble'.

Donald Roy went back to the west coast of Skye, happily spending the night with his friend Lieutenant MacLeod, the man who had been in the dining room with Flora MacDonald while the Prince was sitting on the beach. It was also to MacLeod that Donald Roy had officially surrendered his weapons when he returned to Skye after Culloden. He bought some rough old ones for the purpose, sending his good ones to his brother for safe keeping, which MacLeod probably knew very well. What Lieutenant MacLeod didn't know was that the Prince had waltzed off from under under his nose. He had his men still watching the Minch.

Over the next couple of days, Donald Roy returned the surgeon's horse to him, armed himself with a new pistol and a dirk, and wore himself out and hurt his foot again after walking too many Highland miles. The plan had been that he would go to Raasay to join the Prince, but Charles had moved on. He sent a mysterious stranger with a letter to Donald Roy:

> Sir, I have parted (I thank God) as intended. Make my compliments to all those to whom I have given trouble.
> I am, Sir, your humble servant, James Thomson.

Donald Roy kept this letter, signed with one of Charles's many aliases, until the day his niece, Flora, was arrested. Then, with regret, he destroyed it. He also persuaded Flora to part with the safe conduct her stepfather had written for her and 'one Bettie Burk [*sic*], an Irish girl, who as she tells me is a good spinster'.

Despite his continuing caution, when it came out that he had been seen in Portree in company with the man whom people were now beginning to realize had been the Prince, Donald Roy had to take to the heather. More precisely, he had to take to three different caves in which he spent the next eight weeks, until the fuss had died down.

Lady Margaret MacDonald made sure he had food. Late at night and early in the morning, when no one would see him, he took a bottle to a nearby spring to get water. The surgeon sent dressings for his wounded foot, but Donald Roy was lonely and he was skulking during July and August and the midges and the flies drove him crazy.

He found distraction in writing poetry – in Latin. One is a lament for the slaughter at Culloden, another an ode to his wounded foot. It's not comic. The pain was obviously still too great for that. In his verses, he lamented that his injury was stopping him from doing the things he loved to do, like hunting and swimming. He didn't even feel like 'touching the swelling breasts of girls'. He could only hope and pray that 'the benign Founder of the World' would heal his foot and his situation.

Both did get better. Once it was realized that Charles had left Scotland and things began to quieten down, Donald Roy came out of hiding. He had enough friends in high places, including Lady Margaret's husband, Sir Alexander MacDonald of Sleat, that he was able to quietly get on with his life.

In the fullness of time, his wounded foot healed. When he visited Edinburgh a year or so after Culloden, he walked there from Skye in 12 days.

24

NOT WITHOUT ORDERS: FERGUSSON, LOCKHART & SCOTT

MONSTROUS TRANSACTIONS THAT WERE DELIBERATELY PERPETRATED IN THE FACE OF THE SUN BY GENTLEMEN AND (SHALL I SAY IT?) CHRISTIANS

It's an unpalatable truth that three Redcoat officers who earned themselves an enduring reputation for terrible cruelty after Culloden were all Scotsmen: Captain John Fergusson, Major James Lockhart and Captain Caroline Frederick Scott. In the summer and autumn of 1746, there were plenty of Englishmen running amuck through the Highlands raping, burning and destroying – Captain Cornwallis is one who earned his place in the hall of infamy – but it's these three Scotsmen who are most bitterly remembered.

Captain John Fergusson, master of the Royal Navy's *Furnace*, appears again and again in the stories of horrors committed along the western seaboard and throughout the Hebrides. One of the most dogged of the summer hunters of the Prince, he was afterwards fond of boasting that he had several times come within an hour of finding him.

A native of Oldmeldrum in Aberdeenshire, Fergusson came from a family with a long tradition of enmity towards the Stuarts. He seems also to have been motivated by the price on his quarry's head. After it was all over, a relative in Edinburgh asked him if he would have killed Charles if he had succeeded in capturing him. Fergusson's answer was unequivocal:

> No by God, I would have been so far from doing any such thing that I would have preserved him as the apple of mine eyes, for I would not take any man's word, no, not the Duke of Cumberland's for £30,000 Sterling, though I knew many to be such fools as to do it.

A cruel man by nature, he was also a boor. In pursuit of the Prince on South Uist, he went to Lady Clanranald's house. She was not at home but with the Prince and Flora MacDonald a few miles away on the other side of Loch Uiskevagh, the escape over the sea to Skye in the planning. Fergusson spent the night in Lady Clan's bed. In the eighteenth century, when it was shocking for a gentleman who was not a close relative to even enter a lady's bedroom, this was a deliberate insult.

Dissatisfied with her explanation when she returned home the following morning, that she had spent the night sitting up with a sick child, Fergusson arrested her and her husband. Despite Clanranald being ostensibly a friend of the Government, his wife spent many weary months under house arrest in London.

To add to his many unlovely qualities, Fergusson was a hectoring bully. Some people had the courage to stand up to him. Mrs MacDonald of Kingsburgh was one of them, telling him to his face the word was that he was a 'cruel, hard-hearted man'. Fergusson told her people should not believe everything they hear.

The Prince having once more given him the slip, Fergusson was paying Mrs MacDonald an unwelcome visit in the wake of the 'Betty Burke' episode. In the course of his interrogation, he asked her to show him where her most recent visitors had stayed. Hoping to shock her into an admission of guilt, he asked if she had put the Young Pretender and Flora MacDonald in the same bed. Mrs MacDonald of Kingsburgh remained as cool as a cucumber:

Sir, whom you mean by the Young Pretender I shall
not pretend to guess; but I can assure you it is not the
fashion in the Isle of Skye to lay the mistress and the
maid in the same bed together.

Ferguson observed drily that it was odd the maid seemed then to
have slept in a better bedroom than the mistress. Later that summer,
having failed to capture the Prince, he took some prisoners to
London on the *Furnace*. He kept them half-starved, with the little
food they did get brought to them 'in foul nasty buckets wherein the
sailors used to piss for a piece of ill-natured diversion'.

Before that, Father Alexander Cameron, Jesuit priest, Lochiel's
brother and Catholic chaplain to his regiment, fell into Fergusson's
clutches. Taken prisoner and held on the *Furnace* while the vessel was
still in the Hebrides, he had no bed to lie on other than the coils of
rope in the hold.

When he became ill, some of his friends on shore grew concerned
about his well-being. Getting no response from Fergusson, they went
over his head to the Duke of Albemarle. The Duke of Cumberland had
by now left Scotland, appointing Albemarle commander-in-chief in
his stead. He sent his own physician to examine Alexander Cameron.

The doctor's opinion was that Father Cameron should either be
brought ashore or given better treatment on-board. When Albemarle
sent a platoon of soldiers to pick him up, Fergusson was having none
of it. The man was his prisoner, and he was not obliged to hand him
over unless he had an order from the prime minister or the Lords of
the Admiralty.

A party of Alexander Cameron's friends then rowed out to the
Furnace with a bed, sheets and blankets. Fergusson refused to take these
on-board, threatening the small boat with sinking if its occupants
even tried to unload their cargo. Although Father Cameron was later
transferred to Inverness and away from Captain Fergusson, he did
endure a sea journey to London on a different ship. He died a few
months after he got there on one of the prison hulks moored on the

Thames to accommodate the hundreds of Scottish prisoners who had been shipped south from Inverness.

Felix O'Neil, one of Charles Edward Stuart's companions while he had been hopping about the Hebrides, was also unlucky enough to fall into Fergusson's hands. The captain treated him 'with all the barbarity of a pirate' and ordered him to be flogged when he refused to say where the Prince was. O'Neil was stripped and pinioned, on the point of being lashed, when Lieutenant MacCaghan of the Royal Scots Fusiliers – whose name sounds more Irish than Scottish – stepped forward, drew his sword and told Fergusson 'that he'd sacrifice himself and his detachment rather than to see an officer used after such an infamous manner'. He succeeded in preventing the flogging.

There were others who served under Fergusson who found his cruelty and the brutality he encouraged in others too much to stomach. Marines under his command and that of Captain Duff – another Scotsman who earned himself a notorious reputation – went ashore with the express aim of raping all the women and girls on the island of Canna. One of their number 'who had some grains of Christian principles about him' warned the islanders, thus thwarting this chilling plan.

Major James Lockhart was a senior officer in Cholmondley's Regiment. From their base at Fort Augustus, he and the gang of thugs under his command sallied forth to ravage the surrounding countryside. Lockhart's speciality was encouraging his men to gang-rape women and hang men, whether he had proof they had been in the Jacobite Army or not.

Many of these stories are confirmed by more than one source and many name names. There was Isabel MacDonald in Glenmoriston, raped while her husband, in hiding nearby, had to watch. If he had tried to stop it, Lockhart and his men would undoubtedly have killed him.

One infamous story has Lockhart personally shooting dead two old men and one young lad while they were doing nothing more than working in their fields. Another man, Grant of Daldriggan, was tied up and forced to watch as the dead men were strung up by their feet on a makeshift gallows. Not having jumped quickly enough when Lockhart ordered him to round up some cattle, Daldriggan was set to join them – until once more a man with a conscience stepped forward to stop the barbarity. This time it was a Captain Grant of Lord Loudoun's Regiment.

Like Captain Fergusson, James Lockhart clearly had a cruel streak. He enjoyed seeing people suffer, and he enjoyed watching their growing terror as they realized what he was going to do to them. Yet there's something about Lockhart which gives an even more sinister edge to his exploits: the sense of a man out of control. During these months of bloodletting, all limits were breached. He is reported to have murdered one boy of four by plunging his sword into him 'in at a belly and out at the back'. Something very powerful and very negative was driving James Lockhart.

These reprisals against Jacobite soldiers and the civilian population which had produced them were not only perpetrated by Englishmen and Lowland Scots. Highlanders were also involved. As the Camerons under Lochiel had played such a vital part in the Rebellion, Lochaber was singled out for special treatment. Among those who delivered it were Munro of Culcairn – taking his revenge for being defeated at Inverurie – and Captain Grant of Knockando and Strathspey.

According to John Cameron, Presbyterian minister at Fort William, and another of the chaplains to Lochiel's Regiment, Grant 'burnt and plundered as he marched' and 'stripped men, women and children without distinction of condition or sex'. An officer in Lord Loudoun's Regiment, he did so at the head of a company of 200 men. To know they were heading your way must have been absolutely terrifying.

Someone took revenge, though, shooting Munro of Culcairn dead. The Reverend Cameron knew who it was, knew too that the bullet had been intended for Captain Grant, who was walking beside Munro at the time. Grant had murdered the adult son of the old man who fired the shot which killed Munro.

233

The most infamous of these sadistic Redcoat officers was Captain Caroline Frederick Scott. He served in Guise's, the same regiment as the well-mannered and friendly Captain Sweetenham, but was a man of a very different stamp.

Scott first distinguished himself honourably, conducting a determined, focused and successful defence of Fort William when it was besieged by the Camerons early in 1746. His diary of the siege was published in the *Scots Magazine,* making him something of a hero among the friends of the Government. He was already a personal favourite of the Duke of Cumberland.

After Culloden, Scott led many raiding parties out of Fort William to harry the clan lands which lay around it. He paid particular attention to Appin, whose regiment of Stewarts in the Jacobite Army had been headed by Charles Stewart of Ardsheal.

Ardsheal's strong-minded wife, Isabel Haldane, had encouraged her husband to go out for the Prince. Like many men, he had hesitated, justifiably fearful of the consequences of failure. According to legend, Isabel untied her apron, took it off and handed it to him, saying that if he would not lead the men out, she would, and he could stay at home and look after the house and children. Ardsheal led the men out.

Many of them did not come home again, killed in the desperate charge of the right wing of the Jacobite Army and the subsequent heroic attempts to save the Appin banner. Held now at Edinburgh Castle, it is one of the few Jacobite colours to survive, along with that of Lord Ogilvy's Angus Regiment, kept safe now at the McManus Galleries and Museum in Dundee. In a ritual act of humiliation, the other Jacobite flags and banners were burned in Edinburgh by the public hangman.

Caroline Frederick Scott liked to humiliate his defeated enemies, too. Correctly suspecting that Charles Stewart of Ardsheal was skulking not too far from his home, Scott swooped down on Isabel Haldane and her young children. He took her house and her life apart, in the most literal sense.

Her meagre stores of butter and cheese were taken. On the direct orders of Cumberland himself, most of her livestock had. already been driven off. This confiscation of assets and tools of trades happened to many Highland families after the '45. Ploughs were burned and cows taken to Fort William and elsewhere to be sold to cattle farmers from the south, who journeyed north to buy them at bargain prices, leaving people destitute and with no means of tilling the ground, working the land or feeding themselves.

Many houses were burned, too, leaving a family with no shelter. In August 1746, Caroline Frederick Scott further refined the cruelty of this heartless policy. He stripped Ardsheal House bare, to the extent of having every piece of wood in it removed. Doors were taken off their hinges, panelling removed from the walls, the slates taken off the roof. Under Scott's orders it was all done very slowly and carefully, the nails straightened out so they too could be taken back to Fort William and sold. He even took the children's school books.

The lady of the house was then asked for her keys. Surrounded by her frightened children, pregnant with another, a confused Isabel handed them over. In a parody of gentlemanly behaviour, Caroline Scott offered her his hand, led her to the door and told her to go. She had no business here any more. Ardsheal House was no longer her home.

Isabel Haldane penned a furious letter of protest to Major General John Campbell of Mamore, the father of Colonel Jack of the Argyle Militia. Although both father and son were robust in their treatment of the defeated Rebels, by the standards of their time they were also humane, and she was not the only person who appealed to them for help. Many skulking Jacobites let it be known they were prepared to surrender, but only 'to a Campbell', meaning either Lord Loudoun, Colonel Jack or his father.

Considering the bad press the Campbells have had throughout Scottish history, it's interesting that these defeated clansmen clearly believed they would get better treatment from a Scotsman and fellow Highlander than they would from an Englishman or a Scottish Lowlander.

By birth, that's what Caroline Frederick Scott was, although it might also be fair to call him an Anglo-Scot. His father, George Scott of Bristo in Edinburgh, was British Ambassador to the Hanoverian Court during the reign of Queen Anne, before the House of Hanover succeeded to the British throne.

When George Scott's wife, Marion Steuart of Goodtrees, gave birth to a son, his godmother was Princess Caroline. As the wife of George II, she was to become Queen Caroline and the mother of the Duke of Cumberland. Caroline Frederick Scott was named in her honour, thus acquiring a first name which was as unusual for a man in his own day as it would be in ours.

Through both his father and his mother – whose surviving letters show that she believed in raising children with kindness – Caroline Frederick Scott was very 'weel-connecktit' in Scotland, too. In this he was not unusual. Sometimes it can seem that everyone involved in the '45 was related to everyone else.

Like many people, Scott had relatives who were friends of the Government, others who kept their opinions to themselves and others again who gave him a bad case of Embarrassing Jacobite Relatives Syndrome. One of his cousins was Provost Archibald Stewart of Edinburgh, whom Alexander Carlyle and John Home and their friends suspected of collusion with the Prince and his army. The provost's wife was the sister of Lord Elcho, colonel of one of the cavalry regiments in the Jacobite Army. For Caroline Frederick Scott, there weren't even seven degrees of separation in it.

Isabel Haldane of Ardsheal also belonged to the Scotland-wide network of friends and closely related families. This crossed the Highland–Lowland divide. She herself was one of the Haldanes of Lanrick, near Doune, just north of Stirling. Besides which, the Highland gentry often had houses in Edinburgh, where Flora MacDonald went to boarding school, or at least paid regular visits there.

The chances that Isabel and Caroline Frederick Scott knew one another are therefore pretty high. Tellingly, in her letter to John Campbell of Mamore senior, she said she could hardly believe 'that any man especially bred in a civilized country and good company could be so free of compassion or anything at all of the gentleman to descend to such a low degree of meanness'.

There's a strong implication here that Isabel knew the 'good company' which her ruthlessly cool and cruel tormentor had kept. She and Captain Scott were around the same age, in their early thirties in the mid-1740s. Could he have been a rejected suitor? Or had they simply already met and taken a hearty dislike to one another before their encounters in the summer of 1746?

The eighteenth century was a robust age, especially when it came to crime and punishment. Clan justice could be as brutal as any. When Angus MacDonell of Glengarry was accidentally shot in the streets of Falkirk by a man cleaning his gun, the man was immediately shot dead in reprisal. Captain Fergusson persuaded some of those he captured to talk by means of an instrument of torture which had been invented by MacDonald of Barisdale. It was a sort of rack, and Barisdale had previously used it to punish thieves.

Nevertheless, the idea that the Jacobite Army as a whole acted humanely to those whom it defeated and did not wage war on women and children is not just a romantic notion. The evidence is there in story after story. They were ferociously brutal in battle but merciful afterwards. There are stories of cruelties committed by Jacobites, but you have to look hard to find them, which does not, of course, excuse those which did take place.

There is Mrs Grossett of Alloa, whose husband, Walter, was an exciseman who detested smugglers and Jacobites and did much to thwart the plans of both. The revenge the latter took on him makes for unpleasant reading, with echoes of what happened to Isabel Haldane and her family:

> The Rebells robbed and plundered his house at Alloa
> and his house in the country to such a degree that they
> did not leave his infant children even a shirt to shift them,
> and pursued his wife and daughter to an uncle's house,
> to whose estate they knew Mr. Grosett was to succeed,

plundered that house, stript his wife and daughter of the
very clothes they had upon their backs and used them
otherwise in a most cruel and barbarous manner.

Mrs Grossett died not long afterwards. Her husband suffered a second
bereavement when his brother Alexander was killed at Culloden. His
death, too, was claimed as a Jacobite atrocity. A contemporary print
called 'Rebell Ingratitude' shows him being shot by a Jacobite soldier
whose face is twisted with malice. Caught at the moment of death,
falling backwards off his horse, Captain Grossett's neat white military
wig has slipped off his head. Behind him, two other Redcoats rush
forward to avenge their captain. The text under the picture tells the
story:

> Or a **Representation** *of the Treachery and Barbarity of*
> Two **Rebell Officers**, *at the* **Battle** *of* **Culloden,**
> *who had their Lives Generously given them by the* **Earl of**
> **Ancram**, *(who had a considerable Command that Day)* and
> by **Captain Grosett** *Engineer & Aid De Camp to the*
> *General.*
>
> *The One attempted to shoot His Lordship behind his back,*
> *with a* **Pistol,** *which he had kept concealed & which luckily*
> *only Flash'd in the Pan. The Other Shot* **Captain Grosett**
> **Dead** *with his own* **Pistol,** *which happened Accidentally*
> *to fall from his as he was on* **Horseback,** *under pretence of*
> *restoring the same to the Captain.*
>
> *These* **Rebells** *received the Just reward of their* **Perfidy**,
> *By being immediatly cut to pieces by the* **King's Troops**.
> *And it is Generally believed that this their Ingratitude and*
> *Treachery greatly heightened the Slaughter that was that Day*
> *made of their Party.*
>
> *Captain Grossett left behind him a Distressed Widow, with*
> *Six young Children.*

Captain Alexander Grossett was indeed killed at Culloden, but there is
no other detailed account of how he died. It's interesting that his death

was being used as justification for '*the Slaughter that was that Day made of their Party*'. It did not take long for people in Edinburgh, London and elsewhere to begin to think that, in stamping out the Rebellion, too many Government officers had gone too far. Robust punishment had tipped over into sadistic cruelty.

Leading the storm of fire, rape and death which raged through the Highlands and Islands in the summer and autumn of 1746, none of the men responsible thought they were going too far. Yet Fergusson, Lockhart and Scott would all have called themselves gentlemen, and would not have dared behave in Edinburgh as they did while they were north of the Highland Line.

When one of his officers remonstrated with him, telling him he *was* going too far, Caroline Frederick Scott told him he knew very well what he was doing, which was 'not without orders'. Close as he was to the Duke of Cumberland, he knew better than anyone what was wanted: Scotland was to suffer. It never seems to have occurred to Cumberland, as it occurred to others, that such harsh and profoundly unfair reprisals might be counter-productive, as they have been – to this very day.

In their own minds, Fergusson, Lockhart and Scott, as much as many of their English fellow officers, seem to have felt themselves in the Highlands to be in a land of savages. The people they hounded were not people like them and, as such, did not deserve to treated with humanity. The class structure of the time forced them to rein in their more violent impulses when dealing with the Highland gentry. The common man, woman or child had no such protection.

Yet Caroline Frederick Scott spoke, or at least understood, Gaelic. Was it a form of self-hatred which propelled him? As red-coated Scotsmen did he, Fergusson, Lockhart and the others feel they had something to prove? In putting down this 'Scotch Rebellion' were they trying to show not only that they could be as rigorous as any Englishman but also how much they despised so many of their fellow Scots?

In the case of Major James Lockhart, there may have been more to it even than that.

25

THE SHAH OF PERSIA,
THE MAGIC PENNY &
EMBARRASSING RELATIVES:
THE LOCKHARTS OF CARNWATH

THEY OFFER'D TO LET ME GO IF I WOULD GIVE MY PAROLE
OF HONOUR, WCH I UTTERLY REFUSED TO DO

The Lockharts of Lee and Carnwath were Jacobites to their
fingertips. Sir George Lockhart was a member of the Scottish
Parliament before the Union in 1707 and a Jacobite plotter in the
run-up to the Rising of 1715. It was he who first made it public
that many of his fellow Members of the old Scottish Parliament had
accepted English bribes to vote in favour of the Union, publishing a
list of their names. King James VIII's agent in Scotland, his extensive
correspondence and his *Memoirs of the Affairs of Scotland* were later
published as *The Lockhart Papers*.

Sir George died in 1731, but several of his children and grandchildren
played their part in the '45, if not necessarily in ways of which he
would have approved. He would undoubtedly have been proud of his
son-in-law and two of his grandsons. Married to Lockhart's daughter
Mary, the former was John Rattray, golfer, doctor and personal

physician to Charles Edward Stuart. The grandsons were George and James. George, known in 1745 as Young Carnwath, was one of Charles Edward Stuart's aides-de-camp. His younger brother, James, was also in the Jacobite Army. Both fought at Culloden and subsequently spent many years in exile in Europe.

James was only 18 at the time of the battle, which did not stop him from undertaking an epic journey afterwards, crossing Europe and hiring out his sword and his soldiering skills to the Shah of Persia. Nobody knows how he got there. He fetched up a year or so later fighting in the War of the Austrian Succession in the army of the Empress Maria Theresa. He rose to become a general and was ennobled by her as Count Lockhart-Wishart, taking his mother's name in his title as well as his father's, in the Austrian style.

The Empress also gave him a very special box to house a very special object, whose origin may indicate that James had felt some sort of pull towards the Middle East. An ancestor had fought in the Crusades, acquiring there what has been known throughout history as the Lee Penny. A silver coin with a red stone in its centre, it was credited with healing sickness in humans and animals, and remains in the possession of the Lockhart family today. Sir Walter Scott took inspiration from it to write his novel *The Talisman*.

The figure which stands on top of the memorial at Glenfinnan that commemorates the Raising of the Standard is James Lockhart's brother, George, the aide-de-camp to the Prince. It was sculpted by John Greenshields of Carluke. Told there was a painting of Charles Edward Stuart at Lee Castle, Greenshields went to have a look at it. Only the housekeeper was at home, and she showed him two paintings of two young men, which hung side by side, and left him to it.

When Greenshields discovered he had assumed Young Carnwath was the Prince and modelled his statue accordingly, he was philosophical. He thought George Lockhart junior looked a lot better than 'the Prince in tartan pantaloons'. So the '45, inextricably associated with the Highlands, is marked at its birthplace in one of the most beautiful glens in the Highlands by the figure of a

Lowlander. There's a yet more intriguing twist to the story of the Jacobite Lockharts of Carnwath.

Major James Lockhart, Government officer and brutal persecutor of Jacobite fugitives and Highlanders, fought with his regiment, Cholmondley's, at Falkirk. As his men panicked, he did his utmost to rally them but fell from his horse and hurt his hip and thigh, which, as he later wrote when required to answer for his conduct at Falkirk, 'swell'd prodigiously, & made me very Lame'. Forced into 'resting on Captn Websters shoulder', he was helped onto another horse, his own presumably having bolted, but found he could hardly sit on it because of the pain in his leg.

They had to move. Everyone had now realized the Jacobites had won the battle. Despite his injury, Major Lockhart was ordered to see to the collecting of tents from the Government camp. He issued orders in his turn for that to be done and was helped onto his third horse of the afternoon. It was not to be third time lucky. He 'had not rode a few Yards, when the Horse fell & tumbled Over me'. The pain of it made him lose consciousness.

When he came to, he found himself in nearby Callendar House, home of the Jacobite Lord and Lady Kilmarnock. They'd had him put to bed, and a doctor was bleeding him. It was very difficult to get Lockhart's boot off, and the pain was so great he was shouting out and crying with it.

Once the doctor had done what he could to make his patient comfortable – Lockhart told the maid the next day when she enquired that he was 'a little easier' – Lord and Lady Kilmarnock promised not to hand the major over as a prisoner of war. It's very possible that they all knew each other. One of the Kilmarnocks' sons, James, Lord Boyd, was a serving British officer, a 2nd lieutenant in the Royal Scots Fusiliers.

Yet the very next day they broke their promise. The major was handed over to Mr Murray, possibly John Murray of Broughton, the Prince's secretary, who:

after much insignificant Discourse, Offer'd to Let me go, If I would give my Parole of Honour, not to Serve Against Them for 12 Months, wch I utterly refus'd to do; On wch they ordered a Guard into the Room wth me & next day was offer'd my Liberty, on the above Terms, wch I absolutely refus'd; On which, Though I was then Extremely Ill, I was forc'd down Stairs, with Half my Cloths on, in Presence Of Lord, Lady Kilmarnock & Son, who told me, as I had refus'd my Parole, & show'd so little Respect to them I deserv'd no Favour.

They put him in a chaise, which took him to Stirling where Jacobite commander Lord John Drummond again asked him to give his parole and Lockhart again refused to do so. He was then asked to write to General Hawley to ask for the release of 'Kinloch Moidart or some such Person', as he later haughtily put it, in exchange for himself. He wouldn't do that, either.

Held at Stirling, he and other Government prisoners were later moved out to Doune Castle by a company of Jacobites commanded by John Roy Stuart. The colonel of the Edinburgh Regiment also asked for their parole of honour but required of them only that they would not try to escape on the way to their new prison. If they gave their parole, they could march like officers.

This time Lockhart agreed to make the promise and was outraged to find himself 'betwixt A Party of Men, wth Fix'd Bayonets, & all Kinds of Pris^rs'. He called up to John Roy in protest and the two men threw angry words at one another, John Roy threatening to have Lockhart tied with ropes. Although the threat was not carried out, the major was clearly outraged. The account he wrote bristles with indignation that an officer and a gentleman such as himself should have been so insulted.

And what does he have to do with the Lockharts of Carnwath? Well, possibly rather a lot. While he was a prisoner of the Jacobites, he was locked up with John Gray of Rogart, the cattle drover from

Sutherland who gave evidence at Lord Lovat's trial. Major Lockhart had a visitor, and, when he left, Gray asked who he was. Lockhart replied that it was Young Carnwath.

This was George Lockhart, aide-de-camp to Prince Charles. Frustratingly, John Gray said nothing about their conversation, even whether it had been cordial or aggressive. The family tree of the Lockharts shows that Old Carnwath, the Sir George Lockhart who had been King James's agent in Scotland, had a son called James. Born in 1707, he died in 1749 while serving as lieutenant colonel of 'Hacket's Regiment in the Dutch service'.

There's a misprint here. Hacket's Regiment was stationed for many years on the island of Menorca. The Mediterranean island had been captured by the British Navy in 1708 during the War of the Spanish Succession and, with interruptions, remained in British hands until 1802.

If Lockhart died in Holland, he may well have done so as lieutenant colonel of *Halkett's* Regiment. This was commanded by Sir Peter Halkett of Pitfirrane in Fife, the man who asked the Jacobite doctor John Rattray if he could help Lee's Regiment's inexperienced young surgeon after the Battle of Prestonpans.

Was Young Carnwath visiting his Uncle James at Stirling, offering to see what he could do for him? It seems highly likely. It's clear from his written defence of himself that James Lockhart felt humiliated and insulted by what had happened to him at Falkirk. It's also clear he thought his conduct as an officer and his honour as a gentleman were being called into question.

Was this because he felt he always had to defend himself from allegations that he was a secret Jacobite? Was that why he kept refusing to give his parole? In the angry final paragraph of his passionate defence of himself, he states that his colonel will speak up for him as to his character and his conduct. The final lines he wrote were these:

> As to my Principles, & Education, from my Youth
> They are Notorious, to all the World, & I beg my Coll;
> will inform Himself, as to Them, from His Majesty's
> Sollicitor, Lord Justice Clerk, or any Other Person He
> Pleases.

He may have been born and reared a Jacobite but had he decided very early on in life that he would not grow up one? Given what we know about his character, when his nephew came to visit him in Stirling, did he angrily tell him to get lost?

There may be a revealing glimpse of the boy who was to become the dreaded Major Lockhart in a letter Sir George Lockhart wrote to another of his sons:

> Jamie hath been ane undutiful child, and shows no
> inclinations to do well, but hes young and not to be
> dispaird of, and he must be cherishd or discouraged
> according to his good or bad behaviour.

Just as we sagely nod our heads at this clue as to why James Lockhart turned out the way he did, we read in *The Lockhart Papers* that a note 'in a feeble hand' was added to this letter: 'Jamie, since writing this letter, having alterd his way and behaved to my satisfaction, I have intirely forgot all offences in his younger years.'

All the same, did he perhaps continue to rebel against his family and their commitment to the Stuart Cause? Was he getting back at them when he acted so cruelly in the west Highlands? It's an intriguing possibility.

Lockhart suffered another mishap at Falkirk. A man called Dunbar, a deserter to the Jacobites at Prestonpans, stole 'a suit of laced clothes' from the major's baggage. When Dunbar was hanged at Inverness, he was dressed in Lockhart's fine clothes. He hung in them, twisting in the wind and the streets of Inverness, for two days.

The account which gives this story also confirms the brawl between

Scottish and English Redcoats in those same streets which took place after the hanging of young Malcolm Forbes of Pitcalnie.

If Major Lockhart was involved in that, I think we can probably guess on which side of the street he lined up.

26

THE ESCAPE OF JOHN ROY STUART

GREAT IS THE CAUSE OF MY SORROW,
AS I MOURN FOR THE WOUNDS OF MY LAND

After Culloden, John Roy Stuart marched with the survivors of the Edinburgh Regiment to Ruthven Barracks near Kingussie. There is no record of this having been an agreed rendezvous point in the event of a Jacobite defeat, but it seems it must have been. Two to three thousand men who had escaped the battlefield met up there.

Nowadays we see Culloden as a decisive final blow, the death knell to the '45, the Jacobites and any further hope of a restoration of the Stuarts. This wasn't necessarily how they saw it at the time. When James Johnstone reached Ruthven, he was 'delighted to see the gaiety of the Highlanders, who seemed to have returned from a ball rather than a defeat'.

Next day, the mood underwent a drastic change. A letter from the Prince reached those assembled at Ruthven. It was read out to them, very probably by John Roy, who seems to have taken charge. By this time Lord George Murray had already sent a bitter letter to the Prince resigning his commission. The last order to the men who had followed Charles Edward Stuart to hell and back was succinct, if nothing else: 'Let every man seek his own safety the best way he can.'

It was John Roy Stuart who disbanded the Jacobite Army, telling everyone it was time to go. It was a painful farewell, men in tears at the realization that it was all over. They were fearful too of the reprisals they rightly anticipated were going to be meted out to them, their families and the Highlands.

Now a notorious Jacobite, John Roy would have been entitled to be scared, too. Yet he was one of those who still had the stomach to continue the fight, one of those who hadn't yet lost hope.

Two weeks later, on 2 May 1746, two French ships sailed into Loch nan Uamh, running the gauntlet of a flotilla of British warships. The Frenchmen unloaded gunpowder and six casks of gold coins and took some fugitives away with them. The louis-d'or they left behind had an estimated value of £38,000: a huge sum of money in those days. It didn't take long for it to cause dissension, the remnants of the Jacobite leadership arguing bitterly over how the money should be used. At the time, it gave encouragement to those who were left. Some of the money was used to help those who were now destitute.

John Roy Stuart, Lord Lovat, Cameron of Lochiel, Gordon of Glenbucket and Clanranald met with some others a couple of days later at Murlaggan near the head of Loch Arkaig. The meeting broke up without any decision having been taken on what to do next. The bulk of the French money was stashed away, possibly buried, possibly hidden away in a cave. The now legendary Jacobite gold has never been found, but it's still out there somewhere.

Redcoat military patrols were now spreading out across the Highlands and Islands. Unsurprisingly, the movements of the mercurial Mr Stuart once again become a little hazy. Some historians claim he was dispatched by the Prince to France with the news of the defeat and then returned to Scotland, which sounds both highly unlikely and highly risky.

The evidence of his own poetry and the traditions of Badenoch and Strathspey are that he spent much of the next four months there, moving from one hiding place to another, including a cave where he held his foot under a waterfall in the hope of relieving the pain of a sprained ankle. The pain of the defeat he poured out into poetry. Translated from the Gaelic, his '*Latha Chuil-Lodair*' or 'Culloden Day' begins: 'Great is the cause of my sorrow, / As I mourn for the wounds of my land' and continues:

> Woe is me for the host of the tartan
> Scattered and spread everywhere,
> At the hands of England's base rascals
> Who met us unfairly in war;
> Though they conquered us in the battle,
> 'Twas due to no courage or merit of theirs,
> But the wind and the rain blowing westwards
> Coming on us up from the Lowlands.

After lamenting the white bodies of the dead lying unburied on the hillsides and that those 'who survived the disaster are carried to exile o'erseas by the winds', the poem throws some bitter words at Lord George Murray. John Roy was one of many who believed he had betrayed the Cause.

John Roy's poems and songs are full of Biblical references, comparing the Jacobites to the Children of Israel being delivered from slavery in Egypt. In John Roy's 'Prayer', he bemoans the injury to his foot:

> By a streamlet, worn and tired,
> The poor Christian John Roy sits.
> A warrior still lacking rest,
> His ankle sprained, and wretched the time.

He continues by invoking the charms and incantations which had been chanted in the Highlands for centuries as an aid to healing:

> I'll make the charm Peter made for Paul
> When his foot was sprained leaping a bank,
> Seven prayers in name of Priest and of Pope
> As plaster to put round about.

One charm more for Mary of grace
Who can a believer soon heal:
I believe, without doubt or delay,
That we shall discomfort our foes.

Perhaps his most well-known poem is a parody of the 23rd psalm:

The Lord's my targe, I will be stout,
With dirk and trusty blade,
Though Campbells come in flocks about
I will not be afraid.

Either the waterfall or the incantations must have done the trick as far as his ankle was concerned. An old story has it that Marjory Stewart of Abernethy, who died at the age of 100 in 1830, remembered that as a young girl in her teens she had danced with John Roy Stuart at a wedding in Balnagown.

In September 1746, back on the mainland after his adventures in the Hebrides, the Prince was asking if anyone knew where John Roy was. Charles was at this point with Cluny Macpherson, skulking in a bothy on Ben Alder which was 'superlatively bad and smockie'. This was before they decamped to the hiding place on the same mountain known as Cluny's Cage. A kind of tree-house woven into a rockface, an account thought to have been written by Cluny himself describes it as 'a very romantic comical habitation'. Intriguingly, this account at one point refers to 'John Roy Stewart (whom the Prince used to call THE BODY)'. Sadly, the writer does not explain how or why the nickname had been earned.

Back at the smoky bothy, John Roy Stuart had been found but not told who he was going to meet there. Alerted to his approach and wanting to surprise him, Charles wrapped himself in his plaid and lay down. As John Roy entered the hut, the Prince showed his face. Astonished and overwhelmed with relief that he was alive and well, John Roy cried out, 'O Lord! My master!' and promptly fainted. He ended up in the puddle of water in the doorway, causing great hilarity all round.

A week later, having crossed over to the west coast, Charles Edward Stuart stepped on to *L'Heureux,* the French privateer which had anchored in Loch nan Uamh. Those who were with him as he left Scotland, never to return, included Cameron of Lochiel, his brother Dr Archie Cameron, Neil MacEachainn and John Roy Stuart.

Once back in France, the former colonel of the Edinburgh Regiment soon exited stage left. Yet again the accounts differ. One story has him dying in 1747, leaving his wife and young daughter to the charity of the Stuart court in exile. Another says he died in 1752, offering as his place of death only as somewhere in Europe. The man whose light shone so brightly during the '45 steps back into the shadows and vanishes.

A roadside cairn placed there by the 1745 Association marks his birthplace at Knock of Kincardine. His poetry and songs live on.

27

FORTUNE'S TRICKS IN FORTY-SIX: DONALD MACDONELL OF TIRNADRIS

LUDICROUS WITH HIS FETTERS . . .

Fortune played the cruellest of tricks on Donald MacDonell of Tirnadris, the man who kicked off the '45 by taking Captain Sweetenham prisoner and ambushing the Royal Scots at High Bridge. In the growing darkness and torrential rain which accompanied the Battle of Falkirk in January 1746, he mistook a group of Government officers for Jacobites and walked right up to them.

Thinking on his feet, Donald MacDonell tried to pass himself off as a Campbell, the white cockade he wore being so dirty from heavy rain and gunsmoke that 'there was no discovering the colour of it'. General Huske of Barrell's Regiment was having none of it. He pointed at MacDonell's sword, which was 'covered over with blood and hair', and immediately shouted out 'to shoot the dog instantly'. Seven or eight muskets were raised, all aimed at Tirnadris's chest.

They would have killed him there and then if Lord Robert Kerr had not intervened, 'beating down the muskets'. Tirnadris admitted defeat and said he would hand over his weapons to General Huske.

The Government commander angrily said he would 'not do the Major that honour'. Once more Lord Robert Kerr intervened:

> Upon which Lord Robert Ker politely stept forwards to receive the Major's arms. When the Major was pulling off his pistol from his belt he happened to do it with such an air that Husk swore the dog was going to shoot him. To which the Major replied, 'I am more of a gentleman, Sir, than to do any such thing, I am only pulling off my pistol to deliver it up.' When the Major at any time spoke to a friend about delivering up his good claymore and his fine pistol, he used to sigh and to mention Lord Robert Ker with great affection for his generous and singular civilities.

Lord Robert was killed at Culloden, another of those men who was mourned by friend and foe alike.

Tirnadris was at first imprisoned in Edinburgh Castle where one of the sentries was an Irishman called Trapeau, a lieutenant in Bligh's Regiment. Trapeau went to some pains to ingratiate himself with the prisoners, particularly Donald MacDonell and Mrs Jean Cameron. This was the famous Jenny Cameron of the '45, who had led the Camerons of Glendessary to the Raising of the Standard at Glenfinnan.

When the sentry's regiment was ordered to sail to Aberdeen in February to join the Duke of Cumberland, 'the said Trapeau took care to have recommendatory letters to Keppoch and Lochiel from Major MacDonell and Mrs Jean Cameron, for fear of the worst'. At this stage it was not clear to anyone who was going to win this war. Trapeau changed his tune after Culloden, being in favour of severe measures while at the same time denying that Cumberland was capable of inflicting the cruelties of which he stood accused. The duke apparently had 'a soul much above these things'.

Tirnadris spent six months and more in Edinburgh Castle. Another of his fellow captives was MacDonald of Kingsburgh, accused of helping the Prince escape when the net was closing around him in the Hebrides. The prisoners were all glad to have company but found their confinement intolerable, 'waiting the freak and humour of an officer to be let out when he thinks fit to walk for an hour or so within the narrow bounds of the Half-moon', this being the battery from which those of the castle's guns which pointed at Edinburgh were fired.

The trials of Jacobite officers were held in London, Carlisle and York between August and November 1746. They were charged with high treason 'in compassing and imagining the king's death, adhering to his majesty's enemies, and levying (with other false traitors) a cruel and destructive war in these kingdoms, &c.'

Because of Cumberland's fears that Scottish juries would be too lenient, no cases were held north of the border. Brothers Alexander and Charles Kinloch, on trial in London, argued that as they were born in Scotland they ought to be tried under the laws of Scotland. Their plea was unsuccessful and they were both sentenced to death, although later reprieved. They had friends in high places, including, bizarrely, the Sardinian Ambassador.

Donald MacDonell of Tirnadris was not so lucky. As the man who had lit the spark at High Bridge which ignited the fire, he was probably always going to hang. On 24 August 1746, he wrote from Carlisle Castle to Robert Forbes in Edinburgh, 'making offer of my compliments to yourself and the Leith ladies'.

It's very possible that Tirnadris met Forbes while the latter was also imprisoned in Edinburgh Castle, in his case merely on suspicion of being on his way to join the Prince. The 'Leith ladies' may have visited them there, especially if Trapeau had allowed them access while he had been trying to ingratiate himself. Donald MacDonell might also have met the women while the Jacobites occupied Edinburgh in September and October of the previous year, although not Robert Forbes, who was already a prisoner by then.

Donald MacDonell's letter to Forbes is polite and cheerful, yet what he is relating is awful, describing how there are 100 'gentlemen who came from Scotland' all crowded in together. Not everyone is manacled, but he himself is. Typically, he makes a joke of it, asking Robert Forbes to make those compliments 'especially to Miss Mally Clerk, and tell her that notwithstanding of my irons I could dance a Highland reel with her'. Other people said he was 'ludicrous with his fetters'.

Robert Forbes wrote back, returning the compliments and telling Tirnadris that people in Edinburgh were collecting money to send to them in Carlisle in the hope it would buy them some comforts. Forbes also wanted to pass on his regards to one of Tirnadris's fellow prisoners, Robert Lyon. Both young men were ministers of the Episcopalian Church. In a P. S., Robert Forbes let Tirnadris know that 'The lady prisoners in the Castle are well.' The picture which emerges is of a group of friends all desperately worried about one another.

Three weeks later, Donald MacDonell wrote a joint letter to Robert Forbes and another friend, John Moir, described as a merchant in Edinburgh. He wanted to let them know he had been tried the day before and found guilty of treason. He had not yet been sentenced, but he was hoping for the best and preparing for the worst.

MacDonell's concern was for his 'dear wife'. She wanted to visit him in prison, but he did not think this would be allowed. In any case, he wanted her to go home. He knew he had little hope of a reprieve, and it's clear he was desperate to get her as far away as possible from the impending horror of his execution. He makes the request several times during the course of the short letter to his two friends in Edinburgh: 'I never will forgive either of you if you do not manage this point.' A few lines on, he emphasizes the point yet again: 'And for God's cause, see my wife fairly on her way home.'

He wrote again ten days later to tell Robert Forbes he'd had a bit of a fever but was now once more in good health. If it was his fate to go to the scaffold, 'I dare say that I'll goe as a Christian and a man of honour ought to do.' Once more he asked for his regards to be given to everyone, 'Miss Mally in particular'.

He wrote a farewell letter to his friend John Moir the day before he died. He had written to his wife and his brother, and he asked John Moir to help his wife sort out her finances. She wasn't going to have much money, but Tirnadris had sent 'fourteen pounds sterling and half a dozen shirts':

> I conclude with my blessing to yourself and to all the honourable honest ladies of my acquaintance in Edinburgh, and to all other friends in general, and in particular those in the Castle. And I am, with love and affection, My dear Sir, yours affectionately till death, and wishes we meet in Heaven. Donald MacDonell.
>
> Carlisle Castle, October 17th, 1746.
>
> P. S. Remember me in particular to my dear Mr. Robert Forbes.

His dying speech, which condemned prisoners gave from the scaffold and had been printed to be handed out to the crowd, was solemn and dignified. He had taken part in the Rising out of principle and conviction, believing it to be his duty to take up arms for 'Charles, Prince of Wales' in support of having 'our ancient and only rightful royal family restored'.

He also believed that 'nothing but the king's restoration could make our country flourish, all ranks and degrees of men happy, and free both Church and State from the many evil consequences of Revolution principles'. 'Revolution principles' were held by Whigs and friends of the Government, whose political philosophy stood on the rock of what they called the Glorious Revolution of 1688, when the Stuarts had been deposed and William of Orange had come to the throne.

Tirnadris contrasted the 'publick, cruel, barbarous and (in the eyes of the world) an ignominious and shameful death' with the magnanimous conduct of Charles Edward Stuart and the 'charity and humanity' he himself had shown to 'my enemies, the Elector's troops, when prisoners and in my power'. He died 'an unworthy member of the Roman Catholick Church, in the communion of which I have lived'. He was at pains to point out he had never had any wish to impose this on others:

> But I hereby declare upon the word of a dying man that it was with no view to establish or force that religion upon this nation that made me join my Prince's standard, but purely owing to that duty and allegiance which was due to our only rightful, lawful and natural sovereign, had even he or his family been heathen, Mahometan, or Quaker.

He hoped his 'dear son' would show the same loyalty as his father had to 'his King's, his Prince's and his country's service', and finished:

> I conclude with my blessing to my dearest wife and all my relations and friends, and humbly beg of my God to restore the King, to grant success to the Prince's arms, to forgive my enemies and receive my soul. Come, Lord Jesus, come quickly! Into thy hands I resign my spirit!

He was hanged at Carlisle on Saturday, 18 October 1746.

28

FAITHFUL UNTO DEATH: ROBERT LYON OF PERTH

LET US PRAY WE MAY HAVE A JOYFUL AND HAPPY MEETING IN ANOTHER WORLD

Lord Ogilvy's Regiment had two chaplains, one Church of Scotland and the other Episcopalian. The latter was Robert Lyon of Perth, who joined the Jacobite Army along with many of his parishioners as it swept south in the late summer of 1745. He did not carry arms and took no part in any battle, believing that 'to be inconsistent with my sacred character'.

Despite that, he was arrested in Perth after the defeat at Culloden and taken to Carlisle for trial. Imprisoned with many other Jacobite prisoners, he continued his ministry, leading services, and giving them communion, solace and comfort. He also wrote to their relatives to let them know what had happened to their loved ones.

One of his fellow prisoners was Laurence Mercer of Lethenty. A gentleman volunteer, he had served as a cavalry officer in the troop in the Perthshire Squadron commanded by the nephew of Isabel Haldane of Ardsheal. Tried and condemned to death, he died in Carlisle Castle before the sentence could be carried out. Robert Lyon wrote to Laurence's mother, Lady Mercer, to let her know. His letter is addressed to her at Carlisle, so she cannot have been allowed inside the castle to be with her son as he lay dying. Robert Lyon offered her the comfort of their shared religious beliefs and some very practical suggestions as to what might be done with Laurence Mercer's clothes:

> Your worthy Son Mr Mercer was remov'd from the Miseries of this World about one o'clock this Morning, during which time I was recommending his Soul to God; I hope the Consideration of his Happiness in the other World, will allay in You all immoderate Grief, & make You thoroughly resigned to God in all his wise Disposals.

Telling Lady Mercer that Laurence had died wearing a shirt belonging to a Mr Clark, who understandably did not want it back, Robert Lyon suggested she might send Mr Clark a new nightshirt. The young clergyman had a further suggestion to make:

> I beg leave to suggest to you that Mr Randal has been of great Use to your Son during the time of Distress which shou'd not be forgot, & as your Son had a new big Coat, which I know Mr Randal stands in need of, I presume it wou'd be a very acceptable Compliment to him.

Robert Lyon finished his letter by hoping God would support Lady Mercer in her grief and asking for her prayers for himself, as he believed he, too, would soon be leaving behind the miseries of the world. Three days later, he did.

He had already written his last letter to 'my dear mother and sisters' in Perth, telling them that by the time they received it he would be dead. He was his mother's only son, and his father had died while Robert was still a schoolboy. In his dying speech, he made an illuminating comment about his Protestantism:

I declare upon this aweful occasion, and on the word
of a dying man, that I ever abhor'd and detested and do
now solemnly disclaim the many errors and corruptions
of the Church of Rome; as I do with equal zeal the
distinguishing principles of Presbyterians and other
dissenting sectaries amongst us who are void of every
support in our country but ignorance and usurping
force, and whom I have always considered the shame
and reproach of the happy Reformation, and both alike
uncatholick and dangerous to the soul of a Christian.

For him, his own Episcopalian church was the real Church of Scotland.
He believed, too, in the divine right of kings, in the sense that it was
up to God to decide who ruled, not man.

Robert Lyon was outraged that he had been tried and condemned
to death when he had committed 'no overt act of treason' and deeply
regretted that he had gone against his religious principles and his
commitment to the Stuart Cause by submitting a petition for clemency
to the 'Elector of Hanover'. This he had done because of 'fear, human
frailty, the persuasion of lawyers and the promise and assurance of life'.
He retracted it completely before he died.

In his last letter to his family, he entreated his womenfolk to put
their faith in God and expressed his regret that he was not leaving
them in a better position financially. He was sorry he had spent so
much of his sister Cicie's money but hoped they would all understand
because it had gone not on riotous living but 'on the late glorious
cause of serving my King and country'.

He asked the Lyon women to take care of Stewart Rose, the girl
whom he had hoped to marry and whose first name leaves no doubt
of her family's commitment to the Jacobite Cause. Robert hoped his
family would treat her like a daughter and a sister. He also asked them
to pass on his last good wishes to various friends and every member
of his congregation.

Living up to his vocation, he asked, too, that his mother and sisters would forgive – as he did – George Miller, the Perth town clerk. Miller had earned himself a terrible reputation for vindictiveness, his evidence hanging many of his fellow citizens who had been involved in the Rising.

Robert Lyon finished his 'too long' letter to his family by hoping God would pour down His blessings on them, and gave them his own:

> Farewel, my dear mother! Farewel, my loving sisters! Farewel, every one of you for ever! And let us fervently pray for one another that we may have a joyful and happy meeting in another world, and there continue in holy fellowship and communion with our God and one another, partakers of everlasting bliss and glory to the endless ages of eternity.
>
> The grace of our Lord Jesus Christ and the love of God and the communion of the Holy Ghost be with you all evermore, is the prayer and blessing of, my dear mother, your obedient and affectionate son, and my loving sisters, your affectionate and loving brother.

He wrote that from Carlisle Castle on 23 October 1746 and, after having comforted the dying Laurence Mercer and his bereaved mother, 'stepped into eternity' at Penrith five days later:

> He suffer'd at Penrith upon Tuesday, October 28th, the festival of St. Simon and St. Jude, 1746, and perform'd the whole devotions upon the scaffold, with the same calmness and composure of mind and the same decency of behaviour, as if he had been only a witness of the fatal scene. He delivered every word of his speech to the numerous crowd of spectators.

His sister Cecelia Lyon personally gave that report to Bishop Robert Forbes, and the existence of a macabre piece of mourning jewellery seems to confirm that she personally witnessed her brother's execution. A ring was made in commemoration of Robert Lyon's life and death, its centrepiece a drop of his blood. Someone must have stepped forward to the scaffold and gathered that, perhaps soaking it up in a linen handkerchief. If it was Cicie, then at least Robert Lyon, who had given comfort to so many, was comforted himself in his last moments of life. Perhaps Cicie, the loving and much-loved sister, stood in that numerous crowd of spectators and locked eyes with him until the light dimmed for the last time in his.

29

THE LAST-MINUTE REPRIEVE: FRANCIS FARQUHARSON OF MONALTRIE & FRANCIS BUCHANAN OF ARNPRIOR

AND I'LL BE IN SCOTLAND AFORE YE

Francis Farquharson of Monaltrie on Deeside was said to be the most handsome man in the Jacobite Army. He was tall and fair and, in the parlance of the time, 'wore his own hair' – that is, he did not cover short hair or a balding head with a wig. At the age of 40, he still had a fine head of it, his golden locks falling to his shoulders. These earned him his nickname of 'Baron Ban', *ban* being Gaelic for fair.

He was the nephew of Farquharson of Invercauld, the clan chief, who had fought in the '15 but was too old to take an active part in the '45. With his blessing, Monaltrie led out the clan. Serving with him as the regiment's other colonel was his cousin James Farquharson of Balmoral. Another cousin was Captain Henry Farquharson of Whitehouse. The family relationships do not end there. Yet another of Francis Farquharson's cousins – he was a witness at her wedding in Aberdeen in 1740 – was Lady Anne Mackintosh, the Jacobite 'Colonel' Anne.

Monaltrie and Balmoral's Regiment first joined the Jacobite Army at the shambolic siege of Stirling in January 1746, although they also saw action at the Battle of Falkirk and the skirmish at Inverurie. At Culloden, they fought with the Mackintoshes under Dunmaglass and were in the thick of the fight. Many were killed. Monaltrie himself survived but was taken prisoner on the field.

He later wrote his own account of the battle, a copy of which can be read today in the National Archives of Scotland. It confirms other accounts, detailing the mistakes made in the day and weeks before the battle. Writing of the abortive night march to Nairn, Monaltrie commented on how many of the men had gone off before it in search of food:

> The thing was this; numbers of men went off to all sides, especially towards Inverness and then the officers who were sent on horseback to bring them back came up with them, they could by no persuasion be induced to return again, giving for answer they were starving, and said to the officers they might shoot them if they pleased but they could not go back until they got meat.

Francis Farquharson of Monaltrie made the hellish journey to London on-board one of the overcrowded ships on which Jacobite prisoners suffered so much and was held at the New Gaol at Southwark with several other Jacobite officers, including Andrew Wood, the young Glasgow shoemaker.

Curiously, Charles Gordon of Terpersie, one of the members of Monaltrie's Regiment held at Carlisle, wrote to his wife the night before his execution to tell her how kind Francis Farquharson had been to him. 'I think my butchered body will be taken care of and buried as a Christian, by order of Francis Farquharson, who has acted a father to me.' Although Monaltrie was never held at Carlisle, he must have found a way of sending some money there to pay for that Christian burial. Gordon was the man who had been skulking close to his home near

Alford and whose identity was fatally confirmed when Government soldiers marched him to his own home whereupon his young children ran out calling 'Daddy, Daddy'.

Like most of the prisoners at Southwark, Francis Farquharson was tried, condemned and sentenced to hang. The night before the date set for his execution, a reprieve came for him, a petition for clemency having been submitted and granted. The condition of his release was that he should not return to Scotland but remain in exile in England. He endured this separation from his homeland for almost 20 years.

He had the consolation of the love of a good woman. Elizabeth Eyre of Hassop in Derbyshire, member of a devoutly Catholic and Jacobite family, visited the prisoners in Southwark Gaol, bringing them what comfort she could. She and Francis Farquharson fell in love and married during his period of exile.

He lived for a long time in Berkhamsted, where he applied himself to the study of agriculture. When he was, at last, allowed to return home to Deeside, he put much of what he had learned into practice. He is credited with having initiated the changes which transformed Aberdeenshire from a wild upland place full of bogs and stones into the fruitful farming county it is today. He also developed Ballater as a spa, a place to go to take the waters. In so doing, he might also be credited as being one of the fathers of Scottish tourism.

The story of another Francis, Buchanan of Arnprior, is quite different. Arnprior did not serve in the Jacobite Army and never publicly declared himself for the Prince. Or did he? There's more than one mystery in his case, one of which involves the unexplained death of a man found in Arnprior's house at Leny near Callander with a pistol in his hand.

Shortly before Culloden, when Government forces were once more in charge of southern Scotland, Francis Buchanan was arrested at Leny and taken to Stirling Castle. The case against him seemed thin. There was no hard evidence to say he had been a Rebel, his arrest made on the basis of suspicion only. Thinking it highly unlikely he would be found guilty, the commanding officer of Stirling Castle allowed him the run of the place. The officers who escorted him to Carlisle were equally relaxed:

> These officers knowing well the case of Mr. Buchanan, and having witness'd the usage he had met with in Stirling Castle, treated him in a quite different manner from the other prisoners. In the forenoon, as if he had been only a fellow-traveller, they would have desir'd him to ride forwards to bespeak dinner at a proper place, and to have it ready for them against the time they should come up. In the afternoon they also desir'd him to ride on to take up night quarters and to order supper for them, and all this without any command attending him; so that he had several opportunities every day of making is escape had he dream'd that he ran any risque of his life.

This all changed when they arrived at Carlisle. To the astonishment of Francis Buchanan and the escorting officers, he was immediately thrown into a dungeon and clapped in irons. Shocked by this brutal treatment, Arnprior asked to see Captain James Thomson, one of the soldiers who had brought him to Carlisle. Equally shocked, Thomson came immediately to him and undertook to do what he could for his erstwhile travelling companion.

When Thomson approached the officer in command of Carlisle Castle, he was told the prisoners were now the responsibility of the English Solicitor General, who had come to Carlisle to oversee their trials. The Solicitor General drew a list of names out of his pocket and asked Thomson if the Mr Buchanan of whom he spoke was Francis Buchanan of Arnprior. When Thomson said yes, the Solicitor General said a curious thing: 'Pray, Sir, give yourself no more trouble about that gentleman. I shall take care of him. I have particular orders about him, for HE MUST SUFFER!'

Captain Thomson went back to Arnprior and told him what had happened 'in the softest manner he could'. The story of his interview with the Solicitor General was told to friends of Arnprior's in Edinburgh after his execution by Lieutenant Archibald Campbell, the other officer who had been in charge of escorting the prisoners to Carlisle.

The evidence brought against Francis Buchanan at his trial was flimsy, and, although the jury found him guilty, no one thought he would hang. A reprieve would surely come. Only it didn't, leaving everyone with the distinct impression that Arnprior's fate had been sealed even before he had been arrested.

Although he left no printed dying speech, Francis Buchanan did declare himself before he died:

> as he was persuaded in his conscience King James the 8th had the sole undoubted right to sit on the throne of these realms, so the only action that stared him most in the face was that he had acted the prudent and over-cautious part in not joining the Prince immediately upon his arrival, and drawing his sword in so glorious a cause . . .

Curiously, there is a letter in the National Archives of Scotland which would seem to provide the hard evidence of Arnprior's involvement with the Jacobites. Although the writer refers to 'poor Arnpior', he also writes that: 'they swore him at Glasgow two days between Christmas and the New Year walking with the Rebels in arms highland cloaths and white Cockade.' However, this letter does not seem to have been used as evidence at his trial.

At the time, his case was something of a cause célèbre. Bishop Robert Forbes did his damnedest to get to the bottom of it. He was helped in this by Robert Lyon, who spoke with Arnprior about his case shortly before they both died. Francis Buchanan himself thought people believed him to be guilty of murdering the man found dead in his house and that this, as much as anything, was what was going to hang him. With death staring him in the face, Arnprior was prepared to say what he believed had happened to Stewart of Glenbucky:

> Now I take this opportunity to declare publickly to you and my fellow prisoners that Glenbuckie and I liv'd many years in close friendship together, and altho' he was found dead in my house, yet, upon the word of a dying man, I declare I myself had no hand in his death, nor do I know any other person that had. And I am persuaded that I can likewise answer for every one of my servants, since all of them were acquainted with and had a particular love to that gentleman. So that I declare it to be my opinion that he was the occasion of his own death.

Was Arnprior reluctant to add to the pain Glenbucky's death caused to his family by saying it was suicide? Did this damage his own case? Or did the powers that be have it in for him anyway? Take a bow, Dougal Graham. The rhyming reporter mentions Arnprior in his *History of the Rebellion*.

According to Dougal Graham, while the Prince was marching south and Johnnie Cope was turning round at Inverness, a council of war was held at Leny:

> *While Charles yet, he lay at Down,*
> *And the dragoons at Stirling town:*
> *A council call'd at his desire,*
> *Held in the house of Arnprior,*
> *With chiefs and heads of ev'ry clan,*
> *Their expedition south to plan.*

If Dougal Graham was right, that Arnprior had hosted a meeting of Jacobite leaders at his home, this would certainly have been enough to hang him. And hang he did at Carlisle on 18 October 1746, along with Donald MacDonnell of Tirnadris; Thomas Coppack, the chaplain of the Manchester Regiment; Donald MacDonald of Kinlochmoidart, colonel and aide-de-camp to the Prince; and John MacNaughton. A watchmaker in Edinburgh before the outbreak of hostilities, MacNaughton was accused of having been the man who killed Colonel Gardiner at Prestonpans, which he denied. He was also the messenger instructed by Murray of Broughton, the Prince's secretary, how to steal the mail from the postboy. Although Murray himself betrayed the Cause, turning king's evidence, John MacNaughton refused to do the same.

On the sledge which dragged the prisoners to their execution, he was offered his life and a lifetime's pension if he would give evidence against his former comrades. As Bishop Robert Forbes later recorded in *The Lyon in Mourning*: 'He answered that they had done him much honour in ranking him with gentlemen, and he hoped to let the world see he would suffer like a gentleman.'

One of the Jacobite prisoners hanged at Carlisle is traditionally said to have written the poignant love song 'Loch Lomond'. The singer bids farewell to his friend, who will be returning to Scotland by the high road of life, while he will have to travel on the low road of death, returning home only as a ghost.

It's not known who wrote 'Loch Lomond'. If only on the basis of where he lived, Francis Buchanan of Arnprior would seem to be a likely candidate.

30

THE CAPTAIN'S HALFPENNY:
ANDREW WOOD OF GLASGOW

ALL THAT YOUR FOREFATHERS EVER FOUGHT FOR IS GONE

S hortly before nine o'clock on the morning of Friday, 28 November 1746, a young man in Southwark Gaol, on the south bank of the Thames, was told to prepare himself. In three hours' time, he was to be hanged on nearby Kennington Common. He was Captain Andrew Wood, and he was the man who wasn't there – if only according to Provost Cochrane of Glasgow. There were no Jacobites in his city.

Andrew Wood asked about one of his fellow prisoners, John Hamilton from Huntly, who had been left with Colonel Townley of the Manchester Regiment in the doomed attempt to hold Carlisle Castle after the Jacobite Army's retreat from England. Was he to hang, despite his years? 'Yes,' came the answer, to which Andrew replied, 'I am sorry for that poor old gentleman.'

Wood, Hamilton, Sir John Wedderburn, Captain Alexander Leith, James Lindsay and Jem Bradshaw of the Manchester Regiment were to be executed that day. Before they left the prison, they were offered refreshment. Andrew Wood called for white wine and toasted King James and Prince Charles Edward Stuart, defiantly giving them what he believed to be their proper titles.

The condemned men were to be drawn to Kennington Common on straw-covered sledges pulled by strong shire horses. As they were submitting to having their hands tied, a reprieve came for James Lindsay. He and Andrew Wood knew each other well from the campaign and from their sojourn in Southwark Gaol. They also had a profession in common: they were both shoemakers.

Such last-minute reprieves were not uncommon. Francis Farquharson of Monaltrie had received one just the night before. Jamie Lindsay broke down in tears, unable to do more than embrace his friend before he was led away.

There is a curious little souvenir of the six months or so which Andrew Wood spent in Southwark Gaol. It is a George II halfpenny, with the following inscription on the reverse: 'Given to me by Captain Andrew Wood of the Rebel Army whilst confined at Southward, 1745. Wm. Stapley.'

The year must, of course, have been 1746, but the mistake only adds authenticity to the piece. Anyone faking a Jacobite relic would have made sure to get the date right. The logical assumption is that William Stapley was a prison warder. In those days, prisoners had to pay for their own food and drink, but since Stapley kept the halfpenny it obviously wasn't given in payment. We know, too, that Andrew was short of cash, 'not so plentifully supplied' as some of his fellow prisoners were. The halfpenny must have been a token gift, perhaps for some kindness rendered in a prison whose chief gaoler was known for his greed, brutality and lack of humanity. Stapley must have felt more compassion for the Scotsmen so far from home. Andrew Wood, too, must have made an impression on Stapley, enough for him to have the coin engraved and keep it as a memento of the young Glaswegian.

To the representatives of the Government of King George, whose authority he and every other Jacobite did not recognize, Andrew Wood adopted a policy of non-cooperation. The notes of the official who interrogated him illustrate this. Other than acknowledging his name, time and again it is noted that 'he refuses to answer further'. When asked where he was born, he replied only, 'Scotland, I think.'

Others tried to help him escape his fate. The Glasgow men whom he had saved at Falkirk, seeing them through the Jacobite lines, composed a petition for clemency. As they put it:

> had it not been for his humanity and safe conduct of us
> we should have been carried Prisoners by the Rebells
> further North and should have been stript and robbed
> of all we had if not deprived of our Lives.

Nine men signed the petition: James Steven, John Bannatyne, James McKean, John Buchanan, Alexander Sutherland, Robert Logan, William Thomson, Thomas McKinlay and Robert Philipshill. There were two separate affidavits in support of clemency from William Aitken, a student of divinity, and Joseph McCray, a fencing-master. They, too, believed they owed their lives to Andrew Wood.

Provost Andrew Cochrane, the man who fell over backwards to affirm his city's loyalty to the Government and the House of Hanover, also signed the petition. He was careful not to minute this. There is no reference to Andrew Wood's case in any of the archives of Glasgow from this period. At the same time, Cochrane did make the petition official, affixing to it the seal of the Corporation of Glasgow.

Defiant though he was, Andrew Wood must have hoped against hope that, like Monaltrie, he, too, might receive a last-minute reprieve. As James Lindsay's case shows, hope could last to the steps of the scaffold.

Andrew Wood was distressed the day before his execution but not because of fear. A Presbyterian minister visiting Southwark Gaol had refused to give him communion. He was a Rebel. What's more, he refused to acknowledge that what he had done was wrong.

Bishop Gordon was a Scottish Episcopalian who visited Southwark later that day. With tears in his eyes, Andrew Wood told him the story. According to the other clergyman, Wood was no better than a murderer. He had Christian blood on his hands, and he was guilty of 'rebelling against the wisest, most just, most pious & best of Kings in favour of a Popish Pretender, & with a great deal more of Such like unbecoming Rant'. Unless he repented and asked God's Pardon for what he had done, the minister would not give him communion or have anything more to do with him. At this point Andrew Wood saw red, too angry to care that his words were being overheard by at least a dozen bystanders, including 'those in the Room & those looking in at the Windows'.

First, he was no Rebel. He had taken up arms in support of the lawful king and if he got the chance he would do the same again. Second, Charles Edward Stuart's religion was neither here nor there. Everyone owed him and his father James their allegiance. Third, look at what Scotland had lost:

> I bid him remember too the Massacre of Glencoe, & Destruction of the Scots in Darien; the base & Scandalous Union, the Articles of which had constantly been violated as often as ever it Served the Wicked Purposes of the Usurpers & their infamous Tools; & particularly on the present Occasion with regard to us the poor Prisoners, who are brought up here out of our own Country, the ancient Kingdom, to be tried, condemn'd and murthered by Strangers & Foreigners, who most inhumanly thirst after our Blood.

Andrew's final point to the Presbyterian minister, whose full and silent attention he now had, cited the 'Murders & Massacre in cool Blood after the Battle of Culloden, So barbarous and unchristian, that I verily believe the like had never before been heard of in any civilized, much less Christian Country'.

Recovering at last from the verbal onslaught, the minister told the young man to mind his tongue. He could be endangering his fellow prisoners. Andrew Wood retorted that he had to speak the truth, at which point the clergyman rose to his feet and left without a further word.

Feeling deeply sorry for the young captain, whom he described as being 'in the utmost Distress, quite bewildered', Bishop Gordon sat down and talked it all through with him. A lengthy theological discussion followed, in which the good Bishop convinced Andrew Wood that a Presbyterian minister had no right to give or withhold communion anyway. The only true Church of Scotland was the Episcopalian one.

With Andrew's agreement, he baptized him a member of it and gave him the solace of communion which he so craved. Afterwards, he was 'easy and cheerfull, like a person indeed thoroughly Satisfied in his Mind: And this Ease and Cheerfulness, I have good reason to believe continued with him to the last Moment of his life'.

No reprieve came for him. On the scaffold at Kennington Common, not far from where the Oval cricket ground now stands, he was calm and forgave his enemies. He affirmed his support for the Stuarts and appealed to his fellow Scots to realize that, by uniting with England, 'all ever your forefathers fought for is gone'.

He asked God to bless King James and Prince Charles and committed his spirit to the Lord. He was 23 years old.

31

WARM ALE ON A COLD MORNING: THE ESCAPE OF LORD PITSLIGO

I HAD ATE, AND DRUNK, AND LAUGHED ENOUGH

And then there are the ones who got away. Alexander Forbes, 4th Lord Pitsligo, was one of them. After Culloden, he made it back to Elgin, hiding there for a while before heading east to his home at Pitsligo Castle near Fraserburgh. The plan was to take ship for France. It didn't work out that way.

Alexander Forbes was, after all, one of the most important Jacobite leaders, a man who'd had an enormous influence on his neighbours, not by bullying and coercion but through the strength of his mind and the force of his arguments. A huge military operation swung into place to prevent his escape. This man was dangerous.

This man was also no longer young nor in the best of health, making it all the more remarkable that he eluded his pursuers for so many years. It's a tribute to his own lust for life and the loyalty of his tenants, who sheltered him and shared what they had with him. He shrugged off the discomforts of being a fugitive, saying: 'I had ate, and drunk, and laughed enough.'

Disguised as a beggar and going under the alias of 'Sanny Brown', the noble lord stravaiged the Buchan coast and countryside for several years, occasionally managing a flying visit to see his second wife, Elizabeth Allan, whom he had married after Rebecca's death in 1731. Often he hid in a cave a mile or two west of Rosehearty and on other occasions concealed himself under the arches of the old bridge at Craigmaud, several miles inland. The latter he found extremely uncomfortable, the arches being low and the space beneath them very cramped.

His narrow escapes while he was skulking are the stuff of legend. On one occasion, he was taken badly by an asthma attack on the road at the very moment that a troop of Government soldiers were marching past. Unable to move, he played his beggar's role so well the men gave him some coins and sympathized with him about his illness. Another time, sleeping at one of his tenant's houses, he was surprised by cavalrymen searching for him. In his disguise, he conducted them around the house himself, carrying a lantern to help them see better. Satisfied their quarry was not there, the soldiers departed, giving their guide a shilling for his pains.

While he was in hiding, his friend the Countess of Erroll kept in touch with him via messages carried by Jamie Fleeman. We know him as the Laird of Udny's fool, but he was a loyal and discreet messenger.

At last, after four years of this exhausting way of life, Alexander Forbes was able to seek the shelter of his son's house at Auchiries, inland from Fraserburgh to the north of the Mormond Hill, Buchan's famous landmark. The search for him was periodically renewed. A full ten years after Culloden, when he was seventy-eight, the household was disturbed by an early morning raid in search of the infamous Lord Pitsligo.

Hurriedly bundled into a small recess behind the wood panelling of one of the bedchambers, the dust, confinement and anxiety provoked an asthma attack. The young lady occupying the room, Miss Gordon of Towie, pretended she was having a coughing fit to mask the noise coming from behind the wall. Despite the soldiers getting close enough to assure themselves she wasn't a man in a woman's nightdress, her ruse worked.

Safely tucked up in his own bed, the exhausted Lord Pitsligo asked his servant James to see to the Redcoats, who were still outside the house. It was March, and a cold morning, and James was to make sure that 'the poor fellows', who, after all, had only been doing their duty, got some breakfast and warm ale.

Gradually the search eased off. It seems many of those ostensibly looking for him had little real desire to catch him. He was a man respected as much by his enemies as his friends.

In his final years, he turned once more to his beloved books and produced another series of moral and philosophical essays. His message was a positive one. He wrote of the joys of friendship and the beauty of the world: its trees, flowers, rivers and seas.

Surrounded by his family and friends, he died shortly before Christmas, 1762. He was 84 years old and a free man still. He is buried in Old Pitsligo church on the hill above Rosehearty.

32

SORE FEET & TENDER KISSES:
THE ESCAPE OF JAMES JOHNSTONE

I PITY HIS SITUATION. WILL YOU TAKE AN OAR?

James Johnstone was 26 years old in 1745. Well off and well connected, his father had despaired of his only son, who seemed interested only in the pursuit of pleasure and the pursuit of the opposite sex. Mr Johnstone senior, an Edinburgh merchant, dispatched James to stay with two uncles in Russia for a while, in the hope the experience would broaden his horizons.

Back in Scotland in September 1745, when James found a cause he could believe in, his father was appalled. Jacobite in sympathy though Mr Johnstone senior was, he was violently opposed to James joining the Prince's army. James went all the same.

His family connections secured him an introduction to the Duke of Perth and Lord George Murray, and he acted for a while as aide-de-camp to the latter. He was to become a passionate supporter of Lord George and was accordingly sometimes highly critical of the Prince.

On the battlefield, fighting on the left wing next to Donald MacDonald of Scotus, Johnstone was momentarily stunned when he saw him fall. Then he deployed the blunderbuss Sergeant Dickson had used to such effect in Manchester:

> I remained for a time motionless, and lost in astonishment;
> then in a rage, I discharged my blunderbuss and pistols at
> the enemy and immediately endeavoured to save myself
> like the rest. But having charged on foot and in boots
> I was so overcome by the marshy ground, the water on
> which reached to the middle of the leg, that instead of
> running, I could scarcely walk.

He had left his servant, a man called Robertson, on a little rise about 600 yards behind where the battle was being fought. This was near to where the Prince stood, and Johnstone had told Robertson to stay there with their horses so he would be sure of finding him afterwards. When Johnstone looked for Robertson, he was gone.

Spotting what he thought was a riderless horse, he ran up to it. Unfortunately, its rider, though lying on the ground, was still holding onto its bridle. A ridiculous argument over possession of the horse then ensued. Even when they were showered with mud from grapeshot from the Government cannons, it continued until Johnstone called on a friend by the name of Finlay Cameron who was also making his escape from the field.

Finlay 'flew to me like lightning, immediately presented his pistol to the head of this man and threatened to blow out his brains if he hesitated a moment to let go the bridle'. The man let go of the bridle and ran off. Since the 'cowardly poltroon ... had the appearance of a servant', Johnstone obviously felt he was more entitled to his horse than he was. At times, young Captain Johnstone could be the most awful snob.

The day after the battle, he reached Ruthven Barracks. When the order came that each man should seek his own safety, the survivors were devastated:

> Our separation at Ruthven was truly affecting. We bade
> one another an eternal adieu. No one could tell whether
> the scaffold would not be his fate. The Highlanders gave

vent to their grief in wild howlings and lamentations; the tears flowed down their cheeks when they thought that their country was now at the discretion of the duke of Cumberland and on the point of being plundered, whilst they and their children would be reduced to slavery and plunged, without resource, into a state of remediless distress.

James Johnstone was highly critical of the Prince for abandoning the fight when he did. Considering the situation years later, he still believed, as he always had done, that many of the Scottish officers in the Government army could have been persuaded by national pride to come over to the Jacobites. He could not understand why the Prince 'preferred to wander up and down the mountains alone' when he might have been 'at the head of a body of brave and determined men, of whose fidelity and attachment he was secure, and all of whom would have shed the last drop of their blood in his defence'.

Had distance lent a romantic glow to James Johnstone's memories? It's hard to know. In his memoirs, he wrote of his confidence that the regrouped Jacobite Army could have marched back to Inverness and fought the Duke of Cumberland again within the space of a fortnight – and won.

Failing that, Johnstone suggested something that has often been speculated on since: that they could have melted away into the hills and emerged from them to wage a guerrilla campaign against the Government forces, what he described as 'mountain-warfare'. His summing-up of what happened instead has huge resonance. His 'last war' in the following passage was the Seven Years War of 1756–63:

> in a revolt, 'when we draw the sword we ought to throw away the scabbard'. There is no medium; we must conquer or die. This would have spared much of the blood which was afterwards shed on the scaffold in England, and would have prevented the almost total

extermination of the race of Highlanders which has
since taken place, either from the policy of the English
government, the emigration of their families to the
colonies, or from the numerous Highland regiments
which have been raised, and which have been often cut
to pieces during the last war.

Johnstone was to spend the next few months wandering up and
down the mountains himself, seeing them as the most secure hiding
place he could find. He had been at school with one of the Grants
of Rothiemurchus and, although his old school friend was in the
Government army, both he and his father had assured James that he
would always find a welcome under their roof.

At a time when mountains and untamed nature were not admired
as they are today, James Johnstone loved them. Waxing lyrical
about the waterfalls and the glens, he described the Grants' home
at Rothiemurchus as being in 'one of the most beautiful valleys
imaginable' and 'on the banks of a very beautiful river, the Spey'.

He found other fugitives at Rothiemurchus, including Sir
William Gordon of Park and Gordon of Avochie. They had resolved
to head home to Banffshire, and Johnstone decided to go with them.
His brother-in-law lived in Banff, 'where he had the inspection of
merchant-ships, in virtue of an office lately obtained by him from
the government', and he thought he would help him to escape. The
group didn't go far on the first day of their journey, spending the
night at a friend's house 'near a mountain called Cairngorm':

> These gentlemen yielded to the entreaties of their friend
> to stay a day at his house, and I was not displeased at it.
> Forgetting our disasters for a moment, I rose at an early
> hour and flew immediately to the mountains among
> the herdsmen, where I found some pretty and beautiful
> topazes, two of which, sufficiently large to serve for seals,
> I afterwards presented to the Duke of York, at Paris.

This Duke of York was the Jacobite holder of that title: Henry, Bonnie Prince Charlie's brother, a cardinal in the Roman Catholic Church. When he came back in with a bag of cairngorms, Johnstone's friends burst out laughing and suggested he ought to be concentrating on saving himself from being hanged rather than on 'collecting pebbles'.

It's obvious, however, that he found his stravaig through the hills searching for cairngorms soothing and distracting. His head must have been full of the terrible sights and sounds of Culloden. Only too well aware of the danger they were all in, he was also haunted by thoughts of the scaffold on which he was likely to end his days if he were captured. These thoughts were to torment his imagination in the weary weeks and months of flight which followed.

They reached William Gordon's home at Castle of Park, halfway between Huntly and Banff, four days after they left Rothiemurchus. On the way, they spent one night with a Reverend Stuart. A Church of Scotland minister, he was a covert Jacobite. The minister's servant swapped clothes with James Johnstone, so that instead of a 'laced Highland dress' he now wore 'an old labourer's dress, quite ragged and exhaling a pestilential odour'. He assumed the man must have worn the clothes only when he mucked out the minister's stables, because they reeked of manure. Despite his appalled distaste, Johnstone was happy to admit that 'these rags were to contribute to save my life'.

Banff was swarming with English soldiers, a good 400 of them, but the clothes with the pestilential odour kept them away. It was a crushing disappointment when Johnstone's brother-in-law refused to help him. Every ship leaving Banff was being searched for escaping Jacobites, and he would not risk smuggling a fugitive on-board.

Johnstone decided there was nothing for it but to head overland towards Edinburgh. It took him weeks to get there. Every port and every river was being watched, and getting across the Tay was to be a major problem. Persuaded it might help if he bided his time until the fuss had died down a bit, he spent more than a fortnight with two other fugitives in the humble home of a man called Samuel in Glenprosen, near Cortachy.

Samuel, his wife and their married daughter, who lived nearby and kept a lookout for any approaching Redcoat patrols, risked their lives for James Johnstone, and he was profoundly grateful to them. He did get bored with their diet, although he had to admit it was healthy:

> Samuel was a very honest man but extremely poor. We remained seventeen days in his house, eating at the same table with himself and his family, who had no other food than oatmeal and no other drink than the water of the stream which ran through the glen. We breakfasted every morning on a piece of oatmeal bread, which we were enabled to swallow by draughts of water; for dinner we boiled oatmeal with water, till it acquired a consistency, and we ate it with horn-spoons; in the evening, we poured boiling water on this meal in a dish for our supper. I must own that the time during which I was confined to this diet appeared to pass very slowly, though none of us seemed to suffer in our health from it; on the contrary we were all exceedingly well.

Johnstone had the money to be able to send Samuel to buy some food or drink to vary this monotonous regime, but everyone was scared this might arouse suspicion. There were too many Government soldiers patrolling the area. A similar problem arose when the 'very honest man' at last guided Johnstone to Broughty Ferry, from where he hoped to cross the Tay. When James offered him the horse on which he had ridden away from Culloden as a present, Samuel refused. If people saw him in possession of such a fine horse that would arouse suspicion, too.

So James threw the saddle and tack down a well and sent the horse off into a field. Someone was bound to find him, take him for a stray and give him a home. It took the faithful cuddy some time to get the message that, for him, the war was over: 'We had great difficulty in getting quit of this animal, for he followed us for some time like a dog.'

A combination of Samuel's local knowledge and Johnstone's social network produced the fugitive's next helper. Leaving him in a field where he was concealed by a mass of broom bushes, Samuel returned with Mr Graham of Duntroon. He asked James Johnstone what he would like for breakfast. His answer is not hard to guess: anything as long as it's not oatmeal and water:

> He left me and soon after sent me his gardener, in whose fidelity he could confide, with new-laid eggs, butter, cheese, a bottle of white wine and another of beer. I never ate with so much voracity, and devoured seven or eight eggs in a moment, with a great quantity of bread, butter and cheese.

Johnstone gave Samuel a generous tip – he still had six or seven guineas on him – said his farewells and lay down for a sleep among the broom. Mr Graham woke him at midday to take his order for dinner and with the good news that he could get him across the Tay that evening. 'He mentioned a piece of beef, and I begged he would send me nothing else.' Graham brought it back himself, plus a good bottle of claret, which the two of them shared.

When James arrived at the pub in Broughty Ferry to which he had been covertly led, the boatmen who were to row him across the Tay reneged on the deal, fearful of what might happen to them if anyone ever found out they had helped a Jacobite fugitive to escape. The landlady's daughters, 'who were as beautiful as Venus' and clearly as charmed by James Johnstone as he was by them, were a lot bolder:

> The beautiful and charming Mally Burn, the eldest of the two, disgusted at length, and indignant at their obstinacy, said to her sister, 'O, Jenny! they are despicable cowards and poltroons, I would not for the world that

this unfortunate gentleman was taken in our house. I
pity his situation. Will you take an oar?'

James 'clasped them in my arms and covered them in turns with a
thousand tender kisses'. For the sake of Mally and Jenny, hopefully
the stay at Samuel's had allowed his smelly clothes to become a little
fresher.

It took two hours to row across the river, and they reached the
other side at midnight. Affectionate farewells were exchanged under
the stars. More tender kisses, one assumes. The girls would take no
money from him, but he slipped ten shillings into Mally's pocket
without her realizing he had done it.

Heading through Fife towards St Andrews, where he had another
relative, he stopped by a burn to bathe his feet, which were blistered
and bleeding. After the romantic drama and the kindness of the girls
the previous night, it's here that he reached his lowest point, suddenly
swamped by images of himself being hung, drawn and quartered.

He wished he had died with his comrades at Culloden. He saw his
current situation as hopeless. How on earth was he to reach safety?
As he sat on the banks of the burn, he mulled it all over and seriously
considered taking his own life.

A spark of hope and a prayer to God that one way or another his
troubles might soon be over stayed his hand. His shoes and stockings
were encrusted with dried blood. He soaked them in the burn for
half an hour, put them on again and continued to St Andrew's to his
cousin, Mrs Spence.

She sent him to one of her tenants, with a note that the man should
give James a horse and conduct him to Wemyss, where he could get
a boat to cross to Edinburgh. However, Mrs Spence's tenant was not
willing to cooperate:

> I delivered the letter to the farmer and the answer I
> received from this brute petrified me. 'Mrs. Spence,' said
> he, 'may take her farm from me and give it to whom she

pleases, but she cannot make me profane the Lord's day by giving my horse to one who means to travel upon the Sabbath.'

James got his revenge on this man in his memoirs, going into full rant mode about the hypocrisy of this 'holy rabble' who 'never scrupled to deceive their neighbours on the Lord's day, as well as other days'. At the time, the man's refusal to give him the horse was a disaster. Johnstone's feet were in a terrible state, every step bringing fresh agony.

He remembered that a former maid to his mother had married a gardener who worked for Mr Beaton of Balfour, whose home was ten miles away. His feet were so sore by the time he got there that he had to hold onto the doorpost to stop himself from falling over. Even if it was to save himself from being hanged, he could not have walked another step.

The gardener was horrified when he realized his visitor was a Jacobite fugitive, but his wife immediately said, 'Good God, I know him; quick – shut the door!' Like many people in Scotland at the time, her husband fortunately drew a distinction between disliking someone's politics and not wanting to see a fellow Scotsman hanged. He bathed James's feet in whisky before applying salve to them, his wife cooked him steak for his supper and James Johnstone slept the clock round.

His troubles were by no means over. The only fisherman who might even consider taking him across to Edinburgh when he went to Leith to sell his fish the following morning was 'a very zealous Calvinist and a violent enemy of the house of Stuart' by the name of Salmon. He would do James no harm, he said, and was not capable of informing against him, but he would not help. Money could not persuade him either.

As well as being a fisherman, Salmon kept an alehouse. James suggested they all have a beer together. After an hour of matching him 'glass for glass', during which he did not mention the lift to Leith, Salmon suddenly changed his mind, exclaiming to the gardener:

'What a pity, that this poor young man should have been debauched and perverted by this worthless rebel crew! He is a fine lad!'

And so it went on. In Leith, his old governess sheltered him. He saw his father but could not risk seeing his mother, who was very ill and not fit enough to leave the family home, which everyone feared was too risky for James to visit. Being persuaded out of running that risk was something he was to regret for the rest of his life. He never saw his mother again, as she died soon afterwards.

He travelled overland to London and, at last, after several narrow escapes, made it to the Continent. He was to spend his life in exile in France, soldiering in Europe and in Canada, becoming known as the Chevalier de Johnstone.

In old age, he published *A Memoir of the 'Forty-Five*. It's sharply observed, intelligently and well written, and his descriptions leap off the page. Few who write about the '45 can resist quoting him.

He never came home to Scotland.

33

A CHIEL AMANG YE TAKIN' NOTES: BISHOP ROBERT FORBES

I LOVE TRUTH

It's not much to look at: ten small notebooks bound in dark brown leather. Over the two and a half centuries since a man with a quill pen first wrote in them, some of the covers have come off. They are secured now to the handwritten pages they protect by linen tape tied in a bow. You can hold one of them in your hand for a moment or two without realizing what you have. This is *The Lyon in Mourning*, and there are riches beyond measure in here.

When its compiler, Robert Forbes, designed, drew and wrote the title page in 1747, he was committing an act of treason for which he could have been sentenced to death. Over the next 30 years, he kept his notebooks carefully hidden when he was not copying letters, poems, dying speeches and eyewitness accounts of events and personalities of the '45 into them.

Born in Old Rayne in Aberdeenshire, Robert Forbes was 37 in 1745, an Episcopalian for whom commitment to the House of Stuart was bound up inextricably with his religious faith. With a group of friends, he was arrested at Stirling on his way to join the Prince. He was held captive in the castle there and subsequently at Edinburgh

Castle from the beginning of September 1745 until the end of May 1746.

So he never met Charles Edward Stuart, and he never knew what it was like to be in Edinburgh while a Stuart prince held court at Holyroodhouse. He must have been so frustrated by that.

He seems to have met Donald MacDonell of Tirnadris after the latter was taken prisoner at the Battle of Falkirk on 17 January. Although they cannot have spent more than a few weeks together, the friendship forged under such circumstances ran deep. Robert Forbes and the men with whom he'd been captured were transferred to Edinburgh Castle in February 1746, on the orders of the Duke of Cumberland, who was then at Stirling. Taken out of the castle at nine o'clock in the morning, Forbes and his fellow prisoners stood in the street till the middle of the afternoon 'as so many spectacles to be gazed at'.

When the Duke of Albemarle came riding up and 'with a volley of oaths' demanded to know why the prisoners weren't tied, Captain Hamilton, who was in charge of them, said it was because they were gentlemen. 'Gentlemen,' snarled Albemarle, 'damn them for rebels. Get ropes and rope them immediately.'

Hamilton demurred. The gentlemen had been arrested on suspicion only. He didn't think they had actually committed any rebellious acts. Albemarle roared his head off and insisted on the ropes. 'Tied two and two by the arms, the gentlemen laughing at the farce,' Captain Hamilton apologized as it was done. Once they were away from Stirling, he told them to throw away the ropes. Might this have been the same Captain Hamilton who rescued Ranald MacDonald of Belfinlay on the battlefield at Culloden?

Writing in the third person about this incident, Bishop Forbes added a discreet footnote to the story: 'This account about the prisoners I wrote from my own eyesight and experience.' The modesty is typical of the man, as is his acknowledgement of the reluctance of Captain Hamilton to rope his prisoners. *The Lyon* contains searing accounts of cruelties perpetrated by Government troops and commanders, but where credit is due to them for restraint and kindness, Bishop Forbes is always scrupulous to give it. 'I love truth,' he wrote, 'let who will be either justified or condemned by it. I would not wish to advance a falsehood upon any subject, not even on Cumberland himself, for any consideration whatsoever.'

In May 1746, he was released from Edinburgh Castle without charge and went to stay in Leith with a wealthy parishioner, Dame Magdalene Scott, Lady Bruce of Kinross, well known for her Jacobite sympathies. He married twice, his first wife dying after only a year. His second wife was Rachel Houston and they seem to have been devoted to one another. She shared her husband's politics and was as committed as him to the compilation of *The Lyon in Mourning*.

Charles Edward Stuart was aware of both of them. Rachel often sent the Prince little presents, and he said of her husband that he was an honest man and that he held him in high esteem. Robert Forbes' collection does not include only words. There are Jacobite relics, too.

They include a scrap of the flowery material of Betty Burke's dress and a tiny piece of wood from one of the oars of the boat which carried Charles, Flora MacDonald and Neil MacEachainn to Skye. There's a large strip of tartan material, its reds, greens and yellows still jewel bright after 250 years. As ever, the Bishop was careful to record in writing where this piece of tartan came from: a waistcoat which MacDonald of Kingsburgh gave the Prince after he changed out of his female clothes. Unfortunately, since the waistcoat was 'too fine for a Servant', Charles had to discard it.

Compiling *The Lyon in Mourning* was Robert Forbes' life's work. He went on gathering information until a month before his death in 1778. By this time, Jacobitism was a spent force, no longer viewed as a danger to the status quo. The Episcopalian church was to officially separate itself from the Cause two years later. Despite a gradual easing of attitudes towards the vanquished Jacobites, the Bishop could never be persuaded to allow his collection to be published.

He may have been right to continue to view it as containing too many 'truths of so much delicacy and danger' or perhaps it had simply become too precious to him. His wife Rachel survived him by 30 years. Short of money, she sold the notebooks in 1806, but it was to be another 25 years before some of the information in them was released to the public between the covers of writer and publisher Robert Chambers' *History of the Rebellion of 1745–6*.

The Lyon in Mourning in its entirety was subsequently published by the Scottish History Society. It gave a great boost to writers investigating the '45 in the late nineteenth and early twentieth centuries and continues to be an amazing resource for anyone fascinated by the events of 1745–6.

Some people don't like it. Academic historians accuse Bishop Forbes of having a bias towards the Jacobites. Revisionist historians who try to persuade us that the cruelties encouraged by the Duke of Cumberland and perpetrated by some of the officers and men in his army are exaggerated accuse the Bishop of peddling Jacobite propaganda.

Of course Robert Forbes had a bias towards the Jacobites. He was impelled to start compiling *The Lyon in Mourning* because of a sense of burning injustice over how defeated Jacobites were being treated: they were being hanged and hounded and persecuted. Those are hard facts, not propaganda.

The Bishop, as he said, loved the truth. Read *The Lyon in Mourning* and you keep coming across letters from him to the people who were sending him information. He always wants the truth, he always wants to check if there are other sources to corroborate a story, as he is scrupulous about recording the names of those Government soldiers who acted to stop cruelty.

All history is selective. What we leave out is as important as what we leave in. Robert Forbes did his absolute best, working with a quill pen by candlelight, to put everything in.

EPILOGUE: ON CULLODEN MOOR

BEHAVE YOURSELF. PEOPLE DIED HERE

Scotland's broken heart lies here. Even the name hurts. The vicious battle fought on this windswept moor four miles east of Inverness meant the death of the Jacobite dream, the end of the line for the House of Stuart and the abandonment of any hope of Scotland, the ancient Kingdom, regaining her centuries-old status as an independent European country. This is where the clocks stopped.

The massacre of wounded Jacobites by the victorious Government forces initiated that devastating summer of bloodletting and reprisals. Throughout the Highlands and Islands, men and boys were shot, women and girls were raped, houses, farm buildings and chapels were burned. The treatment meted out to Jacobite prisoners who survived Culloden and its aftermath is a chilling example of man's inhumanity to man.

Many of the thousands carried south in the holds of filthy, overcrowded and disease-ridden ships did not survive the journey, their bodies flung overboard into the chilly waters of the North Sea. Those who did survive endured incarceration on prison hulks moored on the Thames or were cooped up in Tilbury Fort, where excursions were run so people could gawp at them. Hundreds of men, women and children were transported to the West Indies to work as forced labour on the sugar plantations.

Thirty-six men were hanged in the streets of Inverness. Eighty-four more suffered the medieval barbarity of being hung, drawn and quartered in Carlisle, York and London. Their heads were placed on spikes as a terrible warning to anyone who might ever again contemplate delivering such a shock to the British state as the Jacobites did.

After Culloden, there was a determined effort to diminish and marginalize the culture which was seen to have nurtured the 'unnatural rebellion'. Highlanders were no longer allowed to carry weapons. The wearing of kilts and tartan was banned. One of the men sent to enforce this prohibition was Captain Sweetenham. Whether he thought it was suitable work for an engineer is debatable.

Culloden symbolizes the end of the clan system and is bound up irrevocably with the Highland Clearances, which were to see the emigration of hundreds of thousands of Scots to the farthest ends of the Earth.

For so many sad reasons, it's easy to understand why so many of those who visit the battlefield today do so in a spirit of solemn pilgrimage and can be overheard admonishing their children to 'Behave yourself. People died here.'

Each year, at the annual commemoration of this last full-scale battle fought on British soil, flowers are laid to remember the sons, fathers, brothers and friends who fought and died here. Nobody ever lays flowers for the Redcoats.

The men whose choices led them to this place to fight under the Standard of Prince Charles Edward Stuart did so for a variety of reasons. Some had no choice.

Many on the Government side were in the army through economic necessity. Many on the Jacobite side were here because their clan chiefs, lairds and landlords had demanded it. That rigorous obedience was mirrored in those among their leaders whose mystical, near-religious loyalty to Scotland's royal house evokes so much admiration in those who take the romantic view of the Jacobite Cause.

For the men who felt this unswerving loyalty to the Stuarts, the '45 was the final act in the War of the British Succession, the culmination of all the other failed attempts to regain the British crown and throne for the ruling house to whom they believed it rightfully belonged. As they saw it, this right was God-given, not to be questioned or usurped by man.

For them and many others, what they were also fighting for was their country's nationhood. They were to be bitterly disappointed when it became clear that Scotland alone was not enough for Charles Edward Stuart. Nevertheless, at the start of the great adventure, he gave all those disaffected to the status quo a focus for their discontent and a leader they could follow. In the days before democracy and universal suffrage, it was one of the few ways ordinary people might hope to change things.

On the field and off it, there were Scots who sincerely believed Scotland's best hopes for peace and prosperity were dependent on remaining in the Union. Others, with regret for the loss of nationhood, were unwilling to plunge their country into bloodshed and turmoil for the sake of which royal house sat on the throne in a conflict between a German king and a Polish-Italian prince.

Yet that European dimension meant the stage on which the drama of the '45 was acted out was as big as it could be. If the attempt to regain the throne for the Stuarts had succeeded – and there were certain pivotal moments when it might have done – the subsequent history of Britain, Europe and the world would have been very different.

Once the Jacobites had been so comprehensively defeated, the French no longer had the opportunity to meddle in Britain's affairs and cause trouble for their old rival, England. With Scotland on-board, reluctantly or not, there was now the freedom to concentrate on the building of the British Empire. The Highland warriors who might have destroyed a united Britain ended up putting their swords, fighting spirit and loyalty at its disposal.

Culloden is often presented as a mythic Last Battle, the final conflict between the old Scotland and the new. Even as they line up on that windswept moor four miles east of Inverness, ready to run into the history books, a hundred sentimental songs and Scotland's collective memory, the Jacobites are the romantic but doomed warriors of a way of life already fading into the mists of time and legend. Their loyalty and courage is lauded, their suffering condemned, but essentially they are consigned to the footnotes of history.

According to this scenario, modern Scotland – the Enlightenment, the Industrial Revolution, Scots seizing their opportunities as so many did in Britain and the British Empire – could only be born out of the death throes of old Scotland.

Culloden does symbolize the death of an ancient way of life, but it was changing anyway. It had to, and the people living it understood that better than anybody. The Jacobite ranks were filled with men who were looking not to the past but the future.

There were Highlanders and Lowlanders who had lived through the famines which ravaged Scotland in the early 1740s. They were passionate about the planting of trees and other long-overdue improvements to agriculture and the land which would enable the country to feed itself and make such periodic catastrophes as famine a thing of the past.

Many of the committed Jacobites and Episcopalians of Scotland's east coast were involved in trade with Scandinavia, Europe and the Baltic which had been going on for hundreds of years. There was a trade in ideas, too. Catholic Scots were not permitted to attend their own universities and although they were also banned by law from going abroad to seek a Catholic education, many of them did, studying in Rome, Paris and Leyden.

Presbyterians and Episcopalians studied on the Continent, too, as a matter of course acquiring the necessary language skills. Among the merchants, doctors, lawyers, students, clergymen and poets who stood at Culloden were many fluent in several languages over and above their native Gaelic, Scots and English.

When they came home to Scotland, they kept their fluency up

by reading Voltaire in the original and corresponding with men and women throughout Europe on religion, philosophy, engineering, science and every other subject under the sun.

Scottish Jacobites were in the mainstream of contemporary European thought. In their attitudes to women, personal liberty and religious freedom they were light years ahead of their adversaries. These were modern men. They were also individuals who had thought long and hard about what they were doing and who understood only too well the consequences of failure.

That they were prepared to risk those consequences shows they could see a different path stretching forward into the future, one they thought was worth fighting for. At a time when Scotland stood at a crossroads of history, they were prepared to stand up and be counted. They have inspired Scotsmen and women to do the same ever since.

Two hundred and fifty years ago, the *Gentleman's Magazine* reported the Battle of Culloden under the headline 'Rebels Totally Defeated'.

In Scotland? How wrong can you be?

SELECT BIBLIOGRAPHY

MANUSCRIPT SOURCES

PUBLIC RECORD OFFICE, LONDON *State Papers Domestic George II, Treasury Solicitors Papers (TS11), The 1745 Rebellion Papers (TS20), Court of King's Bench Papers (Baga de Secretis), Patent Rolls*

NATIONAL ARCHIVES OF SCOTLAND NAS mss including *GD12 Records of the Episcopal Church of Scotland, GD158 Hume of Polwarth Earls of Marchmont Papers (Lady Jane Nimmo's letters), GD220 Papers of the Graham Family, Dukes of Montrose (Montrose Muniments), GD498 Records Relating to Colonel James Gardiner*

KING'S COLLEGE SPECIAL COLLECTIONS, ABERDEEN UNIVERSITY LIBRARY *The MacBean Collection*

NATIONAL LIBRARY OF SCOTLAND NLS mss including *The Lyon in Mourning (manuscript originals)* and *The Blaikie Collection*

ROYAL ARCHIVES, WINDSOR *RA/CP/MAIN/10/173* and *RA/CP/MAIN/10/176*, quotations from which are reproduced by the permission of Her Majesty Queen Elizabeth II

PUBLISHED PAPERS

The Albemarle Papers New Spalding Club, Aberdeen, 1902

Blaikie, W.B., *Origins of the 'Forty-Five* Scottish Academic Press, Edinburgh, 1975

The Cochrane Correspondence Regarding The Affairs Of Glasgow 1745–46 Maitland Club, Glasgow, 1836

Cottin, Paul, *Un Protégé de Bachaumont: Correspondance Inédite de Marquis d'Eguilles* Revue Rétrospective, Paris, 1887

Duff, H.R., *Culloden Papers* T. Cadell & W. Davies, London, 1815

Forbes, Bishop Robert, *The Lyon in Mourning* Scottish History Society, Edinburgh, 1895

Howell, T.J. (Compiler), *A Complete Collection of State Trials and Proceedings for High Treason and Other Crimes and Misdemeanours* Longman, London, 1816

Lockhart, George, *The Lockhart Papers* Wm. Anderson, London, 1817

MacGregor, George, *The Collected Writings of Dougal Graham, 'Skellat' Bellman of Glasgow* Thomas D. Morison, Glasgow, 1883

Nicholas, Donald (ed.), *Intercepted Post* Bodley Head, London, 1956

Report of the Proceedings and Opinion of the Board of General Officers on their Examination into the Conduct, Behaviour, and Proceedings of Lieutenant-General Sir John Cope . . . London, 1746

Seton, Sir Bruce Gordon & Arnot, Jean Gordon (eds), *The Prisoners of the '45* Scottish History Society, Edinburgh, 1929

Warrand, D. (ed.), *More Culloden Papers (Vol. III 1725–1745)* Robert Carruthers & Sons, Inverness, 1927

Woodhouselee Manuscript Edinburgh, 1907

OTHER SOURCES (BOOKS, JOURNAL ARTICLES & WEBSITES)

Ainsworth, William Harrison, *The Manchester Rebels* Printwise Publications, Bury & Manchester, 1992

Campbell, John Lorne, *Highland Songs of the Forty-Five* Scottish Academic Press, Edinburgh, 1984

Colley, Linda, *Britons: Forging the Nation 1707–1837* Yale University Press, New Haven & London, 2005

Doddridge, Rev. P., *Some Remarkable Passages in the Life of the Honourable Col. James Gardiner* London, 1791

Doran, Dr, *London in the Jacobite Times* Richard Bentley & Son, London, 1877

Duffy, Christopher, *The '45: Bonnie Prince Charlie and the Untold Story of the Jacobite Rising* Cassell, London, 2003

Eardley-Simpson, L.E., *Derby and the Forty-Five* Philip Allan, London, 1933

Forbes, Alexander (Lord Pitsligo), *Essays Moral and Philosophical on Several Subjects* J. Osborn & T. Longman, London, 1734

Forsyth, William, *In The Shadow of Cairngorm: Chronicles of the United Parishes of Abernethy and Kincardine* Northern Counties Publishing Company, Inverness, 1900

The Gentleman's Magazine for 1745 & 1746

Fergusson, Sir James, *Argyll in the Forty-Five* Faber, London, 1951

Gibson, John S., *Ships of the '45* Hutchinson, London, 1967

Gibson, John S., *The Gentle Lochiel: The Cameron Chief and Bonnie Prince Charlie* NMS Publishing, Edinburgh, 1998

Gordon-Taylor, G. (1945), 'The Medical and Surgical Aspects of the 'Forty-Five', *The British Journal of Surgery*, Vol. 33, Issue 129, pp. 4–16

Hancox, Joy, *The Queen's Chameleon: The Life of John Byrom* Jonathan Cape, London, 1994

Harrington, Peter, *Culloden 1746: The Highland Clans' Last Charge* Osprey Publishing, London, 1991

Home, John, *The History of the Rebellion in Scotland in 1745* Peter Brown, Edinburgh & Ogle, Duncan & Co., London, 1822

Johnstone, James, Chevalier de, *A Memoir of the 'Forty-Five* Folio Society, London, 1958

Lawson, John Parker, *History of the Scottish Episcopal Church* Edinburgh, 1843

Livingstone of Bachuil, Alistair, Aikman, C.W.H. and Stuart Hart, Betty (eds), *No Quarter Given: The Muster Roll of Prince Charles Edward Stuart's Army 1745–46* Neil Wilson Publishing, Glasgow, 2001

MacGregor, Neil (2006), 'John Roy Stuart, Jacobite Bard of Strathspey', *Transactions of the Gaelic Society of Inverness*, Vol. LXIII, pp. 1–24

McKim, Anne, *Defoe in Scotland: A S.P.Y. Among Us* Scottish Cultural Press, Dalkeith, 2006

Maclean, Fitzroy, *Bonnie Prince Charlie* Canongate, Edinburgh, 1988

McLynn, F.J., *The Jacobite Army in England 1745: The Final Campaign* John Donald, Edinburgh, 1983

MacNaughton, P. (1965), 'Medical Heroes of the '45', *Transactions of the Gaelic Society of Inverness,* Vol. XLII

Menary, George, *The Life and Letters of Duncan Forbes of Culloden, Lord President of the Court of Session, 1685–1747* Alexander Maclehose & Co., London, 1936

Monod, Paul Kléber, *Jacobitism and the English People, 1688–1788* Cambridge University Press, Cambridge, 1989

National Trust for Scotland, *Cùil Lodair/Culloden* Edinburgh, 2007

Prebble, John, *Culloden* Penguin, London, 1961

Reid, Stuart, *Cumberland's Army: The British Army at Culloden* Partizan Press, Leigh-on-Sea, 2006

Scots Magazine for 1745 & 1746

Tayler, A. & Tayler, H., *Jacobites of Aberdeenshire & Banffshire in the Forty-Five* Oliver & Boyd, Aberdeen, 1928

Tayler, A. & Tayler, H., *1745 and After* T. Nelson and Sons, London, 1938

Tomasson, Katherine & Buist, Francis, *Battles of the '45* B.T. Batsford Ltd, London, 1962

Watts, John, *Scalan: The Forbidden College, 1716–1799* Tuckwell Press, East Linton, 1999

Watts, John, *Hugh MacDonald, Highland, Jacobite & Bishop* John Donald, Edinburgh, 2002

Whittet, Martin M. (1967), 'Medical Resources of the Forty-Five', *Transactions of the Gaelic Society of Inverness,* Vol. XXIV, pp. 1–41

http://www.battleofprestonpans1745.org

http://www.abdn.ac.uk/historic/actsofunion/ (online exhibition by the University of Aberdeen)

INDEX